BOOK TWO OF THE

MASKS OF THE MISCAM

JOAQUÍN BALDWIN

Copyright © 2024 by Joaquín Baldwin.
Written by Joaquín Baldwin.
Edited by Andrew Corvin.
Cover illustration by Ilse Gort.
Book design and layout by Joaquín Baldwin.
Illustrations and maps by Joaquín Baldwin.
Author's Photograph by Timothy Dahlum.
Typeset in: *Concourse*, by Matthew Butterick; *Cinzel*, by Natanael Gama; *Inknut Antiqua*, by Claus Eggers Sørensen. *ETbb*, by Dmitry Krasny, Bonnie Scranton, Edward Tufte, David J. Perry, Daniel Benjamin Miller, & Michael Sharpe.

This book is a work of fiction. Names, characters, places, and incidents are the product of the author's imagination or are used fictitiously. Any resemblance to actual events, locales, or persons, living or dead, is coincidental.

This is a work of passion and love created by a human, not by an AI.

The scanning, uploading, and distribution of this book without permission, as well as the processing of its contents for Large Language Models or other AI datasets, is a theft of the author's intellectual property. If you would like permission to use material from the book (other than for review purposes), please contact the author. Thank you for your support of the author's rights.

All rights reserved.

Library of Congress Control Number: 2024901830
ISBN: 978-1-961076-04-4 (e-book)
ISBN: 978-1-961076-05-1 (paperback)
ISBN: 978-1-961076-06-8 (hardcover)
ISBN: 978-1-961076-07-5 (audiobook)

First Edition, 2024.
Los Angeles, California.
NS2-H1

"Drifting about among flowers and sunshine, I am like a butterfly or bee, though not half so busy or with so sure an aim. But in the midst of theses methodless rovings I seek to spell out by close inspection things not well understood."

— John Muir

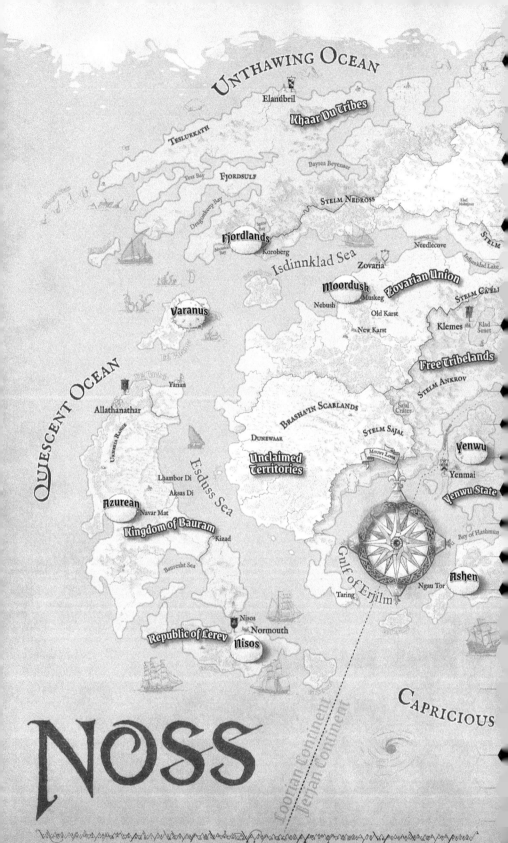

MOORDUSK DOME
MINDRELDROLOM

0 10 20 30 40 50

Zovaria

Provinces
Gwur Pantônil
Gwur Ali
Gwur Lamiish
Gwur Ceseth
Gwur Aalip

Isdinnklad Sea

Elkhorn
Meadowmere

Mirefoot

Moor Gate

Draad

Hills of the Unspoken

Parjuul

Urdanklen
Kiath
Barmu Forest

Mossborough

Loonsad
Hum'Khabab
Gwora Forest
Quolash

Moordusk Bogs

Oälpaskist
Arjum
Akvash Forest
Quas Trell
Barmu Forest

Settler's Hollow

Buchan
Ierno
Hiro Jungle
Dakhüd

Hartedge
Elothi
Ifrenlon
Orin
Jebbur
Humenath
Muskeg
Goubi
Orpieth
Annelo
Saphir
Ibrat

Wayfarer's Bridge

Nebush

Firr

Wuhir Peak

Golem's Cove
Old Karst

Oxal

Karst Forest
Wardne

Boru
Siltlands
Kaolin

Brightbay

Sial
Eastern Karst Forest

Whitefern Forest
Brightbay Run

Lahari
Nightlure Cliffs

Mudflow Ruins
New Karst

Sentic Tower

Seyen Battlefield

Barnoy
Moonbow Timberlands

Conflux Ruins

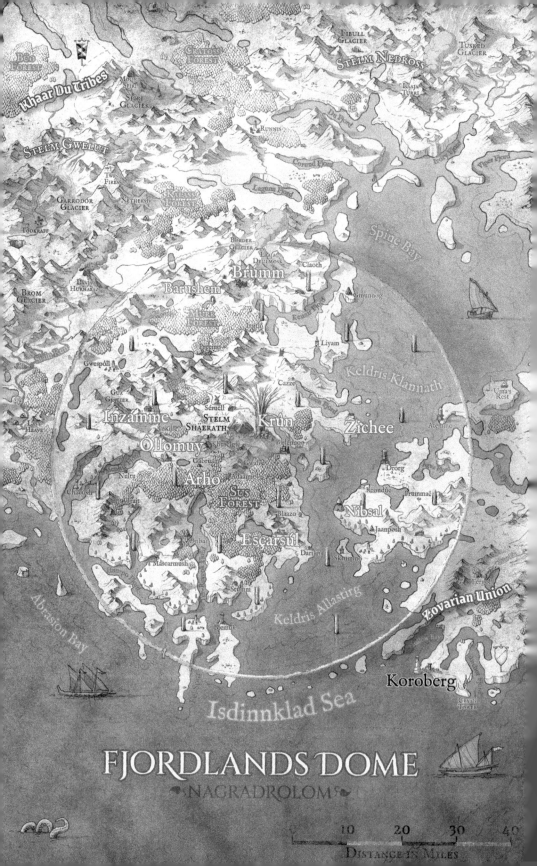

Table of Contents

Quote 5
Maps 6
Table of Contents 12
Author's Note 16
The Story So Far 17
Part One: The Pink Capital 23
  1. River of Fire 25
  2. The Red Tide 33
    Image: Jaxon 47
  3. Successor 51
  4. Isdinnklad 53
  5. Zovaria 57
    Image: The Pink Capital 61
  6. Balstei Woodslav 67
    Image: Map with Glyphs and Clades 78
  7. Respite 81
  8. Betrayal 89
  9. Boglands 97
    Image: Alaia and the Fogbow 106
  10. Lured by the Flame 109
  11. The Moordusk Dome 115
    Image: Mindreldrolom 122
  12. Climb On 127
  13. Grest Miscamish 129
  14. Secret Messages 137
  15. The Legacy 141

Part Two: Mindreldrolom 149

   16. Prince Aio 151

   17. Arjum Promenade 161

      Image: Kulak and Blu 171

   18. The Council of the Six Provinces 173

   18. Fool's Gold 187

   20. Minquoll 195

   21. The Temple of Felids 201

   22. The Second Council 205

   23. Sunu 209

   24. Strike Harder 215

   25. Six Widows 221

   26. Obsidian Moon 227

   27. Summer Solstice 239

   28. Golden Rack 243

   29. Sea Wing 251

   30. Munnji Silos 259

   31. The Company of Nine 265

   32. The Lights of Humenath 269

   33. Threads Pulled Inward 279

   34. Banook's Guest 285

Part Three: Memory 289

   35. Over the Ophidian 291

   36. Lorr of Wings 297

   37. Wuhir Peak 307

   38. Sulphur Moon 311

   39. Giant Redwoods 321

   40. Beyond Six Lands, Beneath Six Seas 329

   41. A Meeting in the Mountains 339

Image: Banook, Bear, and Safís 344

42. Brasha'in Scablands 345

43. Whiskers in the Dark 355

44. Enolv Ruins 359

45. Petroglyphs 369

　　Image: Petroglyphs 387

46. Momsúndosilv 389

47. Sentinel 395

48. Amethyst Moon 401

49. The Final Push 407

50. Hearth Stones 419

51. Fate of the Silvesh 427

52. Gre Ieren 439

53. The Unfolding 449

Part Four: Reawakening 453

54. To Sea 455

55. Tower Maiden 465

56. Adventuress 471

57. Balance from Chaos 479

58. Rilgsilv 485

59. Hold 491

60. A Flower of Deep Time 495

　　Image: Golden Flower 501

61. Fjordlands 503

62. Tusks and Axes 513

63. The Tricolored Mountain 523

64. Nalaníri of the Nagra 531

　　Image: Kitjári and Nalaníri 538

65. Hêsshogo's Bow 545

66. Sea Shanties 551
67. Sea Serpents 557
68. Hallow 569
69. Bayanhong Wars 575
70. Into the Dragon's Lair 581
71. The Drowned Palace 589
72. Kruwenfröa 601
73. The Lashing Ichor 611
74. Braided Threads 615
75. A Candle in the Dark 621
76. Noss 625
    Image: Circle of Six 631
77. Full Change 639
78. The Journey Ahead 649
    Image: End Cladoglyphs 654

Appendices 658
    The Rules of Minquoll 659
    The Eighteen Clades 661
    Glossary of Commonly Used Miscamish Words ... 665
    Characters, Gods, Items, Tribes 669
    Locations 677
    Map: The Journey So Far 688

Acknowledgments 690

About the Author 693

Author's Note

Hello reader; I'm very happy you made it to Book 2 of the *Noss Saga*! This is where the core story really gets started, so there are huge surprises coming. As with the previous installment, I have a few recommendations before you journey onward:

Maps and Illustrations

There are several new maps for this book. To properly read all the details on the maps, I recommend you view them at full resolution and in color. Visit the link below to find all the maps, illustrations, and other goodies.

Guides and Glossary

Characters, locations, and common Miscamish words can be found in the appendices at the end of this book. Previous guides, such as the pronunciation guide that was included in Book 1, are not printed in this installment (the volume is thick enough already!), but they are available on the link below alongside even more extras.

Supplemental Materials

Follow this link to access all the Supplemental Materials, including the color illustrations, maps, glossaries, lists of characters, locations, and more.

JoaquinBaldwin.com/book2/extras

The Story So Far

The *Noss Saga* is a complex tale. It's easy even for me to forget all that happened in previous books. While I try to remind the readers of the preceding events along the way, I recognize the need for a full-on refresher.

The following is not a comprehensive synopsis, so it will not make much sense unless you've read the previous book in this series (you should not be here if you haven't read it yet, either way).

Thank you for joining me for the next part of this queer and epic journey. I hope you enjoy your return to Noss.

May the moon light your path,

— Joaquín Baldwin

Book 1 - Wolf of Withervale

Lago Vaari is entrusted with Agnargsilv—the mask of canids—by a shapeshifting elderly woman named Sontai, who asks him to take the mask to her grandson, Bonmei. Lago tricks Chief Arbalister Fjorna Daro of the Negian Empire, who had been hunting Sontai to acquire the mask. Fearful of the mask and the soldiers pursuing it, Lago and his best friend Alaia hide it away in a coal mine. After his father kicks him out of his home, Lago gets a job at the Mesa Monastery, delivering packages for the Havengall monks and helping Professor Crysta Holt with the monastery's telescope. He falls in love with the stars, the planets, and the moon. A dire wolf, a species thought extinct, is killed near Withervale. The creature is much larger than any in fossil records, and the recent collapse of the Heartpine Dome's roof seems to be related to the giant's appearance.

Six years later, Withervale is attacked by Fjorna Daro and General Alvis Hallow. Lago escapes through the coal mine and retrieves Agnargsilv, aided by a scout from the Free Tribelands named Ockam Radiartis, who considers Bonmei his adopted son. Alaia and Lago's pet dog Bear join them. Lago learns how to see the threads of life with Agnargsilv but knows there are more powers the mask is hiding. Shortly after they arrive at the Thornridge Lookout, Fjorna's squad attacks them, killing Bonmei. Lago defeats Fjorna's soldiers by using Agnargsilv's powers, which let him see in the pure dark and foresee the attacks of his enemies. Platoon Commander Jiara Ascura also joins their party, and the five of them flee by using Agnargsilv to penetrate the wall of vines that surround the Heartpine Dome, hoping that taking the mask away from the Free Tribelands will avert a potential war.

After being imprisoned for some time with a handful of survivors from her squad, Fjorna and her team escape to warn Alvis Hallow. When they find him, Alvis is already in possession of the mask of cervids, which he stole from the Anglass Dome. With Artificer Urcai's aid, Alvis finds his elk half-form. As the Red Stag, he kills the weak Emperor Uvon dus Grei and takes the throne of the Negian Empire under the title of Monarch Hallow.

Inside the Heartpine Dome, Lago and his friends discover that the Negians exterminated the Southern Wutash tribe who lived there. They find strange quaar artifacts at a broken lattice located in a temple at the dome's trunk, and also encounter Safís, a white wolf shapeshifter who is the spirit of canids. They help her escape the dome and then head north, searching for the Firefalls—also known as Minnelvad—where they hope they might find the surviving "cousins" of the Wutash.

After a steamy visit through Brimstowne, they venture up the hot creeks of the Firefalls, where they are struck by a blizzard. Lago is caught in an avalanche and overcome by the toxic fumes of the falls. He hallucinates a huge golden bear coming to save him. He wakes up in a cabin and meets a corpulent giant named Banook, who rescued him and his friends. Lago quickly grows fond of the mountain of a man.

Banook, who is the spirit of ursids, tells the wayfarers the story of the Downfall, and how the domes were grown to protect the eighteen chosen clades from the cataclysm. He reveals that the dome of ursids was never grown, causing the demise of the Northern Wutash tribe. Banook also teaches them about the Nu'irgesh—animal spirits of each major clade—and tells them that the mask of ursids, Urnaadisilv, lays buried under the icy caldera that engulfed the city of Da'áju. He promises to take them there once Winter is over.

With Banook's aid, Lago finds his timber wolf half-form and is gifted with the name of Sterjall, as well as with a dagger named Leif, which Banook and Ockam crafted from a lattice segment and dire wolf fang that Lago took from the Heartpine Dome. Lago-Sterjall and Banook fall in love but are fearful of their future because Banook will not be able to join them—he can only travel where other bears reside, and the bears only live in the mountains of the north.

During an excursion into Brimstowne, Banook sees that Negians are searching for the mask Lago-Sterjall wields. He meets with a ranger named Ardof, who tells him that the Red Stag may be readying to attack Withervale.

The Red Stag has ransacked the Anglass Dome and reshaped the Negian Empire's politics. He captures and mindlocks Sovath, the cervid Nu'irg, forcing her to join his army of enslaved cervids, including the megaloceroses (giant elk) and cervalces (giant moose). The Red Stag ventures to the Lequa Dome. With the aid of Fjorna, he acquires Krostsilv, the mask of musteloids, and gifts it to General Jaxon Remon. He also gifts him with caged jarv wolverines—vicious, bear-sized creatures he captured in the Lequa Dome.

Throughout Winter, Lago and his friends train with Jiara, preparing to journey into Da'áju. Once the Thawing season arrives, they leave Bear in the cabin with two bears who will take care of the mutt, and venture into the Da'áju Caldera. They find the ice-buried temple of ursids and rescue Urnaadisilv from its forsaken depths. Ockam becomes the wearer of Urnaadisilv, although he is not yet able to shapeshift. From a rock-carved map, they learn that there was once another dome in a volcanic desert known as the Brasha'in Scablands; they do not know why it is no longer there. They decide they should travel west, to the Moordusk Dome, in hopes of finding a Miscam tribe who might know why the domes have not opened as they were meant to open, and who might know how to defeat the Red Stag.

Upon exiting the glacier, they spot an orange glow in the distance: Withervale is on fire. Lago-Sterjall needs to help Crysta and his other friends in the city. Banook tries to follow them to Withervale, but once he is too far from his bears, the Nu'irg withers and turns feeble. Unable to follow any longer, he kisses his precious cub goodbye.

MASKS OF THE MISCAM

Part One
THE PINK CAPITAL

Chapter One

River of Fire

Withervale burned.

Lago's eyes reflected the sickly yellow bursts of sapfire blazing in the distance. He could smell the acrid fumes, which billowed like netherflames spewed by a bloodwraith from Khest.

This is all my fault. He held on to the strap of his bag but didn't look down at it, feeling the presence of Agnargsilv inside. *I brought war to my own home,* he thought, although *home* no longer felt like the right word.

The night was dark and starless, lit only by the flashes of malignant light that reflected over the still-distant expanse of the Stiss Malpa, the Great River.

"You need to rest, Gwoli," Alaia said, placing a hand on Lago's shoulder. She stood next to him on the crag's edge and leaned her head on his, blending the darkness of her braided hair with Lago's curls. "We will only get a few hours of sleep tonight," she added, already closing her eyes.

"I can't," Lago said. "It feels so close, as if we could reach it if we push a bit harder." He lifted his binoculars once more, but the dense smoke obscured all landmarks, even the Withervale Mesa itself.

Alaia muffled a yawn, leaning heavily on Lago's side. "Please," she said. "We... You need rest. Use these few hours to gather your strength." She pulled on his arm. "Come, Gwoli."

Lago let himself be dragged. He looked toward the lingering embers of their campfire, which caught a light breeze and brightened suddenly, casting an ominous glow over his sleeping friends. Ockam was blanketed by his green wool cloak, his thin mustache rising and falling under his even breaths. Jiara lay opposite of him, her thick braid snaking over her brawny body looking more red than blonde in the emberlight.

Lago dropped heavily on his bedroll and tucked himself in. The yellow-tinged clouds to the south were too dreary a sight, so he turned to face the rising peaks of the Stelm Wujann to the north, then felt the crushing presence of an absence in his heart.

Banook, he called within him as he closed his eyes.

"Cub! You must wake up!" said a rough yet melodious voice.

Lago felt his shoulders being shaken, but his eyes were too heavy. He could not remember falling asleep.

"Come on cub, you can do this," the mountainous voice rumbled. "We are waiting."

"Banook!" Lago suddenly called, opening his eyes wide to find his lover crouching beside him. Banook had fully returned to his youthful, vibrant self, as if he had never left bearkind behind. "What is happening? Why are you here?" Lago asked. He wanted to kiss him but found he could not move.

Banook placed a hand on Lago's cheek and said, "Jiara said we can make it to the river before dawn. We need to hurry, Gwoli."

"Why are you calling me that?" Lago asked.

"Gwoli, wake up," Banook said, shaking his shoulders. "Wake up!"

Lago inhaled deeply as he opened his eyes. Alaia was crouching beside him, silhouetted by a star-studded sky.

"Gwoli, are you there?" she asked.

He sat up. "I thought we were going to sleep," he mumbled.

"We got two hours of rest," Jiara said from nearby, slinging her backpack over her broad shoulders.

Ockam stepped beside Lago and handed him a strip of dry jerky. "The winds are blowing the smoke south," he said, "leaving nearly enough starlight to see by. Let's hurry while we can see our path."

They journeyed down a barely visible trail and arrived at the coast of the Stiss Malpa moments before Sunnokh made his appearance in the east. The glow of dawn tinted the higher smoke a deep red.

"Thank the watchful eyes of the Great Spider! The city still holds," Ockam said, having borrowed Lago's binoculars to peer at Withervale. "The battle is mostly in the water."

Lago took the instrument and aimed it across the wide river. The core of the city held strong, as did the mesa and the observatory's tower—most of the fires were contained outside the perimeter of Withervale's ramparts.

"They haven't breached through yet," he said. "The Zovarians are blocking passage along the river."

A pink-sailed flotilla cruised eastward to where the heart of the battle raged; there, they were met by sapfire cannon blasts from the red-sailed dromon ships of the Negians. The water itself burned, with the currents dragging the flaming patches westward, toward the Zovarians.

While the dromon ships vomited their bedeviled flames, the much larger war galleys pushed their attacks with ballistae and catapults, hoping to carve a path to unload their troops. The Zovarian navy countered with their powerful ramships and agile trimarans, keeping their advantage in numbers. On land, scores of soldiers clad in pink and bronze mobilized to protect the ramparts.

"We need to find a way across," Lago said.

"There's a fishing village west of here," Alaia suggested. "We could find a boat there."

Ockam nodded, then said to Lago, "Let's keep the masks safely hidden. And anything quaar, too." While wrapping his quaar shield in a blanket, he added, "And just in case, don't use your real name. I'm certain they are still looking for you."

The winds shifted once more, bringing the smoke back over them like a bitter haze. The river vanished in the whiteness.

After a mile's walk along the shore, they encountered a fisherman who had just moored his rickety canoe on a crumbling pier. "Moon lights," he mumbled, squinting his reddened eyes through the smoke.

"Stars guide," Ockam replied, tipping his short-brimmed hat by the tapered crown.

"It's a scary sight, them netherflames swimming the Great River," the old fisherman said, eyeing a patch of sapfire burning downstream; it flowed away like a castaway specter. He pushed his hat back to reveal canyons of wrinkles carving his overly tanned forehead. "Never seen nothing like it in seventy years rowing these waters." He sucked on his cheeks as he inspected the wayfarers.

"Two of you don't seem like you belong around here. I'm hoping this old man is not in trouble, as I have not much trouble to give in return."

"The two of us are from the Free Tribelands," Ockam said, nodding toward Jiara. "You will suffer no trouble from us. But we could sure use your help, if you'd be willing. We need to get to Withervale."

"If death is what you seek, start swimming. The Great River will gladly grant your wishes."

"We were hoping to get there alive," Lago said. "We have friends there who might be in danger. All we need is to get across."

"The currents are pulling the sap downriver, sonny, more so by the southern shores. Even the patches that are not aflame would eat up my mighty vessel's planks and oars. I only made my catch here by the confluence, where the creek pushes the spiteful bile away."

"Please, we beg of you," Lago said. "We'd pay you for your troubles."

The old man picked up the baskets of crappies and eels he'd caught. "I have a family to feed, lad. I'm no use to them dead. There's no amount of Qupi you could offer me to change that."

Lago's eyes brightened. He dropped his bag and searched its depths, careful not to reveal the mask within it. He pulled out the tiny bottle of soot that Khopto had given him seven months earlier, the same day the Negians attacked Withervale and forced him to flee through the limestone caverns. "Do you know what this is?" he asked.

The fisherman stared distrustfully. "Young man, how did you get your hands on that?"

"If I told you, you wouldn't believe me. Either way, it's pure. I can see in your eyes that you know its value."

"I tasted soot in my youth. I know what it's like, and I know its value. But this old soul has been swindled many a time before, and long gone are the days in which I fell for these tricks. I don't believe a sapling like you could afford that bottle, else you wouldn't be here begging for a canoe ride."

"If you don't believe me, then take a sample and see for yourself," Lago said, uncapping the bottle and handing it to him. "You can hold it, so I don't play any tricks on you." The old man plucked a dry blade of grass, dipped it in the bottle, and lifted it to his nose. He inhaled. Those few particles were enough to make his eyes dilate, to flush his ashen face back to a youthful pink. He capped the bottle and held tightly to it, savoring the effect of the drug.

Lago tipped his head toward the canoe. "Does the deal seem fair to you? We are in a hurry."

"I cannot take you, it is too dangerous. But you can have my dear old *Soroley*. That scrappy bundle of wood may still have one more league before she falters. But like I said, I have a family to feed, so you aren't getting away with my catch." The old man leaned into his boat and finished unloading his baskets and fishing tools.

The wayfarers boarded the canoe, which had an extra set of oars. Jiara and Ockam set to rowing.

"May the white-haired sprites of the Stiss Malpa grant you tight lines and a great haul!" the old fisherman yelled, waving his hat.

Lago waved back until the fisherman vanished in the smoke, then turned toward his friends. "Can't even see where we are going," he said, feeling his eyes itch from the particulates in the air.

"The pull of the current tells us where we are headed," Jiara said, thick arms pulling hard on the oars. "You two keep your eyes on the sapfire, burning or not—don't let any of it stick to dear old *Soroley*."

"We'll take care of it," Alaia said, who'd been smart enough to carry a long and leafy branch just for that purpose.

It didn't take long for a burning patch to advance threateningly toward them. Alaia took the initiative, practically dangling from the vessel to catch the sticky substance with her branch. She dragged it around the canoe to divert its path, then tried to shake it off at the opposite side. "Shit, shit!" she called. "It won't come off!"

The branch began to burn even as she shoved it underwater.

"Cast it away," Ockam said. "Sapfire will bind to anything it touches."

Alaia tried to shake the flames off one more time, then hurled the branch away. Ockam handed her one of his oars, then kept the other at the ready while Jiara kept rowing. He spotted a small patch of fire and flicked it away.

"Curse this thing!" he cried as a drip of sapfire clinging to his oar was flung into the canoe. The fire burned intensely, like a tear from a sickened sun. It was only a droplet, so Ockam managed to stomp it out, but not without effort. "Teslur's hex upon you," he spat to the extinguished flame. "Whatever they put in that venomous substance makes the flames burn hotter, brighter, deadlier."

"Another one's coming!" Alaia warned, aiming her oar to divert a patch of fire too bright to directly look at. She caught it, but it had been burning over flotsam and carried too much weight. The bundle slammed against the side of their canoe.

"Keep away from the flames and hold tight!" Jiara said, straining her muscles. "We are nearly there!"

They heard the sounds of metal striking wood coming from the south; they were not the sounds of battle, but of people and machinery at work.

"That sounds like the lumber mill," Lago said, leaning on the side of the canoe to get a better look. "There, I see reeds through the smoke. The docks must be nearby."

They entered a reedy channel and slam-docked on a wooden pier of the Oak Ridge Mill, abandoning the ship in a hurry as it was consumed by fire.

"So long, *Soroley* the brave," Jiara said, kicking the burning canoe away to prevent it from igniting the pier.

Lago was familiar with the screech of spinning tools at the mill, but today the sounds were heightened, hurried, and the mill overflowed with busy workers. The four of them were barely noticed as they rushed past giant saws and lumber cranes. The smell of the oil, woodchips, and sweat overpowered that of the sapfire smoke.

Near the whipsaw, right underneath the water mill, a woman in her early sixties stood, gazing eastward toward the billowing smoke. She had several bags and crates stacked next to her.

"Hey, Lago!" the woman called as loudly as she could. "Lago Vaari, hey! Is that truly you?"

"I guess the whole 'don't use your name' will not be necessary after all," Ockam grumbled.

"Lurr Cherdov?" Lago asked as he approached.

"Where in Takh's two names have you been?" the woman asked. "People have been looking for you everywhere! There was—"

"I'm sorry, I don't have time to tell you the story, but it's nice to see you too. We need to get to the mesa, but we don't know which roads are safe."

"Oh, the mesa is fine, dear. With the reinforcements to the rampart, they haven't gotten close to that area. It's only at the water that the battle is ongoing." She pulled Lago by the shoulder and led the group behind the building, where the sound of the saws wasn't so deafening. "Is this a woman's garment?" she asked distractedly, feeling the silkiness of Lago's gray and black cloak. "Anyway, we are holding tight here, crafting buttresses and bracings for the rampart, even weapons. But if the Negians breach the naval base, I'm ready to flee west. I'm waiting for my husband's signal, who is farther up the road with the horses. It's not safe here, dear, you should head west too."

"We probably will, soon," Lago said, already walking away. "Stay safe, Lurr Cherdov, and say hi to Lorr Cherdov for me."

"Don't get anywhere near the main city! Take the forest road, then go around the south by the mines. May Takhísh's Shield guard you!"

They followed her advice, skipping the Old Pilgrim's Road and heading for the trails that Lago and Alaia knew so well. The mines were also in full operation, providing coal to the war effort.

"Keep the Oldrin at work, even while everything burns," Alaia complained, covering her head with the furred hood of her cloak and signaling for Lago to do the same.

They jumped the fence and continued ascending toward the mesa. Most of the citizens who hadn't fled were gathered at the edges of the sandstone prominence to get the best views from above, leaving Runestone Lane nearly empty. The monastery was just north of them, with the Mesa Observatory's tower silhouetted against a swirling cloud of smoke.

"They haven't called for an evacuation yet," Jiara noted. "That's a good sign, I think. It means they trust they can keep the attack under control."

Lago hurried under the monastery's stone arch and knocked hard on the observatory's door.

"Who goes there?" a voice called.

"Gwil? It's Lago."

The door swung open at once, and Chaplain Gwil came out to wrap his long-sleeved arms around the young man's back. "You stupid, stupid child," the bald monk said. "Where have you been? What in the Haven's name has been going on?"

Chapter Two

The Red Tide

"Is Crysta okay?" Lago inquired. "Khopto? Esum? All the monks?"

"We are fine," Gwil said. "All fine. Some of us are upstairs, waiting for the smoke to clear so we can keep track of the battle using the telescope." He glanced distrustfully at Lago's odd company, holding him protectively.

"They are friends," Lago said. "You can trust them."

"Then let's go up at once."

Lago bolted into the observatory, eyeing the bags packed in the library—the monks were ready for a quick evacuation.

As he ushered the others in, Gwil subtly eyed Alaia—Oldrin were not allowed on the monastery grounds, much less inside their buildings.

"I'm going in too," Alaia said, pushing past him. "Been here before anyway," she mocked.

Gwil shrugged beneath his robes.

Lago rushed up the staircase of the octagonal tower, and as he reached the last steps, he spotted Crysta and Khopto leaning on the northern window next to a small woman with short black hair.

"Crysta!" he said. Crysta turned, dumbfounded. Lago dropped his bag and ran to her, taking her in an embrace.

"Where?" Crysta gasped. "I... I was so worried about you! Where have you been? Are you hurt? Did someone—"

"I'm okay. It's a complicated story, but I'm so happy to see you."

Khopto limped forward, aided by a cane. He put his free arm around Lago. "Glad to see you in one piece! I was certain you died when you fell down the lift. We looked everywhere for you!"

"I'm so sorry, Khopto," Lago said, glancing down at the monk's limp leg. "I'm guessing that was my fault."

"Not your fault, but that of the man who shot the arrow—it sliced right through a tendon, but I'm fine. No one else was hurt, other than Hesefer. She got a black eye when she tried to stop that scumwad from leaving."

"Lago, you have to tell us—" Crysta began, but Lago stopped her.

"Soon. First, I need to know if we are all safe here."

"Safer than in town, that is for certain," the short woman said. "I'm Kedra. Heard a lot about you, Lago." She offered her hand; it was tiny and calloused. Her smile was missing an incisor, making her look rather endearing and childish. "I'm a scout, among other things," she added, while avoiding any mention of her and Crysta's involvement with the military, something they kept confidential. "The attacks haven't made it past the rampart, but catapults have set buildings ablaze beyond the fortifications. We were up here keeping an eye on things, but every time the smoke shifts it makes it impossible to see the battle."

Ockam stepped forward. "Before we get ahead of ourselves, it's time for introductions. My name is Ockam Radiartis. I'm a scout from the Free Tribelands. My brawny companion here is Jiara Ascura. She's a platoon commander, and sometimes high warden, when she's not abandoning her posts."

Jiara punched his shoulder. "We were stationed at Thornridge," she added.

"Essence of one, soul of the many," Gwil said, linking his arms in a circle and bowing over it. "I am the chaplain at this chapter of the Congregation." He tilted his head toward the monk with an aquiline nose. "Khopto is a talented scribe who works with us at the Haven."

"I'm Lago's big sister," Alaia said. "Name's Alaia. Hey, this place looks a lot messier than last time I was here," she pointed out, making Gwil's brow drop suspiciously. Lago elbowed her.

"I'm Professor Holt," Crysta said. "Let's just get on with this."

"Can you tell us what's been happening here?" Lago asked.

"They began the attack over a week ago," Gwil explained, "but they were just testing the waters. They tried one breach at the Loomdinn Gate but quickly retreated about three days ago. They can't properly besiege us, so I believe they are preparing a larger attack."

"I wouldn't worry too much," Crysta said. "The Halfort Rampart has been reinforced—it would be impossible for them to breach it."

Ockam leaned against the northeast window. The light was dimming once more, with the smoke blowing intensely in their direction, and although he could not see all the way to Withervale proper, he could clearly spot the thick line of the newly fortified rampart. "That is one massive wall."

"For the past several months they've been making the rampart taller, thicker, much more secure," Kedra said. "It's well guarded. We are safe here, for now."

"What about the monks?" Lago asked.

"Most are tending the wounded down in the Harrowdale Temple," Gwil replied. "A few remain up here with us, preparing medicine."

"I'm still worried," Lago said. "Do you have any sort of escape plan?"

"We are all packed and ready to flee, if it comes to that," Gwil answered. "The Old Pilgrim's Road could take us out safely, although we'd have to walk, for it might prove hard to find a wagon in these circumstances."

Crysta cut in. "My son, Corben, he has *Skyfarer* docked at the west end of the shipyard."

"*Skyfarer*?" Lago asked.

"His catamaran. It's well hidden behind a wall. He already took his sister and my husband west, to our old home in Needlecove."

"And why haven't you gone with them?" Lago asked.

Crysta did not want to speak of the sunnograph in front of the strangers, wary of revealing the method of communication with light she used to keep Zovaria informed, so instead answered, "Corben has been waiting by the shipyard every evening, in case things take a turn for the worse." She glanced at the entire group. "His catamaran is large enough for all of us, if needed. It's a fast vessel, and he's competed in many races." She looked back at Lago. "Does that ease your worries enough? Will you tell us what is going on now?"

"Maybe," Lago said. "Crysta, could you come with me for a bit?"

He took Crysta halfway down the spiral steps so they could converse privately. "Sorry for being so secretive," he whispered, "but I need to know if we can trust everyone we are with. I trust Jiara and Ockam with my life, and no need to mention Alaia."

"Yes, you can. Kedra is the scout I hired many times in the past, for my research. I've trusted her with things I haven't even trusted *you* with."

"You mean your work for the military?"

"How do you know about that?"

"I'm not daft, your codes aren't hard to figure out. You are simply replacing words and switching your numbers from base ten to base sixteen. And I guess that extra 'calibration' knob on the sunnograph has something to do with that job."

"I'm… so embarrassed. Sorry I had to hide that from you. And was I really being so obvious?"

"Yeah, but I don't think anyone else could notice. They didn't work so closely with you."

"If anything, I didn't tell you because it would have been dangerous." She placed a hand right under his ear. "I'm so relieved to see you are well. My heart broke when you disappeared, and… Sorry, this isn't the time."

"Missed you too," Lago said with an earnest smile. "Anyway, my secrets might be a bit more complicated to explain, but if you say it is safe to talk openly, I'll trust you."

They rejoined the others upstairs and sat around a desk. Lago began to tell their story, with Alaia adding critical details whenever he too hastily skipped over them. When he mentioned Agnargsilv, Kedra perked up.

"You really had it?" she asked, not hiding her surprise or excitement. "They took the mask from you, then?"

"No, we managed to escape."

"But… their new monarch, the Red Stag, they say he has the mask you described. That he used it to kill Emperor Uvon."

"That is Urgsilv, a different mask. There is more than one. Many more."

Lago carried on with his story. He carefully avoided lingering on the subject of Bonmei's death, so as not to upset Ockam, then described how they reached the Stelm Bir temple and later the Firefalls. He explained why they'd been away for so long, waiting for the snow over Da'áju to clear, and how they found Urnaadisilv with the help of Banook, although he did not dare get into the details of his relationship with the bear. When he explained that Banook was a Nu'irg, and mentioned his journey into shapeshifting and his new halfform as Sterjall, he began to lose them to their incredulity.

He glanced to Ockam for support. Ockam nodded to him.

They both reached into their bags and retrieved the two Silvesh. Bewilderment and awe transfixed Crysta, Gwil, Kedra, and Khopto.

"I know you don't believe all the stuff we've told you," Lago said, "I can see it in your faces. So let me show you instead."

He stood, loosened the drawstrings on his collar, stepped out of his boots, and popped the magnetic buttons on the back of his trousers. He put Agnargsilv on and let himself shapeshift slowly. He took his time, just as Banook had done the first time he'd demonstrated for them, letting them all see the threads, the refracting, liquid-like smoke, the way it all coalesced into a new form. His captive audience stared in amazement, frozen in their chairs.

Sterjall took a step forward. "This is also me, Sterjall. It's the name Banook gave me. It means *star-heart*. I thought you might like that, Crysta."

She croaked an incoherent mumble of approval, then leaned forward and mouthed, "May I?"

Sterjall let her inspect his pink-padded handpaws, his long whiskers, the softness of his black tail, then sat back down. Gwil and Khopto reached across the desk to awkwardly feel his fur, but Kedra kept her distance, still uncertain what to think of the black-faced half-wolf.

"It's really—but how can it..." Crysta stammered.

"I know," Sterjall said. "All those stories you read—well, maybe not all of them—they are true. And you can keep staring, but at least close your mouth a little bit."

Ockam pushed Urnaadisilv over the table, always keeping a hand over it, but then pulled it back to his chest. "I will let you hold it if you are careful with it," he said. He pushed the mask out again and let go of it. Khopto was the first to pick it up.

"Just don't put it close to your faces, please," Ockam warned as the mask was passed around. "It would be a most unpleasant mistake."

Crysta reached for a loupe from a nearby shelf and leaned it over the bulging brow of the ursid mask. "This is so finely carved," she said, one eye glued to the brass and glass device, the other still trying to peek at the wolf from time to time. "Or rather, it doesn't look like it was carved, but woven filament by filament, as if they were knotted together like a filigree. This is the most magnificent artifact I've ever seen! I... I have an old friend in Zovaria, Artificer Balstei Woodslav, who studies the aetheric elements. He would strangle Takhísh himself for a chance to study such a marvel."

"So, you also think the aetheric elements have something to do with this?" Sterjall asked.

"At least soot," Khopto said. "Balstei and I were chatting a few months back. He suspects quaar is a crystalline arrangement of pure soot particles. That could mean your mask is made of aetheric carbon, if his guess is correct."

Sterjall had already suspected something of the sort, but now felt the pressure of knowing his mask was even more valuable than he could conceive of. He swallowed, cleared his throat, and said, "That reminds me, thanks for that bottle of soot, Khopto. It bought us the canoe we used to cross the river."

"That was worth a lot more than a canoe!" Khopto grumbled, a bit insulted.

"You gave him what?" Gwil croaked.

"Where were we?" Khopto asked Sterjall.

Kedra had the ursid mask in her hands now. She looked to Ockam and said, "So, if you were to put this on, you'd turn into a bear?"

"Not quite. I've barely begun using it, and I have not had time to find myself in the way Lago has found Sterjall, so you will not see a bear today. But I've learned to control the pain and to see the threads."

"Oh, and there's also this," Sterjall said, unsheathing Leif. "Banook and Ockam made it for me. The hilt is part of that structure I described, from the temple at Stelm Bir the Negians destroyed. Be careful, the blade is extremely sharp."

"Obsidian?" Crysta asked, taking the blade by the pommel carved with the wolf and bear heads.

"Senstregalv," Sterjall answered. "Inserted around a dire wolf fang. It's much more durable than it looks."

As they passed the dagger around, Sterjall saw each of their threads pulled through the black, spiraling tube that made its grip, pushed out the other end as if by a strong current. He described the effect to them.

"So carefully engineered," Crysta said. "You should take this to Balstei as well. I trust him, and he'd be able to run some experiments. He's in Zovaria now, he has a lab at the institute. If you mention my name, he'll lend you a hand. Actually, he knows about you anyway, sort of…"

"How come?" Sterjall asked.

"When you disappeared, we heard rumors about the mask. Well, Gwil did. And it got me curious. I asked Balstei to bring me his papers on quaar and any books mentioning the Silvesh, though they weren't too helpful. I told Bal about you then. If you can, go see him."

"I would not mind a detour through the pink city," Ockam said, "it's on the way to the Moordusk Dome." He peered toward the darkening windows. Sunnokh was already dipping his toes in the Isdinnklad, turning the smoke outside a sinister, saturated red. "But there's something else we thought you could help us with," he said, producing the map of Noss he'd copied at the Da'áju temple. He placed the two pages on the table, lining up the pieces side by side. "This, I think, is something you'll be very interested in," he said, looking at Crysta.

"What is this?" she asked, excited as a child seeing a treasure map.

Ockam pointed at the red markings on his drawing. "If you count the domes on this map—they are these glyphs here—there's a total of eightee—"

BOOM, came a not-so-distant rumble.

"What was that?" Alaia asked, being first to rush to a window.

Through the stinging particulates of the red-tinted smoke, right where the Halfort Rampart rose, a pile of dust was billowing. They couldn't see much detail, other than soldiers fleeing from a cracking portion of the rampart like tiny ants.

"Siege weapons..." Ockam mumbled, pointing at a shadow that crawled slowly through the dust, with a Negian platoon standing at attention behind it.

"What is that thing?" Crysta asked. She aimed the telescope to the weakened section of the rampart and locked the extension tube Artificer Balstei had constructed for it. "That's not a machine, it is... That is..."

Sterjall pushed her out of the way to look through the device. "A giant elk? It's charging toward the wall!"

BOOM!

The wolf stared in awe as the antlerless megaloceros—the largest species of cervid to ever stomp their hooves on Noss—backed away from the cracking wall, head splattered in red, then readied for another attack. She ran at full speed again, but instead of crashing through, she shrunk, pulling with her a cloud of dust and smoke, and in a vanishing blur leapt through the crack in a smaller form, that of a deer covered in flecks of white, only to reform into the giant megaloceros once on the inside.

"It's the cervid Nu'irg!" Sterjall said. *Sovath*, he thought, remembering the name Banook had taught him. *He said her primal form was that of a chital, a spotted deer.*

The others could see her too, no telescope needed: Sovath was trampling the internal defenses of the rampart.

"There are more coming, up there!" Sterjall warned, witnessing a line of giant elk breaking through the smoke, half of them crowned by colossal antlers. Alongside the megaloceroses marched the enormous cervalces stagmoose, a troop of war caribou, and various species of deer. The mindlocked creatures slogged through spasming muscles, as if trying to shake biting insects off their hides.

"She's headed back to the rampart!" Alaia warned, seeing Sovath retreat to the hole she'd made in the wall—she had finished vanquishing her enemies and was now kicking hard at the weakened wall, shattering it further.

Bells from the rampart towers began to toll, joined by horns across the city, then by the louder bells of the Haven.

"That's the signal to evacuate," Gwil said.

"We need to get out of here, now!" Sterjall ordered, picking up his bag.

"Wait!" Jiara said, who had just pushed her way in to look through the telescope, aiming it toward what seemed to be the focus around which all the animals and soldiers gathered. "There is more trouble coming. It's that fucking Red Stain."

There he was. Surrounded by his private guard of arbalisters, the Red Stag was marching toward the toppled rampart, followed by a relentless army of humans and cervids alike.

"It's him. General Hallow," Jiara added, letting Sterjall take a look. "And that group around him looks like—"

"Fjorna and her squad," Sterjall said. "How in the Six Gates did they escape? Lodestar guide us, there's more. The fuck is that thing? Walking next to the Red Stag, there's a man who looks like... what? A giant badger?"

"How did they get another mask?" Alaia asked.

"The Lequa Dome..." Ockam mumbled.

The leading colossi charged, slamming into the rampart and demolishing a substantial portion of it.

"We can't waste time here," Sterjall said. "Hurry, now! We have to flee before too late!"

Crysta grabbed a notebook and began to jot down information. "I have to report this to Zovaria, it's crucial that—"

But Sterjall grabbed Crysta's arm and dragged her toward the stairs. "There's no light for the sunnograph," he said, hurrying them along. "We'll all be dead by the time the sun rises. Let's go, now! Show us to where your son is waiting."

They hurried down the steps, with Khopto taking longer to follow due to his limp leg. Jiara helped Khopto keep his pace, but the monk was still slowing them down.

"Hide your mask," Ockam reminded Sterjall. "But keep it accessible—we might need it."

Lago put his mask away and looked to his side as he ran into the courtyard, spotting several monks fleeing the nearby Haven.

They hurried down Runestone Lane while the bells of the monastery continued tolling their mournful dirge. The few people still left in the mesa scrambled out, dragging bags, children, and pets with them.

Thundering rumbles resounded in the distance; more portions of the rampart collapsing.

"Turn here," Lago said, "we can take the road behind the mines again."

"Wait!" Jiara said, stopping. "Look up on the trails."

On the mountain trail that led behind the mines, which then climbed up to become the Ninn Tago mountain pass, a long line of soldiers was marching. With the sun already so far down the horizon, the troops were barely visible, hiding in the shadows of the oak trees and granite.

"They do not move like Free Tribesfolk," Ockam observed. "Those are Negian soldiers. They'll block access to the road."

"Straight to the shipyard," Crysta said, "it's our only chance."

They ran as fast as their feet would take them. Jiara, Ockam, and Lago took turns helping Khopto, switching multiple times to share the load.

"Move, you have to flee, now!" Alaia called as they rushed through the Hollows. "The rampart has fallen. The Gray Pass is taken. Flee west and warn everyone!" While rushing through Riftside, not too far from the shack she had once shared with Lago and Bear, Alaia saw her friends from the mines in the distance, but they were far behind. She had to keep running, no matter how terrible she felt; she had to push on without putting the others at risk.

As they sped north, they found themselves surrounded from both sides. The Old Pilgrim's Road had just been blocked to the west, where the troops rushing down the Ninn Tago were taking the bridge that was the only safe way across the creek. To the east, massive antlers from megaloceroses rose above the cloud of dust from the toppled rampart, with soldiers pouring in beneath them. And as they got closer to the core of Withervale, up through the clouds they saw catapult-hurled boulders punching through, lit bright and yellow with sickly sapfire.

The city is lost, Lago thought, his eyes following the flaming boulders streaking across the sky, as if the Downfall itself had come to claim his world.

"Corben's ship is on the western end!" Crysta told them. "They haven't breached that far in yet. Stay behind the Zovarian troops!"

They followed a tide of Zovarian soldiers who were rushing to protect the port and the naval base, entering through the Alban Bazaar, where merchants wailed and tried to flee with precious wares weighing them down.

"This way!" Crysta said, stumbling into Fliskel Square, where Lago had seen the dead dire wolf six years earlier. The plaza was festering with a dense smoke that blocked the view, but Crysta knew her way. Cries of battle and the clashing of steel resounded closer now; then suddenly, as if birthed by the light of sapfire, Negian soldiers appeared out of the white fumes.

Ockam uncovered his quaar shield and made an opening by slamming through two soldiers at the same time.

"Keep going!" Jiara urged, landing three consecutive arrows in approaching enemies. She then pulled out her sword, parried an attacker, and kicked him back into the smoke whence he'd come. "Go! I'll cover your backs!"

With piercing spears, the Negians marched in, killing anyone they crossed paths with. Each of their silver breastplates had a red laurel embossed upon it, with a hand-painted red triangle dripping paint below, looking like the bloodied head of an elk. The soldiers exterminated methodically.

"Down this street!" Crysta said, turning left at the Harrowdale Temple, where the injured were being carried away in gurneys by the monks who'd been tending to them.

They did not follow the evacuation route but continued on the path Crysta was guiding them along. A battle raged right within the fortified harbor of the naval base—the Negians had breached through by water as well. Lago caught glimpses of Zovarian ramships going up in flames, their pink sails ablaze like portentous banners of loss and ruination.

"I'll take him now," Jiara said to Ockam, catching up with them and taking her turn helping Khopto.

"No," Lago said, pushing between them and wrapping Khopto's arm around his shoulder. "We need your swords," he told her and Ockam. "I hear more soldiers in front of us."

Both Jiara and Ockam pushed ahead to open a safer path.

They reached the edge of the shipyard, which was overflowing with Zovarian infantry rushing hopelessly in the opposite direction.

They were hurrying past slipways and half-built vessels when war broke out all around them. Ballistae and catapults from the Negian ships released enormous bolts and rocks to shatter the warehouses, the cranes, the docks. A war galley was unloading a platoon of lancers when it was met by a flood of Zovarian soldiers who fought back with passion and fear, but a blast of sapfire spewed out from a dromon ship, sticking to the Zovarians near the water. They fled, covered in flames, lighting up the skeletal ships and splintered structures around them.

"Run with me," Lago told Khopto. "I've got you, let's not lose sight of them." They found a rhythm while running on three legs, and were finally catching up to the others, when a pack of overgrown tufted deer charged straight by them, smashing through a formation of shield-bearing Zovarians. The deer leading the pack shapeshifted into a megaloceros and trampled a dozen more Zovarians before slamming into a shipshed and tearing through the supports of a tall crane. Despite her injuries, the beast continued on to crush the guards at the farther end of the shipyard.

Lago had barely managed to keep Khopto away from the stampede. "Let's go, before they come back," he said, and was just about to hurry ahead when the heavy crane the Nu'irg had crashed through tilted downward, its foundations spraying metal bolts in every direction. The crane fell slowly, but with titanic might, and demolished the shipyard's deck, crashing through the floorboards and into the waters beneath while hurling them all into the air.

Khopto, where is Khopto? Lago thought, dazed by his fall. He had lost sight of his friends.

Negian soldiers poured in, jumping the gap the crane had left in the deck. They were followed by crimson guardians—formidable Negian elite knights—who moved confident in their stride, safe under their thick, red-plated armor. A guardian was slashing his way into the shipyard when he spotted Lago on the ground; he swung his longsword at him. Lago barely rolled out of the way, letting the sword wedge itself into the fractured floorboards. In a quick move, he unsheathed Leif, stabbed the senstregalv blade through the knight's foot, and ran as he pulled the knife free, leaving the screaming knight behind him.

"Khopto!" he called out as he searched, but there was no way anyone could hear him in the chaos. He dodged soldiers—some with swords, some aflame—who could be Zovarian, could be Negian; there was no time to tell.

"Alaia? Ockam?" he asked the smoke.

He lost his sense of direction.

Two more crimson guardians breached through the clouds and came straight at him. Lago felt something push him from behind as a squad of Zovarian spear soldiers jumped over him and pushed the knights back. He landed next to a burning corpse, feeling the superheated flames too close to his face, smelling burned meat and fat.

He stood again, stunned.

"Jiara? Crysta?" he called, barely hearing his own words.

All he knew was that he needed to run away from the fire, but burning bodies were all around, adding to the confusion. He searched for his friends, but couldn't see through the steel, smoke, and jagged floorboards. He suddenly remembered his mask. He ducked behind the rudder of a half-built ship and took Agnargsilv out, immediately shifting into Sterjall.

As the crane impacted the floorboards, Alaia was thrown through the air. She recovered, helped Gwil up to his feet, and tried to find a path through the smoke and fire.

"Move, spur!" A Zovarian soldier slammed her with his shield. "Get out of the way!"

Alaia fell again, catching splinters in her hands. "Gwoli? Lago?" she called while regaining her footing. "Lago!" she yelled louder, hearing no answer. "Where is he?" she asked Gwil.

"I see Crysta ahead of us," Kedra said, appearing through the haze. "Perhaps he's with her. We must get to that boat."

They hurried onward, jumping over burning bodies who wailed at them like wraiths.

Crysta was still leading. She spotted her son next to a wall by the last slipway in the shipyard. She knew his catamaran was behind that wall, hidden from enemy eyes. "Corben!" she called out.

Corben saw her through the thunder of clashing swords and shrieking soldiers.

"Let's go, let's go!" Corben ordered with dread in his eyes. He ran to his mother and hurried her toward his vessel. "Don't stop, Mom!"

"Wait!" she said. "I have friends coming."

Corben recognized Gwil and Kedra, but the other people he didn't know. They all arrived from different directions, at different times.

The group gathered at the slipway and looked around.

"Where is Lago?" Ockam asked.

"I don't know," Alaia said. "I lost him when the crane came down. I thought he might be ahead of us."

"And Khopto?" Gwil asked in despair. "We need to go back for them!"

"We could not possibly see them through the smoke," Jiara said.

"I could," Ockam said. He handed his backpack to Jiara and took out Urnaadisilv. "Wait here and load the boat. Be ready for us." He tightened his grip on his quaar shield and put the mask on. But the pain around him he had not been ready for—he crumbled to his knees, feeling the anguish of so much death and despair. He nearly cried out, but held on, took the pain in, and let it feed his determination.

White-knuckled and tight-jawed, Ockam hastened back toward the massacre, brandishing his short sword as he ran.

Sterjall cowered behind the rudder. With Agnargsilv's sight, he tried to feel where he should go. It was impossible to discern what was going on: threads of connections tied together and broke apart, clouding his vision in a spiderweb of confusion. There was so much pain that he struggled to push it to the side. Behind a pile of eviscerated bodies, he saw a crawling, shaved-headed man.

"Khopto!" he called out. Khopto's ear was bleeding. His left arm seemed broken and torn. The monk dragged himself toward the wolf, using one arm and one leg.

Sterjall was running toward his friend when the hull of a ship exploded as a towering cervalces crashed through. He barely had time to hide behind a pile of splintered timber. The giant stag-moose came to a halt. He had red paint splattered over his wide antlers, dripping down to his head and back. The paint was mixed with blood. His hide quivered as if possessed by angered maggots.

Sterjall froze, afraid to even breathe.

The cervalces sniffed the air, spotted a group of fleeing lancers, and charged at them, followed by a torrent of what at first seemed like bears. But bears they were not—the creatures were a kind of giant musteloid, jarv wolverines, who slammed and slashed through anything that ran away, including Negian soldiers. The barrage of claws vanished through the smoke.

"Help…" pleaded a weak voice from nearby.

Sterjall's sensitive ears perked up. *He's still alive,* he realized, sensing Khopto with his mask. He had just left his cover to help the monk when he recognized the aura of a Silv not too far from him. *Ockam!* He thought. Yet the glow was not golden, but composed of tawny ochres and hazels, like that of rusty sand dunes. The aura moved closer, until a half-human, half-wolverine crashed through the remains of a wrecked hull, clearing the path by swinging a massive mace with his single arm. He was a tall creature covered in fur and armor splattered with blood. Seeing a helpless soldier scrambling to stand, he mercilessly crushed his torso with a clean swing of his spiked mace.

The wolverine spotted Sterjall and stopped, sensing the indigo aura; he hesitated, too surprised to react. Sterjall took the chance to rush past him to get to Khopto, trying to sneak in a stab as he ran, but the beast dodged the attack, then smashed his mace into the ground, splintering the boards and making Sterjall fall in a roll toward the monk.

"Hold tight," the wolf said to Khopto, pulling him over his shoulders as he scrambled away.

The wolverine swung his mace again—but even though Sterjall was facing away, he predicted the attack in the movement of the threads and took cover behind a wooden beam.

The mace crunched through the wood, hurling the beam into Sterjall's side. The mighty blow sent the wolf tumbling into the air, separating him from Khopto once more. Sterjall scraped his torso as he landed, hearing a bone snap out of place in his shoulder. Then the beam crashed into him, pinning his right arm under the devastating weight.

Sterjall clenched his teeth, not yet aware of the pain, failing to free his arm from the wreckage. He felt his shoulder twisting at an impossible angle, then saw blood pooling under the heavy beam.

Khopto had landed nearby, but Sterjall was so stunned that he could not even cry out his friend's name. He looked up and gasped in terror as the one-armed monster approached.

The wolverine leaned casually on his mace and said, "Is that truly you under all that fur, Lago Vaari?" His voice was grinding like a whetstone, heavy as his mace. "Quite an unexpected encounter, I must admit. We have not met, but I can see you in the same way you probably see me. I'm General Jaxon Remon. I believe you have something you stole from us."

Jaxon noticed Sterjall glancing at Khopto, who was trying to drag himself away. "Is this thing distracting you?" he asked. He lifted his mace and lowered it down again, crushing Khopto's head to a pulp.

"No!" Sterjall cried out in pain, for his murdered friend, for his crushed arm, for all the loss that would come from this cruel battle. He picked Leif up from the ground with his non-dominant hand and held it protectively in front of his face. He snarled, trembling with fear.

Jaxon chuckled at the weak display. "Hand the mask over and I'll bring you alive to face the Red Stag. Otherwise, I'll bring you in pieces. Your choice."

A catapult-hurled stone blasted through a nearby warehouse, distracting Jaxon for a heartbeat. Sterjall leaned in and swung Leif toward the wolverine's leg, but the general simply stepped sideways, letting the senstregalv blade cut only air.

"Feisty mongrel," he said. "I guess in pieces it will be." He lifted his mace and brought it down with a vengeance.

A black shield took the hit. Ockam had leapt from the shadows, taking the impact and tumbling out of balance. He immediately recovered and sprinted back toward the wolverine, smashing his shield on Jaxon's armless side.

"Run! To the boat!" he yelled.

"I can't. My arm is caught!" Sterjall cried, trying to pull himself out, wincing from the torture he was inflicting upon his dislocated shoulder.

Jaxon and Ockam parried, both too well trained, both sensing each other's intentions and predicting every move. The mace swung, tolling deafeningly on steel girders. Ockam blocked the sparks with his shield and struck again, but his sword seemed useless against the plated armor. Even with just one arm, this foe was formidable.

Ockam charged with his shield again, but this time the wolverine dodged to the side and let Ockam trip on the shaft of his mace. As Ockam fell, his shield flew away, toppling through cracks on the deck and landing in the water.

Jaxon stood next to Sterjall now, but his eyes were on Ockam, who was getting back to his feet. "Another mask? Where did—never mind, this will make for a very profitable evening."

Ockam rushed forward again, shieldless, fending off Jaxon's controlled attacks. He managed to strike twice on Jaxon's armless side, but the wolverine's magsteel armor did not budge. Jaxon shuffled his feet in a quick dance, spinning around Ockam, then kicked him in the ribs, sending him flying to where the crane had broken through the deck.

Ockam scraped against the floorboards and fell off the edge of the dock, losing his sword, barely holding on to the splintered wood while his feet dragged in the water.

"I see your cloak, Free Tribesman," Jaxon said, spinning his mace as he stared at his nimble assailant. "Who are you? How did you come upon that Silv?"

Ockam pulled his tired body back onto the platform, hands covered in splinters. His lungs had no air left in them after the heavy kick, and his tensed diaphragm refused to provide him with another breath. A rage boiled within him. Rage, fear, and hopelessness. But the rage was taking over.

The wolverine nearly pitied the struggling man, who could barely stay on his knees. "I'll get the answers from you later. But now, I have a bug to squash." He gave Ockam a sadistic, sharp-toothed smirk and slowly lifted his mace, shifting his gaze toward Sterjall.

Sterjall once more tried to yank his arm free. "Ockam!" he called, then looked up and saw the wolverine's swinging mace dropping toward him. He raised Leif to protect himself from the blow.

A roar exploded like a thunderclap as a bear leapt through the air and dug his teeth into Jaxon's swinging arm, taking them both down in a tumbling pile of fur and sparks. The bear slashed with his long claws while chewing on Jaxon's arm, twisting it and cutting through armor and tendons. Ockam's rage, his pain, his fear, they had pushed him not merely into a half-form, but into the full form of a feral grizzly bear. He mauled with manic, rabid anger.

From behind the bloody scuffle came a squad of arbalisters, readying their weapons. Sterjall barely recognized Fjorna Daro among them: the left side of her face had fused in odd angles and overlapping scars, with an eye now sagging lower in its shattered orbit. He had done that, he knew, back at Thornridge.

Fjorna's uneven eyes hadn't noticed him yet, being too focused on the ravaging in front of her.

Sterjall's heart sank like an anchor in the deepest seas when he saw, rising behind Fjorna, the silhouette of sixteen sharp tines from a crown of antlers, dark against the pallid-yellow fires. A crimson aura gleamed downward from the antlers, glossy and viscous, like half-coagulated blood.

The Red Stag stared at the pinned wolf, recognizing the presence of Agnargsilv immediately. He stretched a wicked smile over his long muzzle, then tightened his grip on his blood-streaked, wave-bladed longsword.

"Ockam!" Sterjall called, eyes locked onto the Red Stag's face.

The Red Stag stepped forward, but the wolverine and bear rolled in a clump of violence between him and the wolf, stopping his advance and leaving him confused as to what he was witnessing.

Jaxon hurled the bear away and tumbled backward, trying to lift his mace with his shredded arm. He shoved the mace into the grizzly's ribs, but as he tried to recoup from the strike, the bear snapped his jaws into the wolverine's neck, ripping his trachea in a bloody spray. Jaxon fell to the ground in a gurgle of bone-splintered blood.

The arbalisters loosed their arrows and bolts, lodging them into Ockam's side. The bear winced at the strike of each projectile and turned toward Sterjall, pushing the wooden beam off the wolf with his slamming shoulder, then biting hard into Sterjall's bag, dragging him by the strap. As he scrambled over burning bodies and splintered hulls, the arbalisters shot again, almost perfectly synchronized, piercing arrows and bolts across the ursid's back, thigh, and neck. But the bear ran faster than any human, dragging Sterjall toward the boat. They vanished through the smoke.

Corben saw the grizzly monster racing toward them, the sight of the beast chilling his blood with utter terror. He released the ropes of *Skyfarer* and pushed it off the slipway. The bear sprinted as more arrows dug into him. With a final push, he jumped off the end of the slipway and landed on the boat, pushing it forward as the eastern winds caught on the sails and took them onto the river.

The bear dragged Sterjall to the center of the catamaran and placed him down softly. He groaned, with dozens of projectiles sticking out from his bloodied fur and tattered clothes. He tumbled to his side in a pool of blood, breathing harshly.

Sterjall dragged himself toward his injured friend, his protector, with Alaia holding him from behind. "Ockam, no… Stay with us, please. Turn back to yourself. We will help you, Jiara will take care of you. Just turn back, just turn back."

Jiara kneeled. The bear lifted his head and looked at her, recognizing his old friend. Blood dripped from his thick-furred neck and bubbled through his black nose.

"Hold tight, I'll get you fixed up," Jiara said. She touched the arrows, feeling for a way to remove them, but the bear shook his head and dropped it back down again.

"Ockam, stay strong," Sterjall mumbled as he wept. "We'll get you to safety, just… just hold a bit longer." He caressed the bear's muzzle, then felt a warm tongue tenderly licking his handpaws. "Please, I can't do this without you. You have to be brave, and, and… Don't leave us, please, I can't—"

The bear placed a paw over Sterjall's leg. He looked at the wolf, at the boy, at his son, with proud eyes that were as dark and sparkling as obsidian, and he seemed to smile. He closed his small eyes, then took one last breath before he died, peacefully shifting back to his human form.

Chapter Three

Successor

The Red Stag looked down at the wolverine's shredded throat; once the last gurgle bubbled out from it and the body went limp, the dead general shapeshifted into a pile of human meat. The very moment Jaxon died, all the wolverines he had mindlocked stopped their attacks. They had been conscious all along, but unable to stop, uncertain what the purpose of the bloodshed was. The traumatized animals ran away to freedom, killing anything that tried to stop them.

The Red Stag used the tip of his longsword to turn his friend's head around; the dark, sharp-snouted mask fell softly away from Jaxon's face. He squatted, his red-painted muzzle and antlers shimmering with yellow flames. With a hoofed hand, he picked up the musteloid mask, Krostsilv, which Fjorna had recently procured for him after killing the Jojek leader in the Lequa Dome.

"Jaxon," he mumbled, trying to make sense of his friend's death yet giving not a moment's thought to the countless others who had lost their lives that day. He looked around. Withervale was now his: the naval base, the coal mines, the Ninn Tago pass, they were all in the hands of his army. His fleet would secure all the ports along the Great River, and his slaves would take down the Halfort Rampart and rebuild it on the western edge of the city.

His eyes were drawn to a silhouette breaching through the smoke. Fjorna had returned after having chased the bear through the shipyard. She brought no bear or mask as an offering, but she did bring something wide and dark dangling from her arm: a shield. She stood next to Crescu and the rest of her squad, and said, "They are gone, Monarch Hallow. They escaped in a fast vessel. The attacker dropped this." She held up Ockam's quaar shield.

"Not exactly a Silv, but this is a fascinating artifact," the elk said, marveling at the perfect smoothness and the specular inlays that reflected from the shield's impermeable surface. "And they had two masks with them. The wolf one, and also a bear one. Only Yza's Shade knows where they found that, or this shield, for that matter."

The Red Stag slung the shield's strap over his shoulder, looked at Krostsilv, and then once again at Jaxon's corpse.

"It's a pity," he said. "Jaxon was most perfectly suited for this honor. I was about to surprise him with a new name and title after the battle. *Warmaster Dextral*, I thought. You know, for his right arm." He glanced at the others and got no response. "Well, never mind, I thought it was clever. His mask needs a wielder, swiftly, with no delay." He straightened his back as he faced the arbalister squad. "It's time I pass the honor to someone else I can trust and depend on. We have a long road ahead, and many more riches to uncover. For these tasks, I require loyalty, valor, and strength."

The Red Stag approached Fjorna, holding Krostsilv in his hands. Fjorna stood at attention and held her breath.

"You have been there with me during the last several months," he said, "protecting me, aiding me in taking back the lands that are rightfully ours. And for that, I thank you." He pushed Fjorna out of the way and took two steps behind her, toward Crescu. "Armsmaster Valaran, would you wear Krostsilv and learn to wield it? Would you accept the title of general, and take command of Jaxon's Third Legion?"

"Yes, Monarch Hallow!" Crescu Valaran responded, banging the shaft of his spear on the ground.

The Red Stag handed the mask to Crescu and turned around. "We will begin your training tomorrow. For now, let's move south and check the frontlines." He strutted away, with Ockam's quaar shield protecting his back.

The arbalisters marched behind him.

Fjorna gritted her teeth. Her disfigured temples made it hard to notice, but her jaw muscles were clenched like a vise. Her shaman, Aurélien, approached from behind and cautiously whispered, "Fucking men. It's always fucking men. Not a single woman general. Scorch their flesh, sixteen*thousand*fold. You deserved that mask."

Fjorna stared straight ahead and walked, saying not a word.

Chapter Four

Isdinnklad

The might of Sunnokh rising made the winds pick up, billowing *Skyfarer*'s sails and propelling the vessel farther west. They had mourned all night, unable to sleep. Ockam's body was wrapped in a sheet, laid out in the open over the starboard hull, inescapable to any of their gazes.

Jiara had expertly pulled Lago's humerus back into its socket while avoiding further damaging his torn and inflamed forearm. "You might have a fractured bone, maybe two," she said. "But I'm more worried about infections. We need to get your arm cleaned, pull out those splinters. I'll make a sling for you until we can get a proper splint."

She sat next to Lago, leaning on the crossbar below the mast. Alaia joined them.

Kedra quietly dangled her legs over the port side. She seemed curious but didn't dare ask questions.

Gwil stood alone, his sleeves flowing like banners. He silently mourned the loss of Khopto and prayed that Esum and the remaining monks had escaped Withervale. But he knew that was unlikely.

Crysta conversed with her son, who was still confused. Corben had the same pensive face as his mother, same auburn hair, but trimmed short with an undercut. Crysta had spent all night apologizing to him, explaining the peculiar and tragic situation.

The cliffsides on the southern shore soon began to rise, stretching to hundreds of feet and taking on a powdery white coloration. They had arrived at the Ivory Cliffs of Needlecove, Crysta's birthplace. The chalk promontories dropped into elegant arches, treacherous sea stacks, and sharp points, dotting the Isdinnklad with precarious islets and bridges.

"We are close to my old home now," Crysta said to the group. "My husband and daughter will be there. We can stop to rest. And if you feel it's appropriate, have a funeral for your friend."

As the catamaran skimmed closer to the Ivory Cliffs, Lago thought he could see the ribs of a shipwreck inside a cove. He remembered Crysta's story of how she had found the ancient mariner's astrolabe by a wreck at these same shores, wondering whether that could be the very same ship. He yearned to take this beautiful moment to reminisce with her, but couldn't bring himself to say a word.

Skyfarer coasted toward an eroded channel that dropped steeply to the shore.

"The house is right up this cliff," Corben said as he moored the ship to a dead tree that leaned precariously by the shore. "I'll go grab help," he added, then hurried ahead on his own. Corben soon returned with his father and sister—Rowan and Eddena Holt—who helped them up the powdery-white ramp while carrying the burden of Ockam's body. The Holt family led them to a quaint, pastoral home with a dry stone wall that had been swallowed by moss long ago.

After Crysta's father's death, her elderly neighbor Sarina had moved into the Holts' home. She had kindly agreed to let the Holts stay with her when Rowan arrived a week ago, asking for shelter from the war in Withervale. She waited at her front porch, holding the door open as she leaned on her cane; her eighty years of life had left a toll on her body, but not in her compassionate nature.

Lago paused before setting foot on the porch and looked to the east. Sceres was in her first quarter, rising over the Isdinnklad during the daytime, with the Ilaadrid Shard shining as the Daystar. Her dress was of Pearl, shimmering with muted pastels that harmonized with the milky blue sky.

"She shines brightest when she's mourning," Sarina said, then ushered Lago inside.

The old woman took care of cleaning Lago's wounds, then concocted a splint and sling while Jiara sutured the gashes on his forearm.

"Your ulna is definitely broken," Jiara observed as she wrapped a bandage, "although it seems like a clean break. It'll heal. The radius seems fine, but it might also have a light fracture. You have to take it easy for a few months."

After Lago's wounds were taken care of, they sat around a small dining table. They did not speak of magic, or Silvesh, or quaar, or animal spirits. To protect her family and Sarina, Crysta simply told them she and some old friends had been trapped in the middle of the battle when Corben rescued them with his boat.

Rowan shifted uncomfortably, having recognized Lago's name. He stared at the young man as if wanting to ask about his disappearance, but Crysta subtly shook her head at him, urging her husband to keep quiet.

"Ockam sacrificed himself for me last night," Lago murmured, looking toward the front door; his friend's body had been lowered to the porch. "I would not be here without him. We would like to grant him a proper Tribelands funeral, if there's enough wood for a pyre."

"Of course, dear, back in the shed," Sarina said. "And you are welcome to stay, for as long as you'd like."

"Thank you," Lago said, "it'd be wonderful to get a good night's sleep. But tomorrow we should keep going. We are headed to Zovaria."

"It's a long way away, and you are injured," she questioned.

"I was thinking..." Crysta said. "Corben, if you wouldn't mind—"

"I don't mind," Corben said. "I can drop them off at the capital."

"And myself as well," Crysta said. "I have to introduce them to a colleague of mine at the institute. And there are things we witnessed in Withervale that I should inform some people about while we are there."

"There's no need to continue with that work, Crysta," her husband complained. "Withervale is lost. If you want to accompany them to the capital, I think that would be a kindness, but you and Corben will come back to us right away."

Crysta nodded to appease him.

They gathered firewood from the shed and from dried junipers that haunted the cliffside. They set up a bed of wood overlooking the Isdinnklad, then laid Ockam's body upon it. Once sunset gilded the crests of the waves, they unwrapped the sheet and let it drape over the logs.

Alaia approached the body first, holding her Pliwe figurine, that of the Oldrin goddess with three horns wrapped like crescents around her contorted back. "You were like a father to him, you know?" she said, eyes lingering on Ockam's tranquil face. "Thank you for being there for him. For us." Holding a candle, Alaia chanted a prayer for Ockam, the same prayer she had chanted for Sontai, and then for Bonmei.

Jiara went next, kneeling next to Ockam's body. She had been holding back tears the entire time but let them flow freely as she faced her old friend. She wiped her eyes and nose, then talked to Ockam for a long while, just as if he could hear her, recalling their adventures and thanking him for the most recent memories. While she spoke, she carefully braided ribbons with the five colors of the Free Tribelands: blue, green, gray, ochre, and violet. The knotted ribbons wrapped back into themselves to form a small wreath. She didn't have the proper offerings the Free Tribesfolk gave to the sprites during their funerary rituals or any of the eight sacred rocks the Khaar Du used in their rites, but the looped ribbons would suffice in their stead. She lowered the wreath onto Ockam's chest.

After Jiara walked away, Lago approached. He stood silently for a long while, staring at the sparkles of light across the vast lake.

I will not let your death be for naught. I will carry on, with your strength. He held tightly to a sharp object: it was Ockam's penannular brooch, which Jiara had insisted Lago should keep. The silvery brooch was shaped like a crescent Sceres, with a sixteen-pointed star representing her shard. Lago fastened it to his cloak, wiped his eyes, then took Ockam's cold hand in his. With a broken voice, he recited Ockam's litany:

"A young tree I am, the old forest I am not, yet forest and tree are of one soul. A small fish I am, the vast ocean I am not, yet ocean and fish are of one mind. A frail wolf I am, the strong pack I am not, yet pack and wolf are of one heart. Ockam, you were young and old, small and vast, frail and strong, and with you we all shared one soul, mind, and heart. Thank you, protector, for guiding me, for giving me another chance, for showing me purpose."

Sceres had crested in her heavenly arc, shining her shard directly above them, mingling her Pearl colors with that of sunset, of fire, of the radiance of her beckoning beacon.

Lago placed Ockam's kalimba over his friend's chest. As he let go of it, his fingers scraped the metallic tines, releasing a chord of warm notes. He set the pyre ablaze and walked backward as the flames reached up to the heavens. He was reminded of Bonmei's funeral, during their first day inside the Heartpine Dome. It was the same, but Ockam's music was gone.

Chapter Five

Zovaria

"Thank you, Sarina," Alaia said, picking up her haversack. "You've been too kind, and those drunken mussels were something else!"

"Just an old recipe from when I used to cook aboard trading ships. You are welcome back here anytime, dear. Be careful in the big city," she said, pointing at Alaia's nub.

Alaia nodded, then offered a hand to Lago, seeing him struggling with the strap of his bag and his splinted arm. "I can take that," she said. "You okay?"

"Thanks," he said. "I'm alright. But I might need a hand getting on the boat."

Crysta kissed Eddena and Rowan goodbye, then led the way. Her husband had a look of resignation in his eyes. "We'll be waiting. Don't be too long," he said, knowing better.

Corben walked alongside his mother as they made their way down the slope. "You are not coming back with me, are you?" he whispered.

"I'm sorry. You know it's more complicated than what we could tell them. Please, keep quiet for their protection, and place all the blame on me. Say I got caught up at the institute and decided to stay there a while. Tell your father that they are researching the Moordusk Dome and needed my help."

"It's okay, Mom, I'll handle it," Corben said with a smile. "They seem like good people. I'm sure they'll appreciate your help."

Morning had just broken when *Skyfarer* set sail.

Just ten miles west of Needlecove, the Isdinnklad Lake narrowed into the Northlock Strait, then opened up widely into the Isdinnklad Sea. The sea was choppier, but Corben was an expert navigator. "If the eastern winds keep up, we should arrive in the late afternoon," he said, leaning on the mast.

Zovarian ships passed by them, tacking against the wind as they headed to Withervale. One of them signaled flags for the catamaran to stop, but after seeing that the passengers were mostly fleeing Zovarians, let them through.

"Those must be the fleets from Umarion and Koroberg," Corben said as they sailed onward. "There are so many of them." He waved at the receding fleet. Some of the pink-clad soldiers waved back; the rest stood with blank eyes.

While the catamaran jumped the waves, they sat to discuss what to do next.

"Before the Red Stag breached the rampart," Jiara said, producing Ockam's map, "Ockam was about to show you this. It's a copy of a map from the Da'áju temple." She held the two halves side by side on the deck, protecting them from the wind. "Each glyph represents one of the domes. What we found is that there's one dome here"—she pointed to the Brasha'in Scablands—"that doesn't exist. We think it might've been swallowed by a lava flow."

"These glyphs, I've seen them before," Crysta said. "They were in one of the books Balstei lent to me. They were the names of different animals, I think. It's not phonetic, though they look similar to the runes in the *Miscamish Grimoire*. I have no clue how to read them. I wish I had studied that book before he took it back, but it didn't seem relevant. We'll ask him to fetch it from the library once we get there."

"After Zovaria, we are planning to go to the Moordusk Dome," Lago said. "The Miscam tribe inside the dome could teach us more about the masks. Maybe they know what happened to the missing dome."

"I'm all about pursuing quests for knowledge, but we are at war," Crysta said. "And that sounds awfully dangerous. Why go there now?"

Lago thought for a beat while massaging his throbbing shoulder. "If Monarch Hallow, the Red Stag, whatever you want to call him… if he's already stolen two of the masks, he's going to be searching for more of them. Even with his cervids, the Zovarian Union is too powerful for him to attack directly, but he can easily steal more masks from the Jerjan Continent, so he'll be marching east. He'll be unstoppable after that."

"We need to find out how the Silvesh work," Alaia said. "It's the only way to stop him. If he does to the other domes what he did to Heartpine, it would be a disaster."

"Aren't your two masks as powerful as the two he has?" Kedra asked. "With them and the support of the Zovarian army, we could take him down."

"I don't think using the masks for war is what the Miscam intended," Lago said. "And how can we be certain the Union won't also use them for the wrong purposes? More conquest, more war, it'll never end."

"And so many innocent animals would die," Alaia said. "We can't be using the same methods as the enemy, then we'd be no better than they are."

"On this, I agree with the young lad and gal," Gwil said. "I may not know much about these ancient artifacts, but I can feel the danger in them."

"Besides, if Hallow is going east, we'll never catch him," Jiara said. "Especially now that he holds Withervale and the Ninn Tago. Like Ockam once said, we should focus on learning more about the masks, and maybe find help not just at Moordusk, but the other domes as well."

"I know it's too soon," Alaia said, "but I feel like we should figure out what to do with Urnaadisilv. I think you should learn to use it, Jiara. Ockam would have liked you to be the one."

Jiara smiled tensely. "I'll admit I've always wanted to try it on, but... Ockam was the strongest of us. I always made a show out of being tough, while he didn't need to. The pain he felt when he put the mask on for the first time, it terrifies me."

"I've seen you take big hits without flinching," Lago said.

"It's... You don't understand," Jiara added. "We were captured once, together... And I saw him get tortured in the most horrible ways. He didn't wince, he didn't blink, he didn't give out any information after all those cuts. While I broke down right away."

"Yet you are the strongest warrior among us," Alaia insisted. "You are unstoppable with the bow, and you can climb like a bear already."

Jiara's brows dropped, but she nodded pointedly. "If Lago will teach me, I will," she said.

"I'll do my best," Lago replied, offering a reassuring smile.

"Thank you. Perhaps at a moment when we are in private, and where I can focus, I will try it out."

Corben whistled to get their attention. "Zovaria is right ahead," he said. He adjusted the sails, pointing *Skyfarer* leeward.

All their heads turned to look west. Zovaria, the capital of the Zovarian Union, was glistening pink, like a tourmaline carved out of the rocky cliffsides. The city rose in sixteen climbing levels called the *bulwarks*. The retaining walls of each bulwark were constructed from rose quartz from the Dianthus quarry, which shone a bright pink when the sun hit them directly, showcasing marbled filaments of white through their translucent interiors. Though only a handful of the bulwarks were fortified with towers and bastions, each of the sixteen levels were reminiscent of battlements due to the interspersed buildings, which from afar looked like crenelating merlons and embrasures.

"The institute is under the tall tower on the right," Crysta said, pointing at a spire capped by a golden cone on the north side of the highest bulwark, the tower of the Zovarian Academic Institute's School of Cosmology. A shorter but more opulent dome competed for attention to the south of it, one belonging to the Palace of Representatives, where the sixteen Arch Sedecims signed the many laws that kept the states united and prosperous.

"When you told me about the city before," Lago said, "I never understood how magnificent it was." He marveled at the parks and bridges, at the statues and waterfalls, at the density of structures and height of it all. "How are we getting all the way to the top?"

"We can hire a rickshaw puller," Crysta said.

"I'm not having a slave carry me in a wheelbarrow," Lago said.

"They aren't wheelbarrows. And the pullers aren't slaves. It's hard work, but they make decent Qupi in the big city."

They coasted by the Rose Marina: a set of piers outside the main city, set up for leisure near the white beaches of Zazara. From this close, the marvel of the Cliffside Lifts was on full display. On the promontory jutting out at the northern end of the pink city rose gargantuan columns delineated by a vertical gash in the otherwise natural outcrop. In the space between the columns and the promontory a series of counterweighted lifts were moving up and down, pulled endlessly by packs of Bergsulf bison.

"We'll take the lifts down later," Crysta said, reading the interest in Lago's eyes. "They offer a great view of the Isdinnklad, but not of the city itself."

"It's like the lift we had at the monastery," Lago said.

"Only a thousand feet taller," Gwil said. "Don't fall down this one, lad."

They arrived at the First Bulwark, where pink jetties extended into the Isdinnklad and opened into the enormous Rigmaul Harbor. Corben gracefully maneuvered the catamaran toward the entrance channel of the busy port, where hundreds of vessels danced in and out in an incomprehensible choreography. Gulls called out in their greedy cacophony, fighting for scraps amongst the fishing ships. Buoys littered the waters, indicating zones and directions that seemed arbitrary but that the sailors had no problem following. Lago could not understand how Corben found his way—the port alone felt larger than all of Withervale.

Corben whistled shrilly as he coasted to a dock, luffing the mainsail. "Hey Ben!" he said, tossing a rope to a young man. Ben grabbed it and hitched the bow to a cleat, while Corben secured the stern. The two chatted while the others disembarked. The last one to step onto the dock was Lago—Alaia gave him a hand as he hopped off.

Crysta shot a look at Corben, who patted Ben on the shoulder before joining his mother. "Remember—"

"I know, Mom. I'll stay with Ben for tonight, head back in the morning. You know where to find me if you want to go back. Please stay safe."

"I really don't know how long we'll be. Take care of Sarina. She could use help around the orchard."

"I will." He kissed her cheek and hurried to catch up with friends of his who were gathering down by the harbor.

The enchantment of the big city faded as they wandered in. Lago was stunned by the volume of citizens, but the port was filthy. The alluring scent of sea salt was swiftly overtaken by the stench of fish guts and overused cooking oils. Crysta told him not to worry, that once they entered the main gates, the city was considerably more glamorous.

"But you must be careful," Kedra warned, sharp eyes scanning the crowd. "Keep your bags in front of you, the flaps tied, and your eyes peeled. Those… things you carry are too valuable, and this city is teeming with lowlifes who'd snatch your belongings in a heartbeat."

"Kedra is right," Crysta said. "I will aim to take you through the safest districts, but no area is ever truly safe from muggers. Follow me and keep close."

Alaia was carrying Lago's bag, which she pulled to her chest like a mother protecting a newborn child. "Can you tell us more about the city?" she asked Crysta.

"I was just about to. We are now in the First Bulwark, which we call the Bailey, and it is where most people live. It includes the port and harbor, but also extends way out to the perimeter farmlands in the south. It's much more extensive than the fifteen other levels."

They headed down a main street that emptied into an ample plaza. Awnings, flagpoles, and columns flew pink banners brandishing the Zovarian sigil: sixteen white shields arranged in a four-by-four diamond crossed diagonally by a black spear, to represent the Shield of Creation and the Spear of Undoing.

The thoroughfare directed them to an enormous archway of rose quartz. Two rooted pillars flanked the gateway, carved in the likenesses of the Twin Gods, Takhísh and Takhamún. Vendors, merchants, and swindlers called out for attention all around them, selling quartz-carved trinkets, kitschy jewelry, and empty promises.

"This city was built before the Downfall," Crysta explained, "then dug out from the ashes. Back then, the hill had fifteen levels—the top level was added only seven hundred years ago."

"I've never seen a crystal so big," Lago said, approaching the portal. The keystone above him was a single crystal of rose quartz, marbled, translucent, and sharp in its polygonal splendor. If it hadn't been for the gull droppings coating it, it would have looked undeniably magical.

"That's nothing," Crysta said. "Those sculptures of the Twin Gods are each sculpted from a single block. That's the size *after* they've been cut down. They say the Dianthus Mountain, where the crystals were quarried, used to be sixteenfold more beautiful than the city itself."

"Used to be?" Alaia asked. "What happened to it?"

"It was chopped down and brought here. What's left now is the Dianthus quarry—nothing more than a pink hole in the ground." She walked on. "We are crossing under the Finflayer Arch," she explained, "and entering the Second Bulwark, right into the Artisan's Esplanade. It's much livelier on this northern end, where you can enjoy views of the Isdinnklad all around."

As they crossed the threshold, the landscape changed. The city behind it was vaster and more vertical than Lago had dreamed of. The patterns of the cobblestone roads mixed dark-colored rocks with the ever-present pink. The tall buildings soared too high to see the rooftops. Luxurious plants dangled and tangled from their balconies, bridging over the narrow, curving streets, bathing the cobblestones with ever-dappled light. Every corner had a bakery, a bookseller, a brothel, a guild, a smithy, or a tavern. Narrow hallways—called closes—separated the buildings and led to secret courtyards where children played, lovers groped each other, and old couples sat to read or argue.

It was a vibrant city of exquisite aromas and incessant music, where exotic lands and common folk blended together. They passed guilds on the Third, bazaars on the Fourth, and on the Fifth Bulwark strode across plazas sixteenfold larger than Fliskel Square from Withervale. Courtyards were filled with trees or open lawns, exploding with unnecessarily complicated fountains, or adorned with monuments to great heroes and great despots.

"We are nearly at Mistveil Heights," Crysta remarked as they neared one of many gateways to the Seventh Bulwark. As with all other portals of the city, the pink-carved forms of Takhísh and Takhamún silently framed it, both naked and grand, one with a shield painted white, one with a spear painted black.

"Are you still doing alright?" Crysta asked Lago, seeing him wince as he rolled his shoulder around.

"Yeah," Lago lied. "Well, it's been throbbing a bit, but I want to make it up on my own."

Crysta eyed him apprehensively, then took the matter into her own hands. She hailed a caribou-pulled carriage in which all six of them could fit, then directed the driver to take the scenic routes as much as possible.

Lago was silently thankful.

As they drew close to the grounds of the palace and the institute, the architecture became grander and more sumptuous. A long ramp took them straight into the Sixteenth Bulwark, near the Palace of Representatives and the Takh Basilica. Crysta flagged the driver to stop, gave him a handful of Qupi chips as a tip, and asked the others to follow her on foot again.

The Sixteenth Bulwark was entirely artificial, constructed mostly out of rose quartz, so not only were the retaining walls and the multiple towers and bastions pink, but so were the streets. The thoroughfares were quieter, as if conversations were best had with whispers, looks, and gestures in the academic and gubernatorial grounds. Each monument, archway, bridge, or passage was protected by a Union guard, always robed in light gray and pink. Their helms were tall and shining bronze, their faces bored, their legs fatigued, their swords dull.

A circular road looped around the perimeter of the institute's grounds, guarded by sixteen statues, each holding the emblems of their schools while their concave irises emptily searched for meaning among the clouds. Alchemy, physics, Takheism, and mathematics were followed by sculptures from agriculture, medicine, zoology, and mining. Farther ahead were the schools of metallurgy, the arts, warfare, and architecture, and also those of engineering, law, aetheric theory, and cosmology.

The pink capital was beautiful, grotesque, intimidating, and alluring. If fate or luck had not dropped Agnargsilv at Lago's feet, he would have been starting his first year studying cosmology in just a few more months. *This would've been my life*, he thought, and understood that his fortune could have taken him in such a path, and that he would have found a way to be happy, perhaps successful, or even famous. But now that he had seen so much more of the world—even though he had only witnessed a tiny speck of it—he knew that this was not his path, at least not now. *I don't think I could be happy here, despite it all. Not in this big city, as beautiful as it is.* He thought of the mysteries and unknowns ahead, of the cultures to learn from, the forests to become lost in, the oceans to cruise, the domes to explore, the men to love. He thought of the mountains and of Banook, and of wanting to continue on his journey so that he might someday return to the bear to tell him that he had followed the right path. *I will make you proud of me*, he thought as Banook's mountain song began to play in his mind. *I hope he knows that we can be together all along, when far apart he thinks of me and hears the mountain song.*

"I used to work up there," Crysta said, walking toward the gold-capped tower of the School of Cosmology. "It's a bit more spacious than the one in Withervale, and with such a view. I'll have to speak to the dean about returning to work there—I could help gather news with their sunnograph."

The long shadows of the statues crept up the pink walls of the campus. They were almost there, Crysta had mentioned, but Lago was tired.

They paused to rest against a balcony from which they could observe the city from above. Zovaria was bathed in a deep crepuscular glow. The pink buildings shimmered while the sounds of metropolitan life wafted up in the breeze to blend with the chatter of students, with the clattering of hooves.

Lago watched as Union guards lit the streetlamps using long sticks, their pointed helms shakily reflecting the blue flames.

"I don't see any wicks," he said.

"They are gas lanterns," Kedra said, who was as familiar with Zovaria as Crysta was. "There are vast peat bogs near Mirefoot. The peat builds up gas pockets underground. That's why Mirefoot burned twenty years ago."

"One flatulent explosion took it down," Jiara helpfully added. She had been to the big city before, several years earlier.

"Artificers found a way to pump the gas to Zovaria," Crysta said, "preventing those unpredictable fires while providing light and heat."

As the sky darkened, the city became speckled by the colorful dots of blue streetlights and orange candlelight.

"It's beautiful," Alaia said. "And immense."

"And you've only seen the tiniest portion of it," Crysta said. "Let's get going. Balstei's laboratory is in that round building, conveniently located between the schools of cosmology and aetheric theory. It's Sunnday, but he never stops working—I'm hoping we'll find him there."

The school's double doors were unlocked, as they always were. A few students came in and out, shooting odd stares at the group, particularly toward Alaia; it wasn't common seeing an Oldrin out in the open around the Sixteenth Bulwark. They headed down a curved hallway lined with glass cases showcasing mysterious instruments that had been invented or stolen by academics from the school. They turned a corner, and Crysta knocked on a heavy mahogany door. They heard a shuffle of keys, a click, then the door creaked open.

"Crysta? By Takhísh's Shield, what are you doing here?" the artificer asked. His dark mustache furrowed over his ashen beard as he peeked behind Crysta, scrutinizing her peculiar companions.

"Hey Bal. May we come in?"

Balstei tensed his muscular neck—if it hadn't been for his gray hair and out-of-fashion doublet, the brawny academician could've passed for any thick-muscled student in his thirties, yet he was twice as old and thrice as experienced. He nodded, then stood by the door as they entered, holding a deep frown between his bushy brows. "And Gwil too? So... Withervale?"

"Yes, we had to escape," Gwil said, bowing in the Havengall Congregation manner. "They tore through the new rampart. We barely made it out."

"Where is Khopto?"

Gwil took a deep breath. "Do you mind locking the door behind us? Let's sit down."

Chapter Six

Balstei Woodslav

Artificer Balstei Woodslav put out the light of the microscope he had been working with, then set coffee to brew.

Balstei's lab reminded Lago of the lab at the Mesa Monastery, but on a smaller scale. Optical paraphernalia, blueprints, precision tools, and alchemical reagents lay scattered about. There were sieves, grinders, presses, filters, and dozens more instruments tucked in niches. The black stone walls felt cold, but the space was warmed by the floors of polished, pink quartz. By the door was a corner lounge with creaky couches flanking a short, ornamented table. Books wallpapered the nook, illuminated by five blue-flamed sconces.

After brief introductions, they huddled in the nook and told Balstei the story of their escape. They were not sure how to bring up the issue of the masks yet, but they explained that Withervale was lost and told him of Khopto's death.

Balstei had his eyes closed, chin down. He rubbed on a pendant of a shield crossed by a spear while Crysta poured coffee for him.

"Khopto… this breaks my heart," he said, taking the mug. "Knowing him, he'll already be past all Six Gates. But I'm glad you all made it out. This is so terrible. But… Why are you here? Gwil, why aren't you at the Gaalem Monastery? And Crysta, didn't you say you'd be going to Needlecove if the war broke out?"

"There's something we need help with," Crysta said. "Remember months ago, when you brought those books for me? When we talked about Lago going missing?"

"And I see you've been found," he added, turning to Lago. "We hadn't met, but I saw you running errands in Withervale once or twice. Where had you been? I can tell you lad, Crysta was so worried about you."

"I was fleeing from Negian soldiers, barely escaped," Lago said.

"Glad to see you made it," Balstei said. "Gwil here seemed to think you were involved in something related to the ancient Silv myths. I remember how silly you—"

"I was. I am," Lago replied. "That's why we came to you." He opened his bag and took Agnargsilv out.

Balstei backed his body deep into his leather chair. No words came from his opened mouth.

"It's all true," Crysta said. "This… this is Agnargsilv, the canid mask from the legends."

Balstei darted his eyes around, unglued himself from the chair, and dared to lean in, wordlessly seeking permission.

"Please," Lago said, holding the mask in front of him. "But keep it away from your face."

While Balstei examined the intricate filigrees of the mask, the group quickly recounted how they came upon it and Urnaadisilv as well, then showed him the bear mask, Jiara's quaar rope, and Alaia's quaar helm.

"We thought you could help us understand how the masks work," Lago said, finishing the story.

"This is too much to process," Balstei replied, rising from his chair to pace around like a caged cat. "I'll tell you what I know, which is not much more than what Crysta probably told you. We think… I think quaar is the same as soot. Soot might just be a less organized allotrope of aetheric carbon, while quaar is a structured, crystalline form. How they crafted artifacts out of this rare element, I have no idea. We've only been able to partway purify it into a powder, never made it react in any exceptional ways."

He leaned down to grab his mug. It was empty. He sat again, then continued. "All these forces you talk of, I've glimpsed them, briefly. Or I think I did, because after the fact I could not quite remember what it all had felt like. Khopto would have been able to describe it better. I have journals filled with notes from his descriptions. But when you talk about transformation, you mean that metaphorically, don't you?"

Jiara's eyebrows gave Lago a here-we-go-again look.

Lago demonstrated. Sterjall sat in his stead. Balstei's jaw dropped once more.

After a choked, incoherent mumble and a struggle with a fight-or-flight response, Balstei continued, "I… I don't have any idea how this technology can be possible. It's more like magic, it's too advanced! I thought the stories were hallucinations induced by soot. There's so much to learn here! And this whole time, Lago, you can—"

"Sterjall."

"Sterjall. Sorry. Right now, you can see the threads? Consciously, clearly, this whole time while wearing the mask?"

"Not *see* them, exactly. It's like Khopto would have described it, a different sense, entirely new qualia. The threads are not made of light, but I can feel them, and they somewhat take the same mental space as what my eyes see, though they don't overlap. It's very hard to describe. It's like how you can 'see' where a sound comes from, yet the sound does not change what your eyes see, but the two senses are linked. But yes, the threads are there—yours, theirs, the masks', all present as long as I focus to see them, although they vanish if I stop paying attention."

"It's like an endless supply of soot!" Balstei said with a manic grin. "Could you imagine all we could discover with it? No more need to pay exorbitant amounts for a pinch of powder that will burn your nose and make you cough black phlegm. This would revolutionize our research!" He began to reach for Urnaadisilv, which had been resting on the coffee table. "Do you mind if I—"

"It's not a toy," Jiara said, pulling the mask toward her. "It's not a tool, nor is it something to be passed around to get high on."

Balstei leaned back in his chair, offended. He chewed on the corners of his mustache, but kept his composure.

"There's not much I can tell you," he said, "unless you let me examine them more closely. I'd love to study those carvings with my microscope."

Sterjall looked at Jiara and said, "It's fine, he'll just take a look."

They gathered around the heavy metal microscope. Balstei unscrewed a portion of the bottom platform so that he could fit Urnaadisilv under the lenses.

"Fascinating," he murmured. "These channels and grooves are not carved, but woven from extremely thin filaments, thinner than the softest spider silks. They knot and split back in all sorts of convoluted layers. There's so much complexity in this, and that's just the surface—I can't possibly begin to understand it."

Balstei let each of them have a look.

"There's something peculiar I noticed while looking at the threads," Sterjall said. "Both soot and quaar react with the threads in odd ways, shifting them in a jumble of lines, as if attracted and repelled by them. But when I look at Urnaadisilv, or have Agnargsilv look at itself, the threads interact with them in a perfectly ordered manner, flowing as if they are being consciously driven. I learned to read those shifts—actually, I think Agnargsilv taught me how to do it, if that makes sense. It's oddly intuitive, even if indescribable. And I don't mean I'm reading minds and thoughts, it's not like that, but more like understanding how someone feels and what their immediate intentions are. The same aligning and pushing of the threads happens around my dagger, Leif, though in a more linear way."

Sterjall unsheathed his dagger and handed it to Balstei. "Careful, it's extremely sharp."

"Dorvauros style? It must be ancient," the bewildered artificer said. "Where did you get this?"

"It's quite new, actually." Sterjall briefly explained how he had acquired the quaar tube, and how Banook and Ockam had crafted the dagger for him. "It's a senstregalv blade."

"Real senstregalv? Takh forgive us. How many more wonders have you stolen from the nethervoids? I've been trying to borrow a tiny senstregalv arrowhead from the Lerevi collection for years. It's so precious they will not let me touch it unless I travel there to study it at their museum."

"Agnargsilv shows me there is quaar within the crystal," Sterjall said. "We think that's what makes it so strong. I see filaments within it, and the threads line up to them, giving them a faceted shimmer."

"But obsidian is a compound of silicon and oxygen, not carbon. I don't think soot could crystallize with it. May I look at your blade under the microscope?"

"Be my guest. But don't let it cut your lenses."

Balstei positioned Leif carefully, then focused the mirrors to concentrate a light bright enough to shine through the sharpest end of the dark glass. He increased the magnification once. Twice.

"It is like you described. The glass has a lattice of dark filaments running through it. It's a bit imperfect, seems naturally formed, like the crystal itself. Perhaps not quaar, but something very similar to it. In most instances, aetheric carbon behaves like regular carbon, which makes it so hard to detect. This is a new kind of unique arrangement."

"Crysta told us you study soot," Sterjall said. "It is true th—"

"Crysta, what in the nethervoids?" Balstei complained.

"I thought they should know!" the professor answered defensively.

"The dean would take my research funds if he found out! We don't do no 'mystical nonsense' here on our academic grounds." He looked at Sterjall, then around at all the others. "Yes, I study soot, but don't you let your tongues loose about that. I'm not risking my tenure for anyone. The other aetheric elements are fine to study, according to the institute, but no talking about soot, oh no

Lerrs don't you dare, particularly next to anyone wearing one of these." He shook his Takheist pendant.

"They won't tell anyone," Crysta reassured him. "Don't get too flustered about it."

"What can you tell us about soot?" Sterjall asked. "And the other aetheric elements, how are they related?"

Balstei rubbed a leathery knuckle on his well-trimmed mustache, compressed his face into a knot, then relaxed, exhaling through his teeth. "These are things the academicians do not want to discuss," he said, "because everything related to the aetheric elements makes no sense in the way we understand the rest of the world. The only element they'd teach you about at school is magnium, since we use it for minting Qupi chips, and it's fairly well understood. But there are others, perhaps many more, that remain undiscovered. Each aetheric element is somehow related to one of our common elements. Soot to carbon, magnium to iron, ignium to oxygen, pharos to phosphorus, galvanum to silver, brime to sulphur, aether to hydrogen. There are a few more that are suspected, but it's hard to find any proof because they react almost entirely like their sister common elements, and only in certain combinations behave erratically."

"Please tell me you haven't been inhaling magnium particles," Crysta pleaded.

"I'll neither confirm it nor deny it," the artificer said. "But let's just say aetheric carbon is so far the only one of the aetheric elements that produces hallucinations."

"What do the other elements do?" Kedra asked, for she had never even heard of most of the ones Balstei had mentioned.

"Magnium simply shares magnetic properties with things it's alloyed with," Balstei said, "even if you use only a few particles of it. It's bizarre, because it doesn't change the arrangement of the particles in a Qupi chip, it simply imbues the matrix with its magnetic properties, and that holds it together a bit more tightly, creating a stronger metal."

He paced once more, as if perusing his lab would offer an epiphany. "The others are much harder to come by," he said. "Ignium burns with much more energy than regular oxygen, but it reacts normally in every other circumstance we know of. Dangerous substance, I wouldn't dare study it in a small lab like this one."

"Then there is pharos," he continued. "Pharos is equivalent to phosphorus, but it emits light when exposed to air or water. Although not forever—once it rusts, it takes incredible energy to break the bonds, so it effectively goes dark." He pointed to one of the blue flames that illuminated his laboratory. "If we had enough pharos, we probably would not need lights like these. And there's galvanum, aetheric silver, which has electrical properties. But we can't study galvanum either, since all sixteen crystals we know of are in the bloody scepters of the Arch Sedecims. Which one was I missing?"

"Brime," Sterjall said. "Banook told us about brime. He said it's like a rock that always stays hot."

"Yes, brime, or aetheric sulphur," Balstei said. "Quite rare and precious. They say the dukes of Bauram are so filthy rich that they use the yellow crystals to warm up their bedrooms instead of lighting fires."

"And aether?" Alaia asked, remembering another of the elements Balstei had mentioned.

"Aether is equivalent to hydrogen," Balstei said. "We don't know much about it. We can detect it only by its fluctuating mass, but we haven't been able to isolate it or figure out what properties it carries. You go and try to find some, see how hard it is to separate a few particles of transparent air from other invisible gases, see if they'll offer you grants to study what seems more like ghosts than real particles. It's not an easy field, despite the lofty promises it might inspire."

"Do you think these elements are related to the Silvesh?" Sterjall asked. "Other than soot, I mean."

"I do not know," Balstei answered, deflating a bit. "Not from what I can see on the surface. Your masks look like quaar, and quaar seems more related to soot. But maybe, if it is such a complex machine, its insides might have something to do with the other aetheric elements we know about, or ones we haven't even discovered yet."

Balstei went quiet for a moment, his brain searching for new connections.

"There's another thing we wanted to ask you about," Crysta said, interrupting his thought process. "Lago, do you ha—I'm sorry, Sterjall, I'm still getting used to this. Do you have that map you showed me?"

Sterjall produced Ockam's map and placed it on the table.

"Each of these glyphs marks the position of a dome," Crysta said, pointing at the red-inked symbols. "Do you remember that big, green book you brought me? *Interpreting Early Miscam Symbology* or something of the sort? I saw glyphs just like these listed there. Do you still have it?"

"I returned it already, and the library is closed, but I could get it from Simza in the morning, she's there early. What's this here?" he asked, already noticing the dome that should not be on the map.

"That's one of the things we want to look into," Jiara said. "Another dome was supposedly grown there, but we think it might've been destroyed by the

Laaja Khenukh eruption. We are thinking of going to the Moordusk Dome first, to see if we can learn anything from the Miscam tribe in there."

"You talk about walking into the ancient domes as if taking a stroll around the Third Bulwark!" Balstei said. He leaned down and counted the glyphs. Three times, to be sure. He pointed at the dome that should not be there and said, "I... I'm still confused by this. You say there were seventeen domes, then?"

"Yes, but eighteen masks," Lago said. "Urnaadisilv was at a place where the eighteenth dome was to be grown, but they decided not to do it. Right here." He pointed to the glyph marking the location of the Da'áju Caldera.

"But the Takh Codex speaks of sixteen emanations of Takhamún," Balstei complained. "Like our sixteen states and the divine power of the sixteen Arch Sedecims. Not seventeen, not eighteen."

"Bal, I don't know how to put this," Crysta said. "You know the Codex was written after the Downfall. Since Gweshkamir only saw sixteen domes, that's what he wrote down."

"But it wasn't what Prophet Gweshkamir saw, it was the word of Takhísh himself that was written into the sacred Codex. Gweshkamir was merely the vessel." He held tight to his pendant. "Two pairs twice doubled, that's the divine number. Not two pairs twice doubled plus two."

"Maybe it was a mistranslation," Crysta said to reassure him.

"But either way, we'll be traveling west for more answers," Jiara said.

"Don't you dare leave yet. Give me a few days, let me run some tests." He looked at Sterjall's badly injured arm. "You all look like you could use some rest, time to heal. I can borrow instruments from other labs. I have things to measure, places to probe."

"I could use some time tomorrow to visit Scholar Dashal," Crysta said. "He's the one who receives my sunnograph messages." She shared a look with Sterjall and Kedra, knowing they'd understand that she wanted to report on the military movements in Withervale.

"We could explore around the city a bit," Alaia said. "It'd be nice to take a break, finally. There's so much to see here."

Crysta agreed. "Bal, it's late, and we are tired. Could we stay with you tonight? And tomorrow we can find an inn around the Thirteenth." She put a delicate hand on Balstei's thick arm muscles, then pulled it quickly back.

Sterjall glanced at their tensely awkward interaction, not sure what to make of it.

Balstei softened to Crysta's pleading smile. "I don't have any room in my small dormitory," he said while unnecessarily combing his beard, "but you can stay here if you wish. Although I have no beds, just the few couches and a cold quartz floor."

"You have a roof," Jiara said. "That's a lot more than we've been getting lately. The couches will be a lavish indulgence at this point."

As he left for his dormitory, Balstei asked them to lock the door behind him. He warned them that he had only one key, which he would leave with them, and asked them to never leave the lab unattended.

During morning twilight, before Sunnokh or any of them had awakened, a bang resounded on the heavy mahogany door. They all jolted up, startled. Jiara pulled out her sword.

"Bestir yourselves!" Balstei's voice hollered.

Kedra unlocked the door for him.

"Here it is!" he said as he trampled in, shaking a large green book in his hand. "How are you all not up? Are you not excited to get started with this?" He bit on his lower lip, waiting for a reply.

They all grumbled at him.

"I couldn't sleep myself. There's so much to do, so much to learn. Come on Crysta, get your ass up. I had to fight my way through Simza's gossip to get this from the library."

They begrudgingly peeled their bodies from their bedrolls and couches and sat around the coffee table, spreading Ockam's map over it.

Crysta flipped through the voluminous book until she found the chapter with the glyphs. It was a long list of symbols, all in the same triangular style and complex design. They didn't appear to follow the Miscamish phonetic code but some other kind of seemingly logical pattern. A translation in Common had been inscribed right underneath each glyph, and the corresponding Miscamish phonetic runes below those as well. "Here we go," she said, "now we just need to... Wait, these aren't the names of animals, but the names of *types* of animals."

"It must be the clades Banook taught me about," Lago said.

"Lago, do you mind if I write them down on the map? Or should I use a clean piece of paper?"

"On the map is fine. It might come in handy."

"Good, then let's start with the obvious one, the Heartpine Dome. The runes beneath have four triangles, starting with an upside-down one, meaning a vowel. This is the word *agnarg*, which doesn't mean wolf exactly, but *canids*, like it's written here. Miscamish has some taxonomical underpinnings. From these derive *agnurf*, meaning *wolf*, or *agnist tago*, for *gray fox*."

Crysta slid her finger over the list of glyphs. "Here are the other two we suspected already, *urnaadi* for *ursids*, meaning *bears*, and *urg* for *cervids*." She wrote the two words on the map with very delicate handwriting.

Lago pointed at the glyph closest to Zovaria, which had a crescent-like shape inside the triangular form. "The Moordusk Dome says *felids*. That's exciting. I like cats."

"You are right," Crysta said. "And that's pronounced... min... minre... No, it's *mindrel*."

"I wish you had been with us at Stelm Bir, Da'áju, and Minnelvad," Lago said. "You could've translated all those runes we found."

"I might've been able to translate the sounds, given enough time, but not most of their meanings."

"Same with me," Balstei said. "I can read the phonemes, but only know the root words we use in academia."

"What about the dome that isn't there?" Alaia asked.

Crysta couldn't find it, so she flipped to the next page until she spotted a match. "That one spells *momsúndo*, which is translated as *proboscideans*. I'm not sure what that means. Maybe Mirek will know—he's the head of the School of Zoology, we could ask him later."

"Banook taught me about all eighteen Nu'irgesh," Lago said. "I don't recall him saying anything about"—he tried reading the word under the glyph—"*prob-os-scid-deans*. Or at least he never used that word."

"These are next to each other in the book," Crysta continued, "*avians* and *reptilians*, very different glyphs, yet similar rune spellings for them. They spell *kroowin* and *kruwen*. And kruwen seems to be right over Fel Varanus, the island where the dome grows so irregularly."

"Dragons..." Lago whispered to himself.

"Let's continue in whatever order we find them for the rest," Crysta said. "I'll write only the Common translations for now and do the phonetic pronunciation later. Some are really hard. Hmm"—she bit her pen—"this round one says *glires*, but it's expanded below as *rodents* and *lagomorphs*. I think they are closely related. This here says *suids*, I don't know—"

"That means *boars* and *pigs*," Jiara said.

"Thank you, I should've known that."

"I see one," Alaia said. "This one with horns translates to *bovids*, like bison and such."

It quickly became a game, seeing who could spot them first.

"*Perissodactyls!*" Kedra yelled, and they all looked at her as if she had lost her mind. "That's what it says on this one."

"I see," Crysta said, writing it down. "Hmm. No clue about that. Another one to ask Mirek about."

"This one says *primates*," Lago pointed out, "right in the Tsing Empire. And here's another one, *cetaceans*."

Alaia leaned in. "Isn't that like dolphins? Blessings of the Daystar! That's so thrilling!"

"And right in the middle of the Capricious Ocean, too," Kedra pointed out. "That's the Seafaring Dome. Makes sense."

"I got *musteloids*!" Balstei said, joining in. "What in Khest is a musteloid?"

"Don't know," Lago admitted. "It's over the Lequa Dome, in the Negian Empire."

"I think muste*lids* are otters, badgers and such?" Crysta guessed. "Muste*loid* must be something related."

"Some weasels in the Farsulf are called mustela," Jiara said. "Aren't they related to—"

"Wolverines," Lago interrupted. "That all makes sense now."

Balstei pointed at a new glyph and said, "This one on the Moonrise Dome says *pinnipeds*, another one for Mirek?"

"I know that one," Crysta said. "Those are seals, walruses, that sort of thing. Corben loves them. Just three more to go. I love doing this, actually."

"*Marsupials*!" Gwil shrieked a bit too excitedly—it was his first. "I don't know of these creatures."

"They are an extinct clade of mammals," Balstei said. "The institute has many fossils of them. Quite varied, some small as mice, some large as horses. They used to be widespread across the continents."

"Banook told me about them too," Lago explained, "he said they carried their babies in pockets they cut in their skin."

"That's revolting," Kedra said, then pointed out yet another glyph. "*Caprids* is this one, I think? Like sheep. Right on the Bighorn Dome. Figures."

"I see the last one!" Alaia yelled. "*Chiropterans*. Definitely no clue what that is." All the others shrugged with the same uncertainty.

Crysta finished writing all eighteen clade names next to their corresponding glyphs, then took some time to translate the Miscamish phonemes and wrote their pronunciation right below.

Lago scanned through the updated map. "The only three we aren't certain about are chiropterans, perissodactyls, and pruh-proboscideans. I'm trying to recall all the Nu'irgesh Banook taught me about, and the three we are missing are Estriéggo, the woolly rhinoceros. Fuuriseth, who is some sort of white bat... And Mamóru, who is a mammoth. They have to correspond to those three words, I'm sure."

"We need to make copies of this," Alaia suggested. "Imagine if we lost it. Better to have a few around."

"I'm used to cartography," Kedra said, "just get me some paper and I'll start tracing."

While Kedra made copies of the map, the others continued hypothesizing about the domes and studying the other glyphs in the book.

"There are so many more clades," Alaia said after a long discussion. "Like this one, *umult* for *cephalopods*, or this one for *coleopterans*, and whatever *ctenophores* are. I wonder why only eighteen of them were chosen for the masks."

"Because they are all mammals," Lago said with certainty.

"Have you ever seen a bird breastfeeding?" Jiara said.

"Hey, there is a species called the *voluptuous frigatebirds*," Alaia said. "Your melons would look like lemons next to theirs. But you are right, no milk in there. And reptiles aren't mammals either. Are dolphins mammals?"

"All done!" Kedra boasted. "I made one copy for each of us. Sorry if the outlines are a bit messy, but I think they are good enough." She handed the copies out while Lago safely tucked the original in Ockam's notebook, then announced, "I'm starved. Could we go grab breakfast now, please?"

"Coffee will suffice for me," Balstei said. "Do you mind if I stay here and begin the tests?"

"I don't want to leave my mask behind," Lago said. "Maybe once we come back?"

"Have you lost your senses?" Balstei exclaimed. "Carrying precious things like these in Zovaria? Unless you only stay in the Fifteenth and Sixteenth, you could be mugged at any moment. And I don't see you fighting any thieves with that broken arm."

Crysta noticed Lago's face flaring with distrust. "Bal is right," she said. "Zovaria might be sparkling pink on the outside, but once inside, it can be dangerous. The masks will be safer in here."

"It's true," Kedra agreed. "When I was a kid, I was one of the thieflings prowling the Terrang Harbor. That was until my uncle caught me and punched a tooth right out of my face." She grinned, showing the dark gap in her smile.

"But what if—" Lago started, but Balstei quieted him down with a broad hand gesture.

"I tell you what, I don't need to use the masks for the tests," he said. "I won't touch them, I won't even look at them. You can leave them in your bags, and I'll wait until you return so we can look at them together. But I could examine the dagger, which has the same structure."

"What are you going to do with Leif?" Lago asked.

"Nothing more than watch it through different types of lenses. I want to see if it responds to soot or if it affects the fields magnium creates. No scraping, no sampling, no damaging of any sort."

"He does know what he's doing, Lago," Crysta said. "Bal works with precious artifacts all the time. It's okay."

"Thank you, Professor Holt," Balstei said a bit too formally.

Lago unclipped the cedarwood and brass scabbard and handed it to Balstei with Leif safely tucked inside. He felt uncomfortable parting with it, but he knew he shouldn't need it while going out for a walk in the city—he wouldn't know how to wield it with his left hand anyway.

"There are some instruments I need to borrow from a friend," Balstei said, "and he lives across the bridge on the Third Bulwark, far south side of town. I will have to leave for a while, which means I'll have to lock the doors while I'm gone. I have the only keys, don't worry. Why don't we agree to meet back here at sunset? It'll give you all day to see the city, and I'll be back here long before then."

They agreed. Lago and Jiara made sure the masks were carefully tucked in their bags, then pushed the bags far into a corner where potential visitors would not spot them. Jiara placed a hair under the flap of her backpack, just in case, to check whether anyone had opened it while they were away.

Chapter Seven

Respite

"I prefer the back entrance to the institute better," Crysta said, leading the group down a spiral staircase that emptied into a quieter, hidden path through a rose garden. She pointed beyond the maze of thorny bushes and said, "But I mainly brought you this way because that is the School of Medicine."

They stopped by the apothecary, where Crysta bought medication for pain and inflammation for Lago, as well as a better-fitting splint.

"How about we try the Cliffside Lifts?" Alaia recommended.

Lago loved the idea, and Crysta was glad to comply.

They walked to the northern end of the Sixteenth Bulwark, then waited by the entrance to the lifts. The lines to go down weren't too long in the morning, with most people headed in the opposite direction.

"How much do they cost?" Alaia asked.

"They are free," Crysta answered. "Well, not really free—the taxes in the top fifteen bulwarks are outrageous, so everyone but the farmers in the Bailey pay for the service."

The fast-moving line took them to a tunnel carved into the original rock of the promontory, which was not rose quartz, but darkly textured granite. They were ushered into one of the magsteel-forged lifts. The heavily ornamented gates locked.

They descended in darkness for several levels, but then the view opened up brightly as they breached into the Twelfth Bulwark. They were no longer in a granite tunnel but suspended in the air. North of them was a vertigo-inducing view of the Isdinnklad, framed by two of the four columns that supported the promontory above them. The columns were covered in a mosaic of pink tiles, with missing tiles here and there revealing their true, darker color underneath.

"They didn't raise these columns," Crysta explained. "They were part of the outcrop. All they did was carve the space around them and then covered them in pink tiles so they would look like they were made of the same rose quartz as the retaining walls."

They exited the lift at the Artisan's Esplanade, on the Second Bulwark. They took a stroll along the northern cliffside, where men, women, and allgenders patiently fished for mackerels and groupers, then continued to the upscale Terrang Harbor on the west side, from which they had a clear view of the Moordusk Dome, only sixty miles southwest of the pink city.

They found a cozy cafe named Dee-Ngo's Hideout near the busy Tavern Quarter. They sat in a snug corner filled with colorful cushions and studied the exotic but inexpensive menu. Lago ordered Kam's Special, which consisted of a black-dough waffle with sides of Brilfond basil, goat cheese, and warthog bacon, topped with a fried quail egg. Alaia tried the hotcakes with spicy arson mushrooms and had to order an additional glass of bison milk to put the fire out. Crysta settled for comforting tea and pastries, Gwil for a sweet potato bowl, and Kedra for a savory omelet with lightly brined olives from Lerev.

They almost felt guilty for feeling so relaxed after all the death and pain they had experienced. After all they had endured, they welcomed this moment around a comfortable table, laughing with friends and watching the unfathomable diversity of people passing by. It seemed an inconceivable luxury.

Alaia felt strangely at ease. Up at the institute she'd been getting a lot of dirty looks, and she still got some from a Tharman peddler who had traveled down the lift with them, but at least in this busy cultural watering hole, being an Oldrin wasn't much to be concerned about.

They tipped generously, leaving a whole Horn, two Qupis, and a sprinkle of Lodes for the waiter, then walked out into the jostling street.

"What should we do now?" Alaia asked.

"Children, I must get to the Gaalem Monastery," Gwil said. "My friends there need to hear the sad news. And do not worry, our secret is safe." Gwil looked at Lago. "If you need anything at all, you'll find the monastery in front of the Forlorn Castle Tavern. Big tower, easy to spot. They'll let you in if you show them the bracelet Khopto gave you, which I'm very happy to see you are still wearing."

"You're still not getting me converted, Gwil," Lago replied with good humor.

"The future always holds surprises," Gwil said, then regarded the others. "I do not know if I will be able to return to Balstei's lab before Sunnokh sets, but if you don't see me then, I'll stop by in the morrow. Essence of one, soul of the many."

Gwil tried to offer his Havengall bow over his looped arms, but Lago interrupted him by giving him a hug.

"I have to visit Scholar Dashal, the one I sent the, y-you know, those messages t-to," Crysta stuttered, completely incompetent at being secretive. "I'll meet you at the lab by sundown."

"Gotta go too," Kedra said. "I have family who live at the Arcane District. I have to let them know I'm safe. Moon lights."

"Stars guide," they replied as one. That left just Lago, Jiara, and Alaia, who decided to stick together, like they had before.

They walked the cobblestone streets and explored the closes and courtyards, which led them to long stairs with magnificent views of the sea. Alaia suggested visiting the museums, but they figured it would take too long, so they decided to leave that for another day. Instead, they tasted street foods, listened to bards perform out-of-tune ballads, and watched fish swim in colorful spirals at the ponds of the Third Bulwark.

Their exploratory trek took them in a wide circle, leading them back to the Artisan's Esplanade by the early afternoon. Their tired legs begged for rest.

"Well, this place sounds fun," Jiara said, stopping in front of a rowdy tavern named Surly Gals. She dragged them in for a drink.

"Should we get the sampler?" Alaia recommended. "That way we can try all the ales at once."

Lago and Jiara loved the idea.

"Hey, sweetheart," Jiara said, flirting with a pear-bodied waitress. "One sampler please. I'd like a taste of all that you have to offer."

"I hope you give her a good tip after that," Alaia said.

"I'll give her anything she wants."

They moved to a cozy corner table where Lago could more easily rest his splinted arm. He got a bit buzzed from the sampler, not used to strong drinks. The rumbling and laughter from the crowds, the clinking of glasses, the floral, herbal, and tropical aromas from the mixed drinks; it was all intoxicating. With the safety of the company of his friends and the pounding of his shoulder, Lago felt exhausted and began to doze off. A jumble of thoughts spiraled into a daydream. *A frail wolf I am, the strong pack I am... but wolf and heart are of one... wolf. Wolf and soul... The alpenglow on snowy peaks calls forth... calls...*

belong. Ockam. Listen to the granite, I hear the mountain speak, I hear the... *Wolf song*... I—

The shattering of a bottle shook him awake. It was followed by laughter from the patrons. "You okay?" Alaia asked.

"Yeah, sorry, I'm just so tired," Lago answered, a layer of sweat glistening on his forehead.

"If we can get Jiara off that poor woman's ass, maybe we can head back a bit earlier and take a nap on those comfy couches Balstei has."

"That would be really nice."

They finished their drinks and dropped some chips on the table.

"Come back soon!" said the waitress.

"I'll come for you anytime!" Jiara replied, walking out surprisingly well balanced after having engulfed so many drinks. "Sorry for that spectacle, kids. Lago, are you feeling alright?"

"Just tired, and my arm is hurting. The new splint feels a bit tighter."

"Let's head back then," Jiara said. "The lifts aren't too far. It's early, but I'm guessing Balstei might be back by now. I'm sure he's keeping himself quite busy."

There was a long wait for the lifts, filled with impatient denizens peeking over the shoulders of those ahead of them. After about a wick of waiting in line, an Oldrin with spurs protruding from his muscular shoulders stopped by their side, sensing the wayfarers were not locals. "Something's holding the lifts up at the Sixteenth," he said. He nodded toward his rickshaw and added, "I'll give you a ride for merely two Cups. Make it a Cup and a Hand—a discount for the gal with the charming spur."

Alaia beamed and pulled her friends toward the rickshaw, sitting in the middle.

"Fast or scenic?" the puller asked.

Alaia looked at Lago for confirmation.

"Fast is fine," Lago said. "I'd rather get there quickly so we can take a proper break."

"I'll take you through the side roads then," the man said, pulling the rickshaw with no effort at all. "When you skip the crowds at the main arches, it's much quicker."

The ride up the bulwarks was expedient but relaxed, letting them contemplate the beauty of the city from the western side, where they had not ventured yet. The views of the distant Moordusk Dome were breathtaking, but although Lago's eyes were aimed toward the vastness, he saw none of it. His hand clutched the Sceres-shaped brooch Ockam had given to him, feeling the sharpness of the sixteen-pointed star that represented the Ilaadrid Shard. He pulled at one metallic point with a fingernail to make it click, over and over. *A frail wolf...* Click. *A young tree...* Click. *A small fish—*

"Where have you gone to?" Alaia asked him.

"Huh?"

"Your head is elsewhere."

Lago consciously removed his hand from the brooch, pretending to unwrinkle his cloak. "Just thinking," he said.

The rickshaw turned at a small road and entered the Tenth Bulwark, climbing steadily.

"I know it's silly, but there's this thing many Oldrin believe," Alaia said, unprompted. "They say our spurs are the bones of Noss themself coming back to reclaim us. That once we are past the Sixth Gate—well, actually, in our stories there are only three—that we'll become beings made of nothing but spurs, the bones of the planet themself, becoming one with the essence of everything."

"What does that have to—"

"I don't really believe in all of it," she went on, "but whatever happens after, whether there be three, six, or sixteen thousand gates to cross, I think Ockam has made it past all of them by now, and he's one with all of us."

Lago looked away, hiding his eyes.

"We barely got to know him," he said, choking up. "Yet still... It's like I knew him so well. And he was there for me. And he's... He's gone because of me."

"Not allowed to have such silly thoughts while in my presence," Jiara said, reaching over to ruffle Lago's curls, then giving him a solid yet playful smack.

Lago attempted to smile, but it faded too quickly.

"No, no," Jiara said. "Whenever you think of Ockam, the smile stays plastered to your face. Understand?"

"But if it wasn't for me, he would—"

"The way I see it," Jiara interrupted, leaning forward, "is that *you* are here because of *him*. There's a big difference. And so am I, for that matter. That pube-mustachioed grump saved me a dozen times during the Barujan War, before you tadpoles had even hatched. And I don't think he cared about six or three or however many gates—the idiot did not believe in the Steward, Pliwe, or even the Twin Gods. He believed in the Great Spider of Beyenaar. A big fucking spider." She shook her head while reminiscing, grinning all the while.

"I heard him mention that a few times," Lago said, "but I was too embarrassed to ask."

"What happens to those who are gone and believed in the spider?" Alaia asked.

"*Teslurians* is what they call themselves," Jiara replied, "although Ockam never cared to adopt the title. When they die, they are dissolved into the Great Spider's silk glands, to become part of the infinite thread she's weaving across eternity. Something like that. Back to being spider ass soup. That's what the Khaar Du believe, at least the tribes who don't sing to rocks instead. This giant insect goes around—"

"They are not insects," Alaia corrected, "they are actually—"

"This *ugly insect* goes around," Jiara continued, "weaving her web between all planets, moons, stars, galaxies, using the essences of all those who have departed to connect the entire cosmos into a single, nightmarish sky web."

"I think it sounds beautiful," Alaia said.

"I don't know," Jiara said. "I picture it covered in space moths, in planet-sized gnats. Great Spider must eat, mustn't she? Either way, it's a silly thought, but I like to picture Ockam out there, thin as a maiden's hair, making up one strand of this huge web that connects all of us to each other, that connects us to the stars themselves. And I know he can hold on tight."

Lago flashed another smile, one which stuck for longer. "All these stories sound similar, in weird ways. Some pre-Downfall texts say we are all made of stardust, and we'll all return to stardust."

"*Ster-jall*," Jiara said and reached over to knock on Lago's heart, but her fingers found the brooch of Sceres instead. She tapped it respectfully, then leaned back in her seat.

They sat quietly, watching the people rush by them, hearing the clacking of wheels on cobblestones.

"Where at in the Sixteenth?" the rickshaw puller asked.

"There's this round building between Cosmology and Aetheric Theory," Lago said.

"I know the one," the powerfully built man replied, barely breaking a sweat. As he took them through another shortcut, the passengers noticed that a ramp climbing to the Sixteenth Bulwark was swarming with guards.

Jiara tensed up immediately, leaning forward to get a better look.

The shortcut exited near the top of the Cliffside Lifts, where an even longer line had formed, with a mob screaming at Union guards to hurry up. A scuffle broke out among the crowd.

"What's happening?" Alaia asked.

"No idea," the man pulling their vehicle said. "But now you're glad I offered my services, aren't you?" He turned his head to share a flirty wink.

Farther ahead, toward their destination, four guards were conspicuously patrolling the main thoroughfare.

"Turn right, here," Jiara said.

"Cosmology is just up the—"

"No, turn here, toward the School of Medicine. Now!" she demanded.

The rickshaw turned sharply.

"To the rose garden, over there," Jiara directed.

The rickshaw stopped by the tall hedges.

"Thank you," Jiara said, handing him two Cups and hurrying into the garden, with Lago following behind her.

"Your change," the man said, reaching into his Qupi pouch.

"Keep it," Alaia said, winking at him as she ran behind the others.

They climbed up the spiral stairs at the back of the building, then followed the curved hall. The laboratory's mahogany door was ajar, just a few fingerbreadths. Jiara instinctively put her hand on the pommel of her sword before slowly pushing the door open.

Chapter Eight

Betrayal

Balstei was standing at the back of his lab next to two Union guards and a military man who seemed of a much higher rank; an admiral, Jiara figured from the bronze armor, gold-rimmed blue cape, and the multitude of ribbons over his pauldron. When they heard the door creak open, they turned. In the hands of the admiral was Agnargsilv, while Balstei was holding Urnaadisilv.

"Motherfucker, you sold us out!" Alaia yelled.

"Arrest them, now," the admiral ordered.

The Union guards approached, short swords drawn. Jiara knew their little armor was ornamental and their training pitiful compared to that of the military. She shifted her fingers from her sword's pommel to the grip.

"Don't try anything stupid," the blue-caped man said. "I am Admiral Grinn from the Centennial Fleet. We have sedecim peacekeepers on their way. You don't want to—"

Slam! The admiral fell to the ground. Behind him was Balstei, holding up his heavy microscope, now badly bent after denting the admiral's helm. The Union guards turned toward the noise, and in a moment, Jiara was on top of one, slamming his head against a work desk. The other guard looked around, weighed his odds, and tried to flee out the door.

Alaia stuck out a leg and tripped him, making the guard fall against the doorframe. Lago ran to the door and locked it before the guard could escape.

"Please, please don't…" the Union guard implored, backing into a corner.

Jiara kicked his dull sword away and said, "Sit quietly and we won't hurt you." She felt sorry for the pathetic, inexperienced guard, who nodded compliantly and began to sob.

Jiara turned to Balstei. "Tell us what in Khest is happening, now!"

"It was Kedra!" Balstei yelled. "Admiral Grinn is her uncle. She told him everything and sent these pink pricks to confiscate the masks. They were asking how they work, how they could use them to win the war."

"That piece of shit!" Alaia spat.

"We need to get out," Balstei said. "The admiral wasn't lying—there were more guards here just moments ago. If they bring sedecim peacekeepers, we won't stand a chance."

Admiral Grinn stirred, blood pooling between his helm and cheeks. Balstei crouched by him and pulled the blade from the admiral's scabbard—a fancifully ornamented baselard sword. "Stay down," he ordered, "don't make a move."

"Get your things, now," Jiara told the group, running to get her backpack.

"Here, Lago," Balstei said, returning Leif to him. Lago clipped the dagger to his belt. They packed all their gear, hiding the masks safely inside their bags.

"Here, you carry this," Jiara said, hurling Ockam's backpack to Balstei. He caught it and slung it over his shoulders.

Admiral Grinn turned onto his side. "Think this through," he said. "All through the sixteen bulwarks, the guards have been told to be on the lookout for a Tribeswoman, a cripple, and an Oldrin. There is no way for you to make it out of Zovaria."

He tried to stand, but Balstei put a leg over his back and pressed him back to the ground. "Sorry, Admiral." He used the admiral's sword to cut his belt and remove the scabbard. "It's very pointy, so I'll borrow this too, if you don't mind." He ran to the door, hurrying the others through as he held it open.

"There's no way you'll get out of this," Admiral Grinn mumbled. "The Union guards are being warned, and everyone in the military will know your name, Lago Vaari. Surrender now and the Twin Gods will show you mercy, otherw—"

"Oh, fuck off," Lago interrupted. "Let's go."

Balstei locked the heavy door behind them, then led them down the hall.

"There's a back way Crysta showed us," Lago said, "down the—"

"I know my way," Balstei said, leading them down the same spiral steps they had taken earlier in the day. They exited into the rose garden, startling a group of students and academics.

"Going on an expedition?" a student of Balstei's said as she saw her teacher trot by with a backpack and a sword.

"Where are you taking us?" Jiara asked him.

"To the west side. We have to get out of the city."

"There were guards at the ramps," Lago warned. "And the lifts too."

"I figured, but there are many more paths. They can't cover them all."

They heard the rumbling call from a blown horn, alerting the city guards.

"Where is Kedra?" Lago asked. "We need to be careful with her."

Balstei pushed his way through a gated hedge. "She had gone to show the soldiers where she last saw you."

"That was by that cafe," Jiara said. "Crysta called the area… er… the Tavern Quarter."

"Got it," Balstei said. "We'll avoid it."

There were many ramps connecting the bulwarks, but there were more inconspicuous ways to cross between levels: steps connecting closes in well-hidden corners, shortcuts alongside drainage canals, even residential buildings that shared a level at the top and another at the bottom of the retaining walls. Balstei led them down secret pathways all the way to the Seventh Bulwark, where the lively Yamazu Market was teeming with shoppers and merchants.

"Slow down here," Balstei recommended. "We don't want to appear suspect. The Seventh is quite open, but the crowds will keep us hidden."

"Hide your splint," Jiara told Lago.

Lago covered his splint and the bag where he kept Agnargsilv with his dusky gray cloak.

"And Alaia…" Jiara added.

"I know," Alaia grumbled. It was too warm to wear her furred hood, so she undid her braids so that her frizzy hair would cover up her nub.

They spotted guards running in their direction. Balstei leaned over to look at a crate full of star fruit; the others followed his lead. Lago held his breath, glancing sideways as the guards rushed by, headed to the ramps connecting to higher levels. More guards followed behind those, pushing the citizens around and inspecting their faces.

"Over here, quickly!" Balstei said, pulling them into a close where short steps led into a recessed courtyard. "Let's skip the main streets for a bit."

"Over there!" they heard a shout from behind. "Stop!" A guard bolted down the narrow close to get to them. They turned right at the end of the close, then Balstei waited just around the corner. When the guard came out running and tried to turn, Balstei used the guard's momentum and pushed him toward a handrail, making him topple over it and land at the bottom of the courtyard. A few passersby screamed and scrambled out of the way.

They fled once more, sneaking into hallways and dark passages. More horns blew, to which even more horns replied. They dropped through a dry drainage canal on Enclave West that went all the way from the Fifth to the Third, where the fountains and ponds drew in large crowds even on a Moonday afternoon. Instead of arched gateways, the plaza had enormous stairs leading to the Second Bulwark, with no way for the guards to be checking everyone among the stream of people. They exited the plaza on a touristy street on the west side of the Second. A high pink wall rose in front of them.

"Up these steps," Balstei said.

"Where are you taking us?" Alaia complained, out of breath.

"Just trust me!"

They hurried upward. On top of the wall was a popular viewpoint where vendors sold cheaply carved figurines. Couples and families came to this overlook to lean on the battlements and watch Sunnokh set over the Isdinnklad. The walls of the First and Second bulwarks merged here into a taller fortification, with battlements, towers, and even a few bastions farther southwest. Beyond the wall were the soft sand beaches of the Albite Shores, and farther away was the Moordusk Dome's magnificent curve, looming beyond the horizon like a rising planet.

Balstei made them hurry through the viewpoint, but Jiara pulled at his shoulder. "Careful," she said, leaning on an embrasure while trying to act natural. "There are guards in that tower."

Lago peeked over her thick shoulders and spotted two Union guards. "They are distracted, playing Qu," he said, referring to the popular board game that used Qupi chips as the board pieces.

They walked with the crowd while pretending to admire the view, passing right by the guards. Balstei stopped at the edge of the battlement and looked around.

"Why are we stopping?" Alaia asked. Balstei held up a hand.

Throngs of people walked by. A couple of kids leaned through the thick embrasures. More horns blew to the south. Balstei looked down to the main street and saw nearly a dozen sedecim peacekeepers marching toward the Tavern Quarter, their fully armored bodies glistening.

"Once no one is looking, we jump, right here," Balstei said, keeping his eyes on the Union guards at the tower—they had come out to see what the commotion was about, their eyes following the peacekeepers.

"Jump where?" Lago asked.

"There are sand dunes right below the wall. It's two bulwarks high, but the wall is slanted and smooth, it will slow us down. It's the only way out that doesn't involve the Bailey's gates. Just trust me. Go when I tell you, don't stop to look down."

The guards rushed back to the tower to retrieve their weapons and pocket the chips from their unfinished game.

"Now!" Balstei half-shouted. He climbed through the embrasure and dropped out of sight. Alaia followed next, and then Jiara, who helped Lago up and dragged him off the edge. They slid down a long, smooth wall of pink for what felt like a hundred feet. Lago forced himself to roll as he landed, clutching his splinted arm to protect it, yet still slamming it against the sand once or twice. They tumbled down the dunes until the slope flattened.

"Khest yeah!" a young boy standing next to them exclaimed. He had just jumped down the same way and was waiting for his friends to stop being cowards and follow him down.

Alaia struggled to stand, her breath knocked out of her from the impact. Lago tried to pull her up with his good arm, but only managed to slip in the sand and fall on his face.

Jiara and Balstei helped them scurry behind a dune crested with tall beachgrass; there they caught their breaths.

"I don't think they saw us," Balstei said, shaking off his striped doublet.

"That was just a bit too suicidal," Alaia said, spitting out sand.

"Sorry. We used to take that plunge as a dare when I was a young student at the institute. Hasn't changed, it still hurts like the netherflames when you land."

"What do we do now? It's like we can't catch a break lately," Lago said.

Balstei peeked at the looming wall of pink. "Well, we can't stay here, not after that. Scorch me sixteenfold. My whole career! There's no way back now. Attacking an admiral like that is treason. They'd send me to the gallows!"

"We need to warn Crysta and Gwil," Lago said.

"Too dangerous," Balstei said. "They weren't there when it happened, so they will probably be spared. The admiral did ask about them, and they will certainly be questioned and followed, but there's no reason for them to get in trouble over this." He stood up. "For now, we should get the Khest out of here. We can walk across the dunes for a bit. There are no guards at the beach."

They moved closer to the water, where the compacted sand made it easier to walk. The beach was lively near the pink walls, but the farther west they traveled, the quieter it became, with only the sound of surf and gulls remaining. The smell of the sea was fresher at this end, very different from the rotten aroma near the city. They walked by strange orchids and bromeliads that hid among the beachgrass and dried kelp. Sandpipers piped the sand, skimmers cut silvery trails among the waves, and many species of crabs poked out of holes and dashed madly across the seaside. They even saw a small burrowing owl hunting for insects, bobbing around on two clumsy feet.

Bear would've loved playing on this beach, Lago thought, suddenly feeling distant and melancholy, imagining Bear back in Banook's cabin and yearning to be there with the warmth of the fireplace, of their presence.

Farther ahead, fishermen were pulling their nets at a pink jetty made from discarded blocks of rose quartz that were not translucent enough to be used in the main city. Beyond the jetties, a trail went up a rocky hillside, where humble houses teetered near the edges. Bison-pulled wagons stopped at the top of the trail, ready to load up on the fresh catch to be taken to the city's marketplaces.

They sat on a bench halfway up the hill, where the sound of the wind and surf would grant them privacy even if someone came down the path behind them.

"After Zovaria, your plan was to head to the Moordusk Dome, correct?" Balstei asked.

Lago nodded. "I really wanted Crysta to see the inside, but I guess we can't go back for her."

Balstei shook his head. "No, no. And I don't mean to impose, but imagine yourselves in my precarious situation. I think I just lost everything! My career, my tenure, my lab, my research. But at the same time, this is the most magnificent chance to explore something entirely new *and* related to my field of study. I was born in Muskeg, just south of the dome. I know the area quite well. I'm not much of an outdoorsman, but I could help you out if you let me tag along."

"Sorry I called you a motherfucker," Alaia said. "I really thought you betrayed us. We could use the help. You know the area better, and the city too, if we need to go back there."

"I don't think we could anytime soon. But I know my way around these states of the Union."

Lago pondered guiltily as the salty breeze shook his curly hair. "I'd like to let Crysta know we made it out. Is there a way to send her a letter?"

"She doesn't have an address in Zovaria anymore," Balstei answered. "Sending something to the institute or the congregation would be idiotic at this point. Even her home in Needlecove will be spied upon, no correspondence will make it through unopened. But we need to get moving now. Perhaps in Mirefoot we could find a place to rest before dark. It's an industrial town where I don't think anyone will think of looking for us."

They followed a country road by the sea cliffs, headed toward the bulging magnitude of the Moordusk Dome. About an hour into their walk, they saw a bison-pulled wagon headed southwest and hitched a ride for free. People in these small towns were generous and did not ask to be reciprocated for a simple favor, especially when their wagons reeked of fish.

They arrived in Mirefoot late that night. The town had its own constellation hovering over it, birthed by the blue flames that hundreds of gas flares spewed when lighting up the bog gas at the processing plants.

"They pipe all that gas for the city from here," Jiara said.

"Do you know any place to spend the night around here?" Balstei asked Ralmir, their driver.

"Lotsa temp bog workers stay at the Marsh Willow. Nothing fancy, would suit you travelers fine. I'll drop you off there if it looks like your kinda place."

Ralmir did just that. The Marsh Willow was no proper inn, but more like a bunch of stacked shacks with not much more to offer than cold beds and a complimentary serving of the flatulent aroma of the gas plants. But it was cheap, and Qupi was something they had almost entirely ran out of. Luckily, Balstei always carried an entire Quggon in his Qupi pouch and was able to cover for the cheap room with merely a Horn and a Hand, saving his Hex and remaining chips for later.

They were surprised to discover that their ramshackle room had gas lights and a furnace, something that would have been considered a luxury in any other town. They settled down, tired and ready to collapse, yet Lago struggled to fall asleep—too many thoughts clouded his mind.

Chapter Nine

Boglands

"It's quite busy out there," Alaia said, peeking through the moth-eaten curtains.

"Peat and pipeline workers only," Balstei reassured her. "It should be safe to walk outside."

"I still wish we could let Crysta and Gwil know we are fine," Lago said while he packed his belongings.

"A fool's errand, lad," Balstei warned. "Unless we could fly a herald directly to them, it'd be pointless to risk it—we'd simply get them in trouble or reveal our location." He looked around the decrepit room. "Are we ready to go? I can't stand the smell of this town one moment longer."

Jiara was sitting in her bed. Her backpack's flap was open, with the round ears of the ursid mask poking out attentively. She gazed at them and said, "I've been thinking…"

"Not here," Lago interrupted. "Someone might hear you scream."

"But no one can see us now," she said. "If we run into trouble, being able to control that mask might be what saves us."

"That's what I like to hear!" Balstei said. "I've been wondering how you could resist having this sublime gift tucked inside a bag, blind to all the wonders it can help you discover."

"It's not that easy, though," Jiara said. "Even Ockam barely managed the pain. But I need to learn, sooner or later."

"I don't think this is a good idea," Alaia warned.

"It will be fine. You'll help me get the mask off if anything goes wrong. Just stay close, help me through it."

Lago made sure the curtains were pulled tight enough that no one could peek in, then sat next to Jiara, with Alaia sitting opposite them.

"Stop looking so gloomy," Jiara said to Lago, holding Urnaadisilv on her lap. "I'll handle it. I'm built tough as a ramship's hull." She tightened her pectoral muscles, making her breasts jump up comedically. "And don't try to bore me with instructions, we all know how this goes." She shook the nervousness from her fingertips, lifted the mask up, and stared into its concavity. "You can do this..." she said to herself, then pulled the mask toward her face.

Even before the mask had conformed around her facial features, Jiara felt the unbearable shock of all the threads slamming like a lance through her spine. She reacted violently, swinging her powerful arms out, punching the mask away from her face, and only then realized she had been screaming, and was still screaming.

She backed away over the mattress, slamming her head against the wall and carving a hole in the cheap plaster.

"Calm down!" Lago said. "Stop! Stop screaming!"

"It's alright," Alaia said. "We are with you. Take it easy, we are here."

Jiara's wailing subsided, leaving her panting with eyes wide and white as dinner plates, staring at the mask that had fallen quietly, remorselessly to the ground.

"I couldn't, I couldn't," she mumbled.

"You are fine," Lago comforted her, "just catch your breath."

A knock on the door. "Is everything alright there?"

"Sounds like the innkeeper," Balstei said. "I'll deal with her."

Alaia bolted to hide the mask while Balstei cracked the door open.

"Everything is fine," Balstei said, "our friend suffers dreadful nightmares. We are taking care of her."

The innkeeper peered in suspiciously. She saw Jiara holding onto her head, trying to smile back at her, then noticed the hole she'd smashed in the wall, which had a stain of blood on it.

"We'll pay for that," Balstei said.

The innkeeper left while peeking over her shoulder, making no comment.

"Clean that wall and the blood off your hair," Balstei said. "We better get out of here before they start asking questions."

They hurried out of the Marsh Willow and asked a passerby for directions to the nearest trading post.

"How long was I out for?" Jiara asked as they meandered through the busy town.

"Out?" Lago asked. "You hurled the mask off your face as soon as you put it on. You didn't wear it for more than a heartbeat."

"Shit... I felt like I was trapped in that pain for hours. This is... Never mind, we'll deal with this later."

They dodged around a wagon hauling hefty pipes, then hurried past carts loading peat stacks to be used as fuel in areas where the gas pipes did not reach. The streets were muddy and nearly black, with nonexistent sidewalks. When they reached the corner of a trading post called the Foul Fen Faire, two children of maybe thirteen years approached them, squinting through dark eyebags and sniffling through blackened noses.

"Can cutya good deal Lorr, best moor dust n'all of Mirefoot," one of the scrawny faces said to Balstei.

"Not interested, thank you," the artificer replied, sidestepping around the urchin.

The grimy hands of the other child pulled out a tiny leather pouch and held it up. "Jess one Hand for a taste, Lorr. A Hex for a full pouch."

"A fucking Hex?" Balstei barked. "Why don't you just rob me at knifepoint? It'd be a more honest way to go about it." He brushed the kids aside and walked into the trading post.

"What is moor dust?" Lago asked while choosing provisions for the road.

"It's the shoddy version of soot, which they get from the peat. After they dry the peat stacks and burn them, they can get a tiny fraction of soot particles from them. But they can't purify it like the stuff from the coal mines. It's treacherous stuff, all it does is sizzle your brains till eventually the lights burn out. I feel sorry for them, but I'd wager their parents harvest the peat and force the kids to sell the shit."

"You've tried that stuff?" Alaia asked.

"And regretted it, but don't you dare tell Crysta."

After paying for their goods, they went out to the street and aimed their noses southwest, toward the dome; its snowy top was barely visible, crowned by striped clouds.

Balstei looked at the road signs and said, "This is Traughill Road. It should connect to Mossborough, and from there we can take the Old Pilgrim's Road to—"

"We'll cross through the bogs," Jiara said.

"Have you lost your wits, woman?" he said. "It's miles and miles of nothing but filthy wetlands, there are no roads there."

"Good," she replied. "That's exactly why we should go that way. Kedra knows our plan, she'll have the army watching all the roads, and the navy patrolling the sea routes. She's a professional, she'll know to keep an eye on trails where there could be any trace of us. The bogs would leave no footprints to follow, no witnesses."

"A most execrable idea," Balstei muttered. "Where would we sleep? It would take days! There's no food, there's no shelter."

"It's nothing that has stopped us before," Jiara said as she began to walk southwest, following an overgrown country road.

"Sounds fun, actually," Alaia added, trotting behind her. "Never seen bogs before."

Balstei shook his head. "Maybe we could try to—"

"Are you coming or not?" Lago asked, also walking away.

"Takhísh's Shield protect us." Balstei secured Ockam's bag over his shoulders, then followed.

The road wound through peat farms, where peat cutters were slicing and dicing as if they were cutting pieces off the skin of Noss themself. The peat was old and ran deep; wherever it was cut, it left steep canyons, dark and moist and smelling of methane and ancient soil. The peat was greenish-brown at the top, where the moss was still living, deepening in color to what looked like a coal seam at the bottom.

"That's where they get the moor dust," Balstei said. "The lower layers have a higher concentration of it, but it's still exceedingly low."

They jumped a wood fence and followed wagon tracks through a grassy meadow that adjoined the edge of the untouched bogs. Ahead of them, the usual soil and grass were gone, the land extending into dozens of miles of mossy grounds and ponds.

"It would take us months to cross that far," Balstei said, gaping at the uninterrupted wetlands separating them from the dome.

"I bet we can do it in a week and a half," Jiara calculated. "The bogs look flat, but they are soft, which means we will sink often. It will be hard to stay dry, and we'll get our boots tangled in the peat moss. Whenever we find a flat rock or any surface to rest, we should take the chance to dry up. We can pick up dry peat to start fires."

Balstei stepped onto the spongy moss to test it and felt his leather shoes sink in and soak up the cold water. The moss was drenched underneath, and now his thin socks were too.

"I don't have the gear for this sort of unhinged expedition. Maybe we could go back to Mirefoot and purchase something more fitting?"

"You only have a Hex and some change left," Jiara said, "that won't get you much."

"You can borrow what you need from Ockam's bag," Lago suggested.

Balstei searched through the bag. Among the cooking supplies and other outdoor gear were plenty of good socks. No extra boots—they wouldn't have fit anyway—so his leather shoes would have to do. He swapped his thin trousers for the rugged canvas ones Ockam had worn and buckled the baselard sword he had stolen from the admiral onto a thicker leather belt. Over his fanciful doublet, he put on Ockam's green wool cloak, protecting himself from the already chilly breeze.

"You look just like a sylvan scout," Jiara mocked, glaring at the dressy shoes.

As they trekked through the bog, mists curled at their feet, strange smells and spores wafting through the air whenever they sank into thick pillows of moss.

What had seemed like a sterile and fetid flatland quickly revealed itself to be a marvelous landscape of alien life. Alaia spotted outlandish birds she could not name—small, numerous, and vociferous—who hid in the moss and flew away all at once as the wayfarers stomped on the billowing hills. Carnivorous sundews waited patiently to trap unlucky insects in their curling, bejeweled tentacles. By their feet swam colorful newts and frogs, chasing after insect larvae in their diamond-sparkling universes. The ponds reminded Lago of an aquarium he had once seen when delivering a package to a wealthy allgender in Withervale. The landscape was filled with life, strange and colorful and perfect in every way.

"What a filthy swamp," Balstei grumbled, draining water from his shoes while resting on a lichen-embellished boulder.

They had climbed up a rocky patch to rest, wring their socks, and search for food. The shrubs that clustered around the rocks were those of bilberries and cloudberries, which were delicious, filling, and plentiful. Alaia filled up her quaar helm with them and shared her bounty. They ate until their bellies ached.

"Those were really good," Lago said, "but I might've had too many." He fiddled with his fingers a bit shyly. "Um, I was thinking. We are so far from anywhere now, I don't think anyone could see us. It is alright if I go as Sterjall? I want to better understand this weird landscape."

He encountered no objections.

He hurriedly kicked off his boots, pulled the mask out of his bag, and changed into his wolf half-form. He then groaned painfully. "I'm alright," he said through bared teeth. "The splint tightened with the fur. I should loosen it before shapeshifting."

While the others rested their legs and stomachs, Sterjall walked around the boulders to feel the spongy moss spreading between his paw pads, to better smell the musky and woody epochs below him, to listen to a near-silent cacophony of small organisms swimming, breeding, dying, living. He saw the landscape anew, marveling at the multitude of connections woven by the threads around him.

He kneeled on the moss and observed spiders dancing over the water as if they were skating on ice, salamanders pretending to be rocks, peculiar mushrooms that blossomed like the ribs of a delicate fish, and tadpoles that swarmed in latent expectation of the day they grew legs, so they could travel to the faraway ponds that awaited twenty strides away.

"This whole place is so full of life," Sterjall told them, as he peered underneath rocks without having to lift them. "It's not just the surface. It goes deep, very deep. All these flowing connections feel ancient and intentional. Even the tiniest insects have a place in it."

"They say the Moordusk Bogs are thousands of years old," Balstei told him. "It's layers upon layers of dead stuff. There are no animals around other than birds."

"It's not dead, it's thriving. And there are bigger animals too, like the family of raccoons living under the boulder you are sitting on. Five of them."

Balstei shifted awkwardly on his boulder. "You can see that with the mask?"

"Only if I focus. I have to isolate the threads from each other. It's hard here, since nearly everything is alive, except the insides of rocks. But bigger animals like you and those raccoons stand out. They look… 'brighter,' with threads that loop around themselves, easier to spot."

"Fascinating," Balstei said. "You know, I was halfway through an experiment when that dent-skulled admiral came knocking. I was testing whether your dagger reacted to magnium and soot particles."

"What did you find out?" the wolf asked.

"Didn't have time for much experimenting, but the little that did happen surprised me," the artificer replied. "The quaar tube is not magnetic. However, when I placed particles of soot near it, they aligned like iron filings would near a magnium alloy. Not quite in the same way, mind you. Instead of becoming attracted to the tube, they vibrated and held themselves in the air, like a thin filament of hovering particles past the sharp end of the dagger. Eventually, they vibrated themselves too far, and slid off. Takh smite me, I even lost that little bit of soot I had at the laboratory. I wish I had brought it with me."

"At Stelm Bir, where I took Leif's grip from, there were these faceted quaar spheres that joined the tubes together. I held one, and it did feel like it was magnetized to the tube. They snapped together perfectly. What do you think that means?"

"Beats me. Whatever this force is, it seems to interact with more than just invisible threads. My guess is that your mask operates in some similar fashion. These aetheric elements are a wild mystery. I know that at Hashan—or the City of Bridges, as some call it—they have an entire wing of the Tsing Academy dedicated to such studies. They have knowledge from before the Downfall that they are keeping secret. The Tsing Empire is so far advanced by now, that they'll always stay ahead of us."

Nearly no trees grew in the bogs, but on their second night they found a tight grove of black spruces. They camped between four old trees that offered some protection from the elements.

"It's really hard to light this peat," Jiara said, struggling with the wind, which whipped by to blow away the peat as soon as it started to smoke. "We might have to do without a fire tonight."

She resigned herself and sat down, sheltering under her dark-walnut cloak.

"So, are you ready to give it another try?" Balstei asked.

"It won't light up," she said. "The gusts are too—"

"Not that. The mask. You could be obsessing about stupid water striders and slimy tadpoles, just like our friend has."

"It might be trickier here," Sterjall said. "Wearing the mask becomes much harder with more life around you, where there is more pain to tap into. The bogs seem like a most perfectly inadequate place to attempt it."

Jiara nodded politely, seeming embarrassed by the protectiveness of her friends.

Balstei looked disappointed. "Well, I'm not afraid of it," he said. "Why don't you let me try it?"

Jiara shot him a look that pierced like Takhamún's Spear.

"I'm only kidding!" he said. "Quench those flames off your face, woman, I didn't mean it in a bad way. But like you said, the mask might help us yet, and whether it be upon oozing bogs or in whatever forests we may enter next, you'll have to learn."

"Fine," Jiara said, reaching into her bag.

"Are you sure...?" Alaia was beginning to ask, but Jiara had already placed the mask on her face.

Jiara woke up hours later, her head humming like an endlessly tolling bell. Sterjall and Alaia were sleeping back to back. Balstei was sitting up, shivering as he kept watch. He put a hand on her shoulder and said, "Quiet, let them sleep. Are you feeling better?"

"I don't even remember what happened," she answered, trying to force her mangled memories to resurface.

"I helped you pull the mask off. It was on you for maybe ten whole breaths. You screamed some unintelligible things once it came off, then curled into a ball and passed out."

"Shit…" she said. Then she noticed she had wet herself, but didn't dare mention it. "Maybe I'm not cut out for this. I wish Ockam—"

"It's my fault," Balstei said. "And… And I'm sorry. I sometimes let my curiosity get the best of me. I pushed you when I shouldn't have. I was reckless."

Jiara sat next to him. Her pulse was off, as if her heart was still expecting something unexpected to happen. But the pain was slowly subsiding, vanishing like her memories of the event.

"I don't know how that kid did it," she said, glancing at Sterjall. "Ockam, I understand, but him? And at such a young age? I should be the strong one here. I should be able to bear it. But there's more to strength than muscle."

She deflated, leaning heavily against a spruce's uncomfortable trunk.

Balstei awkwardly placed a hand on her shoulder. "And there's more to wisdom than knowledge. But I believe in you. When the time comes, you'll surprise us all, you'll see. Here, chew on these, I found them yonder by that pool." He handed her a handful of leaves.

"Muckweed?" she asked.

"You know your herbs."

"You know it's mighty inappropriate for a Free Tribeswoman."

"I wasn't calling you a muck! I may curse a bit, but slurs isn't my style. Khopto taught me to steam muckweed to extract the oils, but raw works well if you can tolerate the taste. Try them. They'll dull the ache, but they'll make you sleepy."

"I could use some sleep," she said. "Thank you."

Balstei nodded and stared at the moonlight silvering the edges of the bogs.

Jiara slept uneasily. She kept waking up, or dreaming she was waking up, but the recurring moments faded and blended. She recalled something about silk, about stardust, about pine needles, but the dreams turned elusive, and soon she'd forgotten all about them.

When they awoke, they were lying in a pool of mist a foot thick. They were adrift in a sea of fog, where each movement, each step, cast out curls of ghostly vapors.

They could not see far once they were back on the move, but they could feel the glow of Sunnokh rising, so they kept him at their backs as they walked.

They stopped in their tracks when a strange apparition manifested itself in their path: a perfect half-circle of light shone like a colorless rainbow and hovered whitely before them. They saw their shadows underneath the arch, cast onto the dissipating wall of fog, as if four smoky phantasms were traversing the first of the Six Gates of Felsvad.

"It's... it's a fogbow," Jiara whispered, afraid even her voice would dispel the presence.

"Beautiful," Alaia said, stepping forward, trying to catch it. For her, the fogbow kept moving ahead, perpetually unreachable like the horizon; for the others, it looked as if Alaia had been granted passage into the Supernal Realms, disappearing through an archway of milky light.

A beam of warmth was all that was needed to cast the vapors back to hiding, and so Sunnokh commanded it to be. The mists parted. The transition was sudden and satisfying—the fogbow vanished, leaving Alaia standing in a pool of crystal water, still chasing after phantasms.

The morning was booming with bird, frog, and insect calls. Spring was a mere few weeks away, and the animals were beginning their preparations for the lust-filled season.

During the midafternoon of the following day, they spotted a dark line ahead of them.

"It looks like a black river," Sterjall said, squinting into the distance. "Let's get closer."

The dark line was a patch of bog recently harvested for the peat, stretching left and right to the horizon. They stood at the edge of it. Four strides below them, in an almost too perfectly straight cut, was the dead blackness of the bottom. The chasm was about a mile wide, with a wall mirroring the one they were standing on rising in a thin gradient of muddy colors on the opposite end. The smell of gas was inescapable.

"It makes me sad now," Sterjall said, "after witnessing all the life of the bog, seeing it cut to pieces like this."

"It'll grow back," Balstei said. "Though it'll take hundreds, maybe thousands of years."

Sterjall scowled. "It's sickening. People just taking their share of Noss like they are slicing a piece of pie. If they only knew the beauty they are destroying, the pain they are causing, maybe they'd think twice before shredding an entire landscape for a handful of Qupi. I wish it was possible to make them all see the same things I see with Agnargsilv."

"There's plenty more boglands around, lad," Balstei said as he searched for a way down into the canyon.

Alaia and Balstei slid down a steep ledge, arriving at the bottom streaked with mud. To help Sterjall climb down safely, Jiara lowered him with her quaar rope before hopping down herself. They walked on this new flat and solid ground until, halfway across the chasm, Jiara came to a halt and dropped her bag onto the dark soil.

"I don't think I'll get a better chance than this one," she said. "There is at least a mile of nothingness surrounding us. If any good can come from this destruction, let this be it."

"You sure about this?" Balstei asked. "It hasn't even been two days."

"I'm certain," she said. She took Urnaadisilv out of her bag and found a dry spot to sit down. "Sterjall, would you stay close to me like I did for Ockam?"

"Of course," he said, sitting next to her.

Low, thin clouds were riding gusts of warm air above them, casting transient shadows on the black soil, but the breeze barely penetrated down to where they were. There was nothing else around but the dead crust from the ravaged skin of Noss, their presence, and the air that defined the space that was not them.

"This better be it," Jiara whispered to herself. "You can do this, you can do this and more." She slapped her own face, leaving a red mark on it. "Don't be a blubbering brat, there's no need to cry. You can handle it." She looked to Sterjall. "If I scream, let me scream. Don't pull the mask off me unless you see me trying to do so myself."

"I'm here for you," he assured her.

Jiara exhaled, then put on the mask.

Urnaadisilv quickly adapted to her facial features, filling in all the gaps as if it had been designed for her face alone. Just like the times before, she tensed up, but she did not immediately react by shoving the mask off. Her face turned red under the mask; her jaws clenched like a vise. Once more, she was unable to hold the pain at bay. She fell backward, shaking and wailing uncontrollably. Sterjall had failed to catch her, but he pulled her up and helped her sit again.

Jiara's eyes rolled in their orbits, her white-knuckled hands grasped her sides and clawed at the dirt, her boots kicked and scraped.

"Pull it off her!" Balstei said.

"Wait!" Sterjall replied, holding Jiara but without exerting force. He cradled her while focusing on the pain she was feeling, feeling it himself, hoping the pain within her would stop, willing for it to stop. His eyes began to water; his head pounded.

Jiara kicked and convulsed, then all at once she stopped moving, a breath held halfway in her throat. Her pain had ceased, or rather, she'd found a way to internalize it and not let it control her. She finished drawing her broken breath.

She turned to Sterjall and embraced him, her heart still pounding from the experience.

"Fuck, fuck..." she could barely exhale the words. "I couldn't... By the light of... It was... too much..." She lifted her head and blinked away the tears, realizing she had nothing more to fear.

She focused her attention around her, and suddenly the complexities of all the connections revealed themselves to her, appearing as a second sight that was not one of color or of light.

"I see it now," she said, squishing Sterjall's fluffy cheeks in her hands, staring straight into his amber eyes. "Look at you, Sterjall, how magnificent. You are glowing." She tried to kiss his wet nose, but her mask's muzzle simply bumped into it. She laughed, then rose, breathing in the world. "It's all... so beautiful..."

Chapter Ten

Lured by the Flame

Sterjall was entranced by the sudden change in Jiara; he rejoiced in the childlike process of discovery she was undergoing. He guessed he would have looked just as silly the first times he wore Agnargsilv, if there had been any light in the limestone caverns for his friends to see him by.

"How come you have your blue aura extending down through you?" Jiara asked Sterjall, scrutinizing a bit too closely. "When I 'look' toward myself, I see the golden aura only around my head."

"That's because I'm in my half-form," Sterjall answered.

He loosened his splint, then shapeshifted to show Jiara. To her, it looked as if the sapphire glow from Agnargsilv had retracted back into the canid mask. Then Lago took Sterjall's form again, and the indigo essence extended downward as if coursing through his spine to follow every nerve and vein in his body, diluting itself into a larger yet dimmer glow.

"Strange that with so much changing, your bones are just as broken," Jiara mused, helping him tighten the splint again. "I can see the fractures clearly through your fur."

"Same as it was when I boiled my leg," Sterjall said. "Never could regrow fur there."

"A shame it doesn't fix what's damaged, really," Balstei said, wishing he could see what they were seeing. "Yet even so, a tool such as this could do wonders for medicine. Chirurgeons would stab their eyeballs out in exchange for such a sight."

"Gross," Alaia said.

As they reached the edge of the cut peat, Jiara stared at the layers of time that made up the gradient of diversity. They climbed out of the canyon and walked slowly, letting her savor the complexity of the virgin bogs on top. She was a joy to behold. Her tough demeanor had transformed into wonder, carelessness, and bliss.

"I feel like I'm ready to sing about the bogs, like your big, fat, bear lover would have!" she said. She cleared her throat, and in an objectively terrible caricature of Banook's voice, she recited, "Here the moss caresses our souls, and the peat sings its glorious symphony of sun-drenched memories and crystal lores, for the temples of mist and moonlight have at long last opened to inspire reverence for the gods of time and their timeless bogs."

Sterjall and Alaia laughed out loud.

"Bear lover? What does she mean by that?" Balstei asked, entirely lost.

"She means Banook," Alaia answered.

Balstei creased his brow and squinted at Alaia. "The Nu'irg? You were... dating?"

"I'm not into bears, you nubhead. He's Sterjall's lover."

Balstei forgot how to walk. He was left behind, mouth agape, trying to process the information. He snapped out of it, then clumsily caught up again, sloshing through the life-permeated ponds.

Jiara and Balstei developed a more harmonious relationship over the next few days. She enjoyed describing all her discoveries with the mask, and the artificer was hungry for all the data. She also told him the full story behind Banook and Sterjall, and more about Da'áju and the secrets that still hid in the icy caldera. As the shadows lengthened before sunset, they stopped at a large, flat rock that was perfect for setting up their bedrolls. No wind bothered them, and they decided to start a fire to dry their clothes.

Sterjall was helping Alaia gather berries and pointing out the mushrooms that hid under the moss. They both watched Jiara and Balstei, who were having a lively conversation by the fire.

"Never thought they'd get along like this," Alaia said. "She seems so happy."

"And he's curious. I wonder what they're chatting about."

Before it got dark, they all circled the fire to boil water and begin preparations for dinner.

Jiara took her mask off. She had been wearing it all day, and it had given her a headache.

"Finally, a decent campfire," Balstei said.

"Perfect mood for ghost stories," Jiara added.

"Not here, not a good idea," he warned, then the two went eerily quiet.

"How come?" Alaia asked after a tense pause.

Balstei's face went expressionless. "This is a dark place," he said in a hushed tone. "These bogs are haunted by spirits from those who perished during the Downfall. We should not invite them in, as in the bogs the veil from the Supernal Realms is as thin as the mists of Summer."

"Oh, spare me," Jiara said. "That's hogshit. Those stories are made up to scare children from wandering the bogs at night."

Balstei exhaled derisively. "I'm no fool, woman. I was born in Muskeg, a town at the edge of the Moordusk Bogs. I've been in places like this many a time before, and always with an open but objective mind." He cracked his knuckles and stared at the fire. "I am a scholar, it's in my nature to question things, to be skeptical, yet there are some things I've seen in the bogs that I still can't explain. But that's not something to discuss here."

"Don't be a coward," Lago said. He had also removed his mask, as it made it easier for him to dry up without so much fur. "Now I want to hear about it."

Balstei considered for a moment. "Very well, but I won't raise my voice. Call me superstitious if you will. I would rather have you shame me than take the risk." They scooted in closer to hear him better.

"Beyond six lands, beneath six seas, in the days before the Downfall, a tribe who called themselves the Horumma lived here. This wasn't a bog back then, but a fertile prairieland with oak forests and pristine lakes. Half of the tribe had moved into the mountains, where they dug deep mines to take shelter from whatever horrors befell upon Noss. The other half of the tribe did not believe the prophecies of the Downfall and chose to remain here, right in this very land.

"When the fires from the Downfall came, all who stayed here were scorched and swallowed by flames. Many years later, when the fires ceased, the Horumma from the mountains came back to search for their lost cousins. The sky was still dark with fumes, and there was no sun, or day, or night, only a perpetual penumbra where ash filled the air as thick as the densest fog. It was cold, and dark, and the Horumma carried candles in their trembling hands, searching for their loved ones. Nothing but ashes did they find.

"They came every night with their glimmers of hope, even as it got colder, hoping their lost families would see their lights and join them again. Their flames called out for the lost ones, yet received no reply. One night, during a terrible blizzard, the Horumma's legs weakened, and their feet were frozen to the ground. Their souls surrendered to despair as the snow buried them and soon turned to ice.

"The Moordusk Bogs grew on top of that obscene graveyard of cold sorrow. Sometimes the fire from their candles can still be seen, as flaming sprites moving around the bogs, searching in the night. Those who approach the sprites are following a devilish lure, as the dead that lie below the bog have not entered even the first of the Six Gates and are still yearning for warmth, for the loved ones they lost. They yearn so hard that they will pull anyone down to a mossy grave if they get too close to their trap."

Balstei's lips tightened. He crossed his arms, as if stricken by a sudden chill.

"If they all died, how was there anyone left to tell the story?" Alaia asked.

"I don't know the answer to that," Balstei said. "Perhaps the story is not literally true, but there is truth to be found in it. I have seen the sprites move about the bog, late at night. I lost a dear friend to them. His name was Roche. We were scouting for soot deposits near the edge of the dome, and I felt him getting up in the middle of the night. From my tent I saw him walking alone under the moonlight, so I got up too, wondering where he was going. Then I saw it—the light, like a blue flame floating in malignant air. I have to admit that I too was entranced, but I was more concerned for Roche.

"I hastened after him and called his name, but he didn't answer. Then I sprinted, but the moss was deep and hard to move through, and I tripped and did not reach him in time. I saw him lift his hand to touch the flame, and it was as if his body was pulled down by a magical force, and he was swallowed into the moss. By the time I regained my footing, he was gone. No flame, no Roche. We never saw him again."

Jiara had gotten up distractedly, as if no longer interested in the story, and was walking away from them. Balstei seemed confused, then his eyes widened in terror.

Lago and Alaia turned their heads and saw it too: a blue flame was dancing in the air, and Jiara was headed straight for it. It was glowing dimly, waving like a worm wriggling on a hook, with a fishline at the ready.

Jiara walked toward it faster now, without saying a word.

Balstei got up and screamed. "No! Jiara, stop!" He ran after her.

Lago and Alaia scrambled to their feet, but Jiara was already reaching toward the blue flame, closer and closer, until suddenly she dropped down and was gone.

Balstei ran to where Jiara had been and looked around. "Jiara! Come back!"

Alaia caught up to Balstei as fast as she could, with Lago nearly falling on his face as he bolted behind her, screaming, "No! Where is she?! Jiara!"

And then Jiara got up from the mossy pillow she had dropped on and laughed. Balstei laughed with her. Alaia reached them first and punched Jiara in her right breast.

"Fuck!" Jiara said.

"Yeah, fuck you too!" Alaia said.

Lago arrived a few heartbeats later, struggling to keep up. He kicked sharply into Balstei's shin. "And you too, dammit, you gave me a heart attack!"

Balstei hopped on one leg as he backed off, hands up but still laughing.

"But what just happened?" Alaia asked in confusion. "It was just a joke? But I saw the fire! How…?"

Jiara snorted, still holding her breast—it would probably be bruised in the morning. "So sorry, kids," she said. "Stand back, I'll show you."

She leaned down in the area she had 'fallen' in and suspended her hand over a pocket of dense moss, feeling for an air current. With her flint, she released a spark over the spot, and with a soft *fwhooomp!* a dim, blue flame came to life, hovering in midair.

"It's just a gas vent," she said. "I smelled it earlier and lit it before we made the campfire. You can't see the flames during the day." She swung her cloak over the flame to put it out.

"You fuckers," Alaia muttered, stomping back to the campfire.

They sat to eat their dinner, with dirty conspiratorial looks shifting between them and a few smiles they could not hold back.

"So, is that why you lovebirds were so chatty earlier?" Alaia asked. "All just scheming? And you better tell us whose idea it was." She pointed an accusatory finger.

Balstei and Jiara looked at each other and shook their heads.

"Nah, we'll let you ponder over it," Jiara said.

"And that whole story… you just made it all up?" Lago asked Balstei.

"I borrowed from other spritetales and myths that grow around these fires. However, what Jiara said earlier is true—the myths aren't real, they are just stories to scare little children."

"You are reeeeally pushing it," Alaia said, glaring at him.

"You'll pay for this, someday," Lago added. "I promise you that."

Chapter Eleven

The Moordusk Dome

They were not bothered by sprites, netherbeasts, supernal specters, or malevolent fires that evening. After a restful night, they continued sloshing across the bogs. Balstei detested tromping through the muck, but he kept up—the expectation of what waited inside the dome was too great a motivator for him to overlook.

One twilight, when the dome was finally a mere mile away from them, they saw the glimmer of diaphanous moonlight illuminating the top of it, and they stopped to look back. Sceres was rising in the east, her near-full face stretching their shadows toward the dome. Her nacreous roundness was squashed at the bottom, where the horizon refracted her form as if she was made of liquid opals. She was at the end of her Pearl season, with her iridescent seashell face giving way to the first black tendrils of her Obsidian season, which spread from where the giant crystal of the Ilaadrid Shard grew. Soon she would be veiled in black, even when full.

"She's beginning to turn," Sterjall said to no one in particular. The shard did not shine that night, but the black tendrils made it easy to spot. "I wonder why she turns so black. Down here we are entering Spring, and everything turns green and colorful, but up there…"

"I love her best in Pearl," Alaia said. "She gives such vibrant moonlight to walk by."

"We should arrive at the vines in an hour or two," Jiara said, breaking the spell. "What's our plan?"

"If what Crysta guessed is correct," Sterjall said, "it should be daytime inside the dome while it's nighttime out here. It might be better if we go in now, even if we are tired, so we can see our way and make sure there's no danger."

"I'm so tired…" Balstei complained. "But if it means taking us out of these damnable bogs, let's go."

They followed their shadows.

"Hey look," Alaia said when they reached the towering dome. "The vines are a bit different-colored, don't you think?"

"It's probably just the moonlight," Sterjall said.

"Nuh-uh," she replied. "There's a colder hue to these, even from far away it seemed that way. And the thorns, they have a slight curve, and they are a bit flatter on one side."

She pushed a curved thorn until it pierced a vine next to it, making it bleed white. The sap looked and smelled the same. "Must be like a different subspecies than Heartpine," she added. "I wonder if the other domes are also different from one another."

Sterjall was about to ask the vines to part when he had a better idea. "Why don't you try it?" he asked Jiara. "It'd be useful for you to learn how to do it."

"I can give it a try," she said, cracking her neck. For the past week, she had gotten good practice with Urnaadisilv, and she was eager to learn more.

She stood next to an area with smaller vines and extended her right arm forward. She focused on the vines and saw them clearly, threads shifting, almost as if she was staring at the sap flowing inside. She pictured the vines pushing, shifting, and widening around them, while keeping her eyes focused straight ahead.

Although she had never attempted such a thing, the effect was immediate. Urnaadisilv was a good teacher and had already taught Jiara what to do before she herself had realized it.

"It's working!" Jiara said. Right in front of her, a path slowly opened.

The vines folded away, wrapping themselves tightly around their larger, immovable neighbors until there was a tunnel in front of them, smaller than the ones Sterjall had conjured in the past, but large enough. It was noisier when these vines opened, crackling with the sounds of the thorns snagging on the shifting peat. Jiara took a step forward, and then another, and—"Wait!" Sterjall yelled, pulling her by her cloak. He fell back onto the spongy moss, with Jiara on top of him.

"What's the—"

"Look down," Sterjall said, crawling to the edge of where the vines had parted.

Instead of a solid path, the ground dropped into a dark pit of peat, tangled with shredded roots and loose soil.

Balstei approached and looked into the hole. "This peat grew here after the dome was made, growing higher than the original ground below."

Alaia lit her lantern. "It's not too deep," she said, "we could slide down."

"Let me go down there first," Sterjall said, seeing the vines already closing. "I'll make sure it stays open while you climb down."

Jiara tied her rope around Sterjall's waist and lowered him. It wasn't a straight drop, but slanted, with plenty of roots and mossy tendrils to grab on to.

Once he reached the bottom, Sterjall turned toward the vines and focused to push them further. "All good down here," he said, "I'll keep them open."

Alaia went next, struggling to keep her lantern in one hand, yet she did not need to use the rope at all. She had to slide down the muddy moss for the last few strides, but landed expertly. Balstei sat at the edge and tried to lower himself, facing forward.

"You better turn around and try the other way, or just hold on to my rope," Jiara said.

"I can handle this, I'm fine," he grumbled. He grabbed a handful of moss to aid in his descent, which promptly broke under his weight. He panicked, and instead of grabbing another handful of roots reached for a sturdier-looking vine dangling near him. He didn't even think about the thorns.

His pierced hand recoiled. He lost his footing and slid sideways in a tumble, stopping by slamming his bleeding hand against the ground.

"Imbecile!" he exclaimed to himself. The fall itself had not injured him, as the ground was a soft mixture of soil and moss, but it was still painful.

Jiara slid down fast after Balstei and kneeled next to him. "How deep did those go?" she asked, looking at Balstei's bleeding hand.

"It's not too deep, I think. But it hurts like Takhamún's Spear."

She splashed water from her canteen over Balstei's wound, focusing Urnaadisilv's attention on the red cuts. Her face contorted with agony as she washed off the wound. "Shit, that stings," she said. "It's like Sterjall described. When I focus on the pain, I feel it like it's my own." She pulled back, shaking her hand.

Once the wound was wrapped in a clean bandage, they carried on through the dome's wall, Sterjall and Jiara opening the tunnel together.

Their passage through the wall was much easier this time around. Not only was Sterjall more experienced, but with two Silvesh used at the same time, the opening was larger, and the vines parted faster. He realized he didn't need to raise his handpaws to cast an effect onto the vines; the power was all in his mind. While considering this, he had an idea; he unsheathed Leif and aimed its senstregalv tip toward the vines. The flow of threads intensified, and the vines opened deeper, from a greater distance, scurrying away from wherever the blade was aimed.

"It's like a focusing effect," Jiara said.

"It's interesting," Sterjall noted, putting his dagger away. "But I'd rather have my eyes more broadly focused—I need to be careful with all the holes left by the vines."

A while later, this they felt the environment softly brightening. The light had no apparent source; it was diffused, tinted green from all the vines. Alaia stowed her lamp away. They parted a last curtain of tangles, and a verdant paradise opened up in front of them. They had breached into the dome of the Moordusk Bogs.

"It feels like we stepped into another world," Alaia said, staring at the leaf-covered sky.

They found themselves in a temperate rainforest where bigleaf maples were ornamented with epiphytes, the alders and cottonwoods were slippery with mosses, and the fallen logs of firs and hemlocks cradled nurturing pockets of ferns and exquisite mushrooms.

"How is this possible?" Balstei asked. "How can it be daytime when it was just night?"

It was bright as noon, but the light was strange: it cast no defined shadows and was missing the feel of dappled light they expected for a forest so dense with leaves.

They turned to look at the tunnel they had come in through.

Alaia ran to the vines. "They are glowing!"

The interior wall was coated with seedpod-like tendrils that shimmered in the breeze, like a blanket of fuzzy incandescence. Few of the glowing capsules could be found close to the ground, but as the vines climbed, they became more numerous, until above the tree line the coating of bulbs was so dense that there were no pockets without their presence, creating a continuous, evenly bright surface.

"It's like those husks that rained on us when part of Heartpine collapsed," Alaia observed.

"Just not dried up," Sterjall said, pinching pink pads around an illuminated pod. "And they are hot!"

It was hard to see the sky from within the thickly shaded forest, so they carved a path among the ferns until they reached a clearing with a decent view. The domed ceiling was a radiant white, casting a perfectly neutral light all around. As their eyes adjusted to the brightness, they saw that the vines had variations in their hues, though always tending toward whiteness, turning the sky into a fractal mix of diluted pastels. It reminded Sterjall of the colors of Sceres just as she was before they entered the dome. Plump cumulus clouds hung above them, creating a disconcerting illusion where the clouds seemed tiny due to the vines behind them.

"Look," Alaia said, climbing on a boulder to get a better view, "you can see one of the supporting columns from here."

Balstei climbed after her. "That is impossibly large," he said. The green column did not shine like the rest of the sky, but remained a dark, hazy pillar.

"That's one of the small ones," Alaia said, "the big one is at the center. Let's find a more open view."

Curious flying squirrels glided alongside them as they traversed the forest, territorially shaking their tails. Colorful birds fluttered by, crimson and cobalt and sulphur in their feathers; Alaia recognized almost none of them. The air was dense with moisture, and dew accumulated on the underside of leaves and in the hearts of bromeliads, where tadpoles waited patiently, or funnel spiders set deadly traps.

The forest seemed to never end, no matter how far they traveled. After leaping over a rocky creek, they arrived at an escarpment where they carefully approached the slippery edge of a lichen-splattered rock.

"This view is breathtaking," Jiara said, pulling her mask off to see more widely.

The expanse of the Moordusk Dome was a continuous undulation of verdant mountains, emerald valleys, and blue-hazed plateaus. Endless green spread before them, only interrupted by small streaks of white from monumental waterfalls and from wide rivers that snaked off to where a large portion of the Isdinnklad Sea had been scooped into the dome, reflecting the quaint light in a blurred horizon. The even lighting made the sea look foggy, blending with the sky as if the land ended and dropped off to where only a white void remained.

They recognized more hazed-out columns, all equally spectral. The farthest ones remained unseen.

"I don't see the central trunk," Jiara said. "Shouldn't there be one?"

"It's right in front of you," Sterjall pointed out. "Right at the center, over that tall mesa."

And the trunk was indeed there. It was so far away, and blending so smoothly with the bright sky, that it was nearly imperceptible. Once they learned to spot its blurred edges, its size was unmistakable.

"The trunk shines like the sky," Balstei said. Unlike the smaller columns, the trunk was alight with a soft gradient, fully aglow at its branching top and dimming to darkness at its bottom.

"This is where Ockam would've drawn a map of the area," Jiara said. "I'm no draftswoman, but if you all lend me a hand, I can give it a try."

"I'll handle this one," Balstei said. "I'm used to doing scholarly illustrations. Cells, organelles, stuff seen under a microscope. This dome reminds me of those things, making me feel like we are invasive microbes breaching through the skin of a complex organism."

Other than the supporting columns, a couple of wide rivers, and a few sharp peaks, there were no easy-to-spot landmarks; the forest here extended almost everywhere, and the waterfalls they saw looked very similar to one another. Jiara helped by aiming her compass, giving Balstei clear directions to sketch his landmarks. The artificer did a commendable job. He was not as skilled at guessing distances and scales as Ockam, but he had a steady hand and an eye for details.

"This breeze is making it hard to draw," Balstei said, struggling to keep the paper flat as he crosshatched the shaded side of a mountain. "Which makes me wonder…" He stopped sketching and stared up, as if smelling something. "How is there a wind in here? Where is it coming from?" The pastel sky offered no answers, only more questions. "How can such a massive structure hold its weight? How does it know when to light up? Are there seasons in here? Is the air we are breathing filtered from the outside, or are we breathing in scents trapped here since the Downfall?"

"I'd say you should ask the Miscam," Sterjall said, "but I don't see any cities here." He was searching for signs of habitation with his binoculars, but he found nothing. He passed the device to Balstei.

"What are we going to do once we find them?" Balstei asked. "I only know a handful of Miscamish words."

"Maybe they speak Common?" Jiara replied with a shrug. "We don't even know if they'll be friendly or see us as a threat. They've been stuck here for almost fifteen hundred years—we can't tell how they'll react to strangers showing up all of a sudden."

"Should we keep the masks on?" Sterjall asked.

Jiara gave it some thought. "I think it might be safer to keep them hidden, for now. We can always reveal them when needed. Better to avoid any strong reactions at first."

Sterjall agreed. Lago put his mask away.

"I see a structure!" Balstei excitedly announced. "Down there, see that big waterfall with a square shape on top? And those cuts on the cliff, they must be massive pillars framing the falls."

"That's not too far," Jiara said, "we could arrive in a day or two if we follow the river. But first we should rest. It feels like noon, but it's past midnight outside the dome."

They found fruits and nuts to eat. It was warmer here than it had been on the outside, so they felt no need for a fire. They spread their bedrolls around the escarpment and only then realized how truly tired they were. They sank into their bedrolls and closed their eyes.

Alaia was the first to awaken. "Gwoli, look," she said, shaking Lago's shoulder. "Look at the sky."

Lago sat up. The dome was extinguishing its glow. The smallest vines near the horizon had darkened first, then the next smallest, followed by the large ones, and then the incomprehensibly large, creating a pattern like that of a leaf skeleton. All the lights receded toward the central trunk. It was a very slow process, and they had all risen to watch it as they boiled water for a meal.

"It's like a giant mushroom ungrowing," Balstei said when only half the dome remained lit, leaving a giant, tightening iris above them.

"Looks like a tree made of light to me," Alaia said. "Or like the shapes you see in cracked mud, but with lights shining inside each crack."

After a long while, even the trunk's splitting top went dark, leaving only the trunk itself lit up, a vertical beacon softly transitioning to darkness at its base.

"The light is so strange," Jiara mused, "it feels so different now."

"It's the shadows," Lago said. "There were no shadows in the daytime, and now that all the light comes from one point, the shadows are sharp, all stretching away from the center."

The effect was particularly eerie extending from the supporting columns, which cast radial shadows all the way to the dome's periphery and even onto the now dark-green sky. The light dimmed to what looked like sharp moonlight, then the curved sky darkened further.

Once even the trunk had fallen into its dark slumber, they were left awash in an inky blue sea. The lights on the vines had not darkened entirely but lingered with an ungraspable blueness similar to a rich, post-twilight sky.

"That was magnificent," Jiara half-whispered, eyes locked onto the starless dome.

"See, I told you," Balstei said, releasing them from their spell. He pointed at the structure he had spotted earlier, above the waterfall. Now it was clearly visible, as there were fires burning inside windows. Many other lights soon showed themselves—some orange, some green—clustering toward the center of the dome, with no lights at the dome's periphery.

"The ancient ones still live," Balstei said, "and with them lives the knowledge of times past. What a wonder, what an opportunity."

"Look," Lago said. "The sky is still lighting up." Seven miles above, a couple of branches flickered, illuminating fast, then taking a long moment to dissipate.

"They remind me of lightning bolts," Jiara said. "Ones that imprint your retinas with a lasting afterimage."

"Or like meteors shattering through a sphere of glass in the sky," Alaia added, not knowing where the thought had come from.

"They look like the drawings of constellations to me," Lago said, "those lines that connect the dots on star maps. Just like that, but with no stars."

The eerie flickers continued through the night, albeit rarely, a handful of times each hour. The shards of light were a quaint substitute for the moon and the stars: beautiful in their own way, and massive on an entirely different scale factor, but massive and beautiful nonetheless.

"Although we got enough rest," Jiara said, "we should wait for daylight. We shouldn't risk moving about in the dark."

"And it will reset our bodies," Balstei added, "helping us adapt to this new schedule."

It took them a while, but eventually they fell asleep again, tricked by the darkness, which made them feel more tired than they truly were. They woke up multiple times during the night, startled by the unfamiliar calls of katydids, night birds, and unknown creatures whose eyes elusively shimmered around their camp.

Lago had been shifting in his bedroll, unable to sleep. He kept his half-lidded eyes on the dome, waiting for one of the distant branches to randomly light up. A different kind of light shook him wide awake, like a needle of gold streaking from the sky.

"What is that?" he voiced a bit too loudly.

"What is what?" Alaia croaked, eyes barely opening.

"That light up in the—" But the light was already gone. "It was... it was like a meteor, but held there in the sky, like a thin beam of light that... that..."

"One of the flashing branches?" Jiara groggily said.

"No, not like that. Just a straight line, yellow-colored and extremely bright."

"Perhaps it was a wisp," Balstei conjectured, sitting up, a bit more interested than the rest. "Or rather, a *reverse* wisp. If we can see wisps outside, when the spacing in the vines lines up for the light to exit, then the Miscam must be able to see wisps here on the inside too, from Sunnokh's light coming in."

"That... that would make sense. Except that this one was much brighter, and it disappeared quickly. Wisps normally last for weeks."

"Hmm..." Balstei said, pulling at his mustache. "With that in mind, it makes even more sense. Inside this dome, the entire sky is evenly lit, so the wisps we see from the outside are static and not very concentrated. And if you think of the opposite situation, in here the 'reverse wisps' would show up when Sunnokh is in exactly the right alignment, and since the sun moves through the sky, the wisp could vanish in a heartbeat. It would be much brighter as well, as it would come from a single, direct source."

"I think that makes sense," Lago agreed, trying to picture the angles and intensities of light. *Crysta would be so thrilled to hear about all this*, he thought. *I can't wait to tell her.* He lay back down and kept his eyes on the dome, hoping to see more reverse wisps. He saw none, but the thoughts helped his mind drift happily to sleep.

Morning began at the central trunk, expanding radially like a fountain of light. The radiance ran through the largest vines first, and when reaching the supporting columns, it spread like ripples in a bioluminescent pond. Over the course of an hour, the sky went from twilight blue to a white-streaked green, finally settling into pearlescent pastels.

"It's so uncanny," Lago said. "It never went red or orange, or even yellow like a proper sunrise or sunset." He slung his bag over his shoulder and followed the others, starting their trek toward the river.

The deep forest had a primeval quintessence to it, and though it looked untamed, in its wildness was veiled an unseen order.

"These trees are so huge," Lago remarked, as Jiara helped him climb over a root as high as a wall.

"I think there's a tree growing out of this tree," Alaia said, trying to comprehend the tangles around them.

"It's a strangler fig," Jiara said. "We call them *banyans* in the Free Tribelands. They don't grow anywhere near this size in our forests."

"These trees might've been alive before the Downfall," Balstei said. "This place feels ancient."

They could no longer see the waterfall they were headed toward, but they knew the river would guide them in that direction. The waters dragged a chilled air by their legs, dropping the temperature as if the season had suddenly turned to Umbra. The river splashed and twirled devilishly at the rocky shore, making them glad that they were not planning on crossing the strong current.

As they walked alongside a tumble of cascades, Jiara spotted something on the opposite shore. "Hold. Over there, among the reeds," she said.

"Is that some sort of cat?" Alaia asked, only able to spot a flicking tail within the swaying of reeds.

A rustling sound spooked them as a huge felid flew out of the reeds and into the water. She disappeared briefly, then surfaced with a hefty otter in her jaws.

"What sort of cat is that?" Alaia whispered. "Such beautiful stripes…"

"I don't know," Jiara murmured thoughtfully. "I've seen striped cats before, but never of that size or color."

"I think…" Lago said, still remembering, "I think that's a tiger. Banook once described them to me. He said they went extinct."

"Many giant cat species roamed before the Downfall," Balstei said. "None survived the fires, except for mountain lions, as far as we know."

They snuck away from the tiger and her prey.

"Balstei, can you use a bow?" Jiara asked.

"Maybe? I haven't tried. My arms are strong," he said, tapping a bulky biceps.

"It's more in your back muscles, but those arms will help. Either way, keep Ockam's bow and arrows at the ready. Those tigers look fierce."

"Don't you think their cats might be tame?" Lago asked. "Or maybe not tame, but they at least would not attack humans?"

"Possibly," Jiara answered. "Or maybe they are trained to maul intruders."

They saw other felids along the way, most of which they could not name, but none the size of the tigers. The smaller cats were curious, but careful, slinking around the trees. Their slim frames reminded Lago of pine martens and ferrets.

Once the sky dissolved into its mosaic of blues, they stopped to rest underneath an overhanging rock, where dangling roots provided suitable cover for the night.

"This will do for a shelter." Jiara said. "We can light a fire to scare away any creatures while we sleep."

As they gathered around the campfire, they recounted stories from their travels. Lago was telling Balstei about his first time as Sterjall, how Banook had helped him find his focus, and how staring into a pool of swirling leaves had set him into a different mental state, allowing him to shapeshift for the first time.

Lago enjoyed telling these stories to Balstei, as a way of reliving those happy moments, reawakening the powerful love he felt toward Banook. The melody of Banook's mountain song began to play in his head, and he was glad for its warm company.

I hear the wind caress my fur, sharp claws resound along. The spruce and pine, and cones of fir all join the mountain song. Lago sighed, eyes lost in the flickering flames. *I miss you.*

"And what about you, Jiara?" Balstei asked. "How come you haven't found a way to shapeshift yet?"

"Don't think I haven't tried," she said as she fidgeted with the ursid mask. "Since that day at the bogs, every moment I've had to myself, I've attempted to find that bear within me, but I still haven't figured it out. I've never seen myself as a fierce bear like Banook, it's hard to connect to that. But I will keep trying."

Jiara kept pondering over ursid forms that night. She had placed Urnaadisilv in her backpack, which she was using as a pillow. There was an image somewhere in the back of her mind, something that would make sense for her, but she was unable to draw it out. She dozed off uneasily, trying to recall the image, lulled by the crackling sounds of the fire.

Chapter Twelve

Climb On

Jiara dreamed.

She dreamed she was back in Thornridge, but the trees were taller than ever before, lost above clouds like the tall columns inside the domes. She wanted to get a better view of the forest, so she climbed one of the lookout's watchtowers. From up there, she saw her sister looking for her. Jiara had left the Free Tribelands without saying goodbye. She screamed her sister's name, over and over, but her sister could not hear her.

Fuck her, she thought in her dream, feeling guilty. She turned around and saw that there were more levels to the tower, rising higher than she remembered. She climbed on. The steps were slippery, covered in moss and something that looked like coagulated blood. They led her to a wooden wall with a rope ladder that she held tightly and used to pull her weight up.

The ropes were green and waxy, and she had to avoid the many thorns that grew on them, but she climbed on. She could smell the freshness of pine mixed with the bitterness of white sap and a pungent aroma that reminded her of scorched flesh. She felt a sting, and looked at her injured hands. She had cut herself on the thorns, and her palms were dripping golden pine sap. She licked the sap that bled from her wounds—it tasted like honey.

She climbed on, using her sticky hands to aid her, ignoring the sting on her palms. The vines wept white beneath her tight grip.

The wall she climbed was frozen now, and there was no rope to hold on to, nor were there vines or wooden steps; but bones stuck out from the ice. She climbed on, using a jawbone as a hold, then the protruding ribs of a massive beast as a staircase. She crawled into the eye socket of a half-frozen skull, to keep warm, to take a breath. Inside the eye socket, she found crampons. She attached them to her boots.

Jiara climbed on, kicking her sharp metal crampons into the wall. But the ice was melting, and through the thinning wall a pink substance palpitated. The ice broke, revealing a wall of skin covered in pores and wiry hairs. She touched it, and the hairs tensed with goosebumps. She had to keep climbing, but there was nothing left to hold on to.

She dug her nails into the flesh to pull herself up. The tissue pulsated around her fingers, shivering, spasming. Her nails grew longer, sharper, and she slashed and tore and dug into the column of flesh, ascending while blood sprayed out from the holes she dug. She felt the flesh twitch in pain and stopped. She saw that the wall was covered in scars, and all she was doing was adding fresh wounds on top of them. The new cuts looked painful, but she knew they would also heal in time.

Her claws were long and dark now, like knives. Her wet nose smelled the canopy above her, so she climbed on. The flesh was hardening beneath her grip, crackling like dry mud. It got harder and became a thick, layered bark, fragrant and welcoming. She pushed herself up on branches and burls. Clouds of yellow pollen spiraled in ghostly shapes as she hugged the thinning tree trunk and reached yet higher.

The trunk ended abruptly in a jagged summit, as if it had been split by lightning. She was at the top now, and so high that the sky was not blue but black, and there was no air to breathe.

She tried to look at herself, but she could see only her long claws. She could not even see the color of her own fur, no matter how hard she tried; it was there, but it was beyond her reach. She turned to see the sky-high forest around her. Most of the trees were below her, but two of them rose higher. Atop one of those two trees, she saw herself. No, it was not herself, but her sister, taking a nap on a branch, careless and comfortable. She loved her. She hated her. She missed her.

But there was one tree yet higher than that one. She looked up at it, her eyes sparkling of starlight.

I must reach the top, Jiara thought, *I am not high enough yet*. She dug her claws back into her own tree to begin her descent.

The tallest tree waited for her.

Chapter Thirteen

Grest Miscamish

The fire was dead.

A muffled scream alerted Lago that something was wrong. As he opened his eyes, he felt someone grab him from behind, then choked as something dry was shoved into his mouth. Under the dim light, he saw Jiara, Balstei, and Alaia with their hands tied behind their backs and gags in their mouths. Lago felt a fang-like knife pressed to his throat and gave himself up without struggling, but when his captors bent his injured limb backward, he jolted up with a searing pain burning in his shoulder and forearm.

He collapsed to the ground from the pain. The strange people tried to force him again by pulling on his arm, further injuring him, until they understood the problem. Instead, they tied only Lago's left arm, but as a precaution also his legs. A towering, big-boned man picked Lago up and carried him on his shoulders. Lago suddenly remembered Leif; he looked toward his belt—his dagger wasn't there.

He tried to make himself comfortable, but it was impossible with one arm tied to his back and the other still throbbing and useless. The man carrying him was built like a stone monolith and had no hair on his head; the thick skin around the back of his skull folded in ridges and fissures, like the surface of a brain, and it was decorated with blue patterns that blended with the wavy skin. The man smelled of salt, smoke, and singed leather.

Their captors were fleet of foot. A small group behind them carried all their gear while a group in front scouted the path without a light to guide them. They were completely silent, eyes attentive.

After they were a long way from the camp, the captors relaxed, and Lago at last heard them chatting and laughing their nerves off. He did not understand any of their words.

The sky brightened, or rather, the trunk did, allowing Lago to see them better. They had no tattoos or red-colored skin like Bonmei or Sontai, but fully smooth skin of a lighter hue. Their faces seemed Khaar Du due to their high cheekbones, slanted eyes, and wide noses, but unlike the Khaar Du, their features were rounded instead of angular. Entirely bald they were, not just in the head, but everywhere Lago could see. Each of their scalps was decorated with unique patterns of blue: some simple and organic, some geometric and intricate.

Lago tried gesturing, humming, twisting to get their attention. They ignored his pleas. When he got too loud, they made eye contact and placed fingers over his gagged mouth.

Hours later, they stopped at a clearing where a ring of stones grinned like sharp teeth. They sat their captives down in the circle, backs against the rocks.

Lago looked around, his chest and shoulders throbbing from having been carried. All the warriors wore a peculiar jacket that wrapped around their arms and connected around their backs while leaving their hairless torsos and bellies completely exposed. Around their waists they wore kilts of a variety of muted colors, some made of finely worked leather, others of woven plant fibers that gave them a geometric sheen. Their weapons—knives, spears, and blowguns—seemed to all be made of bones.

A woman squatted in front of Lago and examined his curls, fascinated by them. Her eyes were a piercing green. The blue pigments decorating her scalp were fading, leaving only a washed-out, cold ghost of an image. The woman smiled, made the gesture over Lago's mouth to keep quiet, then removed his gag.

Lago coughed. The gag's fibers had dried up his mouth, leaving it raw. The woman helped Lago take a sip from her waterskin, then looked down at his injured arm and touched it; Lago winced. She then showed him a bright-purple fruit, took a bite from it, and put it in front of his face. Lago was starving. He ate the entire fruit until all that remained was a hard seed at the center.

He saw his friends being given the same treatment.

Once they were done being fed, the rock-bodied man with the folds on his scalp approached menacingly. He pointed his bone spear at them, and asked, "*Jakri ragisse echienn olvet seltäu haabral? Echienn aruss shiörelg, wem shisen?*"

"We don't speak Miscamish," Balstei answered.

The man reacted to the word *Miscamish* and replied directly to Balstei, "*Chienn enuss Miscamish? Ilm laar ah afahuss chiennat?*"

Balstei replied, "*Grest. Grest Miscamish.*" His knowledge of the old Miscam tongue was slim, but he knew the word for *no*. "We speak Common, do you speak Common?"

The tall man lodged his skeletal spear in the ground, then grunted, "*Maalt. Glal maalt. Grest* Commom." He gestured something to his people, who hurried to help the foreigners up to their feet.

"Wait, wait!" Lago cried before the man picked him up again; he pointed his chin to his injured shoulder and rolled it around with a pained expression on his face. The kind woman said something to the man, gesturing with her brows and pursing lips toward Lago's legs. Lago smiled and nodded. She untied Lago's legs and let him walk next to her.

The wayfarers had no gags and were walking close to each other now, but they were still careful not to raise their voices.

"They are treating us too kindly, for kidnappers," Balstei said.

"That large man seemed to understand what Common is," Lago said, "even if he doesn't speak it."

"Common was around before Miscamish," Balstei said, "so it doesn't surprise me it survived inside the domes. Why do you think they are letting us walk with no gags now?"

"Recall how they quietly removed us from the camp and didn't relax until we were far from it," Jiara replied. "They were being careful in case there were more of us we could alert. It's what I would've done."

"It'll be hard to explain why we are here until we're more familiar with their language," Alaia said. "We should try and be friendly to them."

Alaia saw that they were being taken toward the mountain with the waterfall they had been trying to reach before being captured. She whistled to get the attention of the friendly woman marching next to Lago. The woman looked at Alaia, and Alaia said, "*Stelm,*" pointing her nose at the mountain. The woman smiled and repeated, "*Stelm.*"

Alaia then pointed her nose to the waterfall and said, "*Minnel.*" The woman frowned, then corrected her. "*Minnéllo.*"

"*Minnéllo,*" Alaia repeated, and the woman smiled brightly at her.

"Like Minnelvad," she told Lago. "Might as well try to learn what we can."

Next, she pointed at each of her friends in turn, saying, "Lago, Jiara, Balstei," She then pointed her nose at the woman. No response. Alaia repeated the same gestures and words. The woman understood then, put her hand over her blue-patterned scalp, and said, "Givra." Then she pointed her nose to Alaia in the same way she'd done. Alaia grinned and said, "Alaia."

"Lagu, Jara, Baaste, Leia."

Alaia laughed. "Close enough."

"Klosenaf," Givra said, shifting her bag over her shoulder; it was beautiful, made of a plant fiber so thin it looked like silk.

Alaia pointed at it and said, "Bag."

Givra glanced at her bag and said, "*Alsolt*. Beauty." Alaia was happily surprised. Then Givra lifted Alaia's overall straps. The garment had seen better days, being patched up in many places, but still held together.

Alaia said, "Overalls," gesturing at the entire garment, including the straps.

"Obreolls," Givra repeated. She stroked her open-chested jacket, the same style all the members of her party wore, and said, "*Shodog*." She then showed Alaia how her shodog could be used: the sleeves connected by a loose fabric on the back, draping like a small cape down over their buttocks. Givra reached back for the loose bit of fabric and expertly tossed it over her head, creating a hood that covered even her shoulders.

Alaia and Givra kept learning as they walked. The others learned by overhearing their conversation. Pines were *far*; Jiara could've told them that one, as she was born in the Farsulf, or *pine land*. Stones were *cowom*, the sky was *nokh*, the river was *stiss*; that one all of them had known. Food—or perhaps *eating*, Alaia wasn't sure—was *fam*.

They reached the base of the *stelm*, where wide steps, named *gake*, led right into the *cowom* face. Two massive engaged columns rose on either side of the waterfall cliff. Those had been the structures Balstei had spotted, and now that the group was next to them, they were reminded of the columns at the Cliffside Lifts of Zovaria: there were windows in the columns, and through them they could see a lift dropping to meet them, fitted perfectly to the interior of the hollowed rock.

The platform reached the bottom of the column. Three curious onlookers exited it, but the big man yelled something at them and pushed his way in, ushering the entire group into the lift. There were no gates or levers; the lift simply began to ascend.

A wall of mist suddenly sprayed through a passing window. The opening vanished as they kept ascending.

"This makes me wonder," Balstei said, raising his voice so they could hear him over the roar of the waterfall, "if they have rainbows in this world. If all they get is this even sky and no direct sunlight, they might not even know what a rainbow is."

Through a vertical slit, Lago spotted an enormous barrel descending at the same rate as they were ascending. *A counterweight*, he deduced.

The lift stopped at a rock-carved tunnel lit by sconces. They followed it, ignoring many branching passages until the tunnel exited into a square courtyard surrounded by stone arches draped by tree roots. The wayfarers were brought to the center of the courtyard, where two well-armed warriors saluted the leaders of the scouting party with a head-bumping gesture, then stood at attention next to the foreigners.

"*Diathuk*. Wait," one of the warriors said, hand ready on his sheathed knife. Givra and the others exited through a mossy archway.

A crowd gathered at the edges of the courtyard, watching in astonishment. Balstei felt as if they were livestock on display at an auction.

Lago noticed children hiding behind columns: some giggling, others weeping in fear. Not a single soul—neither the children nor adults—grew any sort of head or body hair other than eyebrows and eyelashes. Among the children, he noticed what looked like a tortoiseshell-furred housecat, but the cat was enormous, the size of a wolf. The cat stared at them briefly with a mixture of curiosity and indifference, then leapt over a toppled column and was gone.

Balstei wriggled his arms, trying to free his hands.

"Don't fight it," Jiara said. "It's better if we don't appear threatening to them. Let's just wait and see what they want."

They heard a thundering growl, and from under an archway came six enormous felids much larger than the tiger they had encountered by the river, larger even than draft horses. Each wielded enormous, saber-like fangs, which protruded like stalactites beneath their lower jaws.

"Shit," Balstei said, backing up into one of the warriors. "They'll feed us to their beasts!" He lost his balance, fell on his ass, and tried to worm away.

"Calm down!" Lago told him. "Stay still, hold on."

The warriors walking alongside the beasts laughed. One man repeated, "Shit!" and helped Balstei up. The saber-toothed cats prowled around them, pacing with massive paws that landed soundlessly on the tiny yellow flowers that carpeted the courtyard. Their coats were of a variety of dusky chocolate colors, faded to yellow or white at their bellies, and with very dim rosettes and spots that were only visible when the light hit them at a particular angle. Their round pupils carved dark holes inside hazel irises, while their short tails snapped left and right, judgingly. One of the cats sniffed at Jiara's blonde braid, then huffed and turned, scraping his thick whiskers over her face.

Givra was having a slightly heated conversation with the tall, muscular man. The man spat and seemed to give up. To the warriors behind the foreigners, he commanded, "*Rennuthuk chelefash. Da umbresh grei uth khaleglash.*"

The warriors untied all their hands, but kept their knives pointed at them as a warning. The tall man said, "*Grest egla.* No trouble."

"No trouble," Balstei repeated. He walked closer to his friends and whispered, "These... These saber-toothed cats. I've seen their bones at the Horjalv Museum, we call them smilodons. We have fossils of them, though none of this enormous size."

An allgender joined the group, who had purple pigments on their head instead of blue. They whistled piercingly, and all six of the smilodons dropped to their bellies. Warriors placed saddles on the cats while the allgender fed them a strange-looking paste cut into cubes.

Givra was first to hop onto a saddle. There were no reins to pull, not even a collar. "Leia!" she said and tapped the cat's shoulder blades.

"You are fucking kidding me," Alaia replied.

"Fakin kiddemmi," Givra responded and tapped again. She nodded to the warrior behind Alaia, who picked her up and placed her in front of Givra.

The others followed, each mounting a different animal; some carried two, some three passengers. The largest of the cats—who was bright like a sandy beach, sprinkled in lighter, creamy spots—carried all their gear, along with a heavy bundle of supplies that had been loaded up on her thick back. She needed no rider to guide her. Lago was placed in front of the tall man, who tapped the shoulder of his smilodon and proclaimed, "*Echoss aith melm ve nokh onnäith!*"

They rode under a green archway.

The smilodons were speedier than galloping horses, yet their paws were as silent as a moth's heartbeat. Lago was glad his hands had been granted freedom, as he enjoyed grasping the chocolate fur of the cat while they cut through the air like sharp arrows. The cat's shoulders went up and down rhythmically, undulating like mountains of fur during an earthquake. As the fur folded under his grasp, Lago saw that each of the hairs was striped, creating a unique coloration at deeper levels, old and colorful like sandstone strata.

They rode for hours, covering vast distances with haste and agility, hopping treacherous creeks, crossing through tunnels that snaked underneath the roots of old groves. They were climbing constantly, headed toward the trunk, which became clearer after every long stride.

They briefly stopped at a headland that overlooked the Isdinnklad Sea, which was as still as a sheet of glass. Far below sailed strange ships: green their sails were and shaped like leaves. A vine column rose straight ahead of them, about five miles out into the sea. From this elevation, and with the perfect stillness of the water, the reflected column looked like it continued down forever and became lost in a void where water and sky were the same.

Givra hopped down the smilodon and went to retrieve a basket heavy with food patties. A herd of tiny sand cats followed at her feet, begging for scraps with what sounded more like barks than meows. Givra whistled, then called out, "*Pichi!*"

The largest of the smilodons approached and dropped to her belly before Givra, shushing away the smaller felids as if they were gnats. While Givra loaded the basket atop Pichi's harness, Alaia remembered the word for *felid*, and tapping on the shoulder of the smilodon she was riding, said, "*Mindrel.*"

Givra seemed surprised, as she hadn't taught Alaia that word. She put her hand on Pichi's muscular chest and said, "*Mindrégo.*" Then she pointed at two smilodons, one with each hand, and said, "*Mindrégosh.*" She squatted down and scratched the chin of one of the sand cats, who was still imploring for scraps, and said, "*Mindillli.*" She then stood in a broad gesture, almost like a dance, signaling to all the cats around her, and said, "*Mindrel!*" and laughed.

That gave Lago an idea. He looked up at the towering man sitting behind him and said, "*Mindrelfröa?*"

The man's face grew stern. He looked at Givra questioningly. Givra seemed confused.

"What are you trying to do?" Jiara said near him.

"Maybe it's time we mention the masks. It might help us." He put his hand on his head—as he had seen Givra do—and said, "*Agnargfröa.*"

The tall man's already furrowed brow furrowed further, into chasms. Then his lips widened, he shook with laughter, and said, "*Agnargfröa, fala!*"

Lago tried again. He pointed toward Jiara and said, "*Urnaadifröa.*"

This time, even Givra laughed. They chuckled as they signaled for the smilodons to move, then continued their sprint toward the center of the Moordusk Dome.

Chapter Fourteen

Secret Messages

It had been two weeks since Lago had gone missing again. Crysta and Gwil had been mercilessly interrogated by Admiral Grinn, and they had answered all his questions truthfully—since Kedra already knew everything they knew, they never felt the pressure to lie. Kedra even dared to show her face at the interrogations once, but Crysta's eyes told Kedra everything she'd ever hear from her again. Fortunately, the admiral claimed he hadn't spoken about the masks with the dean of the institute or with the monks at the monastery; the Arch Sedecims had asked Grinn to keep utmost secrecy in these matters.

Crysta was walking back to the School of Cosmology after her latest interrogation when she heard someone running behind her.

"Crysta!" a scholar exhaled, hurrying toward her. "Where in the nethervoids have you been?"

It was Dashal, the scholar who operated the sunnograph at the tower of the School of Cosmology. Crysta had been directed to continue her work while in Zovaria, helping Dashal with the transmission and receipt of messages. She felt more at ease with Dashal, as they could discuss matters related to the military, but she never mentioned her involvement with Lago, Balstei, or the masks.

"I told you I had things to take care of," Crysta said. "What is—"

"We received a message, from Withervale."

"Withervale! How did they—"

"Let's go up together. I'll show you."

They hurried up the interminable spiral staircase. This wasn't like the tower in Withervale: it was much taller, and much more ostentatious in construction, particularly under the golden cone at the spire.

Dashal was out of breath by the time they reached the top. "I haven't shown this… to anyone else yet. I wanted you… to see it first." He adjusted his thick, square spectacles, removed a paperweight from a pile of notes, and handed the top page to Crysta. It read:

> 13-Lustbloom-1455. Negian soldiers took mines and monastery, forcing us all into soot production. Monks okay, except Hailem, they are past the Six Gates. Observatory now used by Negians, spying Isdinnklad with telescope. Port taken, shipyard building ships, rampart down. I stole the sunnograph. Operating from balcony at Haven's chapel, Negians unaware of device. Will report same time, Sunnday. DO NOT REPLY unless you see our light on first. Transmit only while our light shines, keep replies short. If our light blinks during your transmission, stop signal, await instructions. -Esum

"Esum is alive!" Crysta exclaimed. "Thank the Twin Gods. But Hailem? They were so young…" She reread the note. "Was there a message encoded in the spectrum?"

"No, just white light. If Esum gets in trouble and they force her to send a message, I'm sure she'll tell us with an encoded message underneath. At least, I'm hoping she's smart enough to do that. Is she good with the instrument?"

"Slower than I am, but she can handle it." Crysta flopped heavily on a chair. "I need to let Esum know we made it out, that we'll be receiving her messages. Do we have full control of the sunnograph?"

"Yes. Only the two of us will be accessing it, but I'll be reporting back to the agent who hired me. I can't reveal their name, but I will have to be open about our transmissions."

"That is fine, I work the same way. I'll have you read through the messages before sending them." She pointed at the desk behind Dashal. "Do you mind?"

Dashal handed Crysta a quill, ink, and a clean piece of paper. Crysta took her time and wrote:

> C and Gw safe in Z. Kh PTSG. Will watch for signal, safe to transmit. -C

Crysta handed the compact message to Dashal and said, "We'll have to warn the Nedross and Wujann observatories to operate in a new way, keeping the messages ready to be delivered instead of immediately passing them through to Withervale."

Kedra had traveled with Admiral Grinn and a troop of three hundred mounted cavalry to secure the boglands around the city of Muskeg, which was the nearest easy access point to the Moordusk Dome. They met a larger unit of infantry soldiers there, and with their help attempted to create a contained perimeter around the dome. They were forced to focus their efforts near the cities, as their resources didn't allow for more; the battle at Withervale had depleted their forces. Kedra was afraid that Jiara might choose to take her fugitive friends through the Moordusk Bogs. It would be impossible to track them if they took that route, but she had to make do with securing Muskeg and then Nebush.

The admiral had assigned his captains to patrol the waters, checking for stowaways aboard any suspicious ships. Although Grinn felt more comfortable at sea, he now had a much more important mission on land.

Kedra had shared with the admiral her copy of the map, which wasn't of much interest to the Zovarian army, except for the dome that wasn't known to exist. She'd told Grinn that Lago wanted to go to the Brasha'in Scablands after visiting the Moordusk Dome. In this, the Zovarians had the upper hand: with their cavalry, they could cross the dried-up lava fields much faster than the fugitives, and if there was a mask there for the taking—as there had been at Da'áju—they would reach it first.

"They aren't coming this way. That Tribeswoman is too smart," Kedra said to Admiral Grinn as they rode their horses back to the command post from a perimeter check. She felt she must look ridiculous riding the enormous destrier horse that the cavalry had entrusted her with. Her petite body was but an ornament atop the velvety-black coat, flowing mane, and powerful hindquarters of the beast. She couldn't wait to get down—the townsfolk of Muskeg were staring.

To top it off, the admiral had the audacity to try to help her dismount, as if she were a child. She slapped his gauntleted hand away, a gesture that would have garnered severe repercussions if the admiral had not been her uncle. She hopped off on her own and handed the reins to a dragoon at the stables.

"It's been long enough, we need to head to the scablands now," she told him. "They are either in hiding, or already inside the Moordusk Dome. Leave the cavalry here to keep watch. We can take a squad and hire rangers at Alluviar. They have war caribou there, better suited to our mission."

"You, my dear, do not get to give orders to the army," Admiral Grinn said, once again belittling his niece.

"You don't either, uncle, you only command your fleet. Marshal Embercut oversees the ground forces, and I'll have a word with her."

Grinn scowled. He underestimated Kedra, but at least that also meant he would let certain things slide. He knew she was right this time, however, and he had already talked with the marshal about taking a cavalry squadron to the scablands, but he didn't want to give Kedra the satisfaction of agreeing with her.

Two days later, supplies were loaded on the draft horses while a group of forty lancers and dragoons prepared to leave, with Kedra and the admiral joining them. As the horses were readied, Kedra examined the mounts and warned her uncle, "I thought we agreed we'd hire mountain folk and caribou from Alluviar. They are the only ones who can travel that terrain safely."

"We will hire a few," Grinn said, "but our horses will go with us for protection."

Kedra shook her head. "Drop anything metal, bring waterskins instead. There's no need for armor or extra supplies for the mounts. Most won't make it through the lava fields—their hooves will cut on the sharp rocks."

"That's why we are bringing plenty of magsteel horseshoes. The strong alloy can't possibly break, and we can replace them *if* they wear down."

"The black glass will lodge itself like knives between the horseshoes, right into their soles. Be ready to lose the mounts and continue on foot."

"You worry too much. We'll have a shaman with heralds in case we need to send out for more supplies." The admiral was tired of Kedra's insolence and stalked away to add more weight to his mount. Kedra went to her own horse to see how much weight she could remove.

Chapter Fifteen

The Legacy

The Red Stag returned to Hestfell to announce his victory over Withervale to roaring crowds. The entirety of the Negian capital, from the winding mountain paths to the gates of the three mesas, was decorated with his red sigil. Even his newly acquired quaar shield had been emblazoned with the elk-skull laurels; he showcased it to further solidify his rule as a confluence of the powers of Takhísh and Takhamún, referring to it as Gaönir-Bijeor, like the mythical Shield of Creation.

His army had taken charge of Withervale, already utilizing the shipyard and the new port they'd acquired. They had spared most of the Oldrin, who would be needed to work the coal mines, and also spared most of the monks at the Mesa Monastery, who were best trained and equipped to purify soot. Shamans required heavy doses of the aetheric carbon to speak with their heralds and send them to remote lands with which the Empire needed to communicate.

Monarch Hallow had left the First Legion in charge of Withervale, under the command of General Edmar Helm. He'd never liked Edmar, who always over-inflated his achievements while smirking with his stupid, crooked lower lip. This was Hallow's way of keeping his old challenger out of the way, rotting in that wretched border town while he went forth and conquered.

In the months since the taking of the Anglass Dome, the Negian Empire had been flooded with a stream of riches: furs, precious metals, gemstones, spices, magnium ores, quaar relics, and slaves—hordes of slaves.

The Teldebran Miscam slaves were not as productive as the Oldrin ones, for they'd not been broken yet. Yet the Negians found them more appealing. They considered the Teldebran's pale skin and long black hair sensual, and the fact they didn't have spurs on their bodies was very welcome.

Since the attack on Withervale, the Red Stag had thought hard about his order of succession, and how to keep the throne secure during his absence. To maximize his odds of producing an heir, he chose many concubines from different levels of nobility to impregnate. He did not know whether a woman could conceive children with him while he was in his elk half-form, but that did not stop him from trying.

The Red Stag wiped off his long, tapered cock, then got dressed. He had a banquet to attend. He left Ulle dus Grei, sister to the dead Emperor Uvon dus Grei, sobbing as she covered herself with the drenched sheets. If there was one woman who would be ideal to help him ensure his future dynasty, that woman was Ulle.

As he left his bedroom, he said to a servant, "Make sure Ulle gets as good a dinner as we do. She did not want to attend the banquet and will remain in the bedroom."

"As you command, Monarch Hallow," the servant acknowledged with a deep bow.

Viceroy Urcai came running down the hall. His ornate orange-and-gray doublet was partially covered by a half shoulder cape of the darkest silks. The golden embroidery on his new outfit seemed as decadent as the kenzir stones of legend.

"Monarch Hallow, the generals and new ministers are waiting," he said, pulling his slim spectacles down his nose. "I've had the grand chancellor seated next to you, as you should discuss the land registers before he returns to Lamanni. Our new imperial counselor, Duke Leveret Sun, can assist with those matters as well. He will be there to overhear any conversations you may have."

"Urcai, you know I'd prefer to leave these decisions to you. I have more important things to worry about. Feel free to introduce me to these new... bureaucrats"—he nearly choked on that word—"but don't expect me to remember all their names."

"Of course, Monarch Hallow. But we'll still need you to sign the treaties tomorrow."

"Fine."

"And I have good news," Urcai added, "from the Lequa Dome. I will brief you fully after the banquet, but I thought you might want to know about it before—"

"Just spit it out."

"Certainly. General Behler Broadleaf has discovered that the graphite mines inside the dome are of aetheric graphite. A crystalline form of soot."

"Soot from graphite, not coal?" the Red Stag asked, slowing his pace.

"Indeed, Monarch Hallow. And more pure than any source we have access to, even Withervale's mines. It should provide enough soot to supply all our shamans during the war effort. You'll be able to venture into other realms while we solidify our strategy with no delays in communication."

"Splendid. Perhaps this will convince some of those thick-headed ministers of the value of fully committing to our cause. I'll need to learn all the details after this dreadful event is over."

Urcai eyed the monarch's outfit, particularly the sword held by his belt. "Have you considered trading your longsword for a spear? With your new quaar shield, that would certainly draw attention and birth legends on its own."

"Crescu is better with the spear than I. I can't abandon my wave-bladed beauty, it would be like giving up a part of myself."

"But as a tool for command. Visualize the powerful presence you'd project if you were to hold both Gaönir-Bijeor and Tor-Reveo in your hands. Hooves."

"I will give it some thought," the Red Stag said, fixing the dewlap poking from his collar as they neared the end of the hallway.

"I will request that the finest blacksmiths of Gulas Hassol craft a spear worthy of legend," Urcai said, taking charge without waiting for his monarch's confirmation. "We could use the quaar staff from the Gathallar collection as the shaft. It's a beautiful piece of art."

"A quaar shaft? As long as you properly balance its weight, or it'll be impractical."

"It would not be for fighting, but I'll make sure they balance it well. Think of our replica of Tor-Reveo more as a ceremonial scepter. A very deadly and persuasive scepter."

The Red Stag ducked to avoid hitting his antlers on the top of the archway as he entered the banquet hall. Twenty-four chairs were filled by self-righteous dignitaries, newly ordained officials, and power-hungry sycophants. They stood and covered any ranking insignias they possessed, all slightly terrified of the elk's presence, even those who'd seen his half-form before.

A handful of the army's highest-ranked officers were present too: General Gino Baneras, a master of the longbow who commanded the Fourth Legion;

General Korten dus Fer, a fearless strategist from the Sixth; and, of course, General Crescu Valaran, who had just taken command of the Third Legion after Jaxon's death. Crescu was not wearing Krostsilv that evening: the musteloid mask would make eating too cumbersome, and he did not want to present the appearance of challenging the position of Monarch Hallow in front of the dignitaries.

The Red Stag was introduced to the new members of the council that Viceroy Urcai had placed in command of the Empire. There was the Master of Coin, Grand Chancellor, Imperial Counselor, and a new Political Advisor to replace that snake who had 'advised' Emperor Uvon. There was also the new Minister of Worship and Ceremonies to replace the antiquated Inquisitor, the Minister of Guard, Minister of Law, Minister of Commerce, and some—but not all—of the Head Ministers who ruled each of the nine Negian states. By the time the appetizers were served, the Red Stag had entirely forgotten their names.

Dinner was utterly boring. This was not what Monarch Hallow was made for; he didn't care for the politics of provincial jurisdictions, administrative bureaus, irrigation, recordkeeping, or foreign affairs. His heart yearned for conquest, for expanding the rule of his empire and enjoying the spoils of war. He wanted the best for his growing domain, but he knew he could best serve it by leaving these affairs under better care, so he could focus on securing the domes that awaited in the Jerjan Continent. He needed more masks. He needed that power so he could strike Zovaria and even conquer the Takhforsaken Tsing Empire.

The reception dragged on long after the loathsome dinner had concluded. The Red Stag retreated to the balcony with a goblet of red wine and looked at the lights of the city below. All three mesas of the fortified capital were visible from this vantage point. Solid bastions set aglow by great lanterns delineated the fortifications like a fiery constellation.

Crescu approached with a confident stride and said, "What a fun dinner."

"It was categorically atrocious. How can you stand their constant yammering and frivolous gossip? Lurr Faelster would not shut her snout about her negotiations with the archduke, or about her stupid son choosing to study civil law."

"I was merely being polite," Crescu said, flustered with embarrassment. "I was saved since I was sitting between General dus Fer and General Baneras. We talked strategy and numbers, shared tales of the recent battle. Frankly, I felt entirely out of place among the other dignitaries. Don't get me wrong, this dinner is a great honor, but those muck fuckers don't give a shit about expanding the Empire, all they care about is stuffing the pockets of the Lerrs of their fiefdoms."

"Well said, Crescu. I think I picked the right man for this job, after all." The Red Stag finished his wine in a quick gulp. "How is your training going, by the way? I haven't seen you in days."

"I'm making some progress. Shapeshifting has been… elusive. But the rest has become a bit easier for me. The threads are clear, the pain I can fully push away." Crescu grabbed two glasses of sparkling wine from a servant's tray and leaned on the balcony next to the elk, handing him one.

The Red Stag tossed his empty goblet down to the courtyard and accepted the sparkling wine. "It took Jaxon nearly a month to figure it out," he said, "but what an amazing beast he turned out to be."

Crescu furtively stared at the Red Stag's fingertips, which were clinking on the glass while the elk reminisced. Each of his fingers ended in what looked like small hooves, yet the hand still appeared distinctly human. He averted his eyes and, with feigned disinterest, said, "I'm still surprised that you managed to find your new form in just three days. I don't think even the Miscam chief thought that was possible."

The Red Stag looked at Crescu and said, "When a man knows himself, and knows exactly what he wants, he knows exactly how to take it."

Crescu nodded. He rubbed at his left temple and winced. The pink skin was still sensitive from the new tattoos adding to his ranking insignia, those marking his new title of general. He tried to picture Monarch Hallow's complex tattoos beneath the dark-brown coat, wondering whether they'd be visible if the elk shaved the fur off. It had been quite a beautiful insignia, complex and rich, showing that Alvis Hallow had been winning battles since Crescu was but a child.

Crescu ruminated for a moment, then decided to ask, "Why an elk, Monarch Hallow? How did you know that was the right form for you?"

"It was the first large creature I killed, when I was eight. Shot the bastard right through the left eye, with the arrow coming out the right one. Just a lucky shot, but it made an impression. Gorgeous beast."

"I'm struggling to find that right animal for me. I have some ideas, but nothing has clicked into place yet."

"I'd like to say you should take your time with it, but the truth is, I want to leave Hestfell soon. The troops are already gathering in the steppes, and the Fifth Legion is transferring pipe segments from Shaderift to the port of Wyrmwash. We'll soon gather the largest army the Bayanhong Tribes have ever seen, and our attack will take them entirely by surprise."

The Red Stag straightened up. Crescu mimicked his action.

"If I may ask," Crescu said, "what is holding us back? Why not move now if the troops are ready?"

"I like that attitude, and it's what I'd prefer to do as well. But I need to make sure the throne is taken care of while I'm gone. Ulle hasn't gotten pregnant yet—as far as I can tell—and neither have Anja, Fara, Odalys, or any of the others. I'm beginning to wonder if doing it in this way will even produce a child. I may soon have to try the old-fashioned way again."

"You mean to say... You've been trying as the Red Stag?"

"What better way to secure the legacy? There won't be any questioning of my child's provenance and authority if he matures with even an inkling of the power of Urgsilv in him. Sure, it terrifies most of my brides, but I can tell you at least Odalys would not have it any other way."

"I'm... sorry if this is an improper question, but you've only been in Hestfell for a few weeks. How do you know your brides are not pregnant? It hasn't been long enough."

"I know because Urgsilv can show me. I can see the latent eggs in their bellies, and my own seed spreading inside them, and so far it has not taken hold. But I will keep trying. You'll have to try it for yourself, once you find what kind of beast you are. Whatever women we take from our next battle—or men, or children, if that's what you fancy—they can all be yours, and so can any of the Miscam slaves we'll carry with us. Make good use of them, in whichever form you prefer."

Crescu felt sickened by the idea, but he nodded politely. He was genuinely grateful to the monarch for having chosen him to wear Krostsilv, and he had not expected it at all, but the event had immediately changed the relationship between him and his family of arbalisters. Osef, in particular, had remained distant since that day, having mistakenly assumed that Crescu had planned this move behind their backs.

While Crescu and the Red Stag were sharing their dull, upscale banquet, Fjorna and her arbalisters were gathered at the Brass Dagger, a tavern in the eastern quarter of the Mid Mesa that was known for its nightly dagger-throwing shows, which inevitably left someone wounded or dead every week—exactly what the patrons came back for.

They were drinking a potent Dimbali hoary rum to celebrate Shea Lu's promotion from sentryward to armsmaster, as she took over Crescu's old role.

Shea was amenable enough and had the charisma and strength of character to lead as second-in-command in their small squad. Despite their antiquated titles, in the newly restructured army they held a much higher rank than most, partially commanding entire battalions. The arbalisters still functioned as Monarch Hallow's personal guard but had also been tasked with training and directing archers for all legions, not just the Second and Third.

Muriel ordered a round of oysters for the table, then continued with the story she was telling. "In less than a heartbeat, all the sails went *whooomph*. Those sapfire cannons are wicked, but you use them once and they are trash."

"That'sss ruh-right," Shea drawled. "Dare to use them th-wice anda them'll spill ssap over yer own ship and scrorch ya to Khest and beeyond."

Muriel nodded. "After my ship caught fire, I had to dive straight into the water, but the waves were thick with burning sapfire. Got smeared in sap going in but kept swimming until I was away from the flames. That's how I caught the white hives, it took me hours to clean that shit off."

"Why didn't y-you jiss… f-fight from the shore? Had pluh-enty of targets there," Shea questioned.

"Couldn't resist that crow's nest," Muriel answered. "You had to be there, what a view. It was a treat to shoot Zovarians while the whole mast was tilting. And great height to jump from, too."

"Wait, you jumped from the top of the mast?" Trevin asked, leaning toward Muriel, disbelieving the story now. "I thought you were down by the cannons."

"Are you daft?" she said, "I'm not suicidal, I wouldn't get close to those things. I was safer up the mast, jump and all."

"I think… you are full of—full offf shiiit," Shea told Muriel, enjoying the warmth on her drunken cheeks.

"Ask Crescu if you don't believe me. He saw me jump and helped me clean up after."

"I'll do jiss that," Shea said, then took another gulp from her pint. "What d'ya think Crescu will end up as? What sorta animal, I mean."

"A weasel would fit him well," Osef said, bringing a new pitcher of rum for the group. "The scoundrel planned this. Just the day before the battle, I saw him conversing privately with Monarch Hallow. There's something fishy going on."

"If he's into fish, maybe more of an otter than a weasel," Trevin said.

"Weasels eat fish too," Aurélien said matter-of-factly.

Aaaauuurrggh! came a cry from an unlucky target at the dagger-throwing board. They all raised their tankards and clinked them, as was tradition. They hollered as they saw a man being carried out, a dagger sticking from his thigh and probably lodged in a bone. More drinks were ordered.

"I juss want you to know, Fjorna," Shea began to say to the chief arbalister, who had been noticeably quiet most of the night. She leaned in close, her breath overpowering as she slurred her words. "I'll always sssupport you. My allegin… allenian… a-lle-gi-ance lies with you. I don care if Lorr Weasel gets a weasel crown and a weasel palace. Yer still the boss, Chief."

"Hear ye—agreed—I'll drink to that," the voices around the table echoed as tankards were raised once more.

Fjorna smiled through the unbroken half of her face. She was a tad embarrassed, but touched. "Alright, alright, you are all very kind, but don't take it out on Crescu. I don't believe he planned this. He was Hallow's choice, and he's still part of our family. We have a war to win and new lands to conquer—we can't let this split us apart, we are stronger together."

"I don't think we are split," Osef said. "I feel we are more united than ever before. At least among the six of us." Heads nodded around the table. Fjorna wasn't entirely comfortable with the conspiratorial tone, and she wanted to make sure that what she was hearing was correct, but decided not to ask further questions in a crowded tavern filled with loose tongues.

Part Two
MINDRELDROLOM

Chapter Sixteen

Prince Aio

The smilodons became earth-colored blurs as they galloped through the dense greens. Sunset was just beginning; sunset, or whatever name one could give the dimming of the vines, for Sunnokh did not show his face in this realm, and there was no true horizon for the day's light to set over.

As the Miscam and their captives neared the trunk of the Moordusk Dome, they entered a tangled forest of banyan trees. The draping roots had been directed to grow in knotted patterns that wove meshes between stone buildings; some acted as climbable walls and bridges, others as ornamental barriers alongside roads and canals. Roots spilled curtains across the thoroughfares, waterfalls, and down the tongues of beastly sculptures.

There were numerous giant housecats prowling the root-woven dwellings, like the one they had seen earlier in the courtyard. The enormous felids peered down from rooftops, stalked shadows on the streets, or dozed in niches seemingly carved for the sole purpose that the cats might lounge and judge all who passed through their domain.

As night gradually settled inside the dome, holes in the stone walls were set alight with sap flames, lighting the entire city in an ethereal green. This was the city of Arjum, capital of the Gwur Ali province, where forest and architecture were one and the same, where giant housecats made their den of whichever home they so chose that day, and where the Laatu tribe had settled nine thousand years ago, long before they had joined the Miscam and adopted their name.

A tall, woven bridge they crossed, over a rocky chasm that dropped to a river crested in white. The wall of rock at the far side of the chasm was carved with hundreds of windows, many of them glowing orange with fires, none burning green. Strange-sounding horns blew, which could be heard over the rumble of the river. The root bridge emptied into a wide atrium circled by enormous basalt sculptures. The stone carvings were of feline-shaped busts with fangs that dripped tendrils of moss, ears that flowered with orchids, mouths that cradled amphibians, and necks passively strangled by lianas. The feline heads stared with hollow eye sockets that smoked white and burned green.

At the northern end of the atrium, green-flamed lanterns flanked stone steps that climbed up to the trunk of the dome. The steps ended in an archway so ancient that it must have been from a world that had lost memory of itself. This single entrance to the felid temple was sheltered under the largest and oldest of banyan trees, which grasped the colossal bricks in its roots like bony hands and draped its leaves over the entrance and atrium alike, spreading a domed ceiling that aimed to compete with the majesty of the dome in the sky.

The smilodons stopped in the middle of the atrium, and soon hundreds of hairless people gathered around them, though none entered the circle that the felid sculptures demarcated. Warriors helped the wayfarers off their mounts, and before they knew it, their hands were once again tied behind their backs; all except for Lago, who was instead held by his uninjured arm by a fierce-faced woman.

A procession of twenty priests paraded down the temple's steps, lanterns in their left hands, curious staves in their right. They wore long robes woven from strips of vellum-thin leather. Their blue- or purple-pigmented scalps bore designs that reminded Lago of peacock feathers.

The priests stopped at the edge of the circle of sculptures and shuffled to one side, revealing an old woman whose posture and demeanor radiated nobility and rank.

"*Ierun Alúma!*" one of the priests announced.

Balstei tightened his posture and whispered to Lago, "*Ierun* means *queen*. Mind your manners, lad."

A large calico cat circled protectively around the Laatu Miscam queen, rubbing her tricolored head on the ruler's belly and hips. Ierun Alúma took five steps forward and gestured with her lips. The tall man who had been riding with Lago hurried to her. As he spoke to the queen, she constantly spied beyond the man's broad body to inspect the strangers.

After a tense silence, the queen stepped closer. She wore a saffron and peach-colored robe with an open chest. The fabric was embroidered with utmost delicacy, and her breasts decorated with orange, white, and black petals. Her face was wrinkled as much from past smiles as from age; she had narrow eyebrows and thin streaks of blue rising to the top of her scalp, braiding in calligraphic shapes. She held a quaar scepter, which she used to emphasize her speech.

She looked at Jiara, who she perceived to be the leader of the group, and directed the scepter at her accusingly. "*Ejienn pregiss pool glist? Jakri ragisse echienn sulf ust Gwur Ali?*"

The tall man next to her whispered, "*Echelef grest enuth olvet bipri. Echelef enuth Commom.*"

The queen quieted him with a look and said, "*Flam sulfesh uth laantil frerg ejoss igwith he khanarom ust Noss. Fress ragith, fress faith. Jakri echienn mamusse no teäli? Echienn ragiss bralmesh, wem nu'irgesh?*"

"Grest Miscamish," Lago said, remembering the words. That caught Ierun Alúma's attention.

Givra now approached Alúma. While she whispered to the queen, another procession—this one of only half a dozen priests—was reaching the bottom of the steps.

"*Ieron Lepa'olt enn Khuron Aio!*" two priests announced.

"Their king and their prince," Balstei interpreted.

A sad-looking man in his mid-sixties had come down with the priests. He was quiet and detached, hiding under regal-red clothes. The king stepped to the side, revealing a young man about Lago's age, with skin so hairless and smooth that it seemed oiled.

"*Aio, hienn ergothuk od,*" the queen said.

Prince Aio trotted to his mother. He was clad in the open-front jacket, or *shodog*, that most other citizens wore. His shodog was emerald-green embroidered with fiery colors, and he had a dark pauldron fastened to his right shoulder. His leather kilt had embossed Miscamish runes blended with hexagonal motifs and was held in place by a belt adorned with blue stones. His body had average proportions, but was evenly padded with soft fat, just like his tender, almost babylike face.

The prince leaned in close to his mother as they discussed matters in their own tongue. Lago could see the resemblance between them. The prince's bald head was also decorated with pigments, but his blues wove in much simpler, minimalistic patterns starting at the space between his thin eyebrows, branching over his crown, and descending the back of his neck. Lago suddenly recognized that the pauldron on the prince's shoulder was no pauldron at all, but the felid mask.

"Mindrelsilv!" he gasped without meaning to.

The tall man took out his smilodon fang knife and pointed it at Lago's face. *"Tienn grei iuth shiquerag li enuth olv khe Khuron che a ma'ántu!"*

"Hey, watch it!" Alaia barked at him.

Loud voices resounded but were quickly silenced when the queen lifted her scepter.

The prince approached Lago and stood in front of him, almost eye to eye, only a fingerbreadth shorter. His teal eyes held a devious wonder that was mature and disconcertingly inquisitive, never breaking contact—Lago found it hard to be in their presence.

"Mindrelsilv," Lago said, more quietly this time, pointing his nose at the prince's mask. "I don't speak Miscamish, so I don't know how to talk with you. I'm the wearer of Agnargsilv, which used to reside at Stelm Bir. And Jiara is the wearer of Urnaadisilv, from Da'áju."

Khuron Aio looked toward his mother. The mentioning of the Silvesh and Da'áju seemed to resonate with the old queen.

Lago pointed his nose toward their bags, still tied to the harness of the largest smilodon, Pichi. "Agnargsilv," he said, "it's in there. Look in our bags."

"Agnargsilv, *alsolt, mindrégo*," Alaia said to help out, recalling the words for bag and smilodon.

"Urnaadisilv, in *my* alsolt," Jiara added.

Aio's soft face compressed with skepticism. He detached Mindrelsilv from his shoulder and put it on his face. As he did so, he quickly shapeshifted into his half-form of a gorgeous wild cat with black tufts extending up from his ears: a caracal. His coat was sand-colored and lustrous, diluting to soft cream at the neck, exposed belly, and chest. Blackness delineated his rounded mouth, while even rows of dark dots decorated his bewhiskered cheeks, as dark as the markings on his eyebrows and the sides of his nose. His footpaws had extended out from his sandal-like, open-toed shoes, pushing the footwear higher onto his now lifted ankles, making it look almost like shin guards. Below the kilt, Lago saw a black-tipped tail that reached down to the prince's upper calves.

Lago knew that the caracal could see the auras of the masks inside their bags; the widening of his teal eyes made it evident. Lago stared at those eyes; the pupils were not slitted like a housecat's, nor were they round like a mountain lion's, but lay somewhere in-between, in an elongated circle that was piercing and soft at the same time.

The caracal returned to his mother and had a flustered conversation with her. He then extended a sharp, retractable claw, pointing at the bags while yelling a multitude of commands.

The bags were lowered and opened. "Agnargsilv!" a voice called out. The crowd gasped. "Urnaadisilv!" followed another voice.

"*Dufrüethuk welvet finnush ete!*" the queen loudly commanded. "*Echelef uth wukid baargesh!*" Then to Lago, a bit more quietly, with the thickest of accents, she said, "Reegret. Forgiff." She covered her eyes to express her embarrassment as the prisoners' hands were untied.

The caracal ordered the two masks be brought forward, then stared down at Lago. Propped on his feline footpaws, he now stood slightly taller than Lago, and it was obvious that he was fascinated by the curly hair growing from his scalp.

He puckered his lips at Lago and Jiara, making his white whiskers point forward. He then looked at the masks that two bowing warriors held and repeated the gesture. Lago understood. He loosened the drawstrings on his neck, stepped out of his boots with a bit of effort, popped the magnets on his back fly, and then put Agnargsilv on his face. As he shifted into Sterjall, shouts, oohs, and aahs exploded from the crowd.

Sterjall straightened his back, trying to look strong, but his muzzle contorted—he'd forgotten to loosen his splint, and the fur was compressing his injury. He looked at the felid prince through Agnargsilv's sight and saw that Mindrelsilv's glowing aura was like an ageless, viridescent gemstone, or like the translucence of leaves shimmering in a sunlit canopy.

The dark wolf winced in discomfort. The caracal noticed the pained expression, gazed down at Sterjall's arm, and squinted his eyes at it. Sterjall observed his threads spreading toward the prince, as if he was absorbing them into the green glow of his aura. His arm suddenly stopped throbbing, with only a dull, manageable ache remaining.

"What... what did you do?" he asked, stupefied. But the prince wasn't listening, now too distracted by the black-furred animal in front of him.

The caracal paced around, pulling at Sterjall's tail, counting his whiskers, playing with the magnetic buttons Jiara had sewn into his trousers—with a kilt, he had never needed a tail hole. Though the prince's boldness with his hands might have seemed rude to Zovarians, Sterjall guessed this wasn't a strange way to behave for this tribe. The prince then went to Jiara, who put her mask on without waiting for his signal. He waited for more, but Jiara stood there in her human form, no more.

The felid prince lost interest in her and turned to scrutinize Sterjall once more. Mindrelsilv told him that Sterjall was hungry, and tired, and scared, and was not here to hurt them. He placed a handpaw on the top of his own head and said, "Kulak." He then shifted back to human form, reattached the mask to his shoulder, put his hand over the blue lines atop his bald head, and said, "Aio."

Sterjall understood. He repeated the gesture and said, "Sterjall."

At this, Aio laughed, utterly charmed. He pointed up at the sky and then tapped Sterjall's chest with his knuckles and repeated, "Ster-jall!"

Sterjall laughed with him. He then shifted into Lago, took the mask off, and with his hand pressed on his curls, said, "Lago."

Now that the tension had vanished, Aio could not resist playing with Lago's curly hair. He pulled at it, as if expecting to remove a wig. While Aio examined his curls, Lago stared at an octahedral pendant dangling from a leather cord around Aio's neck: the blue sapphire's eight triangular faces were carved with delicate glyphs. He had noticed most other members of the tribe had a pendant of that kind, made from different kinds of rocks, gemstones, or metals.

Aio moved on, first to inspect Jiara's thick braid, then Alaia's more delicate and decorative ones, and finally examining Balstei's salt-and-pepper haircut, while the three introduced themselves. He then pointed to his mother and called her name, Ierun Alúma; then to his father, who had remained quiet with the priests, and who was Ieron Lepa'olt; and then to the tall man with the ridged scalp they had traveled with, Kenondok, who they later learned was a talented weaponsmith. Aio turned to introduce the calico cat who followed his mother, but the felid had become bored with the pleasantries and had quietly left the atrium.

It would take a long while before they could communicate freely, but knowing each other's names eased everyone's spirits and opened up doors. It was a time for celebration.

They were shown down a winding staircase to an ample banquet hall. The chamber's curved ceiling was knotted with banyan tree roots that pierced through the rocks above, growing in tessellated patterns similar to the fractal shapes of the dome. Unusual decorations hung from the roots: skulls, feathers, octahedral crystals, wood carvings, furs. It was cozy, despite the spaciousness. The many fires that kept the hall lit were warm and welcoming, gifting them with fragrant hardwood scents.

As they took their seats around a long table, Aio quickly shapeshifted into Kulak. Lago followed suit as Sterjall, uncertain of what the proper etiquette might be. Jiara had to settle for keeping the ursid mask on her lap while dining.

Servants brought a plethora of exotic foods. They were served juicy fruits that grew in spiral patterns, sour breads that crunched with explosions of floury dust, jams and spreads of every color. They drank a fermented, fizzy drink that had a flavor reminiscent of pineapple; the Laatu Miscam called the drink *braaw*, and it was as refreshing as it was filling. Balstei told them that braaw was an ancient drink from the Jerjan Continent that had recently become popular at taverns in Old Karst and New Karst, but not so much in Zovaria, where meads and ales were preferred.

The main courses comprised variations of cubed, paste-like cakes, each slightly different in color, texture, and flavor, but all obviously coming from the same source. The newcomers could not tell whether they were some sort of cheese, or a plant, or a kind of processed meat.

"What is this?" Sterjall asked, taking a bite out of a Quggon-sized cube—the one he picked was tart and slightly herby in flavor.

"*Munnji,*" Khuron Kulak answered, as if that was enough clarification. He snatched the remains of the cube from Sterjall's handpaw and chomped it down.

They learned new words while they feasted, starting with the obvious things at hand: fruit, meat, table, root, glass, mouth. A man who spoke a bit more Common was asked to sit near them, to interpret what he could.

"Does anyone speak Common fluently around here?" Balstei asked the man.

"Interprertersh, talkish good Crommon. Far house, name Fingrenn. Comesh later, Fingrenn *fedethi* help."

"We need to explain the reason for our visit," Balstei said.

The man quickly interpreted what he understood to Kulak and to Alúma. They exchanged a few words in Miscamish, then the man simply replied, "*Tralt krirg.* Chiefs far province, comesh ilm Fingrenn. Wait. *Echoss ëath diath frulv je hedesh.*"

They had a long process of learning ahead of them, but the three Silvfröash had an advantage: since the masks read the emotions and intentions of others, their wearers could pick up the meanings of words much more easily, as if the essence of the words was communicated along with their sounds as long as that was the intent of the speakers.

When Kulak said something like *voss uth wulem,* Sterjall—and to a slightly lesser degree, Jiara—could feel the word *voss* being spoken with a pull of the threads toward the prince, and in his mind Sterjall understood it to mean *I*. When the word *wulem* was spoken, the Silvesh communicated that the young man was happy, and the word implanted that meaning in the minds of the listeners. Through inference combined with the power of the Silvesh, they could understand the sentence to mean *I am happy.*

Alaia didn't need a mask to learn—she and Givra were picking words up as if it was a game, and Balstei could catch up thanks to his slightly greater knowledge of Miscamish, associating terms he knew from root words, prefixes, and suffixes with their meanings in the language.

While lounging around after dinner was over, Givra approached Alaia to inspect the horn-like bump growing below her hairline. She was fascinated by the spur and loved how the patterns in Alaia's carefully braided hair highlighted its presence.

Alaia examined Givra's blue-pigmented head in turn and smiled widely.

"*Diathuk*," Givra said. She left for a time, then returned with a glass jar that held live snails munching on leaves. She picked up a snail by the shell and placed it on the back of Alaia's hand: the shell was slender and elegant, of matte black highlighted with glossy blue spots. As the snail crawled, it left a trail of mucus that turned Alaia's skin a deep dark blue, hard to see over her already dark skin, though much more noticeable once the snail reached her lighter palms. Givra picked the snail up, touched it with a finger to pick up some mucus, then tapped the finger to her forehead, leaving a blue dot over the fading pattern that had been painted there some time ago.

"*Kupógo grinesht*," she said to Alaia.

Alaia didn't exactly understand the words, but she guessed one of them might mean *snail*.

After digesting the feast, they were taken to their dormitory. It was a spacious guest room with six soft mattresses on bedframes crafted from woven roots. The room had a central open hearth, fire already crackling. Their bags had been placed on a low table next to a tray with drinks and cubed snacks.

Ieron Lepa'olt remained quiet as usual, but Khuron Kulak and Ierun Alúma together said, "*Oset fin uth halvet*," to which Balstei replied, "*Olvet finesh uth velm.*"

The prince and queen smiled fondly at the response. They closed the door, leaving the wayfarers to rest.

Sterjall moved to lock the door, only to find it had no lock. He turned to Balstei and asked, "What does that greeting mean?"

"It loosely translates to *my essence is yours*," Balstei answered as he went to prepare his chosen bed, "with the reply being *our essence is one*. Though the word for *essence* is pronounced the same as the word for *thread*, which I think you might find interesting. The greeting is still often used, at least west of Zovaria."

"Sounds similar to the Havengall Congregation greeting," Lago replied, taking Agnargsilv off and placing it on the table.

"Most of the teachings from the monks aren't exactly original."

Alaia explored the exotic room. "The view from these windows is exquisite," she observed, peering out a window over the deep chasm they had crossed earlier, with the white-capped river beneath. Waterfalls cascaded from the opposite end of the gorge, where treacherous steps descended to a fishing platform. Alaia followed the row of windows around a corner, then screamed, "Khest!"

Jiara rushed to check on her.

"It's one of those giant cats!" Alaia said, eyes focused on the top of an armoire where a giant tabby cat slept, or had been sleeping until Alaia's shriek had caused him to flatten an ear to the side. "Did they forget the cat here?"

"Maybe they come with the rooms," Lago said. "I saw them just about everywhere today. Leave the cats be, we don't really know if they are tame."

"But they are just big kitties," Alaia complained.

"Hey, can I borrow your compass?" Lago asked Jiara. She complied, then watched with confusion as Lago placed the compass on his bed, then pushed the heavy bedframe, making it screech against the stone ground as he tried to rotate it.

"What are you doing?" Jiara asked.

"Just lining it up better," he replied, pushing the bed completely off alignment with the room and the other beds.

"Never mind him," Alaia said, "he's a nubhead. He thinks that if his head doesn't point north when he sleeps, he loses his sense of direction."

Jiara chuckled. "Is that why you always set up your bedroll at such inconvenient angles?" she asked, and with a taunting tone added, "You are afraid you'll get lost?"

"It's not a joke! I do get all confused if—"

"Don't worry, kid. Lodestar guide you, we all have our quirks." She came closer to help Lago with the bed. "Don't force your arm."

"Thank you," Lago said, massaging his shoulder as he sat on the soft mattress. "Oh, I forgot to tell you! When Kulak first saw me as Sterjall, he did something to me. My arm was hurting from shapeshifting, and he somehow made it stop, as if he took the pain away from me."

"He healed your arm?" Alaia asked.

"Not healed, it's still broken. But the pain disappeared, at least for a while. It's back to normal now, but it gave me great relief."

"Fascinating," Jiara said. "We'll have to ask him about this, once we figure out how to ask."

It was late. Their backs were hurting from riding the smilodons, their hands and arms sore from being tied, but now they were warm, and their bellies were full.

They pulled up cushioned chairs around the hearth and sat in them.

"These Laatu people are great hosts," Alaia remarked, "kidnapping and all. Did you notice they only use the green fire outdoors?" She wrapped a soft blanket over her lap. "I'm glad. Orange fires are so much better for cozy spaces like this one."

As if agreeing with her, the large tabby cat hopped down from the armoire and went to sit right at Alaia's feet.

"He's so soft," Alaia mouthed toward Lago, reaching down to pet the giant cat.

"Just be careful with them," Lago insisted.

"So, what should we do now that we made it here?" Jiara asked. "How do we explain to them about the outside world, about the problem with the domes and the Red Stag?"

"We wait for the interpreter," Lago said. "But we'll also have to learn the language while we are here. It will take time, but Agnargsilv has been incredibly useful to me. I'm picking up words very fast."

"Same with me," Jiara agreed.

"I say we take our time," Alaia commented, hands sunken into the cat's fur. "I don't mind being spoiled like this."

The cat tensed his back in a lazy stretch and purred.

Chapter Seventeen

Arjum Promenade

Alaia woke up to the giant tabby crushing her legs. She needed to move, to let her blood circulate, but when she shifted her hips, the cat seemed too bothered. He jumped off the bed, opened the door with a dexterous paw, and left, closing the door behind him in a much too practiced manner.

For breakfast, they were served a milky substance paired with roasted insects and fruits. Alaia didn't want to think about the insects very much and instead focused on the fruits.

Khuron Aio came to see them sometime later. He greeted them by lightly tapping the right side of his forehead to each of theirs. Ierun Alúma and her calico cat arrived after him, as did Ieron Lepa'olt, who remained present yet distant. A dozen warriors and priests shadowed the monarchs—their private guard and servants. The royal family took their guests on a walk around the Arjum Promenade while they worked on better understanding each other's words.

They began at the atrium circled by felid statues. Through the canopy of the mighty banyan tree, they saw the central trunk, dark at the bottom, brightening to the broadening top. Beneath it was the entrance to the felid temple.

"I would love to see that temple," Balstei commented, directing his gaze up the steps. He pointed at the root-covered archway and asked, "Ommo?"

Alúma frowned deeply. *"Pust an neh ommo,"* she replied, then turned, leading them away from the steps and toward the gardens that surrounded the trunk. With the trunk being a mile wide, the promenade was over three miles around, with multiple destinations that Alúma proudly presented as they arrived at each one.

As they made their way clockwise around the trunk, they first entered a dimly lit reliquary where old artifacts were displayed behind glass covers. Balstei immediately recognized quaar tools among the items displayed, but their function remained a mystery to him. He then spotted an ancient tome with a red leather cover filigreed in quaar.

"A *Miscamish Grimoire!*" he exclaimed.

"Miscamish, *haast*," Alúma agreed.

"That must be one of the original tomes from the legends." He wanted to pick the tome up, but the protective glass made it clear that it was not meant to be handled by just any curious hands.

A circular table was the centerpiece of the reliquary; it was a relief map of the Moordusk Dome carved from a single slice of a giant redwood. The map was inscribed with copper-inlaid Miscamish runes that invoked the names of rivers, cities, mountains, and provinces. Their tallest mountain, Stelm Humenath, protruded proudly from the carved surface, but wasn't nearly as tall as the brass pipes that marked the positions of the twenty-three supporting columns or the silver pipe lodged at the center, representing the wider trunk.

Balstei yearned to spend more time in the reliquary, but the queen hurried them on.

Next, they reached a field surrounded by descending, stepped seats. A stadium. The game field was not grass or sand, but soil coated with such a thick covering of pine needles that it was like a pillow. The needles came from two dozen enormous pines, although more had been brought from the forests nearby, for extra padding. The conifers were planted in a regular pattern of six trees by four trees across a rectangular field. Hoops hung vertically at the ends of the rectangle, suspended between tree trunks by ropes. Each side had three hoops, each one higher and smaller than the next. The thick branches of the pines had been carefully trimmed down, probably to give a better view of the game to the audience. Alaia wondered what kind of game would be played in a place like this, but there were no spectators or players at the moment.

After viewing the stadium, they entered the stables, where they saw dozens of saber-toothed cats of breeds different from the ones they had encountered before and other thought-extinct felids that were not quite as massive as the smilodons. Lago recognized the tigers, which Aio called *mindrukh*. Some of the biggest animals were the snow leopards, as well as the dinofelises, who had shorter but no less deadly fangs than the smilodons.

"These stables could not be made to keep the cats in," Jiara said. "They could jump over the fences anytime they wanted."

"Perhaps it's just to help them behave," Alaia said. "They seem to work well with the stable handlers."

On an open field hundreds of feet below the Arjum Promenade, they saw black panthers—or *mindu*, as *du* was the word for *night*—as well as mountain lions, jaguars, cheetahs, and smaller wild cats that were hard to tell apart from a distance.

Lago was curious as to how so many species of ferocious cats walked, played, and worked together without fights breaking out. He knew not all felids were social creatures; this mingling of predatory species was uncanny. He also wondered how they could feed such a large population of carnivores, as he had not seen great herds of ruminants or open fields for them to graze. He wanted to ask about these things, but still lacked the vocabulary to do so.

Before they reached the end of the stables, Aio whistled loudly, and from the fields below, a smilodon ran up the slopes. The giant felid came to Aio and head-butted him a bit too violently, almost sending him to the ground. Aio laughed and petted the cat, who purred in tones as low as a rumbling waterfall.

Aio stood eye-to-eye with the smilodon, put a hand on his vast forehead, and said, "Blu."

It was a simple name, and Lago liked it.

Blu was not as imposing as most others of his species. He was shorter, softly padded, with a friendlier face, a bit like Aio. Blu's coat was a deep burnt umber transitioning to gray toward his belly; instead of rosettes, the umber and gray fur mixed in a marbled pattern that flowed like tendrils of dark smoke. His teal eyes were of a slightly darker hue than Aio-Kulak's.

Alaia stepped forward with a raised hand and asked, "Can I pet him?" Blu came straight to her as if giving more than permission, shoving his fur into her hand and making her giggle. She caressed the big cat's ears, pulled on his whiskers, and even dared to touch the sharp fangs that poked below his cheeks. "Lago, you should rub this kitty's fur, it's lovely," she said.

"Blu," Lago said, fascinated by the creature. He extended a hand, hoping the smilodon would step closer. Blu did, much too fast, hoping for a head bump. The bump was as loving and violent as the one he had given to Aio, shoving Lago to the ground, who landed on his injured arm.

"Blu!" Aio cried. He removed the mask from his shoulder and took his caracal half-form. As Kulak, he mindspoke his admonishment to the smilodon, making the poor creature lower his ears in shame, then helped Lago up and focused his attention on the wounded area. As he'd done before, he slowly removed the pain from Lago's injury until all that was left was a dull, bearable throb.

"He did it again," Lago said to his friends. "He took the pain from my arm, like when we first met him." He directed his attention to Kulak and said, "How did you do that?"

The caracal cocked his head.

"The pain in my arm, how did you make it stop?" Lago asked, nodding toward his splint, trying to emphasize each word to make their meanings transparent to Mindrelsilv. He scrunched his face to pantomime pain, then relaxed and sighed. "How?"

Kulak seemed to understand, although he was confused as to why the Agnargfröa would ask such a basic question. He gestured toward Lago's bag, where he was keeping Agnargsilv, and said, "Sterjall."

Lago complied. Once in his wolf half-form, Sterjall's arm began to hurt again. Kulak pointed to the arm, then to his eyes, and said, "*Chëathuk.* See."

He performed the same feat once more, this time miming with his handpaws as if he were pulling on a rope.

Jiara had put her mask on to watch. "It's like he's dragging your threads into his body," she said.

"Take," Kulak said, gesturing toward himself. "Take, *finesh,* here."

Even the last bits of lingering pain vanished from Sterjall's arm.

Kulak then tapped on Sterjall's furred muzzle and said, "Agnargsilv, *khelef gwihuth däenn.*" And tapping Jiara's quaar muzzle, he added, "Urnaadisilv, *khelef gwihuth däenn.*"

"Th-thank you," Sterjall said. "We will need to learn how to do this. Thank you, Khuron Kulak."

Kulak seemed tired; he was panting slightly, and droplets of sweat had formed on his gray-padded handpaws. But he shook off the discomfort, making the tufts on his ears jiggle.

Blu joined them on the rest of their journey, silently walking next to Kulak, still mortified about having bumped the guests so hard.

Their next stop was a sculpture garden that had animal-shaped monoliths spread over an extensive field of short-trimmed grass. Cobblestones were tightly fitted on the ground, delineating curves that intermixed with the grass in organic, seemingly random patterns. The sculptures in this garden weren't all felids like the ones at the atrium, but there was one felid sculpture among them that was unmissable, for instead of being carved from granite, it was carved out of a single block of obsidian, black as the Silvesh.

"This is another map!" Alaia said excitedly, figuring out the patterns and connections. "The same from Da'áju, but as sculptures. Look! There's a dog, um, wolf thing." She was unsure, as the monoliths were blocky and heavily stylized, but the long muzzle and fangs of a wolf-like creature were distinct enough. "And this here with five claws has to be urnaadi, a bear."

"Urnaadi," Alúma repeated with a smile.

They studied the stones and found a regal-looking creature with antlers, and assumed that's where Urgsilv had come from, the Anglass Dome. They recognized a bird, some winged creature that was perhaps a bat, a dolphin sitting alone at the southern edge, a bull with immense horns, and other strange beings too creative in their interpretations to determine their species.

"I think the cobblestones are water," Jiara noted, "and the grass is the land. See? It's all stones toward the outside."

"We could figure out which corresponds to the missing dome," Sterjall said.

"I can find it," Jiara said. She traced her way back to the obsidian felid and from there looked south and quickly found the sculpture she was looking for. "This one!"

It was the strangest one they had yet seen. It looked like a horse, maybe, but with floppy ears and three long tubes sticking out from the middle of its face: a central one that dropped to the ground, and two others that curved out and then back in.

"What in Khest is that thing?" Sterjall asked.

"The book described them as *presbicedeons* or something like it," Balstei said. "Wish we'd had time to figure them out."

Alúma was intrigued by their curiosity. "Momsúndo," she said, placing a hand on the sculpture.

Sterjall squinted at the carving and remembered Banook's story about a strange beast. "Remember Banook's story about those weird creatures? Elfents, I think he called them. He said they had a nose that dragged on the ground, and tusks that twisted out. And ears like wings, I remember that. I thought it was so funny that I asked Ockam to draw the creature for me. I still have the drawing, it's in his notebook."

"I thought Banook was joking," Alaia said.

"I did too," Jiara concurred.

"So, the missing dome was home to these strange creatures," Sterjall said. "And also to Banook's friend, the mammoth who could take the form of a man. Mamóru."

"Mamóru!" Alúma repeated, tapping on the sculpture's tusks. "Mamóru, Nu'irg ust Momsúndo."

"Yes," Sterjall said, "the Nu'irg's name is Mamóru! Or was, we don't know…"

"Elfents I know nothing about, but mammoths I've heard of," Balstei said. "We have fossils of them in Zovaria. Massive creatures, with a single, enormous eye on their foreheads."

"Weird…" Alaia said.

"If they know about this Nu'irg," Balstei said, "then they likely know a lot more about the times before the Downfall."

"All the Nu'irgesh knew each other back then," Sterjall said. "They likely learned about Mamóru from the Nu'irg ust Mindrel."

Kulak perked up at the mention of those words. He grabbed Sterjall's handpaw and led him to a terrace with a clear view south. Through the haze, a single mountain stood lonely and blue, its snowy cap piercing a blanket of lenticular clouds.

"Nelv. Nu'irg ust Mindrel, *khelef birreth fass*," Kulak said, pointing his whiskers toward the mountain.

Sterjall didn't need his mask to understand what the caracal was saying. *I hope I get to meet her,* he thought.

Givra was waiting for them with drinks when they completed their journey around the trunk. The king and queen, the calico cat, and the trailing warriors and priests left them, but Khuron Kulak, Blu, and Givra remained.

They sat underneath a trellis overgrown with ivies, savoring their chilled drinks. Sterjall rested his tired shoulder. Kulak sat to his side, staring at Sterjall's cumbersome boots, which the wolf had been carrying tied to his belt ever since changing forms. The prince scrunched up his face at the oddness of Sterjall's attire. "*Diathuk*," he said, then put his glass down and ran toward an old tree, where he disappeared between tall roots as he descended cleverly disguised steps.

"Waith, pleese," Givra said. So, they waited.

A few moments later, Kulak returned with a pair of the same type of open-toed shoes he was wearing. "*Enquolv*," he called them, showing that the toes could be left open, like sandals, or a flap could be folded over the front of the shoes and tightened with a drawstring, sealing the toe cap entirely.

He handed a pair to Sterjall, then showed him how to put them on. It was a clever design that allowed for the front of the shoes to open up as the wearer's legs changed shape, sliding up to let them walk on the balls and toes of their footpaws, like any canid or felid should.

"Sliding shoes," Sterjall said, "I like them, they fit well." He thanked Kulak for the new shoes—they were comfortable, although a bit tight. He'd need to break them in.

Kulak then handed Sterjall and Jiara shoulder braces identical to the one he wore, and helped them put them on, although he wrapped Sterjall's on his left shoulder to avoid the injured side.

"So convenient!" Jiara said, easily attaching the bear mask to her shoulder. "Thank you."

"It looks so intimidating," Alaia said to her. Then, to Sterjall, "Aren't you going to try yours?"

"I'll try it out later. My arm is still throbbing, and I don't want to mess with the splint."

"You are in pain again? Good," Jiara said, detaching her mask from the brace and placing it on her face once more. "I've been wanting to give this a try." She scrutinized the threads flowing through Sterjall's injured arm. As Kulak had done before, she unnecessarily mimed the action of pulling the threads toward her, and soon enough she began to feel pain in her own right arm. She stopped, wincing, and rolling her shoulder.

Kulak expelled a brief and sharp exhalation through his nose to show disapproval. "*Aspaloth*," he said, inhaling and gesturing with his handpaws from his nose and down through his entire body.

"I think he means... *spread*," Sterjall said. "To spread it through you."

Jiara breathed in, and in the same way she learned to move vines, willed the threads she had pulled from Sterjall to spread over her. The sharp pain dissipated from her arm and became a dull throb, like a headache throughout her entire body. Uncomfortable, but manageable.

"It feels like shit," she said. "But I hope it's better for you."

Sterjall nodded. "It is, thank you," he said. "I think... I think this is exactly what happened at the bogs, when you first controlled your mask."

"What do you mean?" she asked.

"When you were rolling and screaming on the ground, I was so distraught that I nearly begged for your pain to go away. You stopped screaming then, and I was left with a dull ache all over my body. I thought it was just from being so tense, from all the stress, but I think I might've helped you somehow."

"Don't go taking all the credit, kid. I suffered through that. Let me earn it."

Kulak did not understand their conversation, but he seemed content. He stood, then gestured widely, implying they could walk anywhere they wanted: the city of Arjum was theirs to peruse.

Alaia took the lead and directed them toward the core of the city. They walked across the bridge they had galloped over the night before, admiring the meticulous weaving of banyan roots. They stopped in the middle to look at the river below, where they spotted fisherfolk casting nets and a herd of animals that had to be goats, as they were sticking to the sides of the rocky cliff, defying all laws of physics.

Kulak approached Jiara and grabbed her right arm. He caressed it, feeling her furless skin. Then he did the same on his furred arm and shook his whiskers toward her.

Jiara answered, "Not yet." Kulak understood the essence of what was said and smiled eagerly, as if in anticipation of the moment when Jiara would find her ursid form.

Once across the bridge, Kulak offered his guests a variety of street foods, as it was past lunchtime and they had been walking for a long time. They went from vendor to vendor, picking a wide selection of cube-cut cakes like the ones they had tasted at dinner, although these were all of new colors and flavors. Alaia even found one that tasted like muskberries.

"*Munnji*," Kulak said with a smile. Some munnji cakes were deep fried, others skewered, caramelized to look like jewels, or filled with tasty jams. They had a spongy texture that dissolved satisfyingly in their mouths.

The last cubes of munnji they tasted had been sprinkled with a red powder—they were as spicy as they'd feared.

Kulak noticed their tearing eyes and reddening cheeks. "*Kelithuk*," he said apologetically, rushing with Givra to procure drinks to cool off their mouths.

Givra quickly returned with a tray of braaw goblets. The drink was fizzy and didn't do much to douse the spices, but it was better than nothing. Kulak had stayed by the vendor's cart. He had removed his octahedral pendant and was using the sapphire to stamp glyphs on a scroll of translucent vellum the vendor had unrolled over his counter. Blu took the chance to steal a big bite of meat from the vendor, who glowered at Kulak with eyes that seemed to say, *You owe me for that, too. I don't care if you are the prince.*

"What are they doing?" Sterjall asked.

"He seems to be paying for the food," Balstei said. "My guess is that each of those pendants has unique markings, and the scrolls are ledgers. The old Dorvauros tribes had a similar system, using clay tablets and signet rings."

"So, there's no money?"

"The ledger is the money, it's all written down."

Givra was aware of their curiosity. She took off her own octahedral pendant and mimicked the motion of placing stamps on her arm. She let them inspect it and said, "*Arambukh.*" Instead of a sapphire, hers was a marbled agate. Six of the pendant's triangular faces were carved with unique glyphs, while the remaining two were pierced through so that the leather cord could pass through them.

"These are compound glyphs," Balstei said, rotating the gemstone in his fingers, "similar to the eighteen clade glyphs on the map Ockam copied. Perhaps it represents their initials, or family sigils."

Kulak returned and saw them examining Givra's agate.

Balstei reached into his Qupi pouch and took out the last few chips he had left: a Hex, a Cup, a Qupi, and three Lodes. He showed them to Givra and Kulak and said, "Arambukh."

The two were fascinated by the pull of the magnium-infused chips yet seemed confused as to why one person held more than one arambukh, wondering if Balstei was carrying the ones for Alaia, Jiara, and Sterjall as well. They laughed as they pretend-stamped the gnomon-shaped chips on their arms. Kulak liked the blue Hex the most, while Givra seemed most fond of the copper Cup.

As they continued exploring narrow streets, townspeople gathered near them, but never too intrusively, perhaps because the prince—and Blu—were there. Up a gnarled tree trunk they headed, following carved steps to an ample platform cradled beneath the canopy. Clusters of residential treehouses were nestled among the horizontal branches, which reminded Sterjall of Banook's cabin, but these structures formed an entire multi-leveled treehouse city. Below the treehouses—whose walls were mostly grown from roots—were stone buildings carved directly into the body of the mountain.

Children tagged along, many with small pets on their shoulders: mostly wild cats, but also lemurs and colorful mot-mots.

"I think everything in the treetops is residential," Balstei said. "It looks cozier and more personal, and there are more children around. Reminds me of Zovaria, where taller buildings have businesses below and housing on the upper floors."

They leaned over a bridge to peer at the thoroughfare below. Balstei noted that the smilodons transporting goods were doing so with no human intervention.

Bells tolled in a distant canyon.

"*Jeu hedesh!*" Kulak said and gestured for them to follow him to the lower levels.

A caravan of around eighty people approached; they were riding a varied mix of felids, wearing colors and ornaments representative of their unique provinces.

The caravan stopped when they saw the prince. Kulak exchanged words with the riders at the front. One of them whistled, then yelled a command. An allgender jumped off a snow leopard, gliding gracefully up to them. They were wearing a long, black shodog that draped like a toga, paired with a kilt that reached down to their ankles at the back, where it split like a tailcoat jacket. They had small breasts, and a scalp decorated in purple patterns that were so arbitrary that Sterjall guessed they must've let those snails crawl over their head unattended. The allgender stopped in front of Sterjall.

"Greetings. I am named Fingrenn of house Hi'úmen, from the province of Gwur Úrëath," they said, in a too crisp Common that highlighted the purity of the phonemes but failed to emphasize the right words. "I crossed southern lands with Hod Buil, our chief, to join the chiefs of the six provinces. The ierenesh and khuron summoned us regarding the matter of your mysterious appearance."

"*Oset fin uth halvet,*" Balstei greeted him.

"*Olvet finesh uth velm,*" Fingrenn greeted back. "Although the word is *henet,* not *halvet,* when addressing only one person. I am what in Common you call a scholar. I studied in Humenath, where a mixture of Miscamish and Common is spoken. My presence was requested so I may aid you in interpreting words."

"Thank you, Fingrenn," Sterjall said. "There is so much we need to discuss. We came from outside the dome, and we've been trying to—"

Fingrenn's hand went up. "Your story will be recounted to the chiefs, not to me," they said. "Tomorrow, a council shall meet, and I will be there to aid you, as will other interpreters."

An envoy whispered privately to Kulak, then quickly left. Kulak tapped Sterjall's shoulder and spoke to him in Miscamish.

"I beg you for patience," Fingrenn interpreted, keeping a hand pointed at Kulak so that it was understood it was the prince's words that were being delivered. They even mimicked Kulak's own voice and intonations as they translated the words. "My scalp rejoices with your arrival. It is my honor to show you the beauty of Arjum. But now I must take my leave. We will meet in the morrow after breaking fast, at the Laatu Dacaann, where your tongues will speak your story."

Kulak approached each of them, tapped his left temple on each of theirs, and said to them all, "*Oset fin.*"

Fingrenn replied, "*Olvet finesh,* Khuron."

Kulak hopped onto Blu's back, not worried that the smilodon had no saddle, and rode quickly toward the bridge.

"We have more than a story, we also came with a lot of questions," Jiara said to Fingrenn.

"Your questions will meet their answers. Agnargfröa and Urnaadifröa have that right. It has been many hundreds of years since Mindreldrolom closed. Your arrival is auspicious. Tomorrow we will meet again under the unwavering light of the *arudinn.*"

Chapter Eighteen

The Council of the Six Provinces

They were served the same insects, fruits, and milky drink for breakfast the next morning. Alaia crunched through the insects without much complaint this time, realizing the flavors complimented one another just right, although getting over the crunchy texture would take some time.

After breakfast, four priests showed them the way to the Laatu Dacaann, the Great Hall of the Laatu, where legislative and ceremonial activities were undertaken. An influx of people was hurrying in the same direction, from common citizens to dignitaries covered in too much jewelry and fragrant perfumes.

"Were we supposed to dress up for this?" Lago asked.

"Just go with it," Balstei assured him. "As far as they know, our clothes could be kingly gowns. They've probably never seen anything like them."

Lago looked to his side. Balstei's striped doublet made him look important. Jiara's leather armor gave her the air of a legendary warrior. But at least Alaia's overalls made him feel a bit better about his own garments. He smoothed out his blue tunic and tightened his collar's drawstrings, then made sure Agnargsilv was properly fastened to his shoulder brace. Since it was relatively warm, he wasn't wearing his gray cloak—its leaf-like trims of black might have made him look a bit more regal, although he still felt irrationally uncomfortable knowing the cloak had been fashioned for women.

The Great Hall of the Laatu was an enormous cube of stone sticking out from a sharp cliff of gray-blue mica schist, tinted green by the vegetation growing over it. They walked between two tall, rectangular monoliths that framed the entrance and gazed up at the expansive interior. It was well lit, thanks to angular cuts on the enormous rock, which cast soft, striped shadows across the square hall. The marbled interiors blended grays and deep blues, with warm sparkles of mica all along the polished walls. The gathering audience was already taking their seats at the stepped periphery.

At the center of the hall was a crescent-shaped table. The queen was sitting in a tall-backed chair at the far, widest end of the crescent, flanked by the prince and king. Priests guided the wayfarers to sit to the side of the prince. The chiefs from the other provinces took their seats after them, two on the side of Khuron Aio and the newcomers, and three more on the opposite side, next to Ieron Lepa'olt, who seemed bored and distracted. Nobles and advisors filled the few remaining seats.

Ierun Alúma stood and was the first to speak. Fingrenn—who stood on the inside of the crescent so they could hear everyone and everyone could hear them—interpreted the entirety of the proceedings both ways, speaking with a silky, clear voice. Pointing a hand toward the queen, they said. "We welcome you to our modest hall, Lago-Sterjall, Jiara, Alaia, and Balstei. Your presence brings honor to our six provinces and tingles our scalps with curiosity. We are the Laatu Miscam, descendants of Nish-Ailúr, custodians of Mindrelsilv, the sixth Silv of the Miscam. On this first day of the season of blossoms, I requested the presence of the chiefs of the other five provinces, who guard the white mountain of Humenath, the great mangroves of the Tidal Realms, the fertile terraces of the Stiss Regu-Omen, the black canyons of the Primordial Forest, and the reefs of the Loonsad Islands."

The queen then introduced each of the chiefs. First, on the same side as the guests, was Hud Ilsed. Her long eyelashes and sharp brows gave her a stern-faced look, obscuring her light-brown eyes. Ilsed wore earrings made of coral as red as her painted lips and a shodog to match both in hue and temerity. Her scalp pigments spiraled into a blue maelstrom. She was the chief of Gwur Gomosh, the western province of islands and reefs, where the water was as blue as the feet of the gannets who plunged at their endless shores.

To Ilsed's side was Hod Buil, the chief of Gwur Úrëath, the southern province where Fingrenn themself came from. The perpetually white-crowned Stelm Humenath rose there, in the lands where the Nu'irg ust Mindrel prowled. Buil was short, stocky, and square-jawed. He was a good listener, and seemed the calmest. His scalp patterns resembled a tortoise's shell, with runes within each polygonal scale. Kenondok—who was the head weaponsmith of Gwur Úrëath—sat close to Buil, seeming a lot more regal with his head paint having just been redone the night before, covering his entire scalp in a piercing blue except for six circles that had been left unpigmented.

At the other side of the table sat Hud Quoda, who was the chief of Gwur Pantuul, the northeast territory of headlands overlooking the Isdinnklad; this was the province the wayfarers had first entered when they breached the dome. Quoda wore a headdress that made it seem as if she had rope-like locs or hair, resembling the roots of the mangroves that spread along the edges of her province's shores.

Hod Abjus was introduced next. A fierce warrior, he was taller even than Kenondok, with a thick neck decorated by a tangle of necklaces and dangling talismans. He commanded the eastern province of Gwur Esmukh, the land of the primordial forests, black canyons, and treacherous terrains. Abjus's scalp pigments were angular, like the teeth of a smilodon, extending down to his cheekbones and wrapping around the back of his neck all the way to his clavicles.

Last to be introduced was Hed Lettáni. They were the chief of the southeastern province of Gwur Aalpe. They wore a long shodog like most allgenders did, but theirs was colorful and full of life. Their scalp was crossed by thick parallel scars, and spots of purple pigments were arranged alongside the scarified grooves. Their land was that of floodplains and terraces, where they harvested grains and built raised channels to grow corn together with squash and beans. Lettáni seemed thoughtful and introspective, keeping their hands draped over their lap and their head always slightly cocked.

Ierun Alúma locked eyes with Lago and said, "From your breaths, your story we must hear. Tell us, friends, how you found yourselves in our sealed lands, and what is the fate that you cast upon us."

Lago exchanged looks between Alúma and Fingrenn, then spoke clearly. "We come from lands north of the Stelm Ca'éli, and south of the Stelm Wujann. We have come to the Moordus—to Mindreldrolom to learn about the Silvesh, to understand why the domes remain sealed. We have many questions and worries, for there are troubles in our lands, and we believe we will need your help."

Hod Abjus leaned forward on the table. "You speak names of unfamiliar mountains," he said, piercing Lago with distrustful eyes. "Are those places within Urnaadidrolom and Agnargdrolom?"

"We come from the lands outside the domes," Jiara said, "the lands that burned during the Downfall and are now alive again. We do not belong to any domes. Our homes are the mountains, forests, and valleys outside of them."

Gasps and looks of concern were shared by all the Laatu.

"That cannot be," Abjus said. "If the New World was thriving, Mindreldrolom would not still be closed."

"Yet it is true," Lago said. "The New World, as you call it, has been full of life for many centuries."

"If you do not belong to one of the domes, how is it that you carry the Silvesh of Agnarg and Urnaadi?" Hud Ilsed asked, squinting her long eyelashes. "And why do you not speak the Miscam tongue, as the Acoapóshi intended us to?"

"This is a very long story," Lago said. "If you allow my friends and I, we will have to start at the beginning, and it will take us some time to properly tell it."

Khuron Aio nodded, encouraging Lago to continue. "Our ears will hear your story," he said through Fingrenn. "I ask the chiefs to listen first and ask questions only once the telling has concluded."

Before they recounted their long adventure, the four of them started by telling the chiefs what they knew of the Downfall, and how the continents of Noss had been nearly destroyed by a force they did not understand, by burning and later freezing, killing most of the great animals that had lived outside the domes. The Laatu had been locked inside the Moordusk Dome for nearly fifteen hundred years, not even certain whether any creatures had survived the cataclysm. The wayfarers explained that new cities had been built atop the remnants of the fallen realms, and that nature had reconquered the lands, albeit with fewer species than before. Though most of history was lost in flames or mistranslations, ancient technology had been rediscovered from the ruins and brought to a level similar to that seen during the Equilibrium and Segregation epochs.

After the story of their distant past was recounted, Lago continued with the tale of their own adventures, beginning with the history of the Negian Empire digging under the Heartpine Dome, and the genocide they inflicted upon the Southern Wutash tribe. He told them about Sontai, and how her tragic end had made him the custodian of Agnargsilv, which he used to escape Withervale through the limestone caverns. The crowd became agitated and began whispering amongst themselves, as if a great blasphemy had been spoken.

The queen raised her scepter to bring an end to the chatter, allowing Lago to continue.

"We did what was necessary to survive, to bring Agnargsilv back into the light," Lago said. "If Agnargsilv had wanted to remain forever in the dark, it would've let us perish." He then spoke of Ockam's adopted son, Bonmei, and the promise Lago had made—and briefly fulfilled—of returning the mask to Bonmei. He told of Fjorna's attack and defeat at Thornridge, and how they escaped by walking into the Heartpine Dome. He was again interrupted by the chatter, this time not of anger, but confusion.

Hed Lettáni raised their hand and asked, "Have you not told us the other domes are closed? Or has Agnargdrolom heard the voice of Noss and blossomed open?"

The queen was the one to answer. "Few but the high priests and the royal family know of this aspect of the Silvesh," she said. "A Silvfröa can ask the vines of white blood to step aside to allow them to walk through the dome. It is not something we have ever attempted."

"But why not?" Lago asked. "You would've seen the New World is healthy if you had simply looked outside yourselves."

The queen exhaled sharply. "That power is there as a safeguard. Noss ordered us never to leave this land until either we heard their call, or until after the passing of two millennia, for leaving sooner could bring death to us all. We do not go near the vines, it is forbidden, and—"

She was interrupted when the crowd by the entrance suddenly parted. Everyone at the table stood, including the queen. Between the parting citizens strode a clouded leopard not much bigger than a normal-sized housecat, coated in marbled patterns of gold and black that made her look like she was draped in dappled forest light, both luminous and obscure. She strutted to the space inside the crescent-shaped table, rubbed her tail on Fingrenn's leg as she passed, and jumped up directly in front of the queen, who bowed so that the Nu'irg could bump heads with her. The captivating felid then hopped atop the queen's high chair to roost above them all. Her long tail dangled right over the queen's head, sometimes tickling her blue-inscribed scalp. Once the clouded leopard's slitted eyes relaxed, so did the crowds.

All took their seats, except for Aio. He looked at Jiara and Lago, and said, "Nelv, Nu'irg ust Mindrel, has come to listen and offer advice. We ask that you both wear your Silvesh so that she may see you better."

Aio shapeshifted into Kulak. Lago followed his lead, drawing uncomfortable mumbles from the crowds. Jiara put her mask on and ignored the questioning looks.

Sterjall felt Nelv's gaze scrutinizing him. She was skeptical, constantly assessing, and judicious. They exchanged no words—they could not do so, as felids and canids did not share the same qualia—but they could feel each other's intentions: Sterjall because of the exceptional powers of his Silv, and Nelv because she was old, wise, and knew better.

Sterjall continued his story, doing his best to avoid staring at Nelv. He guessed Kulak was interpreting the words back to her, given the attention he was placing toward her whenever Sterjall spoke. He spoke of the ongoing collapse of the Heartpine Dome, and how he had helped Safís—the canid Nu'irg—escape her doomed land. He could not help but look to Nelv as he spoke of the white wolf. Nelv knew his words were true. She slowly blinked her eyes at Sterjall as a wordless *thank you*.

Sterjall then pulled Leif out from its scabbard and placed it on the table in front of him. "This dagger's hilt was crafted from one of the pieces of the Stelm Bir temple. Many other pieces were taken by the Negians, but most remain in the dome."

Worried faces judged him. Hud Quoda, who came from the province of mangroves, spoke next. "Ommo ust Agnarg was desecrated, and you've crafted a weapon with one of its bones. This is a great impiety toward our eighteen tribes."

Hud Ilsed and Hod Abjus agreed with her, but Hed Lettáni shook their head and said, "Or if you see it from his scalp, Sterjall saved the artifact from destruction. What is left in Agnargdrolom is doomed, and this piece would have been doomed as well. Did your own handpaws craft the dagger?"

"No," Sterjall said, "a Nu'irg forged it for me." This got everyone's attention. He explained then how he'd been saved by Banook, or Kerjaastórgnem, as the Laatu knew him. He did not mention his relationship with Banook, as the Nu'irg had once warned him that their love would not be seen as appropriate among the Miscam. *But he can see right through me,* he thought, failing to avert Kulak's gaze, who could pick up on his half-truths and omissions. He tried to project a sense of wariness so that Kulak would not bring the subject up, yet he could not help but tint his emotions with sorrow and longing.

"And Leif was instrumental in rescuing Urnaadisilv from the ice," Jiara added, taking some heat away from the wolf. She explained how Sterjall had used it to see the threads from much farther away, and how Ockam had inherited the ursid mask. The Laatu did not seem as upset about Ockam wearing the mask as they were about Jiara, given that Ockam was Bonmei's father—even if not related by blood—and it felt somewhat appropriate.

Alaia was next to carry the torch, telling them of the burning of Withervale by the Red Stag. When the wolverine general was mentioned, whispers of *Krostsilv* reverberated across the hall. Alaia then mentioned that they saw the cervid Nu'irg fighting under the Red Stag's orders, mindlocked by him.

Nelv's back hairs stood on end, and her ears flattened. Kulak measured her and said, "Nelv is saddened, and fearful. She hopes Sovath will be saved from that horrendous fate. The atrocities of the Unification Epoch must not be repeated."

Balstei took over next, describing his research on quaar and how that had gotten him in such trouble. At his mention of quaar, the queen raised her scepter, which made him stop talking, but soon he realized she was just displaying a quaar object as an acknowledgment. He then explained his research on the aetheric elements, in particular that of soot.

Fingrenn interjected with their own words, "We are very familiar with the aetheric powder you call soot. *Ustlas* we call it." When Fingrenn spoke for themself, they kept both hands pointed toward their own chest. "Ustlas helps us in our learning as interpreters, and aids our shamans in speaking to the animals. The black canyons of Gwur Esmukh provide a constant supply."

When Fingrenn interpreted to Miscamish what they had just spoken of in Common, Hod Abjus—chief of Gwur Esmukh—responded by proudly raising a row of seedpod-like vials that dangled among his many pendants. Abjus smiled for the first time since he had taken his seat.

"And that's how I lost my laboratory, my equipment," Balstei continued. "And why we had to flee Zovaria before they confiscated the Silvesh from us. Why we came here to ask for your aid."

The queen tightened her brows at the mention of yet another army looking to use the Silvesh for war. "It saddens my scalp that the New World has discovered so much from the past, yet seems to have learned nothing. The Silvesh are meant to unite. They are not weapons of conquest, nor are they artifacts of coercion, of fear. Both your Empire and your Union are misguided and dangerous. My heart is relieved that you kept Agnargsilv and Urnaadisilv safe from their hands."

"These foreigners have brought nothing but war to us," Abjus said.

"Hold your tongue, Chief," the queen reprimanded him. "This gathering has lingered for long hours. We shall break to feed our bellies and rest our scalps, then we shall allow the travelers to ask questions."

Ierun Alúma called for a break for lunch and requested the meeting resume after a customary afternoon nap.

All chiefs and interpreters joined them in the dining hall. The tension and distrust were palpable, even if they did not discuss any subjects related to the meeting.

Sterjall sat between Kulak and Fingrenn. Plates for a Laatu did not act as borders, so Kulak picked a prickly fruit from Sterjall's plate, then in Common said, "Happy, hearing story. Thank you."

Fingrenn took half a munnji cake directly from Sterjall's handpaw and said, "The Khuron has requested I be his tutor. He learns fast, thanks to Mindrelsilv, but he wants to learn faster. Our lessons began last night."

"I'd like to learn Miscamish, too," Sterjall said. "As your guests, we are the ones who should put in the effort."

"Not so," Fingrenn said. "As your hosts, it is our duty to make you feel at home. But if you'd like, we could all learn together, Miscamish *and* Common." Fingrenn then interpreted to Kulak, who was ecstatic about the idea.

"We should take lessons every morning after breakfast!" Kulak said. "With Balstei, and Alaia, and Jiara, and also Givra, and Mother."

"That is a lot of students," Fingrenn said, pointing both hands to their chest. "My scalp may be able to handle that, but not much more. I shall request additional copies of the grimoires."

"I saw the original *Miscamish Grimoire* you keep at the reliquary," Balstei said from across the table. "We only teach from the *Common Grimoire*, while Miscamish is spoken by very few scholars. Your accent is peculiar, but still easy to understand."

"It was the wisdom of the Acoapóshi, or perhaps of Noss himself, that commanded to safeguard the two languages with strict rules of phonetics. My scalp has studied the grimoires for decades, as well as the old tongues of Heiaggálvan and Kuvej. Soot aids greatly in this pursuit—it lets non-Silvfröash feel the connections and understand meanings better."

"You use soot for learning?" Balstei asked. "Then sign me up! I always wanted to understand Miscamish."

Hod Buil then requested Fingrenn's presence, leaving Sterjall and Kulak without an interpreter. They wanted to chat but did not know how. They felt the awkwardness and laughed together. Kulak then said, "*Chienn uss wulem mad?*"

"Yes, I am happy. We all are," Sterjall answered, feeling through the meaning of the words, though not entirely grasping all of them.

"*Um henet jall jirusse lul ti chienn enuthe ust Kerjaastórgnem?*"

Hearing Banook's name made Sterjall tense up. He wasn't sure what Kulak had asked, but it had something to do with Sterjall's sadness. The wolf smiled, embarrassed, and tried to ignore the question; mask or no mask, he knew the caracal could see through him. Kulak put a friendly arm around his shoulders and said, "*Grei aptaoth, henet inkel uth ampalv ilm Aio-Kulak.* No worry."

Sterjall took that kindly and felt he was safe.

They returned to their dormitory after lunch for what was supposed to be a nap, but they had too much on their minds. The room was warm, so they sat by the windows.

"The chiefs don't seem very happy with us wearing the masks," Lago said. The refreshing breeze from the river and falls felt kinder over his smooth skin than over Sterjall's fur.

"We are not Miscam," Jiara said bluntly.

"I don't know what would happen if they asked us to give them up. They don't really belong to us, but I feel as if Agnargsilv is a part of me now. To take it away would be like ripping me in half."

"I'm beginning to feel the same way about Urnaadisilv, and I've only worn it for a few weeks. I would not want to see it come to that."

"It wouldn't be fair," Alaia said, petting the giant tabby cat, who had returned to sprawl by their feet. "But I think they will be more accepting once we are done explaining everything."

"I don't think they all hear us the same way," Lago said. He leaned over the thick windowsill, savoring the feeling of the cold stone on his arms. "It's been strange sitting close to Kulak. He can read straight into me. There's nothing I can hide from him."

"I had the same feeling," Jiara said. "He is keen and clever, but I feel as if he's on our side more than any of the others."

They returned to their seats before the council resumed, including Nelv, perching atop the tall backrest of the queen's chair. She was now in the shape of a lynx, with tufted ears not as long as Kulak's, and with barely a nub for a tail, but with much longer cheek fur.

While Fingrenn interpreted, Ierun Alúma began, "We have asked much of you, guests of Mindreldrolom, and your breaths have given us many answers, but answers we have not provided in return. Your scalps seem as ignorant of the story of the domes as ours are of the story of the New World. Ask now, children, but I warn you that our memories only extend so far."

Sterjall thought it would be best to start at the beginning. "We would like to know why the Silvesh were created. What is their true purpose?"

"We have no answer to that question," Alúma said. "The Acoapóshi tribe, makers of the Silvesh, kept their own secrets and Noss's secrets as well. We know what the Silvesh can do, but we do not know the reason for their creation."

"What about the domes?" Balstei asked. "How do they relate to the calamity that caused the Downfall?"

Alúma signaled for an old allgender to come to her, who seemed to be the oldest person in the room. She whispered to them as they nodded.

"My name is Suque," the elder said with an accent much thicker than Fingrenn's. "I become historian. Forgiveth, not best Common. Little our scalps remembeth. Old tale speaks of star with veil white, seen in dome black by eyetubes of the Yenwu. Star said in five centuries she returneth, to burn Noss. Miscam worked to protect from anger of star, grew *drolomesh*, gathered animals so they would not death. Each tribe grew own drolom, and then closed and waited. Star returneth to fulfill oath of fire. Noss shook in pain—but Laatu were inside, did not see, did not death."

"The veiled star must've been a comet," Sterjall said to his friends.

Fingrenn overheard this and said, "My scalp knows not that word."

"It's a star with a long tail that moves through the sky," Sterjall said, then turned to the queen. "Banook told us—I mean, Kerjaastórgnem told us that the domes were meant to open up again, not keep you trapped forever. It is safe in the New World, it has been for centuries. Why have the domes not opened then?"

Alúma clasped her wrinkled hands and said, "It was Noss who instructed us to wait for their word before opening the dome. We have been waiting, but they have not yet commanded us to do so."

Balstei jumped in, "When you say Noss speaks to you, who do you mean? Do you divine their words in signs from nature? Or from an oracle, perhaps?"

"We mean the planet themself," Alúma said. "My own ears have never heard Noss's voice, none of our ears have. But the Silvfröash who lived long before us did speak to them."

"Was it meant to be some sort of signal?" Sterjall asked. "If you've never heard Noss before, how would you know what to expect?"

"Noss commanded the Mindrelfröash—who was me and my father before me, but who now is my son Kulak—to wait inside Ommo ust Mindrel during the first day of every month. When the day came that it was safe for the dome to open, Noss would inform the Mindrelfröa by means of the Silv. Perhaps it is not safe yet. Perhaps Noss does not think it is wise for us to leave."

Sterjall was confused, as he could not fathom how waiting any longer could make things safer. "Could you open the dome without waiting for Noss's call?"

Alúma's grip tightened on her quaar scepter. "Our laws do not allow such a thing, it goes against the work of generations who fought to keep our home safe."

"But what if Noss is unable to talk to you?" Alaia asked. "You'd be stuck here forever."

"Not so," Alúma said. "Noss had the foresight to prevent such an outcome. If their voice was not heard, Noss asked us to wait for two millennia after the time of the Downfall. Then and only then we would be allowed to use Mindrelsilv in the way you have used Agnargsilv and Urnaadisilv, to cross the wall of vines and judge with our own eyes if the New World was safe for us. If the Mindrelfröa deemed it so, they could begin the process of opening the dome. If not, we would try again every thousand years. It has not yet been twenty centuries since the great closing, and so we wait."

"Something must've gone wrong," Sterjall said, dissatisfied with the answer, but Jiara spoke before he could think of a follow-up question.

"What else can you tell us about the Silvesh?" she asked. "How do they work? We need to find ways to protect ourselves from the Red Stag and from the Silvesh he might be stealing as we speak."

Her demanding tone drew skeptical looks from some of the chiefs.

The queen did not seem as concerned with the question, and she replied, "Our scalps know not the mysteries of the Silvesh. How they work, why they were created. That was a secret of the founding tribe, the Acoapóshi."

"In the New World we have books," Balstei said, "writings, documents that can tell us about things that happened long before. Do you not keep books? A library?"

Historian Suque, who was still standing by the queen, replied in their broken speech, "Laatu keep artifacts in memory of departed. Scrolls in small number, they do province keeping, rules for rituals. Runes in hides, stampeth with arambukh, used for commerce, trade, not history. Only books are grimoires, so that tongues not become lost through time. Books made wasteful, kill trees sacred. History is gifteth from tongue to scalp, words become history. My father, my daughter, they speak history. But history from past far is known little."

"Would Miscam tribes in other domes have answers you do not?" Balstei asked with a bit of snark tinting his tone.

Alúma considered the question and let Fingrenn interpret her reply. "Each dome housed a different Miscam tribe. Each tribe had their own culture and way of being. Each might know something the others do not."

"We need to find out why the domes have not yet received that signal," Jiara said. "We need to warn the other tribes of the threat of the Red Stag, because he *will* come for them."

"Would the New World kingdoms not prevent the Urgfröa from entering their lands?" Hed Lettáni asked with a soft tilt of their head, keeping their composure more than any of the other chiefs.

"They will fight back," Jiara answered, "but the Negian army is strong. In a short time, they have taken two Silvesh and destroyed at least one dome."

"The Miscam in other domes will fight back too," Hod Abjus said, lifting his square chin, "just like we will if they attack us. We have studied the arts of war since before the domes closed, training in sport, battling between provinces, ready in case worst came to pass. The Wutash were weak. We would have fought the intruders, and our companion felids would have battled alongside us."

"I do not doubt it," Jiara said to placate him, "and you seem fiercer than any Negian warrior I've encountered, but their strength is in numbers. I am not talking of thousands, but hundreds of thousands of warriors, and growing."

The chiefs mumbled and shared concerned looks with their advisors.

"Hundreds of thousands?" Hod Buil said, his voice rising way above his stature. "Such numbers we cannot match. We have kept our population under control, for Mindreldrolom was grown not just for us, but for animal and plant species that need room to grow."

"Not even a hundred thousand we could account for between our six provinces," Hud Quoda said, shaking her head and with it her mangrove-like headdress. "And from those, only a small portion could be considered warriors."

"And the Red Stag's army of cervids is growing," Alaia said. "They are common in the New World, and he's mindlocking them wherever he finds them. They are disposable to him. He sends them to die, not caring about them at all."

The Laatu could not comprehend how such cruel measures could be used in war. They were aghast and angered. All animals, and particularly the felids, were sacred to them; the cervids should've been seen as most sacred to the Urgfröa.

"I want to ask about Momsúndodrolom," Sterjall said directly to the queen. "When I spoke Mamóru's name, you seemed to recognize it." At the mention of Mamóru, Nelv stood and focused her lynx eyes on Sterjall.

"Mamóru is spoken of often in tales we tell our children," Alúma responded. "He is the Nu'irg ust Momsúndo, who was known to take a human form like Allamónea of the cetaceans, Kerjaastórgnem of the ursids, and Buujik of the primates. Mamóru was known as smartest of us all, named the Keeper of Memory, the first and oldest of the Nu'irgesh."

"Nelv knew him well before the domes closed," Kulak added, looking up at the felid Nu'irg. "She loved him dearly and hopes to see him again one day."

Alúma raised a hand; the lynx bumped her head on it, but her expression was disconcerting now, as if she was reading the fear in Sterjall's eyes.

"We think... We know that Momsúndodrolom did not survive the Downfall," Sterjall said. "A volcano erupted near it, and where there should be a dome, there is nothing but endless fields of black rock."

The Laatu gasped in horror. Nelv's ears flattened, her whiskers pointing forward while the fur on her back rose; terror filled her eyes, and Sterjall could feel it alongside her helplessness. Nelv shifted into her clouded leopard primal form and hopped down to the chair where Kulak was sitting; the backrest was lower, leaving her at Kulak's shoulder level. She wrapped her long tail around the caracal's neck and stared at Sterjall with interrogating eyes.

"Nelv says her heart can still feel Mamóru," Kulak said. "She does not believe he has died."

"Banook felt the same way," Sterjall said.

"If anyone has answers to our questions, it is Mamóru," Alúma said. "He is the oldest among all kinds. He was there in the times the Silvesh were created, during the Revelation and Unification epochs, and long before then, during the Expansion Epoch. But my aged scalp does not understand how he could still survive if what you said is correct, if his dome was swallowed by Noss's hot blood."

"We could travel there," Sterjall said. "Jiara knows the lands where the lava flowed, and we could use the Silvesh and Leif to locate Mamóru. If he is still there, we'd find him."

"Wolf child, you are injured," Alúma said with honest concern on her face. "Your arm is broken, and you speak of an army waiting outside the white blood vines."

"But one of our chiefs could take Agnargsilv," Abjus said, "so we can journey to the New World and get the answers from the Nu'irg."

"No!" Sterjall said much too loudly. "Agnargsilv stays with me."

"But you are not of the Miscam!" Abjus scolded him.

"And you are not of the Wutash," Sterjall countered. "Or do Laatu laws apply to them too?"

"Your tongue is like a viper. You were not chosen as the voice of canids."

"I know I was not chosen in the same way Aio-Kulak was, but Agnargsilv came to me, and it is my burden to bear."

Hod Abjus stood, the veins on his neck tensing like angered snakes, and yelled, "This broken-armed runt stole the Silv from a dead chief!"

"Abjus!" Alúma exclaimed, not using his honorific.

"And Urnaadisilv too," Abjus spat. "You tossed it like scraps to this woman who can't even wield it properly!"

Alúma rose her frail body, lifted her scepter, and commanded, *"Tienn ëathuk pralloth shiédu, wem voss wäethi henet flaabsam durg ilm teu quollemesh ust va nagrámbe!"*

Fingrenn did not deem it appropriate to interpret the words.

Abjus sat, crossing his thick arms.

Alúma settled into her chair and said, "We will not let our tempers boil our scalps. Lago-Sterjall is the current voice of Agnarg, as Jiara is the voice of Urnaadi, even if she has not found her form yet. It took me a long time to discover mine, and we should not hold that against anyone. Without their help, both Silvesh would have been lost."

"What path should we follow, Ierun?" Hod Buil asked. "Are we to leave Mindreldrolom in this quest?"

Alúma answered, "If Mamóru knows why Noss has not spoken to us, perhaps he will know what to do next. My scalp believes the search for answers is a worthy goal, but there will be danger. We shall not depend on strength in numbers, as we will fall short. We shall plan with cunning and proceed with speed, cleverness, and resourcefulness. We will send only our best warriors, mounted on our finest smilodons."

"Interpreters will be needed too," Buil said, thinking of Fingrenn, who came from his province.

"Perhaps that will not be necessary," Kulak said. "Lago-Sterjall needs time to heal. We can all do our best to learn each other's words while his arm mends, while we craft a sound plan."

"We need to speak of this to our citizens," Hed Lettáni said. "The provinces need to agree on these terms, as we represent their voices, not their wills."

The other chiefs agreed with Lettáni. They conversed for a while longer about what they might expect to need in the outside world, but no fixed decisions were to be made yet. Finally, Alúma spoke again. "My scalp believes we must give ourselves time. Chiefs, return to your provinces and talk to your citizens about what you have learned. We will gather in two weeks' time and decide on a plan. In the meantime, I ask of you to learn what you can of the Common tongue, and if our guests so desire, for them to also learn our Miscamish tongue, so that ears could better hear other voices. In two weeks we shall meet, and in two weeks our fates shall be decided."

She banged her scepter on the ground, then rose, bringing the council session to an end.

Chapter Nineteen

Fool's Gold

Time flowed quickly over the next two weeks. In the mornings they would meet Fingrenn for language lessons, alongside Aio-Kulak and Givra, and were surprised to find that Kenondok also came to study; the tree trunk of a warrior who had been a bit rough with Lago in the past was acting friendlier now, and had a good aptitude for learning the Common tongue.

The chiefs and the queen also took lessons with their own tutors, readying themselves for the potential opening of the dome and the need to communicate clearly with the New World.

What made it all better—particularly for Balstei—was that soot was used to expedite their learning, of a kind purified from the finest seams of the Quas Trell mines. Unlike the relatively impure soot the monks at Withervale could extract, this refined substance did not lead to any headaches, dry sinuses, or lethargy after use, and neither did it make the user cough up black phlegm.

"It's like magic," Balstei said to Sterjall, inhaling an unnecessary second dose. "Imagine having access to this for our studies. I wish Khopto was still with us... He would've been able to teach us so much more."

"I wish he was here too," Sterjall said, feeling both guilty and sorrowful.

Balstei placed an arm over his shoulder. "Cheer up, lad. I'm sure he's past the Sixth Gate and teaching the Steward herself all that he learned in his years of hard work. But *I* still have a lot to learn. I'm beginning to feel something new. It's like the threads are a tingle on my skin, but I don't have the proper means to perceive them. Maybe with more practice." He inhaled a third dose.

The Silv wearers did not need the aid of the aetheric carbon. Alaia insisted that she also did not need any 'alchemical interventions,' and worked herself harder than the others to prove herself right, but soon fell behind. Resigned, she agreed to try it; only for now, and only for learning the language.

Fingrenn told them that soot was the key to the proper handling and balancing of the complex biomes within Mindreldrolom, aiding those who did not wear Mindrelsilv to better communicate with other species.

"Can you mindspeak to animals in the same way Kulak can?" Sterjall asked Fingrenn.

"I cannot. Soot offers but a minuscule portion of the Silvesh's power. It takes many years of training to speak to the animals, a training only shamans endure, and it's as much related to learning through empathy as it is to the use of the black powder. With soot, I can communicate simple emotions to the smarter species, but only shamans have learned how to communicate more complex ideas."

"Can you also use it for non-felids?" Sterjall asked.

"We can. It is the one quality at which soot is better than the Silvesh—it has a broader reach, as it is not bound to a particular clade of animals. Soot is a bridge to empathize with the minds of species of a certain degree of intelligence and self-awareness. It is, however, a one-way mode of communication. Even shamans cannot hear the voices of the animals, for their scalps do not possess the qualia to understand them. That is the greatest gift of the Silvesh—not the ability to talk, but to listen."

Some Laatu Miscam showed a better predisposition to the effects of soot, particularly allgenders. Those who reached mastery of the substance were given the title of shaman, and they were the ones who directed the movement and cycle of animals within the dome, gave them instructions, and trained birds to deliver messages between the provinces, just like the shamans of Wastyr could do.

During a break after a long Miscamish lesson, the tutor and their students sat side by side on a long bench in a shaded tunnel. The tunnel had been carved on the rocks right behind a draping curtain of water. The respite was welcome, for the day was warm, and they had been walking for hours while Fingrenn pointed out new things and named them. The subtle mist from the thin falls cooled their necks and brows, and the murmur of the stream refreshed their minds.

Balstei leaned back against the moist wall, fidgeting with a small vial of soot. He flipped it around, letting the dark powder fall onto the cap like a miniature black waterfall. The vial contained more soot—and of a purer kind—than he had ever been able to afford for his experiments.

"Just how much soot do your mines produce, Fingrenn?" he asked.

"The weight of one *mindu*, or black panther, every year," they said, "which we find is most appropriate, and just enough for our shamans to work with."

"Twin Gods have mercy," the artificer mumbled under his breath. "That must be ten times more than the supply from the Zovarian Union and the Negian Empire combined, including the more illicit sources." He chewed on his lower lip, thinking of the amount of information that could have been transferred via heralds if such a vast quantity of soot had been available to the Union—the balance of powers would have greatly shifted in their favor.

"Say, Fingrenn, I'm curious about something," he said after a while. "You know so much more about soot than anyone in the New World. Do you also study, or perhaps harvest, the other aetheric elements?"

"Yes. The *annudand*, the waverers, those elements who remain uncertain, who rise and fall."

"Yes, exactly," Balstei said, assuming Fingrenn was referring to the peculiar attribute of aetheric elements of having constantly fluctuating, undefined masses.

"Carbon is *las*, soot is *ustlas*," the interpreter explained. "In the same way iron is *kriss*, and magnium is *ustkriss*. Magnium is quite rare in Mindreldrolom. Too much of the knowledge of the waverers was lost to us when the domes closed. With most of them not being found within our dome, with the exception of our *ustlas* and *usteov* mines, we had no chance to learn about them."

"*Usteov*? Balstei asked. Which one is that one?"

"The fire starter. The yellow crystal who holds the warmth of the hearth. How does one say? Brimstone."

"Aetheric sulphur?" Balstei nearly barked. "You have mines of brime in this dome?"

"Yes, we collect the warm rocks near the black canyons of Gwur Esmukh, in the shale stone caverns not too far from the soot mines. They grow in large crystals, easy for our eyes to see, and the mines are always hot, like a campfire after the embers have gone dark."

Fingrenn reached within a pocket of their kilt and pulled out a nearly perfect cube of what looked like gold. The cube was about two fingerbreadths wide on each side, and although the edges were sharp, the corners had been chipped to a brownish dullness.

They handed the brime crystal to Balstei, who took it with reverent, quivering hands.

"I… I can't believe my eyes," he said. "Nor my hands. This must be quite pure. It is warm, too warm." He had to switch hands; although the brime was not hot enough to burn, it became uncomfortable to the touch if held for too long, like a hot bowl of soup. "But it's golden, not yellow. It seems more like pyrite than a pure sulphur crystal. Must be mixed with iron—fool's gold."

"Alright, you fool, let me see!" Alaia barged in, reaching for the rock.

"Careful, gal!" Balstei squawked.

"It *is* hot!" she exclaimed with a smile. "Sterjall, feel this," she said, tossing it over. Sterjall fumbled to catch the cube and dropped it, but Kulak caught it in midair and handed it to him.

Balstei's eyes tracked the precious crystal with palpable tension. He darted his eyes back to Fingrenn and said, "Fingrenn, why do you carry something so precious with you? Is it a talisman of power? Of rank?"

"I can show you why," they said and waved their fingers to ask for the crystal once more. Jiara had been touching the cube to her cheek, feeling it warm up her face. She begrudgingly handed it over.

Fingrenn reached back into their pocket and pulled out a strip of what seemed to be old leather, about as wide as their hand. They placed the object on top of the rocky bench and scraped at it with a sharp edge of the brime crystal, creating a fuzzy pocket of loose fibers, then they lifted their hand.

Balstei's eyes went wide with terror as he saw what Fingrenn was about to do. With one quick motion, Fingrenn struck the crystal onto the wall of stone. The impact released a blinding torrent of sparks, shining white like a magnesium flame, then settling to sparkling yellows and oranges. The sparks were a hundredfold more numerous than those from striking flint to steel, and they lingered for much longer, like timid stars. More than a handful caught onto the fibers, quickly billowing into an eager flame.

"We catch the usteov on the tinder fungus," Fingrenn explained, "or sometimes we let the sparks fly onto birch bark, or dry grasses. Sparks from usteov stay alight for much longer."

The sparks which had not landed onto the tinder fungus were still crackling on the stone bench and on the ground, flickering hotly like embers escaped from a furnace. They released a sharp, metallic scent with soft traces of something like rotten eggs. It took a long while before the sparks fizzled out to darkness.

"We... we didn't know of this effect," Balstei said. "We would never have dared strike such precious rocks."

"It only happens with the golden crystals, not the yellow ones," Fingrenn added, "the kind you called *pyrite*. We find the yellow crystals in our mines as well, as part of the matrix from where these other ones grow, but they are too brittle, and they do not spark, even if they are better at producing heat."

Fingrenn was curious at the manner in which Balstei was transfixed by the simple mineral. They held the cube out toward him and said, "It is yours to keep, if you so wish."

The artificer's heart skipped a few beats. He did not let humility get in the way of accepting the gift; he took it eagerly while mumbling a string of thank-yous under his breath.

"I'm curious," Alaia said, watching Balstei struggle to keep from shaking, "how come the aetheric elements are hard to find? Wouldn't it be easier to tell a hot rock from the others?"

"It's not that simple a matter," Balstei said, rotating the golden cube in his hands. "Brime would be easy to detect, due to the heat, if it was commonplace. But we never found any mines of it, only tiny seams or pockets with scarce specimens. Pharos would be easy to spot too, if it was still glowing, but the few places it's been found in had the rocks already spent, so they were glowing no longer."

"Then how *do* you find them?" Alaia asked.

"It's through their one common property, the fact that their masses fluctuate over time," Balstei answered. "Say you have a particle of aetheric carbon." He held the cube of brime in his thumb and forefinger and placed it on the palm of his other hand. "If you were to weigh it, you'd see peaks and troughs every time the mass goes up and down. Easy, right? Anyone could detect an aetheric element that way."

"Hmm, yes," Alaia said. "That's the opposite—"

"No, gal, now imagine you have *two* particles of soot. When you measure them, their peaks and troughs will not match, so they will, overall, average out to something closer to the middle point. Still easy to detect, however. Now imagine instead of two, you have a thousand of them. No, a million particles. They all vary in mass, but overall, their masses average out to something even tighter to the absolute centerline, making the differences extremely hard to detect."

Alaia nodded, "I think I see it now—"

"No, you don't. Now make it billions of particles. Quadrillions. Even more! And not only that, but mix it up with a bunch of common carbon particles, making it absolutely impossible to tell which ones are which. That's why it's so hard to detect these elements in the wild, even if we might be breathing or eating them from time to time. If we find them, it's by luck, like finding a seam of magnium, or how our friends here live next to a mine of brime jewels and another of nearly pure soot.

"But once we have a pure-enough sample that we suspect might have an aetheric component, we can use sensitive machines to detect its variations in mass. Every once in a while, very rarely, the peaks and troughs of the masses line up, and the shift in the weight can be felt by our machines. It's most peculiar... Those alignments happen all at once, not just in one sample but in samples all across the entirety of Noss. We have measurements with the same fluctuations happening in the Tsing Empire, in Dathereol, Bauram, Elmaren, and Wastyr, all in perfect synchrony."

"Wait, what causes their sizes to fluctuate together like that?" Alaia asked.

"Not sizes, masses. Their size remains the same, but they gain or lose relative weight. We don't have the slightest clue what causes the shift. We *used* to think it was earthquakes, because those shifts tend to coincide with some major tremors. However, nearly two centuries ago, Artificer Tokav proposed that the earthquakes were not the cause, but were *caused by* the shift in the masses. Imagine you have a seam of magnium deep underground, a massive one." He held his brime cube on the palm of his hand as an example once more. "One that in an instant starts to weigh nearly twice as much." Balstei lowered the hand with the brime as if it had suddenly become heavier. "The entire foundation of the crust below the aetheric seam might shift if the seam is large enough."

"They don't shift *because* of earthquakes then," Sterjall said. "So what makes it happen?"

"Who in Khest knows?" Balstei replied with an exaggerated shrug. "Alignment of the planets? Conspiring stars? The heartbeat of demons from the nethervoids? The whims of the Twin Gods? It could be caused by mischievous sprites, for all we know. It makes no sense at all. There seem to be more forces at play than purely natural ones."

"How is it not natural if it happens in nature?" Alaia asked without a hint of mockery in her tone.

"I... Good point. I don't know."

"But what about the ones that aren't solid, then?" she inquired. "How could you possibly find those? How can you weigh them?"

"That is a smart question, gal," he said. "But the procedure is not as hard as it may seem." He looked up toward the curtain of water in front of them; it was shimmering like silver. "We know about the gases—not only of the aetheric kind, mind you—mostly from texts that survived the Downfall. How the ancients knew of their existence, how they measured them and discovered their properties, that we do not know. Too much knowledge was lost then, but what survived has been invaluable for alchemy and aetheric theory."

He held his precious new crystal up again and stared at its golden reflections. "Think of this crystal of brime. It's not just aetheric sulphur, but also iron—if I'm not mistaken—mixed in a perfect cube of pyrite. Most rocks are not just silicon, iron, calcium, and other elements we tend to know as solids. The *major portion* of all rocks is made of oxygen, combined with the other elements. And also hydrogen, another gas you are breathing in and out at this very moment, while unable to see it or detect it."

"Then they find the gases in rocks?" Alaia asked.

"Precisely. Although most rocks tend to be too mixed up, having been melted and reforged a thousandfold inside the bellies of volcanoes. And water is entirely useless, as it runs through cycles, and the particles are always as mixed as they possibly can be. But there are some seams that remain untouched, and also meteors, in which we've managed to find more pristine matrices."

"Meteorites," Sterjall corrected.

"Don't get smart with me, wolf. Anyway, there is a great slab of pallasite that was discovered near Allathanathar, the capital of the Kingdom of Bauram. The oxygen bound to its crystals seems to be entirely of the aetheric kind, pure ignium. When it's separated and set to burn, it releases hundreds of times more energy than regular oxygen would. They have shipped a small chip of the meteorite for our institute to study, but as it happens, I haven't been granted access to it. It's much too precious, and I don't yet have the tenure or the suck-up influence to be granted such honors."

Balstei rubbed his gray beard, then his black mustache, and seemed to scowl beneath it. "Fingrenn, what else can you teach me? I need to know more. How did you find your sources? How do you purify them? Are there other elements your tribe has access to?"

"None other than soot, brime, and a small source of magnium," they said. "As far as how the alchemical process is handled, perhaps you could speak to the sages at Quas Trell, where the purification sanctuaries are. My scalp does not hold the knowledge you seek. I was aiming to teach you what I know of the wavering elements, yet my scalp has learned more from you instead. But let us continue now. There are more words to learn, more knowledge to be gained."

As they walked back out from behind the waterfall, Kulak approached Sterjall, cocking his head. His black ear tufts dangled with curiosity.

Sterjall smiled awkwardly, not knowing what to say or what Kulak wanted.

The caracal reached into a side pouch and pulled out a little cube of brime. Kulak's was smaller than Fingrenn's and had no damage at the corners or edges, perhaps because a prince was not likely to be the one starting a fire for cooking or for any other purpose.

"To you," Kulak said. "Gift."

"Th-thank you," Sterjall said, taking the cube from his handpaws. It was warm and inviting. It felt like holding a beam of sunshine, and he did miss Sunnokh's touch. "I... I have nothing to give in return," he said, embarrassed.

Kulak either did not understand the words, or understood them perfectly but did not understand why they needed saying. He simply smiled, black lips curling to pull his whiskers higher.

Chapter Twenty

Minquoll

Morning came with curling mists and melodious birdsong.

As they walked toward the atrium, Sterjall spun his hot cube of brime in his padded fingertips. It really did shine like gold, and it was so perfectly crystallized that every facet of the cube reflected everything like a polished mirror, but in a warmer shade.

"I don't want to smash mine on a rock," he admitted to Alaia. Both Alaia and Jiara had gotten a cube as well. Brime cubes were nothing special in Mindreldrolom; almost everyone carried one to start fires, but Sterjall felt his was special.

"Fingrenn said they last a long time," Alaia said, scraping hers on a wall. It sparked as if she were a blacksmith pummeling a sledgehammer on a white-hot blade. "And they can get us more if we run out."

"I'll pretend I've spent mine up and ask for a new one every day," Balstei said greedily.

Fingrenn met them at the circle of moss-covered statues for their daily language lesson. The interpreter ushered the group toward the stables to teach them the names of the different felid species.

"There's something I've been curious about," Sterjall said to Fingrenn. "There are so many felids, and they are all predators. How do you feed them all? I have not seen cows, horses, or antelope. I've seen a few goats and wild hogs, but not in great numbers."

Fingrenn approached Blu, who was strutting next to Kulak, and petted the smilodon's head. "The larger the cat, the more they eat, so it would be unsustainable to have them always feed on prey they hunt. Most of our felids feed on *munnji*, but also on fish, which are plentiful in the Isdinnklad."

"What is munnji anyway?" Alaia asked. "We've been eating those cakes all this time but have no clue what they are made of."

"Munnji is the nutritious lifeblood paste, made from the white milk of the sacred vines."

"White sap? Isn't that poisonous?" Sterjall asked.

"Not when treated with a special fungus, mixed with ashborn beans, and cooked with juniper ashes. They serve the strict nutritional needs of many species, and the supply of white blood is inexhaustible. Hed Lettáni manages the plantations of ashborn beans in the province of Gwur Aalpe. You could ask them to show you someday. Their silos process the feed for the cats. Other provinces handle different recipes for non-felid species."

They arrived at the fence bordering the stables and watched as trained shamans directed the felids. It all seemed surprisingly easy, for there were no cages, no locks. All the felids cooperated willingly, even enthusiastically.

Three smilodons were feeding on an enormous block of munnji. Even from a distance, the pungent aroma was overbearing—clearly not the same munnji the humans were fed.

"The smilodons you have here are much larger than any fossils we've found in the New World," Balstei noted. "Not to mention your housecats… They are enormous!"

Fingrenn nodded their purple-pigmented head. "We have chosen three felid kinds to be our companion species—the smilodons, the domestic cats, and the snow leopards. That is why they are so large."

"Companion species?" Alaia asked.

Fingrenn pondered how to best explain. "The companion species are those who help us care for Mindreldrolom, but also those who will help us when the time comes to migrate away from home. They are bigger, as you noticed, but also much smarter, longer-lived, and grow steel-tough bones that we use for tools and structures. We have helped them adapt in this way for centuries, as that is what Noss ordered us to do."

"How is it possible?" Balstei wondered out loud. "Animals don't simply grow bigger. A bit, perhaps, with careful breeding, but like this?"

"It has to do with munnji, the lifeblood paste we were just speaking of. Most felids, humans, and other large creatures feed from common munnji made from sap milked from the twenty-three columns that hold up our skies. But the companion species have been fed with *idshall-munnji*, lifeblood paste made from the sap of the core vine. It is this diet that causes the change, although the change is slow, occurring across generations."

"What is the core vine?" Sterjall asked.

"The vine that sits at the center of the temple of felids and listens to the words of the Mindrelfröa. You could think of it as the spine of the dome, or perhaps its brain, if the analogies hold that far."

"Like the vine at Stelm Bir, the one the Negians chopped to pieces," Jiara said. "No wonder Heartpine is falling apart." She strangled her braid as she considered further. "This all makes sense, the dire wolves too. Remember that murderous taintsmear we found there? Baldo. He told us there used to be other large canids in Heartpine, too. Foxes or coyotes, I think he said, but they all died off."

"Those must be the species the Southern Wutash chose as their companions," Fingrenn remarked. "It is a shame. With no Wutash left, there was no one there to prepare the paste for them."

"That's so sad," Alaia said while scratching behind Blu's chocolate ears. "But that won't happen to these sweet kitties."

Blu offered a soft growl of appreciation, seeming to understand her words.

"They all seem so well behaved," she continued. "Just how smart *do* they get?"

"The companions are as smart as you or I," Fingrenn said, "only in a different manner. They understand many words, but prefer to communicate with gestures, looks, signals, growls, scents, emotions."

"Could Blu learn Common with us?" Alaia asked with a smile.

"We could ask a shaman to teach him some words, but I'd wager he has already picked up some meanings from listening to us speak. Companions cannot speak our tongues, however, their minds do not work the same way."

Fingrenn whistled. From the depths of the stables, a snow leopard came running, leaping unnecessarily high to cross over the fence. She bumped heads with Fingrenn, then with Blu and Kulak. She ignored the others.

"This is Sharíni," Fingrenn said, extending a hand over the snow leopard's shoulders, which reached up to their chest. "She carried me from Humenath. Like all snow leopards, she is resilient, wise, dexterous. We chose three companion species because they hold qualities we value and need. The smilodons are fierce, strong, and clever. The ones you call housecats are not quite as large, but they are much smarter, cunning, and independent. Perhaps too independent—they think they own the city now, and no longer help us much, simply doing as they please. In hindsight, we should've picked a different species. Maybe the servals."

"So why not feed that special mix of munnji to all felid species?" Sterjall asked.

"That would not be wise," the interpreter said. "Too much idshall-munnji would drain the core vine, and the species would grow too big to handle, living longer lives than we can properly support in our limited dome. The companion species are few and chosen with purpose. The day the dome opens, shamans and companions will help other species repopulate the lands and teach them to live in harmony without our constant meddling. This is why our supply of soot, too, is important, for without it, our shamans would not be able to communicate as clearly."

"Say, Fingrenn," Balstei said, narrowing his eyes, "do you think the dome locations were picked based on their reserves of soot?"

Fingrenn considered for a moment. "My scalp does not know the answer," they replied. "Suque might know, but it is a good assumption, as soot would be necessary for any of the domes to function properly."

On Sunnday of the twenty-fourth day of Lustbloom, Kulak said he had a special treat for the guests, requesting their presence at the atrium after lunch. Heavy crowds were crossing the bridges to the Arjum Promenade that day, all wearing either yellow or red shodogs. Kulak, who was wearing red that day, found his friends among the flowing masses, greeted them with a little tap of their right temples, and asked them to follow.

The prince took them to the stadium, where they were given preferential seats right in front of the two dozen massive pines. Being much closer now, Sterjall noticed something peculiar about the six-by-four formation of conifers. "Are those bones curving under the branches?" he asked.

"They must be," Alaia said.

The bone supports were from companion species, which were more durable than most metals and able to hold the weight of the players during the game. Kulak told them the game they were about to watch was called *minquoll*, which literally translated to *cat ball*. He said they had a game every other Sunnday, and that today his province of Gwur Ali was playing against Gwur Gomosh.

They took their seats and waited eagerly. Kulak was trying to explain the rules, but they guessed they'd figure out more from watching the game than from Kulak's expressive handpaw gestures and pointing whiskers.

The two teams entered the field, Gwur Ali wearing red shodogs, and Gwur Gomosh wearing yellow. The teams comprised human players mounted on different species of large cats: mostly jaguars, but also black panthers, tigers, and mountain lions. Smilodons or dinofelises were, unfortunately, too heavy to be hopping about on branches.

Two species of felids carried no riders at all. First were the snow leopards, who, being of a sapient companion species, were smart enough to act as captains, mindspeaking to the other felids on their team to direct their plays in perfect coordination. The other species with no riders were the ocelots. Not much bigger than a New World housecat, ocelots had gorgeous black rosettes over their yellow-to-white fur. The cats seemed excited about the game, particularly the ocelots, who were overflowing with energy and anticipation.

A horn was blown and drums percussed. The human players each inhaled a small dose of soot from their pendants, then asked their cats to climb the trees and take positions among the thicker, lower branches. A white ball the size of a human head was tossed to the striker of the Gwur Ali team—as they were playing home—who lifted the ball above her head and waited. With the metallic clang of a gong, the game began. The Gwur Ali striker had her jaguar climb higher on their tree. All the other cats moved around the field at different heights, but never touching the ground, as that would be a foul.

The striker found a solid branch and tossed the ball to a teammate, who caught it from a protected branch of his tree. His mountain lion jumped to another tree while the player passed the ball in midair. The plays continued in this manner until they got closer to the opposing team's three hoops, hanging vertically at the end of the field. They were within scoring distance, but the ball was stolen during a pass by a leaping snow leopard from Gwur Gomosh.

"Noooo!" Alaia screamed. "Go get that fucker!"

The yellow team advanced, passing the ball from player to player while hopping swiftly among the branches. Gwur Ali seemed to have no defense against the Gwur Gomosh cats, who played at many heights at once. A striker on a black panther was getting close to the red team's triple hoops. Alaia held on to her seat, white-knuckled. The panther climbed higher, trying to get closer to the middle of the three hoops, giving the player a chance to launch the ball. The crowd gasped as the striker hurled the ball toward the central hoop, but the tiny ocelot from Gwur Ali leapt and kicked the ball, sending it flying to the ground. The crowd cheered for the ocelot, who swiftly landed on a branch, eager to go again.

"Go kitty!" Alaia cheered. "We love you!"

Kulak tried to explain that when the ball was knocked to the ground by an ocelot, it went to the ocelot's team, so they were used strategically to steal plays. He wasn't sure if his friends had understood him; they were too focused on the continuing game.

By looking at the scoreboard, they figured out that the lower hoop was worth two points, the middle was four points, and the smallest hoop on top was six points.

Minquoll was intense and fast. Each felid species had a specialty, but the ocelots were everyone's favorites, always jumping to stop the ball in midair. They usually stayed close to the hoops, but sometimes came out to the middle of the field to interrupt plays and steal the ball.

Sterjall was paying close attention to the moves of the players, how they interacted with each other and their mounts. Through Agnargsilv he noticed something peculiar: the threads that connected the players seemed fuzzy somehow, as if they extended past their own bodies, even their cats' bodies, and blended with the spaces between them and the crowds. He felt an odd aura emanating from the two teams, or rather, two auras that subtly combined into one, as if through their competition they acted as a unit, and their very essences combined into two wholes that were one. Sterjall knew that glow; it was like that of a Silv or a Nu'irg, although those were more focused, and had synesthetic colors to them. He recalled when Jiara had gathered honey from a beehive, and how the swarm of bees had kindled a similar, colorless glow. The aura had suddenly vanished after the sweet nectar had been harvested.

Sterjall wondered if this colorless aura was due to the influence of soot, but then realized it wasn't only the players who sprouted connections to each other: the spectators too, in their fervor, shifted threads in ripples, all combining into a powerful essence, though not as clear and concise as that of the players in the field.

The excitement of the crowd was contagious, and Alaia added more intensity to it all. She cheered for every cat on Gwur Ali's team and riled up the crowd behind her. She booed and pouted at the end of the game, when Gwur Gomosh won by seven points. Gwur Ali would have to do better next time. There would be a game again in two weeks, but it would be between Gwur Urëath and Gwur Pantuul—Alaia would have to wait a bit longer to enjoy a satisfactory victory.

Chapter Twenty-One

The Temple of Felids

While taking a break from their lessons with Fingrenn, Sterjall asked Kulak if they could visit Ommo ust Mindrel, the temple of felids. The prince said he needed to ask his mother. When he returned with Ierun Alúma, she told them the temple was forbidden to anyone but the high priests and the Silvfröash. Balstei vehemently protested—and Alaia called it a bullshit rule—but the queen was adamant that she would not break her laws for anyone. The two stayed with Fingrenn to continue their lessons, while Sterjall and Jiara accompanied the queen and prince up the steps.

The titanic banyan tree guarded the entrance to the temple, so thick and gnarly that it wrapped around itself in impossible contortions.

"Ma'u banyan is name," Alúma said, caressing the bulbous growths on the massive trunk. "Sacred, old."

Moss and ferns filled the cracks between the entranceway's stone bricks. Partially obscured within the vegetation, an octahedral keystone sat heavily, its most prominent face deeply carved with a green-glowing triangular glyph representing the clade of felids. Alúma pushed open a curtain of roots and ushered them inside.

They walked slowly, at the queen's pace.

"I wonder why they don't have a proper door," Sterjall whispered, "if they are so strict about no one else entering this place."

"I don't think they have a concept of locks," Jiara said. "I've seen none in our dormitory or anywhere else in Arjum."

A pack of four snow leopards was walking in their direction, pulling a wagon filled with barrels. The rosetted felids offered a courteous blink as they passed by, too busy to be bothered to stop.

"Idshall-munnji," the queen explained, nodding toward the snow leopards. "Food, for companions."

After their half-mile walk up the shallow ramp, they entered the temple. Ommo ust Mindrel was nearly identical to the temple they had visited at Stelm Bir, except that here they could see all that had been missing—or had been destroyed—at the temple of canids. The chamber was well lit with orange-burning lamps, for green fires from vine sap were never burned indoors. Enormous columns supported the tall ceiling, all made of thorny vines interwoven with wood carvings with an angular style characteristic of the Laatu Miscam arts.

Six steps climbed to a central dais which held not a carved map of the continents and domes—like the temple at Da'áju had—but a throne of subtly translucent white marble carved with felid motifs and forms. Behind the throne rose the core vine: thornless, glossier, and somehow greener than all the others. And above it all, orbiting around the central vine, was the polyhedral lattice. Complex and inexplicable, the lattice was a jumble of intersecting polygons, quaar tubes, and articulated geodesic joints. It resembled a chandelier, albeit one with too many arms, prisms, and chains.

"It's like a filigree made of darkness," Sterjall whispered, unsure if he was allowed to speak inside the sacred space—Alúma and Kulak had not said a word since stepping into the temple. "Like a dark diamond of quaar edges."

"Like a black spiderweb," Jiara added. "*The Great Spider bless us eightfold*, Ockam would have said."

Sterjall flashed a sad smile. "I miss him. I wish he could be here to see this."

"Oh, he's watching from somewhere. Besides, if Ockam had been here with the mask, Alúma would not have let me in." She teasingly bumped his shoulders. "Cheer up, kid. And come closer, look at how the threads flow through these. Like on Leif, but on such a massive scale. It looks like the tubes are directing the threads into the vines, right up the trunk."

Sterjall felt as if he was standing within the confines of a crystalline compound, surrounded by invisible forces. "The threads that feed into the lattice, they come from below the ground. But they are so chaotic, it's hard to focus on them." He looked at Leif, wrapped in its scabbard by his side; the threads that flowed through its quaar hilt were immediately pulled into the lattice.

Kulak could see the threads too, and Alúma had seen them many times before, when her name had been Farshálv, and she had been a fierce and beautiful tigress. The queen and prince nodded to their visitors, inviting them to explore the structure.

Sterjall walked around the vast chamber, greeting the six high priests who guarded it. He tentatively stepped up the dais, finding a priest there who was wiping sap from the side of the core vine, covering the wound they had inflicted upon it with a plant fiber; they nodded deferentially and exited like a shadow. Sterjall approached the marble throne and asked Kulak, "What is it?"

Kulak walked to it and sat down. He pointed at his eyes with two retractable claws and said, "*Chëathuk veu finesh.*" He leaned back on the throne and closed his eyes.

Sterjall took a few steps back and watched with Agnargsilv's sight. The chaotic threads that flowed from the underground coalesced through Kulak, then split up into the crystalline shape above, moving through the lattice in a more regular pattern. Kulak was organizing them, controlling them, and making them flow with the aid of the lattice. Sterjall heard a scraping sound above; he looked up and saw the vines slowly shifting in place. The motion was small, but noticeable. Some segments of the lattice shifted as well, subtly reassembling in a new configuration. The intense tangle of threads then unwound and returned to its earlier chaos. The sound of moving vines ceased. Kulak opened his eyes and stood.

"*Ete ommo uth wuglalv,*" he said, then nodded toward the exit.

The four of them returned down the long ramp and pushed the curtain of roots open. Sterjall approached Fingrenn and said, "Could you please ask Kulak what the purpose of the throne is? And the crystal shape above it?"

Fingrenn asked Kulak the question, then pointed a hand toward the prince as they interpreted his response. "The lattice's purpose is to direct the energy of the threads that flow through the ground. It focuses them and gives them power. The quaar conduits, like the one from Leif, are designed to direct the flow."

Kulak puckered his lips, pointing toward Sterjall's hips. Sterjall took Leif out from the scabbard and handed it to him, saying, "Be careful. It's sharp."

Fingrenn continued speaking for Kulak. "Could you show me how you used Leif? You said it helped you find Urnaadisilv."

"Hold it like this," Sterjall said, lifting Kulak's arm so that the dagger was aligned with the caracal's sight.

Kulak's whiskers lifted in a wide smile. He scanned his surroundings, seeing threads much farther than he could see before, then handed the blade back to Sterjall.

"If your scalp understands this blade," Kulak continued, "then it understands the temple. Mindreldrolom is too big. Mindrelsilv cannot reach all the way across the skies, but the lattice makes it possible. The throne, as you call it, is just a marble seat placed where it helps the Silv focus the threads into the lattice. When you become one with the lattice, you see the entire dome at once, just as you can see far with your blade."

"What were you doing with the threads?" Jiara asked.

"I was directing them into the lattice, into the vines, and organizing them, so that the dome stays healthy and keeps growing in the right way. The core vine listens. If no Silv steers the lattice, the dome will suffer, growing in chaos and disorder. It is a complex being who needs a guiding mind."

"That must be what happened to the Varanus Dome," Balstei mused. He explained to Kulak the mystery of Kruwendrolom, and how it had spread out of bounds over the centuries. "If that dome has grown like a spiderweb, what does that mean? Perhaps there's a problem with their Silv? With their temple?"

"Perhaps," Kulak answered. "But my scalp does not know what happens in other domes, only here."

Sterjall nodded and asked, "Kulak, how did you learn to talk to the dome, to make it healthy?"

"It is not taught," the caracal spoke through Fingrenn, "but it is learned with intuition. Like when you make pain go away from someone, by taking their pain and spreading it on your own body. You do that with the dome, and the lattice helps you. You take some of its pain and give it more life. You feel with it and make it grow. The Silv is smart, it teaches you how to do it, when you need to do it."

"Is that how you will open the dome someday?" Jiara asked.

Alúma stepped closer to answer instead of letting Kulak do so. "You understand correctly, child of urnaadi, but you must not take the power lightly. It has never been done because it must not be done until the time is right. Perhaps after we have spoken to Mamóru, we will decide whether it is time to ask Mindreldrolom to unmake itself and lead us into the New World. Perhaps, when that time comes, we will teach you how it is done. Or perhaps you both already know, for Agnargsilv and Urnaadisilv know all that they need to know."

Chapter Twenty-Two

The Second Council

The chiefs of the six provinces returned to Arjum two weeks after the first council session and reconvened in the Great Hall of the Laatu. They took the same seats as before. This time Nelv joined them from the start, taking the friendlier shape of a tiny black-footed cat.

After going through the formalities, Ierun Alúma said, "We entrusted the chiefs to seek the counsel of their people and ask them what the right course of action should be. I will ask each to voice the words of their citizenry before we call for a vote. Hud Ilsed of Gwur Gomosh, if you would please be the first to speak."

Ilsed rose from her seat. She was wearing a red and orange shodog that made her look like a sunset. Framed by the velvety fabrics, her tanned breasts glistened like those of a copper sculpture. "The land of reefs and turquoise waters believes the guests have good intentions and are here out of the kindness of their hearts. Our scalps think that we first need answers, and that if the wisdom of the Nu'irg ust Momsúndo can enlighten us, that we should embark on that path. But we should do so with utmost care. Our guests will be indispensable in this quest, as they are the only ones who can guide our warriors across the New World. Yet our scalps believe the Silvesh belong to the Miscam. The guests were very gracious to return them to us, and we should now find new chiefs to honor with the gift of the voices of Urnaadi and Agnarg."

Sterjall clenched his fist under the table. His jaw, too, was clenched.

Hod Buil from Gwur Úrëath stood next, though his height didn't increase much after he rose to his feet. "The Humenath-Nurr have met under the auspicious shadow of the clouded mountain and have decided to trust the foreigners in this important quest. They see wisdom and good judgment in their hair-covered scalps, but also believe they do not look ready for the task at hand." He pointed a bulky arm at Sterjall's splint. "They ask for patience, time for healing. We need focused training in the arts of battle and time to study the threat of the new kingdoms. The Humenath-Nurr believe Mindrelsilv belongs to the Laatu, but make no claims over Silvesh other than our own. Our scalps believe the Silvesh should remain with the foreigners."

Some onlookers scowled, outraged by this suggestion.

"My eyes see your hesitation and anger," Buil continued. He placed a hand over his tortoiseshell-patterned head. "And my scalp feels uneasy with the thought as well. Our law says only Miscam should wield the Silvesh, but these are strange times, times for change, and other laws are already being broken. We believe the Silvfröash have earned their honor and should retain it, lest a Wutash heir makes themself known."

Hud Quoda from Gwur Pantuul was the next one to stand. She parted the locs of her headdress to expose her milk-white smile before saying, "The people from the headlands and mangroves are not all in agreement, but we have reached a compromise. We think it is best to let the foreigners lead the expedition to the New World, but with the condition that they hand the Silvesh back to the Miscam once they have completed the mission." She said this while looking at Sterjall and Jiara with a non-confrontational smile, simply delivering the message her people had entrusted her with.

As soon as Quoda was finished, Hod Abjus stood, necklaces rattling over his solid chest. "My scalp offers apologies for the rude words I spoke during our previous gathering, but the people of Gwur Esmukh believe the Silvesh should be taken from the foreigners at once, so that we may train Laatu Miscam warriors and have them find their voices before we go out in search of the Nu'irg. We believe that Mindreldrolom should be opened if the New World is as vibrant as the foreigners have claimed, even if we fail to find the Nu'irg ust Momsúndo." Abjus rested back on his seat but kept his chest raised.

Hed Lettáni rose slowly, a colorful, long shodog embroidered with floral patterns draping down their body. Calmly they said, "Across the terraced fields of Gwur Aalpe, our people agree that our guests are appropriate vessels to carry the honor of their Silvesh, at least for now, and that we must seek the counsel of Mamóru. Our scalps believe it is best to wait until Lago-Sterjall has healed and until we have learned more about the dangers that await us. Our scalps also believe that only Jiara is ready for this dangerous task, and that the other guests must be trained properly for battle before departing. On the matter of the future of Agnargsilv and Urnaadisilv, we believe it would be best to discuss our options once the company returns from their quest, as deciding now would be premature." Lettáni sat and folded their shodog over their lap.

Alúma gazed around the table, not finding any unspoken opinions. "There are several matters of concern. There is the matter of undertaking the dangerous quest to find Mamóru, for which all provinces were in favor. If my scalp was mistaken, you must speak now."

No one spoke.

"Then we shall continue with that as our goal. As to how we proceed, there were differing points of view. On the matter of allowing our guests to remain as Silvfröash, the opinions were split. We should vote for what we feel is right for this quest, and separately for what we feel is right after the quest is completed. Should we let Lago-Sterjall, and Jiara, whose second name remains unspoken, remain the Silvfröash of canids and ursids as we search for Mamóru? Stand if this is what you believe."

Three chiefs rose, and Alaia did too, for which Sterjall elbowed her to stop.

"And now those who vote against."

Two chiefs stood. But then the queen rose in the name of the province of Gwur Ali, which made Sterjall feel betrayed.

"We have three votes on each side, which means Khuron Kulak will have the breaking vote. Son, what say you?"

Kulak stood and without hesitation said, "My scalp trusts our friends and believes they deserve the honor of the Silvesh they rescued. They have earned it."

Sterjall took a deep breath of relief. Some of the Gwur Ali guests were shocked that the son would vote against his mother, but Alúma lifted her scepter and said, "Noss's sacred words are law, and the law we obey. Now we come to the matter of when we should undertake this quest. Do we leave now, or do we allow for time for training and healing?"

After a short discussion, the chiefs decided that they would like to leave in three months' time. They would spend those days strategizing their exit route, preparing supplies, and receiving training from their best warriors.

Alúma held up her scepter for silence once more. "As for the matter of the fate of Agnargsilv and Urnaadisilv after the company returns, we could choose to let our guests remain as Silvfröash, we could ask for them to surrender the Silvesh back to the Miscam, or, as Hed Lettáni suggested, we could vote on this decision after their return."

The vote here did not bode well for Sterjall and Jiara. Three chiefs voted for the masks to be taken from them upon their return, two to reevaluate the situation once the mission was completed, and only one to let the masks remain in their possession.

"This is not fair," Kulak interrupted. "They are Silvfröash, they should have a vote as well. If they are allowed to vote, it will be a tie, and I would break the tie in their favor."

"This is a Laatu council, and only Laatu chiefs get to vote," Alúma said, her neck muscles suddenly taut as a bowstring.

"Does a Laatu council vote on Wutash law?" Kulak countered. "Does a Laatu council vote for the New World?"

"If the fate of the Silvesh was decided by their current wielders, then the Red Stag would get a vote too," Hod Abjus said, facing the prince.

"Abjus!" Alúma cried out.

"Mother, we cannot speak for others," Kulak said, ignoring Abjus.

"We speak for ourselves," she chided. "We are of Mindreldrolom, not of the New World, or of the domes of other tribes. We do what we believe is best for the Laatu, for the Miscam, and for Noss. We heard the honored guests and let them voice their opinions, but they are not Laatu or Miscam, and do not get to vote in our council." She faced Sterjall and Jiara and said, "Upon your return you shall surrender the Silvesh to us, and you will do so with great honor. No matter the outcome, we will forever be thankful for your service, and you will always be welcomed as guests in our six provinces."

Kulak slammed his fist on the table.

"Kulak!" his mother warned.

"Laws are not justice, Mother. Sometimes we must do what we think is right."

"And so we have done. The votes are cast, our voices are heard, and the matter is settled."

She stood, seeming to grow tall and magnificent, like an ancient goddess. She stared defiantly at her son, who flattened his tufted ears and averted his own gaze.

Chapter Twenty-Three

Sunu

"And those are the six levels of pronouns and articles," Fingrenn said.

"That's... much too complicated," Jiara complained. "Why have a whole set of pronouns just for Silvesh, wind, bugs, and all that other stuff? Wind isn't even alive."

"It is not about life as you understand it, Lurr Ascura," Fingrenn said. "It is about the level of animation the being spoken of may possess. If it helps your scalps, you could always use the third level, the most common one, and anyone speaking Miscamish will understand what you are trying to say."

"And how come rocks don't get any articles?" Alaia asked. "That's unfair to *the* rocks."

Sterjall noticed Kulak stepping away from the group, seeming tired and distant. He shuffled closer to the prince and said, "Thank you. For trying to help yesterday, at the council."

"I meant words. True words," Kulak said, keeping his eyes lowered.

"Is there something else bothering you? You seem... *Lul*. Sad."

"Good learning word. But... Nothing, not bothering. Not sad."

Sterjall tried to read his expression, but the prince wouldn't meet his eyes. He focused on the caracal's threads, but even those seemed elusive, ungraspable.

An *eihnk-eihnk!* screech broke his focus, followed by a flutter of blue wings. Perched on the tongue of one of the felid statues was an azure-hooded jay, staring impatiently at the group.

"That is Olo, Sunu's herald," Fingrenn said. "Khuron Kulak, would you take our guests to them? We will continue our lessons tomorrow."

The jay flew to perch on a nearby branch, then waited.

"Come, come," Kulak said to his friends, snapping out of his downcast mood.

"What is happening?" Balstei asked.

"Sunu happening," Kulak said. "Wish meet you."

"Who is Sunu?" Sterjall asked.

"Come," Kulak repeated, and followed the jay to a cliffside where streams cascaded into a series of shallow ponds, to then empty into a massive waterfall that joined the Stiss Regu-Omen.

Balancing masterfully while traversing slippery boulders was a shaman wielding a halberd of bone, battling eight warriors at the same time. The allgender spun like leaves caught in a hot wind, using their weapon only to deflect attacks or as a pole to vault from boulder to boulder, never getting their tailcoat kilt wet in the ponds. They kicked and punched sharply but with care, disabling their attackers without harming them. It took but one sequence of measured spins until all the assailants were knocked into the water.

"What a beast!" Jiara said. "Is that—"

"Sunu!" Kulak called from the terrace.

"Khuron! Come down, Sunu has been waiting," Sunu said, in a clear and flowingly accented Common. "Join Sunu at the cascades, Khuron and wandering guests." Sunu's vocabulary was vast, even if their syntax might've been a bit skewed; their first language was neither Common nor Miscamish, but the old Laatu tongue of Heiaggálvan.

They each sat on a different boulder, with Sunu sitting in front of the group, legs crossed under their kilt. Their azure-hooded jay, Olo, perched on their right shoulder. The gorgeously colored bird was feathered in a vibrant indigo, with a black chest and face and a white-framed azure cap.

"Sunu has been tasked with bestowing training," Sunu began, "for battle, for wisdom, for survival. Today, your training begins." Their dark eyes, though nearing blackness, shimmered suddenly with a violet cast that vanished once they were no longer under direct light.

"Sunu will become your teacher," they continued, "but not just in battle. Sunu has chosen a split path in life, encompassing two opposing disciplines. Sunu is both shaman, who preaches respect for all living creatures, and hunter-warrior, who chooses to take life. Sunu shall teach you how the differences do not make the arts incompatible but allow for suffering to be minimized when killing becomes a necessity."

Sunu's skin was heavily freckled, a rare trait among the Laatu. The right half of their scalp was imprinted with purple patterns of leaf skeletons, while their left was stamped with the undersides of mushrooms, tied together by calligraphic knots. Though they were a shaman, Sunu did not wear the customary long shodog but only a compact, more practical one, with long sleeves full of pockets for their blowgun darts.

"Your muscles need learning," Sunu said. "Your scalps, too. Sunu comes from Gwur Pantuul, where the mangroves teach us the stance of the Thousand Feet, showing us balance and grounding. Where the sea teaches us the Tidal Strike, to imbue relentlessness within our cores. Where the winds whisper the song of the Whirlwind Sidestep, to tell us we never move alone, but in a flow with our enemies and allies. Sunu is not acquainted with the ways of battle of the New World. Sunu must learn from you as well."

Sunu rose to their feet, picking up their skeletal halberd. The weapon's long shaft was crafted from a series of smilodon bones joined at the tips by hexagonal cuts much like the quaar conduits at the temple. The halberd had a blade of marbled steel at the top and a blunt cap of iron at the bottom. "First, Sunu needs to see how you fare in battle." They picked up a wooden sword and tossed it toward Balstei. "You first."

"Wh-what why?" Balstei clucked, thrown off balance from grabbing the sword. "I'm not built for this—"

"You carry a heavier sword."

"I stole that from an admiral!"

"And you have thick warrior arms."

"That's from lifting weights!"

Sunu did not understand the concept, so they simply aimed the point of their halberd threateningly.

"I'm no warrior," the artificer pleaded, "I don't need to—"

"Then there is more need," Sunu said. "Attack, and Sunu will learn with you."

The display that followed was embarrassing. At least Sunu did not strike back, but flowed from boulder to boulder, letting their halberd take the hits in a dance that seemed as if they were barely moving at all.

Balstei retreated to sit in shame. Sunu nodded to Alaia, who stood next.

"Hey Sunu, how come you use jays instead of magpies for heralds?" she asked, while measuring the wooden sword's reach and weight.

"Magpies? Not trustworthy birds. Jays are smart, beautiful, and great listeners." They caressed Olo's feathers, then sent him to perch on a rock as they took a defensive stance. "Strike," they commanded.

Alaia was barely more successful than Balstei, but at least she laughed it off when she fell splashing in the water.

Sterjall was next to take the wooden sword. He had the advantage of Agnargsilv and the disadvantage of his splinted arm; to make it fairer, Sunu kept one arm behind their back and also fought with one leg folded up. Even so, Sterjall only managed to fall face first into the water with his own momentum.

Jiara's turn came next. She had been studying Sunu's techniques and was eager to learn from them. She secured Urnaadisilv on her shoulder brace, then spun the wooden sword.

"You may battle with the aid of your Silv," Sunu said.

"I prefer to measure you up this way first," she said. "Do the Laatu wear no armor?" she asked, scrutinizing the weak points left in the open by Sunu's scant garments.

"Sunu has all the armor they need," Sunu said, pointing to their arm bracers, which were made from snow leopard bones and could take a longsword swing without breaking.

Jiara hopped to another boulder, analyzing Sunu's motions without striking. "Those might be good to protect your arms, but what about the rest of your body?" she asked. "Your chest is your weakest point and always in the open."

"Then Sunu will avoid being struck in the rest of their body," was the shaman's simple reply. "Bare chested is the only way, for otherwise, how would Sunu feel the wind upon their skin? To move like the wind, one must feel the wind." Jiara didn't agree—Sunu's small, freckled breasts might not be a problem for them, but Jiara's voluminous ones would not do well in battle unless properly secured.

Jiara leapt from boulder to boulder, like Sunu had been doing, and circled around in a succession of quick strikes. She was not as good with the sword as she was with the bow, but still quite proficient. Although Sunu dodged or deflected all of her attacks, by the end, the shaman had a sheen of sweat covering their purple-pigmented scalp.

"Your turn, Khuron," Sunu said, speaking in Miscamish now.

"I am only an observer," Kulak replied, shrinking into his shoulders.

"No, Khuron, the time to fight might come to all of us," Sunu said. "You must learn, for the future is uncertain, and the mission you will embark on will be dangerous. Strike." They tossed the wooden sword to the prince.

Kulak grabbed it weakly, his expression turning melancholy once more. With ears flattened, he said, "Mother says I will not leave on the mission. She is asking me to stay, to take care of Mindreldrolom."

Sterjall listened to the Miscamish words and could not pick up on any of their meanings, as if Kulak was preventing him from glimpsing into the threads.

"Train the others," Kulak said to Sunu, tossing the sword back. "And say nothing of this. They will go find Mamóru, and I will stay."

"Do you believe that a wise choice, Khuron Kulak?" Sunu asked.

"It does not matter what I believe. Her ears will not listen. Mother is eldest, she enforces the law."

"That may be true, Khuron," Sunu said, "but you are Mindrelfröa. It is your duty to change the law in times of need. Whatever your choice for the future, you must still learn, for even within Mindreldrolom, a battle might be forthcoming." They tossed the sword again. "Strike."

Kulak loosened his tense shoulders, took a deep breath, and gave it his best. The caracal might have had razor claws, sharp fangs, and piercing eyes, but his body was not a warrior's body. He was a little plump in places and indecisive in his steps, too used to having Blu carry him around. By any measure, his attempts to strike at Sunu were a failure. By any measure but Sunu's, that is—the shaman had learned the prince's weaknesses and now knew exactly how to focus their training.

Chapter Twenty-Four

Strike Harder

Aside from their daily language lessons with Fingrenn and battle training with Sunu, each of the wayfarers found additional ways to spend their time while they waited for the day of departure.

Balstei requested to speak with the priests in charge of the production of soot. He learned that despite soot being common, quaar was exceedingly rare inside the Moordusk Dome—the few samples they kept had been manufactured long ago by the original Miscam tribe, the Acoapóshi. He traveled weekly to Quas Trell, where the Laatu had the mines and purification sanctuaries where they harvested and refined soot. He'd been surprised to learn that it was not from a coal seam that the Laatu mined the soot, but from a graphite seam—that was where the purest samples of aetheric carbon were buried.

The purification sanctuaries were not much different from the laboratories of the Havengall Congregation, but their techniques of distillation, separation, and recombination had been perfected for much longer. Their technology looked archaic to Balstei, yet they concocted a superb product. He found himself a new dealer to replace his old friend Khopto: the historian named Suque, who was glad to trade soot for Balstei's knowledge of engineering, optics, aetheric theory, religion, and cosmology. Balstei briefly attempted to convert Suque to Takheism, but since he had no copy of the Takh Codex at hand, he had to verbally recount the tale of the Twin Gods to the historian, forced to confront the inconsistencies related to all they had recently learned. The artificer found inventive ways to disregard such contradictions.

Jiara spent her time meditating, aiming to find focus while she climbed the complexly intercut cliffsides of Arjum, hoping that the vision of her half-form would come to her that way. She found overhangs she could climb without the aid of ropes, knowing a fall would land her in the waters of the Stiss Regu-Omen. She enjoyed the sharp clarity her mind reached when traversing through narrow cracks on a wall, when finding a place to rest upside down, and even when she dragged herself back ashore to start over.

When she wasn't climbing, Jiara helped Sunu train the Laatu warriors, helping them understand how the Zovarian forces fought, what weapons and armor they carried, and what formations their infantry types used when attacking. She had not been a field marshal like her sister, but her experience as a platoon commander had taught her how to handle combat against small squads in tight spaces.

Alaia found two different passions. The first was learning to use a blowgun, which was the primary weapon the Laatu used for hunting. Kenondok, as their most knowledgeable weaponsmith, taught her how to increase her lung capacity, how to identify the right species of baneblood trees, and from which branches to extract their poisonous sap. He showed her how to notch the tips of her darts so that they would break and release the poison better, and how to safely harvest the poison from colorful frogs without hurting them or being killed by them. Alaia learned of deadly saps that could kill in the time it took for a heart to beat, of sticky oils that would knock even a smilodon unconscious, and of flower nectars that would make the victims run away in fear as they suffered terrifying hallucinations, feeling their bodies burn. Kenondok carved a special quiver box that fit exactly into the front pocket of Alaia's overalls, where she organized her darts inside tubes made from a strong reed.

Alaia's second interest was one she had fallen in love with at first sight: minquoll. Givra liked to play as well, although she wasn't good enough to qualify for the Gwur Ali team. She and her friends would bring Alaia to play friendly games with them at the stadium, or when the stadium was occupied, they'd go down to the pine forest, where the game was more chaotic, as the pines weren't aligned on a grid or properly trimmed.

Givra taught Alaia the rules, strategies, and most important of all, how to work with the cats. The cats responded to three kinds of commands: physical moves, such as leaning weight, tapping on the neck, or pressing heels down; vocal commands, including whistles; and empathic commands, which were aided by soot and by a good connection between rider and mount. Alaia was paired up with Moorca, a black panther who made sure Alaia felt safe on her back while also being self-sufficient enough to lead the plays. Alaia was glad that Moorca liked to run on the lower branches—she was not looking forward to a fall from high up, even over the soft padding of pine needles. She always wore the quaar helm Banook had given her, just in case.

Despite his mother's objections, Aio-Kulak had joined the daily training with Sunu, less from his own desires than due to Sunu's insistence. He learned some basic techniques with his smilodon tooth knife, but mostly focused on improving his use of the blowgun, together with Alaia. Sunu taught them which kinds of poison would neutralize the pain of their targets and encouraged Kulak to focus Mindrelsilv on his victims to take away their pain before they died. All Laatu hunters practiced methods to minimize suffering—they even taught their felids to bite to kill as fast and painlessly as possible.

Aio-Kulak pushed himself to learn Common, studying late into the night. Mindrelsilv allowed him to quickly learn the meaning of words, but it did not help with syntax or odd expressions; he had particular trouble with the order of words and with the way Common used gendered instead of animated pronouns, but that did not stop him from swiftly expanding his vocabulary.

He had told his mother that learning Common would become important soon, for he would need to lead diplomatic missions with other realms if their dome was to open. In time, like it or not, he'd become ieron, and his rule would have to be mindful of more than just Mindreldrolom.

Lago-Sterjall could not perform too many physical activities, so he focused on learning more about the Laatu, about the Nu'irgesh, and the ways of the Silvesh. He became very close to Aio-Kulak, who often escaped his royal duties so he could show Lago-Sterjall around his kingdom. They traveled fast on top of Blu, exploring the six provinces, but Alúma insisted they always return in time for dinner.

The training with Sunu had been invigorating for Lago-Sterjall, but also frustrating. One night after dinner, Sterjall asked Sunu if they could have a private session so that he could feel less self-conscious while training; he felt inadequate with his progress and needed to learn more.

Sunu was waiting for him by the light of green-flamed torches at the training ponds, standing one-legged on a mossy boulder, like a night heron with their neck coiled and ready to strike.

Sunu said not a word, but as Sterjall hopped over the boulders to join them, they took a slow swing at him using the Griffon's Whirl, swiping with the blunt end of their halberd. Sterjall took the hit to his hips, losing his balance and falling into the water.

"Hey, I wasn't ready," he protested as he clambered back to his feet.

"Good," Sunu said. "It is only for those attacks we are not ready for that we train." They attacked again, using the Archerfish Gambit, faking an attack by making their halberd splash water on Sterjall's face, then pushing him down with a simple slap of their hand.

Sterjall had sensed the attack coming with Agnargsilv, but being stuck on the boulder, he found no way to dodge it. He fell, then climbed up again.

"You see too much with your Silv," the shaman said. "When you see too much, you think too much. You must react, even when you see no escape." They swung again, swiping with the Twin Crescents. Sterjall felt the attack coming and simply jumped up to let the halberd swoosh under his footpaws, but Sunu carried their swing and let the halberd drop once more.

Sterjall saw no way out. Sunu had not handed him the wooden sword they used to train with, so he used Leif to block the strike, then recovered his balance and aimed the dagger forward to keep Sunu from stepping closer. Sunu stopped.

"Small dagger cannot block Sunu's heavier halberd. If Sunu's Twin Crescents had been at full strength, your handpaw would have lost dagger's grip. If you cannot dodge, use arm bracer to deflect."

Sterjall was wearing the same kind of bone arm bracer the Laatu warriors wore, but only on his non-splinted arm. He knew these were not normal bones at all, just like the core of Leif's blade was not a normal fang, but his mind still told him bone was brittle.

"I can only use one arm," he complained. "And I'm right-handed. I don't have the proper skills on this side."

"A left or a right fang will equally crush through a skull. Your broken arm is teaching you not to depend on it. Teaching you that the left one is equally good if you give it a chance."

Sunu attacked fast with the Fluttering Owlmoth. Sterjall hopped to a larger boulder where he could roll to recover, careful not to put pressure on his injured shoulder. It was an inefficient attempt. He even dropped Leif while rolling, trying not to stab himself with it. He found Sunu's halberd by his neck before he regained his footing—if it had been a real fight, blocking with the bracer would have saved his life.

"Your scalp needs to learn when to block, when to dodge," Sunu said, handing Leif back to him. "Agnargsilv can read Sunu's intentions. Listen to it, not to your fears."

Sunu performed the Fluttering Owlmoth again, in five slower bursts, making it easy for the wolf. Sterjall parried four of the attacks with his bracer and dodged the last one by vaulting out of reach.

"A good escape," Sunu said. "But the longer you dodge Sunu, the longer the battle draws, and the likelier you are to lose your head. The advantage of your shorter blade is speed, efficiency. Your parry must deflect not to escape, but to close the distance."

Sunu thrust with the Soaring Skylark, leaping in a controlled manner that allowed Sterjall to block and then move closer, but Sterjall failed to find an angle with which to strike—Leif had not been aligned the right way to allow him to swing it. He fell back into the water.

"Your handpaw wished to strike," Sunu said, fully in control, "but the strike was counter to the direction of your movement. You needed to strike while pushing through Sunu."

"But I couldn't," Sterjall complained. "I was spinning in the wrong direction for that."

Sunu nodded. "You could have, if you had held the dagger like a smilodon's fang. Its name is Leif, *fang*, wield it like one."

It was the exact same recommendation Banook had once given Sterjall. He felt stupid for not having followed his lover's teachings.

Sterjall spun the dagger around, holding it with uncertainty, with the senstregalv tip aimed toward his footpaws.

"Good," Sunu said. "Next time Sunu strikes, you deflect or dodge as your left leg steps forward to bridge the gap in the same motion, then strike backward before Sunu recovers."

They practiced the motion multiple times, slowly, carefully, with Sunu focusing on Sterjall's stance more than on his strikes.

"Sterjall's goal is always to get closer," Sunu advised, "to pull Sunu in, even by grabbing their elbow, to strike without hesitation."

Sunu advanced once more, not as slowly as in the demonstrations. Instead of striking above, they slashed below with the Blossom Claw. But Sterjall let himself fall and roll around the strike, swinging Leif backward with his spinning momentum. He felt a moment of utter panic as his blade impacted on the shaman. But Sunu had masterfully blocked the attack with their bracer, letting the wolf topple into the water.

"Good," Sunu said, as the wolf resurfaced. "Next time, strike harder, without fear."

Chapter Twenty-Five

Six Widows

One afternoon after a late lunch, Aio brought Lago to one of his favorite spots in the Gwur Ali province: an overlook of the Isdinnklad named Hum Khaabash. Aio had just had his scalp repainted, as his pigments had been slowly fading. The style of patterns he wore were once again very minimal, consisting of simple lines that reminded Lago of Miscamish runes mixed with the flowing lines of Tsing script.

Lago bumped heads with Aio in greeting, then touched the top of Aio's head and said, "I like the new… what do you call it again? Your head paint?"

"Thank you," Aio said with a smile. "We call *grinesht*."

"Who does it for you? I'm guessing you can't paint it yourself."

"Some paint self scalps, but hard reaching. Mother paints mine scalp, she is good paint."

"How long do they last?"

"Long?"

"How much time?"

"Two months, maybe four," Aio answered while he helped Lago onto Blu's saddle. "Depends of how many sweating and bathing."

They rode north, toward the sea. Blu was like a deep chocolate breeze, flowing silently, attuned to the wind. As they ascended into the highlands, the trees became scarce and the ground became dappled with black mosses and green and red grasses. Upon a distant headland, Lago saw six pointy rocks: they were black, shaped like teardrops, perching right at the edge of the cliff, like six sentinels keeping watch side by side.

Blu stopped between two of the six monoliths.

"This are *Hum Khaabash*," Aio said. "She are Six Widows." He helped Lago down, then removed Blu's saddle. Blu promptly dropped onto the grass and stretched under the warm, even light of the dome.

The prince looked to the horizonless edges of the dome and said, "Story speaks she six stood to bump scalps farewell to husbands, before closing of Mindreldrolom. Husbands sailed to beyond Isdinnklad, wanting return before closing. But husbands are late, Isdinnklad fought ships, and deny husbands return. Drolom closed, and six widows weep their love. She six stood here, from evenfall to brightening, until tears cover their kilts, their shodogs, their scalps. So many tears she six weep, that stone became around them, and she now stand here trapped in stone, still she weep."

"That is a very sad story," Lago said. "Do you believe it to be true?"

"My scalp believes story is, like Alaia says, bull shit."

They laughed.

"But is nice story, and is nice place," Aio added.

Dusk was approaching. The vines at the horizon had not begun to extinguish their lights yet, but they were subtly dimming. During his first weeks in Mindreldrolom, Lago had not noticed the tenuous changes, but by now he had learned to feel the moment before dusk arrived as a nearly imperceptible change in the air.

He crept carefully to the edge of the cliff. The sea was a thousand feet below him, sprinkled with tiny ships that dragged white trails behind their green, leaf-shaped sails. One of the supporting columns was only a few miles north, dipping into its own reflection.

A salty breeze cut straight up from the cliff, sometimes carrying feathers from the scores of guillemots, puffins, and razorbills that nested on the wall.

"It's getting close to sunset," Lago said. "We need to be back before dinner."

"Maybe we become late today. Tell me of Sunnokh, and sun set. My scalp not understands what he is like."

"Sunnokh is..." Lago thought out loud. "He is like a flame, up in the sky, even higher than the dome reaches. He is bright and yellow, and the rest of the sky around him is blue."

Blu raised his head at this.

"Not like you, Blu," Lago said, slapping Blu's rump. "Blue as in *esht*."

"My scalp not understands. If sky dome is esht, why everything not esht?"

"I... It's something to do with how light works. People from before the Downfall knew why the sky is blue and left us their knowledge, but I never quite understood those writings. Anyway, colors are the same as here, even though the sky is blue and Sunnokh more yellow."

"What else is he like?" Aio asked.

Lago stared at his feet, thinking. Under the even light of the dome, he barely had any shadow. "When you carry a torch and you look behind you, you see your shadow, right?"

Aio nodded.

"Sunnokh is like that. When you walk under him, you always have a shadow that follows you."

"He is hot, like flame?" Aio asked.

"He is," Lago said. He recalled the cube of brime Aio had gifted him, and took it out of his pouch. He placed the hot crystal over the newly painted patterns on Aio's scalp. "When Sunnokh is high up, you feel him burning your scalp," he said. Aio grinned.

Lago then traced a path across Aio's scalp with the cube. "And he moves like this. And when he is above you, your shadow is small. And when he is down this way"—the brime was now on Aio's forehead—"your shadow stretches far behind you. And at that time, when the shadows are long, that is sunset, when the sky is no longer blue but teal like your eyes, then yellow like daffodils, and later orange like... like oranges. And sometimes even red, like fire."

"My scalp imagines sky red. Must frighten."

"It's beautiful, actually. It's not the sky that shines the reddest, but the clouds. When they turn a deep red, the entire land turns red with them."

"Clouds is water. How is clouds red?"

"It's just the light of the sun that makes them red."

"But is Sunnokh yellow you said?"

He's so curious, Lago thought, *and perceptive.* He felt it was endearing how Aio wanted to learn such complicated ideas without having much grasp of the language yet.

"The sun turns red after it falls beyond the horizon. It has to do with how light works again."

"My scalp smiles with all his colors," Aio said.

Lago noticed the vines at water level losing their light. Dusk always started at the horizon of the dome, while dawn always began at the trunk.

They rested on a toppled boulder overlooking the sea, watching as the horizon dimmed to a crackled line of hazy green.

"Are those dolphins?" Lago said, pointing at the water.

"What is doll fins?"

Lago mimed his best imitation of the cetaceans, making Aio chuckle.

"Yes, *amá'i*, doll fins," Aio said, then tried not to laugh as he emulated their high-pitched squeals.

Lago reached into his bag and took out his binoculars.

"What is metal cups?" Aio asked, touching the binoculars while Lago was trying to find the dolphins, throwing his aim off.

"Binoculars," he answered. "To see far. Look through them," he said and let Aio try them. Aio had never seen such an instrument; he hadn't even thought such a thing possible. He put them up to his eyes, and down again, and up again, and then tried to look at Lago with them and was confused that he'd turned into a blur.

"Only to look far," Lago said. "When I told you about the telescope in Withervale, a telescope is really big binoculars, but only one cup instead of two." He took the instrument back and peered out using only one side to show Aio what he meant.

Aio tried out one side, then both sides again, and said, "My eyes like binoculars, not like telescope." He then found the dolphins with the binoculars. "The amá'i become close!"

"I will show you the telescope one day, and you will like it much more than the binoculars. The amá'i would be even closer, so close you could see their smiles."

Aio smiled in response.

The call of gulls echoed distantly. Lago then smelled the sea spray, and suddenly his eyes fell into grayness. He unconsciously put a hand over the brooch of Sceres pinned to his cloak. *The vast ocean I am not... Yet ocean and fish are of one mind.*

"Eyes become sad," Aio said, holding a stare that was filled with empathy and inquisitiveness.

"Sorry," Lago said. "Just... Memories, that's all."

"What is metal rune in hand?"

Lago pulled his hand away from the brooch. "It's not a rune, it's a brooch." He rotated the penannular brooch to unlock it, then slid the pin off the fabric. "It represents Sceres," he said, handing it to Aio. "This crescent is her, and the star is the Ilaadrid Shard that shines on her face."

"Sceres holds star?"

"Not a real star. It's a crystal that reflects Sunnokh's light."

"My scalp is confused. But tell me more of Sceres, Lago-Sterjall. She is in stories, wears many dresses. What is Sceres like? Tell me."

Lago brightened a little and said, "Sceres is like Sunnokh, but not as bright. The shard I mentioned is a brilliant dot, like a lantern of white light that shines twice every month."

"What are her colors like?" Aio asked, handing the brooch back and focusing instead on Lago's expressions.

"She has six colors, one for each season. When she changes her dress to green, the night is dark but shimmers like a forest. When she is yellow, the night is brown and comforting. When she is pearlescent, the night feels more like day, but not quite as bright. When she is purple, the night is a deeper blue, like an underwater cave. When she is pink, the night is flushed and warm."

"Flushed?" Aio asked, cocking his head.

Lago put a hand on Aio's cheek, "Like when you are embarrassed and your cheeks turn pink. That is flushed."

Aio's cheeks did turn pink at that moment. The prince looked away, suppressing a laugh.

He almost never looks away, Lago thought, studying Aio's gestures.

Aio composed himself and said, "One more dress? You said six."

"Oh, yes. When Sceres is dressed in black, the night is dark as if there was no moon, but you can still see her, because her atmosphere creates a dim halo around her, somewhere between green and cyan, like she is floating in a ripple of clear mountain waters."

Lago seemed lost in memory then, staring at the darkening dome. "I always loved Sceres in Obsidian, which is our Spring. When she is black, you can sometimes see her thin, ghostly clouds. It's my favorite of her seasons."

"Why eyes become sad again?" Aio asked, forcing him to drop his gaze.

"Sorry. It's just that it's already the ninth day of Dustwind. In six more days, Sceres will be fully changed to Sulphur, her yellow season… She's probably already beginning to change. We will not be leaving the dome until after Spring is over, so I will not get to see her dressed in Obsidian this year."

"Perhaps," Aio said. "Perhaps I take you, before Spring over, and you show me."

"We can't do that, it's forbidden. Your mother would kill you."

"Forbidden, yes, but I walk toward wall many times. Mother not know, no one know."

"But it's far. It would take a whole day to get there, even with Blu's help."

"I say excuse. Say we sleep at Parjuul to return day after. But we do no sleep at Parjuul, we go see Sceres together. We go tomorrow, before Spring dies."

"You are going to get us in trouble."

Aio smiled deviously. "Trouble is fun."

Chapter Twenty-Six

Obsidian Moon

The next morning, Lago excused himself from the daily training while Kulak went to talk to his mother. Kulak told Alúma that they wanted to spend the night in Parjuul, the capital of Gwur Pantuul, which was known for its extensive mangroves. Lago had never seen mangroves before, so Kulak insisted that he needed to show Lago the beauty of them. Alúma agreed, but asked Kulak to first meet with the head shaman of Gwur Aalpe, who had come to Arjum to discuss the recent drought in the rice fields. Parjuul was not too far, after all, and the meeting took precedence.

It was midafternoon by the time Kulak was released from the meeting, much later than he had hoped. He rushed to the atrium and found Blu stretching in front of Lago, who was playing with the smilodon's ears, folding them backward and making Blu shake his enormous head to fix them.

"Blu says he eat fingers if you do it again," Kulak said.

Lago quickly pulled his hand away.

"He jokes. He likes it. What is color in your fingers?" Kulak asked.

"Fingernail lacquer," Lago answered, spreading his fingers over Blu's warm fur again. His blue nails sparkled over the burnt umber fur of the large felid. "Like grinesht, but for fingernails."

"My scalp likes it. Why you not fingernail grinesht before?"

"I paint them less often than I used to, because whenever I shift to Sterjall or back, the lacquer breaks apart. It doesn't work the same as the blue pigments on your scalp—mine don't stay on after I shapeshift."

"Then be Lago, for a time, so your hands can be beautiful."

Lago hid a shy smile. "Then Lago Vaari I shall be," he said melodiously.

"What is Vaari?"

"It's my last name."

Kulak's brow whiskers lowered. "How can name be last?"

"It's my family name, coming from my mother. You don't have another name other than Kulak?"

"Aio."

"I mean, other than that."

"No. Alúma is Mother's name, not mine. I am Aio-Kulak, why have more? But my scalp likes your many names. Come, Vaari, we go, it becomes late."

Kulak helped Lago onto Blu's saddle, then they hurried out of Arjum. Lago held tight to Kulak's shodog, staring at the back of the caracal's head, trying to see the blue markings underneath the fur; they were there, but only visible when the wind parted the fur at just the right angles.

It was forty miles on a raven's wing to the northeast edge of the dome, but much longer on paw, and they had to travel stealthily through untrodden paths. They were quiet, and the darkness kept them company.

They arrived at the wall in the half-light of early dawn. Lago had recommended they exit by the shore since he knew there were no towns in those areas, but he primarily chose the location so that Kulak could see the true vastness of the Isdinnklad Sea.

Kulak loosened the belts on Blu's saddle and walked along the rocky shoreline. Night-blue waters crashed into the vines and jagged rocks. The sand was sparkling black, like the color Lago expected to see on the moon's face once they made their way out.

"So, you have been to the wall before?" Lago asked.

"Yes," Kulak answered. "But never before I leave so far with Mindrelsilv. Mother allowed exception because I am with you, and Mindrelsilv helps us speak." He stopped at the dome's wall and caressed the little bulbs that grew on it. "I come to look at arudinn, look at them become bright, like seeds of Sunnokh."

The arudinn were a deep blue, their brightness only perceptible when they did not look at them directly. Daybreak had already started at the trunk. The light would soon branch into spreading tendrils and reach this very wall, setting each of the arudinn aglow.

"I noticed something strange," Lago commented, staring at the patterns of light and shadow that formed in the now green sky of dawn. "Way out here, at the edges of the dome, dusk and dawn create sharp shadows. But in Arjum, there are never any shadows, the light is always too soft."

"Your eyes see smart," Kulak said. "By wall, in new light, shadow sharpens like claw," he said, extending all ten of his retractable claws. "Dim, dangerous. By trunk, light bright, soft like fur," he added, caressing his creamy chest fur. "My scalp better likes sharp, dangerous light." He tapped on the mask attached to Lago's shoulder, and said, "Teach me, how to open the wall."

Lago nodded. As he shifted into Sterjall, he watched his fingernail lacquer shatter and fall in a glittering blue rain. He approached the wall and said, "Mindrelsilv will show you how. Just ask the vines to part. It must be like how you help the vines grow healthy inside the temple. Try it."

Kulak visualized the threads in the vines, seeing them shimmer, almost pulsing. He willed them to move, and they did so almost instantly, pulling from the ground and wrapping tightly around the larger vines. He was already much better than Sterjall at this, and the aperture he created was broadening, eventually spreading wide enough to house a cathedral. It looked like a cathedral.

"H-how did you make them part so wide?" Sterjall asked.

"Time learns," Kulak said.

Kulak tried to push away one of the medium-sized vines, of about fifty feet in diameter, but it wouldn't budge.

"Only the small ones move," Sterjall said. "But we can walk around the big ones. Watch out for the holes they left. The sand fills them back up, but not always."

They entered the dimly lit tunnel and soon found themselves in the dark.

"Kulak eyes still see dark," Kulak said. "Like cat, like owl."

Sterjall was thrilled to hear that. He had wondered whether other Silvesh provided different abilities, just as his sense of hearing was significantly sharper in his wolf half-form.

"Now Kulak eyes see no more," Kulak said once the opening closed behind them. "But Mindrelsilv eyes see."

Blu grew nervous once they sank into pure darkness, but Kulak mindspoke to calm him, guiding him away from any obstacles.

Their footpaws got wet from time to time, as they were walking alongside what was the shoreline within the wall, a transition of vines, sand, and water that was uneven and often interrupted their path.

"We'll be too late for sunset," Lago noted. "Sunnokh would've set by now, but we'll still get to see the night, the moon, and the stars."

"Are your stars like our stars?" Kulak asked. "Vines stuck in sky, like lightning?"

"You mean the flashing vines you sometimes see at night? You call those stars?"

"Yes, *steresh*, what else can we call? They are our stars."

"The outside stars are very different. But I will not tell you what they look like. We are getting close, so I will let you see for yourself."

Kulak's sensitive eyes perceived a dim, cool lightness ahead.

"Wait," Sterjall said. "I'll make a small opening and go out first. Stay inside until I tell you to come out." This was more theatrics than anything else, as Sterjall wanted to make sure the reveal was set up to have the greatest possible impact.

The last few dozen steps had a slight uphill climb, but nothing like the big drop Lago and his friends had to slide down when they entered the dome through the peat bogs. The wolf poked his head out, then his body, and looked around, seeing no one but his own moon shadow. The Isdinnklad was to his left, the black beach in front of him, and the bogs in the distance to his right. He signaled for Kulak and Blu to follow.

Kulak gasped in awestruck joy as he stepped out, whiskers lifted in a sharp-fanged smile. It was a clear night, and the sky was full of stars—the real stars. The beach, the bogs, and the immensity of the Isdinnklad were lit by a piercing, shadowy brightness. The water shimmered at the crest of each wave, like brime sparks caught on an invisible blanket. Kulak looked at the sand between his footpaws and thought it looked so strange. It was the same black sand as that within the dome, but it looked crisper: one side sparkled, while the other side cast deep shadows into the ground. The rocks on the beach also had one bright side and one dark side, with a sharp shadow demarcating cracks and contours. He was surprised at how small his own shadow was, as he was used to shadows from candles and torches, which spread outward, not like these shadows where beams of light traveled parallel and did not change size as he moved.

"Look up," Sterjall said, keeping his eyes on Kulak's expression.

Kulak had been so fascinated by the light at his feet and the stars on the horizon that he had not yet looked above him. As he did so, he was blinded by the brilliance of the Ilaadrid Shard, which shone like a lighthouse within the first-quarter moon. Sceres's dim, aquamarine atmosphere was barely visible, surrounding the piercing moon in an ethereal ring. While one half of Sceres was in shadow, her lit half was nearly as dark, as she was in the late stage of her Obsidian season, when her lit portion was only distinguishable by the glossy highlights around her textured craters and by her thin, wispy clouds. Yellow tendrils were spreading from the shard, signaling the coming of the Sulphur season, of Summer.

"Come here," Sterjall said, taking Kulak's handpaw to break him out of his trance, leading him to a soft and dry spot on the dark sand. They sat, leaning against a rock that faced north. Blu curled up near them, exhausted from the long run, but also entranced by the beauty.

"These are our stars," Sterjall said. "Each one of those dots is like our sun, but much farther, that is why they seem so small." He turned to look to his left, westward. Grazing the northern edge of the Moordusk Dome, in a warmer gradient of sky where Sunnokh's glow still breathed, was a blazing point of light. He pointed at it. "See the bright one near the horizon that looks blurry, like a streak? That one is a planet, called Khumen, from whom we get the name Khuday."

"A planet?" Kulak asked. "Like Noss?"

"Yes. An entire planet like this one. Or rather, very different from this one, but still, a place as big as this entire world. He looks streaky because he has rings around him, like this." Sterjall placed a rock on the sand and drew concentric circles around it. "So when you see him from the side"—he lowered his head almost to the sand—"the rings look flat. We call Khumen the *Dawn Pilgrim*, because he shines the brightest before sunrise, and then vanishes, though he's also there briefly after sunset. The Stelm Ca'éli, which we call the *Pilgrim Sierras*, were named after him. There's a whole song about him."

"Teach me Khumen song. My tufted ears want to hear."

"I'm not good at singing, I couldn't do it justice," Sterjall replied sheepishly; he actually did want to sing, but was feeling shy about it.

"Teach me," Kulak said, his eyes locked on the distant planet. "Laatu rare to sing. Teach me."

"Let me try to remember... It's been a while since Crysta taught me this one." He cleared his throat, then sang a marching melody:

> By your own you partake in the call of the road,
>
> Through the sierras in darkness you roam.
>
> When the sun shines his face, your progression is slowed
>
> And your bedroll and camp become home.

Tell me Pilgrim, where plod you so late in the night?
What's the purpose of journeying 'fore dawn?
> I know not where I travel to, not in the slight,
> But the road says the walk must go on.

When the blackness returns and your march starts anew,
You sing songs to the stars and the moon.
With your walking stick tapping the rhythms ring true,
To the twilight your soul does attune.

Tell me Khumen, why voyage with nowhere in mind?
Will you all destinations decry?
> I prefer to experience the world unconfined,
> That's the end to which I set my eye.

With exhaustion you shamble through lands far and wide
Dragging feet till your muscles burn sore.
With no purpose you slog, with no friends by your side,
All you carry is senseless resolve.

Tell me migrant who wanders and trudges alone,
Why must loneliness walk by your side?
> I'm not lonely, not even when I'm on my own,
> For the stars always travel with I.

> You know nothing, old Khumen, you mustn't go on
> With pretenses that home can't be found.
> Fantasizing of starlight, your dreams all forgone,
> Would you find no relief if homebound?
>
> All I know's that no verses can force me to shame
> When the day to go home comes along,
> For the person returning would not be the same
> As the Pilgrim who's singing this song.

Kulak beamed as brightly as the shard. The song had been a jumble of too many words he had not yet learned but which somehow, when sang, shared their compounded meaning more directly, as if the tune itself drove the emotions into his heart.

"He sings lonely, but sings happy," Kulak said. "My scalp does not understand all words, but I like Khumen. Are there more planets like him?"

"I don't think they are visible right now, but there's also the Enchantress, Iskimesh, who is green and blue. And Ongumar, who we call *Amberlight*, and he's fiery orange. And Senstrell too. She's a small, dark planet who can only be seen with telescopes. And that's only the planets we know of, there might be many more. Each of those stars might have planets of their own, but we can't see them, because they are so far."

"My scalp not understands how planet so big can look so small."

Sterjall dug into his bag and took out the binoculars. "Look at Sceres," he said.

Kulak did so. "Like beacon diamond she shines! Her face becomes ridges, valleys, like Gwur Úrëath looks from eyes on top of Stelm Humenath."

"They *are* mountains and valleys, as big as any in this world. The shard grows from the Segnar Crater, where the yellow tendrils are growing from."

"Crater?"

"A huge hole, much larger than Mindreldrolom. That yellow will spread from there until she changes her entire dress to Sulphur, and no more black remains."

Kulak put the binoculars down and rubbed his eyes. Sterjall saw then that he was crying.

"Thank you, Sterjall," he said, pointing at Sterjall's heart, then at the skies. "My eyes never see such beauty, not know Noss was so vast, sky so tall, Sceres so bright."

He wrapped an arm around Sterjall and leaned his head over the wolf's shoulder, watching the sparkles of darkness, listening to the cycle of the waves lapping on the shore, and inhaling the scents of a foreign world that had always been just beyond his reach.

"We should lean back," Sterjall said, "so we can see the sky better. Would Blu mind?"

Blu did not mind. Kulak and Sterjall walked over to him and leaned on the smilodon's pillow-like belly. Blu stirred, exhaled a mixture of a purr and a sigh, and dozed off again.

"Blu says he is much tired," Kulak said. "But he also gives thank you. He likes stars, he likes smell of new air."

"He's a lovely cat," Sterjall said. "But keep your eyes on the sky, I want to show you something."

"More planets?"

"Not planets, but something that—there! There's one!" Sterjall said. "Did you see the meteor?"

"Yes! Star that became line bright?"

"That one. They go by really fast."

"We have meteors, but slow meteors. Named *abaawe*. Meteors hang from sky for many heartbeats, much brighter, and if night is haze they caress the ground."

"I've seen one of those before! During our first night in Mindreldrolom, I couldn't sleep and was staring at the dome, and I saw a long streak of light. We call those *wisps* here on the outside, though out here they are not as bright and last much longer."

"You also see them in your sky?" Kulak asked, squinting at the starry dome.

"No, sorry, what I said must be confusing. We see them on the dome." He pointed toward the Moordusk Dome. "We see the light from your daytime while it's nighttime out here. They aren't meteors, but holes between vines. When you see them from the inside, it's because the light of the sun shines through those holes."

"Our eyes see Sunnokh inside Mindreldrolom?"

"Just a tiny streak of light from him. You will see him fully sometime soon, I promise."

"Now my scalp understands. You said sunset is orange and red. Sometimes meteors, wisps, also orange, also red, when soon after evenfall or soon before brightening. Red meteors are, how you say? Bad things come."

"Bad omens?"

"Bad omens, remnants of Downfall fire, it is what priests say. But if meteors are Sunnokh, I think priests say bull shit." Kulak chuckled, his eyes still glued to the sky. "Where come your meteors?"

"Ours are falling stars. Well, that's what people call them, but they are actually small rocks that fall from the sky, which burn in the air before they touch the ground."

"Falling star?" Kulak repeated. With a tinge of concern on his face, he asked, "Was it falling star that became Downfall?"

"Something similar to a falling star, but much, much bigger. I'm quite sure it was a comet, because Suque said it was a star with a veil, and a comet looks like one of the bright stars, but with a long tail behind it."

"Not short like caracal tail. Long tail like wolf?" he said, pulling at Sterjall's bushy tail.

Sterjall laughed. "Something like my tail, but white instead of black."

"My scalp now understands your name, *Ster-jall*. It sees why your heart loves stars. Banook chose good name. He knows your heart."

"He does," Sterjall said with a quiet sigh, and could not hide the melancholy in his voice.

"Do you love him?" Kulak asked, quite unashamedly, turning his head to scrutinize Sterjall.

Sterjall swallowed and felt suddenly afraid.

"Why your eyes become fear?" Kulak inquired.

Sterjall took a long while to reply. "Sometimes you understand too much. It's like I can't hide anything from you."

Kulak sat up, shifted into Aio, and placed Mindrelsilv over the dark sand, where the colors blended together and it seemed as if the mask had emerged from the very substance beneath it.

"No Silvesh, better for talk. Fair."

Lago did the same. As they sat side by side under the sharp radiance of the Ilaadrid Shard, Lago for the first time noticed why Aio's skin seemed so uncannily smooth: it was as if the prince had no follicles at all, not even the peach fuzz that grew on Lago's beardless face. The curves of his chin made it even more obvious as they softly transitioned down his sinuous neck, to his pillowy chest, and his tender belly.

Lago stopped staring and leaned back into Blu's belly again. Aio followed.

"Do you love him?" Aio asked once more.

"Yes, I love him. And I'm afraid because... I don't know what others will think, how they will react."

"My scalp knows your fear. Understands."

"What would the other Laatu Miscam think?"

"They would throw you down cliff, feed you to belly of Isdinnklad for your soul to drown, and no Six Widows would cry for you. But they would take Agnargsilv first."

Lago wasn't sure whether Aio was trying to be funny or not, his unease etched on his face.

"No joking," Aio clarified, turning to face him. "Bad thing, to Laatu. Two men, two women, no good together. Man and Nu'irg together, much worse. And man with man Nu'irg? May Noss forgive."

Lago's pulse quickened. *I shouldn't have said a thing,* he thought. *This could only get me in trouble. But why is he so curious? Why do I feel the need to be so open about it?*

"You fear me, I need no Silv to see," Aio said, his eyes locked on Lago's. "I keep your secrets, I have secrets too. But never secret so big like loving Nu'irg!" He guffawed while slapping his thighs, not helping Lago relax at all. Aio took a few breaths to compose himself, noticing he had been insensitive. "You love Banook. Why leave him?"

"It's part of the story I did not fully tell during the council. I would still like to be with him, but I had to leave to save my friends, to find a way to stop the Red Stag. I could not forgive myself if I hadn't done that. And bears only live in the northern mountains, so Banook could not leave with us. So I had to say goodbye. At least for now."

They stared as a thin cirrostratus cloud passed between them and Sceres, birthing a temporary halo of oily colors around the shard's beam. Aio wanted to ask about the glowing halo but did not wish to interrupt Lago's thoughts. The halo vanished as quickly as it had appeared.

"I wish I didn't have to hide it," Lago continued. "Banook told me the Wutash Miscam would not be okay with a man and a Nu'irg being together, but at the same time, they had no problems with lerrkins of any kind."

"Lerrkins?"

"Men who love other men, or women who love other women, or… there are many variations, but it's just the way some people are. Why can't the Laatu be accepting like the Wutash?"

"Tradition," Aio said simply. "Each tribe, different tradition. Many Laatu laws, all bull shit. What we do now, walk outside, all happiness you gifted me, tradition thinks wrong."

"I can see why that rule existed. It's to prevent anyone from leaving the dome until the time is right."

"Many laws. Some good, some bad. Some much more bad. What you call, bad things you not talk about, to do never?"

"We call things that are forbidden like that *taboos*."

"Taboos, many Laatu have. Many about Silvesh, many about things that should not concern, like rituals, and learning, and loving, and food. We do no growing, remain same for fifty-six generations. We become stuck."

"It is not very different out here. We have similar taboos in the Union, and much worse ones in the Negian Empire."

"But your scalps believe in learning, growing. You do artificers, make binoculars, learn stars."

"And we have wars, kill each other, make slaves out of other tribes, and destroy beautiful places like these bogs. Not everything that comes from our knowledge is good. A lot of it is as bad or worse than the rules you live by."

"I never live by rules. I live outside them," Aio said, putting a soft hand on Lago's cheek to make him turn his head. He planted a solid kiss on his lips, then pulled back and looked up at the stars once more, as if the kiss had been merely a gesture of defiance and not one of love, not even desire.

Aio continued talking as if nothing of significance had occurred. "My eyes wish seeing more New World. Laatu can learn from seeing."

Lago was still stunned. Did a kiss on the lips hold a different meaning in Aio's culture? His heart stumbled. He did not know what to think, yet he tried to carry on with the conversation. "Wuh-what will happen once... I m-mean, once Mindreldrolom opens? What happens to all the animals and people?"

"People stay, or go, they choose. Companion species help others spread, make new homes. I think I choose to go."

"But you have the Silv. Wouldn't they need you in Arjum?"

"Unknown. Laws become confusing after drolom is open. Khuren or ieren or hed make laws no more. For long years, we only follow laws made in time before. New laws need decided. World is changing, old and new is one."

Blu stretched and shook his thick limbs, spreading his paws and claws in the air. He plopped back down with a deeply satisfied grunt.

"Poor Blu becomes tired," Aio said. "Road is long like river. My scalp wants here with you, but we have to begin road."

Lago agreed. They lifted their masks from the dark sand and returned to their wolf and caracal selves. Kulak helped Sterjall up, then hurled himself on top of Blu's chest and pulled at his ears, trying to shake the smilodon awake. The big cat growled a complaint and rolled around, burying Kulak between his heavy torso and the sand.

"Lazy mindrégo, we need go!" Kulak said, squeezing out from underneath the trap, then shaking the sand from his fur. Blu dragged himself to his feet and yawned; his huge fangs and deep maw looked terrifying in the sharp light of the moon, but soon the jaws were closed again and all that remained was a sleepy cat's face.

Sterjall took care of opening the vines this time, letting Kulak savor the final moments as he walked backward into the portal and received one last caress of moonlight upon his whiskers.

Chapter Twenty-Seven

Summer Solstice

"Going to bed so early?" Alaia asked.

"Sorry, really tired," Sterjall answered, tucking himself under his blankets. He had just returned from his long trip with Aio-Kulak, having gotten no sleep at all the previous night. He had barely been able to hold on to the prince's shodog to keep himself from falling off Blu's saddle.

"How were the mangroves?"

"Very… wet. Beautiful, but scary, full of alligators. Lots of frogs too, they wouldn't let me sleep. I just need to catch up and get some rest."

"Sounds dangerous. You've never been a light sleeper, those must've been really loud frogs. Oh, I scored two goals against Gao's team today. One on the lower hoop, one on the middle one. Six points total! One of these days I'll score on the high hoop, by Pliwe's horns I will. I tried three times, but that sneaky ocelot—her name is Hobáshi—blocked me. Every. Single. Time. Did you know ocelots don't meow or growl? They make the cutest sound, a bit like…" She mimicked the sounds ocelots make, almost like a chuckle mixed with a purr, and was quite good at it. "They are so cute!" she continued. "And they let me pet them this time! Did you—hey. Sterjall. Are you even listening?"

But the wolf was fast asleep.

Lago-Sterjall noticed that the days were growing longer while the nights became shorter, just like they did outside the dome. Fingrenn explained they were nearing the Summer Solstice, the longest day of the year.

"On the outside, it's Sunnokh's angle that determines how long the days are," Sterjall said to Fingrenn. "How are the days made longer here? Who controls for how long the dome is alight?"

"And how would my scalp know such a thing?" Fingrenn answered. "The dome is mysterious enough as it is."

Balstei overheard them and pondered the mystery. "I think the domes simply do the best they can," he theorized. "They have to gather energy like any other plant, and since they get more sunlight in Summer, their arudinn can shine for longer."

"I bet Crysta would agree with that," Sterjall said. "How long until the Summer Solstice? What day is it today, anyway?"

"Today is *Schereur, ferrcháilio Baurámbra*, or Moonday, on the thirteenth day of Dustwind, fourteen hundred and fifty-five years after the Downfall, or the year fourteen hundred and fifty-six for the Laatu, since we began counting on the day Mindreldrolom closed. In two days, the Solstice will herald the arrival of Summer. And that will be a day for celebration."

When the day of the Solstice came, the denizens of the city dressed in vibrant yellow, green, and orange, and placed unlit lanterns in every crevice of every public space. The lanterns were woven from thin, knotted banyan roots, reminding Lago and Alaia of the woven masks Zovarians wore for the Feast of Plenitude. Drinking parties sprouted up around Arjum; the braaw flowed freely, and the shouting did as well.

"Looks better on that side," Alaia said, watching Lago get ready for the festival.

Fully healed, Lago had shifted his shoulder brace to his right side, attaching Agnargsilv over it. He used his Sceres brooch to pin his cloak around his neck and let it cover only his left shoulder, leaving the right one just for his mask.

"I'm ready," he said, content with his asymmetrical look. "Let's go find the others."

Lago and Alaia found Jiara and Balstei at the marketplace just past the bridge that crossed the Stiss Regu-Omen; they'd been waiting with Givra, Kenondok, Sunu, and Aio.

"No more broken!" Aio said, noticing Lago's new look.

"Good place to watch," Givra said, making room for Lago and Alaia at their viewpoint. "Best place for Solstice."

From this overlook, they could see the very top of the trunk, the cliff that plunged into the river, and a great portion of the levels of the city. The dome was already dimming at the horizon, and people were hurrying to their positions, waiting by their unlit lanterns with brime cubes at the ready.

It was loud, and getting louder. People cheered as each of the vines of the dome darkened; the larger the vine, the more vociferous the cheers it received. The receding umbellate shape of light looked like a titanic barnacle with feathered cirri crawling inward to feed its calcareous plates.

They waited in suspense among the cacophony. The last branch dimmed, leaving only the mile-wide cylinder of the trunk alight. They readied themselves to hear an explosion of screams at the moment its light extinguished, but it was the opposite: as the trunk went dark, everyone went completely quiet. Not even a whisper dared break the silence. Every citizen then struck their brime cubes to light their lanterns, one by one, until thousands of fires of red, green, and yellow sprouted like fireflies upon the trees, along thoroughfares, behind waterfalls, and far away in the cities of distant provinces.

It was a moment of contemplation, when everyone silently thanked the dome for bringing warmth and light each year, when they implored it to provide them with one more cycle of renewal and hope. People began to walk in silence, in an aimless procession to nowhere, admiring the points of colorful light from different perspectives. After all prayers had been silently voiced, whispers could be heard once more.

Lago and his friends leaned over a woven root railing to look toward the province of Gwur Úrëath and the peak of Stelm Humenath, where a green beacon had been lit at the snowy summit, visible from any of the six provinces. The city of Humenath at the base of the mountain glowed too, in much smaller points of light.

"Fires look like stars outside Mindreldrolom," Aio whispered to Lago. "And big fire on Stelm Humenath like light on face of Sceres."

"How can Khuron Aio know?" Kenondok asked, easily overhearing the conversation in the quiet that enveloped them.

"Lago told me," Aio said. "Said stars are points, not branches. Tiny points, very far. Sometimes stars fall to cut lines in black dome, but they are rocks, named meteors."

"Lago took me on a date once, to see a meteor shower," Alaia said. "It's still one of the best nights I ever had."

"Meteor shower?" Aio asked. "Like bathing in waterfall, but burning rocks?"

"It's just the name we give them," Lago explained. "Most nights you can see only a few meteors, but on some special nights, there can be thousands, and bright ones, too, of different colors. We call those meteor showers. It's like standing in the rain, but instead of drops of water, you see bright lights falling."

"Falling rocks do not hurt?" Kenondok asked.

"No, no," Lago said. "They are way up in the sky. They burn before they can touch the ground. It's totally safe."

"New World rocks are weak," Kenondok said. "Mindreldrolom rocks do not burn in the air."

"What is date?" Aio asked Alaia.

"It's when two doves go frolicking alone, to get romantic," she said, leaning uncomfortably close to Lago and pursing her lips.

Lago contorted away from her. "We all make mistakes," he replied with a mocking cringe.

"You must take me to where the shower is," Aio said to Lago. "You must promise to show me."

"I will try to show you, but it's not a place. It's something that happens everywhere around the New World at once, no matter where you are. Some small showers happen once a year, and though they are not so full of meteors, they are still beautiful. The one I showed Alaia was the Quindecims, which happens every fifteen years. We saw it only last year, so you will have to wait a long time before it happens again."

"Then I begin to wait fourteen years," Aio said, staring at the distant lights.

Chapter Twenty-Eight

Golden Rack

"A raccoon?" Shea asked. "You jesting with me?"

Fjorna shrugged. "That's what Urcai wrote. We'll see for ourselves soon enough."

"Suits him right," Osef scowled. "Just the type of sneaky critter he is."

"I thought you said he would be a weasel, not a raccoon," Shea retorted.

"Well. Yes. I mean, any of those mustelids are the same, really."

"Musteloids," Aurélien corrected.

"That's what I said," Osef said.

"Nuh-uh," Aurélien said, shaking her head. "Raccoons are procyonids, weasels are mustelids. But both of them are muste*loids*."

"They all stink the same to me," Osef snorted, not giving a damn.

The arbalisters, minus Crescu Valaran, were riding back north toward Hestfell. They had spent the last few months in the city of Terne, training recruits and strategizing with the new officers who had joined them. It was there that the Arbalisters' Commons were located, the training grounds where Fjorna and her squad had perfected their skills.

They rode under Halarvelm—the first of three great gates—while continuing their conversation.

"And he really went for Ulle dus Grei, huh?" Aurélien asked, red hair glistening with streaks of sweat—it was hot outside, being the longest day of the year.

"It's a bit cruel, but yes," Fjorna answered. "He is marrying the sister of the emperor he killed. It's a good way to assure the head ministers don't contest his right to the throne."

"I'm sure Ulle will look delighted at the wedding," Trevin said, scratching his long nose.

They rode through the farmlands of the Low Mesa and over the ramp that crossed beneath Halartarv—the second gate—into Mid Mesa, where the Old City was located. It was a sprawling and lively community, second in size on the Loorian Continent only to Zovaria. It lacked the particularities of the rose quartz of the competing capital, but made up for it with a quaint and rustic charm that gave the city an air of sophisticated, historical grandeur.

The deceased Emperor Uvon dus Grei had not done a great job at managing his empire, except for when it came to Hestfell. The Negian capital was their symbol of pride, a city of richness, of power. Viceroy Urcai hoped to do a better job for the entirety of the citizenry, but the oncoming war meant that a great portion of the state taxes would end up allocated to the army, and it would take a long time to recover from the expenses. At least the domes they had pillaged were providing invaluable goods and slaves. With more domes cracked open, the war would pay for itself, all the while expanding Negian territory.

The arbalisters rode under the heavily guarded gate of Halarchail, into the Top Mesa, where the fortress of Hestfell resided. They left their horses with a hostler and headed toward the Laurus Palace. They saw a strange figure coming to meet them as they crossed the bridge.

"You are late!" General Crescu Valaran said. But it was not just the old Crescu; he was in his new half-form of a raccoon. Wide-faced and long-whiskered, he lifted his bright-white eyebrows over his deeply shadowed fur mask.

"So you finally came to accept the vermin you truly are?" Fjorna said as she went in for a strong Iesmari arm shake, grasping Crescu at the elbows. "Look at you, you finally did it. Took you a fucking while."

"It's not as easy as Hallow made it seem," the raccoon muttered as he went around shaking arms with the other arbalisters. "I used to have a pet raccoon as a kid. I guess she left an impression on me."

"Did you get a fancy name as well?" Fjorna asked. "Like the Masked Marauder?"

"Or the Rabid Rat!" Shea offered.

"Raccoons aren't rodents," Aurélien pointed out pointlessly.

"Funny. But no. Sort of," he said. "I think this was Urcai's idea—it's always Urcai—but while in my half-form, I'm to be referred to as Silv-Thaar Valaran, or just Valaran. Family name for the half-form, given name otherwise. Monarch Hallow likes this better than the old Miscam traditions."

"But didn't he come up with a name for General Remon, before he got mauled?" Fjorna questioned snidely. "What was it, Captain Dexterity?"

"Warmaster Dextral would've been it," Silv-Thaar Valaran replied. "I guess him and Jaxon had a more personal relationship. But I like this system. He's thinking of keeping it consistent for his army, already planning on getting more masks, more Silv-Thaars under his command."

"Silv-Thaar Valaran," Aurélien said. "It means *Mask Vanguard*. I like it too. Silv-Thaars…" She savored the words and smiled, making the scarified patterns on her face stretch in odd shapes. "But shouldn't it be *Silv-Thaaresh* if the roots are in Miscamish?"

"Do you think he gives a shit about the Miscam?" Valaran countered.

"But what is going on with your armor?" Muriel asked. "That mail is noisy as the bells of Umaagi."

Valaran's armor had been refashioned for his new form, and it was no longer the light, tactical leather the arbalisters normally wore. He was now clad in a lightly plated chainmail over a colorful green tunic, outfitted with expensive-looking arm, shin, and shoulder guards of lacquered silver.

"By Khest, I hate it," he said, "but it's what the generals wear. It's all about portraying a powerful presence. And it will be useful for hand-to-hand combat, I hope, or I'll die of boredom in this job. The damn metal links snag on my fur whenever the sleeves pull up, it's maddening! But enough about me, the ceremony is about to start."

"Are you going to go like that?" Shea asked. "As the Rabid Rat, I mean?"

"Watch it, Shea—if it sticks, I'll tear your tongue out with my very claws. And yes, Hallow asked me to attend in my half-form. Gets the crowds used to our presence. Let's hurry now."

They followed Valaran's striped, swishing tail and entered the long hall of the throne room. Valaran sat at the front with the other generals, while the arbalisters were asked to seat themselves several rows behind.

The marble and rhodonite throne was empty, but around it were offerings from the head ministers of the nine Negian states, who had brought fist-sized gemstones, art from masters old and new, legendary weapons, rare spices, and rugs of the finest silks. The giant statues of Takhísh and Takhamún stood naked and black as quaar on either side of the throne, eyes empty and condemnatory.

"Why did they have to hurry us so much?" Muriel asked, keeping her voice down. "They should've had the ceremony on a Sunnday, like everyone does."

"They wanted the consecration of the Summer Solstice," Aurélien answered. "But it seems the decision was made in haste. It's odd."

Trumpets blared a regal tune, and soon Monarch Hallow emerged wearing a meticulously crafted imperial mantle of yellow and black. His muzzle was not painted red in the way he normally presented himself, but gilded with a delicate filigree, and the tips of his sixteen-pointed rack had been dipped in gold. Thin gold chains hung and tangled from his rack, like gossamer backlit by scraping daybreak light. He was flanked by Ulle dus Grei, who looked as miserable as she looked beautiful in her gold-and-white dress, and Viceroy Urcai, who was wearing a purple cloak over a yellow doublet.

Long speeches were given, and affirmations of allegiance were solidified for both the groom and bride by the head ministers. A Takheist high priest sanctified the union by looping a golden rope through six rings, and under the ever-witnessing stone eyes of Takhísh and Takhamún, the treaties were signed. The ceremony was over, but the gold-crowned monarch asked everyone to sit down again.

Monarch Hallow waited until the room quieted, then said, "Before we move on to the banquet, we have a wonderful announcement to make." He put an arm around Ulle, who smiled more at the crowd than at him, even if awkwardly. "My dear bride, Ulle, my wife, is pregnant. We will soon have an heir to the throne!"

The spectators cheered and clapped. Ulle stood to the side and blushed, forcing out a wretched smile. She was torn, earnestly wanting the best for her child, but trying to forget the memory of having conceived it with a monster.

Monarch Hallow continued his rehearsed speech. "The Twin Brothers will grant us a new prince in the coming year. Lands to the east and south will have been conquered by my army by then, to stretch my heir's empire over the Jerjan Continent, to bring prosperity and riches to our nine states such as we have not seen since the late Reconstitution Epoch." He clenched a hoofed fist in front of his muzzle. "The sixteen emanations of Takhamún will be gathered by my army, bringing the Twin Brothers together, so that they may grant divinity to our races and good fortune to our lands."

Two crimson guardians approached from behind the twin statues. The first held Ockam's quaar shield. The second held a black spear, arresting and grandiose, crafted from a quaar shaft and a magsteel tip that was equally dark. The spear had been commissioned by Urcai, referencing the ancient illuminations of the Codex from the Lost Scribes. It would be instantly recognizable by the faithful and instantly commanding of their reverence.

Monarch Hallow picked up the shield with his left hand, the spear with his right, and stood in front of the throne while flanked by the Twin Gods themselves. "Soon I will command my armies to cross the Ophidian, and I will ride to war with them, aided by the Spear of Undoing and the Shield of Creation. The Shade of Yza will guide us, and the Red Hand of Yaumenn will tighten over the corrupt tribes to bring them retribution for their cowardly actions. I promise you greatness. With Gaönir-Bijeor and Tor-Reveo in my hands, I promise you a rebirth not just for our empire, but for humankind. To glory, and divinity!"

Two weeks later, the legions were marching east from Terne, taking the wide Via Lamanni toward the extensive port of Khoomalith.

The army was a most peculiar sight. Most of it was not human, but composed of platoons of deer, elk, and caribou, each following a cervalces—the stag moose officers leading the units—who were splattered with bright-red paint so as to be easily spotted by those who followed them, and to be more easily seen by the Red Stag so he could issue them commands.

In front of the cervid platoons marched the megaloceroses, who trampled ahead on their own like a wall of sharp antlers. As the army marched on, the Red Stag was always at the head, so that if any wild cervids showed themselves, he could recruit them into his army. The cervids served as convenient mounts for the human troops, but only while traveling; they were unsuitable mounts for battle, as they responded not to human commands—they merely trampled and died for Urgsilv.

Just like the cervalces, the Red Stag's antlers and part of his muzzle were glossy with a fresh coat of red paint. His shield, too, had been embellished with his sigil in shining vermillion paints. His new spear, Tor-Reveo, was tied to the front of the shield as a symbol of the unifying power of the Twin Gods. He thought the weapon looked majestic but would prove useless in battle.

The Red Stag rode on Tremor, a Jartadi horse with thick hooves and a velvet-black coat. Plodding behind him for further protection was Sovath, the cervid Nu'irg, always following in her largest form of an antlerless megaloceros. Next to him rode his private guard of arbalisters and Silv-Thaar Valaran. The raccoon general was supposed to be miles away at the front of his own legion, but the Red Stag had called for him so they could speak while they traveled.

"Say, Monarch Hallow, wouldn't you be better off riding one of your elk?" Silv-Thaar Valaran asked, furrowing his masked brow. "Maybe even a megaloceros? Why a horse? It's so... commonplace."

"It's about projecting an image," the Red Stag answered. "One set of antlers is enough. And a horse portrays a different sort of nobility and strength. And what you call *commonplace*, I see as *commonality*, a way for my subjects to find something to identify with. Besides, the cervids follow my every whim, making it so easy that it becomes boring. I like to crack the whip, pull on the reins, kick my heels into this Jartadi beast until his ribs are sore. It is a more satisfying form of control."

Valaran had a tiny yellow-throated marten slinking over his shoulders. It wasn't a pet, but a tool for him to practice his skills at handling musteloids. A cage was filled with other species—a wolverine, pine marten, polecat, badger, and a sea otter—that were available for him to train with as well. All the animals respected Valaran and became tame next to him, yet he still could not issue orders in the same way the Red Stag could.

The tiny marten dug her way under Valaran's chainmail, making him flinch and spasm. She stuck her head out by Valaran's neck.

"It's too bad you haven't gotten a hold of that yet," the Red Stag said, eyeing the flexible creature, then recoiling at the unpleasant odor his sensitive muzzle detected.

Valaran had become used to the musk of the marten by now, which was particularly easy to tolerate while in his raccoon half-form, but he pulled his horse a few feet away after noticing the revulsion on the stag's face. "Every time I try to control them," he said, "there's this connection I feel toward the stupid creatures. It keeps distracting me. But either way, I don't think a few dozen ferrets would wreak havoc like your megaloceroses could."

"True, though it'd be an amusing skirmish to watch. Yet those giant otters from the Lequa Dome, by Yza they were vicious, agile, and sharp toothed. They would have been a beauty to behold at your side."

"That would've been quite a sight. But a mountain path is not the best place for a giant otter. It's too bad those wolverines ran away after Jaxon died."

The Red Stag smiled, having manipulated the conversation just to reach this point. "Well, I may have good news for you, my Masked Vanguard," he said. "I asked Behler to capture more jarv wolverines before leaving the Lequa Dome, if he can find them. His scouts say they've spotted some tracks. I'm sure he hates me for it, and I hope he won't lose too many soldiers to them. If he catches some, they will come in handy for you."

"Oh, I bet Behler was pissed!" Valaran said, cackling earnestly. "But those are glad tidings indeed. What of the Nu'irg? Was he found at last?"

"No, the musteloid spirit is still on the loose. Perhaps he escaped the dome in a smaller form, we do not know."

"A shame, that is. But no matter, I'll be glad to have those giants on my side. And now I better figure out a way to control them."

"And you will. And there's more you will need to do, Silv-Thaar—once you learn to master your skill, you will need to set up a chain of command, like I do with the cervalces who lead my units."

"I know, Urcai has taught me all there is to it."

"And you must never take your human form again, lest you lose the mind-lock on all your creatures. So, get used to the fur, and be glad you don't have an inconvenient rack over your head the entire time."

"Well, perhaps there is a way to still—"

"No. Your assets are not yours to waste. If you are committed to this path, if you wish to command the title and honors that come with the mask, commit fully." He stared at Valaran with black eyes, reading a flicker of doubt. "Valaran…"

"I will, Monarch Hallow. I will do as you order." He straightened his back and nodded with a bit more conviction, then asked, "Have you truly been only the Red Stag for all these months? Never once back to plain-old Alvis?"

The Red Stag glanced back at the empty-eyed megaloceros who followed him. "I have. Ever since I took control of Sovath. She is too dangerous. I cannot risk her or the other giants turning against me. And you will do the same. Your jarv wolverines will be your most powerful weapon. The creatures follow commands eagerly, but once they've done so, they simply stand there and wait for further instructions, so it's easy to forget about them and leave them behind. I almost lost a pack of tufted deer that way, back near Lamanni. They were drinking by a stream, and I had not told them we needed to continue on. They simply lingered there and did not follow our troops. A soldier found them and warned me to pick them up before we traveled too far."

"I'll be careful," Valaran said. "And I better keep the wolverines in Behler's cages until I have it truly figured out. I promise it won't be long."

The Red Stag smiled, pleased yet also eager, an expression that looked particularly conniving upon his long, dark lips. "And I have some *other* good news," he said with a hushed tone, "of something I found out only hours before we departed."

"What news is that?" Valaran asked, riding closer to him now.

"It's a boy," the Red Stag whispered. "I will be having a son."

"Really? But how? How can you tell it's a boy?"

"The same way I could tell Ulle was pregnant. I saw him through Urgsilv, deep in her belly. For the first few months I could only see an indistinct fetus, but now he has finally changed, and he is definitely a boy."

"Well, congratulations, Monarch Hallow! And I'm curious, but will he be like you? Like you as the Red Stag, I mean."

"That I cannot yet tell. Perhaps in a few months I would have been able to see, but we'll be far away by then. If not, there's always Odalys and Anja, who are both pregnant as well. They will hold substitutes, though no one is to know about them. It's not something I like to think about, but there's a chance Ulle's pregnancy won't come to term. Who knows how any of this works? But I hope that out of three, at least one makes it out safely."

"Are the other two boys as well?"

"Too early to tell with them. But either way, I'll have to think of a good name for a boy, for a prince, for a ruler of the empire I will be building. That I'll be building for him."

Chapter Twenty-Nine

Sea Wing

"There she waits," Kulak said to Sterjall, Jiara, Balstei, and Alaia, leading them down a stone-carved pier where opulent ships were docked.

Hud Ilsed, the chief of Gwur Gomosh, waited at the end of the pier, wearing a red shodog embroidered in pink as well as a new kilt mosaicked with opalescent shells.

"Thank you for joining me in Oälpaskist, the great port capital of my province," Hud Ilsed told them in Common, clearly having rehearsed the words.

She led them up a ramp onto the most majestic vessel the Laatu had yet crafted, one for which she was captain. "Ship is named *Drolvisdinn*," she said, stepping barefoot on the nacre-inlaid deck. "Words become playful, for *drolvisdinn* means *Light of Eternity*, and *drolv-isdinn* means *Sea Wing*."

"This ship is gorgeous," Alaia said, caressing the knotted patterns of the railings. Banyan roots had been grown in complex curves across the entirety of the hull and deck, even up the masts, wrapping the construction in a functional and decorative design. "How do you make the wood grow like this?"

"Good ustlas, priests ask banyan grow in sacred shapes," Ilsed answered. "But time ship needs, like coral reef needs time to grow. Priests direct *finesh*, essence, growing through paths cut in ship. Long work becomes, centuries growing. Few ships become made in *sheijir* way."

Ilsed showed them the masterfully carved details on the deck. The luxurious ship was built for speed, to be handled by a relatively small crew. It was smaller than the Zovarian ramships, but still had two levels below the main deck and lavish quarters at its forecastle and quarterdeck.

"No other than captain, crew, and royal guests allowed aboard *Drolvisdinn*," Ilsed said, continuing with her rehearsed lines. "Sacred vessel. But you... You I welcome, so you may help us in this short mission."

A few days back, Hud Ilsed had proposed to the queen the need for assessing whether the vines could be opened at sea as easily as on land, and also to measure if a ship the size of *Drolvisdinn* would fit through such an aperture, readying themselves for the possibility of a future departure by water. To create the widest opening, all three Silvesh would be required, forcing the queen to allow Kulak to go on the trip.

Ilsed called the signal to cast off all lines. The green, leaf-shaped sails stretched and billowed, pulling them westward. The waters of Gwur Gomosh were a mixture of turquoise, azure, and aquamarine, refracting rainbow reefs under the surface. Sterjall had never seen such colors before; coral reefs did not grow at the far end of the Isdinnklad, where the Stiss Malpa emptied in murky browns.

The ship wove a meandering path around islets that loomed jaggedly, each crowned by windswept spruces and raucous sea birds. Alaia spotted willowsheens, sandlashes, rubylocks, dollycranes, and even sighted a pair of voluptuous frigatebirds who were inflating their pink gular pouches for their mating season displays.

"I'm gonna spot so many new species," she said to Sterjall, "that even Hefra-fucking-Boarmane will be jealous."

They left behind the last of the sea stacks and entered the open waters, arriving at the western edge of the Moordusk Dome when the dimming edges of the wall were beginning to create a reflected, dark horizon. The arudinn reached all the way into the water at the sea wall, glowing partially beneath the waves, at least where no algae were coating them.

"I never become so near to wall before," Ilsed said, staring straight up. "It scares. Too big. Flat like green sea that goes up, endless."

"We'll lose the light very soon," Sterjall said. "Should we attempt this before it gets too dark?"

Ilsed called for all sails to be reefed, while oars and push poles were extended to more carefully direct the ship's movement.

Sterjall, Kulak, and Jiara stood at the bow of the ship and together began to will the vines to part.

"They spread much easier while over water," Sterjall observed. He knew Kulak noticed it too, but the prince could say nothing lest he reveal their secret outing.

Once the opening was large enough, the crew began rowing. The tunnel deepened as the ship moved forward, as if *Drolvisdinn* itself was repelling the vines with the ripples it cast. The Silvfröash at the front redoubled their efforts, aiming to widen the opening as much as possible. The ship had enough room to turn now, and ample space above its mainmast and beneath the keel.

"It works better when we each focus in a different direction," Jiara noted, having changed her focus to keep the opening behind them from closing. "But the space is large enough to fit one ship, maybe two."

"Good," Ilsed said. "Big room. Success." She issued a series of commands; the crew responded by rowing until the ship had turned around. They exited the tunnel, bobbing into the dim and sharp-shadowed light of the dome—only the trunk remained alight. The entire ordeal felt a bit anticlimactic despite their success, but once they were safely back inside, Ilsed approached her guests and spoke quietly, "More my scalp wishes to ask, requiring caution, secrecy. Khuron Kulak, tell?"

"Hud Ilsed wishes seeing Sunnokh," Kulak added. "But wishes we tell no others. Only crew knows. Mother not know, other chiefs not know."

"It could be dangerous to venture out like that," Jiara warned. "What if Zovarian ships spot us? What if we get tired, lose focus, and the vines snag on the mast?"

"Not *Drolvisdinn*," Kulak replied. "Small ship." He pointed his whiskers toward the cockboat. "We do not tell, if you do not tell."

Ilsed widened her red lips in a cunning and assertive manner. Kulak had told Ilsed everything he'd learned about the New World from Lago-Sterjall, all while avoiding any mention of their excursion to the outside. Ilsed had been enchanted by the stories, particularly those of Sunnokh, and had conspired with Kulak to give themselves a chance to see the life-giving star, even if covertly.

"If you really want to see Sunnokh," Sterjall said, "I propose we venture out just before dawn."

"Why dawn?" she asked.

"We are on the west side of the dome, so he will be setting right in front of us then, reflecting his beauty onto the Isdinnklad."

"Then we now rest, and tomorrow we row across the white blood vines," Ilsed declared. "My soul awaits."

They lowered the cockboat in the shimmering darkness before dawn.

"How many people can we fit?" Sterjall asked Ilsed.

"*Uirin kenesh*. Boat for eight," Ilsed said.

Balstei chose to remain aboard *Drolvisdinn* to allow for one more Laatu to experience the sun setting. Alaia was about to offer her spot too, but Sterjall asked her to keep them company.

"Ninc fits, too," Ilsed said to Alaia, "please stay." She then called for four of her crew members to join them in the cockboat and take to the oars.

Sterjall sensed a near-imperceptible change in the dim-blue arudinn light, a feeling he learned to associate with the approach of dawn. "We best hurry, or we'll miss it," he said.

The Laatu rowed hastily.

Ilsed took a deep breath, inhaling the rejuvenating sea breeze. "You gift kindness," she said as the cockboat began to cut through the newly made opening. "My heart gives gratitude until Endfall. My eyes weep thinking outside beauty."

A detachable mast was lifted and locked at the center of the boat, and a lantern was hung from it, casting distorted shadows from the passengers.

Jiara once more focused her attention on the back of the boat, so that it remained clear of vines, while Kulak and Sterjall stood at the bow, holding on to the curved stempost. Even this small boat was decorated with banyan roots, and the stempost was the most luxurious part of all, with the roots knotted and carved in shapes of dolphins jumping among tendrils of kelp.

Sterjall sensed they were nearing the edge of the wall, both through Agnargsilv's sight and through his keen ears, which heard the sound of gulls filtered through the vines. Though he wanted this to be a beautiful surprise, first and foremost, he needed them all to be safe. He volunteered to swim the rest of the way alone, planning to exit through a small aperture to make sure it was safe.

"It's okay, my arm is all healed up, I can swim fine," Sterjall insisted after Alaia questioned his decision to go swimming in the dark, surrounded by millions of sharp thorns, with soldiers looking for them, in an unknown sea, with a recently broken limb.

It was only as he unpinned his cloak that Sterjall realized that the logical thing to do before jumping in the water was to take off all of his clothes. He wasn't sure how nudity was perceived among the Laatu Miscam; they had their own private showers in their dormitories, so they hadn't seen how their hosts chose to bathe.

He leaned in close to Kulak and whispered, "I'm not sure what is proper with Laatu culture. Should I keep my clothes on when I go in the water?"

Kulak snickered but tried to be discreet about it. "Laatu swim naked," he answered. "Take off clothes, then swim."

Sterjall's old fear of being naked in front of strangers rushed to haunt him, his heart suddenly beating too fast.

Alaia noticed his expression and came to the rescue. "We should douse the lantern before you jump in. We don't want boats outside the dome to see our light, and you can see without it." She reached up the mast and extinguished the light. Sterjall let out a sigh of relief—he would thank her later.

He wriggled out of his tunic and dropped it next to his cloak, then removed his open-toed, sliding shoes, and dropped his trousers. He sat on the edge of the boat, dipping his footpaws into the water. It was cold. Painfully cold. The sunlight didn't reach through the vines, keeping the water in constant shade. He chose to deal with it and took the plunge.

The dark-furred wolf swam toward the far end of the wall, concentrating on the vines and making an opening just big enough for him to fit through comfortably. He soon saw a brightening ahead of him and heard his friends chattering excitedly—a beam of golden light was making the water shimmer.

Sterjall emerged from the dome and was bathed in the warmth of a glorious sunset. He glanced around quickly and could spot no boats or dangerous terrain in the vicinity. He didn't want his friends to miss the spectacle, so he hurried back. Even before reaching the boat, he said, "Row, now, it's a gorgeous sunset! Row, before Sunnokh sinks away!"

They picked Sterjall up along the way. He scrambled up the side of the boat, shook some of the water from his fur, then stood naked and shivering upon the deck. Kulak wrapped a blanket around him, then focused on spreading the vines once more.

"Don't look at Sunnokh directly, he could hurt your eyes," Sterjall remembered to warn them.

The small vessel left the dome as the sun began to dip into the chilly waters of the Isdinnklad Sea.

Ilsed and her crew stared toward the mighty star: it looked as if an orb of fire was swimming in the sea, sparkling in saturated radiance. The cockboat crossed the threshold, and the Laatu gasped as the blue sky was revealed, feathered by wispy cirrus clouds ablaze in bright yellow.

"The clouds are burning," Ilsed said almost inaudibly, "the clouds are burning…" She covered her mouth with delicate fingers, forgetting to breathe. Kulak wrapped an arm around Sterjall's shoulder and beamed.

The calm waters floated the boat out to sea. The sun dipped lower, turning a deep bronze while the clouds above flamed in radiant tangerines.

The sun blinked one last time, then disappeared, but the spectacle above them had barely just begun. The wispy vapors flowed and shone pink, then magenta, and then turned the color of sap from a baneblood tree. The lightblue dome that had no distance or scale darkened into a cavernous indigo. The entirety of the splendor was twofold, as it was reflected on the sea, leaving them floating in a field of colors they would have to invent new names for.

They stared in silence as the darkness deepened. Sterjall was shivering, his fur still soaking wet. Kulak pulled the blanket from his shoulders and said, "Be Lago, easier to dry." And so he did, but Lago felt even more embarrassed by his mostly smooth, naked body, with not even fur to conceal him. He kept his mask on and the blanket over him, a shield against Kulak's scrutinizing eyes.

"Behold, diamonds come to greet us," Ilsed said, awestruck, pointing at a blurry streak near the horizon. It was the planet Khumen, his rings streaking brightly in the dimming sky. Only then did she notice a diaphanous, dim glow not too far from the ringed planet. Sceres was there too, as the thinnest of Sulphur-yellow crescents, only visible due to her thin atmosphere.

"That is Sceres," Alaia told them. "Isn't she magical?"

"It's a Hollow Moon tomorrow," Lago said, "so she is nearly empty. But she will be back."

Distant dots of light were beginning to prick the sky. They could have spent all night watching the stars awakening, but Jiara, who had been keeping watch with Lago's binoculars, sounded the alarm. "Time to go. I see pink sails to the south. Three trimarans, sailing fast."

Ilsed kept her eyes locked upon the reflected stars while the cockboat turned and made its way back through the opening. She watched unblinking as the vines closed behind them. "Thank you," she said in the darkness. "I owe you much for gifting me this happiness. My scalp and my ship are forever at your service."

The dome was fully alight when they returned. The Laatu crew pulled the cockboat back up, then they sailed due east.

"I still don't understand how there is wind inside these domes," Balstei said to Ilsed. He had asked the question to others before, but no one could give him a good answer.

"Wind is change," Ilsed replied. "Arudinn warm, air moves. Clouds cold, air moves. Wind is breath, life."

"I think it makes sense," Alaia said, climbing the ratlines just above them. "I read once that plants breathe in and breathe out. The domes are giant plants. And if they let light through sometimes, like when we see wisps, they must let air in and out too. Maybe they have giant lungs up in the sky, somewhere we can't see them."

"Just where do you get your smarts, Oldrin gal?" Balstei asked, looking up at her. "Sorry, I didn't mean for that to sound so impolite. It's just that... Most Oldrin you find in the Union aren't exactly well read. That sounded horrible again, but I'm just pointing out something of statistical significance, nothing more."

"I get it," Alaia said. "Most of my friends at the mines never read much either, but that's because they don't let Oldrin inside libraries. But my Gwoli here borrowed books from the monastery just for me, every single week."

"She read three for each book I read," Sterjall said. "Crysta thought it was me doing all the reading."

He watched as Alaia climbed all the way to the crow's nest, where Jiara was enjoying the sea spray that the winds often carried even that high up.

Drolvisdinn skipped across a tall wave. The inner sea, too, had its cycles, responding to the changes of the weather and tides, to the warmth of the crust compressed beneath it, to the motion of Noss themself.

Kulak casually stepped behind Sterjall and said, "Come. I show you more *Drolvisdinn*. My scalp knows it well." The prince led him down a hatch, and as they entered the 'tween deck added, "Twenty years ago, with Mother aboard ship, my baby scalp became outside."

"Wait, you mean you were born on this ship?"

"Yes, born. Out from Mother." He gestured toward his kilt, then spread his arms down and wide, laughing.

They passed by stores of dried grains, where beds had been set up for the crew members who did not sleep on the hammocks outside. Sterjall sensed something playful in Kulak's demeanor as they continued down to the orlop deck, where extra cables were stowed.

"This ship is small, yet it feels so big," Sterjall remarked.

"It becomes bigger. We are above water. More, under water."

They kept descending until they reached the hold, which was mostly empty.

"Now our scalps are under water," Kulak said. "But goes still more deep. Look down." Kulak asked Sterjall to move his footpaws out of the way, then lifted a hatch. He leaned a lantern over the hole and let Sterjall have a look. A ladder went down; about three steps below, there was water.

Sterjall was confused. "Is the ship open at the bottom? How does it not sink?"

"Not open. Down is locked water, heavy, keeps *Drolvisdinn* straight."

"Like a ballast?" Sterjall asked.

Kulak shrugged, not knowing what the word meant, but sensing the meaning was correct.

"Huh," Sterjall mumbled. "We use rocks to weigh down our ships, not water."

"Easier to find water than rocks, when in water." Kulak said. "But do not swim. Water stinks like *rilgéreo khar*, I not help you dry this time."

Sterjall laughed. "Sorry about that awkward moment. I did not know if it was proper to take my clothes off, especially in front of a prince and a chief. I still don't know all your rules."

"My lips spoke truth, that bathing naked is Laatu way." He paused, then while closing the hatch, added, "It is kind, what you do for us, showing us sunset, showing me stars again. I had a nice view. And I saw a lot more, too." He stared at Sterjall, measuring.

Sterjall felt nervous, felt aroused. *Can he feel me?* he wondered. *And why can't I feel him? It's like his emotions are invisible to my mask.* He kept his eyes locked on Kulak's while his heart thumped louder in his chest.

The caracal watched with calculating eyes, saying nothing, waiting for a reaction.

He must be able to sense I'm nervous, Sterjall thought. *But he's the prince, I shouldn't even be thinking of this.* He tried to shove the thoughts away, lest an erection begin to push on his trousers, something he would not be able to hide. *Why is he still staring? What if—*

"Are you down here?" Alaia's voice called from above. Her skipping footsteps were followed by the swinging shadows from her lantern. "There you are. Ilsed says we're stopping at the port of Loonsad, we are almost there. You should come see. It's a gorgeous area, full of these tiny birds holding on to the reeds."

Sterjall broke eye contact with Kulak, then followed Alaia.

"I show you more, next time," Kulak said.

Chapter Thirty

Munnji Silos

The time to depart the dome was quickly encroaching upon them, leaving the wayfarers with only a week more to prepare.

Balstei had been wanting to learn more about how the Laatu used the sap to prepare munnji, so he had asked Hed Lettáni, chief of Gwur Aalpe, whether they would be willing to show them the process. Lettáni happily obliged, asking Balstei to bring his friends to the munnji silos built around a supporting column just west of Dakhud, the capital of their province.

"It's enormous," Balstei said reverently, gazing up at the monumental structures that drained sap and stored it in cylindrical pools.

"We saw silos like these in the Heartpine Dome," Jiara mentioned, "but they were in ruins, shattered by quakes from when the roof started to collapse."

"One column for each province become wrapped in silos," Hed Lettáni explained in their smoothly accented Common. They were not an interpreter, but had studied the tongue during their scholarly upbringing, then forced themself to learn more after the arrival of the New World travelers. "Dakhud silos are best. Dakhud harvests are best. Follow me inside." They walked in front of the group with their long shodog billowing like a rainbowy sail.

The building was warm and dimly lit on the inside. The acrid scent of sap tingled their noses, but they soon got used to it.

"Ashborn beans are most important of our crops," Hed Lettáni said, pointing at a group of farmers separating beans from their pods. "Though us rarely eat ashborn beans, they become critical ingredient for munnji. Noss taught us, long time past, how to prepare munnji, but soot helped us find ways new. Feeling the threads, we learn what works, what is needed, what is not."

A farmer emptied a bag of chaff into what seemed like a well, to be processed as fertilizer, while nearby a treadwheel-powered mill was grinding the beans.

"In silos we pump white blood," Lettáni continued, showing them a vast pool of milky white. "Mix with ground beans, nutrition. Moisture births taloncyst fungus." The next vat was overgrown with a thick layer of spore-drenched filaments, covered with a protective mesh. "Dangerous, poisonous fungus," Lettáni warned, then pointed at a series of octahedral furnaces resembling the arambukh dangling from their necklace. "Juniper ashes made here. Quenches anger of fungus, makes edible after cooked. Together they birth raw munnji paste."

A smilodon-pulled cart rolled by them with a cargo of unprocessed munnji that looked like blocks harvested from a gelatinous quarry. "Many mixes, many other ingredients," Lettáni said. "These for carnivore kinds. Others for other diets, other palates."

"Do you also make the special munnji that comes from the core vine?" Balstei asked.

"Not here, in Arjum only," Lettáni replied, taking them up to a corridor that wrapped outside the building and offered a view of the terraced fields where the beans were grown. "Smilodons, domestic cats, and snow leopards are only mindrel who feed on core vine blood. But we are weaning them out of it. Mindrel have grown large and intelligent enough."

The chief stopped at a balcony and pointed at a herd of jaguars who were plowing a field, following instructions from a shaman. "Long ago, Laatu predecessors fed tigers, jaguars, panthers, and mountain lions with idshall-munnji, but for short time."

"The same species used to play minquoll?" Alaia asked.

"*Haast*. Growth and hard bones made good for riding, clever brains good for sports, placid mood good for farming. Enough idshall-munnji we fed them so that harsh temperament become subdued, so that mindrel understand Laatu better. Too much idshall-munnji makes bodies too larger, behavior too different from natural behavior they need for when Mindreldrolom opens. Feeding stopped when it was meant to stop."

"Ever since we learned about idshall-munnji, I've been curious," Alaia said. "What would happen if a person ate it?"

"Person would vomit. Not good for human, becomes us sick. Even if swallow, person has to eat for entire life, then make children, then repeat for many generations. Human already smart enough, big enough, long-lived enough.

Noss did not create idshall-munnji for human. Mindrel not happy when eating idshall-munnji, but we teach them flavor from moment they become birthed. Many years it takes to overcome strong flavor. Companion species hated us in past, but now that they are smart, they understand why it needed done."

That evening, a banquet was served at the terraced rotunda of Dakhud. The twenty-four octahedral spires of the capital had been set alight with green flames for the occasion. No idshall-munnji was served to human guests, but normal munnji cakes of all different flavors were available.

Sterjall had been chatting with a group of overeager Laatu children when he lost sight of Alaia, Kulak, and his other friends. He began to meander around the rotunda, tasting the munnji cakes the youngsters dared him to try, when he spotted Hed Lettáni in the distance having a conversation with Sunu and an old allgender shaman wearing a hat much too large for their head—hats of any kind were already a rare sight in Mindreldrolom, but this one was obscene in scale, round and white like a feathery turban. Sterjall nearly choked on his munnji when he saw the hat suddenly expand enormous white wings, flapping madly while emitting a sound much like a nasal moan. It was an albatross, clinging tightly to the allgender's scalp.

He kept his distance as he watched. The shaman spread wide their arms—although not nearly as wide as the albatross' wingspan of two whole strides—then bellowed, "*Va jambradikh frulv halvet alrull!*" summoning five jays from out of their long shodog's sleeves, who flew away at once. Both the old shaman and Sunu left, leaving Lettáni alone at the edge of a terrace. Sterjall awkwardly excused himself from the children following him and went to stand by the chief.

"Who was that?" he asked.

"Shaman Klaawich," Lettáni answered. "And Pei, their albatross. Old as the *sheinokhlom* trees they both are. They flew heralds to other chiefs, asking them to gather at Arjum in three days' time. Council gathers anew, then you depart."

"Will you be going with us?"

"No. I am chief, not warrior. Members for company will be proposed during council. I will remain in Dakhud to make farms work as they must." They plucked a munnji cake from a servant's tray and took a delicate bite from it, then offered the other half to Sterjall. "Is your hunger for knowledge of munnji sated?" they asked.

"I think so. I was surprised to see how many people work at the silos. I'm still curious about something, though. What will happen when the domes finally open? Will the silos collapse with them?"

"Perhaps, perhaps not," Lettáni replied. "We not know what happens when Mindreldrolom is no more, but munnji is meant to provide nutrients during great migrations. In which form, we not know. We will store in caves in case more is needed—munnji lives long life."

Sterjall nodded. "By the way, you speak very good Common. How did you learn?"

"Most allgenders learn jobs where understanding differences is required. Learning tongues, such as Common, is common."

"Is that why all the interpreters are allgender?"

"Not all, but most, like shamans," Lettáni said. "I grew up learning history. Suque taught me. My scalp believes you met them at council. Love for history became love for tongues, though few tongues we learn within our limited dome. Miscamish and Common share sacred grimoires, while other tongues become learned only by oral traditions. Learning of tongues, of history, led me to chiefdom, which is not what my scalp expected. But chiefdom is also good role for allgender."

"Why is that?"

"Because chief's main role is to listen."

"How does being allgender help in that?"

"Like interpreter has to be of multiple minds, we embody many sides at once. Not two sides, but all sides, including spaces in between. All equally important. By not settling in one place, one stands closer to all places." Lettáni turned, facing the crowd once more. "Your friend calls for you."

Sterjall followed their gaze. Alaia was sitting at a table, waving her arms in their direction. "Gwoli! You have to try these!" she called.

Lettáni blinked slowly at him, then took their leave.

Sterjall sat next to Alaia. "Aren't those the spicy ones?" he asked, watching Alaia engulf an ember-orange cube.

"You have no idea," she said through a mouthful and a few tears. "Here, taste it. It's like cubed netherflames. Like a brime crystal just rescued from the pits of a volcano."

"And just why are you putting them in your mouth, then?"

"Just try one!" she insisted, pushing an ominously orange cake toward him. She watched him ponder the hostile snack, and as soon as he took a courageous bite, said, "So, I was chatting with Kulak the other day."

Sterjall swallowed.

"I asked him how big alligators get here," she added, watching his expression shift.

Sterjall downed a glass of goat milk, then through a heaving gasp said, "Probably not as big as the ones in the Stiss Malpa." His nose became exceedingly moist, his eyes reddening.

"Yes, I'd agree with that. Because there are *no alligators* in this dome. None, zero. He had no clue what sort of creature I was talking about. He'd never seen a lizard bigger than an iguana."

"Gators aren't lizards, actually. They—"

"You are missing the point."

"Could you hand me that glass of—"

"Don't change the subject," Alaia snapped, pulling her glass away while glaring at him. "No alligators. That time when you said you and Aio had gone to see the mangroves in Parjuul, you said you found 'so many alligators.'"

Beneath his fur, Sterjall's skin was burning. He began to pant, tongue lolling, eyes searching for something to douse the fire with.

"So, where in the sixteen nethervoids were you?" she asked. She pushed her glass forward.

Sterjall snatched it with his sweaty palms and lapped at the milk, feeling some relief with each strike of his tongue. He peered around them, seeing too many people within earshot. He swallowed, then whispered as quietly as possible, "Kulak wanted... He wanted to see the moon and the stars. And so I showed him."

Alaia covered her gaping mouth. "But someone could've spotted you!" she whispered even more quietly than Sterjall had spoken.

"We stayed hidden, and it was night anyway."

"But the Laatu would kill you if they found out! Both of you."

"I know, but no one needs to find out." He gulped the last bit of milk, swirling it in his mouth before swallowing. "It's just another secret, like when we took Hud Ilsed out to see the sunset. Although thinking back on it, I think Kulak might've incited that outing too..."

Alaia relaxed a little. She squinted at him as if fumingly angry, but a little smile curled her lips.

"Sorry," Sterjall said, panting again. "I didn't want you to worry. And... And... My tongue, it feels like it's covered in angry scorpions."

"Here, have this," she offered, handing him a munnji cake that was robin-egg blue. "It helps with the heat."

Sterjall wolfed the cube down. It helped, much more than the milk had.

"I remember you being awfully tired when you returned from your 'mangrove' trip," Alaia said. "Now it makes a bit more sense."

Sterjall licked his chops through a sigh and said, "We had to ride all night to get back in time, didn't get any sleep. Poor Blu was so worn out, we let him pass out and used him as a pillow so we could look up at the stars."

"That's... um... stupidly romantic, actually. Almost sounds like a date. On your backs, watching the stars like we once did. Which I really enjoyed, by the way, even though I never got a kiss."

"Well, we... um—"

"No! You did what?" she said, loud as a parrot.

"Keep your voice down! I didn't, he did. He kissed me, but not in the way you think. He is rebellious and impulsive sometimes. He kissed me as though saying, *Fuck the rules*, and then kept talking as if nothing had happened. I don't really understand him."

"When I said they would kill you, I meant it. But now they would *enjoy* killing you. Lodestar guide us, he's the prince! And these people don't like lorrkins, lurrkins, or lerrkins, you should know that!"

"Never stopped me before," Sterjall murmured, smirking awkwardly.

Alaia shook her head. "So, you are saying you like him?"

"I don't know. Maybe if I understood him better. He's handsome, though, can't deny that."

"Softly padded, but much smaller than your usual type. I'd say the exact opposite of Banook. And what would he—"

"I talked to Banook about that possibility. If I did something, or if he did, it would not be an issue."

"Figures... Still, if anyone found out about this, we'd all be in huge trouble. Was it just a kiss, or did anything else happen between you two?"

"Not really. Well, maybe, but not that day. I think you might've... interrupted something."

"No! Down inside *Drolvisdinn*?"

"Yeah, I don't know where that was headed, but it seemed like he was flirting with me. If you hadn't come down, well..."

"You dog."

Sterjall shrugged.

"Just... whatever you do, be careful," she pleaded.

"I will. I promise. Just don't tell anyone, even Jiara. It's better if this stays between us."

Chapter Thirty-One

The Company of Nine

The council reconvened three days later, although Nelv did not attend—the felid Nu'irg could not be found when she did not care to be found. Fingrenn once again interpreted the proceedings, standing at the center of the crescent-shaped table in the great hall.

The members of the council discussed at length the supplies and weapons they'd been preparing, then carefully studied a map drawn by Balstei and Jiara to plan their path into the distant desert. Once there was clarity on their plan of action, the time to decide who would go on the expedition arrived.

"We have decided that nine shall be the members traveling in this company," Alúma said, holding high her scepter. "Four from the New World, five more from Mindreldrolom. Each chief has been tasked with choosing a member to represent their province, except for my own province—Gwur Ali shall not have a representative in this mission."

"Wait," Sterjall interjected, "what about Kulak?"

"Khuron Kulak has duties at the temple," the queen replied, stern as a statue, while not even glancing toward her son. "He will stay to keep the dome healthy."

Sterjall looked toward the prince, who held an impassive expression over his crossed arms, saying nothing, staring at nothing.

"But we could use his help," Jiara said. "The Silvesh allow us to see things we'd miss otherwise."

"And two Silvesh you shall carry with you," Alúma said with finality, "while the third remains here as a safeguard in case something goes wrong with the mission. This has long since been decided. I shall name no member, as is my right as chief of Gwur Ali."

Sterjall could not understand why Kulak would not voice an objection, but once again, he could not read the prince's threads at all. He was about to try again when the queen interrupted him.

"Hud Quoda of Gwur Pantuul, I believe I know who you have chosen for the mission, but it is your word that shall officially name the member."

"The province of mangroves had an easy choice to make, Ierun Alúma," Hud Quoda said, bowing her root-like headdress. "Sunu shall join the company, for they are a fierce warrior and caring healer, and can also act as interpreter and language tutor during Fingrenn's absence."

Sunu, who had been sitting with the audience at the periphery, stood up while pushing their freckled chest forward proudly.

"And if you would so allow," Hud Quoda continued, "Olo too shall join, for my scalp does not believe he will encumber the smilodons."

"Sunu and Olo so are chosen," Alúma acknowledged, then looked at the most intimidating of the chiefs. "Hod Abjus of Gwur Esmukh, have you made your choice?"

The mighty warrior stood as if ready to punch something, anything, and while lifting a smilodon-tooth knife said, "The province of sacred waverers and primordial forests chooses their own chief. I shall embark on this mission to protect those weaker than I, to help find the Nu'irg who has been lost to time."

Sterjall must have let his utter displeasure show on his face, as Alaia sharply elbowed him.

"Hod Abjus is so chosen," Alúma intoned. "Hed Lettáni of Gwur Aalpe, you may now speak your choice."

Lettáni stood as elegant and colorful as always. "The province of terraces and white blood chooses Givra to aid in this mission, for she is a masterful scout and is well fond of her new friends."

Givra, who had been sitting by Sunu's side, stood up and smiled. Alaia smiled with her, glad that she would be joining them.

"Givra is so chosen," Alúma said. "Hod Buil of Gwur Úrëath, who is your choice in this matter?"

The stocky chief stood and confidently answered, "The province of the white peak chooses a weaponsmith to travel with the company, one who is also well acquainted with the group. Kenondok, we thus name."

Kenondok had been sitting next to the chief. He rose to his feet, towering at twice Buil's height, then grunted like a bison.

"Kenondok is so chosen," Alúma said. "And last, Hud Ilsed of Gwur Gomosh, who shall be the ninth member of this company?"

As she rose, Ilsed made a seductive gesture as of someone pushing a strand of hair away from their eyes, although she was as hairless as all Laatu. "The province of black islands and turquoise reefs appoints Khuron Aio-Kulak as the ninth and final member of the company."

The queen immediately came to her feet, silencing the whispers that had begun to seep around the chamber. "Hud Ilsed," she said through tightened lips, "you are meant to choose a representative from your own province. No person from Gwur Ali is to travel with the company, for that was my choice as chief."

"My scalp believes that in matters of diplomacy, having a representative who speaks for our tribe will be important. Khuron Kulak is the ideal representative."

"It matters not," the queen said quietly, "for we agreed that your choice must come from your province."

"Was Khuron Kulak not born in Oälpaskist?" Ilsed countered. "I was merely a sailor and not captain then, but I too was aboard *Drolvisdinn* when the prince decided it was his time to breathe in the air of the sea. He now lives in Arjum, but it was in my province that his eyes first saw the light of the arudinn."

The queen looked toward her son, who still said nothing, but seemed to have grown a faint smile on his black lips. "Did you persuade her to do this?" she whispered down to him.

"Hud Ilsed's choice is her own," Kulak whispered back, then stood up. "I accept," he said triumphantly, even though his handpaws were trembling a bit. "And now the company of nine is settled."

The queen held tight to her emotions, composed herself, then said, "Aio-Kulak is so chosen. But he and I will have a talk after this meeting is concluded."

Chapter Thirty-Two

The Lights of Humenath

The day after the council meeting was a day of rest for all except Aio-Kulak, who had to endure off-calendar duties at the temple while being reprimanded by his mother.

The following morning, on Moonday of the twenty-fifth day of Highsun, the nine members of the company gathered between the felid sculptures at the atrium. Humming chants reverberated as their scalps were anointed with sacred oils from the core vine, which had to be rubbed through fur and hair for the representatives of the New World.

"It smells wonderful," Alaia mockingly whispered to Sterjall, scrunching up her nose.

The queen delivered an impassive speech, then withdrew from the ceremonies as the nine hopped on their mounts.

Four smilodons had been chosen for the mission. Kulak, Sterjall, and Sunu—with Olo on their shoulder—rode on the back of Blu. Kenondok, Balstei, and Jiara rode on Fulm, a night-furred smilodon with long legs and a bit of a hissy attitude. Hod Abjus, Givra, and Alaia rode on Kobos, a muscular smilodon-tiger hybrid with sharp stripes along his back.

The last smilodon was the largest, and one Sterjall and his friends had met before; her name was Pichi, and she had carried their bags when they were abducted long ago. Pichi's size was striking. When standing in front of her, Sterjall's shoulders barely met her braided chin tufts. When Pichi shifted her body weight around, Sterjall could feel the displaced air around her rippling chest and leg muscles. Pichi was the color of yellow-sand beaches flecked with sun-bleached seashells. Her long fangs were serrated, much better for cutting and tearing than piercing. She needed neither instructions nor riders and could handle herself perfectly well.

Pichi's harness held their weapons, clothing, tarps, stakes, ropes, skins to later fill with water, and bundles of non-perishable foods. She carried two substantial stashes of munnji cakes—one for humans, another for felids—which they knew they'd need in the desert of black rocks. Munnji was highly nutritious, and a small serving could provide sustenance for them to survive the direst circumstances.

The company arrived at the base of the white-peaked Stelm Humenath in the late evening, taking their time so as to not overwork their cats. Hod Buil welcomed them to the city of Humenath and treated them and their cats to a fine dinner, having them taste salted meats from the goats and sheep that inhabited the great mountain.

The next morning, Kulak requested they venture partially up the mountain, for that was where Nelv usually prowled, and he wanted to speak to the Nu'irg before departing. They stopped to grill fruits and mushrooms for lunch and set the cats loose to hunt caprids on the slopes.

"Nelv will not show her spots to so many voices," Kulak said. "You wait here, find rest, for the arudinn might be dark before I find her. I will take Blu. And Sterjall."

Sterjall was not expecting to be named, yet he was excited about the chance to see Nelv again.

After Blu returned from his hunt, Kulak and Sterjall mounted the smilodon and rode higher up the mountain through a dense forest of ferns and tangled ivies.

"Did you get in trouble?" Sterjall asked now that it was just the two of them. "With your mother, I mean."

"Yes. Angered Mother. She still wants me stay, but also respects rules, respects Ilsed choice."

"Did… Did she punish you?"

Kulak exhaled sharply, then said, "Mother's eyes punish. Mother's words sharper than claw. But my scalp makes no regret. New World is beauty, and my eyes wish more beauty."

Sterjall considered whether he was inquiring too far, but he dared ask another question. "When we took Ilsed out to see the sunset… Did you plan that all along to gain her favor?"

Kulak remained silent. After a long while, he said, "Mother's ways are set. My scalp does what needs done. Now make eyes look for Nelv, we enter her forest."

Sterjall held on to Kulak's shodog as they rode and searched, sometimes aiming Leif in random directions to see farther, hoping to be the first to spot her aura. "Can you feel when she is near?"

"Sometimes, if Nelv wants to be felt. Not form of thread, but glow. Like feeling Silv, but more... Not know word."

"Elusive?" Sterjall tried, having felt the meaning Kulak was trying to convey. Kulak understood the meaning in turn and knew it to be the correct word.

"Yes. Elusive. Hard finding. But if she becomes aware of me, and me of her, we mindspeak and know where we are."

"I need to practice mindspeech, but there are no canids around here for me to do that."

"Foxes, some," Kulak said. "On Gwur Esmukh. Timid."

"How does it feel when you mindspeak with the felids? Do you hear full sentences?"

"Like you guess my words," Kulak answered. "Meaning shared, meaning understood. Nelv not speaks sentences, but says many emotions, one after other, sometimes on top of other. I interpret, like Fingrenn, and make words."

Sterjall couldn't understand how Kulak was navigating the labyrinthine jungle, which grew denser the higher they climbed, but the prince was at ease, not worrying about the direction in which they headed.

Kulak tapped on Blu's shoulders, making him stop. "Ahead," he murmured.

Sterjall couldn't sense anything yet.

Kulak jumped off Blu and helped Sterjall down. Blu dropped to the mossy ground and watched as the young men walked into a tunnel of leaves and pine needles, buried to their knees in ferns.

Deeper within the tunnel, Sterjall at last sensed Nelv's emerald-green aura. Though it was the same 'color' as Mindrelsilv's, hers somehow tasted different. Sterjall found this difficult to rationalize, as there were no colors or flavors associated with these qualia, but he could only think of them in terms he was familiar with. The tunnel widened into a grotto beneath a gnarly banyan tree with a dome-like canopy of tangled roots. Nelv perched just above them in her clouded leopard primal form. Her nebulous coat shimmered darkly, like the essence of dusk and dappled light. Her tail swooshed around like an impatient pendulum.

"Stay here," Kulak said. Once he was right below Nelv, he jumped up to playfully touch her tail, then laughed. Nelv tried to scratch his handpaws like a kitten, swiping first with her left claws, then right. She stood on the branch, then jumped down, using Kulak's shoulders as a step down to the ground.

Sterjall could feel Kulak and Nelv communing. Their threads and auras stretched to share the same space, vibrating together when ideas were exchanged. They prowled around each other in a synchronized dance of paws and tails. Nelv wove around Kulak's furry legs and bumped her head on his lifted ankles. He squatted and presented his handpaws with his claws partially extended, letting her walk underneath so she could choose when and where to scratch herself.

Nelv stopped and stared at Sterjall with pupils as dark as the blotches on her fur. She held still as the statues at Arjum's atrium, except for her swishing tail. Sterjall swallowed.

"Nelv says she sees you," Kulak said. "Nelv says she trusts you, wolf loved by two Nu'irgesh. She says maybe you will gain her love too, and then she will let you brush her shoulders, and perhaps her tail, and your handpaws will not bleed."

"That's... very kind of her," Sterjall said. "Tell her I will do all I can to find Mamóru, to find her old friend."

Kulak communicated Sterjall's feelings with no more than a gaze.

Nelv blinked slowly. She then took the form of a cheetah and ambled in circles with her back bent down in a sensual curve, shoulder blades lifting and dropping in an exaggerated manner. She jumped onto a low branch and in midair she became a flat-headed cat, a species Sterjall had never seen, reminding him more of a loris or a lemur. The cat balanced on the branch and stopped in front of Sterjall's chest. Her eyes were like varnished wooden spheres, reflecting the mottled patterns of the canopy. She stared at Sterjall and seemed to speak without words. The light vibrations of her whiskers shared yearning, hope, and kinship.

Although Sterjall could not hear the felid's thoughts, Agnargsilv did allow him to feel—in an abstracted way—her intentions. He felt they were benevolent, even if confused and alien.

He wanted to say *thank you*, but his was the mask of canids, not felids, and Nelv was out of reach of his mind. Instead, he extended a handpaw to caress Nelv's head, as he would have done with Bear. Nelv shifted into a tiny sand cat, and with her ears flattened, scurried away, jumping up the trunk in the form of a dinofelis and disappearing through the leaves and tangled branches.

"Be thankful you still have arm. And head," Kulak chastised. "Never try that again, not unless Nelv asks."

Sterjall kept his head down as they walked back toward Blu. "So, what did Nelv tell you?" he finally asked.

"Nelv told many things. About hunt, about health of Stelm Humenath, health of all felids. She told she still believes Mamóru lives, though she does not know how she knows. She is hopeful, perhaps naive."

It was nearing dusk by the time they got back on Blu's saddle. They rode in silence until Sterjall noticed something amiss.

"We're going the wrong way," he said. "The camp should be that way."

"Your scalp good sensing direction," Kulak admitted. "But not worry, my scalp knows where we are going. You wait, you see."

Sterjall was curious, so he tried to use Agnargsilv to read Kulak's motives, to feel his frame of mind, but again he could not. "I... I have a strange question," he said.

"Ask, Lago-Sterjall."

"I don't mean to pry, but I noticed that sometimes Agnargsilv won't show me your emotions, not in the way I'm used to sensing others. Do you know what I mean?"

"My scalp understands. When Silv speaks to you, it tells you feelings others may not want you to know. But not all people, some people know to hide. If you know to hide, you keep better secrets."

"But... how do you do it?"

"Do not think of threads of others, but of your own. Look at them, understand them, wrap them inside you. Like when you ask vines to move, ask threads to move, not leave you. When I lie to Mother, she finds out. But if I lie and hold my threads in grasp, she does not notice. I lie to you now, I hide, for reason, and you do not see me lie."

Sterjall pondered. There was more to reading people than the connection Agnargsilv provided. There was a more natural intuition as well, and somehow they all related back to those mysterious threads. Suppressing his own threads meant he could, in theory, keep his intentions hidden not just from other Silvfröash, but from anyone.

They reached a glade covered in grass and fragrant herbs. The clearing sloped down in front of them, then dropped to a cliff, providing an ample view over the canopy. The vista extended uninterrupted all the way to the trunk, which was still alight, with branches of lit arudinn slowly fading.

"This is it," Kulak said, dismounting Blu and holding his arms up to help Sterjall down.

"This is what? What are we doing here?"

"Come. I show you." They walked together over the grass, with Blu's silent steps following.

"That brightness"—Kulak pointed to lights down the mountain's slope—"is Humenath city, where we slept the night. And right of trunk, though too far to see, is Parjuul, where we did not sleep the night, one night." Kulak smiled. "But now, we wait." He patted Blu's head, who dropped onto the grass, stretched his thick limbs, and curled into a comfortable position. "Take seat. Or belly pillow."

They sat on the grass and leaned back on Blu's gray and brown belly.

"Blu says to relax. He feels you become tense."

Sterjall doubted those were Blu's words and not just Kulak's. "I still don't know what we are doing…" he said, earnestly confused.

"We wait for meteor shower."

"What do you mean?"

"We wait, with no more questions."

They waited for a long while, accompanied by the sound of crickets and waking night birds, until only the last shimmer of light around the trunk remained.

They found themselves in that ephemeral moment of dusk in which sharp shadows existed within the dome, all emanating from the brightness of the trunk. Each blade of grass, each pointed conifer, each summit and each vine column stretched shadows in a radial burst. Once the last light of the trunk faded, and as the green sky turned to a dark blue, the true magic began.

"Look, meteor shower started," Kulak said, pointing to the grass near him. A little dot of light flashed and streaked up in phosphorescent greenness.

"Was that a—"

"Quiet, watch."

Soon they were surrounded by thousands of blinking and drifting fireflies. They were everywhere, weaving over Blu's fur, dangling from Sterjall's whiskers, bouncing atop Kulak's ear tufts. Sterjall smiled so widely he feared swallowing the luminous insects. An intermittent dance enveloped them, speaking in a blinking code of motion and light, saturating their view and flowing with its own winds and invisible forces.

"Not same as your falling stars, but still good stars," Kulak said, breaking the silence. "Happy birthday, Lago-Sterjall."

"What? How?"

"Alaia told me. Twenty-sixth of Highsun. I wanted to gift something special. You took Alaia on date, gave her meteor shower for her birthday. I give you my meteor shower."

"Thank you," Sterjall said. "This is perfect. This is beautiful." He didn't know what else to say.

"My scalp does not understand birthday. Laatu count years on first day of year, not on same day mothers birth us. But my scalp learns. Today we are same age, *ferrlárgo*, nineteen, even if I was older yesterday, because that is how things are in New World."

They watched for an hour, maybe two, until the fireflies began to tire. Some still went on signaling their wishes into the dark, helping Sterjall briefly see Kulak's face. Kulak did not need the aid of their light. They spoke of what they thought might happen after this long trip, what might happen to the dome, if it were to open. They had no answers, but it felt good to ponder, to wonder.

"It's too perfect, this meteor shower," Sterjall said, "as it matches the color of the one I showed Alaia. Most meteors outside are of varied colors, but during the Quindecims, they are all green, just like your fireflies."

"Good," Kulak said, satisfied. "Because my scalp does not know where to find orange fireflies." He drew in a deep breath, then continued, "Tomorrow we reach the white blood vines. And then I live life outside, perhaps for months. My soul is excited, my heart is scared. So many sunsets, sunrises, so many stars every night. And then we come back, and we do not know the future."

"I'm not afraid of going out, but I'm afraid of coming back here. I don't want to lose Agnargsilv. Most of the chiefs want to take it away from me. Even your mother."

"Mother likes tradition, follows rules. Mother likes you, but you are not Miscam, that matters to Mother. If not for votes of other provinces, Mother would say we go out never. Agnargsilv and Urnaadisilv become taken, living useless in drolom with few foxes and no bears. We do not even know bears."

"I don't want to upset her. I'm still afraid, if she ever finds out we went outside the dome that night—"

"She will not. I will not tell. Alaia will not tell," Kulak said, turning to face Sterjall with a devious smirk on his face.

"You mean…"

"Alaia told me you told her. It is good, my scalp trusts her. You make good to trust her."

Sterjall turned his face to him. "I'm sorry, she figured it out on her own and—"

"Alley-gaters, yes, it was funny. She is smart. You told her I kissed you."

Kulak looked deeply into Sterjall's eyes again, scrutinizing every expression with quick, saccadic motions of his oval pupils.

"Why are you still afraid of me?" Kulak asked. His eyes broke no contact, not even for a blink.

"I'm not afraid, I'm just—"

"You are. My scalp feels your worry."

Sterjall suddenly wanted to run away. In his mind he heard Banook's mountain song, and he lost himself in the melody and memory of those happy moments. *The alpenglow on snowy peaks calls forth where... I... I hope he knows that we can be... Why does this bother me so? Banook said it would be alright. When far apart he thinks of me... I hear the mountain, I sing the mountain, I...* He pushed the thoughts away before his yearning became too obvious. He paid attention to his own threads and noticed how visibly conflicted they looked, looping so tightly back onto themselves as if shivering. He remembered Kulak's words about suppressing them and tried to keep them in place, willing them to shrink inward. He felt a sudden change, as if he had closed up, becoming self-contained.

"Your scalp went someplace else," Kulak observed. "You learn fast. You do not want me to see." He waited for a breath, then asked again, "Why are you afraid of me?"

"I'm afraid because... It's the things we talked about," Sterjall replied, trying to avoid the other subject on his mind. "The Laatu are so extreme about these taboos. And you are their prince, and if they were to find out that—"

Kulak planted a solid kiss on Sterjall's lips. He didn't pull back right away this time; he held his lips there, dragging his handpaws over Sterjall's face, flattening his ears, rubbing down to his neck, pulling him tighter.

Last time it had been Aio kissing Lago, but this time it was muzzle upon muzzle, a sensation new and thrilling that made Sterjall freeze in blissful terror.

Kulak released him abruptly and proclaimed, "Now *that* is good taboo, caracal and wolf, lip to lip. Wish they could all see, could do nothing about it, and go cry to their grandmothers."

"See? This is what I mean, I can't figure out what you want. You kiss me and then—"

Kulak kissed him again, then rolled his body on top of Sterjall's while locking their muzzles together. It was a deep kiss, with the disconcerting scratch of Kulak's sandpapery tongue. The prince eased their muzzles apart and sat up, enveloping Sterjall's lap with his open kilt. "What my scalp wants is for you to stop fearing what *you* want," he said, then put his sharp index claw under Sterjall's chin and slowly dragged it down his neck, stopping at his jugular notch. He retracted the claw and spread his fingers, weaving his pads over Sterjall's chest, then his belly, below his navel—and there he stopped, a fingerbreadth away from Sterjall's throbbing sheath.

Kulak stood up. "We must go if we want sleep tonight." He smacked Blu's butt, making him lethargically rise, then grabbed Sterjall's handpaws and helped him up. Before letting go of them, he added, "You tell me what you want, when you are ready."

They rode back in darkness. Sterjall said nothing, but instead of holding on to Kulak's shodog, he held on to the soft fur on the caracal's exposed chest.

All was quiet when they arrived at the camp. Sunu was sitting cross-legged, leaning against a boulder; they always slept sitting up, making it hard to tell whether they were meditating or dreaming. "*Oset fin,*" Sunu said without opening their eyes.

"*Olvet finesh,*" Kulak quietly replied. He helped Sterjall down, removed Blu's saddle, and curled up to sleep next to the smilodon, as he always did when outside. Sterjall thought he seemed happy, despite the awkwardness of their last words together, yet Kulak was still holding his threads inward.

Sterjall was tucking himself under his blankets when he heard Alaia turn on her bedroll. Alaia opened her eyes and mouthed, "Happy birthday," before turning back around.

Chapter Thirty-Three

Threads Pulled Inward

Sunu woke the entire company before the break of dawn, asking them to circle around the campfire for their daily lessons.

"This early?" Alaia complained. "Could we not skip this while we are on the mission?"

"Learning never stops," Sunu said. Aside from being their battle instructor, they had taken on Fingrenn's role as a language tutor.

All but the Silvfröash inhaled a small dose of soot, to ready their minds.

"It's strange how things have changed since getting access to pure soot," Balstei observed as they waited for the drug to take effect. "The powder is becoming something else for me—not merely a way to learn about the nature of the aetheric elements, but to learn about the nature of nature." He leaned against the thick roots of a kapok tree and sighed.

"I'm glad I don't have to use it now," Jiara said, muffled from behind her ursid mask. "I mean, I enjoyed a hit or two in my youth, of probably filthier stuff than the moor dust those kids tried to sell us in Mirefoot, and though I enjoyed the effect, it burned through my sinuses for days. Urnaadisilv is much more convenient, thank you."

"And a tad more versatile," Balstei said. "Although the threads remain elusive, I'm beginning to somehow feel them. Like, up on this enormous tree, they're just… there, somehow."

"I've been having the same feeling," Alaia said. "It's like getting goosebumps out of nowhere. It's disconcerting."

"*Kharalvshoth* we name in Miscamish," Givra said. "Means when walk into spider's web." She mimed wiping invisible silk off her arms.

"Is it any different when you are in your half-form?" Balstei asked Sterjall.

"Somewhat. It's more... cohesive? With just the mask, the threads feel separate from my other senses. As a wolf, it's like they all merge into a compound sensation."

"I can't wait to see what you see, kid," Jiara said. "But that witless bear remains elusive to me. I know I have her in me, but it's just like those threads—they are right there, but I can't really grab onto them."

"If the effect has now settled into your bodies," Sunu said, "Sunu will begin a short lesson."

They nodded to the shaman.

"Sunu would like to speak of the terrain our feet and paws will soon cast their prints upon," they began, pulling out the rough-sketched map. "Our first destination, *olvet vermio hurg*, is named Wuhir Peak. The name combines Miscamish with a Common noun that translates to *trod*. *Hir* means *leaf*, and *wu* extracts its essence. So *Wuhir Trod* becomes *Leafy Peak*. If Noss had granted the peak yet more leaves, *Mahuhir* would its name be, or *Dunhir* if Noss's wishes had been for it to be leafless. But Sunu's scalp guesses that Noss knew exactly how many leaves the peak was meant to have, and that it has neither one leaf more, nor one leaf fewer."

"It should take us about a day to get to Wuhir Peak," Balstei interjected. "There are gorgeous views from the top."

"That gives me an idea," Sterjall said, looking at Sunu. "We have a friend in Zovaria, Crysta, who I'd like to send a message to. If you were to send Olo to her, could she send a message back?"

"She could. Sunu can help you write instructions in the letter. But Zovaria is far, from what this map shows. Olo could get lost, unable to find us when he returns if we are not in the same place as before."

"I have an idea for that. Let me think this through, and we can focus on the details later."

After the language lesson concluded, as the combat lessons were about to begin, Sterjall asked if he could attempt a new move he'd been thinking of trying.

"Try any move you wish," Sunu said.

The wolf picked up a dagger-length stick. "Jiara, can I try this with you? I want to know how it feels to someone with a mask."

"Sure, kid," she said through a chuckle. "But you can use your real dagger."

"Let me try it this way first. Just try to block my attack."

Jiara unsheathed her short sword and readied herself.

Sterjall held the stick point down and rushed in a quick attack. Jiara masterfully disabled him, feeling embarrassed by how easy it was to anticipate his moves.

"Let's try that again," Sterjall said. Before striking, he took in a deep breath, willing more than just air to flow into his body. He clenched his muscles and tucked his threads inward, feeling Jiara's intention to block. He slid forward and twisted around the ball of his footpaw, twirling around her and slamming the blunt stick on her waist as he did so.

"What in the cuntvoids was that?" she asked. "Urnaadisilv... it did... I wasn't able to predict that move. What did you do?"

"It's something Kulak taught me."

"I taught when?" Kulak asked in surprise, being the least experienced with any type of blade.

"Yesterday, when we were... looking for Nelv. You taught me to hide my own threads. I was thinking, if Jiara can't see them, she can't predict how I'll attack."

"Sunu, too, was confused," Sunu said. "Sunu has learned to see, not in the same way you see, Lago-Sterjall, but perhaps in a similar way. Sunu did not predict your motion. You must teach Sunu now, teach us all."

The wall of vines was at a stone's throw away when the company dismounted the smilodons and began to tread with caution, seeming fearful of the looming ends of their land.

"Other than Khuron Kulak, none of us Laatu have been this close to the vines before," Sunu said, although that was not entirely true—Givra had broken that rule as a teenager and had even touched the wall on a dare once.

"Scalps tingle with unease," Hod Abjus said.

"What if vines close, die inside?" Kenondok asked.

"There's nothing to fear," Sterjall said, feeling odd at seeing two brawny men showing fear so openly. "We'll make sure the vines stay open."

They set up to cook a late lunch before venturing through the wall. Sunu struck their brime cube, releasing a torrent of sparks on a bundle of birch bark. Givra was seasoning munnji cakes, while Balstei and Jiara discussed possible routes over the map. Kulak was having a quiet conversation with Kenondok and Abjus.

Sterjall meandered off to ponder without interruptions. He shapeshifted back to Lago in order to better feel the cold moisture over his skin and attached the mask over his right shoulder. He shuffled his feet over the pebbles of a gurgling creek, keeping the toecaps of his sliding shoes open, like sandals. His eyes followed the paths of leaves in the water and of the silvery fish that swam beneath the surface.

"Hey, catch," Alaia said, having snuck up behind him. She tossed him what looked like a pebble of pure light.

Lago caught it—it was an arudinn bulb, still glowing. "It's hot!" he exclaimed, feeling it burn his hands like a bean that had just finished cooking. It soon cooled, and as it did, the light faded. "Maybe you shouldn't pluck these," he warned, squishing the bulb until it popped, producing one last flash of light. "They are sacred, or whatever."

"You are probably right," she said. She checked around her; there was no one but the constellation of arudinn on the wall and the silvery fish by their feet to keep them company. "So, how was it?" she finally asked.

Lago couldn't help but smile. "It was truly magnificent, never seen anything like it. And what were you thinking? Setting me up like that."

"You did something nice for my birthday, and I thought I'd return the favor. Aio was telling me about these fireflies, and I thought you'd enjoy seeing them."

"You would have, too. Why didn't you come?"

"I didn't wanna intrude between you two, I already interrupted you once. We won't get much privacy the rest of the way."

Lago sighed.

"So? What happened?" she inquired, leaning in.

"After we found Nelv, he took me to this overlook. He wouldn't say what he was planning, but asked that we lean back on Blu's belly and wait. And as the trunk went dark, they all came out, as many fireflies as the lanterns we saw during the Solstice. They lit up the entire glade. It was so wonderful…"

He paused for much too long, his wide smile fading.

"And?" she prompted.

"And… it happened again. He kissed me. He was much rougher this time, but he defused the whole thing with a joke and a dare for me to take the next step. He knows I'm afraid, and it almost feels as if he enjoys that. I think he should be more afraid, too."

"What do you plan to do?"

"Like you said, there won't be much privacy, so I better stay out of trouble, especially with Abjus around. But I do like Aio, I think."

"You think?"

Lago half nodded, half shook his head, watching the creek flow.

"I… It's complicated," he said. "I don't really want to talk about it."

The silvery fish kept swimming against the current.

Lago felt a disconcerting breeze blowing through the vines, as if the dome itself was breathing. The cold air carried particles of silt and pollen that made him smell distant lands. His mind drifted away then, as if he was back in the mountains.

Chapter Thirty-Four

Banook's Guest

Banook trudged solemnly in his lonesome procession. He had felt himself age and weaken as he left the mountains, and even more so as his friends left him, but now that he was back among bearkind, he had returned to his former self, although the vibrant and joyous vitality of his steps was missing.

It took him a long time to arrive back at his cabin. It had been over a month since he—since they—had left.

Bear was beyond delighted upon seeing Banook return. The dog jumped and licked and yipped with joy, though he kept searching for Lago and the others and soon lost his energy, cocking his head in confusion. Sabikh and Frud, the bear mother and cub, were there too; Banook thanked them for taking care of Bear during his absence.

During the following months, Banook focused on upgrading his cabin and on spending time alone in distant lands, though he was never entirely alone now, because Bear followed by his heels wherever he went. Banook was glad for the company of the silly mutt, but his heart still ached for Lago-Sterjall.

On the twenty-sixth day of Highsun, Banook took a stroll to Unemar Lake, and from there followed the trail up Drann Trodesh. He climbed up the middle of the five peaks and found the spot where he and Lago had first held hands on a moonlit night seemingly ages ago. Back then, Banook had been too cowardly to express his true feelings for Lago, and he was now feeling remorseful for not following the path his heart had told him was the right one for him.

"I should've made the best out of the short time Lago and I had," he said to no one, but Bear was there to listen.

He had chosen to hike to Unemar Lake that night because it was Lago's nineteenth birthday, and he needed the space to ponder.

"I hope Lago will be thinking of the mountains at this very moment," he said as he watched the last glow of Sunnokh fading in the west. He then began to quietly sing:

> I hope he knows that we can be together all along
>
> When far apart he thinks of me and hears the mountain song.

He reached down to pet Bear's head, who was a curled bundle of brown and white next to Banook's thick thighs. The dog's ears suddenly perked up, then his head rose.

"What's the matter, silly Bear?" Banook asked him.

Rrrouwwff, Bear replied. His head tilted to one side, flopping one of his ears.

Banook lifted his weight from the rocks. As he stood, he felt the hopeful rays of Sceres on him, leading his gaze eastward. He was struck by the radiance of the moon's Sulphur fullness, who was ascending proudly over the Stelm Khull, shining more amber than yellow. She was flattened, melting her edges on the mountain range like thick syrup, reflecting onto the tributaries that fed the Stiss Khull. The creeks looked like golden snakes chasing after a purple twilight.

Far in the distance, Banook heard a muted howl.

"Oh, I hear what your sharp ears caught. It's all swell, it's just Lago's friends serenading Sceres, for she is looking sweet as honey right now. And how come *you* never howl?"

Grrwuff, Bear answered, then jumped atop the rocks to scour the distance.

More howls joined the nocturnal chant; some closer, some immeasurably farther. From the nearest of the five peaks, a louder call resounded into the mountainy crags, sadder yet sweeter, full of sorrow, yearning, and hope.

Banook jumped up in recognition, and excitedly exclaimed, "I know this voice! Could it be? Truly?"

He climbed onto the rocks next to Bear and howled loud as a typhoon. Bear stared at him in distressed bewilderment, taking several steps back. Banook howled again, and from the nearby peak, he heard the reply. It wasn't a song to Sceres this time, but a response directed at him, loud and clear.

"Let's go, boy, my old friend is back!"

Their moonlit hike was punctuated by stops to howl and find their bearings. Once they reached the next summit, they stopped at the glorious sight that awaited there, that of a proud tundra wolf. She waited, motionless except for her flowing fur, which glistened like topaz under the yellow moonlight.

"Safis!" Banook cried, then rushed to embrace her. The canid Nu'irg let him—despite the indignity of it all—because she had also missed him, as she had missed all of her Nu'irgesh family.

Banook placed the wolf down with a smile as full as the moon, and from deep within his soul he mindspoke tender words to her. «My beautiful white lady,» he communicated in a language older than the snowmelt of the first mountains, «how wonderful to gaze upon your golden eyes!»

«Long has it been, Kerjaastórgnem of the ursids,» she expressed with a thought. «Long as the glacial epochs that carved these mountains.»

Although the qualia of ursids and canid consciousnesses differed, their bonds ran deeper in the ways that mattered most, allowing Nu'irgesh from disparate clades to mindspeak with one another. But Bear was lost with no translations.

"Apologies, Bear," Banook said out loud. "This is my old friend, Safis. And Safis, this is Bear."

Bear had recognized the white wolf's scent and approached excitedly to greet her, but Safis gave him a displeased look followed by a single, deep growl that put him in his place; she had suffered enough indignities for one night. Bear hid behind Banook with his tail between his legs.

"My lady of tundra and meadows," Banook said both aloud and in mindspeech, so that Bear would not feel excluded, "I heard you met a friend of mine, by the name of Lago."

Safis cocked her head in recognition. «That name is one I've heard before,» she communicated. «It was spoken by humans who helped me escape Agnargdrolom. That is what they called the boy wielding the Miscam mask.»

With her wordless words, Safis had expressed more than just meanings, but also images, smells, and sounds. For a moment, Banook could hear Lago's laughter and smell the sweetness of his curls.

"That is him," Banook replied, choking up a bit. "And he is not just any friend." He shook the melancholy off and smiled. "Come with me, graceful lady, there is much we need to discuss. And you should see the home I've built for myself and my dear guests!"

During the two days it took for them to walk to the cabin, they mindspoke at length about all that they had experienced since the closing of the domes and the advent of the Downfall. Long were their stories, filled with tragedy, joy, and longing. They both understood that uncertain times loomed ahead, and that a lot was at peril: for the Nu'irgesh, for the wild animals, for the humans, and for the planet themself.

"You said the Anglass Dome looks different?" Banook asked the wolf. The three were sitting out on the cabin's terrace, watching Sunnokh's last rays caress the snow-covered top of the dome. "It is looking the same as always to me."

«The vines are turning unruly, more gnarled,» she explained. «Like Agnargdrolom's vines before its demise began.» She had spent months around the periphery of the Anglass Dome, searching for the few dire wolves who had escaped the Heartpine Dome, and during that time had noticed the subtle change. «I fear wrongness within Urgdrolom. I fear its end, like the end that came to my lands.»

Banook nervously combed his beard. "Dire news you bring, Safis," he said. "If Anglass suffers the same fate as Heartpine, it could come down crashing on all the creatures still within."

Safis agreed by saying nothing.

"I think this is important information that Lago should know," Banook said, "and though I cannot leave these mountains, I have thought of a way to get the message to reach him."

He stood up decisively. "Come now, both of you. Off we go before too late."

Bear straightened up next to him, uncertain of where they were going or why, but ready for their next adventure.

Part Three
MEMORY

Chapter Thirty-Five

Over the Ophidian

It took the Red Stag's forces several weeks to reach the port of Khoomalith. They had traveled sluggishly due to the enormous sizes of their legions, but they were well supplied, and the inexhaustible mounts helped provide transport as well as plentiful meat.

Merchant vessels had been repurposed to carry his army across. The Red Stag directed six of his mindlocked megaloceroses to climb the reinforced ramps, ordered them to stay put, then boarded his flagship, the *Black Spear*.

"Those were the last of them," he said to his private guard of arbalisters and Silv-Thaar Valaran, who had followed him aboard.

"The fleet is ready to sail," Fjorna said.

The Red Stag subtly tipped down his red-streaked antlers. "Inform the captain we are to depart at once."

War galleys and dromons from the navy, joined by galleys and crayers from the salt and potash mines, began to sail across the narrow sea, keels dipping heavily from the legions of cervids and humans. More troops had made it across during the previous days, gathering in Kayamur and Montano, both important trade cities in the only state of the Negian Empire located in the Jerjan Continent.

The Red Stag felt a flutter of green at the edge of his vision—a jade stealer, landing on Aurélien Knivlar's shoulder, green wings contrasting against the shaman's red hair.

"Islav brings a message for you, Monarch Hallow," Aurélien said, retrieving a tightly rolled letter from the herald's harness.

"But we just heard from Urcai this morning," he replied, taking the paper and unrolling it with his hoofed fingertips.

"Not from Viceroy Urcai, but from General Behler Broadleaf of the Fifth Legion," Aurélien said. "Aness I sent to Urcai, but Islav I sent across the sea."

Silv-Thaar Valaran swished his striped tail nearby, anxious to hear the news. His pet marten poked out from his collar, also staring curiously at the Red Stag.

The Red Stag turned toward Valaran. "Good," he said. "Broadleaf has already reached the Brinelaar mines. He is unloading pipe segments by our planned entry point, and once done, he'll send a few platoons northeast, to Duajash."

"Whatever for?" Valaran asked. "That's on the Bayani coast."

"It was Shea's idea," Fjorna answered. "She's coordinating an attack with the admirals. It's merely a distraction to draw the Bayani out. They know we are coming, but they have no clue what's really coming to them, or from where."

"But it's suicidal," Valaran said. "Why would Shea—"

"She knows what she's doing," Fjorna said. "She's leading the fleet to strike from a distance. By land, Broadleaf's platoons will likely not survive, but the fleet should suffer few casualties."

The Red Stag finished reading the missive, rolled up the paper, and pocketed it with a smile. "There's more news here you might be interested in," he said to Valaran, but did not elaborate.

"Good or bad?" Valaran asked, unable to discern the Red Stag's mood or intentions. "You are hiding yourself again, so I can't tell."

The elk chuckled, having made himself fully unreadable. He had recently discovered how he could pull his threads inward to make them imperceptible to others. The skill presented itself naturally to those who wore the Silvesh, as an instinct that surfaced the more they learned to control the threads.

"You will find out soon," the Red Stag said. "It has to do with Broadleaf. Once we dock, you'll see."

The legions disembarked and marched over the wide road from Montano to Brinelaar, arriving at the entrance to the salt mines, where rows of wagons loaded with giant pipe segments waited. For the Negians, the pipeline was the way of the future. It still created a bottleneck, but as long as they marched unnoticed, they could assemble inside the Bighorn Dome in the tens of thousands before mobilizing their attacks.

A snub-nosed man waved at the arriving group.

"General Broadleaf," the Red Stag said, shaking the general's armored arm, "I must thank you for bringing these heavy pipes across so many miles."

"These are not the ones I brought, Monarch Hallow, but the ones cast and fired at Caerlye. Brand new. The ones I carried are already by the wall." He peered over the Red Stag's shoulder, then shook arms with the raccoon. "Armsmaster Crescu Valaran. Last time I saw you, you were clean-shaven."

"It's Silv-Thaar Valaran now," he replied. "But it's nice to see you again, General Broadleaf."

"Indeed, a pleasure. And there's something you should see, Silv-Thaar Valaran. Come and I'll show you." Broadleaf ordered the Oldrin slaves to pull open the enormous gates marking the entrance to the mines. "The mines are not operational right now," he explained as the gates screeched on their rails. "Most miners have been reassigned to work on the pipes, north of here. We already have enough segments to make it into the dome, but we'll need additional ones to make it out the other end."

"What a surprise that will be for the Bayani," the Red Stag said. "An army cutting straight through to take On Khurderen from behind. They will stand no chance."

They marched through the ample portal, feeling a dry breeze that carried a briny scent. Weapon racks were lined up at the sides of the shaft; wagons weighed down by salt blocks lay immobile in the side tunnels, waiting for operations to restart.

The Red Stag gazed at the huge tunnel carved through pink salt, which was wide enough to fit three of his megaloceroses abreast, antlers and all. "It's a bit of an irony," he mused, "that such a strong mining force could have also been used to dig under the Bighorn Dome the old-fashioned way. Although that gutless Emperor Uvon would've never approved such an expense."

Guttural growls echoed in the depths, as if the shafts were haunted by rabid wraiths. As they got nearer the source, the flames from the hanging lanterns revealed a row of wheeled cages, each holding a bear-sized wolverine; all of them had their limbs bound by thick ropes. The presence of Krostsilv seemed to douse their wrath—they quieted and stared, perhaps with hope, more likely with fear.

"A present, from the Fifth Legion to the Third," Broadleaf said, lightly bowing toward Silv-Thaar Valaran.

"Jarv wolverines..." Valaran mumbled. "How did you—"

"A scouting squad found them hiding in a cave in the Lequa Dome. I ordered they be captured alive, for you. I lost a handful of good soldiers fetching them."

"Thank you, General," Valaran said, stepping close enough to touch one of the cages, but still keeping his hands at a safe distance. "But why tie them up if they are already caged?"

"We had to bind them after the last one escaped," Broadleaf explained. "They aren't strong enough to break through the magsteel bars, but they are too smart—one threw his weight against it and sent the wagon down a cliff, and another seemed to be trying to pick the lock with a stick."

"We'll need their aid once inside the Bighorn Dome," the Red Stag said. "Valaran, you better stay here and practice with them. The sooner we can have them out of their cages, the better."

Crescu Valaran paced around a spacious room where the walls were decorated with too many head trophies from thick-horned caprids. He'd been housed in a mansion from a wealthy mine owner for his short stay in Brinelaar, and he'd been unable to fall asleep—the flames from the fireplace reflecting on all the glassy eyes were making him nervous.

A knock on the door.

He quickly reached for his mask, put it on, and took his half-form before answering.

"Fjorna," he said after cracking open the door. "It's a bit late."

"May I?" she asked, showing him the bottle of aged braaw she was holding.

Valaran let her in and locked the door behind her.

"I see they put you in the fancy room," Fjorna noted, admiring the decor with a crooked, half-dangling smile on the broken half of her face. "They placed the rest of us in the servants' room," she added, although her tone did not betray any disappointment; it was just an observation. She uncorked the bottle and poured the fizzy drink into two brass goblets.

"I'd rather be in the bunks than with these horned monsters for company," Valaran said, taking a goblet and dropping into a fur-upholstered armchair. He stood up again awkwardly, moved his tail out of the way, and sat back down.

"You don't need to fake it in front of me," Fjorna said, taking the armchair in front of him. "I know you don't like to wear it at night. Until you have those creatures under your control, there's no need for you to force it."

Valaran tensed up, but then quickly relaxed. He shapeshifted back to his human self and placed the mask on a side table. "I just don't know when that's going to happen," he admitted. "I tried for hours tonight. I can mindspeak with the fuckers, even if they don't want to say much to me. But when I finally take them under my control and try to issue orders, I lose them."

"I've been talking to Aurélien about this. It's similar to how she handles her heralds. She says she sometimes feels their tiredness, or hunger, and her own body pains with theirs. But she's learned to not push the pain aside, but to find a way to understand it."

"I know... but it's more than hunger. Those caged wolverines are suffering like you could not comprehend. It just... snaps me out. And Hallow... I think he feeds on the pain of his cervids, he enjoys it, so it's easier for him."

Fjorna leaned back in her armchair and crossed her legs, then abruptly hopped out of her seat, spilling her drink as she felt something wriggle behind her back. "The fuck is that?" she cried. On her backrest was the yellow-throated marten, who called with a shrill yowl.

"It's just Dishu," Crescu said calmly.

"You gave it a name?"

"Her. She's friendly. She tolerates me even when I'm not wearing the mask." He clicked his tongue; the marten hopped onto his arm and hid in his sleeve. "But anyway, I almost got it figured out, the rest will come with practice. But you aren't here to talk about wolverines or martens, are you?"

Fjorna paced toward the wall of trophies and stared upward. The mounted head of a gold-furred takin stared back. "I'm concerned about where we're headed," she murmured.

"The Bighorn Dome?"

"No, not that. Not us. The Empire as a whole. Did you notice the enmity of the citizens as we rode from Montano to here?"

"To be frank, I don't get to speak much with the common folk nowadays."

"Figures," Fjorna said. She took out her white-hilted dagger and began to clean her nails with it. "This state is proud of their exports. Salt, potash—they are a major economic power. They do not like being told to halt their work to make pipes that could bring potential wars to their lands. It's not just them who suffer, but all the farms across the Ophidian."

"But the war effort comes first," Crescu said. "They have to think of the long-term benefits."

"I do agree that taking the domes is most important. Yet the way Monarch Hallow goes about doing it is making his subjects lose trust in him."

Crescu shook his head. "Viceroy Urcai is shrewd. He is the one who recommended this move with the mines. He wouldn't have done so unless he had a good strategy."

"Perhaps he does," Fjorna said, resting her elbows on the back of her chair. "I think Urcai planned this too well. Once Monarch Hallow returns from this war, if he does not hold the support of the head ministers, it could start a war of its own. And if Hallow dies, it would be Urcai to take the throne. At least until his heir comes of age."

"I think you are reading too much into it," Crescu said. He stood and poured himself another drink. "Hallow is the only hope this wretched empire has left. Uvon left us in ruins. If it wasn't for Hallow's initiative, the states would've quickly seceded or joined our enemies."

"I'm not disagreeing with you, Crescu." She turned and walked toward the door. "Just don't forget the reason why we are fighting. It's not for the masks, it's not to conquer lands beyond—those goals are merely incidental. We fight to make our land thrive again, to bring prosperity back to the citizens who took us in, fed us, trained us, and made us who we are today. I was nothing when Father died, when I sailed away from Fjarmallen. You were nothing when the Bergsulfi abandoned you in that burning village. The Negian Empire birthed us anew. It will outlive us, outlive the Red Stag, and we will always have a duty toward it."

"I get it, I get it. But just what are you asking me to do?"

Fjorna cracked the door open, then stood there facing away from him. "I don't know. Just don't forget about us, we are still your family."

"Even Shea and Osef?"

Fjorna turned. "They love you as well, but they are confused. Show them you are still with us, and they'll see reason. Now get some rest, and take a bath—that worm you carry in your sleeves is rubbing her musk on you."

She closed the door, leaving Crescu with a half-empty goblet in his hands.

Chapter Thirty-Six

Lorr of Wings

Dusk was nigh when the company began their journey through the vines, meaning that dawn would soon arrive in the outside world. Although their plan was to travel at night as much as possible, they needed light to find their bearings before venturing too far.

As they traversed through the wall, Sterjall and Jiara noticed their skills had increased, allowing them to make larger openings. Still, Kulak's adeptness surpassed theirs, and he was able to control the vines better than the two of them combined.

"We are almost there," Jiara said. "I can see trees past this last cluster of vines."

"Hold here a moment," Sterjall said, pulling out Leif. He aimed the senstregalv blade and scanned through the vines, seeing farther than Jiara or Kulak could. "Looks safe," he said. "Just trees, ferns, squirrels, and birds."

"What kind of birds?" Alaia asked.

"Focus."

Despite the enveloping darkness, a warm light filtered through as they exited among dark-leafed alders and papery birches. All the Laatu tried to catch glimpses of the colored sky but could only see dappled patches of it.

"Over here!" Alaia called. "Climb up, there's a clear view!"

They scrambled up a balding hillock, and from its top the Laatu gasped, their faces reflecting their fear and delight. Their hearts stammered when they saw the ember-red clouds that burned ominously in the east. The sky above was already a blue more intense than they'd ever seen, and it mixed with magenta and yellow hues that defied reason.

"What you are about to see is called a sunrise," Jiara said to reassure them. "Don't be afraid, it's just Sunnokh awakening."

"*Ve nokh uth ëovad*," Sunu whispered with wonderment in their eyes, marveling at the dome of fire that enveloped them. Olo looked up as well, sharply cocking his head.

Sunnokh suddenly made himself visible, and in a flaring streak lit up all their faces. Kenondok fell to his knees, struck by spears of yellow light.

"Don't look at him directly!" Sterjall warned a bit too late, then in Miscamish called, "*Grei evelithuk uanfill olv te wast ust Sunnokh!*"

The command made the Laatu avert their gazes, but afterimages still burned their supplicating eyes.

"I see his face, no matter where!" Kenondok said, turning his head around, trying to avoid the stare of the star.

"You will be fine," Jiara said, placing a hand on Kenondok's ridged scalp. "His image will go away soon. Just don't look at him again, or he could burn your eyes."

"My eyes wish to watch him forever," Givra muttered, trying but failing to close her eyes.

Hod Abjus had no words, but his expression was that of a prayer cast in the winds.

The Laatu soon regained their sight, but they could not be prevented from sneaking a furtive glance or two toward Sunnokh. Sterjall could not blame them; he, too, had missed the sun.

While the others recovered from their daze, Sterjall, Alaia, Balstei, and Jiara studied the landscape.

"All of this is the Karst Forest," Balstei said. "It should provide ample shelter all the way to the Nightlure Cliffs. After that, the Moonbow Timberlands should keep us hidden until we arrive at the edge of the scablands."

The forest spread southeast from the dome's wall, pinching up into a green peak that seemed nearly a mile high and about twenty miles away.

"That's Wuhir Peak," Balstei said. "From there, we'll be able to scout our path."

"Hey, Sunu," Sterjall said, tapping on their shoulder. "Do you think Olo is ready? This would be the best place to send the letter from." He produced the tightly rolled paper from his pocket.

Sunu snapped out of their daydream, eyes still aglow. "Yes," they answered, looking up toward Olo, who had been floating about in the warming air currents. "Olo is well rested, eager."

"Remember the instructions?"

"Woman with auburn hair. Find her by the window of tallest, gold-tipped tower at the pink city."

"Exactly. The pink city will be easy for Olo to spot from the air," Sterjall said. "Make sure Olo gives the message only to the woman with auburn hair. No one else. And have him meet us there"—he pointed to Wuhir Peak—"tomorrow at dawn, at the top of the green mountain."

Sunu nodded and called for Olo; the jay perched on their left hand.

Sunu stuffed the letter in the pocket of Olo's tiny harness, then sifted through the multiple pendants on their necklaces: there were vials of unguents, herbs, and colorful powders, as well as the octahedral arambukh that they used as a money stamp—theirs was a fire opal. They popped open a pendant that seemed like a walnut rimmed with copper and lifted the pod to their nose. They inhaled sharply.

Sunu's eyes went dark, both empty and full at the same time, while their freckled breasts flushed with blood. They moved Olo close to their lips and seemed to talk, though no sounds came from their mouth. Then they lifted Olo above their purple-pigmented head and intoned, "*Va jambradikh frulv henet alrull.*"

Olo flew like an arrow, searching for the pink beacon.

Crysta clinked her nails on her teacup as she waited. She was expecting a message from Withervale that day, but Esum had kept in touch inconsistently and at unknowable intervals, forcing Crysta to spend most of her time here in the tower. She and Scholar Dashal had been taking turns in case a sunnograph transmission was received, for the messages often needed to be replied to immediately.

Esum was among the monks spared during the battle, but she was only spared to help the Negians with processing soot. She had more covert jobs, however, and conspired with three spies who reported to her. The first was an innocent-looking Oldrin named Mellorie, who made high-purity coal deliveries for the monastery to refine. The second was a Negian soldier named Maitane, who was stationed to guard the monastery's gate; originally of

Tharman blood, Maitane had always opposed the war and hated having been drafted. The third was a ranger named Ardof, who was not in Withervale, but traveled between Brimstowne and Anglass. Once he gathered enough gossip, Ardof would hike all the way up Mount Fogra to deliver messages directly to the scholar operating the Wujann Observatory's sunnograph. Ardof provided the most critical information to Esum and to Zovaria as a whole, but his deliveries took months at a time, as there were long hikes involved.

Luckily, the Negians had not found out about the Zovarians' method of communicating with light. A lot of information was being exchanged, practically every day, as long as the sun was shining. Esum—who had hidden the sunnograph before the Negians reached the mesa—waited until the monastery grounds were cleared before taking the device out to the Haven's balcony, from where she could use it without being seen. Maitane helped keep the operation safe, guarding the entrance to the monastery at the end of Runestone Lane. If Maitane held her poleaxe in her right hand, a monk on the Haven's second floor would cough three times, and another monk would run to the opposite end of the cloister to tell Esum to hurry and send a message. If Maitane switched her poleaxe to her left hand, any transmissions had to be stopped at once. Due to the high elevation of the mesa, no one outside of the monastery would ever notice the little blinking light shining from the distant Wujann Observatory.

But maybe they got into trouble, Crysta thought. *How would I know if they did?* She sipped her cold tea. She had no way to heat water in the room, and taking the spiral staircase and walking all the way to that dreadful kitchen full of parroting scholars was out of the question. Dashal would bring her lunch soon, and with it, hopefully, a fresh pot of tea as well.

It was sunny out that Summer afternoon; messages could arrive at any moment. She sat by the northern window, keeping an eye out for blinking lights from the Nedross Observatory, the one that received the signals from Wujann. As she stared across the Isdinnklad, a strange bird fluttered by and landed right on the western windowsill, staring at her with beady, dark-red eyes. It was a gorgeous bird; Crysta had never seen one like it. She slowly reached for a notepad and pencil to take notes. She figured that Hefra Boarmane, her old naturalist friend, would be very interested in hearing the details of this peculiar species. She hurriedly scribbled down:

Dark blue. Black head and chest. Fancy cap, sky blue with white edge. Reddish eyes? Dark legs and bill. Foot long or so, corvid? Jay? Friendly. Odd brown feathers on back. Or missing feathers?

She stopped and stared. The brown wasn't feathers, but some sort of harness wrapped around the bird's body, with a little pouch tied to the back. The bird emitted a shrilling *eihnk-eihnk* and hopped into the room, right onto Crysta's desk. The professor reached toward the bird, confounded, as she had never seen birds other than magpies or cormorants used as heralds, and never with a harness as ornate as this one. The bird did not flinch as Crysta untied the red thread that held the pouch closed. She removed a rolled piece of paper, then hastily read:

> Crysta, this is Lago. No, I did not turn into a bird. I mean it's Lago writing this letter. Before you do anything else, immediately speak these words out loud to Olo, the jay delivering this message: "*Diathuk frulv oset enue, Lorrdrolvesh.*" Do not wait, do not hesitate, do it now and read the rest of this message after.

Crysta read the words in her head a few times, making sure she understood the pronunciation, and then, in a very self-conscious manner, she said to Olo, "*Diathuk frulv oset enue, Lorrdrolvesh.*"

Olo cocked his head so that one eye peered directly at her, responded with *eihnk-eihnk-eihnk*, and stood there, examining the room in quick head motions.

Crysta unrolled the letter again and continued reading:

> Next thing: give him some food, preferably seeds or berries, but I guess bread will do, too. Don't wait, Olo will be hungry. This is important, do it right away.

What in the Six Gates is this? What am I doing? she thought, feeling like the target of a prank. She had no berries or nuts, but had a piece of stale fig pastry on her desk. *I hope this is enough.* She placed the porcelain plate next to Olo, who began to peck at the sweet crumbs. She read on:

> After you've done those things, you can be certain that Olo will not fly away from you, as long as you keep feeding him. He'll only leave after six hours have passed, or once you say some special words. More on that later. Now, please close the door, lock it, and don't let anyone come in until you're done with this letter.

"When will this end?" she grumbled out loud. There was no door to the top of the tower—the only door was at the very bottom. She let out an exasperated sigh, then hurried down the long spiral staircase and locked the door before dragging herself all the way back up. She dropped to her seat in a sweat to finally read the rest of the letter:

> First, sorry that we had to leave in a hurry, again. Balstei helped us escape. We made it out of Zovaria, and we have the X. Kedra betrayed us. She thought the X would be in better hands with the Zovarian Union. Kedra brought her uncle, Admiral Grinn, to search Balstei's lab while we were away (be wary of Admiral Grinn: Balstei bashed his head in with a microscope, stole his sword, then locked him in his lab. He's likely not in a good mood). I'm sure Grinn must've interrogated you and Gwil by now, but Kedra told him everything already, so there's no point in lying if he comes to you.
>
> I cannot give you any information about us, in case someone else gets a hold of this letter, but I want you to know we are all safe. Safe, but could still be in trouble. We need you to send a letter back to us describing all you know about the Red Stag's army. Have they made any moves to strike the Union since we vanished? How did Withervale fare? Also, it'd be most useful to know anything about the Zovarian troops searching for us. You know what we are after; you know what will be most useful.
>
> If it's safe to do so, send our love to Gwil. We may contact you this way again, but will not write the instructions on how to deal with Olo, just to be safe. Memorize them before you burn this letter.
>
> You have up to six hours to write down the information you want to send us, then Olo will fly back. If you are done before then, place your letter in his pouch, say the words, "*Va jambradikh frulv henet alrull,*" and Olo will return to us.
>
> At the end of your letter and any future ones, write the name of the song you once sang to me that night. You know the one. If you write any of your responses under duress, skip that, or write the wrong song name, and I'll know you are in trouble.
>
> Balstei, Alaia, Jiara, and I miss you a lot. Please stay safe.
> Love,
> - Lago-Sterjall

Crysta covered her face and rubbed her temples. *Just what have you gotten yourselves into?* she thought. First things first, she had to memorize the instructions Lago had provided. She reread the letter five times, then picked up a Miscamish dictionary, figuring that knowing the meaning of the words would help her memorize them.

Diath means... wait... Hmm. Lorr is quite obvious, and this... is a possessive determiner. Wait for their, no, my... Wait for my word, Lorrwing? Lorr of Wings, perhaps? She memorized the first sentence, repeating it in her head over and over. She then worked on the next one, careful not to speak even a single one of the Miscamish words out loud. *A tailwind for your journey,* she concluded after some work, satisfied with her translation.

A bell rang right by her face, making her scramble and nearly hurl the paper out the window—someone was downstairs tugging on the bell pull. *Scholar Dashal is back already.* She trusted Dashal with certain things, but not with everything. She could not place her friends in jeopardy again; it had been her trust in Kedra that had landed them all in trouble. She was afraid to burn the letter just yet, in case she forgot the words, so she tucked it in her blouse before heading down.

She unlocked the door and cracked it open.

"Why did you lock the door?" Dashal asked, holding a tray with a pot of tea and a pear salad. Crysta awkwardly took the tray from him with one hand while holding the door with the other.

"Can I come—"

"Thank you, I can take this. Sorry, I'm having a hard time focusing today. Do you mind if I—"

"But I'm supposed to take the next shift."

"I just have to finish this one message. I have such a foul headache and haven't been able to focus."

"I can do it for you—"

"It's okay, I'll take care of it," she said, closing the door and locking it again.

"You are the lousiest liar, you know?" the muffled voice said behind the door.

"It's... um... It's a woman's thing."

"Oh, sorry, I didn't mean to..." the voice mumbled.

"Thank you for lunch, and for the tea," she said, already hurrying back upstairs. She'd think of a better excuse later.

Lago said I have six hours, she thought, reaching the top of the tower. *Maybe I could lock the bird in to get more time.* She looked at Olo and pondered, then thought better of it. *Either way, Brenna will be around tonight to use her shitty little telescope.* She didn't like Brenna, who took the evening shift to observe wisps on the Moordusk Dome. Brenna didn't like her either; she'd make a scandal about the door being locked.

Crysta leaned over the desk, wolfing down her lunch while jotting down information she thought might be helpful to Lago. She plucked the walnuts from her salad and gave them to Olo, who enjoyed breaking them apart with his highly utilitarian beak.

She remembered the letter in her blouse. She reread it ten more times, made sure she had it memorized, then burned it.

She had plenty of firsthand information about Withervale and the Negian forces, but not much about the Zovarians who were after Lago. She'd have to find that out fast. She closed the tower's windows in case Olo decided to fly away, left him water and a few breadcrumbs she found on the floor, then walked out of the tower, locking the door behind her.

She didn't know what to do or where to go for information, so she went to the only person she could fully trust: Gwil. She found him at the Gaalem Monastery, which she visited often to share news about the monks in Withervale. Gwil welcomed her and took her to a private study room.

Crysta told him all she could, though in a hurry, as she had to be back that evening or Brenna would call the dean to unlock the door. Once she was done relating the story of her avian visitor, she said, "Oh Gwil, what do I do? I don't have much to tell them, at least not about the people chasing after them."

"Maybe... hmm... This might be dangerous to try, but I know an ex-monk who enlisted in the navy. I greet him whenever I pick up fresh fish at the wharf. But just by asking him, we might risk getting both of us sent back to Admiral Grinn, and perhaps to the gallows this time."

He thought for a short while, then continued, "I'll tell you what. Let's go there together, right now. If he's there, I'll tell him the people we are trying to protect are the ones who saved me and almost died trying to save Khopto, who was a good friend of his. I'll ask you to watch from a safe location. If I put my hood on, it means he's not cooperating and will turn me in to Admiral Grinn. If that happens, you run away to send what you can before your time is up. I won't mention your name, whether he cooperates or not. If he gives me any information, I'll walk away from the wharf, to meet you past the Finflayer Arch. We hurry into the Artisan's Esplanade and take the Cliffside Lifts from there."

Crysta agreed with the plan. They hastened to the wharf.

Crysta sat down at the Stranded Nautilus, ordered pink wine and a greasy appetizer, and watched as Gwil ambled around the wharf, searching for his friend. *We are wasting so much time,* she thought, but she had no better chance than this. When her deep-fried calamari finally arrived, she chomped it down;

the light lunch and her nerves had left her starved. By the time she looked back at Gwil, he was already talking to not just a lowly recruit, but a commander or captain or something; Crysta didn't know their ranks and titles, but the officer looked important with those ribbons on his bronze pauldrons. She waited with her toes curled in an uncomfortable position, ready to sneak away if Gwil put his hood up.

The sunlight was reddening in the west. *Hurry, Gwil, hurry,* she urged. *Sunnokh will soon set, and Brenna will show up at the tower and ruin everything.*

A hand landed on her shoulder. "Takh!" she yelped.

"More wine?" the waiter asked.

"I wasn't... Yes, fine. Thank you."

She clinked her nails on the refilled glass, listening to the passersby as if trying to pick up on clandestine whispers, but she could tell none of their conversations apart.

After a long while, she saw Gwil and his friend take a seat on a bench, with their backs to her. They seemed to be jotting something down. As she waited, Crysta thought about what to write, and how to best condense the information, as the letter could only be so big and her handwriting only so small.

She saw Gwil and the officer stand up, then perform the Havengall Congregation bow. She dropped a Hex on the table. *That should cover it,* she thought, then gulped down the rest of her wine and hurried out as sneakily as she could. She waited conspicuously past the crystal arch, behind the judgmental statues of Takhísh and Takhamún.

Gwil stepped through the portal, grabbed her arm, and strode quickly with her toward the Cliffside Lifts. He placed a piece of paper in her hands and let her read it as they walked.

"Thank you, Gwil," she said, tucking the paper away. "This might be helpful to them. I hope it's helpful to them."

"I think it might be," he said, "but I'm afraid there's not much more we can provide. Hurry now, Sunnokh is already setting. Write your letter and send that bird before too late."

He nearly shoved her into one of the lifts and closed the metal gate.

"Essence of one, soul of the many," he said, bowing deeply.

Crysta watched him recede as her lift climbed toward the Sixteenth Bulwark.

Chapter Thirty-Seven

Wuhir Peak

The snowcapped top of the Moordusk Dome burned orange, warmed by the first beam of direct sunlight. Sunnokh emerged from a hazy horizon, yawning through the glow of the morning's mists. The Laatu had seen a sunrise the previous day, yet still the spectacle filled their eyes with sparkling tears.

The company had traveled all night and had arrived at the top of Wuhir Peak just in time for Olo's return. Sunu screeched a shrill *eihnk-eihnk!* The sound was repeated like an echo from the firmament. They lifted a hand toward the fiery dome, and Olo flew down to perch on it.

"Poor thing must've been flying all night," Alaia said. She took out a handful of berries and let Olo pick his favorites.

"Sunu's eyes see a letter in the harness," Sunu said, pulling out a tiny roll of paper and handing it to Sterjall.

"It's very tightly rolled," Sterjall said, struggling to flatten the letter with his paw pads. He immediately recognized Crysta's neat handwriting, though she'd used much smaller characters than her usual style.

"My eyes want to read what Crysta wrote," Kulak said from behind him, "but my eyes do not know your runes. Read for us, Lago-Sterjall."

Sterjall read the letter out loud:

> Dear Lago,
> You never cease to amaze me… and scare me. I'll be brief, as space is limited, but I'm thrilled you are all safe (Gwil and I are fine too).

Withervale: monks and mine workers who didn't fight back were spared, thank the Twin Gods. They are being forced to manufacture soot. Seems that's their main goal for the city, as well as protecting the pass into the Stiss Malpa and Ninn Tago. City is under control of General Edmar Helm of the First Legion, but seems like he has no plans to push west—their numbers are not large enough to threaten the Union from within.

Red Stag: Source in Anglass says a new general by the name Crescu Valaran took over the mask from the general Ockam killed. Crescu and Stag recalled their legions and sent them east. Unsure of plans, but they are likely crossing the Ophidian to take the Bighorn Dome. Their army and herd have grown immensely. Smaller towns in Negian states are rioting—they can't hunt for deer or elk; Stag has taken most of them away.

Esum says that Anglass Dome is being emptied out of resources, trying to distribute to towns to compensate for missing animals, but high taxes are keeping the Empire unruly. Temple inside Anglass has not been touched, as far as our source could find out, but they are quickly killing off most animals there and burning the prairies (not sure what for?).

Sterjall flipped the paper around and continued reading.

Regarding Zovarians, I procured a good tip from navy source: if you ever need to venture out by sea, it will be very difficult. Navy is patrolling dome area day and night. But… There is one day, the fourteenth of Fireleaf, when the full navy returns to Zovaria for the annual Sail Parade, to showcase their fleets to the Arch Sedecims. There will be no navy ships on patrol that day. It is four months away, but might be a useful date to keep in mind.

Source said Kedra and Grinn traveled to scablands months ago, probably searching for you or for that proboscidean mask. They have infantry and cavalry stationed in Muskeg, Nebush, and New Karst. Lots more patrolling the main roads and rivers. There's a reward for your heads, all four of you, so be wary of anyone you meet.

I'm working at the tower for now. Sunnograph messages from Withervale arrive almost daily. If you have a way to find me again with your bird friend, I'll be here, and I will remember the instructions. Stay safe, all of you.

The song is *Oh, Iskimesh*.

Love,

- Crysta

"This is extremely valuable," Sterjall said, folding the letter. "We could exit by sea now, if we needed to."

"You have good friends," Kenondok said.

"I would like to meet Crysta, some day," Kulak added.

"But that traitorous little leech, Kedra," Balstei mumbled. "Takhamún smite her. Do you think we are too late?"

"Perhaps, but Kedra knows nothing about Mamóru," Sterjall said, "she only went to the scablands because there might be another mask there."

"Either way, they got there before us," Jiara said. "And there's a reward for our heads? I hope it's a respectable amount of Quggons."

"We should get moving, find a place to rest farther down the slopes," Balstei said, "just in case any travelers decide to hike up the peak. But first, get a good look at the landscape. Those canyons to the west are the Siltlands—it would've been much faster to travel that way, but the path is utterly exposed. We'd be spotted faster than you can say *Takh*. We need to aim toward those saw-toothed edges to the south, the Nightlure Cliffs. There's a ford there that will help us cross the Brightbay Run."

"Could Olo help us by scouting the path for us?" Alaia asked.

"If there is light and no fog, he could point to a clear path the smilodons could follow," Sunu said.

"And could he tell us of potential dangers?" Jiara inquired.

"Olo does not speak back to Sunu. Sunu's scalp speaks to him, to tell Olo where to go. If Sunu's scalp sends Olo to look, Olo will look, but he cannot tell Sunu what he saw. Olo can track, if provided with enough information, flying close to target, or high above target, so Sunu's eyes may see the blue sparkle of his wings and know where target is. But Olo is too tired now. We should find a place to shelter until nightfall."

"Good hide," Hod Abjus declared when they found a comfortable gully to rest in. "Sleep day." He was still a bit behind in his Common, but had learned a respectable amount. "First watch becomes my eyes," he added, unsheathing a smilodon-tooth knife.

"I'm so glad Crysta got the message," Lago said, preparing his bedroll.

"The face she must've made when she read the letter," Balstei said. "I bet you she even translated those Miscamish texts into Common." He tucked his Takheist pendant against his hairy chest and lay down.

"I wish I had learned Miscamish in school," Lago continued, "it would've come in handy. But they didn't teach it at Birth-Light School."

"You could've asked Crysta to enroll you at the Fliskel Academy, in Withervale proper. Would have cost her almost the same as your old school."

"My costs were covered because of my grades, I couldn't just transfer that program to another school."

Balstei propped himself up on his elbow and cocked his head at Lago. He chewed on his lower lip, trying to figure out what was wrong with the young man. He made a dismissive gesture with his hands, then lay back down.

"What?" Lago asked. "What is it?"

"You're telling me you didn't even know?"

"Know what?"

Balstei put a hand to his forehead. "You clueless lad. There is no free tuition program, Crysta was paying for your studies."

"What? But she told me..." Lago sat there, staring at the ground. "All these years?" he asked the grass.

Chapter Thirty-Eight

Sulphur Moon

When darkness swallowed them, they resumed their journey, confident in the night-adapted eyes of the smilodons. They kept close to streams to obscure the sound of their steps, even though the cats' paws fell silent as snowflakes. Olo guided them often, hovering over safe paths when there was moonlight for him to scout by. The forest changed around them, with the deciduous trees giving way to hemlocks and spruces.

Days passed in sleep, nights in unceasing travel. Through the Karst Forest they rode, beyond the Nightlure Cliffs, and crossed over the Old Pilgrim's Road when no wagons were in sight. Through wetlands they strode, between groves of red firs, cedars, and sugar pines, until they reached a wide river.

"The Brightbay Run," Balstei said. "Farther west, by New Karst, it deepens even more, then empties out to sea." He pointed at an island between a confluence of rivers. "Up there, the Brightbay and the Lindee join up. The point widens the waters, making them more shallow, less deadly. It would be the only safe place to cross, other than at the New Karst bridge."

They held tight to their saddles and asked the cats to wade in. The smilodons were good swimmers, even if they did not enjoy the water. Blu growled a bit, Kobos and Pichi remained disgruntledly quiet, and Fulm bubbled hisses at the sky. It took an arduous effort to cross the first segment of the confluence. Once at the sandy isle, Givra pointed to recent footprints. They kept their eyes peeled but found no fisherfolk around. They forded the next branch of the river, then continued into the beginnings of the Moonbow Timberlands.

Creeks entwined with hillocks crowned by glacier-deposited erratic boulders, which patiently held their ground since time immemorial. Through the rocks and water, the smilodons wove like transient blurs, venturing deeper into the pristine forest. Passing a gurgling stream replete with colorful pebbles, they spotted rectangular boulders entirely covered in moss.

"Downfall ruins," Sterjall said to Kulak. The prince lit up with anticipation.

The toppled remains of a building were cradled between overgrown roots, ferns, and purple-flowering ivies. Its stone walls stood mostly erect, though more greenery than rock was visible. The structure was three stories tall, offering good shelter from the sun, and with signs of having been used as a camping spot, though not recently. They deemed it a good place to rest.

Since they had missed their language lessons the previous day, Sunu asked them to join in for a quick session. Hod Abjus, Kenondok, and Givra refused this time, preferring to go straight to sleep, but the others sat down to listen.

Sunu concluded the lesson as Sunnokh was rising. "And that is why important roles, such as titles and ranks, are gendered in our tongue," they finished.

"*Ierun* for *queen* and *ieron* for *king* we knew already," Sterjall recalled. "So an allgender royal would be *ieren*?"

"Since the *udácuënn*, allgenders, are not allowed ranks above hed," Sunu said, "we reserve *ieren* for when referring to royalty of undefined gender. As in speaking of *either* a king or queen."

"Why can't allgenders be ieren?" Alaia questioned.

"*Ierenesh*," Sunu corrected. "The plural form still applies."

Alaia waited. Hearing no response, she raised a demanding eyebrow.

"It is not the way of things," Sunu answered.

"Yet you seem to have a lot more allgenders among the Laatu," Sterjall noted. "They are not as common in the New World. I only knew one closely when I lived in Withervale. A botanist from Bauram. Lerr Holfster, we called them."

Sterjall suddenly remembered the treasured ruby-flecked stoneleaf Lerr Holfster had gifted to him, but the memory was tainted by the image of the succulent lying in a puddle of blood and blue Baurami sands, and a dead soldier next to the toppled plant: the first man he had ever killed. He could almost hear the crunching of the man's spine as he saw himself remove his dagger from the soldier's neck. *I hope Lerr Holfster escaped the war*, he thought, shaking the image away. *They were always so kind to me.*

"Come back to us, Lago-Sterjall," Sunu said, snapping Sterjall out of his gruesome daydream.

Sterjall lifted his muzzle. He squinted at Sunu and said, "Sorry if this is an odd question… But… do allgenders have children?"

"No," Sunu answered. "For we are not meant to procreate, or touch ourselves or others in that manner. It would be a transgression of sacred laws, as only men and women are meant to bind together, and we have chosen neither path."

"But... you could, if the law was different," Sterjall probed further.

"Law is there for reasons," Kenondok interjected, rising from his slumber. "Let us sleep now. Sunnokh's face shines. Speak no more of this."

Sunu walked to a corner of the ruins and sat cross-legged, readying to fall asleep. "Sunu's eyes have seen it happen once," they quietly answered, eyes already closed. "And as the law called for, before the fourth month of pregnancy, the priests had to release the allgender from their affliction and let the Isdinnklad carry their sin."

Sterjall didn't want to ask what that implied; it seemed dreadful enough without knowing. He felt sad, mostly because Sunu showed no sign of being upset, seeming perfectly accepting of their fate.

I don't understand, he thought. *How can someone in their position, with such high regard for understanding different points of view, hold such skewed beliefs?* But each culture carried their own burdens, and he couldn't blame Sunu for their upbringing or the situation they found themself in. He only hoped that the Laatu allowed room for change.

The others had all fallen asleep, but Sterjall stirred, feeling something was off. He cracked open his eyes and noticed Kulak was not at the entrance to the ruins—he was supposed to be keeping first watch. He focused Agnargsilv in a wide area and sensed Kulak above him, on the top level of the ruins. He snuck out from under his covers, followed what remained of the ruined steps, and climbed on mossy walls the rest of the way up.

He found Kulak sitting on a toppled column, leather kilt wrapped around the mossy pillar. A clear view of the forest spread before them, and now that they were far enough south, even the beginnings of the Stelm Sajal were visible.

"Hey," Sterjall said. "Why are you not keeping watch?"

Kulak's eyes were focused west, toward the descending moon. Sceres's saturated yellow dress perfectly matched the brightness of the sky, deeply blurring the colors together, like an elusive optical illusion.

"What is wrong with Sceres?" Kulak asked.

"Wrong with her? What did you see?" Sterjall replied, sitting by his side.

"My scalp did not know Sceres woke up in the daytime, but my eyes saw her, through trees. I climbed high to see her better, and grew scared. Part of her is missing."

"That's... I guess it would be confusing. It's not missing, it's in shadows. Sceres comes out during the day too, and when it's daytime, her shadow side looks like that."

"Why not black, if in shadow? Looks broken to my eyes."

"Her shadow can only be as dark as the sky is dark. Like a mountain far away, its shadows will look blue, not black."

"Far shadows always gray in Mindreldrolom. Only blue out here, sometimes purple."

"I... never noticed that. Well, Sceres is like mountains, only much farther away, so her shadows take those colors. You will see her sometimes like this, sometimes full, or even fully empty during a Hollow Moon. If it was night, you'd notice her atmosphere completing the circle."

"I still do not fully understand, but she remains beautiful," Kulak said, holding his teal eyes on her.

Sterjall was sleepy, but he was enjoying the fascination Kulak found in these simple moments. He hadn't had a chance to be alone with Kulak for the past week, nor had he gotten any proper rest during their journey; even while he slept, he felt anxious beneath the sun's light, which reached them no matter how deeply they hid in forests.

Sterjall pulled at his chin whiskers as he pondered. "Do you like it better out here?" he asked.

"Yes. Home is beautiful, but my scalp feels there is more out here, for me."

"I'm afraid of going back to the dome, to be done with this mission. If your mother takes Agnargsilv from me, it will be like ripping a part of me away."

"We find solution. Perhaps Mother thinks differently, once she sees we succeeded."

"Do you believe that?"

Kulak thought for a moment. "No. Mother's scalp cannot be changed. But perhaps we find another solution. Have hope."

"I can't imagine giving up the mask willingly. Your mother must've been strong to do that when she gave it to you. What was that like? When do they decide to pass it on?"

"It does not matter age of old Silvfröa, it matters age of heir, at least that is the way of the Laatu Miscam. Happened when my age became fifteen, and I became man. Mother was shining proud, but I saw sadness veil her eyes. It was last day of tigress, of Farshálv, when Mother left half of her soul behind. Always I knew Mother as strong tigress, but that day she was only old woman. Mother knew she was doing right, and was happy for me, and that was enough for her. Mother is a good chief, even if too strict sometimes. She cares for Laatu, cares for me."

"What about you? Will you give up Mindrelsilv when the time comes?"

"Time does not come for me, not in same way. I do not wish children, and that is thought I cannot share with Mother. At year's end, when my age turns twenty, each province will present one candidate, a woman to bride me, so we can make an heir and gift them Mindrelsilv one day. Same way Mother chose Father, long time past. One woman I make forced to pick, like picking cut of meat from butcher. It does not matter what I want, only what tradition wants. Perhaps escaping Mindreldrolom, breaking old rules, is only way for me."

"But Mindrelsilv is needed, to open the dome, to help control the felids. No matter what, you are tied to those responsibilities."

"Those my scalp minds not. Also this mission, this quest we share together, my scalp learns and my soul grows from it, so my scalp minds not. When more far paths take me, I become more alive, doing something different. One day I die, and I hope I am Aio-Kulak until that day, and no one takes caracal from me. But now I see wonderful world to discover, to learn from. Look at this beauty, and tell me you prefer to live trapped in cage instead."

"I really missed the moon, the stars, the sun. In the dome, I felt disoriented. I always guide myself by looking at the constellations, by seeing the directions in which shadows fall, or by feeling which side of the sky is brighter. Out here Sceres tells me how far we are into the year, just with her colors."

"A lot to be learned in your world. To me, I know shape and color of each great vine, position of each of twenty-three columns. Looking up, or to sides, my scalp knows where I am, because vines are always there, painting sky map. And seasons make day longer, and color of arudinn changes, only little, but I learn to feel changes, I learn sounds that come with time passing. Our stars—the ones that are not stars—I learn them too. It is always same ones who brighten and hide again. Why they do it? No one knows, but maybe they try speaking us something, and we are not enough smart to understand. Mindreldrolom can be beautiful, complex, but still incomplete."

"I can see its beauty too," Sterjall said, looking at Kulak. "Hey, you are getting really good at Common, you seem so much more comfortable with it now."

"*Chienn uthir akhól olv Miscamish inn.*"

"Not as much, but I'm learning."

Kulak lowered his sight to the canopy in front of them, studying the many rivers they still had to cross. He lowered his gaze further to examine the stone bricks that made up the old ruins and caressed the toppled column they were sitting on.

"Ruins are sad, but my scalp likes them. They are broken, yet they hold on."

"The Downfall left entire cities buried under sand, under forests. Most of our cities are built on top of them, but many more are still out there waiting to be found. An old friend used to tell me about the black and blue sand dunes of the Kingdom of Bauram, where entire temples are still undiscovered, whole palaces that reveal themselves when the sand blows away, just to be covered up again in the night."

"My eyes yearn to see blue sand, buried temples." Kulak scraped his claws on old runes carved on the column, right below Sterjall's legs. He then ran his handpaw over Sterjall's scars. "Your leg. Why missing fur?"

"That happened when we were at Minnelvad, climbing by the falls. Bear, my dog, was about to jump into a pool of boiling water, so I ran to rescue him. On the way back, my leg broke through the ice and sank into the water, and I burned it really badly."

"How is ice water boiling?"

"It's not. There are hot springs, and then there's an icy wind that freezes their tops, so you have a sheet of ice over the hot water."

"Strange world you travel, where ice water boils, and dogs are bears. We do not have hot water, unless we burn *ëovad* beneath it, or fill pool with brime cubes. Like blue sand, you also must show me hot waters."

"I will! They are one of my favorite things to do, visiting hot springs, I mean. They are like any creek or pond, but when the water comes out, it comes out hot. Boiling hot, and acidic, and it would kill you if you fell into it."

"Then why do you like doing hot spring?"

"Oh, not all of them are that hot. But all hot springs are colorful and magical. Maybe we'll find one in the mountains near here, you'll see."

"As long as caracal legs can keep fur, I will try," Kulak said, sliding his handpaw higher, past Sterjall's scars and up to his thigh.

Sterjall twitched. *I know he can feel my nervousness,* he thought, *so there's no point in hiding it.* He took Kulak's handpaw in his and entwined their fingers together. Kulak held tight and smiled, looking into Sterjall's eyes.

"I like you," Kulak said. "You teach me things my scalp can never know otherwise. Like hot spring, like blue sand, like stars and meteors and sunsets. I am sorry if I make pressure on you, or make you feel like it is a game to me. It is not. My heart is also afraid, sometimes, of many things. I try to keep fear from controlling me, but fear is good, too."

Sterjall tried to keep his eyes on the prince's, but Kulak's gaze was overpowering. "What sort of things are you afraid of?" he asked.

"You will think it is funny. I am afraid of Mother, of Father."

"Your mother can be awfully intimidating," Sterjall said. "But your father? I don't think I ever even heard him talk. He just stands so distant that I don't even notice him sometimes."

"Many things you not know about them, about me."

"Like what?"

Kulak pulled their entwined hands closer to his chest and examined them, contemplating something that wasn't what he was looking at. "Tell me most hidden secret, Lago-Sterjall, and I will tell you mine. If you trust me."

"I... What sort of secret?"

Kulak looked deeply into Sterjall's eyes. "Secret you have not told anyone."

Sterjall felt compelled by the prince's gaze. He considered the request. All the secrets related to his adventures, Kulak already knew. *He knows about Banook, the mask, the Diamond Cave, Sontai. What doesn't he already know?* He recalled the time when his schoolmate Deon wasn't at the shop, so he ended up fucking Deon's father instead. *That was wild and risky, but I did tell Alaia about it.* He thought about his own father, and how he had been mistreated by him. *No, that's not a secret, it's just life—others have had it much worse than I.* Thinking of his father made him feel embarrassed and hurt, so he thought about his mother instead. *I don't tell people about her, but I never met her. There's no mystery there, only emptiness.* Then, instead of thinking of things that had happened to him, he thought about things he himself had done, and immediately an old memory surfaced to haunt him.

"There's something I haven't told anyone, not even Alaia," he whispered, not sure why he was suddenly trusting Kulak more than his childhood friend. "I feel she would hate me if she found out, so you must promise never to tell her."

"I promise."

Sterjall tightened his tail around the pillar. "When I was... about ten, I think, I was making deliveries at the Alban Bazaar, a marketplace in Withervale that is full of shops and tight alleys. As I reached up to grab a package from a merchant, someone took my bag and ran. I chased after him, followed him into an empty alley. It was an Oldrin kid, like Alaia, with spurs on his arms and one on his nose. Oldrin aren't treated well in Zovaria, people call them *spurs* to say they are lesser than them. It's hard to explain—"

"Alaia told me. I understand."

"Well, he tried to jump up a wall and climb away, but I grabbed his leg and pulled him down. And I just beat him up. I used to be so violent... It's something I've worked hard to overcome, but sometimes I still lose it and can't hold back. That poor kid, I hit him so hard, over and over until he was bleeding on the ground, begging me to stop. The spur on his nose seemed broken, and my hands were all bloody, and... and I..."

Sterjall was looking down at his handpaws but seeing bloodied human hands. "And I... I called him a *fucking spur* as I hit him. I still don't know why I said that. I felt dirty, and evil. And I left him there bleeding, and went home and cried."

Sterjall silently wept. Kulak placed an arm around him; the wolf reacted by flinching back, feeling undeserving of the comfort.

"I couldn't face Alaia after that," Sterjall said as he fought more tears. "I avoided her for months, and never told her why." He had bottled this up inside himself for so long, and it was painful, but good to finally let it out.

"People say things they do not mean," Kulak said after a long moment. "Say things they do not understand. But if you learn they are bad, you change, you are not bad. We make mistakes, we fix them."

"Thank you. And I'm sorry, I didn't mean for this to get so intense. I just... never thought I'd tell anyone about it."

"Sorry to upset you. Perhaps I tell my story another day, it also upsets."

"No, no." Sterjall wiped his nose. "Sorry. I want to hear it. I want to know more about you."

"If you want." Kulak stood, lifted a leg, and straddled the column to fully face Sterjall. "Story has more to do with Mother and Father. And with Brother."

"Brother?"

"Older brother. Like I never tell Alaia, you must never tell anyone, because it is not me who gets in trouble, but parents. Mother made a son, two years before she birth me. Mother was not Alúma, but Farshálv, when she became pregnant. When Brother was birthed, he had long tail, orange fur, just like Mother.

"Uncle told me, years later. He told me as warning. He was there when Brother was born. Mother wanted to keep him, but knew Laatu would take Mindrelsilv from her and maybe kill her for great sin. Father did not want him. He took baby and drowned him, said to tribe that baby died at birthing." His handpaws tensed, his claws extending and briefly scraping the moss-covered column. He retracted his claws and added, "Uncle says that since that day father is quiet, and that I must never do same sins of Mother, or I will suffer like she suffered."

Kulak's brow was furrowed, his eyelids tight, almost closed. He held the stiff expression, not giving away more than what his words said. "My scalp thinks Mother is afraid of breaking rules because of cruel pain Father gave her heart. Mother does not want people to suffer pain, and forces chiefs to obey laws, to do what she thinks is best for all Laatu. My heart wishes I could know

Brother's name, but uncle did not know what name they gave him. I could never ask Mother, or Father—they do not know I know."

"I wish your brother had been given a chance," Sterjall said gently.

"My scalp does too. I would have liked to know him, grow with him and play together. But it makes me also guilty, because sometimes I think it is better Brother is dead, because if not, I would never become Kulak, only Aio. Kulak is me, and Aio is me, and thinking bad thoughts makes me sad, thinking I would trade Brother, innocent baby, for one part of myself. Selfish. I do not deserve Mindrelsilv. He would been strong, proud leader, and I am not good at weapons, not good at politics, only good at breaking rules."

Kulak's eyes had drifted to the ground.

Sterjall placed a handpaw on his shoulder. "Perhaps you are not meant to be a leader in the same way the ones before you were. You are different, and that is your strength. If you were not a good person, you would not feel bad about having those thoughts. I think everything will change, for Arjum, for Mindreldrolom, and even for the New World, very soon. You seem more ready to face what's coming than any other Laatu I've met."

"Thank you. I hope so. I am glad I told you. It is easier with the Silvesh, but also harder, because we cannot hide, we can only trust, and I trust you."

"I trust you, too. Even if sometimes I seem confused. It's only fear, nothing else. I'm not as brave as you are."

Kulak stood up and helped Sterjall to his feet.

They held handpaws for a moment. Sterjall gave Kulak a soft kiss on the lips, then embraced him and said, "I will learn to be less afraid, for us. I promise." Sterjall let go of the prince, then led him down the steps of the ruins.

Sceres's yellow eye watched them both, like a slit of golden curiosity in the firmament.

Chapter Thirty-Nine

Giant Redwoods

A week passed as the company rode through the Moonbow Timberlands, climbing higher each day. The forests offered no trails other than those of deer, wild hogs, and the occasional moose, but Olo always helped by spotting paths with fewer treacherous chasms to leap over.

While they rested during the day, coyotes would sometimes sneak into their camp looking for scraps. Sterjall took the opportunity to practice his skills with the sharp-eared canids, and although he was able to more clearly feel their emotions, he could not yet find a way to truly mindspeak to them.

They kept on riding, now through a conifer forest that kept stretching ever higher.

"What are you doing?" Kulak whispered, tensely perking up.

Sterjall had been holding a bit too confidently to Kulak's bare chest. "Counting," he whispered back. "Sunu is asleep. And the others can't see us right now, don't worry."

"Counting?"

"Seven... Eight... That's all, I think. You have eight nipples?"

"Yes. Very small. Also very sensitive."

"I only got six," Sterjall said with palpable disappointment. "I was excited the first time I discovered them, but now I feel cheated."

"I will count them myself, sometime. Not now, sometime."

A cacophony of birds announced the arrival of morning. They had been crossing the forest all night and had finally stopped in a grove of giant redwoods. This high-elevation area would be covered in snow later in the year, but in mid-Summer it was dusty and hot, forcing Lago and Aio to remain in their human forms to keep from overheating.

"It's so massive," Alaia said, staring at the towering trunk of a giant tree. There were no branches at the bottom of it, only the thickest, reddest bark Alaia had ever seen, and a trunk so wide that all of them together could not have linked their hands around it.

"Look at these ones over here!" Lago called out, running as he let the breeze dry off his sweat.

"This tree biggest," Givra said by a tree with a hollow trunk. "You walk inside." She spread her arms wide and could barely reach the edges of the portal. Sunu, Kenondok and Abjus walked inside the tree and looked up in astonishment: the space rose for thirty more feet, where beams of light shone through from cuts on the sides of the trunk.

"These groves are magnificent," Jiara said. "We can rest here before it gets too hot." She had seen giant redwoods before, in a valley east of the Sajal Crater, but they had not been of this remarkable scale. She looked up as far as she could see, but it was impossible to spot the tops of the tallest trees.

Givra, Balstei, and Abjus slept within the hollowed-out redwood. Sunu slept cross-legged between two conjoined trunks that rose at a slight angle. Jiara found a redwood with an incomprehensibly wide trunk that had a hole just big enough for one person to cradle in. The others rested on the soft mulch, in a spot that Lago calculated would remain in the shade even later in the day.

They let their sweat drip and evaporate as they dozed off.

Within the hollow core of the largest tree, Jiara dreamed.

Jiara was a fetus sleeping in a womb of granite. Her amniotic fluid was pine needles, dried sap globules, cicada larvae, and seeds from shattered cones. Sustenance, vigor—she breathed it all in.

Her umbilical cord was a quaar rope, feeding her the threads around her, driving them into her bowels and bone marrow. Rocks split above, letting spikes of crystalline light cut through. The rift above her was a cracking geode, with tooth-like shards of amethyst smiling a jagged taunt. The crevice widened further, and out of the serrated fracture erupted rotten logs and moist soil, like a dark and humid volcano, but Jiara remained under the granitic crust, holding her ground stubbornly with raw fingers. Her naked body curled into a ball as the torrent of latent soil rushed by her, filling every orifice, from her crotch, to her nostrils, mouth, and eyes. A beam of sunlight caressed the bumps of her spine, and she felt like opening up like a lotus flower, but still did not want to let go.

The quaar rope tied to her navel split into black roots, grasping the rocks yet tighter, offering respite to her bruised arms and scraped fingers. Her back suddenly split open, as seven waxy-green needles poked out from her ribs, yearning for light, for moisture. The needles smelled the sunlight, shivered, and pulled up.

Jiara's bleeding fingers lost their grip.

Her body rose while the quaar roots below her grew, feeding her energy from deep within the molten mantle of rock. Higher she ascended, and taller she grew, until she was one of the redwoods, the tallest of them all. She was up so high that no air remained, but her lungs only needed the sun, and her belly only needed the soil at her roots.

She looked down at the forest. On top of one of the trees, she saw a blonde woman much like herself, but who wasn't herself, and would never be herself. She looked to another tree next to it—one with a jagged tip, as if cracked by lighting—and there she saw a cinnamon-colored black bear looking up at her. The bear's reddish fur glistened with starlight; her dark-mahogany eyes sparkled like huckleberries sprinkled in dew. Jiara knew then that she was seeing her true self, the missing part of her being, so she asked the bear who was her to come close, to climb up on her, so that they could meet at last.

Jiara woke up in a sweat, tasting fresh soil. The memory of the dream pulsed through her entire body. The light outside was yellowed with the encroaching sunset. She didn't entirely know why, but she took off all her clothes, then put Urnaadisilv on her face. She felt the verticality of the threads beckoning her up the tree that had sheltered her. *I must reach the top,* she thought, then crawled out of her hole. Without the aid of any rope or shoes, she grasped the thick bark of the tree and began her ascent.

The breeze was soothing, evaporating the sweat beneath her breasts, under her hairy armpits, in her crotch. Her thick-woven braid bounced over her tight back muscles, which tensed and rippled as her hands found holds in the cuts of the bark. She placed her trust in tree hollows, branches, and galls. Her nipples scraped over the red bark, turning raw and sensitive, flushing rhythmically after every heartbeat. Halfway up the tree, the tree began to narrow. Higher yet, it was thin enough for her arms to nearly wrap around the trunk, and the branches were numerous, letting her walk up them as if ascending a spiral staircase.

She reached the top as Sunnokh was hesitatingly dipping his toes on the horizon. The rest of the forest expanded beneath her, and far beyond it stretched the treacherous cinder cones and lava flows of the Brasha'in Scablands.

She straddled a thick branch, leaned back against the trunk, and watched as Sunnokh sank into his own heat haze. She thought of her dream, of that cinnamon bear, of her cream-colored muzzle and dark-brown ears. She pictured the bear's sparkling mahogany eyes, clutching the image in her mind as she stared at the last fingers of Sunnokh waving their farewells. The last thing she saw was a brief flash of viridian light. She blinked hard, and the tenuous afterimage followed her vision into darkness.

When she opened her eyes, the dark muzzle of Urnaadisilv had been replaced by one of creamy fur.

Jiara looked down at her strong handpaws, her fierce claws, her silky cinnamon fur, and felt rejuvenated and pure. She squeezed her powerful arm muscles, her dexterous muzzle, her tenderly round ears. She dragged her handpaws over her three pairs of furry breasts and felt a thrill as each of her six nipples hardened beneath her leathery pads. She stood on the branch and pinched at her nub of a tail—as delicate as her ears.

I am a bear, she thought, *a fucking bear…* She inhaled deeply. *The smells.* The scents of the forest were so clear, so full, so vibrant that she could taste them. *It smells so old. But it also smells of newness, like my new body. This is me… This, this is who I truly am.*

Her proportions had slightly changed: her legs felt shorter, her arms and torso longer, her neck and hips fuller, but the rest felt about the same. Her halfform looked more bear-like than Sterjall's looked wolf-like, as bears could walk on their hind legs more naturally, and they did so with feet flat on the ground instead of on their toes.

It will soon be dark, she thought, seeing her cinnamon fur turn red under the sunset clouds.

She began her descent, renewed and whole.

"Where is Jiara?" Lago asked Alaia, searching inside the tree Jiara had slept in. "Aren't these her clothes?"

Aio was shaking Blu awake while all the others packed up camp. Blu suddenly hissed, looking upward with whiskers pricked forward.

"*Gwen chëass henet welvesh*, Blu?" Aio asked and followed his gaze. From high up in the wide tree, a bulky shadow was descending.

Lago and Alaia turned in time to see the half-bear sliding the rest of her way down.

"*Ggrrowllm*," the bear said, unable to use her new vocal cords yet. She lumbered toward them on two clawed feet.

"Jiara!" Alaia screamed, running to steal a warm bear hug. "Lodestar have mercy! You are packing more now!" She laughed, staring at the six furry teats adorning Jiara's muscular chest and abdomen.

Lago wasn't sure whether a hug was appropriate, with Jiara being naked and all, but Jiara took him into a smothering hug before he could overthink it.

That night, instead of hurrying back to the mission, they celebrated. They were not afraid of being spotted, not this far from any inhabited areas, so they made a campfire for the first time since leaving the dome. It was still hot out, and a fire wasn't needed, but a fire was the only way to properly tell stories at night.

Jiara plopped her bottom on a log. Other than for some parts of her leather armor, she had managed to fit her clothes back on, although she had needed to roll up her too long trousers, and she had to switch the prong of her belt a few notches wider. She had cut a tiny hole in her trousers so that her nubby tail could poke out, but didn't need anything as drastic as Sterjall's alterations. Even her boots fit, as her footpaws were about the same length as her human feet, after a bit of careful claw trimming. At least she wouldn't have to shred through her boots mid-transformation, like Banook would have.

Jiara tried to recount her experience, all the while working on regaining control of her voice. Her friends listened intently, yet still laughed at her fumbling tongue and insecure growls. She started with what she recalled from her dreams, then told them about her real climb, her transformation, and her descent as a bear.

Once Jiara was done, Lago said, "Well, you took your sweet time with it."

The bear shrugged. "Iss not sorrhmthing you khan pusch."

"True words," Aio said. "How much time to find Sterjall?"

"Just one week," Lago said.

"Bull. Shit," Alaia clarified. "You had been wearing the mask for *months* before Banook helped you out."

"But I didn't know how the whole thing worked yet!"

"And you had the mask for *six years* before that."

"Hey, that definitely doesn't count," Lago retorted. "And what about you, Aio?"

"On fifth day I found caracal," he answered.

Lago was stunned. "How did you manage so fast?"

"My scalp had considered it long before Mother gifted me Mindrelsilv. But it took more time to tolerate pain, I did not like it. Two weeks, tried, could not wear Silv. In the *Laatu Tarvio Loom Tikhálv*, ceremony of second birth, we perform it one night, and if new Mindrelfröa cannot tolerate pain, Silv is taken, and ceremony begins again next night. Many nights I tried, many nights I failed."

"Because of how young you were?" Lago guessed.

"Not all because of youth. There is learning to understand pain, which my scalp did not understand yet. But tales say it is common thing to happen, different for every scalp. Mother wore Mindrelsilv on same day, then two months she took to find her voice."

"Three," Kenondok corrected him. "Ierun Alúma says two, but my eyes witnessed. Three months. Young boy I was, but my scalp remembers clear as breath."

"Seeh? I didnnth do sow bahd," the bear said.

Aio stood. "There is something Laatu must discuss," he declared. "Kenondok, Givra, Sunu, Abjus." He nodded to them, and they seemed to know what was happening. All the Laatu walked away, disappearing into a pocket of dark forest. They returned a wick later and took their seats by the campfire.

Sunu remained standing, their violet-cast eyes sparkling with firelight. They picked up their bone halberd and slammed the iron-capped, bludgeoning end on the ground. With the overly formal voice of someone not used to public speaking, they said, "Sunu asks for your attention. We are honored to have you, Jiara, as embodiment of Urnaadifröa, the voice of ursids. As Miscam law is written, we have chosen a new name for your half-form. As Holy Shaman, as *Galv Eilejen*, Sunu is proud to gift this name to you."

Sunu gestured with their free hand over their purple-pigmented scalp, as if grasping an invisible tendril of their consciousness, then released the thought into the air with a flick of their wrist. "Among our eighteen tribes, your name shall be Kitjári, *wood-claw*, the one whose paws can hold on to bark and is master of heights, of trees, of mountains. Do you accept this name, and swear to uphold the sacred laws of the Silvesh, to bring honor, balance, and longevity to bearkind?"

"I... I d-don'th knouw wat d'laws of the Silfessh arr," Jiara stammered, looking around for help.

"Just say yes," Aio whispered close to her.

"Yesh, sure. I do."

"Then rise, Kitjári!" Sunu continued, building up theatrical flair. They lifted their halberd to the skies. "Rise and pride yourself on your two selves, for now you are more than one."

Kitjári rose. With a sharp-fanged smile, she said, "Kithjáarri. I really like id. Hankyuu, Sunu." And she did like it. It was a true name, and it was hers, and she would be as much Kitjári as she was Jiara now that a part of her that had been missing for so long had awakened.

Chapter Forty

Beyond Six Lands, Beneath Six Seas

Before leaving the redwood forest, the company filled their bellies and canteens, gathering as much food as they could, for they did not expect to find anything to eat or drink in the dreaded scablands.

As she hunted for provisions, Kitjári found it even more important to minimize the amount of suffering she inflicted, in the way Kulak and Sunu had taught her. The deaths somehow felt more personal while in her half-form, as if each one left a lingering bruise in her heart. She avoided loosing her arrows until she was certain the killing would be swift, then rushed to her victims and used Urnaadisilv to take all the pain she could into herself before the animals died.

They crossed what remained of the forest and arrived at a long line of cinder cones. Some vegetation still clung here: short junipers, brambly slopebrushes, and long grasses tangled with prickly tumblethorns that had been desiccated by the scorching Summer.

The cats attempted to plod up the dusty cone, but their heavy paws dislodged the powdery ash, foamy pumice, and bladelets of obsidian that made up the bulbous hills. They quickly understood that the rest of the journey would be much harder than they'd expected. The company decided it would be best to dismount the smilodons and travel in a switchback line. Each step they took made them sink and slide, making for slow progress. Their boots constantly filled up with pebbles and sand, to the point they had to learn to ignore it and live with the annoyance.

They arrived at the top of the cone covered in sweat and plastered in silt. A jaundiced, waning crescent was rising in the east, which, together with the stars, provided just enough light to see the barren wastes by. The chain of cinder cones extended for miles, like burial mounds where flowers blossomed no longer. Past this point, nearly no trees grew. Shrubs and brambles clung bitterly to the loose stones, with withered branches that rattled under the sporadic, dry winds. Behind the last line of cones loomed jagged peaks, darkly obscuring the much vaster, true scablands.

They slid down the tall cone, careful not to cut themselves on the fragments of obsidian poking out from the slopes. They carried onward, weaving around the troughs of the formations instead of powering up to their crests. The cats grew frustrated and tired, often slumping on their sides as the soft ashes swallowed their wide paws.

Kitjári tottered up the powdery edges of a cone and pointed her claws west. "Past those peaks the terrain drops into the dry lava beds," she said, having regained full control of her tongue; other than for tiny grunts that surfaced from time to time, she sounded just the same as Jiara. "From that vantage point, we could scout the scablands."

"What eyes look for? How can us know?" Abjus asked.

Kitjári slid back down, shook the ashes off her fur, and said, "So far at Stelm Bir, Da'áju, and Arjum, the temples were on high ground. We should search for the highest point we can and hope for the best."

Once morning brightened the skies, it did not care to brighten the terrain as much, as the wasteland was charred and choked with dark dust, heating quickly beneath the broiling breath of Sunnokh.

A single, anguished juniper was all the shelter they could find, so they used it to tie up shading tarps as a refuge. They shared a small meal, eating only that which would spoil in the heat while saving their munnji, dried fruits, nuts, and cured meats for later. They were all too close together for comfort under the tarps, with the cats taking up an enormous amount of space, but they needed the shade in order to sleep through the hot day. The air became stale and suffocating.

"At least the ash is soft," Lago whispered, lying on his back next to Aio. They were resting their heads on Blu's forelegs, having trouble finding sleep. It was close to noon, and Sunnokh was unyielding, manifesting as an orb through the thickness of the tarp.

"My scalp never feel so much heat," Aio said. "Hot days in Mindreldrolom, scalp sweats, but the arudinn do not burn one side of you until skin peels like birch bark."

"I hope the hottest part of Summer is behind us," Lago said, rolling to his side to face Aio. He saw Aio's brow, neck, and chest dripping with sweat. His smooth skin glistened where the dark sediments hadn't plastered over.

Aio was rolling his octahedral pendant over his breastbone, leaving tiny, triangular indentations.

Lago ran a finger over the pendant's leather cord, lightly brushing Aio's chest. Then his fingers reached Aio's. He knew his friends were mere feet away, but right now they were all lying down beneath the tarps, and no one could see their secret gesture.

"It's beautiful," Lago murmured.

Aio's brow furrowed.

"Your pendant. Is it a sapphire?"

"That is what Fingrenn said Common name is. We call them all *arambukh*, no matter if stone or metal."

"Sapphires are highly valuable in Zovaria. Especially ones with strong colors, like yours."

"My scalp does not think I could stamp it in Zovaria. They do not share our ledgers."

"No, I mean it's valuable on its own." Lago lifted the sapphire. It shimmered, tinting his fingertips blue. "We trade colorful gemstones like this one, like I told you we trade Qupi chips, but the stones are worth a lot more."

"Is Zovaria not built of pink stones?"

"Yes, but those are relatively common, so they aren't that valuable. I find it funny that you think they are all the same, yet yours is such a precious stone, while Abjus's is only made of granite."

"I like granite, it makes bigger mountains. Just because it is common, it does not make it less precious."

Lago could smell Aio's salty sweat mixing with the silty scent of Blu's fur. *I wish I could hold him right now*, he thought, *even in the heat, sweating as one*. He dropped the sapphire and turned to lie on his back.

Aio had his hand down by his side, and Lago took it in his own, tenderly, with their palms now sweating together. Aio smiled and closed his eyes.

They awoke to a thunderous slapping sound. Lago pulled his hand back in a fearful reflex, but Aio had rolled over in his sleep long ago, and they were holding hands no longer. The tarps were crackling in the strong winds, which had picked up as soon as Sunnokh set. Although the wind was refreshing to their sweating bodies, the air blown was still hot and dense with particulates.

Abjus and Sunu quickly packed the tarps before they flew away. When twilight asked for the winds to abate, they navigated by following the path dictated by the stars. They had traveled at night for two weeks, but almost entirely under the cover of the forests. Now that they finally walked under clear skies, Lago thought it would be a good chance to teach the Laatu about the constellations and how to follow the stars.

"The most important constellation you should learn," Lago said, "and also a very easy one to spot, is the Sword of Zeiheim." He pointed north and upward. "It's the one that looks like a cross with a blurred jewel at its core. They say the sword's blade was forged from lightning, that it was so sharp it could cut a person's soul in two, leaving them in anguish, always searching for their missing half."

"Sword of Dseiheim," Givra repeated, unable to figure out how to voice the *zee* sound, as it was not a phoneme used in the Miscamish tongue.

"It's the sword the great hero Dravéll carried in his adventures in the *Barlum Saga*," Lago said.

"Is hero Dravéll friend of Lago-Sterjall?" Kenondok asked.

"Oh no, it's fiction. He's one of the Wayfarers of the Sixteen Realms, an adventurer in a series of books by Ansko Loregem, all made-up stories. But Ansko didn't invent the Sword of Zeiheim—that came from legends from before the Downfall, he just added it to his tales. The pink jewel at the center of the sword is the Lodestar, who we call Pellámbri. She is actually a nebula, who always stays in the north. All the other stars spin around her, including the blade, pommel, and guard of the sword."

"What is nebula?" Aio asked.

"It's like a cloud, with many stars inside, that's why it looks blurry. Pre-Downfall texts claim that stars are born in nebulas. With a telescope you can see dozens of stars inside Pellámbri, and she looks even more pink and colorful." Lago pointed his right arm at the sword while speaking. "When you walk, if you keep the sword to your right hand, you are traveling west. And if you follow the sword, you are traveling north, though you will never get any closer to it."

Lago came to a stop and pointed directly south toward a bright point of light flickering in and out of view through the ash clouds of Laaja Khenukh, who had been dormantly smoking for at least a thousand years. "That is Eo-Nuk," he said, "they are the brightest of all stars. Eo-Nuk is not a nebula, not like Pellámbri, but six stars that happen to be aligned."

"The star who hides in smoke?" Kenondok asked.

"That one. Look closer, you'll see they are really six."

"How to look closer?" Kenondok asked, leaning his head forward as if that would help.

"Actually, here," Lago said, handing Kenondok his binoculars. Gazing through the instrument, the Laatu warrior understood. He passed the glass around for the others to observe the six stars in one.

"Eo-Nuk is only visible in Summer," Lago proudly added. "In the next few days, they'll sink under the volcano and not show up again for a long while. They are some sort of allgender Tsing god. Their creator or something, like Takhísh and Takhamún, but all in one. Don't know much about them, but they are the smallest of all constellations."

"What else do your keen eyes see?" Sunu asked.

Lago searched the heavens. "There's another weapon up there, Dunokh Sull, the mystical bow," he said, pointing left of Eo-Nuk's six stars. "They call it the *Arc of the Night Sky*. It's the one with the seven stars making a half circle, with a dim line of stars that look like a taut string."

"Like the legendary bow the dauntless Hed Mauvenel wielded?" Sunu asked.

"You've heard of it! Yes, though we call them Lerr Mauvenel in the Zovarian Union. They are the only allgender hero in any of the stories I've read."

Sunu concurred. "They say Dunokh Sull needed no arrows. When Hed Mauvenel plucked its string, a shard of obsidian would appear in midair and chase after its target, missing not ever. They say the bow was so dangerous, that Mauvenel took it to their own grave."

"The Oldrin have tales of this hero too," Alaia said. "In our version, Lerr Mauvenel shot spears instead of arrows, but during the great battle of Oskirin they ran out of spears, so instead they started shooting out pine trees with their bow. They used up an entire forest to defeat the hordes of xenolith giants. That's how Dorhond became so barren, how the White Desert came to be."

"How do you even shoot a pine tree? That makes no sense," Lago teased.

Alaia glared. "Hey, don't question *my* stories, they are as likely as your own."

"What other great legends are written upon your black dome?" Sunu asked.

"Hmm, let's see." Lago pointed straight up. "That snaking line of stars there, we call Lummukem. It's supposed to be a winged dragon, but I don't know the story behind it."

"The Laatu know Lummukem's tragic story," Sunu said, excited to share. "Tale is old as roots of Ma'u banyan. Sunu will tell you. Beyond six lands, beneath six seas, when Noss was young as a tadpole, the two continents were one, known as the lands of Illid. To protect all life on Illid, Lummukem soared, by day, by night, swallowing fires that fell from endless sky. Big as the trunk of Mindreldrolom was the dragon, and nothing could hurt him. But humans nonetheless tried. They blew poisoned darts at him, and hurled spears, and spat at his shadow.

"Lummukem wanted human tribes to stop hating his gentle wings, so one day he asked Noss for help. Noss reached deep within their ocean and brought out the tear of a star. *This tear will allow you to become human for one day,* said Noss, *so you may tell the founding tribes of Illid that dragons are benevolent, not evil.* Lummukem thanked Noss and drank the tear, and so he became human. But the tribes of Illid did not listen to his strange words, because dragons speak two tongues at once, neither of which humans can understand. When day turned to night, and back to day again, Lummukem's body began to shift. The tribes saw his skin turn purple, and yellow, and full of scales. They pierced his back with lances and cut off his head, not allowing him to become tall like the trunk and invincible once more. That is the tale of Lummukem, Sky Dragon of Illid. Thread unravels, cut, and sewn, and so the story goes."

"Poor Lummukem," Alaia said ruefully. "So unfair."

Sunu pointed northeast. "What story tell those stars?"

Lago knew exactly the ones they meant, as those stars made a bright and clear shape. "That constellation is Gara'ébra's Hourglass. See how one side looks like it's more filled with stars than the other? As the seasons pass, the hourglass becomes inverted."

"Yet the sands never fall," Balstei said. "The hourglass is stuck in time."

"Sunu does not know this legend," Sunu said to the artificer.

"I don't either," Lago added, "I just know the name of the constellation."

"I don't much care for spritetales," Balstei said, "but I know of this one because it deals with a mythical aetheric element, *caesura*, the aetheric variant of calcium, which is said to control time. Caesura doesn't exist, as far as we know, other than in tales. The story is about an artificer named Gara'ébra, who was growing old and was fearful of not having enough time left to finish learning the secrets of the world. Beyond six lands, beneath six seas, Gara'ébra ventured to Norviria, far in the northern Khaar Du Wastes, where deep in the ice a giant from beyond time was buried."

"Another dragon?" Alaia asked.

"No, a giant squid," Balstei said. "Gara'ébra dug into the ice and pulled out the squid's chitinous beak. She ground it up and separated the aetheric calcium from it, obtaining pure sands of caesura. With these magical sands, she crafted an hourglass that would allow her to stop aging. When the artifact was finished and her enchantment cast, the caesura sands began to drop, one grain at a time.

All the artificer needed to do was turn the hourglass every hour, before the last grain of sand fell, and she would gain those four wicks of time back. Unfortunately, it also meant she had to keep turning the hourglass, hour after hour. She grew tired of this hourly ritual, for it constantly interrupted her studies and her sleep. More fatigued she grew until one night she fell asleep and did not wake up in time to turn the hourglass. When the last grain of caesura fell, time stopped not just for Gara'ébra, but also for the hourglass, leaving them both stranded that way for eternity, never moving forward or backward. And so the story goes."

"I wonder why so many of these stories are depressing," Alaia grumbled. "But I have a happy one for you. Look right over there." She pointed at a cluster of thirteen golden stars. "Those are the thirteen sisters of Muhmele, who I named my back spurs after."

"Back spurs?" Abjus asked.

Alaia dropped the straps of her overalls and lifted her shirt. Aio, Givra, and Sunu had seen her back spurs before, but Abjus and Kenondok had not. They leaned closer to inspect the thirteen bones protruding from her spine.

"Tell the story of your beautiful spine," Givra requested.

Alaia fixed her clothing and began, "My friend Mellorie told me this one. By Pliwe, I hope she made it out of Withervale... Anyway, beyond six lands, beneath six seas, was this range called the Thirteen Peaks—actually, it's still there, south of the White Desert—where thirteen princesses once lived. Their yellow hairs were shinier than gold, their faces blacker than coal. Their wicked father wanted them forever pure, so the fucker kept his daughters locked at the stupas atop each of the peaks, and the princesses were unable to see or talk to each other. An allgender caretaker would bring them food, clothing, jewels, books, and anything their princessy hearts desired, as long as they remained locked up and accepted their fate."

Alaia slowed her pace, allowing herself to recall the story. "The youngest of the sisters, Vulu, felt lonely, and asked the caretaker for a companion, a bird. She said she wanted the most beautiful bird of all, with fairest of feathers and a song so sweet only a princess like herself could hear it. Her caretaker scoured the ends of the bazaars of Tsenhanuur until they found this old woman of sparse but bright-red hair. The Crone of Ukhagar she was, but the caretaker didn't know this. She's like this trickster? Shows up in many Dorhond legends. Anyway, the Crone of Ukhagar gave the caretaker a golden cage, and inside it was this gorgeous, gold-feathered bird—an aureate thrush.

"*This golden bird will sing only to a princess, but what she will sing, I cannot tell,* said the Crone of Ukhagar with a devious, sharp-toothed smile. *I cast a spell on* her so she can never fly away, not unless she is told to. She will be a perfect companion, even if she has a mind of her own. And then she laughed." Alaia cackled like a demented magpie.

Pichi recoiled in surprise and lost her footing, falling on her enormous rump.

"Sorry, Pichi," Alaia apologized, then continued her tale once the smilodon had gotten back on her paws.

"The Crone of Ukhagar sold the aureate thrush—for a fortune, I bet you—and the caretaker carried the bird and her golden cage to Vulu. The aureate thrush was beautiful, but she did not sing for Vulu. The lonely princess wept then, and told the bird all of her woes, about wanting to be with her sisters, to talk to them. The golden bird listened… and suddenly spoke. *I will be your herald*, said the bird. And Vulu could hear her, for only a princess like herself could hear the words of an aureate thrush. *I will fly to the stupas and talk for you, and for your sisters, if you grant me my freedom after the season of sandstorms is over.*

"Vulu promised she would let the bird fly free come the end of the season of sandstorms. From that day on, the thirteen sisters could tell each other everything by sending their words with the golden herald, and they no longer felt so lonely. But six weeks later, the season of sandstorms came to an end, and the sisters did not want to let the aureate thrush go.

"The oldest of the sisters, Finnashvell, had an idea. She asked the aureate thrush to fly away and find the Crone of Ukhagar, to ask her if she knew of a way they could escape the stupas without their father being able to chase after them. The herald flew beyond six lands, deserts, and seas, and at last in Fel Mellanolv she found the old woman and asked her the question. The old woman was a princess too, you see, and could perfectly hear the bird's words. The thrush flew back to Finnashvell, carrying with her thirteen grains of barley, and said, *This is as the Old Crone commands. On a Summer's night, when the Ilaadrid Shard shines upon Sceres's Sulphur face, you and your sisters must each swallow one of these grains. If you do, you will all fly free and be together at last.*"

"I see where this is going," Kitjári interrupted.

"Then shut your muzzle," Alaia replied before continuing. "So, what happened was, the aureate thrush flew the message and a grain of barley to each of the other sisters, and they waited for six moon cycles until Sceres changed to Sulphur, until a night when her shard shone bright. *What will happen once we swallow the grains?* The oldest sister asked the bird. *The light will come and carry you away*, answered the golden herald. Sceres and her shining beacon rose in the east, gilding each grain of sand of the White Desert. Up in the thirteen stupas, the sisters swallowed their grains of barley all at the same time. All except for Finnashvell. As she lifted the grain to her mouth, the golden bird snatched the grain from her slender fingers and swallowed it at once."

"Oh," Kitjári interjected. "Didn't see that betrayal coming."

"There's more," Alaia said. "The light did come, to carry the sisters away. The stupas glowed from the inside, like beacons of radiant gold, shining brighter than Sceres and her shard. From as far as Wastyr, the glow of the Thirteen Peaks could be seen. When the caretaker climbed to each of the stupas and unlocked each of the thirteen doors, they found the princesses' rooms burnt and empty of anything but charcoal. Once they exited the last stupa—the one that used to house Finnashvell—the caretaker looked up and saw thirteen new stars, together, in the sky. Thread unravels, cut, and sewn."

"Wait, so what happened to the older sister?" Kitjári asked.

"Finnashvell burned," Alaia casually answered. "Blackened bones were all that remained of her. The aureate thrush took her place and is now free, up in the sky, with the princesses."

"That's fucking dreadful," Kitjári said. "I thought this was a happy story."

"Twelve out of thirteen is quite a good ratio," Lago opined.

"Exactly!" Alaia said, bumping shoulders with him. "And the bird was freed too. No longer needed to be caged or used for princessy errands."

"What happens to Crone of Ukhagar?" Aio asked. "My scalp likes her, even if it does not understand her."

"Dunno," Alaia replied. "She shows up and messes with stories, but there's never a conclusion to her own."

"I find this story, um…" Abjus paused, trying to think of the word. He looked at Sunu and scraped his tongue with his nails.

"*Dunanfid.* Unpalatable," Sunu suggested.

"Yes. Unpalatable," Abjus repeated. "Lago. Tell me more stars, stories to cleanse stomach."

Lago looked around, trying to find the most obvious constellations. "That one with the curving line of stars, with the red one at the center, that is Panmaskroon, the tamarin monkey."

"This we know about, we tell tales of Panmaskroon," Givra said. "We tell children about monkey, mischievous creature. One of our *ster,* flashing vines in our drolom, we call it Panmaskroon, because he also has four legs and long tail."

Lago continued, pointing out the black-tongued Wyrm of Arkánni, the hexagonal perfection of Zahiir's Apiary, the lengthy penis of the Horse of Malazzari, the sinuous neck of the Alabaster Swan, the three purple eyes of Jawsplitter, the two yellow eyes of Kerjaastórgnem.

"Some stars have Miscam names, some Common, some are Nu'irgesh, some we know not," Kenondok keenly observed.

"The old star maps were modified after the Downfall," Lago said. "I'm still not familiar with a lot of the old names, too many of them changed."

"Do they all have stories?"

"I think so, but I don't know the stories behind all the constellations," Lago admitted. "But I'd like to learn them, every single one of them, someday."

Chapter Forty-One

A Meeting in the Mountains

"Are you ready to go, Bear?" Banook asked.

Bear yipped uncontrollably, then swiftly quieted when Safis gave him a stare colder than the bergs of Teslurkath.

"Although I appreciate when he's quiet, try not to be so rough on the poor mutt," Banook said to the white wolf, both out loud and through mindspeaking, as he always did so Bear would not feel left out.

«No promises,» she mindspoke back. «His impulses are too unrestrained.»

"It's only because he misses Lago-Sterjall as much as I do, and this mission will bring us closer in heart if not in distance. I'm eager to depart, eager to send him the news that you brought from the Anglass Dome."

Banook slung a small backpack over his shoulder and opened wide the cabin's door. "Alright, you two, I'm ready as a sail unfurled in the wind. We won't be venturing into icy crevasses or spectral cities this time. This will be but a short hike."

Their short hike took a bit over three weeks.

Deep in the southwestern Stelm Wujann was Mount Fogra, rising high before cresting in an arrowhead-shaped peak. Atop its perpetually white-crowned summit, the Wujann Observatory perched.

Banook held tight to the chains that served as handholds for the narrow trail, where one side was a steep granite wall while the other was a sheer drop to a jagged oblivion. The path was clearly not built for someone his size, but they had made it safely across thus far. Up ahead, the spiraling tower of the old observatory waited.

Banook looked to Safis, who followed closely behind. "If you don't mind," he said, wincing uncomfortably with what he was about to ask, "could you perchance pick a more domestic form for the time being? Just like our friend, Bear, so that people don't get too suspicious."

Safis did mind, but complied, shapeshifting into a white greyhound. They stepped off the treacherous trail and entered a courtyard of boulders with snowy caps. A trail with recent footprints serpentined toward the stone tower. The Wujann Observatory was a perfectly preserved relic from a distant past, as no damage from the Downfall had reached these inhospitable peaks. Banook slammed the Sceres-shaped knocker into the metal door.

Mere heartbeats later, the door creaked open. Wearing an expression of utter confusion, a man stepped out. His clothes were those of a ranger, one who knew his way up the mountains and beyond. He was light-brown of beard, of coppery skin, with green eyes as sharp as his mind and his long dagger. He held his black cape tightly across his chest, to keep the cold at bay. The ranger's face was shadowed under a wide-brimmed hat and showed that he clearly had not expected visitors.

"Banook?" the ranger asked.

"Ardof?" Banook replied, mimicking the ranger's incredulous tone.

Ardof—one of Esum's secret informants—had recently traveled to the Wujann Observatory to deliver sensitive information he'd acquired around Anglass and Brimstowne.

"You needed not chase me all the way up the tallest peak in the Wujann to trade books with me, pal," Ardof said. "Although my intuition tells me you aren't here to trade books, or to inquire about a certain elk of bad blood, not like when last we met."

"Sorry, friend," Banook affirmed. "I carry no books with me this time. It's... How to explain it? I have a message to deliver, although not for you—I had not expected to find you here."

Ardof's eyes narrowed suspiciously. He ushered the big man and the dogs into the observatory, locking the door behind him.

"You are a wild mystery, man of the mountains," Ardof said, hanging his cape on a hook, revealing the white wraps that covered both his arms. He hung his hat as well, then ran a hand over his receding hairline. "Your curious eyes tell me you haven't been inside this tower before."

"I have not," Banook said hesitantly. "But I've heard of a device used to send messages across long distances. Do you perchance operate it? I would like to—"

"Save your breath, pal," Ardof said, climbing up the steps of the spiraling tower. "You'll have to tell Idefel. I am not the one in charge here."

As they reached the top of the steps, a woman's voice called out, "Did I hear something falling downsta—"

"We have a peculiar visitor," Ardof interrupted.

Behind him came Banook, who ducked under the arch and had to keep ducking, as his nearly nine feet of height were too much for the low ceilings of the old building. Ardof introduced Banook to an elderly Iesmari scholar named Idefel. She tried to shake arms in the Iesmari way, by grasping at the elbows instead of hands, but had to heartily laugh at the impossibility of the situation, struggling with Banook's tree trunk of a forearm.

"Please, sit down, you'll hurt your neck, young man," Idefel said, letting Banook sprawl out on an ample couch in front of a fireplace. Ardof and Idefel pulled up chairs beside him, while Safis sat herself on a tall-backed chair in a distant corner, watching over them as if she owned the observatory. Bear went to sniff at every crevice in the circular room.

Banook explained that there was a message he needed to send to Crysta, a professor who worked at the Mesa Observatory.

"I know of her, of course," Idefel said. "But this is most unusual, for many reasons. How do you know Professor Holt?"

"I, um, I don't know her directly, but only through an old student of hers."

"What is the student's name?" Ardof asked, as he sliced his switchblade through an apple. He offered a slice to Banook.

"He, um, his name is, uh... L-Luras, Luras Varum."

"I'm still confused," Idefel said. "No one is supposed to know of... of our way of communicating with Withervale. Crysta would never reveal such a secret, not to anyone. At least not on purpose. No offense, big fella, but I don't know why I should trust you."

"Luras told me of the reflecting device," Banook said, a bit flustered, "though he probably shouldn't have. He bumped into Crysta while she was using the... I don't know the device's name. I just, um, I—"

"I'll vouch for Banook," Ardof jumped in. "If you think he's a Negian spy, you can't be further from the truth. The poor hermit lives alone in the mountains, he probably doesn't even know what's been going on in Withervale. Do you, pal?"

Banook was surprised by Ardof's interjection, but also glad for it. He admitted he knew Withervale had been attacked but didn't know any details. He was heartbroken when Idefel told him what had happened in Lago's hometown, but his heart pumped with vigor when she said that Crysta and some of her friends had managed to escape, and that she was now communicating with them from all the way in Zovaria.

Banook wanted to ask whether Lago had been one of the people who escaped with the professor, but didn't know how to ask without revealing his true name. "I am glad to hear Crysta made it out safely," was all he said.

"And what sort of message did you want to send to her?" Idefel asked.

"Well, Crysta has always been interested in the domes. I happen to have some information she might find useful, for something strange is festering in Anglass."

"We know of the Red Stag," Idefel said. "That is old news by now."

"Not that, at least not directly," Banook said. "The vines of Anglass, they seem to be twisting out of shape, just like they did at Heartpine long ago, before the dome began to collapse."

"I was there just a few months back," Ardof said, "and noticed no such thing."

"You would not have," Banook said. "A friend of mine was living there, who recently came to visit me. Her name is Safis." He tried not to look at Safis, who still perched on her throne-like chair, but failed. He forced himself to look away, and added, "She used to live by Heartpine, and clearly remembers how the dome began to change, six years back, just in the same way Anglass is now changing. She said the motion is nearly imperceptible, too slow to be noticed by anyone who isn't living near the vines for months at a time, but she's certain something ill is brewing in that nether pit."

"That's peculiar indeed," Idefel remarked, adjusting her round spectacles. Her light-gray eyes were enormously magnified behind them. "I think Crysta would be keenly interested to learn about that."

"Perhaps we could also ask Crysta for a small favor," Banook said. "She could let her old student, Luras, know that Safis is safe and living with me in my cabin now."

"You could add that to the note," Idefel said. "I'm sure Luras will be delighted to hear his friend is out of that wretched cesspit." She handed a logbook and quill to Banook and asked him to write down the message. "I'll send it out tomorrow, if that is alright. We send messages on Sunndays, unless it's an emergency."

"That would be most kind, gracious Idefel. I thank you." Banook bowed from within his couch.

Idefel told Banook that he and his dogs were welcome to spend the night at the observatory. Ardof was meant to leave that day, but he asked to spend one more night, saying he'd be leaving to Brimstowne in the morning, though his path would take him south, through Cragfoot, and not across the rocky heart of the Wujann.

By dawnbreak, Ardof had his bag packed, and he walked out with Banook while Idefel held the metal door open.

"Might be three months till next time," Ardof said to Idefel, boots crunching on the fresh snow of the courtyard. "I'll bring you more nutmeg from Nool. Whole, not ground this time."

"And pink peppercorns from Dimbali."

"If my wanderings carry me that far, but it'll cost ya."

The ranger led the way across the hazardous path with the chain handholds. Past that, the less-deadly portion of the trail would keep them together for a few more hours before they parted ways—just as Ardof had planned.

"Well, my dear pal," Ardof said, "now that we find ourselves alone… are you going to tell me the truth about this friend of yours?"

"Wuh-what do you mean?" Banook asked.

"Luras Varum. Crysta's mysterious student. The name sounds oddly similar to another name you seemed to be struggling to keep from speaking."

Chapter Forty-Two

Brasha'in Scablands

The never-ending cinder cones finally ended. The company found themselves in front of the black peaks they had seen from the top of the first cinder cone. The rocky ground had fragmented into hexagonal chunks, each about a dozen feet wide; they extruded up and down into pillars and steps, like a gargantuan honeycomb turned to stone. These were the Steps of Odrásmunn, a wall that separated the dry lava desert from the range of cinder cones they had traversed.

Jiara scouted for a path up the smooth-faced formations of basalt. "They say that Hashan, the Tsing capital, is built entirely from columnar rocks like these."

"Then why do they call it the City of Bridges and not the City of Columns?" Lago asked.

"Because of the bridges, of course," Balstei replied, jumping into the conversation. "I have not been to Hashan myself, but I have seen colorful depictions of it and heard tales from the scholars who studied at the Tsing Academy. If you were to view a map, you'd notice that all their city blocks—or their plateaus, as they call them—are elevated, separated by canals and connected by bridges. Bridges everywhere, even from home to home. Their columnar rocks rise like dark crystals to form their buildings, with their tops sliced to sharpened facets that resemble cut jewels."

"A friend of mine said that from afar, Hashan looks like a cracked geode," Jiara added. "*A city of incomparable splendor,* he claimed, *and largest in all the realms.*"

They advanced over the flat-topped columns. The polygonal steps were eroded from a much more ancient volcanic event that had acted as a barrier, containing the flow of hot lava into the wasteland known as the Brasha'in Scablands. The sun rose as they climbed the Steps of Odrásmunn, casting their sharp shadows onto the polished, nearly black columns. It was easy for the saber-toothed cats to climb these rocks: they simply jumped from pillar to pillar, step to step, until they reached the top. There they all stopped to revel in the austere vastness that sprawled to the south and west.

Though the sun was out, most of the volcanic lands still sat in the penumbra of the Stelm Sajal's long shadows, which were further darkened by the billowing smoke from the slumbering Laaja Khenukh. The entire stretch ahead was black, glossy, and looked almost liquefied, as if a gangrenous wound had suppurated and the vile, dark fluids had coagulated into a jagged crust, scarring hundreds of miles. No sign of anything alive remained, save for the few kestrels who sometimes took on the hot updrafts, lifting to the skies to observe the scarified lands from high above.

"The rocks at the bottom won't be smooth like these columns," Jiara cautioned. "They will be sharp, full of pointed shards. They will often roll under your feet and want to trap your ankles, and they'll be hot as a frying pan during the day."

"Great," Lago said. "And how are we going to get down there?" He peered down at the abyss of shadow. The Steps of Odrásmunn rose slowly from the east, but once they reached the highest point, they dropped sharply for hundreds of feet on the western side.

"The steps are less steep in some areas," Jiara said. "We'll find a path for the cats to climb down." Jiara looked different up here at the edge of the cliff; her hair was loose instead of tied into her usual thick braid, letting the ash-blonde strands flow like a weightless silk in the warm wind. She had begun to leave her hair loose like this, as every time she shifted into Kitjári and back, her braids would come undone. But it was more than a practical choice—the change felt good.

She asked to borrow Lago's binoculars, then stared at the solidified lava. The landscape was so homogeneous, and the air so dry, that scales and distances were nearly impossible to judge. "There is only one prominent-enough peak in this whole wasteland," she said. "There, to the southwest." She pointed to a blackened bulge on the horizon. "That would be the most likely location for a Miscam temple. As far as I know, no one has traveled that far into the scablands."

"What about those other bumps closer to us?" Balstei asked.

"They seem smaller in comparison, but maybe. We can explore them on the way to the tallest point. The nearest of them is not too far away, maybe thirty miles on a raven's wing."

"Thirty miles?" Alaia asked. "It looks more like three miles to me."

"Do not trust your eyes in these hazeless deserts," Jiara said. "I'm calculating based on the angles and sizes of shadows from the range, and on some details I can only see with the binoculars."

"Is there any spot that wasn't covered by lava?" Balstei asked.

Jiara kept scanning. "Not that I can see. It seems blanketed all the way to the horizon."

"It's time to bring out Ockam's notebook again," Lago said, approaching Pichi, who was carrying all their equipment. He removed the notebook and a pencil from his bag. "Mind helping us again?" he asked Balstei. The artificer nodded, then began to draw a rough map of the area using a makeshift ruler to get the distances close to Jiara's estimations.

"We shelter now," Hod Abjus said once Balstei was done. "Wait day away before trip to frying pan."

They spread the tarps across a ring of columns, locking them in place by wedging metal stakes in the cracks. This time they had more room to spread out, but the ground was hard as could be. It was windy, with a constant updraft from the west twirling at the cusp of the columns. The wind provided some comfort, but also made them realize that hot air would be all that they would be breathing in the days to come.

They awoke when the gusts grew fiercest, summoned by dusk. They stowed the tarps and rode the smilodons, soon finding a path that descended to the lava beds. The shift from the columns to the lava rock was softened by a smooth curve of maroon sand that had piled up over centuries, a grain at a time. The cats jumped off the columns and slid down the slope to the bottom of the field.

The lava flow here had moved more slowly, forming smooth, undulating ripples that clustered like the fossils of intestines. The flow was black, but lined with oxidized edges that glimmered red. When light hit the oxides at certain angles, it looked as if liquid lava was still smoldering within the crusted ropes.

These fields were easy to traverse thanks to the sand that filled the gaps between the cords of rock. There was even a bit of life here, clustering wherever the sediments clung to a pitiful amount of moisture. Tangling and stabbing cacti grew in deep cracks, next to writhing shrubs with hooked barbs and shriveled branches.

The three Silvfröash changed into their half-forms. It had cooled down enough that their fur would not make them overheat, and their Silvesh helped them navigate in the dark.

"Very little lives here," Kulak noted. "Mindrelsilv cannot see much."

"Let's follow next to the wall for now," Sterjall said. "Some plants still grow here. Perhaps we'll find a last source of food or water."

They had switched their seating on the smilodons, deciding the three Silvfröash should be riding in front. Kulak stayed with his trusted Blu, Sterjall with Kobos, and Kitjári with Fulm, visibly uncomfortable with handling the hissy cat.

Sterjall missed the contact with Aio-Kulak, as riding behind him was a way to be intimate without arousing suspicion, but he was also happy to have Alaia close to him now, as they could chat for hours and make time pass more quickly.

They kept close to the columns, walking on the soft sand. The three Silvfröash searched for signs of life and quickly spotted dark beetles, a few scorpions, and tiny mice that hid in holes under the ropy rocks. It would take great effort to get the mice out, and they would not offer much sustenance, so they passed them by.

"I think I smell something," Kitjári said, slapping Fulm's black shoulders to make him stop. Fulm turned his head and hissed at her.

Kenondok hushed the smilodon, then to Kitjári said, "No slapping. Soft rub between shoulders."

Kitjári hopped down, sniffing the air. "Just a moment," she said, and left the others waiting as she made her way into the lava field. About thirty strides away, she kneeled and dug in a pocket of compressed sand. Then she went for another pocket nearby, and another, and soon returned with three large roots skewered on her claws.

"What have you unearthed?" Sunu asked her.

"Igneous verbena roots. Truly delicious if you fry them. Could also boil them, but better not to waste our water."

"How did you spot them from so far away?" Balstei asked her.

"My nose is much more sensitive now. In the forest it was overbearing. Now that there's little to smell, I quickly picked up on the scent."

"One with good ears, one with good eyes, one with good nose," Sunu remarked.

Kitjári stored the roots in Pichi's food bag, then signaled to keep moving. From time to time, she would ask Fulm to stop again, careful to only use light touches between his shoulders. She gathered as many roots as possible, until there were none left to find as they moved deeper into the lava field.

That first night they treaded swiftly and made good progress, taking advantage of the flat ground. By morning, they had slowed down significantly; the lava in this area had flowed faster, lifting shards of rock that stuck out like knives as tall as the smilodons. When the sun finally shone directly on the scablands, they were in a barren field of ruinous rocks, with no place to take shelter, balancing upon uneven grounds that were incisive and vindictive.

"We need to keep moving, even in the daytime," Jiara said, wiping sweat off her brow. "We have to find a spot to pitch our tarps before the heat becomes intolerable."

To protect their scalps from the biting sun, the Laatu covered their heads by pulling up the dangling fabrics at the backs of their shodogs. They arrived at a ravine that had likely once been a river canyon, where the lava flow had filled the bottom more evenly. Sunnokh was already scorching their backs, but the ravine was deep enough to cast protective shadows. They climbed down loose boulders before noon blistered their skin.

Even the ravine would offer no shelter at midday on Highsun, so they nailed the tarps into the rocks diagonally, one end on the smooth ground, another on the jagged wall, and they waited for the heat to pass over them.

Lago crawled closer to Alaia.

"Hey. I know this isn't as pretty a view as last time," he said, looking up at the tarp, "but happy birthday, I guess?"

"Khest," she cursed. "I didn't even realize. The days are all blending together. Is it really?"

"Yeah. Big one and twenty."

"Well, it's certainly not as fancy as a meteor shower. No wine, even—*that* I can't forgive. But you can pretend you brought me to the desert for my birthday, which is something I always wanted to see. Though I pictured white sand dunes, not a bed of black rocks."

"Balstei told me there are enormous dunes on the far west of the scablands. As tall as mountains, and he said they sing in the winds, though I'm not sure what that meant. But that's hundreds of miles west."

"I'll take what I can get."

"Then you owe me one, again."

"I'll set you up on another date next year. I'm curious to see who with, you pick very odd ones lately. Do they need to be of a new species every time?"

"Might as well be," Lago replied.

Abjus woke them hours before sunset, with the heat not yet having abated. "We march before dusk," he declared. "Sleep not priority, little food, little water. We march, fast, find Nu'irg ust Momsúndo."

They plodded along. The rocks were hot, but the jagged landscape cast enough shadows that the crevices were not hot enough to burn the paws of the smilodons. By sundown, they reached the nearest of the hills they had spotted from the Steps of Odrásmunn.

The Silvfröash shifted into their half-forms and began scouting the hill. There was barely anything alive. They could see the threads of flecks of pollen, of dormant tardigrades hibernating in crevices, of wind-blown seeds that would never sprout, but not much more.

"I doubt this will lead to anything," Sterjall said, holding Leif up to scan farther. "This looks like another cinder cone."

Indeed, as they reached the top of the pumice-like bubble of rock, they found a crater's edge. All that remained in the concavity was a patch of foam-like rock streaked with glassy fibers. They found no signs of Mamóru, found no place to shelter.

By the time the pre-dawn sky began to brighten, they reached a long depression where the molten rocks had spilled down.

They stood at the cliff's edge and looked to the left, and then to the right. The bluff receded interminably for miles and miles.

"I couldn't see this drop at all from the steps," Kitjári said. "Do you think this could be—"

"Come, all of you!" Sunu called from farther down the edge. "Cast your sights below."

They pointed to a few prominences beyond the cliff, perhaps old buttes or stacks that seemed to have diverted the lava flow, with their tops made of a different kind of untampered rocks. Atop one of them was a tangle of knotted forms, covering an area a hamlet wide.

"Are those vines?" Balstei asked.

Sterjall stared through his binoculars. "They look like vines," he said, "but there's something odd about them. They also look like rocks." He used Leif to scan the forms. "They don't have any threads," he said. "Whatever they are, they're dead."

The sky was bright and blue by the time they reached the vines, finding they sprouted from a pocket of clean soil that had been spared the wrath of the fiery deluge.

Sterjall dismounted Kobos. His footpaws were delighted to once again settle on soft dirt and soil, as for days they had felt nothing but harsh rocks.

"They are all dead," he said, entering what seemed like a cathedral of dry, grayish vines. The forms extended up into twisted loops and humped galls. The fossilized vines were covered in a craquelure that peeled like the shedding skin of snakes. Sterjall scratched at one of the vines with a dark claw, and its brittle surface collapsed to the ground, exploding in chalky clouds. The revealed interior was congealed into a cloudy crystal, like amber, but smokey and yellow. The dry sap was glass hard, marbled with linear inclusions of tubules, like varicose veins.

"I think this is the edge of the dome," Kitjári said, "where the wall used to be."

"Or maybe one of the supporting columns," Balstei noted.

"Not likely," Kulak said. "Columns only have big vines. These are small, like ones found by perimeter." He found a thorn on the side of a vine and tried to bend it; it collapsed like a burnt incense stick.

Sterjall climbed up a thick arch of yellow glass to get a better view. "If this was the wall, it means the center of the dome, where the temple is, must be forty miles away." He looked southwest to where the lonely pinnacle broke the horizon of the scablands.

"That peak seems to be about forty miles out," Kitjári said. She produced the map Balstei had drawn. "We should scout the hills that are on the way to it, to better plan our route from their vantage points. But for now, we need rest, and the shade of these vines is much too tempting."

They took cover inside the crystallized forest, where they remained cool and got decent rest, at least until noon hit and the hot stillness crawled on them, drenched them, and dried them up again. Abjus woke them up before sundown once more, and they continued onward.

The path took them over a field of obsidian shards that screeched beneath every step of the smilodons, sounding like constantly sharpening knives. It took them all night with no rest before they arrived at the next hill.

Unfortunately, the hill was nothing but an enormous obsidian bubble that had surfaced from beneath the crust, pierced through the lava flow, and hardened into a cracked top, exposing its gloomy heart of glass. The hillside was made of loose shards of black glass that slid under their weight like bloodthirsty dunes—they agreed it would be best not to climb it.

"We need to keep moving, even in daylight, until we find shelter," Lago said, attaching his mask to his shoulder brace before it got too hot again.

The shadows from the Stelm Sajal were sheltering them this early in the morning, yet the air was searing and still. They were exhausted, their mouths parched, their stomachs complaining about the reduced rations. The cats were particularly upset now, as their paw pads felt raw and uncomfortable, and each mile made them more bitter.

They kept pushing with no sleep. The smilodons plodded over a land that rolled up and down in mounds of glass; some shattered, some perfectly smooth, and some foamy and light and quick to bite when touched. Luckily, shade had reached them once more; not from the mountains this time, but from the ashen clouds of Laaja Khenukh.

Fulm began to hiss at the air.

Aio shifted into Kulak and asked, *"Gwen uss melban, iskbia ust du?"*

Fulm hissed again, then growled.

"Fulm says his paws are injured. We need to stop."

They dismounted the cats.

"Sunu sees cuts along his pads," Sunu said, holding up Fulm's bleeding paw and pulling out dozens of glass needles. "We cannot force him, he is hurt."

They checked Pichi's, Kobos's, and Blu's paws: all had suffered cuts from the insidious glass, though none as badly as Fulm.

"We cannot keep them hurting," Kulak said. "But we cannot stop here, or Sunnokh's breath will burn us. We walk, next to mindrégosh, look for shelter."

Lago put Agnargsilv on but did not shift into Sterjall. "Poor cats," he said, sensing their threads. "We need to take their pain away."

"No," Sunu said, putting a hand on Lago's shoulder. "Not yet. Pain is Noss's blessing. Without pain, damaging would continue. Let smilodons feel their wounds and be guided by them until we find a refuge."

Givra and Kenondok scouted ahead for paths that seemed less likely to inflict more injuries. The company walked side by side, paying attention to the cats' behaviors, checking for blood on their trail.

The endless field of glass made it impossible to discern how far they had traveled or how much farther there was still. Laaja Khenukh's plumes suddenly drifted south, leaving them exposed to the scorching light. The glass heated up beneath them, and the reflections on the glossy surfaces made it hard to see their way forward.

Fulm roared and became erratic, trying to chew at his paws. Sunu calmed him, checked for injuries, and removed any new bladelets of glass they found.

It was a rough-going, pathless endeavor. They hobbled, stumbled, and sweated at a monotonous pace. Fulm kept complaining, but nothing could be done to help him; there was no place to rest, nowhere to hide from the heat. His dark coat was heating up quickly, so he stopped his protests, saving his energy to pant.

The peak they were seeking after was not too far away now. Numerous hills surrounded the outskirts of the prominence, which looked much smaller than they had expected now that they were closer. It was early afternoon, and the sun was beating down mercilessly on them. Givra hurried ahead to explore the nearest hills, and from way in the distance called out, *"Olvet khanarom uth paengoleth!* Shelter! Bring mindrégosh, away from Sunnokh, now!"

They hurried toward the hill, glad to see it was not glassy, but made of bulky boulders of dry lava. Givra had found a cave where the long hill had collapsed. The path of fallen boulders was loose, with rocks shifting under their weight, but they were not too hard to scramble down on. Soon they reached the shade of a tunnel that extended deeper, though they could not tell how deep. The ground was mostly flat, covered with a textured rock similar to the ropey ones they had found at the beginning of the scablands.

"It's a lava tube," Jiara said. She shifted into Kitjári to better sense the space. "Like the one at the Emen Ruins, but untouched." She explained to the Laatu how lava sometimes cooled on the outside while the insides flowed out, leaving underground tunnels that could run for miles. As she explained, the others set the tarps and bedrolls on the ground.

The cats dropped onto the tarps and let Sunu tend their wounded paws. The shaman used some of their precious water to cleanse the deeper wounds, then applied an ointment and wrapped the pads with cuts of the tarps, sewing makeshift shoes to prevent the paws from getting cut or dirty again.

Sterjall, Kulak, and Kitjári gathered around the injured cats. They focused on the pain and absorbed the sharp anguish, distributing the ache across their entire bodies. Despite the dull soreness they inflicted on themselves, their hearts felt glad that the cats were no longer wincing or hissing.

Sterjall stood up, feeling relief from the shade, but also worn down by the pain he'd taken. He looked at the deepening tunnel: it was about ten strides at the mouth and mostly in shadow, except for the few cracks in the ceiling that speared down shafts of sunlight. "Should we explore it?" he asked.

"You might get lost, it could go for miles," Kitjári warned. "If Mamóru or Momsúndosilv are nearby, we could sense them from above without risking going deeper. Either way, we should first rest, and hope the cats are able to walk again tonight."

They ate little and drank even less, yet they gave a decent portion of munnji and water to the cats that day. The lava tube was cool, maintaining an even temperature once they ventured deep enough. They had not slept the previous day or night, so now they were glad to have found a place to rest their heads and fall unconscious.

Chapter Forty-Three

Whiskers in the Dark

Abjus shook them awake at sunset, after allowing them only a handful of hours of sleep. "We keep going," he said. "Peak close."

"Will the mindrégosh walk?" Sunu asked. But the cats protested, even Pichi. They did not want to move yet, and everyone was still fatigued.

"*Alg*. Rest, then," Abjus said, glad they had made that decision, for he too was bone-tired but did not want to let it show.

They finally rose at midmorning of the following day.

Sterjall went for a walk atop the snaking lava tube, but even when using Leif, he found no signs of life.

He returned to the shade to wait out the hottest part of the afternoon.

"My eyes want to see deeper in the tunnel," Kulak said.

"Too dangerous," Kitjári said, listening in. "These caves can have multiple levels, they quickly become a labyrinth of passages."

"No worry. Will not go deep," Kulak reassured her. "Only to where my eyes can still see. Sterjall, come with me."

"Uh, okay," Sterjall replied, and followed Kulak into the dark tunnel.

Kitjári stayed behind, arms crossed disapprovingly.

The wolf and caracal hopped over toppled boulders, ducked under short stalactites that looked like melting spines from a reptilian beast, and rounded a craggy bend. At that point, Sterjall could not even see the dim glow from the corner they had just turned. The darkness was absolute, at least to him.

"I can't see anything anymore," he said to Kulak.

He tried to sense the cave through Agnargsilv, but all he saw was himself, Kulak, and here and there a tiny tendril of a thread that was probably a bacterium clinging stubbornly to a fissure. The lifeless void was invisible to him.

"My eyes see three tunnels," Kulak said. "Ceiling drops farther down, so go not there, or you will cut your scalp. But Kitjári was right, farther would be dangerous, unnecessary."

What is he planning? Sterjall wondered. *I can tell he is scheming, but he's unreadable again.*

Kulak walked farther into the cave. "Can your eyes see this deep?" he asked, turning around to face Sterjall.

"All I see is your threads and aura looping back on themselves. It's very eerie, like you are a ghost suspended in nothingness. It's a bit spooky down here."

"Come to me. It is safe, if you walk straight," Kulak said.

"Are you sure?"

"Yes, come to me. Trust me."

Sterjall walked with his shoulders hunched, ears flattened, head kept low.

"No, no crouching. Trust, walk normal."

"Okay, okay." He closed his eyes, as they were useless anyway, and walked toward the spectral aura of Kulak. He trusted his steps and walked normally, stopping right in front of the caracal.

"Now take Agnargsilv off, give to me," Kulak said.

"What? Why?"

"Because I asked."

"Just what are you planning?"

"Give it, then you know," Kulak said mischievously.

Sterjall could not see Kulak's face, but he could feel that self-satisfied smirk in his threads. "You are acting weird again," he said.

"Yes, and you like it. Your tail is wagging."

Sterjall consciously made his tail stop.

"Agnargsilv," Kulak said. "Give."

"Okay, fine," Sterjall said, shapeshifting to Lago and handing his mask over. He was now in full darkness, no threads, no light, surrounded only by echoes chilled by the gloomy air. He turned sharply, hearing a rustling far behind him—he hadn't even noticed Kulak had walked away. He must've been pacing around quietly, like a cat.

"Stand still, put arms up," Kulak commanded. "Hold ceiling, it is low."

"But—"

"Hold ceiling. And do not move."

Lago obeyed. He reached up and put pressure on the textured ceiling of the cave. He thought Kulak was still a great distance behind him and flinched when he felt his breath near his face.

"Be still," a whisper said.

Lago felt handpaws unbuckling his belt, unbuttoning his trousers, and dropping them to the ground. Lago's tunic went next, and he found himself standing in the perfect dark, completely naked, while a predator paced around him and inspected his body. *I feel like he's going to eat me,* he thought, feeling a tingling thrill. Kulak circled, brushing his handpaws over Lago's bare skin, sometimes with a hint of a claw tenderly scraping. Lago became aroused. He lowered a hand to cover his erection.

"No, arms up."

Lago obeyed once more, breath shaky as if he was feeling cold.

Kulak continued prowling, feeling, making Lago quiver, but not giving him enough satisfaction. He teased a short-lived kiss, then vanished. He came from behind and tenderly bit on Lago's ear, letting his tail wrap around Lago's legs like a snake, caressing his balls. After disappearing for ten deafening heartbeats, his warmth returned. Lago felt Kulak's hot breath by his armpits, followed by the caracal's whiskers tickling his nipples. He was immersed in pure tactile pleasure, forgetting about the tunnel, about the darkness, about his tired body, about anything beyond his skin. Kulak was all there was, menacing and sensual, pacing around his vulnerable body and making him quietly moan in pleasure.

Kulak scraped his sandpapery tongue over Lago's quivering navel, and as he pulled back, he let his fur rub lightly on Lago's shaft, leaving him throbbing.

A long moment passed, stretching uncomfortably. Lago's breathing evened out. He felt a drop of his own precum land on his toe, then looked around blindly, searching in the darkness.

"K-Kulak?" he asked, feeling utterly alone. But then a warmth enveloped him from behind, making him jump and nearly hit his head on the ceiling.

Kulak had played enough—he went down on Lago. Mindful of his sharp teeth, the caracal devoured the young man's cock, letting him have his release. He swallowed the last drop, then rose to his feet.

Lago felt lightheaded. He lowered his arms as he exhaled. Kulak embraced him, letting Lago lean his weight onto his shoulders. He placed Agnargsilv back in Lago's hands.

"Now you can be wolf again," Kulak said.

Lago obeyed.

"I did... I... I thought..." Sterjall mumbled. "I thought I was meant to take the next step."

"I am bad at patience," Kulak said wryly. "But next time is your time, I promise." He stood aside and watched as Sterjall fumbled at getting dressed.

They quietly exited the depths of the lava tube, sharing an impish glow about them. The others were readying to depart. After the long rest, the smilodons seemed to have recovered a bit; the medicine Sunu applied on their paws had helped the wounds seal while keeping infections at bay.

Sterjall was wrapping his gear in a corner of the cave when Jiara approached.

"So, what was that all about?" she asked privately.

"What was what?"

"The two of you sneaking out," she said, holding an impassive stare.

"Oh, nothing. We didn't go too deep, just around the corner."

"I know. You are aware I can see through Urnaadisilv too, quite far if I focus in one direction."

"Shit... What did you—"

"I saw enough, then took the mask off. It didn't feel right to intrude more." She paused. "So?"

"Well... I guess you know what it was, then."

"This could be very dangerous. Lerrkins and Laatu don't mix. And he's their prince! And while in his half-form, you horned-up little fuckers!"

"I know!" Sterjall replied a bit too loudly. Then, more quietly, "We have been careful. And will continue to be, if anything else happens."

"Seems like you are *planning* for more to happen," Jiara said. "Just don't risk your balls. I know you feel lonely, but how do you think he would feel if—"

"This is not about Banook," Sterjall interrupted. "I know he would be alright with this, he even encouraged it. Besides, Banook is too special to me, and Aio is... He's different, means something else entirely."

Jiara tried to read the wolf's shifting expressions. She cocked her head and pulled his muzzle up. "Kid, I'm not worried about your big bear. I was asking how *Aio* would react. Whatever you do, however you feel, keep in mind that Aio's feelings might be different. You've made quite an impression on him. When you are not around, all he talks about is how passionate he feels about the world when he's near you. Just be aware of it, and play fair."

"I'm being fair. If anything, it's Aio who is pushing for more."

"Perhaps. But my advice still stands. Don't let things get out of hand, okay?"

"Okay," Sterjall exhaled, resigned. "But you can't tell anyone either."

"Of course," she said, twice tapping her knuckles together as a vow of secrecy. Then, more cheerfully, she added. "Now let's finish packing up. And just so we are clear, I am happy for you both. I'm just trying to make sure you don't get us into more trouble."

She smacked Sterjall's butt and walked away.

Chapter Forty-Four

Enolv Ruins

The peak they'd been struggling toward was only a handful of miles away, and they could now see that it, too, had been covered by lava, which had climbed up its shallow slopes to coat the entire prominence in draping black rocks. The cats could walk at their normal pace now that the ground was not made of blades, though they still had to be careful of the shifting boulders.

As they were halfway up the prominence, with night starting to yield to daybreak, they encountered some ground that was not pure dry lava, but a sort of granitic mix with lighter veins. The higher they ventured, the more of the base rock they encountered.

The sun was almost peeking over the Stelm Sajal.

"What is that smell?" Kitjári asked, lifting her muzzle. "Something is rotten. It's coming from this direction. Follow me."

They crested a mound of slate-like sheets of igneous rock, and behind it found the carcass of a horse. A black-and-white hide wrapped tightly around the skeleton, describing the hollow eye sockets, the ribbed torso, the thin limbs. Insects had devoured the meaty parts, and the ever-thirsty Sunnokh had desiccated the rest.

"Horses look much uglier than you described," Kenondok observed.

"It's a bit past its prime," Kitjári said. "Feathered hooves and wide bones, must be a draft horse. How long ago do you think it died?"

"Two months, maybe three months," Abjus answered. "Is long-faced beast from Dsovaria?"

"The saddle's leatherwork looks like from the Zovarian cavalry. Also, look at the horseshoes," she said, bending one of the dried legs up. "Thick, but very worn. And there are shards of obsidian stuck in the soles. This poor thing must've been unable to walk, so they left it for dead."

"The skin in the neck has a long cut," Balstei pointed out. "And there's another cut in the rump and leg."

Kitjári lifted the flap of leather over the rump; it was crusty and hard, and made a crackling sound as it bent, releasing particles that reached the noses of the entire group. It was no longer a rotting smell, but a dusty, moldy, aged one, like meat that had cured for far too long. The surface underneath was clean, cut with a knife, and there were scrapes over the femur.

"Seems like they ate some of it, then left the rest to rot," Kitjári said. "Let's keep searching."

They found traces of the troop that had abandoned the horse: broken shards of rock a bit glossier at the new cuts, long hairs from around the draft horses' hooves, abandoned bones from a meal, and even an entire chainmail hauberk heavily draped around a pointed rock, like a miniature snow peak.

"Why would they bring armor to a place like this?" Sterjall asked.

Kitjári shrugged. "They might've expected to find us. What a stupid idea, this is so heavy and cumbersome." She tossed the chainmail to the ground. It fell fast and heavy, without bouncing.

The company returned to their cats, searching for clues on the terrain. As they neared the top of the hill, they scrambled up a long mound that reminded them of a lava tube but seemed much too smooth. The sun had finally crested over the sierras, shining right by Sterjall's footpaws.

He stopped, noticing a glint amongst the blackness. He crouched down and pulled a sheet of igneous rock out of the way. Underneath it was a smoky, glassy substance encrusted with veiny tendrils. He scratched at it with his claws. *It looks... It looks like...*

"This mound we are on, it's a dried vine," Alaia said just up ahead. "There is crystallized sap right underneath us. Some of it must've dried up without burning."

"Bricks!" Givra said nearby. "Square stone!" She kicked at a too perfect rock that was stuck in the lava. It didn't budge.

They found more bricks swallowed by the flow as they ascended to the summit. As they neared the peak, they encountered a tangle of drooping shapes near the edge. More vines, smaller ones, clustering in a thicket that grasped a patch of soil that had remained unburnt. The clump grew disorderly, struggling to find sustenance from any crevice.

"Some of these are still alive," Sterjall noted.

"There must be a source of moisture under the rock," Alaia said. "Maybe there's a creek underground." The very idea made their mouths feel even more parched, as they had not had a drink since they departed the night before.

They circled the thicket and at last came to the edge of the hill, finding a sprawling view to the west. This highest point dropped vertically for a thousand feet, where more vines extended from a shelf, then dropped again for a thousand feet more, and again until it reached the bottom where the thickest lava flow had pooled. From here they could envision the paths the flow had taken, and how two currents must have gushed on either side of the peak to collide at the bottom, creating a compression point where a dark ravine formed. The solidified flows were bumpy and extruded, covered in snaking mounds.

"May I have your binoculars?" Balstei asked Sterjall, then studied the rippled rocks. "The flow is much thicker down there. Each of those curves seems to be a lava tube. Must be thousands of them."

"There are more vines on that ledge below us," Kitjári said. "Maybe they'll lead us to Mamóru, or to the temple, if there's anything left of it."

They searched for a safe way to the next level. There was no easy way down; once they reached it, their energy was drained and their muscles sore. The thicket they found was much denser, with some vines as thick as four strides wide; half of them alive, half crusted to glassy sculptures. They asked the vines to part so they could pass, and some answered, but most were unable to move. Amongst the tangle, they found the foundation of a long-burnt building, but no hints of any sort of temple.

Farther into the terraced level was a shaded grotto where a massive rock had been displaced by vines. They did not need to set up their tarps that day, finding plenty of shade behind the cracked rock. Usually, the heat would force Lago to stay in his human form, but today he decided to sleep as Sterjall. He wanted to feel this landscape better, to understand the clues around him. He sensed small grasses, insects, and even worms that lived in the bit of soil nearby, but felt no other presence. He drifted off to sleep with his mind still searching.

Sterjall had a vague and abstract dream. It had to do with the vines: large, vertical, and waxy. But the vines were also columns and had hooves at the bottom, or were they nails? The images were indistinct and confusing. He woke up trying to understand them, but the memories were too ephemeral. *They reminded me of something, what was it?* The more he thought about them, the quicker the memories vanished.

The sun was not yet too low in the west. All his friends were fast asleep. Sterjall sat up on his bedroll and tried not to think about how thirsty he was. They still had some water and munnji cakes, but they had to save most of it for the smilodons. In a few days, they would run out and have to cross the rest of the desert without a drop or bite more.

We need to explore the next level before we lose the light, Sterjall thought. He shook his friends awake.

The next terrace was a thousand feet below. The sun was setting by the time they arrived, glowing behind a yellow-white band of clouds.

"A helm," Kitjári said, kicking a heavy piece of metal. "And more food scraps. Kedra and Grinn made it all the way here. And look, boot prints."

In the areas where soil was exposed, clear prints were still visible.

"Only boots, no hooves," Balstei noted. "Horses would never make it up this steeper end."

"Room opens here," Givra said, calling them ahead. She had found an old doorway cut right into the gray rock. As the light was fading, they lit lamps, then walked through the forsaken archway.

The room did not extend too deep. Vines had broken through the ceiling of the dwelling and spilled onto the ground. A rotten bedframe lay in a corner, collapsed by time. Five human skeletons piled mournfully against a wall, ancient and pale, wearing clothing that had disintegrated into tattered tendrils, indistinguishable from the dried skin that clung to their bones. There were traces of a recent fire at the center of the room.

Kitjári kicked at an apricot seed that had been discarded only months earlier.

"At least it seems the Zovarians have been gone for a while," Sterjall mused. He unsheathed Leif and began scanning carefully.

"But the question is," Kitjári said, "did they leave because they found nothing? Or because they found what they were looking—"

"There! Do you feel that?" Sterjall asked, pointing his dagger directly at the rock.

"I see nothing," Kulak said.

"There's a white aura, very dim, through the rock."

"I don't feel it either," Kitjári said. "Could it be the Silv?"

Sterjall adjusted his arm and scanned again. "Wait... I don't... I swear I saw something in that direction, but it felt beyond Agnargsilv's normal reach." He adjusted his aim, feeling confused. "Maybe it was only—there it is again! It's moving!"

"Mamóru..." Kulak whispered. "Nelv was right, he lives."

Sterjall hurried out of the room. "Let's go, there must be a tunnel somewhere."

They went back out and searched the walls on the terraced cliff, finding other rock-carved dwellings inhabited by skeletons. Hurrying past a tangle of fossilized vines, they reached an enormous doorway carved with Miscamish runes and abstract images. It opened straight into the cliff, but most of it had collapsed due to vines breaking through the rocks.

Sterjall kept on scanning with Leif. "The glow is coming from within the hill. It's still moving."

They searched the toppled entrance and found that rubble had been piled out of the way to create a gap. They ducked through the opening, but asked the smilodons to wait outside, as the entryway was not wide enough for their thick bodies.

Past the rubble was a long tunnel that went slightly uphill, which was again a good sign, reminding them of the temples they had visited before. But this place felt different: the tunnel was wider, and instead of being a single, long path, it split into many side passages and chambers. Wall sconces waited in disuse. Banners that had lost all pigment clung bitterly, proclaiming allegiance to no one. Skeletons littered the hallways, some lonely, some clutching to other bones. It was a dreadful sight. *They must've died from starvation, thirst, or the heat,* Sterjall thought, not looking at them directly. *They sat together and waited for the end.*

The company walked solemnly, following Sterjall's lead. Cracks spiderwebbed the walls. Some fractured rooms had resettled at precarious angles, while others had entirely collapsed.

They found more evidence of Zovarian meddling, this time in the form of abandoned weapons. "Sap corroded these swords," Kitjári noted in a whisper.

They strode past teetering bed chambers, dining halls, workshops, cellars, and rooms for which they could not guess their function, but all had three things in common: the numerous cracks, the vines creeping through them, and the piles of bones.

The glowing aura was close enough that Kitjári and Kulak could now sense it as well. It had stopped moving. Sterjall felt the aura as unfocused, of a pearlescent-white color, like ivory dust falling between moonlit snowflakes. It was dim, weak, and barely perceptible, but still present. They stopped in front of an archway opening into a vast hall of many columns. Enormous bones littered the mosaicked ground, from dozens of towering creatures who had perished within. Behind a toppled column, the white aura concealed itself and trembled.

"Why is he hiding?" Sterjall whispered.

"It makes my scalp feel... sad," Kulak said.

"The three of us should go in," Kitjári muttered. "The rest of you, wait by the doorway."

Sterjall, Kulak, and Kitjári entered. Kitjári carried a lamp, which projected shifting shadows from the columns, barring the walls. They passed by the gargantuan bones; Sterjall thought they looked like skeletons of overgrown horses, but their skulls were malformed and enormous, growing long tusks that curved back toward themselves.

Feeling the presence just behind the collapsed column, they slowed their approach.

Sterjall had expected to find one of the proboscidean creatures, or at least a monumental and imposing man, like Banook, but instead found a shriveled, long-bearded old man, shorter than himself, trembling on the ground and covering his eyes from the glare of the lamp. The old man tried to remain still, hoping he hadn't been spotted.

"Nu'irg ust Momsúndo?" Kulak quietly asked.

The man lowered his arm and saw them clearly. He widened his eyes and exclaimed, "Silvfröash! *Noss iltuthir wet khalivesh! Wuolkilm Mindrel, Urnaadi, enn Agnarg, li changrad immitheoeo.*"

Sterjall understood most of the Miscamish words, but not all. He felt sad for the derelict figure, for his weak and pallid glow. He took a step forward.

"I am Sterjall," he said in Common. "Are you Mamóru?"

"I... I have not heard that name in ages," the old man replied in perfect Common speech embellished by an antiquated and melodious accent. "For fourteen hundred and fifty-five years, to be precise. I am Mamóru, Nu'irg ust Momsúndo, my great Agnargfröa. It is a pleasure to see you again, although you are not one of the Agnargfröash I once knew."

The old man tried to speak once more, but his eyes filled with tears. "I thought... I... I thought I had been lost here, and would remain lost, for all days."

Kulak helped Mamóru up from the stone floor. The Nu'irg stood slowly, leaning on a knotted, blackthorn cane.

Kitjári invited the others to step closer.

Sterjall introduced his friends and asked them to gather in a circle, sitting on the rubble that lay scattered about.

"Thank you for your kindness," Mamóru said as Alaia helped him sit. He wiped his nose on his decrepit, leathery tunic, then asked, "Has Noss sent for me, at last?"

"Not exactly," Sterjall replied. "Noss has not spoken since the Downfall. We came to find you with the hope that you could enlighten us with answers, but also hoping we could help you in turn."

"Noss speaks no longer? Yet they called for your domes to open?"

"The domes are still closed," Kitjári said.

Mamóru's long white eyebrows compressed, summoning even more wrinkles. His thin lips parted slightly, but said nothing.

"It's a complicated story," Sterjall said. "We will tell you all of it, but it will take hours."

Kulak smiled and said, "Nelv, *wuhasim mindrel galassuë*, felt deep in spotted heart of hers that the Downfall did not usher you through the Six Gates. So we came, seeking for you."

Mamóru's face lit up. "Nelv! How gracious of her. A more kind and savage spirit this world has never seen."

"Could you tell us what happened here?" Sterjall asked, gesturing toward their surroundings.

"Just as with your story, mine is one that could take long to tell. Where shall I start?"

"Sorry," Sterjall said. "To start with, could you tell us why you were hiding from us?"

"Ah, this account is brief, agnurf son, and can be told with a mouse's single breath. Alone I've been, alone and hopeless, through epochs for which names I have not learned. Months back, the flame of optimism lit in my heart, for I heard the clapping of hooves. But when I saw the newcomers arrive, my hope shriveled like bluebells in Dustwind, for they were dressed for war, and their faces seethed with a lust for dominance. As a precaution, I concealed my presence, waiting first to overhear them palaver. From Zovaria they claimed to be, a realm I am unfamiliar with. The soldiers were not searching for me, but for Momsúndosilv. Searching for its power so they may wield it at war. Do you know whom I speak of?"

"Yes," Sterjall said, "we have been on the run from the Zovarians for many months. They are after our Silvesh too. They want to use them as weapons against a neighboring empire. I am afraid to ask, but did the soldiers find Momsúndosilv?"

Mamóru seemed suspicious of this question, uncertain if the interest these strangers showed in the Silv was benign.

Kitjári felt his hesitation and intervened, "We are not here for Momsúndosilv, but for answers, and to help you. Though if the Silv has been taken by the Zovarians, we believe it to be in the wrong hands."

"Urnaarell daughter, the fact that I'm talking to you should provide a clue. The only reason I still live is because the Silv of proboscideans is near, being the only source of energy for my withering body, the last remaining essence of my kind, other than myself. Full of youth and vigor I once stood, before the members of my clade perished in the cataclysm. Even the few that hid in these halls did not survive long." He pointed his cane at the skeletons surrounding them. Sterjall noticed the cane's blackthorn handle embraced a fossil, an ammonite, spiraling darkly at its core.

"Your clade is no more, yet you still live?" Kulak asked.

"I remain Mamóru, held together by the threads of Momsúndosilv, which resides at the Enolv Temple. I have not been able to leave this black wasteland because I am bound to the Silv, as the Silv is bound to me."

Mamóru glanced toward the great hall's exit. "Your enemies searched for a way into the temple, day and night, while I concealed myself in secret tunnels, away from their eyes. They cleared the rubble to the temple's passageway only to find a tangle of vines behind it. They diligently cut through, but the white blood splattered their faces, stuck to their boots, and dulled their swords. Little progress they made, then gave up once the hives began to eat at their skin. Their leader sought for more than Momsúndosilv—he was also searching for a young man by the name Lago Vaari. He seemed to be expecting to find him here. Are you familiar with this person?"

"It is me," Sterjall said, "my name is Lago, when I'm not Sterjall."

"Great trouble you drag behind you, Lago-Sterjall, but I am glad to see the trouble has not caught up with your heels quite yet. Thankfully, the soldiers did not secure the proboscidean Silv, but their ambition—and the words I overheard—tell me they may return, better supplied, dragging machinery that can break through rocks and slash the remaining vines. I pray you can tell me your story next, for my mouth tires and my tongue dries up, and I yet lack context as to how this old man, the very last of steppe mammoths, could possibly be of help to you."

They shared their dwindling supply of water with Mamóru and recounted their long story, explaining how ignorant they were of their own past, of the reason the Silvesh were made, even of the true nature of the Downfall. They spoke of the domes, of how they had acquired the Silvesh, then described the threat of the Red Stag and his growing army. Mamóru's heart seemed to shatter at the mention of the cervid Nu'irg, Sovath, and her enslavement by Urgsilv, but he let them continue with the tale.

They spoke of their escape from Zovaria and how they came to meet Khuron Aio-Kulak. They told Mamóru that Mindreldrolom's provinces had voted to find answers before deciding whether to open their dome, and that was how they arrived at this moment.

Sterjall paused and licked his dry lips. "We were told that they called you the Keeper of Memory, and that if anyone would know the history that we seek to understand, what is happening to Noss, how to defeat the Red Stag, it would be you."

"*Khalbaalith ust Mewenn*," Mamóru murmured, rubbing his long, braided beard. "Some of the answers you seek I will reveal with my story, but not all. You have shared your water with me. Now it's time I share mine, as you seem parched and ready for it. I will lead you to a special place, and there I will tell you some of the things you seek to know, and some you don't yet know you need to know."

Mamóru pushed against his cane and rose to his frail feet. They followed him out of the chamber and down the sloped hallway. The old man seemed weary, yet resolute in his step.

"What beautiful kitties you have," he told Kulak once they exited the mountain. "They are much larger than the smilodons I once knew. They seem parched too, they should come with us."

They helped Mamóru up on top of Pichi and set to ride. Mamóru directed them to the bottom level of the prominence, where the two lava flows had collided and formed the snaking mounds they had seen from the top. Aided by the keen night sight of the cats, they quickly arrived at a concealed cave-in. As Mamóru led the way through a secret entrance, their arid skin felt something they had not felt in a long time: moisture in the air. They smelled the silty musk of wet rocks as well as an herbal fragrance that was fresh and invigorating. They would have salivated at once if they could've, but their mouths were too dry.

At the entrance were a handful of lanterns. Mamóru stabbed the side of a vine that was tangled in the rocks and filled a lantern with its white sap. He struck a piece of flint and handed the green-flaming lantern to Sterjall. He did the same with five other lanterns, keeping the last one in his hands. He led them into the narrow lava tube.

The passage was cramped, barely wide enough for the smilodons to fit, but soon the tunnel widened, and the fire seemed to burn an even deeper green. The walls were covered in moss, touched by drops of water that sparkled verdantly. They heard the miraculous gurgling of running water, and their hearts leapt with joy, as they could wait no longer.

Mamóru stepped aside to expose a chamber with a crystalline pool fed by a cascading stream. "Go, drink, my children," he intoned.

They dropped to their knees in supplication and sank their faces into the pool, nearly inhaling the divine liquid. The smilodons lapped up their share too, although Blu simply launched himself into the largest pool, unleashing a refreshing tidal wave on all of them.

Mamóru released a coarse chuckle. "There is enough water for all," he said. "This spring is named Istrilm. It has been providing life since the dawn of this land. Many more springs used to seep from the mountain above you, which the Toldask Miscam knew by the name of Enolv. Well, it used to be a mountain, now only its top remains uncovered. If you venture into the depths of these endless tunnels, you might get lucky and find other creeks, but you are more likely to become lost in the labyrinth."

Mamóru took a long drink from a thin cascade. The room was covered not just in moss, but in curling ferns, plump herbs, and bright mushrooms. The ceiling was bearded with lichens, dripping around circular skylights that glowed in a lush, star-pricked blue.

Mamóru wrung his beard and said, "I have adapted to live only on these mineral waters and the moss and mushrooms that grow in these caves. You are welcome to eat them too, but they will make your stomachs churn. But it's more than this meager sustenance that keeps me alive… Being close to Momsúndosilv provides me with energy and spiritual sustenance. Without it—or too far from it—I would perish, as any Nu'irg would if they left their kind behind."

Once their thirsts were sated, Mamóru guided them deeper still. He followed the streams that branched from Istrilm, which through the centuries had softened the lava tube's floor. The tunnel narrowed, but after ducking through a gap, they found themselves in a chamber so large that the light of their combined lanterns could barely scrape the walls and ceiling.

Mamóru stopped, and while looking up at the darkness proclaimed, "This, travelers from faraway realms, is the Istrilm Sanctum."

Chapter Forty-Five

Petroglyphs

"This chamber is enormous," Alaia remarked. "It feels like we are outside during a starless night."

She looked down at her reflections. The creek pooled in countless pockets that gurgled and dripped to levels unseen. With no gaps in the ceiling to let sunshine in, no moss or ferns grew in the chamber, but the rocks were stippled with golden bacteria. The gilded surfaces collected droplets of moisture, as if sprinkled in dew, and reflected the lantern light in a starscape of green and gold.

Mamóru carefully traversed the slippery surfaces. "I have brought you here because you asked to hear my story, which is also, in part, your story. As the Keeper of Memory, I have worked tirelessly to make sure that if I were to perish, our shared history would be preserved."

He walked toward the southern wall of the immense tunnel, where his lantern revealed petroglyphs carved into the rock face. The pictorial representations were surrounded by shorthand Miscamish runes, crawling from the base of the wall to dozens of feet above.

"Y-you wrote all this?" Balstei asked, awestruck by the secret knowledge displayed before them.

"That I have. What is written upon these walls is all I could remember."

"It must've taken ages," Alaia said, mouth agape.

"And ages I had at my disposal," the old man added. "Each portion of these long tunnels is lined with the stories of great rulers, forgotten lands, evil tyrants, vanished species, monumental discoveries, and tender moments. Alas, my memory fades with the epochs, but these rocks will take longer to crumble. My hope is that all I've inscribed throughout these lonely centuries will find a more permanent home someday.

"I am unable to relate to you the full story, as we'd be walking in the dark for months. I will start not at the beginning, but at the beginning of the times that relate to what may aid you in your quest." He walked onward, skipping a large portion of the petroglyphs. They passed by a tall ladder, and eventually arrived at a bend where it seemed a new chapter began. Mamóru pointed his cane at runes carved up where the ceiling curved. "It all begins with the story of the Silvesh."

They lifted their lanterns to see better. Mamóru's simplified runes were impossible to read, but the pictorial representations added some context.

"Beyond six lands, beneath six seas," he began, "around ten thousand years before the Downfall, the lands of Noss were in disarray. Human tribes had displaced the native animals, dooming many species that would never again breathe a Spring's breeze. Among these tribes were the Acoapóshi. They were simple people with simple rituals, but they were curious. The Acoapóshi lived in a mountain land they called Eba, a thousand miles east of where we find ourselves now, and it was in those mountains that they found a rich seam of graphite with an intense concentration of a type of carbon with exceptional properties."

"We know of aetheric carbon," Balstei interjected. "Nowadays, we call it *soot*. The aetheric elements are the focus of my studies, although they are quite rare."

"As it has been for eons," Mamóru continued. "*Shummori* the Acoapóshi called this carbon in the long-forgotten Ulv tongue, and later *ustlas*. The graphite found in the seams of Eba was of a most pure aetheric carbon. Unknowing of its power, the Acoapóshi mined the inexhaustible seam simply because they liked the hard and pliable material, as it was easy to carve and had a beautiful sheen. But their artisans began experiencing visions when carving it, and soon they deemed the graphite a sacred material. They crafted sculptures and decorative artifacts, and they also carved masks, the *Enwennsilvesh*, precursors to the Silvesh you now wield."

As he told the story, Mamóru used the ammonite handle of his cane to cast a shadow pointing at different images. The shadow landed on figures that looked like animal faces.

"The masks were sometimes animal-like, sometimes inspired by more abstract visions. When the Acoapóshi priests wore them for their rituals, the graphite dust would turn their skin glossy and gray, and it would sometimes be inadvertently inhaled by them. Visions began to cloud—or enlighten—their awareness. Their understanding of the world was reshaped, and their spiritual relationship to all life took a turn. The soot they inhaled was potent enough, but the masks had an even deeper effect on their minds—their crystalline makeup was so pristine that it focused the threads right into their brains.

"Inside the mines they built a temple, which they named Ommo ust Enwenn, carved entirely into the graphite seam. One day, six priests sat in a circle inside the temple, praying as one while wearing their graphite masks. As they chanted and inhaled the soot in the air, they all joined in a common vision. They had not been aware that the number six was important in how the material behaved, that the presence of six masks was critical."

"Why six?" Balstei asked.

"It has something to do with the structure of carbon itself. You could, perhaps, imagine the threads being pushed from one mask into the next, and then again around the circle to create an endless loop, driving itself into itself, perceiving itself. In this state of subconscious drift, each of the priests dreamt the same dream—that Noss themself was alive, and conscious.

"They did not hear words from the planet, but they sensed their emotion, their peril, and their concern. They began performing a daily ritual, always with six priests and six masks, to better understand the pleas of the planet. In time, they learned to mindspeak with them, in a similar way all Silvfröash commune with those of their own clades."

Kulak nodded, and although Sterjall and Kitjári had not learned that skill yet, they nodded as well to avoid getting pulled into a tangent.

"Noss told the Acoapóshi that they were hurting, that in the same way humans needed a healthy body to survive, the planet needed a body that was balanced, in which myriad species could thrive, and change, and diversify in harmony. Noss had pondered alone for billions of years, but now that they had someone to talk to, they finally learned about themself, about the creatures that made up their conscious mind."

"You mean the animals are part of their consciousness?" Sterjall interrupted.

"Not just the animals, but everything alive. Plants, microbes, fungi. From the tiniest bacterium to the grandest of the ocean's blue whales. In the same way that your body is composed of minute cells and your thoughts are neurons exchanging signals, so Noss is made of all living organisms and of the way they connect with one another.

"The more self-aware, or what some would call more 'conscious' species, embody the thought process of the planet, but all other species have their own critical functions. Your brain cannot operate with just neurons—it needs blood to breathe, an immune system to protect it, skin to keep it warm. So Noss depends on all their small parts, but in a much more complex system than any of us can imagine.

"The intelligence of Noss was vaster than any single human mind. Noss, however, had no eyes, no proper ears, no mechanism of proprioception analogous to our own—they could only introspect. But now they had found new eyes, new ears, by speaking to the Acoapóshi and reading into their memories. Armed with this new knowledge, Noss understood themselves and the particles they were made of, but just like you may be aware that you are made of cells, you cannot will a single muscle cell to contract, nor can you tell two particles to combine or break apart. Noss had no control over their own body or the creatures that inhabited it.

"Noss made a bargain then, choosing to take the tribe under their wing. In exchange for the knowledge and sight of the Acoapóshi, Noss taught them the true power behind soot, directed them to craft the Silvesh, and taught them about the threads and the forces that controlled them."

"I've always been curious about what the threads are," Sterjall said. "But no one has been able to explain it."

"Are you still unsure, agnurf son? I thought it would be obvious to you by now."

"I... I really don't know. I guess they are life?"

"Not quite, but close. The threads are consciousness, levels of self-awareness."

"Consciousness?" Sterjall repeated, taken aback. "But... I see them in the smallest of things, in worms digging underground, in pollen floating in the air."

"Indeed, you do. Consciousness is a gradient of infinite levels. The smallest amoeba can perceive its surroundings, even if it is unaware of its own existence. When these threads bind to one another, more complex minds are born."

Sterjall was confused, still processing the idea. "When I use Agnargsilv, it's like I can manipulate these threads, shape them together. How is that possible if they are made of consciousness?"

"There is a force that allows that to happen, which you yourself have, Silv or not. But your Silv lets you better control it. Are you also unaware of this force?"

"I can use it, but I don't understand it," Sterjall admitted. "Is it a type of energy, like magnetism?"

"No, agnurf son," Mamóru said. "The force within you, within your mask, that which binds all these disparate threads of consciousness, is empathy."

Sterjall's mind lit up. *The pain I feel it is the pain of others,* he understood. *The love I place unto others, that is what binds us together. Feeling what others feel, sharing their pain, seeing through another's eyes, therein lies the true power... It resides in being connected, in understanding one another.*

"Your amber eyes are glistening, and they tell me you've finally made the connection," Mamóru said. "Allow me to tell you more about the *empathic focus*, which is how the Silvesh control these threads. It is by means of the empathic focus that they unlock a greater level of empathy, by allowing the Silvfröash to put themselves in the minds of those they connect to, by acquiring their qualia, and thus comprehending what it means to *be* them.

"Aetheric carbon—and to a much greater degree, the Silvesh—allows for empathy to be increased exponentially, to be controlled willfully. Empathy is the key to how all conscious beings become greater than the sum of their parts, as without it, the threads from disparate beings would never interact. And once multiple minds connect, an even larger consciousness can be born. Most of us are but ants, unaware that it is the colony who is the higher-level consciousness."

Sterjall remembered the time he saw an aura around a beehive, and then again around a pack of kiuons in the Stelm Wujann. *I was seeing the manifestation of a higher-level consciousness,* he realized, which to him had looked more like a glow instead of a series of threads. The hive had been alive, at a different level, but still as alive as each of the bees that buzzed it into being. It was like how the players in a game of minquoll created a temporary manifestation of a higher order, or how he himself was a higher order assembled from the living pieces of his complex body.

"Is that..." Sterjall was struggling to find the right words, overwhelmed by the new connections linking in his mind. "Is that why, when I look at a beehive, it looks like it glows?"

"Indeed, it is. When you experience consciousness as threads, they are in your same or lower levels. But levels higher than your own become blurred to your perception."

"So the Silvesh, and you as a Nu'irg, does that mean—"

"Exactly. I am a manifestation of all the consciousnesses that made up my clade, the proboscideans. Kerjaastórgnem and Nelv are manifestations of their own collective kinds. I have, a few times in the past, worn a graphite mask, and under its influence, I could see the threads in a similar way as how you've described them. But instead of a glow, for me the other Nu'irgesh were also made of threads, because I was perceiving them from my same level. Yet the

Silvesh... The Silvesh to me have always had that strange aura about them. They may even be alive, or self-aware in some manner we cannot comprehend."

"Aura is big thread," Kulak said. "Another form of consciousness?"

"It would be analogous to one, but at a level beyond your understanding. Instead of seeing its full complexity, you are seeing its shadow, a simplification of the whole."

"You mentioned they needed six priests to talk to the planet," Balstei said. "Were they creating their own higher-level consciousness?"

"I think that is precisely what was happening," Mamóru noted. "Those who wield the Silvesh—or the graphite masks of yore—provide intention, introspection, and direction to manipulate the empathic focus. Once six of them combine, something new is born, even if ephemeral."

"I don't get it," Alaia muttered. "If this force you mentioned is empathy, how could someone like the Red Stag even remotely wield a Silv? There's not a droplet of empathy in sadistic scum like him."

"Cruel people do feel the pain of others, but it fuels them. The Silvesh were made as tools to facilitate connection, and what the wicked do with those connections can be as vile and rotten as their souls."

"How long ago were the Silvesh made?" Sterjall asked.

"The first Silv, Hoombusilv, was finished eight thousand two hundred and thirty-two years before the Downfall. Being the first of many, it was not as powerful as the ones that came after, unable to mindlock creatures from its clade in the way the other Silvesh can."

"By Takh's mercy," Balstei interrupted in a jolt of realization, "for if it could, all of us primates could've been enslaved. It would've been much too dangerous."

"Too dangerous indeed," Mamóru replied. "Yet Hoombusilv was treasured by the Acoapóshi above all other Silvesh. The tribe remained the wardens of it, as well as the wardens of its secrets. But Hoombusilv was merely the first of many.

"Noss believed the Silvesh would bring balance to their biomes. Many clades of animals had developed to such a high level of intelligence that, with the aid of soot, they could understand and cooperate with humans. Those animals would be key in securing this balance. Their anatomy was analogous to that of humans, up to a point, which eased in the process of shapeshifting. Primates, therefore, were the obvious choice for the first experiment."

Sterjall cocked his head. "How does shapeshifting come into these plans?"

"You could rationalize much with your human brain, but you could never truly feel what another species feels. Shapeshifting provides you with different qualia, not only externally but also internally, so that you can experience the same senses, same ways of thinking, and same grief as your second kind. That is why Noss picked those clades better suited for half-forms, then directed the creation of one mask for each."

Mamóru was now pointing to a cluster of eighteen triangular glyphs, ones they were by now quite familiar with. Instead of being spread on a map, on this wall they were arranged in a large hexagon, with curving lines connecting all symbols in a design reminiscent of the branching roots of a tree.

"This cladogram represents the eighteen clades, arranged by ancestry. Of course, countless more clades exist, but these are the ones for which the eighteen Silvesh were crafted. How the Silvesh were constructed is something far beyond anyone's comprehension, but stories tell about their creation as if the Acoapóshi had been controlling microscopic fibers, braiding and knotting them one at a time. I'd conjecture it was Noss themself doing the weaving, using humans as mediums."

"Under a microscope, the masks seem to be made of complex filaments, just as you describe," Balstei said.

"I have seen them myself. Yet still, those filaments you can see under a microscope are more akin to ropes composed of many thousands of even thinner strands, which even our most advanced instruments at the time could not accurately observe. Once Kroowinsilv, the eighteenth and final mask, was finished, eight thousand and three years before the Downfall, the Unification Epoch began. Noss instructed the Acoapóshi to spread across the two great continents to find other cultures to whom they could gift the masks. Diversity in ways of thought was key, Noss implored, not wanting the Acoapóshi tribe to undertake the burden alone. They found seventeen tribes they felt were trustworthy, with whom they shared a common goal despite their vast differences.

"The eighteen tribes asked the animals of their respective clades to migrate to new biomes, as directed by Noss, to alleviate the destruction caused by humankind. Species from disparate lands mixed and worked with the tribes to establish a new equilibrium. These tribes named themselves the Miscam, and with the shared understanding that came from the Silvesh, they crafted their own language, Miscamish. The tongue was developed with a phonetic lexicon of strict rules, so that it could endure through the ages. That way, tribes who settled apart from one another could communicate once again every time they met. For thousands of years, the tribes and species tirelessly worked, spreading far and wide, helping the planet heal."

Mamóru pointed to carvings of coats of arms from ancient realms that were no more; he had added crude pigments to them, giving them a hint of color. "But not all went well," he continued. "Other rulers did not take kindly to the Miscam intruding on their lands, as balance for nature could mean chaos for their farms, cities, and dams. Wars ravaged the territories, and untold struggle was suffered by all sides. But the ideals of the Miscam spread wide and rooted stubbornly."

"If they were so widespread," Sterjall asked, "how come there's so little of their culture remaining? Other than inside the domes."

"There are two reasons," Mamóru replied. "The first is that the Miscam were flawed in their shared thinking and had faith in nature alone. They did not believe in technology, because what some realms called 'progress' had been the lead cause of Noss's ailments. They were insulated, rarely learning from the books of other realms, and almost never keeping historical records in writing, depending almost entirely on oral traditions."

Mamóru paused for a long moment, feeling that the words he was about to speak were out of order, that he needed to untangle the thread of his thoughts. "The second reason is that the Miscam hid the truth on purpose, but I will get to that in a moment, as it has to do with the next part of the story." He cleared his throat and continued down the tunnel.

"The Miscam tribes always pretended to be weaker than they truly were, but they *were* indeed lagging when it came to technology. Though the Silvesh were advanced in their own way, the technology of all eighteen tribes was rudimentary, unable to compete with the neighboring realms except where it related to their knowledge of the natural world. But the time came for the Miscam to realize that if it hadn't been for the advancements they rejected, they would have perished."

"Because of the Downfall?" Alaia guessed.

Mamóru nodded. "And they would not have seen it coming. It was a cosmologist by the name of Jiu Zezi who made the discovery, from the Stelm Yenwu Observatory."

"Yenwu? Like in the Yenwu Peninsula, where the Yenwu Dome is located?" Sterjall asked.

"If that is what the New World calls Kroowindrolom, then yes, we must be referring to the same place. The observatory was built atop the tallest peak of the Stelm Yenwu, on a mighty range of blade-like rocks that rises like the exposed ribs of a fallen god."

"The observatory still exists inside the dome, then?" Sterjall nearly squealed. "I need to visit that place!"

"And that's the dome of avians," Alaia added. "I need to go there more than you do."

"The observatory may be there, it may not," Mamóru demurred, trying to hold back their expectations. "A long time has passed since the dome closed. But you may be in luck, as even before Kroowindrolom was grown, the Murtégo Miscam deemed the observatory a sacred place. The Yenwu were ruled by a powerful theocracy, one that had developed an advanced understanding of mathematics and optics."

"And they still have the best optics anyone knows of," Sterjall noted. "Most of it was rescued from old ruins."

"They must've salvaged a great deal then, including their own culture," Mamóru said. "The Yenwu Theocracy occupied most of the Jerjan Continent at the time. It was through their technological advancements that five hundred and fifty-six years before the Downfall, Jiu Zezi spotted a comet."

"A comet, I knew it!" Sterjall exclaimed. He felt a bit embarrassed about the silly interruption and let Mamóru carry on.

"The comet was nothing but a tiny dot of aquamarine light, but as months passed, it grew and became a long-veiled streak in the sky, visible even in the daytime. Dangerously close to Noss did it pass. The tail of dust it left was dense, and as Noss crossed through it, the dust ignited the most wonderful—and I must admit, frightening—meteor shower this planet has ever seen. I watched it myself, from these lands, which were a fertile savannah in those olden times."

"Is that the meteor shower we saw?" Alaia asked. "The one that happens every fifteen years?"

"Every five thousand four hundred and twenty-four days, to be precise," Mamóru corrected. "I counted."

"It is the meteors you promised to show me," Kulak reminded Sterjall. "My scalp keeps waiting."

"We call that meteor shower the *Quindecims*," Sterjall said to Mamóru.

"An apt name. I have seen the meteor shower every single time. Ninety-five times so far—never do I miss one. It was not a cyclical meteor shower, not until the Downfall came and the comet's ejected debris became trapped in a strange orbit."

"So, we were watching pieces of the comet that caused the Downfall?" Alaia asked. "Two thousand years after it first passed by us? That's fucking phenomenal."

"Gloriously so," Mamóru chuckled. "Jiu Zezi had taken precise measurements of the comet's trajectory, seeing it wrap around Sunnokh and move back away from our orbit. With painstaking precision, she calculated the comet would orbit back in five hundred and fifty-six years, and very likely would collide with Noss when it returned. The cosmologists she worked with did not believe her, thinking the trajectory was too complex to calculate with such precision, but her methods were too revolutionary for anyone else to understand. She knew almost for a fact that this would happen—it was just a matter of time."

Carved next to an illustration of the comet, Sterjall saw what he understood to be some sort of mathematical equation. The symbols were new to him, some reminding him of the notches embossed on Qupi chips.

"Zezi tried to summon help from the Yenwu Theocracy," the old Nu'irg said, "but the archbishops cared not for her story, as their own oracles prophesied of a doomsday that would not arrive for seventeen thousand more years, a prophecy that was much more convenient to believe in. She tried to convince rulers of remote realms, but not a one paid heed to her pleas. For five years she traveled with her incomprehensible papers, finding no scholars who could grasp the complexities of her calculations.

"Discouraged, she wandered purposelessly east of the peninsula, and by chance happened upon a caravan of Acoapóshi Miscam who took her to their village in the Stelm Tai-Du. Though Zezi knew they would not understand her equations, she nonetheless told them of her findings as a way to vent her frustrations.

"The leader of the Acoapóshi Miscam at the time, a king named Ieron Ulmed, paid heed to every word of Zezi's story. The next time Ulmed visited Ommo ust Enwenn, he mentioned the story to Noss, who listened, then thought long and hard. Noss requested Zezi be brought to the temple, so that they might converse with her."

At this point, the rune-covered wall opened into a new tunnel. More writings were condensed inside the narrower passage, but Mamóru continued down the wall of the main lava tube instead.

"Zezi did not believe in the mystical ways of the Miscam, but she accepted the offer, as it would have been impolite to refuse. Ieron Ulmed invited Zezi to wear one of the graphite masks while he wore the mask of primates, Hoombusilv, although I am certain he did not show his tarsier half-form to her. Four other priests closed the circle of six, then began to chant. Zezi soon became one with them, and within their combined consciousness heard the voice of Noss. Zezi spoke as the six, explaining her observations, her equations, her predicament. Noss's unmatched intelligence found no flaw in the arithmetic; the planet even offered improvements, further precision. Noss warned the six in one that all life would be in peril unless drastic measures were taken.

"The leaders of the eighteen Miscam tribes were summoned, and a year later, they convened. We, the Nu'irgesh, were also present, although only myself, Buujik, and Allamónea could understand the Miscamish words, for

Allamónea and I had found our human forms thousands of years since, and Buujik had always known her own."

"Wait, who are Buujik and Allamónea?" Balstei interrupted.

"Buujik is the Nu'irg of all primates. Allamónea was the Nu'irg of cetaceans, but she is no more—she was killed by whaling ships long before the Downfall, and a new Nu'irg ust Amá'a has emerged to take her place, one I have not yet had the pleasure to meet. But so it was that all of us found ourselves in this greatest of councils. The eighteen Silvfröash formed one great circle, began their chanting, and had a lengthy conversation with Noss. By then, the planet had already devised a plan, one that would take generations to execute. Each of the tribes was tasked with bringing together a set of species that could cohabitate in synchrony. Helped by the clades tied to their Silvesh, and by a great deal of soot from Ommo ust Enwenn, shamans, priests, and chiefs gathered the animals and plants requested by Noss, then led them to the lands where the eighteen domes were to be grown. Some of these lands had already been settled by their original tribes, while the locations of the others were chosen due to their proximity to sources of soot."

On the wall was carved a map of all known lands, with eighteen glyphs marking the positions of the domes, almost identical to the one at Da'áju. It was not as precise, but they still found it admirable that Mamóru had been able to etch all the coastlines so accurately.

"Did the other realms object to the Miscam taking all their soot?" Balstei asked.

"They found no objections, as they did not understand the value of aetheric carbon. The Miscam kept that secret, as well as that of the true motives for securing those lands. This is where I come to the second reason why the memory of the Miscam tribes is not widespread, but rather obscured. As I had mentioned earlier, the Miscam hid the truth on purpose."

"But why would they do that?" Sterjall asked. "Wouldn't they be better off working with everyone else?"

"Not as they saw it, or as Noss saw it. They believed that if the other realms found out the truth, their need for self-preservation would overcome them, ruining the plan Noss had set in motion. The Miscam worked with misinformation, spreading false stories, sending spies to burn or tamper with books, securing deceitful alliances, so that no one would know the truth or fear the oncoming cataclysm. At the same time, they made themselves look weak and foolish in the eyes of outsiders."

"All that we can find about the Miscam tribes is so obscure and contradictory," Balstei said. "Now it makes sense. But why would the other realms give out their lands to begin with?"

"Since the other realms knew not of the Miscam's ultimate goal, they did not object to trading portions of their lands for more valuable territories the Miscam controlled. They were interested in metals, strategic locations for warfare, gemstones, trading routes. The trade seemed a fair one to them, a bargain, even."

Mamóru pointed his cane toward inscriptions listing dated events.

"Not all transactions were peaceful, however," he said. "The Miscam lured in wildlife, throwing off the balance of biological systems that they themselves had brought to stability thousands of years earlier. They also demanded some lands that had already been settled, and though avaricious rulers were quick to trade those provinces for enough profit, their inhabitants were not as happy. The transactions and migrations threw the continents into chaos, causing wars that lasted for centuries.

"I believe that if the old realms had known about the Silvesh, they would have fought to obtain their power and never would have given up their lands. Luckily, the Miscam kept the masks a secret. Mostly. A few of the masks fell into the wrong hands during the Unification Epoch, such as Gwonlesilv, which was temporarily lost to a mad prince. But that was millennia before the discovery of the comet, so the stories of the Gorgellath Kingdom faded into myth and were mostly forgotten.

"In the end, the eighteen locations were settled, amiably and not so amiably, and from within their temples the Silvfröash began the arduous task of growing the vines. It took generations, as the vines grew slowly, needing nourishment, time, and sunlight. How the Silvfröash managed to create such amazing structures is beyond me, but I know they did so with the aid of their Silvesh and with direction only Noss could have provided."

"What were drolomesh like when they grew?" Kulak asked, trying to imagine his own home during those foregone times.

"Oh, a magnificent sight they were, from their very inception. At first, only the central trunk grew, from a sprout no bigger than a blade of grass. It soon stretched like a braided monolith, faster than any other plant had before. The twenty-three columns sprung up next, splitting at their tops to mesh together in the sky, casting a spiderweb of shadows over mountains and seas. I found the sight most awe-inspiring during moonless nights, seeing the firmament shattered into polygonal segments with stars sparkling through it. It made me feel so small, as if I was watching the cosmos through the compound eyes of a fly."

"My scalp feels homesick for beauty of a time before," Kulak whispered.

"It was particularly majestic on hazy days, when the sun cast down golden columns through the thousands of skylights of the tessellated sky. Sometime before the heavens closed, the arudinn lit up to help the plants below keep growing. Strange times those were, when during the day the sky was dark, but with holes of blue light, and during the night it was bright, but flecked with voids of pure darkness.

"The lower perimeters of the domes were kept open to let animals come in and out while resources were gathered, and more species were brought in. The wars intensified when the domes were nearly finished. Hoombudrolom, the dome of the Acoapóshi tribe, was well defended from such strikes by a mighty rampart erected with the help of the Tjardur Miscam, a neighboring tribe who grew their own dome far southwest of them. I presume both those domes must have fared well, though I was not there to witness the final outcome."

"Did you encounter trouble here?" Alaia asked. "Wars and all?"

"That we did. Despite the false stories the Miscam tribes had spread, a spy from the nearby Dunewaar Queendom heard about Zezi's prophecy and informed their queen. She sent legions to break into our dome, but her efforts were futile. Mammoths, elephants, and mastodons protected the dome as much as the human warriors did."

Mamóru's wrinkled eyes narrowed. "There was so much death and pointless suffering back then. Looking back, I am unsure how it could've been avoided."

He sighed deeply, then continued.

"But the time came for the domes to close, exactly one year before Zezi predicted the comet would strike. The perimeter arches dropped and narrowed, and soon we were confined to our enormously small new homes. Not all the Miscam could be saved. There was not enough room in the domes for so many humans, not if a healthy population of other species was to thrive. Countless martyrs remained outside, knowing they would soon die, holding the line from invading forces until the moment the last vine arches had sealed.

"The largest of species—such as dire wolves, megaloceroses, kubanochoeruses, and paraceratheriums—were the hardest to upkeep, yet the most helpful for keeping the domes in order, given that they had already reached a complex level of self-awareness. Due to this, the giant species settled exclusively in their own domes, never in others. This, unfortunately, brought doom to my kind, as our species were as large in bodies as in spirits, so all of us proboscideans were either confined to Momsúndodrolom or to the outside world. Both would prove equally fatal."

Balstei used the pause to make an observation. "We have found fossils of all these animals you mentioned, what we call our pre-Downfall megafauna. They all went extinct in the New World."

"It is truly a pity that the gentle giants did not survive in the outside world, but it surprises me not."

"What came to be once the dome of proboscideans sealed its fate?" Sunu asked.

"It was a sad time when the last arches closed. It broke my heart to see friends left on the outside, human and proboscidean alike. Most accepted their fate, as the tribes had worked together for this moment for centuries. Only a few rebelled at the last moment, causing skirmishes to flare up at the perimeters. I only saw one such battle, but I guess the same must have happened everywhere. Some of the Toldask clans that were to remain outside forced their way in and built their own fortress on the western flanks. Stubborn they were, and held their ground until the dome closed. Perhaps fate would've been kinder to them if they had remained outside—at least they would've stood a chance to run away when the cataclysm arrived."

Mamóru gestured toward cryptic illustrations and symbols that exuded a sense of dread.

"A year later, exactly as predicted, came the Downfall. We all stood atop the mountain of Enolv and looked up at our bright sky, as it was daytime in this dome when it happened. We felt a great tremor and held the ground while a deafening rumble shook us for an hour that seemed like an eternity. The lights of the arudinn dimmed, but soon returned to normal. We thought we'd been spared, but then the eastern vines began to buckle. The arudinn once more flickered, then entirely lost their light.

"But the darkness didn't last. Through cracks in the walls, molten rocks seeped through, setting even the largest of vines ablaze. It was unspeakably frightening. Green fire rose from the spilling sap while red death flowed underneath. The smoke billowed and filled the top of the dome, and bolts of lightning raged within the ashen clouds, shining blue amid the red and green glows. Burning vines rained down from the roof to splatter limply onto the landscape, setting forests ablaze. The river of fire soon reached the first columns, which bowed in submission and brought down their judgment upon our lands, making all of Enolv tremble. Humans and animals fled for cover toward the western perimeter, away from the flames, while some of us remained on high ground. Our chief, Kewarg, sat with Momsúndosilv at the Enolv Temple, trying to heal the vines that were burning and bending above us, but his Silv's power was not enough to contain the wrath."

A tear streaked Mamóru's cheek, his frail hands trembling as he pointed at runes that seemed to be a list of names.

"I hid in the same room you found me in, with a dozen friends of my own kind whose bones now rest there. I did not see all that happened next, as I was too scared. Fear spared my life, in the end. The entire mountain shook and bent, not once, but dozens of times, perhaps once for each of the columns that fell. The largest of all tremors came when the trunk toppled over, shattering rocks deep within the core of the mountain.

"It must have been days later when we finally dared to leave our shelter. I first tried to go to the temple to ask for Kewarg's counsel, but rocks had blocked the path, trapping him, the priests, and Momsúndosilv. I decided to venture outside then, and face the heat and the thick smoke. The entire world was burning, from horizon to dark horizon. A small portion of Enolv had been spared, but all around there was nothing but an endless ocean of molten rock. Some of the vines were still burning, like green-flamed rivers drifting atop the lava."

Mamóru closed his eyes and spoke more quietly. "The humans of Enolv died first, rather quickly, mostly due to the toxic air and the heat. All of my kindred died soon after, from starvation, loneliness, or despair. I was kept alive by my connection with Momsúndosilv and the energy it fed me, and by the stores of food and drink the humans had stockpiled deep in the halls of the mountain. They did not need the caches of food in the end, but they helped me endure.

"The sea of rocks took an entire year to cool off. Once the heat abated enough to walk upon the new crust, I ventured down for the first time, searching for hope. A cloud of steam beckoned me, and I found the waters of Istrilm, boiling hot at the time. It kept me alive. I barely survived those years, eating only the minimum necessary to hold on to life. Some tenacious plants began to sprout again, and fed me, and Istrilm soon blossomed with obstinate lifeforms, but not much else was to be found. I tried walking away, but each time I moved too far from the Silv, my energy waned, my matter became less corporeal, and I felt as if I was slowly unbecoming. So, I stayed here, waiting, unable to leave, unwilling to die.

"Decades after the Downfall, the lava tubes had cooled enough to wander inside them. That was when I began exploring them, at least the ones that are not too far from Enolv. These tunnels gave me a new reason to live. I inscribed these runes so that others would someday read and learn from them, so that my memory could reach across the chasm of deep time."

A jagged crack on the wall punctuated a pause; another series of petroglyphs began right after, like a page waiting to be turned. Without stepping past the crack in the wall, the old man continued, "What I've shown you so far is the brief, condensed version of the story, abridged in the segment of wall we saw during our walk. The full story, with all the names, equations, timelines, extinctions, and heartbreaks, lies deeper still. The tunnels continue for dozens of miles, in labyrinths of rocks sprawling multiple levels. Each and every wall is filled with the memory of the past one hundred thousand years or so, from the human migrations of the Expansion Epoch to the fall of Momsúndodrolom. Of course, history reaches back much farther than that, depending on where you choose to begin counting. Although my memory is as vast as these tunnels, just like them, it is also limited, and I can only remember so far back."

Mamóru leaned on his cane and studied the group. "My body is frail and tired, children," he said. "We best make our return while I still have some energy to spare. But now that you know the truth, you will better know how to ask the right questions and how to understand my answers. So, ask as we make our way back."

Mamóru began his walk toward the exit. The clicking of the tip of his cane pointedly marked the unhurried passage of time. The others felt uncomfortable asking more questions after hearing such a tragic story, even though Mamóru had remained stoic through most of the telling. Perhaps the length of time he'd had to process the events had allowed him to distance himself from his emotions. Perhaps he was simply good at hiding them.

"I wonder…" Sterjall said, hesitating. "Do you know how Noss was meant to send the signal once the domes were to open again?"

"What I know is that the signal—their word—was to be heard within the temples, across all of them at the same time. But Noss also devised a failsafe in case they were unable to deliver such a signal, asking the tribes to wait for two thousand years before making their exit, to evaluate whether the outside was safe once more."

"But life out here is thriving," Alaia exclaimed. "Well, not in the scablands, but everywhere else. What's stopping Noss from sending that signal?"

"I'm afraid the answer is one I do not like to think about," the old man said. "I cannot be certain, but all clues point to one conclusion—Noss is dead."

Hod Abjus stopped abruptly. "Dead? What say you?" he spat.

Mamóru kept on walking. "Noss is, or was, the collection of patterns of every living being that made them up. From what you've told me about how widespread the Downfall was, one can estimate that most life that made up the Noss consciousness was destroyed. Most, but not all. Parts of them still live in each of the surviving domes. Imagine if a substantial portion of your brain had been removed and destroyed, while the pieces that remained were left disconnected, as separate entities, unable to talk to each other."

"But what about the new life that has sprouted since the cataclysm?" Balstei asked. "Wouldn't that mean Noss is alive once more?"

"Not Noss, but a new being, perhaps. We cannot expect them to have the same memories, the same goals. But there may be aspects of old Noss we can still salvage."

"By opening the domes," Kulak said.

"Precisely, mindahim son. The more domes that are opened, and the more we can spread the diversity that was entrusted to their domains, the closer we'll be to bringing back the old Noss, though I don't presume they will ever be the same. Such is life. I can't know for certain if that is the right answer, so I would prefer to ask the planet themself, whatever their new name may be."

"What do you mean? How would we do that?" Sterjall asked.

"In the manner the Miscam of old would have. By combining the strength of six Silvesh, we could mindspeak to whatever is left of Noss, or whatever was birthed in their stead. Perhaps in their rekindled memory we'll find the answers to our quandaries."

"But we only have three Silvesh," Kitjári pointed out.

"Four, if you can help me reach Momsúndosilv. I believe you will have a better chance at it than the soldiers who came for it, as you can control the vines, while they could only foolishly try to cut through them."

They arrived at the narrow gap once more. Far to their left was the opposite wall of the immense tunnel, and they saw it was also covered in drawings and runes. The largest of the drawings was a map, an index of the hundreds of tunnels and their contents.

"Is that where the story you wrote ends?" Balstei asked, staring at the wall.

"It is," Mamóru answered. "If you were to follow along this tunnel, always keeping your left hand on the wall, you'd walk chronologically through myriad different tales. In some parts, the story is not quite linear, as multiple tunnels split up or down, but eventually you'd end up back where you started, and that's here, where it all begins and it all ends."

Balstei was in awe at the scale of it all. "How long did it take you to write this?"

"I spent the first hundred years planning, drawing and erasing in the sand alone, and recalling as best as I could by telling the story to myself. Once I had an outline, I measured the walls and separated all the chapters by tunnels. Only then I got to carving. The rocks are not easy to etch, but I had time to spare, so I worked on these pages of stone for nine hundred years or so. After that, once a year, I'd go back down to make minor corrections or additions, but it's been a long time since anything has changed."

"Nine hundred years…" Balstei repeated.

"Did you give your work a title, like in a book?" Sterjall asked.

"Glad you asked, agnurf son. I did. I titled it *Masks of the Miscam*. Someday I hope it can take a more practical form, such as a proper book that can be transcribed at a scriptorium. In this way, the entirety of this compendium of history and knowledge might be preserved, so that future generations may learn from our mistakes."

Chapter Forty-Six

Momsúndosilv

After replenishing their bodies, souls, and waterskins with Istrilm's mineral waters, the group mounted the smilodons and rode back up to the entrance on the mountainside. They left the cats outside and marched down the long tunnel, avoiding the cracks and fallen rocks.

"I've been meaning to ask," Balstei said as they ventured deeper, "do you happen to know more about how quaar was manufactured?"

"Very little," Mamóru answered. "It was a secret the Acoapóshi priests kept tightly guarded, a secret never revealed outside their tribe. My knowledge of the alchemical intricacies of quaar is limited, but I have some guesses and a few formulas written in the Istrilm Sanctum."

"I would love to study your writings, if you'd let me," Balstei said excitedly. He bit his lower lip, hoping for an encouraging answer.

"Once your mission is not so pressing, perhaps that would be a fine challenge to undertake. If your focus of study has been the aetheric elements, you should be able to make sense of most of what I have written in the lower caves." Mamóru looked toward Sterjall's belt. "Agnurfson, that blade of yours, may I see it?"

Sterjall unsheathed Leif and handed it to him.

"Where did you procure this marvelous artifact?" the old man asked, careful not to touch the obsidian edges.

"Banook and my friend Ockam crafted it for me."

"Indeed. I see Kerjaastórgnem's tender sensibilities permeating through it, as well as Dorvauros influences. And it does not surprise me that he would know where to find senstregalv. But the conduit on the grip, how did he come to possess one? I thought they never built a lattice at Da'áju." He handed the dagger back.

"Conduit? Oh… No, the quaar tube is from Agnargdrolom, where the lattice was destroyed. I took one from there. Many more were scattered on the ground."

Sterjall demonstrated how he could use the dagger to extend Agnargsilv's sight and explained how he'd used it to find Mamóru himself.

"Fascinating," the Nu'irg said. "What you hold is a quaar conduit. I was not aware they could be used in the fashion you've shown, but in hindsight it does not surprise me, as all they do is carve an empathic channel through which the threads can travel. The conduits are similar in nature to the Silvesh, though more simple-minded, to put it somehow. Relatively new artifacts, not nearly as old as the Silvesh, crafted by the Acoapóshi merely to grow and sustain the domes. I believe we may soon encounter more of them."

They passed the large chamber in which Mamóru had been hiding.

"This is but one level of the mountain city of Enolv," Mamóru explained. "The lower levels filled up with lava, and most of the upper ones collapsed when the trunk fell."

"Did the Zovarian soldiers explore it all?" Sterjall asked.

"All they could find. They did not know about my secret passageways. But once they saw the entrance to the temple, they focused all their attention on it."

"How many soldiers were there?"

"Forty, give or take. A few of their horses died near here, and I'm guessing many more died on their return path. I had my first taste of meat in a long time after they left, and realized I had lost the stomach for it—it only made me sick."

"Did you see a small woman with the soldiers?" Kitjári asked. "A scout, short hair, pointed chin, missing a front tooth. Would've looked a bit out of place."

"I did. A feisty one, and smart too. She's the one I heard mention Lago's name. But here we are, at last." Mamóru stopped in front of an archway of rock embellished by etched runes. Two flanking columns had been carved in the shape of the skulls of the tusked creatures. On the ground, partially covered by rubble, was a ten-feet-wide carving of the proboscidean glyph. Liquid silver had been poured in the grooves, making the triangular glyph shimmer.

Mamóru pointed at a portion of the silver that had been recently picked at. "Those greedy ruffians tried to remove the silver from our sacred glyph. The scout lady reprimanded them, telling them they'd die if they carried more weight across the desert." He stepped over the glyph and into a long hallway. "This goes much deeper. The soldiers cleared the fallen rocks, but it was a hopeless endeavor either way. You will see why."

Farther into the tunnel, the ground was streaked by dry sap. They did their best to avoid it, but soon enough, the entire floor was covered in a sticky layer, tugging at their boots and footpaws. Slashed vines lay scattered about, withering but not yet fully dry. They found dulled swords and useless axes, all being eaten by the sap. The soldiers had slashed their way through fifty feet of vines; a commendable feat, but not nearly sufficient. Unlike the healthy vines of an intact dome, these vines didn't seem to have the energy to grow back, at least not rapidly enough to make a difference.

"The roots of these vines run deep into the cracks," Mamóru said, "feeding on the many underground streams. All the vines you see here are one single, stubborn organism that has lost its purpose and merely grows where it still can grow."

They reached the spot where the Zovarians had given up. Nearly no walls were visible, as the hallway was wide, and the soldiers had cut only enough to fit their bodies. Sterjall, Kulak, and Kitjári used the empathic focus their Silvesh granted them to push the rest of the vines out of the way; they crackled and groaned, but obediently parted.

"At least there is no sap on the ground here," Sterjall said, stepping farther in and making a wider opening. "But I still don't—" *Slam!* A portion of a wall collapsed, almost crushing Sterjall.

"Careful, kid!" Kitjári said, pulling him back. "The walls are weak, moving the vines is taking a toll on them. Proceed slowly."

They carried on with more caution, distressing the structure as little as possible. Segments of the vaulted ceiling were dislodged from time to time, but the passage was wide enough to walk around them. Deeper still, the vines spread farther to the sides, indicating that they were now in a bigger chamber.

"Please, step in," Mamóru said, "and gaze upon the vastness of the Enolv Temple, Ommo ust Momsúndo. Or what is left of it."

They stood in a bubble of green covered in thorns, obscuring a much larger room. The entire temple had been overtaken by the tangles, but they did not dare open the vines much wider, fearing a collapse. The ground was tilted, making it difficult to stand without slipping.

"Mindrelsilv sees no Silv aura," Kulak said, disappointed.

"I know it's in here," Mamóru said. "I cannot see it, not in the way you can, but there's a presence, an energy exhaled by it. The closer I am to it, the more whole I feel."

"I don't see the Silv either," Kitjári said, "but there must be pieces of the lattice all around, because something is making a jumble out of the threads I *can* see. It's hard to focus."

"Feels like a broken mirror," Kulak observed.

Sterjall focused his gaze higher, following the tangle of threads that the quaar conduits propelled all about, and noticed the dimmest of glows. "Up there!" he said. "Among the vines, that must be the mask! But… It's such a weak aura, it feels nothing like our Silvesh."

The other Silvfröash spotted the presence as well.

"Let vines open," Kulak said, "ask to bring Silv down to us."

"But be careful," Kitjári added. "This temple is big, and has a lot less support than the hallway. Only lower the vines that we need."

They took a few steps back and projected their empathic focus to make a handful of vines glide toward the ground. Rubble dislodged and slammed in front of them, cracking on the ground in sharp notes.

"Slower," Kitjári warned.

They walked over the rubble, and as they pushed more vines out of the way, all three of them saw a spinning jet of threads descending to hit the ground. It landed in front of them almost soundlessly.

Kulak quickly snatched the artifact before it rolled away. "Lattice conduit," he said.

"Khuron, must not desecrate house of Momsúndo," Hod Abjus whispered tensely.

"Momsúndo does not mind," Mamóru interjected. "If they are of use to you, be my guest, as they are not needed in this temple any longer."

Kulak stowed the conduit in his kilt pocket.

The vines in front of them kept descending. They could feel it clearly now, an aura the same synesthetic color as Mamóru's: a pearlescent white, but with less of a sparkle. More rocks were dislodged, so they took their time, not letting the vines slide too far. At last, white bones and tattered clothes were lowered and displayed in full. Cradled in a nest of thorny vines was the gaunt skeleton of the Toldask chief, with the blackness of Momsúndosilv still clasped to the leathery skin of his skull.

Mamóru stepped toward the osseous display. "Mighty Kewarg, what fate the stars have inflicted upon you. Till your last moments you fought to protect the dome, till your last breath you clutched the mask and wept for your people. For long have you safeguarded this Silv, but the time has come for it to serve a new purpose. Surrender it now, long-tusked warrior of the Dai-Gamár. Surrender it, and be at peace."

He reached forward and pulled the mask away. The skull cracked dryly and was freed from it. Mamóru held the mask up and inspected it. Its long trunk drooped languidly, while its curved tusks reached outward like nocturnal tentacles. It seemed much larger than the other Silvesh—peculiarly monstrous, yet regal.

But it is dim, Sterjall thought. *So dim. Its glow is nothing compared to the others.*

As if reading Sterjall's mind, Balstei turned to Mamóru and asked, "Will Momsúndosilv still work? Given that your own kind is no more? Except for yourself, that is."

"Perhaps not in the same way," Mamóru said. "It is weak, like I am weak, but for as long as I am alive, Momsúndosilv will still have something to connect to."

While they had been talking, the vines had slowly shifted again. More rubble got dislodged, and yet another quaar artifact fell near them—it was not a tubular conduit, but one of the hollow, geodesic spheres that acted as joints. Alaia rushed to grab it.

"There is more lattice above," Kulak said. "We could take more, do more with it."

"Khuron, *baakiag*," Abjus pleaded. "Not proper. *Wuartam*. We must go."

Kulak began to will more vines to shift, slowly and carefully.

"Kulak is right," Sterjall said, "Leif has been invaluable to me. Who knows what else we could do with more of these pieces?" He helped Kulak, keeping an eye on the structure above.

Kitjári remained alert, keeping the exit tunnel open. She ushered the others into the safer space.

A strut from the vault above fell in front of Kulak, dragging with it dozens more conduits and joint segments.

"That should be enough," Kulak said, picking up the artifacts that were within reach, aided by Sterjall and Alaia.

They hurried to safety once they had grabbed enough, letting the rest of the segments roll away on the slanted floor. Behind them, more struts became dislodged, and with them a rain of conduits came down, each of them landing weightlessly, contrasting with the loud and heavy boulders.

"The more the better," Balstei said, and hurried to grab them.

"Stop," Abjus said. "We have enough."

Balstei was filling his pockets with conduits when he felt something impact his neck. When he looked up, his eyes were stung by falling dust. As he tried to wipe the dust off, he heard rubble pelting around him, followed by a piercing crack. He tried to scramble out of the way, but felt something hitting him in the back and slamming him to the ground. It was Kenondok, who had launched himself forward and pushed the artificer away just before Balstei could be crushed by a stone column.

Kenondok dragged the artificer out by a leg. Balstei's hands quickly reached to grab one more geodesic sphere, but it rolled off his fingertips.

"We go now," Kenondok said, dropping Balstei's leg. "Stupid *wuerle almbia*."

"Th-thank you," Balstei mumbled and stood up, eyes still caked with dust. "I... I just..."

"Enough. Go," Abjus demanded.

As they moved into the hallway, a huge wedge of stone tipped over.

"Go, move!" Kitjári urged, pushing them all into the tunnel. Abjus picked up Mamóru, who couldn't move as quickly, and they all bolted out of the tunnel as the mass of rock crumbled behind them. A blast of dust-filled wind shoved them to the ground.

"Lodestar guide us," Alaia said, looking back. The light of her lantern did not reach very far through the gray particles.

Kulak coughed and wiped his nose. "Four masks we have now," he said. "What to do next?"

Mamóru was still cradled in Abjus's arms. He pointed ahead into the vine-wrapped hallway. "Now you lead me to your lands, as there is much that needs to be discussed with the chiefs of Mindreldrolom. We have a dangerous journey ahead, to lands more remote than this."

Chapter Forty-Seven

Sentinel

They slept through the daylight hours in the chamber with the proboscidean bones, then headed to the cliff's edge to scout their potential exit routes. Mamóru pointed out the path he'd seen the soldiers take, and it looked like a much easier trail than the hills and chasms they had recently traveled through.

Before departing, they prepared a meal that consisted of a few nuts and herbs paired with thrice-steeped tea.

Alaia played with a geodesic sphere she'd rescued, making it attach to a quaar conduit as if magnetized. They separated and rejoined satisfyingly. "What do you think we can do with these?" she asked.

"If nothing else, we can use them to see threads from farther away," Sterjall answered. "There's no need to craft a fancy blade for that." He stuck a pinky inside the hole, watching his threads be propelled through it.

"I'm keeping at least a couple of each," Balstei said. "I'd like to study the artifacts, and I was the one who grabbed most of them to begin with," he self-righteously added.

Sterjall joined three conduits to one sphere, which acted as a sort of snapping ball joint as he slid them over the surface. "Kulak, look," he said, sliding the pieces around. "The threads cluster inside the sphere and push out the other tubes." He clicked the conduits into different configurations; as their orientations changed, the threads that split from them drew new patterns in the air.

Kulak stared intently. He had been playing with two long conduits at the same time. He lined them up end to end by their notches, and with a soft twist, locked them together with such mechanical precision and tightness that they were indistinguishable from a single piece. He showed his friends. "I found what we can do," he said. He picked up another segment and attached it to the first two. "Look. Quaar telescope," he exclaimed, grinning sharply as he looked through the hole.

"Does it work?" Sterjall asked, scooting closer. He took the extended conduit from Kulak and aimed it at the rocky fields. "There's almost nothing alive to look at, but I sense some very distant threads, farther away than Leif could see. It's probably bacteria growing underground." He cocked his head, twisting his lips in a strange expression. "It's very odd, speaking of how far away something seems, because there's no perspective to anything. Two parallel threads don't converge on a point on the horizon, instead they keep their same thickness and relative position, but I *know* when they are farther out. And when they are behind one another, they don't overlap, but I know which one is in front."

"It's a different sense altogether," Balstei said. "Does a sound sound smaller to you in the distance? Or does it just have a quality of being distant? You can't think of it in terms of a visual field. I felt the same effect with soot, though it's more of a pull, a gut feeling—I just wish I could actually see those threads."

While Sterjall was trying to determine the reach of the extended conduit, Alaia snapped together three more. "Wait wait wait… This is no telescope," she said. She put the long tube to her lips and blew. "It's a blowgun."

Kenondok stopped stirring the over-steeped tea leaves and looked at her. As their expert weaponsmith, he immediately lit up with curiosity and gestured to Alaia, who tossed him the three lattice segments. Kenondok found the instrument fascinating, as the conduits could be disassembled to compactly stow the weapon, yet when put back together, the pieces sealed together so tightly that it was too perfect to be believed.

"Blowgun *and* telescope," Kulak said, watching Kenondok's expression.

"My lips think it too rough," Kenondok said, testing out the instrument. "Three pieces do enough. Five or six for far targets. Too tight for mink fur darts. Maybe bull thistle or chipmunk fur becomes better fletching."

"We have enough to make a blowgun for you too," Alaia offered.

Kenondok rubbed the fading pigments on his ribbed scalp, then handed the conduits back to Alaia. "Makes my scalp shiver with unease," he said. "Sacred instruments, wrong place. But I craft mouthpieces so your lips will not cut. And I trim darts to fit, once back in Mindreldrolom."

They let the smilodons chomp down a generous portion of munnji cakes, then packed up and headed out. Mamóru rode alone on Pichi's back, cradled among the many bags she carried in her harness. The Nu'irg's emaciated body weighed nearly nothing, so Pichi did not even notice a difference. As before, they traveled by night to conceal themselves from enemies and from the heat. Luckily, the Autumn winds had begun to blow over the Stelm Sajal, bringing with them a chill mountain air.

As they traversed the ruinous landscape, they encountered a dozen more dead horses, discarded pieces of armor, and heavy cooking supplies. A substantial wedge of pure silver ripped from the proboscidean glyph had been cast aside to shimmer uselessly among the shards of black rock.

After three cycles of the stars, the Steps of Odrásmunn came into sight. Sunnokh was readying himself to rise, the brightening sky drawing a stark contrast with the silhouette of dark polygonal columns.

They were plodding through a ravine scored by parallel lava flows, still at a distance from where the steps rose, when Abjus pulled hard on Fulm's saddle. "Hold!" he warned. "Something moves on the steps."

"Be one with shadows," Sunu whispered urgently. "Our scalps are still unseen."

They ducked behind a slanted crust of rocks. Sterjall spied through his binoculars. "They are infantry, Zovarian armor. They seem to be searching."

"That's very close to where we made our descent," Kitjári said, taking the binoculars. "We left many prints in the sand. Maybe they'll follow our old tracks that way."

"And how do we get our hinds out of here now?" Balstei asked.

Kitjári surveyed the area. "We'll have to hide here the rest of the day, then keep moving under the cover of night. If we are spotted, our only choice is to fight before they alert more soldiers. Scout troops tend to travel in squads of three, but I only see two of them up at the—"

Eihnk-eihnk! Olo suddenly called out, his eyes focused toward brightening clouds. Sunu squinted their eyes and above them saw a gyring bird.

"Sentinel!" they warned.

"Can we shoot it?" Alaia asked, reaching in her overalls pocket for a dart.

"Too high," Kenondok answered. The bird kept circling.

Sunu popped open a soot-filled seedpod, inhaled, then spoke to Olo almost apologetically. The jay listened, giving one stern *eihnk* in response. The black-and-blue bird lifted like a hurled spear, aided by the rising, warm currents. He picked up speed, flipped his talons outward, and tangled with the intruding herald in midair, feathers exploding everywhere. The birds locked talons and fell from the sky together.

Sunu rushed to catch them before they hit the ground, then mercilessly snapped the intruder's neck and tossed it to one of the cats to eat. They kneeled, placed Olo carefully on their lap, and spread his wings. "Sunu is sorry," they said. Olo had scratches on his torso and was missing a few feathers, but did not seem gravely injured. "Sunu will deal with your injuries soon. Be patient, Olo."

"Do you think they spotted what happened?" Sterjall asked.

A distant whistle answered his question. Atop the steps, flanked by the two soldiers, was a shaman calling for his bird, with another herald circling over him.

"Fuck, they have another one," Alaia muttered. "We need to stop them before they send for reinforcements."

"To smilodons," Hod Abjus said. "We fight."

They mounted the cats and rushed toward the wall of black columns. Two arrows sparked by the fast-moving paws, but only two—the terrified soldiers quickly turned around and fled.

"Up the wall, before they get away!" Kitjári yelled. The smilodons struggled through their run over the jagged ground, then had to push themselves hard as they scratched their way up the columns.

"There!" Givra said, pointing north—three horses, blasting away at full gallop.

They gave chase, making headway once the horses lost speed on a gray sand dune. But the smilodons were much too tired and had not the stamina to keep going for long.

Kitjári stood atop her saddle, and with one expertly aimed arrow, struck one of the horses in the hip, making the beast crash into the pumice and silt. A dart from Kenondok stopped another horse, while Sunu's hurled halberd took care of the last one.

Blu, Kobos, and Fulm pounced, each of them sinking their saber-like fangs into the fallen horses, assuming they were more dangerous enemies than their riders.

"Mindrégosh, *lu*!" Kulak ordered.

The smilodons opened their jaws and pulled back.

Abjus and Kenondok had already jumped off their saddles and were holding smilodon-tooth knives over the throats of two pink-clad soldiers. The third rider, the shaman, was screaming, trying to free his broken leg from beneath his dying mount.

Sunu hopped off their cat and pricked a poisoned dart into each of the horses, granting them a quicker death. They then pulled the trapped shaman from under the dead horse, holding his arms tightly behind his back.

"No, please," the man implored. Unlike the other two, he was not wearing a pink uniform, but a beet-red robe.

The company dismounted, except for Mamóru, who still held on weakly to Pichi's harness. Kitjári stepped in front of the shaman and asked, "The herald, where is it?"

"Don't speak to them," one of the soldiers said, "they will—"

Abjus pressed his knife to the soldier's neck, drawing just enough blood to make them quiet.

"Where is the herald?" Kitjári repeated.

"What are you? We thought, I thought, this cannot be..." His Wastyrian accent was thick and throaty, but the man tried his best to enunciate properly.

"The herald," she demanded, waving five claws in front of the shaman's face.

"North! North... She flew north, she is no longer with me," he cried, bouncing on his unbroken leg.

"Call her back!"

"She is too far, too far and too fast. I am sorry, I am sorry." The man wept, tears leaving muddy streaks on his cheeks.

"What message did you send with her?" Sterjall asked. "And be precise, because the markings on my friends' scalps allow them to read minds. They will know if you are lying, and then they'll feed you to their cats."

Kenondok played along, nodding savagely while sliding his fingers across Fulm's bloodied fangs.

"Please! By the Divine Archdruids of the triple capital, I swear I will not lie."

"Then speak," Kitjári demanded. "How did you find us? What was written in the message that you sent with your herald?"

"Your... your creatures were spotted by a pilgrim, swimming across the Brightbay Run, near the Nightlure Cliffs. They had been looking for you everywhere, even before you were spotted, we are only one of a dozen scout squads. We were sent to track you and followed your trail up to here. And my herald... The missive was hastily written, there was not much time for me to—"

Kenondok tapped on his ridged scalp and rolled his eyes back to white, pretending to read the shaman's mind.

"I am not lying! I am telling you everything. I wrote that we followed your tracks to here. That we just spotted you in the lava beds. I asked for reinforcements. Nothing else, I swear. There was no time for more than that. I knew no more than that."

"Where are reinforcements?" Kulak asked.

"At N-Nebush, the troops are stationed at Nebush, southwest of the dome."

"They'll have days to prepare and set a perimeter," Balstei said to Kitjári. "We can't go back the same way."

"You are th-the artificer," the shaman said. "Lorr Balstei Woodslav. Please, have mercy. I trained at the institute under—"

"I don't give a tick on Takh's cocks where you studied," Balstei said. "Tell us how to make it back, or we are done with you."

"You may make it through the Moonbow Timberlands unseen, but not through the Brightbay Run. The Arch Sedecims sent ships to patrol the river, and I'm sure they will send more now."

"This wretched laggard might be right," Balstei said. "We can't cross the Brightbay like this, not with ships ready to take us."

"We'll find another way," Kitjári said. She then turned to face the rest of the group, and in Miscamish said, "We can't go back to Mindreldrolom. I can show you a path east, into Tephra, by the Sajal Crater. The Free Tribelands will grant us refuge."

"But my scalp needs to return," Kulak complained, also speaking in Miscamish.

"Not for a while," Kitjári said. "It's the only way we can keep safe."

"And what to do with them?" Kulak asked.

Kitjári stared at the wounded shaman, then at the two soldiers, thinking.

They let the smilodons feed on the horses, then cooked what was left. While the others ate, Sunu took care of Olo's wounds, apologizing all the while.

Before the oppressive heat of noon struck, they set off east, past the basalt columns of the Steps of Odrásmunn, in the direction of the Sajal Crater. They left the shaman and soldiers tied up, with a blade a hundred strides away that they could use to cut their bindings once they wormed their way over to it.

"My scalp confuses why you let them live," Kenondok complained.

"My knife wishes it had tasted their throats," Hod Abjus said. "But Kitjári thought careful. We must not make enemies with the New World."

"This is true," Kulak said. "Mindreldrolom might soon open. Laatu and Zovarians will work as one. Our scalps do not want war."

Once they were deep in the land of ash and cinder cones, far beyond the eyes of the abandoned Zovarians, Kitjári said, "Now we can turn north again. That daftwad shaman is from Wastyr, where they all learn at least basic Miscamish. I know he understood what we said."

"He'll lead the Zovarians the wrong way," Alaia realized, nodding her approval. "So, where are we going, then?"

"Straight to the Moordusk Dome," the bear replied. "It will take us several days, but let's hope they don't have too many reinforcements waiting."

"But how will we cross the river?" Sterjall asked.

"The fastest way, one too obvious for them to expect us to try—over the New Karst bridge."

Chapter Forty-Eight

Amethyst Moon

They left the land of cinder cones behind and crested a hill to set up camp, hiding in a copse of alders. They slept through the day, taking turns to keep watch.

It was past sunset by the time Sterjall awoke. He was surprised Hod Abjus wasn't pushing them to get going. He stood to check on the camp and saw Sunu sitting cross-legged on a tall rock.

"Abjus and Givra have set out to look for hazards," Sunu said, answering the unasked question. "Sunu is keeping watch. A scout troop passed by not too far from us, following the fake trail we set. We will leave once twilight wanes."

Sterjall walked around the hilltop, keeping within the protective circle of trees. He saw Alaia and Kulak reclining their heads on Blu's belly, whispering in each other's ears. He spotted Kitjári in a gulch far below, sniffing for berries and tubers, with Balstei and Kenondok at her heels. He felt suddenly alone, standing with no purpose. He noticed Mamóru then, who was leaning his aching back on the trunk of an alder, looking toward the southeast. Sterjall ambled silently, then sat against a twin tree next to Mamóru's.

"How are you feeling?" he asked.

"Broken, old," Mamóru intoned in his melodious voice. "But so full of hope." He pointed his cane toward the mountains. "The Stelm Sajal also look broken. There is an unsightly gap between the mountains, to the left of Laaja Khenukh. This was not so, back when my kind used to saunter over these domains."

"That must be where the Sajal Crater is," Sterjall said. "Kitjári says it's like an enormous hole in the ground, forming a round lake with waters that are always hot, and hotter the deeper one dives. Our guess is that the comet must've struck there."

"By the time the comet hit," Mamóru said, "we had been locked inside our domes for an entire year, so none of us saw the point of impact. It came close to falling right on our heads."

The old man's eyes glistened under the Amethyst moonlight. The twilight sky glimmered blue and black, while the desolate lands they had just left behind seemed to throb with purples.

"I'm still surprised you survived out there for so long," Sterjall murmured.

"Only thanks to the energy of Momsúndosilv. And I guess also thanks to my own memory, which provided me with a sense of purpose. I am curious, however, how it is that this so-called New World managed to recover from the fires that came. Would you tell me more?"

"There's not much to it, really. During the Downfall Epoch, first came the fire, then the ice. They say people survived in caves, or in distant islands that didn't suffer as greatly. It took a few hundred years until the ice melted and people began to dig out the lost cities, trying to understand what had been left behind. That was the Reconstitution Epoch. Honestly, we still don't understand most of the artifacts and writings found, we just accept them as truths since we know those who came before us were more advanced."

"Yet not all writings were truthful," Mamóru said.

"I guess not. And only recently I learned about all the species we lost. Yet others endured and spread all over again, as if the Downfall never happened. The scablands is the only place I've seen that is not filled with greenery and birdsong."

"Nature can be stubborn like that, resilient as a mammoth's tusks. The coming and going of species is a series of cycles, much like the seasons of Sceres, each with its own flavors and colors."

Sterjall looked up at the purple crescent. "Did the moon always have six seasons?" he asked.

"As far as I can recall, even back in the Gestation Epoch."

"Do you know what they are? What they mean?"

"What the colors are, I do not know, but they mean different things to different people. Poets and bards from all cultures wrote songs to better understand her mysteries."

"Yeah, but those tales are all made up. I wonder what the colors *really* mean."

"Have you been to the moon before?" Mamóru asked.

"I don't und—"

"I will assume you have not. If you were a person who lived on the moon, what her seasons 'really mean' would perhaps be something objective, concrete. But moon people we are not. We live in Noss, and so for us, whatever meanings we dream for her colorful displays are the meanings that matter, as they shape our culture, our stories, our aspirations. They may be spritetales, but they are as real as anything else in the sense that they affect us daily, nightly, whether consciously or subconsciously. In that same way, we imbue meaning to the stars and allow them to guide us, even though they are unreachable to us."

Sterjall gazed up and saw the brightest constellations making their appearance. He spotted Kerjaastórgnem, the golden bear, and could not hide his sorrowful expression.

"You seem to know what that constellation represents," Mamóru said, noticing the two yellow stars where Sterjall's eyes had locked.

"I do. And I know yours too, though it's below the horizon at this moment," Sterjall replied, trying to sidestep the subject.

"Smart wolf. Yes, all Nu'irgesh have one. As I was just saying, all the stories we make up about the stars are real, as real as the melancholy I saw crossing your face when you looked up at Kerjaastórgnem. Does he mean that much to you?"

Sterjall found himself exposed and did not know how to respond.

"I see," Mamóru said after a moment. "And does he feel the same way about you?"

Sterjall simply nodded. There was no need to say more.

"Worry not, agnurf son. I understand better than you can ever know. I've seen your face brighten when you talk about him, glowing as bright as the Ilaadrid Shard. I may be old, but I'm not senile or blind. I've lived as a man for much longer than Banook has, and through the millennia I've fallen in love with many women, though none ever satisfied me as much as the mammoths and mastodons I married in my past."

"Married?"

"In a manner of speaking. We had no ceremonies, but we mated for life, unlike with elephants, who I also dearly enjoyed, but who never did want to commit for quite as long. And when I say *for life*, I mean for the length of *their* life, as I have the curse of always outliving all of my mates. But back to Banook… I first met him perhaps sixty thousand years ago, when—"

"Sixty thousand?! I thought he was only about ten thousand years old."

"Perhaps he only *remembers* as far back as ten thousand years, but he has been around for much longer. I, however, can recall much farther into the past.

Kerjaastórgnem came to be after his predecessor—a polar bear who the northern tribes called Gwunenhauk—died tragically during the Third Great Thawing."

"I... don't know anything about the Great Thawing...s," Sterjall admitted.

"How appalling!" Mamóru teased, slapping a wrinkled hand on Sterjall's knee. "I merely jest, there is no way you could have known about the thawings. Before I return to Banook, let me tell you about the formidable Gwunenhauk. She was a mighty polar bear Nu'irg who loved fishing narwhals and hunting walruses in the Unthawing Ocean, which has quite a misnomer of a name, given that it has thawed on and off through the epochs. She was far north, prowling the ice sheet of the polar continent which is not a true continent, when the third of the great thawings began and the ice sheet broke apart. She was a proud bear, and was certain she could survive on her icy raft. But through many decades her continent-sized raft shrunk until it melted off entirely, abandoning Gwunenhauk near the north pole of Noss, too far for even a Nu'irg to swim back to land. And there she drowned."

"Is that when Banook was born?"

"That was when Gwunenhauk died. Death and life are intertwined, but Banook's life is his own. We Nu'irgesh don't know exactly the moment at which we are born, but some years after Gwunenhauk drowned, I felt the presence of Kerjaastórgnem, of Banook—who had no names yet—beginning to stir. It was a slow, gradual process, like an idea that brews in one's mind and takes a long time to coalesce. All Nu'irgesh felt him slowly becoming, until one day, as I sauntered through the mountains you now know as the Stelm Nedross, Banook and I crossed paths.

"Even in his early years, he was already a kind-spirited, selfless, loving bear. He cared so much for bearkind, and was so enthralled by all manner of creatures, big and small. He also felt a powerful kinship to humankind, though he did not yet know how to express it. I saw him countless more times after that, including one time after he had taken his human form, during the Great Migrations, when the Miscam tribes were settling the lands upon which they'd grow their domes. And what a big man he turned out to be! Banook told me then how he came to find his human form. Has he told you?"

"Yes, he has, of course."

"Then you know about Khaambe, and their forbidden love."

Sterjall nodded.

"It is a heart-rending story," the old Nu'irg said, "but it helped me understand Banook more profoundly. I see what he sees in you, Lago-Sterjall. I see why you fear and hurt when you look up at his stars. I, too, have fallen in love with a Silvfröa before. Her name was Agrum when in her half-form of a zebra, or Kivv, when she chose not to wear Almelsilv." Mamóru seemed suddenly lost in thought. He blinked hard, as if that'd help him wipe off an old memory, then continued, "But that is a story for another time. What I wanted to say was that I understand why Banook feels drawn to you. You can see us the way we see you. You understand what it is like to be of two kinds, yet be one. There is something special about sharing that deepmost way of being, of learning how to find our hidden natures, to elevate them and let them become all that they can be."

"It's true. From my very first moment as Sterjall, I saw Banook differently, fully. I felt I understood him, and I knew he saw the same in me."

"Those kinds of relationships are ones to truly treasure," Mamóru said. "Do not take them for granted."

"I wouldn't. He's too special to me."

Mamóru paused, combing his long beard. He looked straight at Sterjall and pointedly said, "Do not take *any* of those relationships for granted. Someone who can see you for who you truly are is rare and precious. Don't let misconceived cultural norms brew fear within your heart. Be cautious, but stand proud and fight for what you love."

Sterjall pondered the Nu'irg's words as he strolled quietly back into the copse. The others had not yet returned from their scouting expedition, and even Alaia had gone away, following Kitjári to help gather berries.

Kulak was resting on a pile of dry leaves, head leaning on Blu's warm belly, their fur dappled with the light of Sceres.

"She is most beautiful in purple," Kulak said, feeling Sterjall approach. He kept his slitted eyes on the sharp crescent. "My scalp wishes we could stay and see all her dresses, but soon we return inside Mindreldrolom."

"We'll see all of her seasons at some point," Sterjall said. "Together."

He sat next to Kulak, leaned over, and kissed him without fear, holding on to the moment.

When Sterjall pulled back, Kulak sat up and looked around, worried about anyone who might have seen them. "What was kiss about?" he asked.

"Nothing in particular," Sterjall answered. "I'm just happy we have each other." He held on to Kulak's handpaw and leaned back on Blu's belly.

Chapter Forty-Nine

The Final Push

After a few more nights of travel, the company made it back to the Old Pilgrim's Road, but forty miles west from where they had crossed it before, between the Stiss Tungeo and the Brightbay Run. They followed the road northeast, keeping far enough away from it to avoid any night-traveling caravans, until they reached the exposed farmlands on the western edge of New Karst. With daytime nearing, they decided to camp within the protection of a birch forest.

"We need to rush past these farmlands tonight," Kitjári said, spying through leaves with the binoculars. "We do it in one move, so we can make it across the bridge before anyone knows we are here."

The flat farms gave them a clear view of the distant city. The Brightbay Run spread to either side before them, bisected by a majestic bridge that separated a large town from the city rising on the far side of the river.

"Mindreldrolom is still too far," Kulak said. "Smilodons are tired. They cannot run without rest."

"We'll stop when we have to," Kitjári said. "I just hope that we've diverted enough of their resources the wrong way, and that we can find shelter past the city."

They waited until the silence of midnight before bolting through the farmlands. They were only spied by a few dogs who barked while they were crossing the open fields, but by the time the farm owners came out to see what the commotion was about, the cats and riders were long gone.

They stopped at the periphery of the town, hiding behind a half-collapsed barn. "We do not rush unless we are spotted," Kitjári said. "We can approach the bridge slowly to avoid tiring our cats, then attempt to cross it unseen. I doubt it will happen, but there's no point in running until it's necessary."

"Make blowguns ready," Kenondok said.

"Only darts to make them fall unconscious," Alaia said. "Don't kill anyone."

"If they become close, my knife tastes their throats," Abjus warned.

"Then don't let them get too close," she replied.

Weapons readied, they rode through the darkest alleys they could find, letting the smilodons navigate by instinct.

The west side of New Karst was quiet this late at night. Their path toward the bridge led them by a tavern where a drunk man came stumbling out, rambling to himself as he loitered by the front door. As he turned to piss on the wall, they took the chance to sneak behind him. They dodged a pair of shady merchants lurking in a corner and moved toward the bridge, stopping in a tree-filled square right in front of the bridge's tall arches.

"Bridge is so long..." Kulak marveled.

"Half a mile long," Balstei said. "Second longest in the Loorian Continent."

The stone and metal bridge stretched mightily, tall enough at its center to let three-decker warships sail under it. It was guarded by an extensive barbican that climbed into curved steps on either side of a massive gateway.

"At least it seems mostly empty this late at night," Alaia said. "Except for those two."

Two guards gossiped by the barbican steps, looking bored.

Alaia and Givra lifted their blowguns. With a muted *ffwhoop* they took down the two guards at the same time. Blu and Pichi trotted toward the opening while Fulm and Kobos grabbed the guards by their uniforms and tossed the unconscious bodies into nearby bushes. They hurried under the threshold and onto the bridge.

Sterjall had never felt so exposed in his life. The bridge was the longest single structure he'd ever seen, it was well lit, they were riding giant cats, he had the face of a wolf, and they were headed to another barbican with likely more soldiers guarding it.

When they were only a dozen strides across the bridge, they heard a sharp whistle behind them.

"Hey!" a guard called out. "What sort of... What in the Nethervo*aagghh—*"

Abjus's dart pierced the man's neck. He toppled over, but another had already come down the barbican steps. She saw her friend on the ground and jumped backward to take cover, screaming for help.

"They'll sound the alarm!" Kitjári warned. "Move!"

The smilodons galloped across the bridge, scaring dozens of fisherfolk and night workers, some of whom simply leapt into the raging river. Metal gates dropped, sealing the western exit, then a brassy horn blared from the barbican behind them, alerting a twin barbican at the eastern end of the bridge.

The cats raced forward, but the bridge was too long, allowing time for the guards at the city to prepare. Pink-sailed ships in the Brightbay lit up their lanterns and turned toward them, while far over the next barbican figures scurried about, taking positions in windows and parapets.

A distant call was issued, then a clang reverberated.

"Eastern gate has closed!" Sunu cried, seeing the vertical bars of metal obstructing their path.

A wall of armored guards formed in front of the blocked exit, some on horseback, holding long lances.

"Down to the docks!" Kulak commanded.

Blu stepped up on the stone parapet to their left, balancing expertly as he sprinted on it, then aimed for a large fishing boat moored below. The height was substantial, but Blu jumped with no hesitation, slicing his claws through the sails to slow his drop. He tore through the canvas and landed on the deck, spraying a racket of sleepy gulls, then jumped onto a floating dock. The others followed and together rushed into the port, making their way up to street level.

They heard guards calling to their right, then the clopping of hooves.

"To the roofs!" Balstei yelled. "Their horses can't follow us there!"

The houses on this side of the bridge were predominantly constructed with turf roofs, making it look as if the towers of the city grew from a patchwork of grassy mounds.

The four cats jumped onto the nearest roof. Pichi's weight made her sink into it, but she clambered out and hastened to the top ridge, where the structure was more sound. Taking a brief pause, they studied the expanse of the city of New Karst. The turf roofs rose and fell in levels, making it hard to guess the best routes.

"Up on that roof!" a guard called nearby.

"Just head to the dome!" Kitjári shouted. "Now!"

They hurried north, trampling over the turf as much as possible, leaping over narrow alleyways. Menacing bells tolled, waking the entire city.

Horses galloped on streets parallel to them. Across more roofs they leapt, past chimneys, over fences, ignoring the people who screamed near them. *Fwip. Fwip.* Two arrows flew by their heads. Fulm leapt down, his blurry shadow smashing against an archer on horseback, then led the group into the alleys to avoid any more projectiles. They followed winding streets, jumping closed gates and stomping through courtyards, until they reached a less-guarded end of the city.

They vaulted over a tall hedge, through a sheep corral, and then over a stockade into a peach orchard. A canyon sloped downhill from there, at a shallow angle that led directly toward the dome, following the long stretch of the moonlit Siltlands.

The cavalry had stopped at the farmlands, unable to pursue them through all the fences and hedges. Half of the troop broke away, hurrying north on the main road.

"They are going to alert the soldiers ahead," Kitjári said. "We'll find a lot more resistance by the dome."

"We can lose them in the forest," Alaia said.

"No easy way there now," Balstei said. "And it would take us five times longer." He looked east toward the Karst Forest, which was several miles away, climbing up a treacherous cliff.

"Then we take the shortest route," Sterjall declared. "The canyons will keep us hidden, at least for a while."

Even though the size of the Moordusk Dome made it seem as if it was near, it was still over fifty miles away. The smilodons could cover that distance, but it would take all the endurance they had left. At least the dry riverbeds of the Siltlands were flat with compacted sand and relatively easy to navigate.

The cats were fatigued, but now that they had left the horses behind, they could slow to a trot to catch their breaths. Everyone gripped their weapons tightly as the cats padded silently over the purple-lit sand. For dozens of miles, they kept going, until the cats were too worn down to continue.

Sunnokh was rising as they paused to rest, extending a sharp edge of orange light on the western canyon wall.

They let the smilodons feast on the few rations they had left, encouraged them to drink most of their water, then allowed them a short nap to recover.

Eihnk-eihnk! Olo warned, waking them all up. Three birds circled above them.

"Lodestar guide us," Kitjári said. "They know exactly where we are. All we can do is hurry now."

A fourth bird joined the rest, while one who had been circling flew toward the northwest.

While the heralds kept track of their position, the smilodons hastened over the Siltlands. The canyon walls began to tighten, feeling less like a form of protection and more like a trap.

"Over right rim!" Givra warned.

Five horses trotted above them, following the edge of the canyon. The leading rider blew on a bugle. Another bugle replied from the left, the shrill echo bouncing between the vertical walls. Five more horses encroached from that side.

"In the name of the Arch Sedecims of our divine Union, I command you to stop!" a voice from the right rim called out. "Obey, or we shall cast a rain of arrows upon you." Bows were raised and readied by all the soldiers.

"Into that narrower canyon, go!" Kitjári said.

The cats bolted, spraying a cloud of dust behind them.

"Release!"

Fwip! Whap! Thud!

Most of the arrows landed in the sand, but one hit Kobos in his shoulder, and another lodged itself into Givra's thigh. Givra quickly removed the arrow from Kobos's thick fur and pressed her hand over the wound, but she left the arrow in her leg untouched—it had buried deep, and she could not pull it out safely while they bounced so hard.

More arrows fell. One bounced off Alaia's quaar helm, another scraped Abjus's shoulder, but none stuck this time. The soldiers were now trying to shoot at them while at full gallop, and the canyon was narrower and hard to see into, throwing their aim off.

"Push!" Sunu commanded. "Our home is only a few miles ahead!"

The path weaved and narrowed further.

"Shit, stop!" Kitjári said as they turned around a bend. In front of them, an infantry line was marching. Ten long pikes sparkled at the front, covering the entire width of the canyon, ten more on a line behind, followed by twenty spears at the back. The soldiers stopped as soon as they saw the group. The front line kneeled and dropped their pikes forward, locking them against the ground. The second line held their pikes aimed higher. Kite shields behind the pike soldiers were drawn, forming a barrier. Behind the troop, the ten horses that had chased above them converged and joined the formation.

Sterjall felt angry. He did not want to relive the massacre from the time he had to fight against Fjorna's soldiers. *But we can't go back now,* he thought, *there were no splits in the canyon for miles.*

The wall of soldiers briefly parted, making way for five sedecim peacekeepers—the knights were heavily armored, wielding longswords with both hands.

The four smilodons huffed and hissed, fifty feet in front of the fifty-five soldiers. The sedecim peacekeeper at the center of the group—whose ribbon-embellished pauldrons were golden and not bronze-colored—advanced in front of the others and stopped between two piercing pikes. She lifted her helm's visor with a gauntleted hand.

"You have nowhere to run, so be smart, and listen," the knight said, sinking the heavy tip of her longsword into the compacted sand. "I am Marshal Thurann Embercut of Nebush, commander of the Ninth Battalion. I am here with orders from the Arch Sedecims to take you to Zovaria, dead or alive, but I am not eager to spill the blood of my prisoners or that of my comrades. Though your beasts look fierce, they will not be able to battle our numbers. Surrender yourselves, tame your beasts, avoid needless bloodshed, and we will grant you a fair trial."

Givra took the chance to finally pull the arrow from her leg. She hurled the bloodied stick in the Marshal's direction and said, "*Khuluthuk henet khar ilm cha tuun!*"

The marshal was unimpressed. "Which one of you is Lago Vaari?" she asked.

"It's me," Sterjall said, "but I'm not interested in negotiations. You have no right to the masks, and we have importa—"

"I'm not interested in negotiations either. You either do as I command, or you die."

"What do we do?" Kitjári whispered. "The cats will get impaled if they try to jump over those pikes, and we can't fight this many soldiers."

"I will count down from sixteen," Marshal Embercut warned, "and if you do not surrender, my soldiers will attack. Ready!" All ten cavalry soldiers lifted their bows and nocked their arrows. The twenty spear fighters moved their shields slightly to the side and pointed their spears. The pikes tightened their grip on the sand.

"Sixteen!" she began to count down.

Sterjall looked around, heart stumbling.

"Fifteen!"

"What if we try to run?" Balstei asked.

"Fourteen!"

"There will be more of them coming from the canyon," Kitjári said. "And those archers can't miss their shots now."

"Thirteen!"

"Sunu's halberd is ready," Sunu said, holding a reassuring hand over Olo's injured wings.

"Twelve!"

"If we die, we die," Hod Abjus proclaimed. "But we not surrender."

"Eleven!"

Kenondok loaded a dart into his blowgun, saying nothing.

"Ten!"

Kulak's eyes were fully dilated. He mindspoke to the smilodons, trying to calm them down.

"Nine!"

"Let me negotiate," Mamóru said, climbing down from Pichi's harness.

"Eight!"

Sterjall shook his head. "What are you—"

"They will listen to an old man," Mamóru interrupted. "Keep your weapons ready."—*Seven!*—"I will give a signal, and when I do, you will attack."—*Six!*—"Tell your cats to fight like the netherbeasts of Khest."

"Five!"

"Don't, please!" Sterjall implored.

"Four!"

Mamóru walked forward, arms raised. He stumbled weakly, looking as decrepit and harmless as anyone could look.

"Good," Marshal Embercut said. "Old man, ask your friends to do the same."

"I will," Mamóru said. "Take me as your prisoner, and they will surrender."

Two of the pike soldiers dropped their weapons, grabbed Mamóru's arms, and carried him toward the back of the line.

"We have your friend now," the marshal said. "Either you all surrender like he asked you to, or the old man will suff—"

A trumpeting blast erupted from behind the lines, followed by the snap of crushed bones and the whinnying of horses. A spray of soldiers flew right above the Marshal while behind her an enormous steppe mammoth rose. The mammoth's swinging tusks flung a horse right into the enemy formation, taking down a dozen soldiers. Although gaunt and weary, the massive creature had enough power to pick up enemies with his trunk; he hurled them like boulders.

"Now!" Sterjall said. The line of pikes had been shattered, so the cats jumped and tore into the Zovarians as the riders swung their blades and blew their darts. But Fulm was struck, a pike impaled in his chest—the smilodon toppled over, dropping Abjus, Kitjári, and Balstei to the ground. While Balstei cowered trying to unsheathe his sword, the other two protected him, clashing blades with the incoming attackers.

Thurann Embercut slashed forward with her longsword. With Urnaadisilv, Kitjári saw the swing approach, performed a Carapace Lurch to block, then smashed her short sword against Thurann's chest, denting her armor in a blast of sparks. Spear soldiers rushed to protect their commander, but Kitjári's senses were attuned to their threads, like a spider reading each vibration of her deadly web. With the Blossom Claw technique she had learned from Sunu, she tore them apart, then chomped at an unlucky soldier with her mighty jaws, pulling his clavicle out through muscle and armor.

Fulm was on the ground growling, biting off limbs from any soldier who got too close, but more pikes were pushed on him, piercing the struggling animal's ribs.

Kulak heard the unnerving cries of distress and blew a dart toward a soldier torturing Fulm, but the projectile bounced off her armor. "I must help him!" he shouted as he jumped off Blu. Sterjall followed him down while Sunu took control of the saddle, expertly swinging with the Cyclone Orchid, sinking their halberd in and out of bodies in a smooth dance of strikes.

Fulm was tearing through the armor of a sedecim peacekeeper when three more Zovarians pushed their pikes into his ribs. Kulak faltered then, too focused on Fulm, feeling the smilodon's pain as if it were his own. He stumbled, holding his chest.

Thurann sensed an opportunity and prepared to swing her sword.

"Kulak!" Sterjall yelled, trying to reach him, but three soldiers blocked his path.

Thurann swung her blade toward the caracal's exposed neck, but Kenondok jumped from Kobos's back, pushing Kulak out of the way. The marshal's sword cut fast through the air and sliced Kulak's left shoulder, leaving a red gash in his fur. Sterjall saw the spray of blood and leapt forward, stabbing two of the soldiers and dodging the third. His eyes met the marshal's, and with a Whisker Glide he tried to bridge the distance to sink Leif into her. But the marshal kept the momentum of her turn and let Sterjall slide past her, making him trip on a dead body. The wolf slammed into the ground.

The marshal sliced quickly downward. Sterjall lifted his arm instinctively, deflecting the attack with Leif but losing the dagger to the impact.

Thurann lifted her helm's visor and approached confidently. The wolf looked to his side—Leif was out of reach, and his friends were too far away to help him. His right arm was throbbing, as if his recently healed wound had resurfaced like boiling magma.

As the marshal lifted her sword, Sterjall pulled out the little cube of brime Kulak had given to him and struck it on the armor of the fallen soldier next to him, shooting a torrent of white-hot sparks toward Thurann's open visor. The armored woman flinched, half-blinded, striking her longsword on the dirt.

Sterjall rolled out of the way, retrieved Leif with his left hand and stood up. His recent injury, his training with Sunu, they had taught him that left hand or right mattered not, so he held the blade confidently with the point down, like a smilodon's fang. Like a dire wolf's fang. Thurann recovered from the blinding strike and brandished her sword once more; instead of moving out of the way, Sterjall pushed through to place himself behind the marshal, and from there he pulled his arm backward, piercing his dagger into the marshal's breastplate. The senstregalv blade found her lungs.

Thurann Embercut hunched awkwardly, trying to pull the dagger out, but her armor did not let her bend far enough. Sterjall kicked her hips, sending her tumbling, then jumped on her. He punched at her helm over and over, until the visor buckled inward and cut through the marshal's nose. He kept slamming like a hammer; denting, breaking, knuckles bleeding, wanting her spine to crack, not caring about the pain flaring in his right arm. He came to his senses when he heard Kulak's voice calling for help—the caracal was pinned to a wall by a sedecim peacekeeper, with no one around to help him.

No, not Kulak, he thought. *I won't let you hurt him.* He pulled Leif out of the marshal's side and rose to help his friend. The armored soldier followed Kulak's gaze and knew to turn around; he swung at Sterjall, but Agnargsilv foresaw his movement. The wolf closed the distance by grabbing on to the peacekeeper's elbow, then slid his blade into the man's neck. They toppled down together, weighted heavily by the knight's armor.

While Sterjall tried to free himself from the weight, another peacekeeper attacked, followed by two more Zovarians wielding spears and shields. The two in the back were taken down by Blu: one by his claws, the other by his fangs. Then a clean swing cut through the air—the sedecim peacekeeper simply stood there as his head rolled off, sliced cleanly by Sunu's halberd, gorget and all. Sunu continued on atop Blu, relentless as a hurricane.

A hurled horse splattered on a cliffside, rider and all.

A bloodied arm landed by Sterjall's face.

Kulak pushed the dead peacekeeper off Sterjall and helped him to his feet. Sterjall saw Kitjári and Abjus fighting fiercely nearby, but he was not worried about them. He saw Pichi swatting down a horse as if it was a bothersome moth, then tearing apart his neck with her massive fangs. He saw Kenondok protecting Balstei while the artificer tried his best at swinging the baselard sword he had stolen from Admiral Grinn. Sterjall saw Alaia and Givra masterfully disabling soldiers with their blowguns while still riding atop Kobos, the smilodon-tiger hybrid whom no soldiers had dared approach.

He sensed a horse charging from behind him, carrying a woman with a curved sword. She swung at Sterjall, but Kobos intercepted the horse midgallop, tumbling with the beast and dropping Givra and Alaia to the ground.

Givra tried to stand, but her wounded leg made her stumble. As she finally rose, a pike was buried in her stomach.

"Givra!" Alaia screamed. She jumped at the pike soldier before he could remove the polearm from Givra's body and rolled on the ground with him, no weapon in hand.

"Get off, fucking spur!" the soldier spat, rolling over Alaia. He unsheathed a dagger from his belt. Alaia quickly reached into her front pocket, took out the first dart her fingers found, and stuck it into the soldier's armpit. The soldier brought his dagger down, but Alaia held on to his wrists, watching as the man's eyes widened with fear. He let go of his weapon and began waving his hands as if they were aflame. He wailed through nightmarish hallucinations, scrambled up, and fled in terror. Kenondok's knife made him quiet.

Alaia rushed to help Givra, who was twisting on the ground, barely breathing, pike still stuck under her sternum.

Nearby, the mammoth kept crushing and smashing, sending a spray of blood and bones gushing forth with every step. Like macabre decorations, a collection of pikes dangled from his body.

Fulm had stopped fighting and growled weakly while on the ground. Sterjall and Kulak defended the cat while their friends took care of the remaining enemies. Many surrendered, dropping their weapons and backing into the wall. A few ran away, including two on horseback who fled north for reinforcements.

The fight was over.

There were no cheers, no exultations of glory.

Givra was dead—Alaia cried over her body.

"I carry Givra home," Kenondok said tersely. "We mourn later." He picked Givra's body up, placing her across his broad back.

Kulak had a ghastly gash on his shoulder, Blu an arrow in his hind leg, and Kobos was still bleeding from the wound on his shoulder blade. The rest were bruised but not badly hurt, except for Fulm. The night-colored smilodon was not dead, but soon would be. Kulak, Kitjári, and Sterjall approached him and with their Silvesh took some of his pain away, letting him breathe more evenly. Sunu squatted next to the dying feline and from a pocket on their long-sleeved shodog pulled out a small dart. As they caressed Fulm's neck, they pierced the dart painlessly through his skin. Fulm moaned softly, then closed his eyes.

Once Fulm stopped breathing, Mamóru picked him up with his trunk and let him drape over his ivory tusks. The group stumbled onward, marching side by side with the three surviving smilodons. The dome lay straight ahead of them, but the worn-out company was slow moving, and more soldiers were flanking them. Archers. As the archers readied their bows, Mamóru positioned himself between the enemy and his friends. The arrows fell in bursts, but most simply bounced off the mammoth's thick fur. Most, but not all;

Mamóru's trunk, forehead, and parts of his legs were not entirely shielded by the protective fur.

"Open the tunnel before we get there," Kitjári said, aiming a quaar conduit at the distant vines, willing them to part. Kulak followed her lead, and then Sterjall using Leif. With their combined empathic focus, the three Silvfröash pushed open a tunnel and hurried toward it. But more soldiers were moving within range, some on foot and some by horse.

"You two keep it open!" Kitjári ordered, trading her quaar conduit for a bow and arrow. She shot an arrow into a rider's head, then another into an infantryman's leg. The others helped her with a rain of darts, breaking the enemy lines.

"Get in, now!" Kitjári called.

They hastened into the opening, but even though the vines had opened deep enough, the space was not wide enough to fit a mammoth.

Mamóru stayed behind, limping and weak, trying to deflect the heavier attacks. He defended the entrance as the vines unhurriedly widened to fit his frame. Like an uncompromising wall, he took arrows and pikes and swords, then backed off slowly once the opening had widened enough.

Careless soldiers rushed forward in one final, foolish attempt. Mamóru swung his trunk and knocked them into the thorny vines. More arrows came, but the vines were closing, then at last sealed like an iris in front of Mamóru's tusks. The steppe mammoth kept backing off, one earth-quaking step at a time, until the darkness of the wall swallowed them all.

Chapter Fifty

Hearth Stones

"Hold the lamp close," Sunu said to Alaia. "We must take all arrows and pikes out before Mamóru changes forms, or they will cut deeper."

Mamóru had already been tired and sluggish, and the fight had drained the last bits of energy from him. He simply stood there, eyes unfocused, looking much too skeletal and feeble for such a massive creature. Once they finished removing the pikes stuck in his belly, Sterjall asked, "Can you drop to the floor for us?"

Mamóru blared a crackled, trumpeting sigh and slowly lowered himself to his knees, then to his belly. Luckily, most of the weapons had stuck in the wiry fur, but some had pierced deeply. Six more pikes they removed, and over forty arrows, most from Mamóru's trunk and face. His legs were streaked with red, having been exposed to the Zovarians' slashing blades. Although he was losing a lot of blood, the relative scale of the wounds was not exceedingly large, just exceedingly numerous.

"Take your human form now," Sunu told him, "so Sunu may tend to your wounds."

The mammoth's body became foggy and smokey, revealing a web of threads through the uncertain haze. In the center of the mammoth-shaped enormity, a frail human figure floated like a primeval fetus. The flickering lamplight refracted into the liquid smoke, delineating the silhouette and the long-stretching threads connecting the analogous anatomical parts. The old man suspended in the center looked like a gaunt puppet held by thousands of wires.

Slowly, the mass of the mammoth receded, the cloudy fog coalesced, until only the naked old man was left, kneeling, shaking, and bleeding from dozens of small wounds.

Sunu worked their medicine, cleaning Mamóru, applying unguents, stitching, and bandaging. They wrapped a cloak around him and made a comfortable bed on top of Pichi's harness so he could rest.

The nightly interior of the dome was cloudy, with not even the dim blues of the arudinn showing through. The company entered the dome from the province of Gwur Úrëath and stopped at an overlook with a view of Stelm Humenath; its summit was lost in dark clouds.

Kenondok and Abjus gathered wood, then struck their brime cubes over the pile, lighting a beacon visible for miles. Wounded and fatigued, the company quickly drifted into sleep.

They were found in the early morning by scouts, who came riding on medium-sized tigers, black panthers, and snow leopards from Stelm Humenath. Help arrived later that day with food and medicine, and with more mounts. A scout told them that jays had been sent out to notify the provinces, calling for all the chiefs to gather in Arjum as soon as possible.

The company was escorted north. Hod Buil, chief of Gwur Úrëath, welcomed them to Humenath and offered to ride with them the next day. The chief asked for no information on what they had learned through their journey, as those were matters to be discussed in the presence of all the chiefs, but he was glad to see that Mamóru was with them and that the mission had been a success, despite the tragic losses of Givra and Fulm.

That evening, after they were served a feast at the spiraling courtyard of the Humenath Palace, Sterjall went to check on Mamóru, who had been resting his maimed body in a nearby hut.

As Sterjall approached, he saw Mamóru standing weakly at the doorway, and was about to rush to aid him when he caught sight of Nelv bolting toward the old man as a proud lioness, grunting with happiness and relief. Mamóru kneeled to embrace her, whispering secret and tender words in her ears.

Sterjall watched as their emerald and pearl auras merged and blossomed like wildflowers. He felt his own eyes watering as he witnessed the old man crying openly with joy, holding his dear friend at long last, after hundreds of lonesome years.

The tired travelers allowed themselves a few days to mourn and rest. Mamóru, in particular, needed time to recover before speaking at the council.

Fulm and Givra had earned the honor of being interred at the Tombs of Ootárne, an underground sepulcher beneath Arjum's Ma'u banyan. There, their bodies would decompose and be cradled by the roots of the most ancient of trees, feeding the trunk of Mindreldrolom itself.

Givra's and Fulm's bodies were laid alongside honored sages and ancient Mindrelfröash, whose bones were now tightly embraced by tangles of roots. Before the last prayers of parting were chanted, a priest placed warm cubes of brime inside the mouths of the woman and the smilodon, so that the heat would remain with them in the Supernal Realms, a hearth for their souls.

Alaia was the last to say her prayers at the vigil, chanting them in front of her Pliwe figurine, the same one she'd prayed to during Ockam's, Bonmei's, and Sontai's funerals.

Sterjall retreated to the training ponds after the ceremony was over.

He sat alone, watching the cascades tumble into the ponds while he fidgeted with the brime cube Kulak had gifted him, feeling its sharp corners as he spun it in his padded fingers. Sunu came to sit next to him. They eyed the cube and said, "Sunu saw you use brime during the battle. That was brave, that was smart."

"It was luck, it was cowardly," Sterjall corrected them, hiding the cube in his pouch. "It's fighting dirty, like throwing sand in someone's eyes."

"Sand makes dirt, but Sunu cannot see how sparks make dirt," Sunu said, a bit confused.

"I mean it was not a fair fight. It was spineless, weak."

"Then you must take Agnargsilv off for your next battle. Make it fair, show you care more about fairness than living, that you care more about looking strong than the lives of your friends."

Sterjall had no response to that.

"Do not let your furred scalp worry," Sunu added. "Fairness is not for battles where innocent lives are at stake." They paused, letting Olo peck at seeds from their freckled hands, then abruptly said, "Something occurred to Sunu, something that might help you in future battles, fair or unfair ones. Sunu will show you if you join them at the sculpture garden at evenfall, for training."

"Training? We just came back. Can't we give it a rest?"

"Others will rest. But Lago-Sterjall will come, will learn," Sunu said, making sure their command was not phrased as a question.

It was gloomy when Sterjall arrived at the sculpture garden, where each of the carved monoliths represented one of the domes, one of the clades, one chip on an enormous map. The only light came from the sculptures' eyes and mouths, which glowed a menacing green, their hollow skulls boiling with burning sap.

"Sunu has been waiting," Sunu's voice came out of the darkness, making Sterjall jump back in surprise. They had been leaning against the sculpture representing the clade of avians, which loomed at the center of the map. Their bald head was right beneath the green-flaming beak of granite, purple pigments looking flat and colorless under the firelight. A long highlight of green was all that was visible of their deadly bone halberd.

"Why do you have to look so ominous?" Sterjall complained. "What is it you wanted to show me?"

"You have taught Sunu something new, and Sunu wants to express their gratitude with a gift. Sunu will present the gift to you after you parry with them and show them your improvement." They picked up their halberd. "Attack, Lago-Sterjall."

"But my right arm is still throbbing, I don't think I—"

Sunu lunged in the Jumping Spider strike. Sterjall had no time to take Leif out of its sheath, and instead opted to roll sideways, taking cover behind the statue that represented bovids. He peeked out from around a curved horn and said, "You are scaring me a little, you know?"

"Fear keeps you alive, Lago-Sterjall," the shadow replied.

Sterjall felt protected next to the statue, for he knew Sunu would not swing close to it and risk damaging it.

Clang!

The halberd struck the horn Sterjall was hiding behind. The wolf scurried out of the way, with Leif at the ready in his left hand. He sensed Sunu's presence by the multiple shadows the green flames summoned, but even more clearly through Agnargsilv. He focused, tightening his hold around his own threads so that his intentions would be less obvious to his attacker. Sunu's halberd whistled as they thrust with the Widow's Lament, but Sterjall swiftly dodged, then parried a secondary assault with Shield of Thorns.

He took cover behind the statue of the clade of primates—the head of the badly carved ape looked more like a deprecating skull.

"Shield of Thorns is a good block," Sunu said. "But you should have aimed to deflect, not block. Do not take the impact into your arm. Send it into the ground with a Fluke Ward, or into the sky with a Damselfly Roll, for the ground and the sky can withstand much more than your frail bones."

Sunu quickly circled the sculpture and attacked once more, this time with an Arudinn Storm, using the iron cap of their halberd. Sterjall knew better than to back away from a piercing attack, so instead he stepped in and crossed behind Sunu. He did a decent job, but not smoothly or closely enough to strike back.

"Dodging around the statue would have proved more convenient," Sunu advised. "But you did well." They stood straight, letting the blunt end of their weapon rest by their feet. They stared at Sterjall, knowing Sterjall was trying to anticipate their next move.

"I still don't understand what we are doing here," Sterjall admitted, taking a position between the sculptures of primates and chiropterans. He felt with his footpaws the cobbled surface that represented water in this strange map, and somewhere in the back of his mind understood he was standing atop the Alommo Sea.

"Prepare for this next attack. Sunu will strike with the bottom of their halberd with the Rising Scorpion," they warned, and in a slow motion showed Sterjall exactly how they would swing their halberd, with the blunt end moving forward and up in a curving uppercut. "Show them how you would block this attack."

Sterjall was ready. He knew the direction and angle of the strike—or at least he assumed Sunu wasn't lying about it—and knew the countering strategy: bending his knees, he would let his body drop backward, allowing the strike to pass right above him before he swung Leif in a Hornbill Buckler, propelling the halberd in an even faster swing away from him.

He watched the blunt tip of the halberd eagerly and kept his knees slightly bent, his footpaws a careful distance apart.

Sunu's muscles tensed. Sterjall could feel their threads signaling the move. He reckoned Sunu had even exaggerated their anticipation a bit, so that Sterjall could tell exactly when the strike would come. When Sunu swung, their weapon scraped the cobbled ground and unleashed a hailstorm of white-hot sparks, blinding Sterjall. The iron cap of the halberd—in which a cube of brime had been embedded—struck the wolf's left hip, sending him to the ground.

"Ow!" he complained, holding tightly to his side. "I can't see!" he cried out, although he could see—quite clearly—the afterimages that the sparks had imprinted on his retinas.

"Your eyes will see another sunrise, another sunset," Sunu said, helping Sterjall up by pulling on his arm.

Sterjall blinked widely, confusing the images on his retinas with those of the real sparks, which were glowing on the ground, slowly fading from white, to yellow, to a dusky red. He could smell the burnt grass and the sharp aetheric sulphur.

"Why didn't you just tell me what you were going to do?" Sterjall protested.

Sunu took a few steps back. "Because Sunu wants you to know exactly how your enemies will feel the first time you use a strike of this sort. The first time it will be a surprise, but then—" they swung a Rising Scorpion again, scraping the brime onto the cobbles to spray a new torrent of sparks.

As soon as he felt the strike, Sterjall closed his eyes and looked only through his Silv's sight. He sensed redness as the light shone through his closed lids, but it was not enough to blind him. He dodged the attack with a Whirlwind Sidestep and recovered a safe distance back.

"Well done, Lago-Sterjall," Sunu said. "Now you understand. There is only one first time for every thing, be it the sight of a sunrise, a first kiss, or one's death. You fight well, but your short blade imposes limitations. One well-planned strike is all you require to defeat a foe, and a surprise can give you the advantage you need."

Sunu leaned their halberd against the primate monolith, and under the unsightly light of its eyes said, "Step closer, Sunu will grant you your boon."

Sterjall approached, perhaps a bit too cautiously, and waited a few feet in front of Sunu.

"Let Sunu see your left forearm," they said.

Sterjall lifted his left arm. Sunu removed an object from their side bag and wrapped it around Sterjall's forearm. It was an arm bracer crafted with magsteel-tough snow leopard bones upon which was embedded a row of cubes of brime, like bricks down a golden path.

"Brime bracer," Sunu said. "Fits well, but could fit better. Kenondok crafted it, per Sunu's request."

"It looks… nice," Sterjall said, not knowing exactly how else to describe it. "It's a bit warm," he noted, even though the brime was cleverly insulated from his arm. The piece of armor was rustic in its construction, strictly functional, but Sterjall could not yet visualize how exactly it functioned.

"Your eyes are confused," Sunu said. "Sunu will show you. Assume Stalking Jaguar stance."

Sterjall stood with his legs apart, knees bent. He held Leif up with his right handpaw, tip pointing to the ground. His left handpaw was down and in front, ready to pull on an unsuspecting enemy or to be used for support during a roll.

Sunu changed two things in Sterjall's posture: they rotated Leif so that the tip was facing outward, to the front; and placed Sterjall's left arm higher, with the line of brime cubes right under Leif's steel pommel.

"This is now your first move, the Brime Strike," Sunu said, then mimed the action of scraping the pommel over the bracer. "First move is to blind, to confuse, to let you step closer. Second move is to kill. Try it, pretend ugly sculpture is the Red Stag."

Sterjall stared at the ghastly sculpture of the ape, as if measuring an enemy. He stepped forward and in one quick swipe slid Leif's pommel over the crystals of aetheric sulphur, extending a tail of sparks as effulgent as that of a comet.

"Shit!" he cried out. "I forgot to close my eyes!"

"This is also a first time," Sunu said. "And there is only one first time. Unless you are a fool and you do that again."

"I think I'll remember next time around," Sterjall said, blinking as if trying to coax a swarm of fireflies from behind his eyelids. He could smell the rotten eggs from the sulphur, but another sharp scent wafted into his keen nose— burnt fur.

"Fuck, shit!" he cried, and tried to douse the fire that was blazing on his left wrist. The fire was extinguished, but it left a sore, furless spot right below the bracer.

"Sunu will ask Kenondok for modifications," Sunu said, sounding unusually apologetic. "They will make sure there is better insulation, and that there is an extension over your wrist to deflect sparks. You will be a better fighter if you are not on fire."

Chapter Fifty-One

Fate of the Silvesh

Two days after Sterjall's training session, the council of the six provinces reconvened at the Great Hall of the Laatu.

Sterjall pushed his tail out of the way and took a seat. He shook his leg impatiently underneath the crescent-shaped table, studying the faces of the chiefs, who seemed eager to learn the details of the excursion. He then looked up at Nelv, who sat in her clouded leopard form atop the queen's chair. He found it impossible to hold eye contact with the Nu'irg, so he instead inspected the blistered, bald patch on the dorsal side of his handpaw, pushing the fur apart with his dark claws—he could still smell the burnt hairs.

"Will Kenondok fix it?" Kulak asked, already having heard the story of Sterjall's encounter with Sunu.

"Yes, he's fixing it," Sterjall replied, covering up his wrist. "I think it will work better next time."

Mamóru took the empty seat between Kulak and Sterjall, a seat reserved for the guest holding the highest honor. The old man looked indisputably more ancient and wiser than he had before. Aside from his innumerable, still-healing cuts, he was wearing a beautifully embroidered white robe and a black scarf that contrasted against his light-gray beard, which had been braided and adorned with beads of muted colors.

After Alúma called for the council to begin, Mamóru told everyone an abbreviated version of his story.

Fingrenn stood at the center of the crescent next to a map, interpreting Mamóru's long story while Momsúndosilv was passed around to be inspected by the chiefs. Once Mamóru finished speaking, the members of the returned company recounted their adventure and findings.

Ierun Alúma sat in silence for a long while, then at last said, "Nu'irg ust Momsúndo, Tusked Sage of Illid, our ears heard your tale of loss. We now better understand our past, but we are still lost. Our people grow doubt in their scalps and fear in their bones. What counsel can you offer us?"

Mamóru stood and spoke, exuding a persuasive gravitas through his melodious voice. "All we so far know points to the tragic likelihood that the Noss we knew epochs ago may be no more. But lose not hope, for portions of them still exist. Portions that may remember their past, remember their goals, remember the Silvesh and the domes. We find ourselves within the bounds of this old memory, at this very moment. We are a part of that memory. I believe that to help our planet, so the parts of Noss that remain here can be reconstituted with the whole, Mindreldrolom needs to open. The best time to open the domes was centuries ago. The second-best time is now."

"If we open Mindreldrolom, we will be attacked by the outsiders," Hud Quoda interjected. "Our people will not be safe. The New World is longing for war."

Kitjári stood to get a better view of the map and said, "What Mamóru suggests is wise, but Hud Quoda is also wise to recommend caution. We need to plan this carefully and find a way to open the dome without risking the Silvesh being taken by our enemies."

"What will happen to our cities, to our farms, once the dome opens?" Hed Lettáni asked.

"That we cannot know," Mamóru answered. "None of the eighteen Miscam tribes chose this path so they could protect their cities or their lands. They chose this path to protect Noss and the future of the core species. The domes were meant to reopen, forcing the lands to change and adapt to an unknowable future. Mindreldrolom has no owners, only stewards."

"But their armies," Hod Abjus started. "What we saw was nothing, there are tens of thousands more."

Mamóru tightened his grip on his gnarly cane. "There will be war ahead. My instinct tells me the Zovarians will continue chasing after the masks, but if we were to carry the masks away from here, perhaps your six provinces would remain safe."

"They would still come looking for them," Hed Lettáni said. "But they will come today, or tomorrow, or a century from now if that is when we choose for Mindreldrolom to open. We must ready ourselves to fight either way."

"Perhaps not to fight," Hod Buil suggested. "We will be neighbors who cannot afford being at odds with one another. We must aim to work with them."

The other chiefs disagreed, except for Alúma, who kept quiet, not wanting to influence the others at the table.

"We must stop seeing them as the enemy," Buil continued. "We should become trade partners, establish an alliance that will allow our species to endure the long future that awaits."

"Or we could keep the dome sealed as Noss ordered us to," Hud Quoda proposed. "It has not been two thousand years since the closing. Perhaps Noss knew something we do not."

"Perhaps they did," Mamóru said, "but if you wait here any longer, you can be certain that war will still come to you. Not from the Zovarians, but from the Red Stag, once he takes control of these lands and beyond."

"But the Zovarians are after blood!" Abjus snapped.

"No," Balstei said. "The Zovarians are after power and riches. So, give them some to appease them."

"What is it you mean?" Abjus asked.

"Soot," Balstei said. "Soot and brime. Use them for trade. Not with the military, but with the cities of Muskeg, Nebush, and the neighboring states. As Hod Buil said, becoming trade partners will be the only way to establish a lasting peace. You have other resources that the Union would trade extensively for. Munnji, precious minerals, and even the tough bones of your companion species."

"It's true," Kitjári added. "If you use the aetheric elements to foster alliances, you will gain the favor of the locals. Landowners will not take kindly to your animals roaming their farms, eating their crops and cattle, or scaring their game—yet Zovarians are greedy and can be easily bargained with."

"But you must be careful," Balstei continued. "Do not reveal how much soot and brime you have at your disposal. Use it wisely and keep it hidden."

"We can close access to the Quas Trell mines," Hod Abjus said, "to make sure no one discovers our source. We have enough at the ready, we do not need to mine for more."

"It sounds like we have a tool at our disposal to aid with these concerns," Ierun Alúma said, "yet still the risk is great for our children, for our felids, for all that we've safeguarded for generations."

"The risk is yet greater," Mamóru said, "for we may be risking all other domes, not just this one, if we do nothing but wait."

"What is it you propose, wise Nu'irg?" Hud Ilsed asked as she leaned her tanned back against her seat.

"What I propose is simple, yet may prove more complex," Mamóru replied. "If anyone could offer answers to our quandaries, that would be Noss themself. In the past, a circle of six, twelve, or eighteen Silvesh was necessary to commune with the Noss consciousness. At this moment, only four Silvesh have we at our disposal."

He leaned in, pointing the ammonite-encrusted end of his cane toward the map. "Two domes await west of these lands, both reachable by sea. Nagradrolom, which the New World calls the Fjordlands Dome, is home to the suids. There the fearless Puqua Miscam are stewards of Nagrasilv and live with the company of my old javelina friend, Probo. The other is Kruwendrolom, known in the New World as the Varanus Dome, where the perplexing Mo'óto Miscam have kept watch of Kruwensilv, the mask of the reptilian clade. The Nu'irg ust Kruwen, Ishke'ísuk, unblinkingly guards those lands. To both domes we should sail. With both tribes we should ally, and ask for their domes to open."

"It is not yet time!" Hud Quoda countered. "Our feet must not stray from the path we have been following."

"But the lands have regained their vigor," Hod Buil said.

"Heed the word of Noss!" someone screamed from the audience.

Mamóru struck his cane on the table and rising his voice proclaimed, "The time has come to fulfill our oath. Let us help Noss regain what is left of their consciousness. They will have answers for us that I do not, that none of us could envision. Let us help them find a new equilibrium for all living beings."

The crowd broke into a tumult of disagreement and fear, with citizens and chiefs speaking over one another.

Alúma lifted her scepter for silence, but no silence could she summon. "We sought the wisdom of the Nu'irg, and he has spoken!" she yelled, but no one could hear her over their own loud voices. Then Nelv hopped down from the chair, landing in the form of a dinofelis, and roared like a thunderclap.

The crowd covered their ears and shrunk into their shoulders. The commotion subsided immediately, but the tension remained palpable.

Alúma scanned the room, with Nelv pacing menacingly behind her. The queen waited for everyone to sit and for all mouths to close, then proclaimed, "We risked much to hear the words of the Nu'irg ust Momsúndo. His voice is wisdom, and to it we are to listen. What say you, chiefs? The decision is yours to make. Rise if you choose to follow the path the Nu'irg has laid out for us."

Alúma stood herself, for once aiming to influence the votes. Three chiefs rose with her, while two others remained seated.

"Noss wills it so!" she then declared. "The culmination of our long mission looms before us, but the end only brings forth a new beginning. We were entrusted not only to keep Mindreldrolom in balance, but to maintain the balance once the walls of white blood were gone. We need to think thoroughly of our options."

"How long would the dome take to open?" Sterjall asked.

"The vines move as slow as their white blood flows," Alúma answered. "The small vines will shrivel first. In a matter of weeks, the holes left by them will allow the Laatu to venture out, as well as let outsiders venture in. The largest vines will take longer, perhaps years to diminish and seep back into the crust."

Sterjall swallowed, losing hope. "We can't have Kulak tied up at the temple for years."

Alúma offered an understanding smile. "Khuron Aio-Kulak needs only start the process at the temple. Mindreldrolom will ungrow itself after that, needing no further aid."

"Once I travel away, Nelv will help the companion species continue with the plan," Kulak said. Nelv slowly blinked her approval, still pacing around to make sure the crowd remained silent.

"We should make our way out by sea," Kitjári suggested, "before the Zovarians are alerted that the dome has begun opening."

"That date Crysta mentioned in her letter," Sterjall said, "the fourteenth of Fireleaf, the day of the annual Sail Parade. We could make our exit then—there will be no Zovarian ships nearby to chase after us."

"That's only two weeks away," Alaia noted.

"Then we better get started quickly," Kitjári said.

"*Drolvisdinn* will be honored to assist," Hud Ilsed offered, "if you show us the way and teach us how the stars help you navigate. At full sail, she flies faster than the wind. Enough supplies can be loaded for a long trip without weighing the ship down."

"That is most kind of you, Hud Ilsed," Sterjall said. "We'll wait until *Drolvisdinn* is readied, then sail as soon as the dome is set to open."

"I believe this is a more prudent plan than the one I hastily proposed," Mamóru said. "Prudent, expedient, and sound."

"Are the chiefs confident with this plan and vow to see it succeed?" Alúma asked.

All chiefs agreed, feeling there was no time to waste.

"Then we shall strategize our departure at once," Alúma proclaimed, banging her quaar scepter.

For a while longer they discussed the plan, which would require gathering all the felids, closing the mines, preparing the ship, teaching the Laatu about the customs of the outsiders, and much more.

Once they were satisfied with their strategy, Ierun Alúma said, "Now comes the time for us to vote on who will be the new voices of canids and ursids. Sterjall and Kitjári, as we had agreed, would you please surrender Agnargsilv and Urnaadisilv to us, so that the Miscam may once more carry their honor? As Lago and Jiara, you shall be welcome—and needed—in this mission. Your knowledge is essential to our mutual success."

Mamóru was baffled by this new development and did not know what to say.

Kulak stood up and raised his voice. "Mother, they have proven themselves worthy! They saved us, guided us well, and they deserve to wield their Silvesh. Why must you always—"

"We will honor our council's votes!" Alúma said. "The Silvesh are of the Miscam. No matter how much honor our guests carry, Miscam they are not. Our vote was already cast, our decision already made."

"But the Wutash are no more!" Kulak complained. "If there is anyone who is—"

"Enough!" Alúma snapped. "We will not break with tradition. Sit down, Aio-Kulak."

Kulak dropped down heavily, arms crossed, whiskers scrunched and pointed forward.

"If you'd permit me to speak, Ierun Alúma," Mamóru said quietly, yet still commanding everyone to listen.

Alúma nodded to him.

"The Miscam are not one people," he continued softly. "The Miscam are those who help Noss and further the Miscam ideals. Lago-Sterjall and Jiara-Kitjári fight for the same cause you do, they believe in the same tenets, as do Alaia and Balstei. Without their aid perhaps no hope for Noss would remain, or hope for the other Miscam tribes."

"We hear you, wise Momsúndo," Alúma said. "We respect your counsel and respect their sacrifice. But we must also respect our laws."

"This is unfair!" Alaia yelled, standing up.

Sterjall pulled at her arm. "Alaia, don't—"

She yanked her arm free and spoke directly to Alúma. "Didn't you say that the Nu'irg's word is wisdom? That we should listen to him? That we risked much to seek his counsel?"

Recognizing her own words, Alúma said, "Oldrin child, this is about law. Our ears took heed of Mamóru's words. But when it comes to Miscam law, not even the Nu'irgesh may intervene."

"Actually…" Mamóru mused aloud, twining his fingers through his braided beard. "The Toldask Miscam had a way of welcoming outsiders into their tribe. I myself am Toldask Miscam, as they performed the ceremony in my honor during the times in which Momsúndodrolom was closing. Not only am I of the Miscam, but as the last living member of the Toldask Miscam, I can perform the same ceremony to welcome our friends into my tribe."

"Sunu, Kenondok, Hod Abjus—you fought by their side," Kulak said, standing up again. "Tell everyone how you would proudly welcome them, as Toldask Miscam they will be, and no objection could then be voiced."

"They are leaders of judiciousness, courage, and passion," Sunu declared. "It was Sunu's honor to ride alongside them, to wet their halberd in the necks of our mutual enemies. Laatu and Toldask are one. Nu'irg ust Momsúndo, if you welcome them into your tribe, Sunu will welcome them into ours."

"My scalp did not believe Jiara was ready," Kenondok added earnestly, "but she proved me wrong. She is tough and smart, and her claws and teeth are sharp and terrifying. Kitjári's even more so," he added, and everyone laughed. "The Nu'irg is wise. We must respect the word of our Toldask sibling."

Hod Abjus got up from his seat and flatly said, "If Mamóru is willing to perform this ceremony, I would voice no objection." He sat back down wearing an impassive expression.

A visible relief washed over the hall. Even those Laatu who'd been in favor of letting Sterjall and Kitjári keep their masks had clutched on to an unspoken insecurity; the thought of formalizing their identities as true Miscam made their worries vanish, as if their ancestors would no longer be judging them for their law-bending decisions.

"Then this evening I shall welcome our four heroes into my tribe!" Mamóru belted out. "The ceremony is one that I need to perform in private, with no interruptions. I ask that you provide me with five items. I will need a large silk rug, decorated in branching patterns like those of the dome itself. Then a long-stemmed briar pipe, but meerschaum will do if briar is not available. A pouch of aged, silver-tipped mistleaf, which you may know as tannic smokefrond. I'll also need a selection of strong spirits, and—" Mamóru paused for a moment, considering. "And last," he continued, "I'll need a single crystal of amethyst, the largest you can manage."

A scribe took careful notes, then nodded toward the queen. Alúma looked toward Mamóru and slowly closed her eyes in agreement.

Mamóru cleared his throat and said, "By the time the arudinn relight atop Mindreldrolom's trunk, Lago-Sterjall Vaari, Jiara-Kitjári Ascura, Alaia, and Balstei Woodslav will be recognized as Toldask Miscam, from now until the last days of Sceres and Sunnokh, past the foretold Ascension Epoch, until the Endfall and the culmination of all things."

"And we will welcome them as such," Alúma said, banging her scepter, "for Noss speaks through the law, and the law we obey. As for the matter of Momsúndosilv, a Silvfröa must be chosen."

"I am afraid that Momsúndosilv will have to remain unworn," Mamóru said quietly.

The queen was surprised, as were the other chiefs. Before they could speak, Mamóru picked up the tusked mask and said, "The Silvesh tap into the energy of those animals of their own clades. As I am the last remaining proboscidean, if someone were to wear Momsúndosilv, it would likely drain me and kill me. I am already feeble enough as it is, and no other proboscideans remain to feed Momsúndosilv's hunger."

"Then we will be one Silvfröa short," Kitjári fretted. "We'll need to travel much farther to find a sixth mask."

"Not necessarily," Mamóru said. "Once the time comes, as the eldest of the Toldask, I will accept the honor and duty of wearing Momsúndosilv myself."

The chiefs gasped and protested—they found it a preposterous suggestion for a Nu'irg to wear a Silv.

"Honorable Nu'irg, you must understand," Hod Abjus began, veins about to pop but still keeping calm, "the Silvesh were made for humans to wear, not for your kind."

"My kind? What is 'my kind,' valiant and honorable Hod Abjus, if not who I am? I am as human as any of you, just as Nelv is as much a clouded leopard as any clouded leopard in your dense forests, and as much a tigress as any of your tigers. We Nu'irgesh can take certain forms *only because* they are our true forms. I have been human for longer than any of you have been alive—it is who I truly am."

He leaned back in his chair, seeming tired and perhaps even scared. "I do not make this request lightly—it is not something I want, nor is it something I ever sought after. I do so because Momsúndosilv is tied to me, and I cannot leave it behind. It is the reason I was trapped in that desert for so many centuries. If the Silv were removed from me, I would perish. It feeds me, and I feed it."

"You speak bravely," Hud Ilsed said, "but we do not know if such a thing may work. What you speak of is unprecedented."

"Not so," Mamóru said. He looked toward Nelv for a moment, who had returned to her primal form, perching above the queen's tall chair. He mindspoke quietly with her as if asking for permission. Nelv blinked slowly back at him. "Not unprecedented. Another Nu'irg, one who perished in the times before the Downfall, wore her own Silv. Her name was Allamónea, first of the Nu'irgesh to ever take a human form, then first and only to take a half-form, for those in-between forms are unnatural to us otherwise. She ruled as chief of the Isdinnuk Miscam for many years, helping them recover from a fiery cataclysm that swallowed their atoll homeland. But that is a story for another time. What matters is that the Silv *can* be worn by me, and perhaps *only* by me."

"Nelv says the story is true," Kulak interpreted. "That she was a good friend of Allamónea, the sperm whale who sometimes was secretly a woman."

"Good friends they were," Mamóru said. "And if my suppositions are correct, and Noss's memory has been shattered, my own memory might be the key to allow them to remember more. That is also why I should be one of the six who speaks with them."

"But would that be safe for you?" Sterjall asked, clutching the edge of the table a bit too tightly.

Mamóru shook his tired head. "I do not think so, agnurf son. It might take all that is left in me. But I am willing to take the risk, as the planet is in need."

"Then it shall be so," Alúma declared. "The last of the Toldask shall determine what to do with the Silv entrusted to the Toldask. You shall be the custodian of your own Silv, as it is inextricably tied to yourself, and so your future is sealed by your own voice and will. And I hope no chiefs further object."

Tense silence spread across the great hall. No one dared question the authority of the Nu'irg or the queen.

"Noss wills it so!" Alúma proclaimed. "From tomorrow on, we begin our preparations with unwavering resolve. Two weeks from today, the walls of Mindreldrolom will begin to open!"

They had dinner in the streets of Arjum, sampling munnji cakes from a diverse mix of street vendors. Kenondok joined them and gave the modified brime bracer back to Sterjall—it now fit comfortably around his forearm, had better insulation, and had a sloped edge of bone over the wrist to deflect any sparks cast from it.

While on their way back to their rooms, Mamóru reminded Alúma that he would need all five ingredients to perform the ceremony that evening.

"Worry not, wise Momsúndo," Alúma said in Common, having grown considerably more proficient. "Attendant fulfills items. To room become delivered."

They walked down the steps, through the cold hallway of stone, and stopped in front of the entrance to the dormitory.

"*Unnith. Oset fin uth halvet,*" Mamóru said.

"*Olvet finesh uth velm,*" Ierun Alúma replied, then she and Kulak left.

Mamóru closed the door behind them, and not finding a way to lock it, wedged a chair under the doorknob.

The central fireplace was already lit. In front of it was a short table with the items Mamóru had requested. The giant tabby cat who frequented the room was there too, dozing by the fireplace. He lifted an annoyed whisker or two at seeing Mamóru locking the door with the chair, but then went right back to sleep.

"When I asked for a large amethyst, I didn't expect the entire Corundum Monolith," Mamóru half-complained. "My words might have overdone it."

The single crystal upon the table was two feet tall, equally wide, beautifully faceted, and filled with a deep purple essence.

Lago took off his mask and put it on his bed, then reconsidered. "Should we be wearing the masks for the ceremony? What does it entail?"

"It entails for you all to pull up chairs while I examine these items. Come sit by the fire, masks or no masks, please."

They sat and watched Mamóru scrutinize the objects. He unfolded the silk rug, which was elegantly patterned, just like the branching trunk and vines of the dome. He refolded it and placed it at the foot of his bed.

Servants had left three carafes of spirits in different shades of deep ambers, sitting next to half a dozen crystal goblets. Mamóru unstopped them, letting the scents of the liqueurs transport him to faraway times.

He picked up the four leather pouches, each with a different flavor variant of silver-tipped mistleaf. He smelled each of them and seemed to be most attracted to one with muskier, cedarwood-scented leaves.

He examined the long-stemmed pipe. It was made of briar but lined with a meerschaum bowl—a solid, indecisive compromise that Mamóru did not object to.

Mamóru didn't attempt to move the amethyst—it was far too unwieldy. He placed Momsúndosilv atop the crystal, where it shimmered eerily, darkly reflecting the flames while being rimmed by purple refractions.

Mamóru packed three pinches of mistleaf into the pipe, lit it, poured the darkest of the three liqueurs, and handed each of them a goblet. "They provided a sophisticated selection," he noted as he leaned back to smoke and drink.

The smoking mistleaf gave off a translucent veil that smelled of a wet forest and roasted nuts.

"Come on, taste it," he encouraged, noticing that the others had not yet sampled the drink. They all did, Lago wincing at the strong flavor—the liqueur was potent, made from sour cherries with hints of thyme and coriander, clutching to memories of old oak barrels.

Mamóru finished his drink, then slammed the goblet down on the arm of his chair. "And now"—he theatrically lifted the pipe over his head—"you are all Toldask Miscam."

"That's it?" Balstei asked, finishing his small goblet in a quick gulp.

"That's it," Mamóru affirmed, then poured Balstei and himself a refill. "There is no ceremony. I made it all up. Though I was greatly honored by the Toldask, even revered by them, I was never officially welcomed into their tribe. I'm not sure they had any proper way of doing that. The Toldask were as strict about following rules as the Laatu. I thought this would offer a way to appease our hosts and make them bury their irrational doubts."

Alaia's jaw dropped. "So, the liqueur and mistleaf?" she asked.

"I had been a guest at Arjum a long time ago, and tasted some of their fine spirits then," he replied from the side of his mouth while dangling the long pipe. "I wanted to relish in their flavors again. They have aged stupendously. And I smelled someone smoking mistleaf earlier, saw she had a nice pipe, and wanted to taste the smooth smoke once more."

Balstei nodded his approval, finishing a second goblet that failed to conceal his wide grin.

"And the silk rug?" Jiara asked.

"My corner of the room gets a bit cold at night," Mamóru said with a shrug. "I spotted vendors selling rugs with that pattern and knew it'd be easy for them to procure me one."

"What about the crystal?" Lago asked incredulously.

"Well... I needed something that sounded mystical. It's the best I could think of in a pinch. I didn't expect them to deliver such a hefty boulder. We can leave it here as a centerpiece. It sparkles gorgeously by the fire."

Lago chuckled while taking a sip of his drink. He then choked and coughed.

"Were you also lying about Momsúndosilv?" Balstei asked.

"I was not. What I said about the Silv is true." He picked up the mask and held it over his lap. "I witnessed so many Silvfröash find their voices with this mask. They would put it on and struggle to become something else, trying to learn something about my kind they could bring into themselves."

He took a few more puffs and let them waft upward in ethereal forms.

"All Silvfröash start the same way, making the same mistake. They try to hide themselves behind the mask. It is the one thing people most misunderstand about masks—they don't hide who you are, but reveal the truth within you. You both know what I mean," he said, looking at Lago and Jiara. "Those parts of yourselves that the mask uncovered had always been there. They merely needed a way to blossom."

"You said that…" Lago began, then he swallowed. "You said that wearing the mask might take the last bits of energy out of you. Does that mean you might die?"

"It does. And I want you all to be ready and not feel sorrowful if that happens. I've lived the longest life of anyone other than the planet themself, and though I yearn to see how the world has changed, and how your own stories will shape yourselves and the world around you, I have also grown tired and lonely without my own kind around me."

He held the proboscidean form in his bony hands and stared at the essence of himself. His wrinkled face looked worn down by more than age. The cuts over his cheeks, nose, and forehead glistened in the red firelight. His eyes sparkled, reflecting an unreachably distant time.

"But that day is not yet come," he declared. "We have more adventures ahead of us!" He refilled his goblet, then raised it high. "Today, we rejoice together, for tomorrow is knocking on our doors, and the fate of the Silvesh shall soon be revealed."

Chapter Fifty-Two

Gre Ieren

Kulak sat next to his friends while they shared a sumptuous breakfast the next morning. "Is the ceremony finished?" he asked. "Are you Toldask Miscam now?"

"Yup," Alaia said.

"Never felt more Miscam in my life," Balstei answered.

"Toldask up to my tits," Kitjári said while chewing.

"Same," Sterjall agreed. "I'll tell you about the ceremony sometime later."

After breakfast, Kulak asked his friends to join him at the stables, up the escarpment that overlooked the vast meadows. The companion felids and Nelv had been busy herding cats of all species into the open fields—thousands of felids of all colors and sizes had gathered, while more kept arriving from every direction.

"So many kitties!" Alaia exclaimed.

"What an extraordinary sight," Balstei mused.

They stood attentively, watching Kulak, who had Nelv, the queen, and the withdrawn king by his side. Kulak was there to speak truth to the felids, to ask for their help now that this part of their long mission was coming to an end. Their ancestors had helped build this place, and now it was their turn to unmake it and thrive in the outside world once more.

Kulak felt deeply intimidated. He had no problem mindspeaking with his kind, but he had never dealt with them in such numbers or with a goal that was so critical. His mother held his shoulders and walked to the edge of the cliff with him. She had once been the Mindrelfröa—her presence alone was enough to make the felids feel at ease and that helped her son find more courage.

Kulak gave a speech in wordless sentences, and the felids listened. Nelv prowled by his side, sometimes rubbing on his legs, changing shapes through all of her forms, from the heftiest smilodon to the smallest rusty-spotted cat. She echoed Kulak's thoughts and emotions so that the felids would all pay heed, so that they would remember.

Over the next two weeks, many things happened.

Given that the Laatu only knew how to navigate by following vines and columns, Balstei taught the sailors how to read a compass, and built one with the Hex he had left in his Qupi pouch, installing it on *Drolvisdinn*. He also speedily put together a mariner's quadrant with a plumb line, in case they needed to measure angles or distances. Fortunately, the domes were so tall that from about two hundred miles away, at sea level, one could already see their curved tops poking over the horizon, so it would not be hard to know in which direction to navigate.

Kitjári taught the tribe about Zovarian customs, meeting daily with shamans from the six provinces, many of whom had at least a passable understanding of Common. She made them memorize names of towns and important people, while Sterjall explained how to use Sunnokh, Sceres, and the stars to find their path. They taught the Laatu the irrational value of Qupi and Quggons, and how their colorful denominations compared to the relative value of soot and brime.

Alaia joined most of the meetings, as she had a lot more street-smarts than the others. The Laatu would fare best knowing how to deal with swindlers and bullies, and they needed to know how to best behave so that they would not defame the wrong people. Alaia also took the opportunity to play one last game of minquoll, riding on Moorca and scoring her first goal in the highest hoop, for six points. She was sad to say goodbye to the black panther—although Moorca was strong and agile, she wasn't the kind of mount to be taken into the adventures they would soon embark upon.

Mamóru used the time to teach the Laatu Miscam all he could about their past, so that they could better understand their mission and what might happen after more domes opened. He asked Balstei and Fingrenn to be the first to travel with a caravan that was to settle in the untamed lands of the Udarbans Forest, southwest of the scablands. Balstei gladly agreed to travel that way, mostly because he was interested in transcribing Mamóru's writings at the

Istrilm Sanctum. Fingrenn was curious to join this research as well, and to help with translations.

The largest Laatu caravan was to depart toward the Sajal Crater, to settle lands tucked between hot lakes and steaming peaks. Hod Buil from Gwur Úrëath volunteered to lead that mission, knowing those lands would be inhospitable yet well positioned for trade.

Kenondok took care of supplying weapons for the trip, including a generous supply of darts and poisons. He had carved perfectly fitted mouthpieces for the quaar blowguns they'd built with the conduits rescued from the Enolv Temple, and handed one each to Aio-Kulak, Alaia, and Sunu.

The combat training with Sunu continued daily and would continue even once at sea. With their aid, Lago-Sterjall quickly mastered the Brime Strike, managing to only burn his fur thrice more in the process.

Only four days remained before the dome was to be opened.

Everyone was busy every day. And everyone was scared.

Lago and Aio were at the sculpture garden map, taking much needed time for themselves. It had been a stressful week for everyone, after equally stressful months. Aio walked around the oversized map, trying to picture the astronomical scale of the outside world. He had gotten a small glimpse of it, but still could not comprehend the vast distances represented by those parts of the map he had not yet visited.

"I think this one is my favorite one yet," Lago said, staring at Aio.

"Favorite what?"

"Your grinesht. Your scalp painting."

Aio's scalp pigments had faded quicker than usual after so much sweating and exposure to direct sunlight, so his mother had painted a new pattern for him. His current painting looked like a minimalistic sapling rooted at the base of his neck, climbing to branch into geometric knots over his crown. The roots wrapped around his neck and flowed over his clavicles, with tendrils stretching down to almost touch his nipples. The winding lines had a graceful and sensual asymmetry to them.

Lago traced a finger down one of the blue lines and stopped on Aio's left nipple.

Aio flinched backward with a smile. "Careful, many priests walk this path." He seemed wary, but the coy smile stuck to his face. He walked from the granitic sculpture of the proboscidean to the felid one made of obsidian, trying to retrace their recent journey. The black sculpture was sitting halfway into the grass, halfway into the tight cobblestones which represented water.

Aio ambled silently over the cobblestoned Isdinnklad Sea, then stopped. "This is Zovaria?" he asked.

"Just a smidge ahead," Lago corrected him. "About there."

"And your home, Withervale," he continued, taking a few more steps. "Here?"

"Very close!" Lago said. He grabbed Aio's shoulders to move him a bit farther.

"Careful," Aio hissed, wincing. His bandages had come off, but the ghastly cut Marshal Thurann Embercut had carved on his shoulder was still crisscrossed by sutures.

"Sorry, I forgot." Lago removed his hands. "How is your wound?"

"Better. But hurts. Sunu says it will become big scar."

"You could shift your mask over your left shoulder to protect it in the meantime."

"Tried, but shoulder brace rubs on stitches."

Lago more carefully grabbed onto Aio's waist and moved him forward one more step. "The Isdinnklad ends here, and it turns into the Stiss Malpa, but this map shows no rivers, only seas. Withervale would be just around here"—he squatted to touch Aio's left big toe—"and the Withervale Mesa would be here," he said, touching the right big toe.

"Sorry for stepping on your home. I hope my eyes see it one day. And I hope that it goes back to how it used to be."

"It probably won't ever be the same. But I'd like to show you, the observatory more than anything."

"I should show you my home, too. You have not been to Gre Ieren, where my parents and myself rest our scalps at night."

"Am I allowed in there?"

"Probably not. But parents do not need to know."

They circled the trunk through the Arjum Promenade, then took the steps that led to the guest rooms, but continued farther down the stone hallway. They passed by an ample kitchen and snuck past an auditorium where dignitaries were at work. A door opened into a wider hall with vast windows on the right side, overlooking the white river below. The windows were carved in a tessellation of holes that generated shifting silhouettes as they passed by. A row of dozens of carved busts extended down the center of the wide hallway.

"Faces are all the Mindrelfröash who lived here since the great closing," Aio explained as they walked past the figures. The busts were confounding, carved with a human face on the left side, looking toward the wall, and a halfform face on the right, gravely staring out the windows.

Lago walked to the right, more fascinated by the feline aspects of the busts. He saw a proud lion, a wide-eared serval, another caracal like Kulak, a lynx with regal cheeks, a thick-browed mountain lion, an entitled-looking housecat, and many more felids, many of them from species he could not name.

Last in the row of busts was a sad-eyed manul cat. Lago walked around the bust, noticing the features of the human side bore a striking resemblance to Aio, only more solidified.

"Father of Mother," Aio said. "Ieron Aulbo-Damiish. He was simple, funny man. Carving shows not his eye color. Yellow like leaves eager for Autumn."

"I don't see one of Alúma here," Lago observed.

"Not yet. Next year will be sixty-six cycles of the seasons since Mother's birth. They will sculpt a bust of Alúma-Farshálv then. And someday, there might be one of Aio-Kulak as well, but that is many cycles away."

The door at the end of the hallway opened into an octagonal room with a door at each of the sides, except for one side that held a bright, circular window where a giant housecat sprawled much too perfectly, as if the curves had been designed just for her. It was the calico cat who followed Alúma sometimes—she paid no attention to the young men.

At the center of the room, an ancient banyan tree grew. The tree's top was nowhere in sight, for here was merely a portion of the trunk, shooting out roots that had been directed to grow like a staircase, extending sideways before sudden drops, albeit in random intervals instead of a regular spiral.

"What's up there?" Lago asked, trying to peek at where the trunk led.

"Mother and Father's room," Aio said, climbing up the stepped roots. "Want to see?"

"I don't know, will we get in trouble?" Lago murmured, holding on to a root but not daring to go up.

"Maybe," Aio replied, stopping right above him. "Come, just take a peek," he added. He was holding on to the trunk while his legs were spread along two roots, widening his kilt to fully showcase himself. Lago had not yet seen Aio's naked crotch and couldn't resist glancing upward—it was uncannily smooth, like the rest of his body.

Aio smiled deviously and kept climbing. "Follow quick, I show you," he said.

Lago followed, feeling aroused but too nervous for it to show through his trousers.

The royal chamber had lavishly knotted root walls that divided the space into four quadrants. Two beds occupied the first quadrant, with frames rising from the knotted patterns and extending into a domed canopy; the next quadrant was a dressing room, with lush and colorful shodogs and robes, and an oval mirror; next was a study with a solid wooden desk, ample chairs, and intimidating stone carvings as decorations; and the last quadrant was a bathing chamber with a tub carved into the stone floor. The exotic opulence was something Lago had never seen before—it was minimal, functional, even rustic, yet the roots wove so intricately that it felt unapologetically palatial and extravagant.

"Now I show you my room," Aio said, stepping back down the tree. "Not as pretty as parents' room, but still nice."

He turned the knob of one of the seven doors below. It opened quietly. He led Lago in.

The floor plan was an odd polygon, like an octagon cut in half. Immediately to their right was another door, leading to a small lavatory. Farther in was a stack of nine circular windows, each decorated with a different stuffed animal—Lago spotted a wolf among them. Aio hurried him ahead, flushing with embarrassment as they passed by his old toys.

At the far end was Aio's bed, with a frame constructed not from woven banyan roots but from a simple platform of dark-stained wood. Above it opened a large, circular window with a view down the canyon that carried the white waters of the Stiss Regu-Omen.

"Best view is up here," Aio said, crawling up onto his bed, then kneeling on his pillow to peer out the window.

Lago kneeled by Aio's side, enjoying the vista. The opposing cliffsides of the canyon delineated a vertical rift, revealing the Isdinnklad in the far distance where one of the supporting columns stuck out like a frozen waterspout.

"It's beautiful," Lago said. "But I think the best view was down here." He reached under Aio's kilt and felt his smooth crotch. Aio's cock was small, soft, and warm. Lago kept a hold of it while using his right hand to bring Aio's face closer. He bridged the distance between them, lips nearly touching, feeling Aio's pulse as he became erect in his hand. He gave the prince a forceful kiss, then toppled with him onto the bed, laughing all the way.

The Silvesh attached to their shoulder braces were hard and clunky, so they removed them and let them fall silently onto the bedsheets. Aio hurriedly reached for Lago's belt, trying to unclasp it, but Lago straddled him and held him down with his kiss. Aio's breath tasted fresh, like a meadow. Lago let his tongue drift down Aio's neck, to his smooth armpits, then used it to tickle the sides of his ribcage.

Aio let out a sound halfway between laugher and a moan, then tensed up as he felt Lago's wet finger stroking across his tight sphincter.

"My ears knew they heard you return," Alúma's voice came from the door. "Did you have a chance to—" she stopped, wide-eyed. Aio and Lago quickly sat up at the edge of the bed, perplexed and petrified.

"Khuron Aio!" the queen wailed, holding both the door and her mouth open.

Aio could only briefly dart his eyes toward Lago, too terrified to react. He swallowed.

In rough and broken Miscamish, through gritted teeth, Alúma rasped, "Wh-what disgrace have you brought... brought upon our lineage? You... How—"

"Mother, please, do not—"

"My baby, my kitten, how could you..." Her face contorted, torn between anger and sadness.

"Mother," Aio placated, "we can explain. Please do not misunder—"

"Ierun Alúma," Lago said hurriedly, rising to his feet. "It was not Aio's fault, but mine. I was—"

But Aio pushed him back down onto the bed and stood up for himself. "My scalp is sorry you are hurting, Mother. But there should be no shame in love. You brought me up to—"

"I brought you up to lead by example!" Alúma cried, inching closer, her small figure seeming larger with every step. "I brought you up to follow the laws that have kept our tribe alive for fifteen centuries. I brought you up so that you could carry on the legacy that will lead us into the unknown future."

"And what if no heir comes from me? Have you not thought about my own wishes?"

"*How dare you* disrespect our family in this way?" she questioned spitefully. "Your words are sacrilege, a betrayal to our ancestors. What would they think if they could hear—"

"Our ancestors did not have all the answers. They were flawed, as we all are."

"Do not speak of your progenitors in this matter, Aio-Kulak. They were wise, where you are stubborn. They were proud, where you bring shame. I will not allow you to commit such mistakes, to sully our legacy with... with..." She turned toward Lago. "You have done enough, wolf child." She grabbed Lago by the arm and pulled him up. Lago barely had time to grab his mask before the queen dragged him toward the exit. "Leave us. Gre Ieren is no place for your wickedness."

"Do not touch him!" Aio said, standing in front of them. "This matter is between you and me, Mother."

Alúma let go of Lago's arm and stepped directly toward her son, making him shrink beneath her shadow. "You will not tell your own mother what to do. I am chief, I am Ierun. You too are to be Ieron one day, but not if you continue to commit such abhorrent mistakes."

"It is not like you have not made mistakes of your own, Mother. Perhaps much bigger mistakes."

"My ears will hear none of your nonsense," she said, then grabbed onto Lago's arm once more and dragged him out of the room, slamming the door behind him.

Lago leaned against the cold wall, his chest thumping, uncertain whether he should leave or wait for Aio. He cowered near the door, hearing only muted mumbles behind it. He noticed he was clutching tightly to his mask, so he put it on and took his wolf half-form. *I should leave,* he thought, but his curiosity got the best of him. With his keen ears, feeling guilty and helpless, he eavesdropped on the voices in the next room.

"… disrespect, such mockery you make of your responsibilities," Alúma's bileful voice continued striking. "You shame yourself and seek to shame me in front of the Agnargfröa."

"Whatever shame you hold is your own to carry," Aio replied, using powerful words, but sounding muted and weak.

"You know not what you speak of. Our traditions are sacred for a reason, and you, you defile them with your—"

"Do not speak about defiling our traditions. What do you know about—"

"I am your mother!" she yelled.

Sterjall heard a sharp slap, then a sniffle. He focused to bring their threads into his perception; they pulsed, bound to each other while also seeming to repel one another. The threads tasted of fright, anxiety, and also love. He could sense Aio holding a hand to his cheek and felt the pain on his own cheek while doing so. He saw Alúma holding her hand to her chest as if to keep it from striking again, and felt her shame at what she'd done, but also a fervent determination.

"Aio…" Alúma whispered. "This is for your own good, my son."

Aio exhaled sharply. "Your hand strikes me, for my own good."

"This is not a game. But you need to learn to obey. I am doing this to protect you."

"To protect me. What else will you do to protect me, Mother? Perhaps drown me, like you drowned my brother?"

Alúma froze. Her rage turned to fear, and fear turned to sadness and impotence.

"I know about my dead brother," Aio pushed on, "about what father did to him, what *you* let him do to him. To hide your own shame, to protect yourself. Do not talk to me about doing what is right, because what you chose was wrong, and evil. What I choose is to love who I want, nothing more."

In the threads, Sterjall saw Alúma drop, languishing on a chair as she sobbed, unable to face Aio.

"What was his name?" Aio asked, standing above her. Alúma cried and did not respond. "His name! Tell me my brother's name!"

"Ashaskem!" she yelled back in tears. "Ashaskem... I am sorry. His name was Ashaskem. I am so sorry. Please stop, son, please..."

Aio's tense threads seemed to shrivel at his mother's sobs. "Mother?" he tested out, but his mother would not look at him. "Mother?"

"Stop... Just... No more," she pleaded.

"I am... not going to tell anyone. My scalp wanted to... all these years, just wanted to know my brother's name."

"I could not stop him, I'm sorry, I could not stop him."

Aio squatted next to his mother and embraced her, then began to cry over her shoulder, and she wept with him. Their threads wove with each other and became one tense and sorrowful presence. Sterjall could not stand the pain, the disappointment, the worry and uncertainty the threads carried with them. He walked away slowly, trying to find his way back.

Aio found Sterjall leaning over the root bridge that crossed the Stiss Regu-Omen. The night was cloudy, filled with the roar of the white-capped river and the unceasing serenade of insects. Aio leaned next to the wolf, keeping his head down.

A nighthawk croaked a toad-like dirge. The light of green torches flickered.

"My scalp is sorry for what happened," Aio murmured.

"It wasn't your fault," Sterjall replied, his voice thick with sadness.

"It was. Always breaking rules, always upsetting others. Unlike the Mindrelfröash whose busts are carved in long hallway, my scalp is not worthy of honor."

"You know better than that. There is nothing wrong in what we did. It's your mother who is the problem, not—"

"She does what she does out of love," Aio interjected. "She fears. For me. For what she did before I was birthed."

Sterjall sighed. "I... heard some things, after the door closed. About your brother. I heard what you said to her."

"Ashaskem..." Aio whispered. "My scalp is filled with shame. I wished to hurt her. And I hurt her. And I hurt myself."

"What happened there? After that. I couldn't stand waiting there."

Aio moved closer, letting their elbows touch. "We talked. Long talk. She took me to her room, showed me secret she keeps there."

"What secret?"

"A tuft of orange fur. Short. Small. Brother's fur. She let me touch it, let me purr a prayer for him. She loved him." After a sorrowful pause, he continued, "Mother said what happened to Brother, to Ashaskem, was unfair. She is afraid of same thing happening to me. She grew guilt all these years and hated herself, hated Father for what he did, hated that he would never speak Ashaskem's name, or speak much at all after that day."

Aio's eyes scanned the darkness, red and uncertain. Sterjall put an arm around his shoulder and let Aio lean on him.

"Mother will not tell," Aio finally said. "About us, she will not tell. Even so, she does not approve of what she saw, thinks I will someday see better and change. She does not understand us. My scalp thinks she never will. My scalp thinks none of my people ever will."

Chapter Fifty-Three

The Unfolding

The day of the Moordusk Dome's opening at last arrived. The shamans were waiting with their warriors and cats near the vines. The graphite and sulphur mine had been closed and well hidden, and all the soot and brime packed and distributed. *Drolvisdinn* was ready at the Oälpaskist Port, and almost everyone who was to go on the trip was waiting to board it, except for the Silvfröash, who had gathered at Arjum's atrium in front of the temple's steps.

Ierun Alúma was there with the high priests of the six provinces. King Lepa'olt had not shown up, making Kulak wonder about the absence of his dim presence; he hadn't seen his father since the fight with his mother. He hadn't talked much to his mother either, perhaps out of guilt, or most likely fear. Alúma remained impassive.

The four Silvfröash, the queen, and the high priests walked up the steps under the watch of the ancient Ma'u banyan. Alúma stopped to chant a short prayer toward the green-glowing glyph of felids above their heads, then pushed the curtain of roots out of the way, leading them through the archway. They strode up the long hallway in silence. All the lanterns were lit, showing in detail the runes carved on the walls and the textures of the vines and thorns that grew behind stone openings. The air was moist inside, the walls nearly drenched, sparkling with droplets of condensation.

They reached the vast, circular temple. The high priests retreated to the periphery of the chamber, watching disquietly. Orange-flamed sconces flickered, summoning quivering shadows from the carved pillars and the vine columns. The glossy, thornless core vine at the center of the room sparkled like polished olivine.

Alúma walked toward the throne beneath the polyhedral lattice.

"It is time, son. You know what needs to be done," she said in Miscamish. She switched to Common next and said, "Mamóru, Sterjall, Kitjári, keep scalps focused on lattice, on sacred vine, and on movement of threads. Once lattice is set in motion, great opening shall begin, and not even the Endfall may stop it. Learn from this moment. Learn and remember."

Mamóru inhaled from a substantial vial of soot so that he could partially perceive what the others sensed with their Silvesh.

Kulak stood in front of the marble throne, turned, and sat down. His eyes closed, and he seemed to stop breathing. After an indecisive pause, his substance turned ethereal and smoky, then coalesced into his human form. Aio stood, and with Mindrelsilv in his hands said, "Mother, my scalp thinks it should be Farshálv who carries this honor. My eyes would like to see her warm fur once more, before the sails carry us away."

Alúma stood still, brow furrowed. A glint of memory coated her eyes. "I am no longer the Mindrelfröa, son. That time has passed."

"You are always Mindrelfröa, like those who came before you," Aio insisted, stepping toward her with the mask held in front of him. "Do this for me, and the stories we tell about this day will sing your name in them. I want to remember them that way."

Alúma considered in quiet solitude. It had been five years since she had last taken the shape of the tigress. She missed that part of herself dearly, but she had also learned to move past it. It would bring her much joy, but also pain. She closed her eyes, nodded, then opened them again. She took Mindrelsilv and carried it up toward the throne.

Alúma turned around and put the mask on. She shapeshifted slowly, savoring the feeling one last time, and soon Farshálv stood in her stead, coated in fur as fiery as a sunset, holding up her milk-white chest, embraced by stripes of obsidian black. Her long tail wrapped around her legs as she sat. She put her handpaws on the armrests, with her claws extended. Her round pupils were dilated, leaving only an edge of greenish gold around the black voids.

Aio, Kitjári, Sterjall, and Mamóru stood at the base of the steps and looked to the throne.

Aio could not see the threads now, but he knew what he would see if he was wearing the Silv. The threads that connected the lattice were sucked into Mindrelsilv and pulled toward the core vine. It wasn't just the threads that moved, however, but the segments of the lattice itself, which began to collapse into each other, inching closer and closer to the center.

The quaar pipes detached from the geodesic spheres and reattached in new arrangements, reducing the volume of the lattice in a mechanical, angular fashion. In not much time at all, the entirety of the conduits and joints had assembled around the core vine. The conduits slightly twisted and snapped together, forming much longer shafts that wrapped the vine in an impenetrable armor of blackness. The threads all coalesced upward from there, as if a loud signal was being blared up to the skies.

The core vine, along with the wrapping lattice, slowly shifted downward, and together they sank into the hole the vine was sprouting from. Bit by bit, the vine and the lattice disappeared. After a prolonged moment, the entire pillar of black descended below ground, and the hole it had left behind began to fill with sap. The white blood reached the edges of the aperture and stilled, waiting to coagulate into a crystal in the days to come.

A tremor shook from within the deeper crust. The smaller vines above shifted slowly, almost imperceptibly, except for sudden jerks when a thorn was snagged and jolted free. They could feel everything moving, almost as if they could sense the rotation of Noss themself.

"It is done," Farshálv intoned, rising from the throne. She stepped down and stood before her son. "Thank you, Aio, for letting me be whole once more. Thank you, and I am sorry for the pain I caused you."

They held a long embrace. Aio savored the warmth of his mother's fur, the soft caress of her whiskers, and the feeling of her long tail wrapping behind his back.

Alúma returned the mask to him and said, "Go now, my kitten. Your ship awaits. Sail forth and restore what was lost. Sail forth and help the other tribes fulfill their oaths. Go now, and be free."

Part Four
REAWAKENING

Chapter Fifty-Four

To Sea

"I will be fine," Balstei reassured his friends as he mounted on Kobos's saddle. "Fingrenn is already waiting by the southern wall, I should not make them wait any longer."

"We'll miss you, sort of," Kitjári said through a grin.

"Do be careful at the Istrilm Sanctum," Mamóru offered. "It gets slippery between the third and fifth levels. And the rocks are sharp."

"I won't get to the lava tubes for months and months," Balstei said. "First, the settlement needs… settled. But I will be careful, and I will make you all proud. May the moon light your paths." He tapped on Kobos's striped back and hurried away, eager to embark on his own journey in search of the deeper knowledge that lay buried in the scablands.

Sterjall and Kulak mounted on Blu, while Kitjári helped Mamóru up on Pichi's back. The smilodons hastily carried them toward the seafaring province of Gwur Gomosh. They arrived at the Oälpaskist Port in the evening, where Hud Ilsed greeted them and welcomed them aboard *Drolvisdinn*. Ilsed was wearing a magenta shodog that evening, paired with a twilight-blue kilt decorated with pearls and shards of nacre—they made her look like both a sunset and a star-flecked sky.

"There you are," Alaia said to Sterjall. She had been waiting on the deck next to Kenondok, Sunu, and Hod Abjus, who would travel with them as well. "I dropped your bags in the 'tween deck. It's not as fancy as the captain's quarters, but it's comfortable."

Hud Ilsed, the captain of the ship, called out a signal. Her small crew of sailors pulled on the lines, setting the ship's leaf-shaped sails to spread radially, like wings to the wind. The green canvas caught the Isdinnklad's breeze, pulling the wayfarers to sea.

Drolvisdinn skimmed swiftly over the cerulean waters, weaving around the sea stacks that rose from their depths. During the voyage, the humans slept as soundly as the arudinn, but Blu and Pichi did not find the night so restful—unhappy with the swaying vessel, they drowsily hid belowdecks, dreaming of the day their paws would trot over solid ground again. By early the next morning, the travelers had made it to the northernmost point of the dome.

"We should wait until at least midday," Kitjári recommended while they gathered in the luxurious captain's quarters. "That will be midnight in the New World. The annual Sail Parade will start in the afternoon, so most navy ships should've sailed way beyond this point come midnight. Most are likely already at the capital now."

"That'll give me some time to finish the letter," Sterjall said. He had insisted he needed to send one more letter to Crysta and had recommended they exit at the northernmost point of the dome so that Olo would not have to fly so far to reach Zovaria.

Time passed slowly but eagerly.

As the ship held its position near the wall, the passengers carefully watched the wall of vines near them. The arudinn-covered tendrils partially glowed underwater, like sparkling tentacles.

With the constant bobbing of the ship, it was hard to see the vines move, but every once in a while, they could feel something shifting or see an odd splash where there should have been none. They wondered how long it would take for the Zovarians to notice something strange was happening.

Sterjall had just finished writing the letter when they weighed anchor and lined up the ship. The green sails were reefed to avoid potential snags, and the oars were extended.

Kulak stood at the bow, focusing on opening the path forward, being the one with the most experience handling the threads. The massive concavity that opened before them was more than tall enough to fit the ship, with room to spare.

Sterjall stood next to Kulak, and using Leif glimpsed deeper into the wall, trying to spot the wider, unmovable vines, so that they could more easily avoid bumping into them. Kitjári stood atop the quarterdeck, making sure the vines did not close too quickly behind them and that they did not suddenly reappear under their keel.

Once the ship was fully inside the wall of the dome, a quarter of the rowers traded their oars for long push poles, which they used for propulsion and to avoid the ship snagging too close to anything dangerous. Following the Hex-crafted needle of the compass Balstei had built for the ship, they followed the pathless void.

All lanterns were extinguished as they drew near the outer edge of the dome. They came to a stop in the darkness and sent the small cockboat to scout.

The path was clear.

The leaf-shaped sails spread once more, and to the open sea the wind took them. Zovaria could not be spotted from so far away, but its lights shone an amber glow on the horizon's lowest clouds.

Sterjall handed his letter to Sunu. "Make sure Olo hurries," he said. "Tell him we'll sail slow for now, so that he can catch up to us."

Sunu placed the letter in the jay's harness. *"Va jambradikh frulv henet alrull!"* they said, sending the herald to once more find the auburn-haired woman beneath the gold-tipped spire.

"I haven't seen the Sail Parade in over twenty years," Crysta said nostalgically, leaning on the northern window of the School of Cosmology's tower. "All those pink sails, they remind me of cherry blossoms drifting on the Stiss Ashmaarg."

"It is a pointless display of wealth and power to appease the Arch Sedecims," Scholar Dashal replied, ignoring the festival as his eyes scanned the sunnograph for any incoming transmissions.

From their high viewpoint, they could clearly see the Cliffside Lifts. On a terrace above the lifts, all sixteen Arch Sedecims had gathered, leaning on their galvanum scepters as they marveled at the sight of the Isdinnklad, which shone a luminescent blue in the late morning light, sparkling pink with the might of the Zovarian navy.

"At least this pointless display of power has kept the Negians at bay," Crysta said, reaching for a morseleaf roll she'd left on the work desk. She flushed it down with a gulp of emberwood tea and added, "If it wasn't for our navy, the Red Stag would have tried pushing past Withervale by now."

"They have no need for that," Dashal said. "They will hold on to Withervale and the Ninn Tago, that's all they care about, that's why they are rebuilding the rampart west of the city. It's a long-term strategy, it might be years before they attack the Union."

"At least the core army seems to be moving away," Crysta observed. "Whoever Esum's informants are, they know what they are talking about. Even our sources at the Free Tribelands are reporting the same, and they are not at all connected to each other—not now that the Ninn Tago is under control of the Empire."

Crysta was about to pour more tea for herself when she felt a shadow flutter by the west window. *Couldn't be, not now*, she thought. But it was. A bird was circling the tower. She recognized the same *eihnk-eihnk* from her previous encounter with the herald.

Crysta hurled her pot of tea toward the spiral stairs. It shattered, wetting the carpet and the stone floor.

Dashal unbent his back and lifted his brows. "What just—"

"I'm sorry, could you please help me clean up? My arm spasmed and, and—"

"Don't worry," Dashal said, crouching down to pick up the glass.

"I'll handle that!" Crysta said. "Just get me some towels from downstairs, please."

Dashal stepped around the glass and started down the steps.

Crysta knew it was a long way to the bottom, but she still had to hurry. As soon as Olo landed on the windowsill, she quickly said, "*Diathuk frulv oset enue, Lorrdrolvesh.*"

Olo answered with *eihnk-eihnk-eihnk*.

She tossed him a handful of seeds and berries, which she had kept available in her satchel ever since their last meeting, then removed the letter from Olo's harness and began to read it.

> Dear Crysta,
> We are still alive! What you sent us has been extremely—

"I just realized, you could use the cleaning rags in the chest of—" Dashal began, coming back up the steps and stopping cold. Crysta crumpled the letter as she hid it behind her back, then darted her eyes to the windowsill and took an awkward sideways step to block Dashal's view of the bird.

"Crysta…" Dashal grumbled, lowering his square spectacles. "Explain yourself, now."

"This… This is a private matter," she weakly replied. "I would like some privacy, if you please."

Dashal craned his neck to get a better view of Olo, who had jumped onto the desk to search for crumbs. "What kind of herald is—no, I cannot let this slide, Crysta. Tell me what is happening, or I will be forced to—"

"My agent requires this matter be kept solely between myself and my client in the military."

"That is not how this works, and you know it. We both have access to the same information now. And our messages come by sunnograph, not by... by whatever this creature is. Do you have dealings with the Triumvirate? With Afhora perhaps? This bird is not one of our own."

"I am not authorized to speak any further about this, lest I—"

"Lest I ask the dean what the proper procedure is in this matter," Dashal interjected, stepping forward.

"There is no need to involve her in this," she replied, knowing that having to deal with that draconian, octogenarian dean would not go well for her.

The shattered glass from the teapot cracked under Dashal's leather soles, making him look down. Crysta reached toward Olo to run away with him, but the bird fluttered away from her grasp and settled on a tall shelf. She stared at the bird, then at the steps, and was about to bolt when Dashal blocked her way.

"You are done playing games, Crysta," he said sternly. "You will follow me to Dean Tarruken's office, and she will be the one to question you further." He grabbed Crysta's arm and closed the tower's windows, then led her down the long steps.

"Please, Dashal. You know me, you know I would not lie to you unless—"

"Unless you were working with the enemy. I heard some rumors. They say you went to visit Artificer Balstei Woodslav just before his treasonous escape. What you and that soot-snorting leech had going on is likely related to this... incident. But you will have a chance to explain yourself to the dean. Move along."

They reached the bottom of the steps. Dashal opened the door, which led to one of the hallways of the School of Cosmology, and pushed Crysta through it.

With a clumsy twist, Crysta freed herself from Dashal's grasp and tumbled back in through the doorway. She kicked at the door, slamming it in Dashal's face, then locked it and stowed the key in her pocket.

"Crysta!" Dashal screamed from behind the door. "There's nowhere to run to, and you know it. Stop this madness!"

"I will explain... later!" she said.

"Get Dean Tarruken here at once!" Dashal ordered to someone. "Tell her to bring her spare key!"

Crysta hurried up the tower's steps, already uncrumpling the letter and reading it as she ran.

> Dear Crysta,
> We are still alive! What you sent us has been extremely helpful. Again, I can't tell you exactly what we are currently up to, but I wanted to tell you about some other things.
> First, you were right! It was a comet that caused the Downfall. It seems it landed where the Sajal Crater is today. Do you still have that bet with Scholar Mawari? Time for him to hand over that Quggon. A Yenwu cosmologist named Jiu Zezi predicted the impact hundreds of years before it happened. And the original observatory she spotted the comet from might still be intact inside the Yenwu Dome! We have a new friend who is a treasure trove of information from ages past. We are learning from him every day.
> By now, the Zovarian army knows we made it into the Moordusk Dome. We've learned a lot more about how the masks work, and how important it is to keep them safe and not used for war like the Union wants. You will not believe how incredible the dome is on the inside! Like you guessed, their day is our night, and that's why wisps are visible at night for us. And they have wisps of their own, in reverse! They are so much brighter, and they take orange and red colors if they happen at sunrise or sunset. There's so much more about the domes that I want to tell you about, but it would take too many pages. So, I was thinking... why don't you see it for yourself?

Crack. A shard of broken teapot shattered under Crysta's shoes. She stepped into the tower's top room and breathlessly searched around—Olo was still there, looking confused while perched on a crossbeam. "Hold just a moment," she told the bird, then continued reading the letter.

> If you can, travel southwest, right *now*. The Moordusk Dome is slowly opening, at this very moment, as I write this. The perimeter of the dome will open up for anyone to walk through in a matter of days or weeks—don't know the timeline exactly, but it won't be long. I recommend you take a small boat (is Corben around?) and travel to the northeast shore. There's a beautiful beach of black sands at the edge of the bogs, which should be clear of soldiers and inhabitants. From there, you could enter the dome

and see it in its full glory, at least until too many of the vines disappear and it is transformed forever.

The entire world will change after this, for the better, I hope, and all of us will have to adapt. I'm afraid the soldiers by Muskeg and Nebush might fight the Laatu Miscam (the tribe inside), some of whom will be slowly migrating to settle in unclaimed lands. We must find a way to coexist, but there likely will be bloodshed before that happens. We will be staying away from that, except for Balstei, who is traveling with one of those caravans—let's hope he doesn't get into too much trouble.

Back to what we might need from you, if you can still help. First, you must send Olo back straight away. Not in six hours, but in the next wick if possible; otherwise he'll lose track of us and we won't get your message. All we care for is any information you have regarding movements of the Red Stag and the Negian Empire. Nothing more. If you don't have any new information, please just tell us how you are doing.

Oh, and Jiara found herself at last! Next time you see her, she might be in the shape of a gorgeous black bear. Well, a cinnamon-colored black bear, to be more accurate. Her new name is Kitjári.

We all miss you. Stay safe, and hurry! Olo is waiting.
Love,
- Lago-Sterjall

Shit, shit, shit, Crysta thought. *Only a wick of time? If I even have that long. What do I tell him? And how do I get out of this mess?* She then smiled brightly as the Ilaadrid Shard, thinking of the ancient comet, of the nature of wisps, imagining a huge observatory hiding somewhere inside the Yenwu Dome. Her smile faded as she pulled out a quill and ink and hastily wrote.

Bang!

Crysta smeared her signature, startled by the noise. *They are back already? No time to waste.* She folded the still-wet letter, tucked it in Olo's harness, and while opening the window said, *"Va jambradikh frulv henet alrull."*

Olo flew out at once, like a sapphire meteor.

Dear Lago,
Sorry for the hasty missive. Gwil and I are well, excited for all you are telling me.

Withervale is still under Negian control, but they haven't tried pushing west of the city. The Red Stag marched east a long while back, to cross the Ophidian. He might've breached the Bighorn Dome by now, but I can't get confirmation. They say his new general, Silv-Thaar Valaran, has found his half-form of a raccoon.

I'm afraid of what might happen there. Your map said this was the caprid dome, or "rilg," and those mountains are filled with wild sheep and goats with terrifying horns. If they steal Rilgsilv, they will amass an enormous army that could take down the Bayanhong Tribes.

Very strange update: about a month ago, Banook showed up at the Wujann Observatory to deliver a message for some student of mine called *Luras Varum*. I'm guessing that might be you? He said that Luras's friend, Safis, (don't think you mentioned her?) is now staying with him. Safis was living near the Anglass Dome and noticed that it was slowly changing shape: vines are twisting in weird ways, just like the Heartpine vines did before it started to dry up. I asked a source to confirm it, and they agreed it's subtle, but true. The Negian forces in there want to evacuate, but so far there's no sign of that happening. Same source confirmed that the other mask—the musteloid one—came from the Lequa Dome. That dome has also begun to slowly grow out of shape, but to a lesser degree.

The Heartpine Dome has continued to collapse. Only half of the roof still stands, and side walls are buckling inward. The central trunk still holds, but who knows for how much longer. It's just a matter of time before it comes down.

A colleague saw Olo land on the window, and I don't know how to deal with him. Don't send him to the tower again; it's no longer safe. I may have to consider your recommendation to travel to the Moordusk Dome.

Oh, and I told you! A comet! That is the best news of all.

Stay safe and send my love to all. The song is still *Oh, Iskimesh*.

- Crysta

Sterjall folded the letter after he finished reading it to his friends. He had a huge smile on his muzzle, but it was faltering.

"Is she in trouble?" Alaia asked.

"I... I don't know. Her writing is untidy, smeared, like she was being forced. But she wrote the right song name at the end, which means she was not under duress. Yet I'm so happy to hear from Banook! And Safis is with him, how amazing! I wonder why he sent that message, the stuff about the domes growing out of shape."

Kitjári thought for a moment. "Hey, Lorr Luras Varum, remember that twatbadger, Baldo, at Stelm Bir? When he told us about the dome collapsing on them, it dried up and began to fall very shortly after they destroyed the temple. But the Red Stag took over Anglass last year. Whatever is happening there, it's something different, or at least something much slower."

Kulak nodded. "My scalp's guess is that if no Silv helps dome grow, dome grows however it pleases. Is why I had to sit at Ommo ust Mindrel once every month, or Mindreldrolom would have sickened. Not as bad as burning temple, not as bad as killing the core vine. Then the dome dies and falls."

"What will happen if those domes are left without a mask for longer?" Sterjall asked.

"No one knows," Kulak replied. "But perhaps as bad as collapse."

"Or they might go the way of the Varanus Dome," Kitjári said, "and keep growing out of control."

"If that is what happened at Varanus," Mamóru said, "I guess we will soon find out."

Chapter Fifty-Five

Tower Maiden

"Unlock the door, Crysta. This is your last warning." Dashal's voice was strained and bitter.

Crysta stopped at the bottom of the steps and stared at the door. *Takhish and Takhamún, Twin Brothers of light and dark, I implore you both come to my aid.* She took the key out of her pocket. *Maybe if I shove the door open, I could run past him.* She tiptoed forward, hoping Dashal still thought she was at the top of the tower, and lined the key up to the keyhole. A shadow blocked the keyhole's light before she slid it inside.

"She's hiding in there," Dashal's voice grumbled. "She had a herald from another realm with her."

"We won't let her escape," came the rattly voice of Dean Tarruken.

Fuck me sixteenfold, Crysta thought, pulling the key away.

"Guards, follow close behind me," Tarruken said. The lock clicked open. "If she makes a move, disable her, but do not cause any visible injuries. I'd rather keep this matter quiet."

Crysta bolted behind a bookcase just as the door creaked open.

The dean, Dashal, and three Union guards hurried in, rushing up the steps. Crysta watched them go, then ran to the door, tripping on clumsy feet.

"She's behind us!" Dashal called out, stopping only a few steps up.

Crysta scrambled to the door and slammed it closed, holding on to the doorknob while someone on the other side tried to twist it open.

"Treason!" hissed the malign voice of the old dean, muted by the heavy door. "This is treason!"

Crysta noticed the dean's key was still in the lock. She turned it quickly, stowed the key away, then let go of the doorknob. Four students were staring at her—they all took careful steps back.

"This is not what it looks like!" she yelled at them, then rushed down the hallway.

Hefra Boarmane, a most distinguished naturalist at the School of Zoology, was tying a tag around the foot of a warbler specimen she had recently collected in the Moordusk Bogs. She placed the warbler in a drawer amongst dozens of others in the collection; they were all tagged with different species names, although they would have seemed entirely identical to untrained eyes.

She reached into her preposterously oversized backpack, removed a stack of luna and leopard moths, and returned to work. Hefra was a short, stocky woman, with black hair tied in a practical ponytail. Despite having returned from her fieldwork the night before, she was still wearing the same outdoorsy clothes. As she lined a lepidopteran to pin it to a drawer, a barking cry made her toss the insect away.

"Hefra!"

"Fudgevoids! Crysta? What in the nether—"

"I'm so glad…" Crysta said breathlessly, "so glad to f-find you." A drop of sweat fell from her face to land on Hefra's shoulder. "I need your help, now. Right now."

"What's gotten to you, sweet plum? It's been so long, but I'm glad to see you made it out of Withery—"

"No time. I need you to come with me, to take me out of here. Now."

"Out of where? Of the stacks? It's not as labyrinthine as the students make it sound."

"Out of the institute. Out of Zovaria. You need to come to the dome with me, but quietly."

"To the Moordusk Dome?"

"Keep your voice down, please!" Crysta stressed in a whisper, spying down the stacked lines of drawers. Only one lonely intern worked at the far end, cataloging tiny vertebrae to exhaustion. He hadn't heard them.

Crysta leaned in close to Hefra. "The dome is opening. The vines, they are slowly spreading apart. Right this moment. If you ever wanted to see what it's like on the inside, we need to go. Now."

"Sugarloaf, have spiders nested inside your skull?" Hefra asked, not bothering to look at Crysta. She pinned a moth into its shallow sepulcher and picked up another. "I was there a week ago. The only unusual thing around the bogs is the incredibly disrespectful soldiers galloping like direbeasts, scaring all my precious birds and leaving horse dung all around the perimeter. I would've noticed if the dome was 'opening.'"

"Please, Hefra, I just need you to listen to me."

"I did, unfortunately. And I have work to do. Do you mind?"

"I might've... uhm... locked Dean Tarruken in the tower. And Dashal, too. And some Union guards. I'm in big fucking trouble, Hefra."

Hefra lit up, at last interested in whatever Crysta was mumbling about.

"This was written by your old disciple?" Hefra questioned as they traversed the undoubtedly labyrinthine tunnels that housed the School of Zoology's immense collections.

"Student. Yes. Lago used to help me at the Mesa Observatory."

"And you say he's inside the dome? And has one of those spritetale masks? And you believe all this nonsense?"

"It's not nonsense, I've seen the—"

"The institute once sent me all the way to Baysea Beyenaar," Hefra interjected, handing the letter back to Crysta, "to investigate the sighting of a nethervoid dragon swimming among the icebergs."

Crysta cocked her head. "What does that have to do with—"

"It was some Khaar Du teenagers. They dressed giant bladders and driftwood to make it look like a creature from the voids and dragged it out into the bay at night." She peeked around a corner, saw no one passing by, and continued down the hallway. "My point is, your old student is playing a prank on you. And you are being gullible as a toddler."

"This is no prank, Hefra," Crysta said. "I've seen the mask with my own eyes. I've seen Lago grow a tail! I've even communicated with one of the animal spirits of old... In a manner of speaking."

"Here, behind this stack," Hefra said, shoving Crysta out of sight. She pretended to dig through a wall of index cards as a scholar passed by, blocking his view with her enormous backpack. She then gestured for Crysta to come out.

"All I'm saying is..." Crysta began, then stopped. "I... I thought you might want to join me. I thought it'd be perfect for you, honestly, the chance of a lifetime. The chance of an epoch, for Takh's sake. I don't know anything about surviving in the wilderness, but I know how to take field notes, and I know more about the dome than most people around here."

"Did you really lock Dean Tarruken in the tower?"

Crysta shrugged her admission, then pulled the two keys from her pocket. "I don't think they have another copy. They'll have to break the door down."

"Atta girl. I hate that harpy as much as any sentient scholar. She's cut my funding in half since last term." She lifted a stern finger to Crysta's face. "Just because I sympathize with your actions, I might consider helping you. And to be clear, I still don't believe you, even if I do believe that you are naively convinced."

"That will do. Just help me get out of here. I think I might know a way out, by sea. Can you find a safe way to the Rigmaul Harbor?"

"Just hide among the crowds. No one will notice us with the parade going on. What's at the harbor?"

"My son, Corben. He'll be watching the parade. I know where to find him."

Hefra nodded, turned into a dark hallway, and pushed Crysta into a hiding spot once more. "Give me just a minute," she said.

Crysta hid silently. Hefra lowered her backpack and began to unload her recently collected specimens, tucking them into a dusty shelf for later recovery. She then opened a drawer and began to load her backpack with supplies.

"What are you doing?" Crysta whispered.

"Stuffing my bag for the trip, of course."

"With what?"

"With tools to properly collect specimens."

"I thought we were trying to escape!"

"Not yet, muffin. I dragged us to this tunnel to get fresh supplies. If what you are saying is true—and I still don't believe it's true—how else am I supposed to collect samples?"

The last items clinked into place. Hefra cinched the flaps tight, lifted her sarcophagus-sized sack, and led them down a different set of tunnels.

"Put this on," she ordered, handing Crysta a musky and mud-splattered leather jacket.

"It's filthy!"

"I just got back from the bogs! Put it on. And tie down your hair. Make yourself look less... Crysta-like."

Crysta obeyed, holding her breath as she put the mucky garment on.

When they exited the underground stacks, they emerged at the eastern side of the Fourteenth Bulwark, two levels down from the main institute grounds.

The bulwark was swarming with crowds trying to find a good viewpoint to watch the Sail Parade. No one paid attention to the two women, not even when Hefra pushed them around to make way. She led Crysta down the stairs and closes to the Artisan's Esplanade, where the professor told her to stop.

"He should be here somewhere," Crysta muttered as she glanced around. "We used to climb onto these walls when he was a toddler, to watch the parade together. He's always in the same—there! Corben!" She yelled over the crowd, but the young man could not hear her. Crysta shoved her way through the throngs, failed at climbing the wall, then felt Hefra's hands giving her a boost. She scrambled up and embraced her son from behind.

"Gah! Get off my—Mom? What in Takh's two names are you wearing?"

"*Skyfarer*. Can it take us out of the city?"

"What is going on?"

"Take us, now, I'll explain."

Very few people were at the Rigmaul Harbor—the tall walls around the enclosed docks did not provide a view of the parade.

Hefra lowered her burdensome backpack by the catamaran's mast. It made a clinking, glassy sound.

"What do you carry in there?" Corben asked, seeing his boat tip uncomfortably. "It's huge."

"Specimen boxes, cotton, alcohol, notebooks, glassine envelopes, wooden press and paper for botanical samples, lots and lots of glass vials. The usual."

"Let's just hurry," Crysta said, eyes always looking over her shoulders.

Corben unhitched the rope from the cleat and hopped on board, pushing off the dock as he did so. "So, they made it into the dome?" he asked as they sailed between buoys.

"You believe your mother's rubbish?" Hefra asked.

"I was there. I saw Sterjall myself," he answered. "But I don't blame you— I barely believed it even when I saw him with my own eyes."

As they exited the harbor, they had to circle around an enormous perimeter of trimarans from the navy, which were blocking any interference with the parade. The horizon of pink sails was resplendent, but more resplendent was the sixteen-leveled city and its promontory jutting out at the northern end, suspended by the gargantuan columns of the Cliffside Lifts. Streamers and painted leaves were raining from all sixteen levels, landing over the rose quartz bulwarks like colorful snowflakes.

Corben pulled on a line, secured it, then looked back toward Crysta. "Mom, I was thinking... Is it alright if I—"

"Don't even think of it," Crysta stopped him. "You promised your father you'd be back in Needlecove by Onguday. And you need to find Gwil. He will be at the Gaalem Monastery. Approach him carefully, tell him why I had to leave, and offer my apologies."

"I guess," he replied, unamused.

Crysta looked at Hefra. "It will be just the two of us, old pal," she said, forcing herself to sound more excited than afraid. "It will be like our old field trips."

Chapter Fifty-Six

Adventuress

Corben moored *Skyfarer* to a jagged rock, then helped Crysta and Hefra down to the black-sand beach. There was only starlight to see by, but the Moordusk Dome seemed normal, with no magical portal opening for the visitors, no glowing wisps illuminating an entrance.

"As I said," Hefra complained while holding up a lamp, "this whole thing is nonsense. But prove me wrong, Crysta, I want to see you walk through this tangle of thorns."

"Do you want me to take us back home?" Corben asked. "These waters are dangerous—I'll have to move her before low tide."

"Her?" his mother questioned.

Corben grinned awkwardly.

"Let's be patient," Crysta said. "Lago said it would be very slow. Let me try something."

She borrowed Hefra's lamp, and with its aid found a few chunks of driftwood. She placed them very precisely between the vines, then pierced little leaves on the thorns closest to the driftwood.

"Remember the relative position of these leaves to the wood," she instructed. "Let's look around in the meantime."

They hiked for half a mile around the dome's perimeter, finding nothing but the sloshing beginnings of the bogs. The wall seemed as impenetrable as always, with only a few pockets they could walk into, but that was a natural occurrence in all the domes, given the variety of vine sizes.

When they returned to the shore, all three of them squatted next to the driftwood. The thorns behind them had shifted—they were whole finger-breadths away from where they had been earlier.

"See?" Crysta exclaimed. "And look at the sand. There's more moisture on one side, as if the vines were sliding away and leaving marks."

"Sweet pie," Hefra began, "you know the vines constantly move. That's why you get wisps."

"They do, but never this fast. Let's place more markers and check again in a wick or two."

They set more pieces of wood and leaves in place and prepared a very late dinner, taking cover from the evening winds behind black boulders.

Later, under the light of a rising purple crescent, they confirmed the vines had further receded. Some of the driftwood had even snagged on the thorns, leaving a clear trail behind them. Crysta carefully walked into a newly created grotto, inspecting the vines.

"Yeouch!" she suddenly screamed, dropping to the ground.

"Are you alright love?" Hefra asked, hurrying to help her.

"I'm fine," she groused. "Watch where you step. The vines left holes everywhere."

"They look almost like fox dens," Hefra observed.

As Crysta stood back up, her silk shirt caught on the thorns, ripping a long cut in her sleeve.

"You shouldn't have taken my precious jacket off," Hefra snidely remarked.

"No…" she bemoaned. "This was my favorite shirt." She then stared at her muddy skirt.

"I'll let you borrow a set of trousers, too," Hefra said. "And a belt."

Crysta changed her clothes. Now that the rising moon had ushered in the cold western winds, she was thankful for Hefra's grimy jacket, plaid cotton shirt, and wool trousers.

Corben had been readying *Skyfarer*, concerned that the low tide could strand them. Crysta approached him.

"Got everything you need, adventuress?" he asked, smirking at his mother's attire.

"Ugh. Yes, sweetie," she said, then gave him a kiss on the forehead. "Thank you, again."

She paused for a few breaths.

"I guess… I don't know," she said, "maybe you can tell your father the truth, if you want to. I don't know that he'll believe you either way."

"I may. We'll see. I'm proud of you, Mom. I'll come by here in a week's time. If I don't find you, I'll assume you're well on your way."

"You be careful!"

"I will." He pushed the catamaran off the shore and hopped aboard. "And I may do some exploring of my own!" he yelled.

"Don't you dare!"

Corben shrugged. "May the moon light your path!"

"May the stars guide your heart, son."

As Crysta watched her son depart toward the brightening eastern skies, she felt a tremor.

"Earthquake?" Hefra asked. "So far from the mountains?" It was uncommon for the ground to shake near the Isdinnklad except much farther east, where the Stelm Wujann and Stelm Ca'éli pinched close to one another. "I want to try an experiment now," she said, taking the initiative.

Hefra dug into her backpack, then tied small, colorful labels to a selection of thorns, color coding them based on the size and branching pattern of the vines they were attached to. She made sure all the markers were at eye level, then noted them in one of her many field notebooks.

"We can check them in the daytime," she said.

"Come, see!" Hefra called, shaking Crysta's shoulders.

Crysta sat up, her drool sticking black grains of sand to her cheeks. "But... sleep..." she protested.

"You'll get your chance. Come now, quickly!"

Enveloped by the bog's morning mists, Hefra studied the labels. "See, this makes *some* sense at least," she said more to herself than to the somnambulant professor. "The largest vines haven't shifted. Well, maybe a bit, hard to tell, but some small vines are now dozens of feet above!" She pointed up to a yellow label barely within eyesight. "And some seem to have sunk underground, but most are wrapping themselves tighter to the larger vines."

The grotto they had entered the night before dug much deeper now. The sand around the wall had a strange turbulence to it, as if groundhogs had been busily digging at it all night.

Another tremor shook their feet, more prominent than the last one.

"Look over here," Hefra said, exploring a narrow path between the vines. It was a vertical cut barely two feet wide, sinking into full darkness. She slid in carefully, mindful of the threatening thorns.

"Please don't go so deep," Crysta urged. "It's like I'm watching you crawl into a carnivorous flytrap."

"How thick did your student say the wall was?" Hefra asked.

"Half a mile or so."

"Let's hope it opens faster than this, or it'll take us weeks to find our way through. Bring me my lamp, sweet plum."

The channel connected to several other paths. There were no straight trails to follow, but Hefra had come prepared with a compass and found a pathway heading in the southwestern direction they needed to travel.

Once they reached an impasse, where they had no choice but to wait for the vines to further open, Hefra found plenty of ways to keep herself busy by studying the interior structure of the dome's wall. She sampled sand, thorns, sap, and small vines, taking careful measurements and notes.

"There are nearly no holes in the ground deeper in," she observed. "And the vines have fewer thorns. Look over here, where the tunnel ends."

The vines she pointed to still had plenty of sharp thorns, but most of the structure between the vines was filled by fibrous tendrils that looked more like a dense sponge. Hefra plucked a sample and inspected it under the green light of her lantern. "Almost like a fungus, or a beard lichen."

Crysta wrinkled her nose. "Do we need to use sap for the lantern? It stinks, and the green light gives me the creeps."

"I'm not wasting my good oil until it's strictly necessary. We have unlimited sap, and this is a sacrificial lantern. Once we are through, I'll toss it away. The sap will ruin it anyhow. Lookie here, Crysta." She took a white cloth and wiped it on the surface of the sponge-like wall. The cloth became smeared with a black streak. Hefra smelled it, then tasted it.

"I think the tendrils act like a filter. To regulate the air, and perhaps the temperature or moisture within the dome. The thorns outside are for a different kind of protection. These filtering fibers are the first to move out of the way, see?" Hefra pointed at a vine where the fibers had collapsed into a mesh-like cover. "Then the smaller vines wrap around the bigger ones, and then..." She put her hand onto a wide vine, one so large it looked like a flat wall covered in thorns. "And then... I guess these largest babies will either sink underground or move upward. But where do they go?" She kept her hand on the waxy wall, as if waiting for it to move and provide an answer.

Crysta grew tired of waiting and began to walk back toward the beach. The vines were not opening fast enough either way, so there was plenty of time to spare.

"I want to try another experiment," Hefra said, trotting out behind her. "Help me find a large vine that is exposed. One we could walk around without any obstacles."

They found a vine to Hefra's specifications, which she measured by wrapping her climbing rope tightly around it, making a mark where the rope ended, and continuing around to mark the next segment. She measured three hundred and fifty-eight feet in circumference.

"We'll measure it again tomorrow," she declared, hands resting on her hips.

As time passed, Hefra's anticipation turned her more and more ecstatic. Her doubts had entirely vanished, and she was in full-on data-gathering mode, seeing an opportunity no naturalist in history had ever had the chance to experience. The next morning, she measured the large vine in the exact same spot, though her marks were no longer at eye level, but down by her waist.

"Three hundred and forty-nine feet," Hefra said. "Almost seventy strides even. Three strides smaller than the day before. Our range of error was merely a foot or two, this is too big a difference to be a simple mismeasurement."

"The large vines are thinning down," Crysta said, pointing out the obvious. "Where does all that mass go?"

"Underground, is my guess. Hence the tremors."

The following day, they discovered that many of the smaller vines were drying up; the filtering tendrils became brittle and would disintegrate at the slightest touch. And stranger yet, some of the burrows left behind were being filled by white sap. Hefra took samples of every stage of the process.

I feel like we are about to breach through, Crysta thought. *It can't be much longer.* The tunnels went deeper now, but still they were too convoluted and impassable.

Three nights later, they spotted a couple of wisps from deep within the forest of vines, hinting that the end of the wall was near, but the labyrinth was not yet clear in the direction they needed to travel. More holes opened treacherously in the ground, most covered by sap, their tops drying to brittle, crystalline caps.

Hefra used a stick to lift a layer of dried sap; it pulled off the hole like a circular lid. "We must be nearing the internal edge of the dome," she hypothesized. "There are many more of these holes here, just like at the outer edge."

It was past midnight, and they were exhausted, but they kept meandering.

"Another wisp, up ahead," Crysta noted. Subtle light bounced from the vines, coming not just from a single light source. They circled around a columnar vine and saw a bright hole in front of them, one too small for them to fit through.

"To the netherflames with this, I can't wait any longer!" Hefra exclaimed, taking out her cutlass and slashing the last few vines that blocked their path. She quickly lit her cutlass on fire to burn the sap before it ate at the steel, then broke away the brittle, crystallized sap while it was still hot. They waited until the aperture of vines stopped dripping, then jumped through the hole.

The sky caught their gaze first, a brightly skeletal pattern of pastels that blended into whiteness. Then their eyes lowered, following the dark silhouette of the nearest supporting column, and landed upon green mountains streaked by waterfalls. Farther back, more columns rose, hazy and remote, like rifts of purple haze cutting into the fabric of the dome.

"Unbelievable," Hefra muttered in awe. She held her breath to listen to the unrecognizable bird, mammal, and insect calls. She kneeled to caress the petals of a spiraling, cyan-colored flower of a kind she had never seen before, then plucked the flower mercilessly, for later study.

"Hefra, look behind you," Crysta whispered.

Hefra turned to gaze upon the dome's wall with its billions of arudinn covering its surface. Not many arudinn grew close to the ground, but they found some, plucked the seedpod-like bulbs, and watched their light and heat extinguish between their fingers.

Hefra's entranced eyes followed the dark vines upward as they turned to full brightness in a gradual transition. "The entire dome glows..." she mumbled. "It's like the inside of a giant, bioluminescent jellyfish."

Hefra realized she could run out of vials and envelopes by collecting everything she found within a radius of a few strides, so she had to keep her composure and be picky about picking. Since the dome was soon to vanish—according to Crysta's old student—samples of the dome itself became her priority.

"Look at the different species of mosses here," she told Crysta, feeling the textures with her expert fingers. "Some are attracted by these vines with the curled thorns, some by the ones with a higher concentration of the shining pods." She pricked a vine with her cutlass. "And this vine, its sap smells more... coriander-like."

She took more notes, then looked up again as though in a trance. "This dome is a massive, complex organism," she preached to the skies. "Each of the larger vines feels like an organ with a specific function, and even the small vines must adapt and specialize in their own way. On the outside, they are all the same, nothing more than a thorny barrier, but in here they have slight variations—perhaps invisible to untrained eyes—but I feel they each have a purpose. It makes me sad to think this creature will soon die and simply vanish."

Once Hefra had collected enough samples from the interior wall, they decided the next obvious step would be to study the nearest supporting column, which waited about a dozen miles ahead of them, through the dense rainforest. Their progress was sluggish, interrupted by constant stops to write about new discoveries. A few miles into the forest, they climbed a rocky outcrop. The haze had cleared up, and in the distance, almost directly behind the supporting column they were aiming for, they finally saw the central trunk.

"That must be it," Crysta said. "That's where their temple must be." She turned to Hefra, who had just captured an impossibly slender-winged plume moth. "Let's be careful, Hefra. We don't know how they'll react if they encounter foreigners stealing small pieces of their sacred land."

"I'll try, love, but I can't make any promises," Hefra replied absently, stuffing the now dead moth into a glass vial.

Crysta noticed something strange about the light, but it wasn't immediately clear to her what was happening. "Look at the wall," she said, looking back toward where they'd entered the dome. "Some of the vines are dimming."

One by one, beginning at the false horizon, the vines lost their light. The smaller ones faded first, leaving enormous columns of light framing the spaces that had darkened. After an hour, only the largest of vines remained alight, drafting a craquelured pattern across the sky. Then those vines dimmed as well, until only the trunk and its branching top remained, a lighthouse the size of a mountain. The branches of light receded into the trunk, leaving a resplendent column that dimmed until it was nothing but an afterimage. Darkness washed upon them; not of a pure black, but of a twilight blue that would accompany them for the rest of the night.

Two days of travel later, as they neared the supporting column, they encountered a cobblestone path leading in the same direction. They followed it into a land of mangroves, where floating docks and bridges took the place of roads. It wasn't long before a group of Laatu scouts spotted them, tied their hands together, and escorted them into the city of Parjuul, the capital of Gwur Pantuul.

Reaching the wooden platform of the capital's central courtyard, the scouting party halted.

A woman of obvious rank approached and reprimanded the warriors. Unlike all the other bald heads around, she was wearing a highly ornamented headdress of mangrove-like locs covered in shells and colorful wires. While the warriors untied the foreigners, the woman spoke in a flowing mix of Common and Miscamish. "*Lakho, khus lakho...* My scalp begs *ejienn* forgive mistreatment. Hud Quoda I am named, chief of Gwur Pantuul. We not were expecting visitors, not so soon. The *munnashkrull* have been... hasty."

"Thanks for untying us, sweet Lurr," Hefra said. "And don't worry, I would've done the same. I'm Hefra." She extended a hand to shake, but Hud

Quoda did not know the gesture. She stepped closer and tapped right temples with Hefra.

"*Frum.* We are honored to breathe with you, Hefra," Quoda said, then bumped heads with Crysta.

"Sorry, I'm..." Crysta began, a bit lost. "My name is Crysta, Crysta Holt, a pleasure to—"

"Crysta?" Hud Quoda said, eyes sparkling with curiosity. "The professor who looks at the stars?"

"Yes? Excuse me? How did you—"

"*Outhuk.* Come with me, Crysta of the Withering Vale, there is much you need to learn."

Chapter Fifty-Seven

Balance from Chaos

Till long after the arudinn dimmed, Hud Quoda spoke, answering Crysta's questions about Lago's journey, all the while being shamelessly interrogated by Hefra about the natural world inside Mindreldrolom. Although Quoda would not mention where Lago and the others had gone, she told them that Balstei had not traveled with the others and would be with the caravans to the south, on his way out of the dome somewhere near his hometown of Muskeg.

"I would love to see Bal," Crysta said.

"Bun, are you drunk?" Hefra complained. "We just got here, there's so much to explore."

"But I want to catch up with him before he gets too far away and we lose our chance to see him."

"His whereabouts known, for us," Hud Quoda said. "Three powerful shamans follow *welvet*... convoy. Birds they carry, in contact with Arjum, *osgral kroovoish*. We show where to find Balstei. Your scalps become not hurry. Breathe Mindreldrolom. Become home."

For the next few weeks, Crysta and Hefra explored the province, learned about the Laatu, and watched the Parjuul fleet depart the mighty mangrove city. Hud Quoda could not join her fleet or the two women, as she had many responsibilities in her own province, but she notified Alúma of the travelers' arrival, telling the queen they would soon be making their way to Arjum. Each cycle of the arudinn brought more wisps into the night sky, until one evening, a patch of blue shone directly through the dark tendrils of the dome.

"It won't be long until it's all gone," Crysta said.

"The trunk is where this whole thing started," Hefra said. "I'd like to learn more about it. Maybe if we ask nicely, they will let us see their temple."

Alúma did not let them see the temple.

The queen met the guests at the atrium in front of Ommo ust Mindrel. She had heard much about Crysta and considered her a potential asset, an ambassador of sorts, who could be trusted to learn from their culture and ease the transition that was inevitably coming. Although the temple was off limits, the queen told them all that she had observed in the sacred room ever since setting the dome to open. As they were conversing, birds perching on the ancient Ma'u banyan suddenly took flight, forecasting a small tremor that shook the felid statues in the atrium.

"White blood vines dig under Arjum," Ierun Alúma said, "like worms escaping a night heron." She held a tensed hand down so that a giant calico cat could scratch her back on it, then continued, "Tremors shaken us while we rest our scalps, but we fear them not—they are Mindreldrolom saying farewell. We hear them, we thank them for allowing Laatu culture to thrive across time, for keeping a part of Noss alive within us all."

A shaman interrupted their meeting, taking the queen away for a stretched moment. When she returned, the queen faced the two visitors and said, "Heralds have flown news from Fingrenn, who travels with the mighty warrior Balstei."

Crysta snickered. "Mighty warrior?"

"Yes," Alúma continued. "War begins, confusion, and bloodshed. As Lago-Sterjall feared, Zovarian warriors awaited by the wall, some searching for Silvesh, some thirsty for revenge. Silvesh they will not find, so only revenge will sate them."

"Oh, by Noss... Is Balstei alright?"

"He is, for he is smart, he told our warriors to fight but not kill. Bravely they fought, protected by the Nu'irg ust Mindrel. After battling, Laatu exchanged valuables with defeated soldiers, asked for truces, spoke our story, and only then proceeded with their southbound journey. Laatu representatives become summoned to the capital of pink stones. Alliances soon take form. Did Hud Quoda tell you about your friend's mission?"

"She said he would travel to help settle forests in the Unclaimed Territories."

"That is one truth, but more truths are untold. Balstei was entrusted with sacred mission by wise Nu'irg ust Momsúndo."

Alúma explained to Crysta and Hefra about the lava tubes waiting in the depths of the scablands, and how Balstei and Fingrenn were to work on transcribing and interpreting the writings Mamóru had etched in their walls.

"To safeguard the history of the last hundred thousand years," the queen concluded.

"What an incredible opportunity," Crysta said, her voice lowered in awe. "What an honor. I'm envious."

"Mamóru trusts your gray-faced friend, so we trust him, too. Convoy first shall settle lands for Laatu, find homes for our species, and only then your friend shall commence his other mission."

"All these species mixing up will cause complete chaos," Hefra observed. "I don't understand how this will work."

"Chaos breeds balance, given time. Laatu shamans have trained for this moment since Mindreldrolom was but a sapling. Noss provided us knowledge, great foresight. With companion species aiding, animals will spread diversity through your ravaged lands. Companion scalps know which niches to fill, which to avoid, which species to carry to aid in their mutual survival." She looked down at the big housecat. "Well, perhaps not all companions. Too many cats decided to stay here. Lazy. Useless." She smacked the calico a bit playfully, a bit petulantly. The cat huffed.

"Many creatures inevitably shall die," she continued. "Hopefully, enough thrive, in same way your people thrived centuries after Downfall consumed your cities. Perhaps the children of Mindreldrolom find balance sooner, in fewer than fifteen centuries. Though I will not be alive to see this story end, my heart is happy that I am alive to see it begin."

Crysta and Hefra spent their days walking around Arjum, studying, collecting, sharing. Ierun Alúma received constant updates from Balstei's convoy, which had already traveled over a hundred miles and was approaching the city of Alluviar. Soon they would circle around the western side of the Brasha'in Scablands, continue south past the sand-filled shores of the Esduss Sea, until they reached the uninhabited Udarbans Forest at the southern end of the Loorian Continent.

The pilgrims were faring well, despite some skirmishes and deaths. After the Laatu representatives met with the Arch Sedecims—exchanging plentiful soot and brime along with their stories—the rulers of the Zovarian Union decreed that instead of attacking the Laatu, cavalry and infantry troops were to follow the convoys merely to ensure order was maintained while the Laatu passed near populated areas.

On the twenty-eighth day of Dewrest, after a month had passed since Crysta and Hefra arrived in Arjum, the two of them met at the banyan root bridge over the Stiss Regu-Omen. It was nearing noon in the dome; above them, the bright arudinn shone in a tessellated mosaic, outlining polygonal holes that clutched the pure blackness of the night sky. Though they knew it was nearly midnight outside the dome, they could see no stars, as the bright vines obscured the subtleties of the darkness that hid beyond. The Moordusk Dome was caught in an in-between time, a transition period where day and night would blend for months to come, until only a spiderweb of vines connected the heavens.

"I asked that priest earlier about the changes in the weather," Hefra said.

Crysta nodded distractedly.

Hefra continued, "Like I'd guessed, there was something within the vines that kept the cycles of seasons and winds in check. Those branching growths we saw receding in the sky a few days back? I think they were some kind of mechanism to circulate air from the outside, perhaps blowing like giant bellows. I wish we'd had a telescope to study them before they shrunk away."

"Interesting," Crysta mumbled automatically. Her eyes were locked on the roaring river below them, but her mind was elsewhere.

Hefra didn't notice the dullness in her tone. "That priest said that the wind always used to come from the same places in the walls, that they used to be more predictable until the dome began to open. They knew the dome was breathing, that it was making its own clouds in some way. I think I want to visit Gwur Esmukh next. Did you know they grew an entire stadium of roots to play minquoll over? Imagine cats running in a spider's giant funnel web. Each province has their own field style, like the—"

"I think it's time," Crysta declared, straightening her back.

"Huh?" Hefra replied in confusion.

"This has been a wonder to behold, but it will take many months, maybe years for the rest of the dome to shrink and vanish. I've seen what I needed to see, and I'm happy I did."

"Honestly, I could stay in this city forever, if they'd let me," Hefra said. "I'd never run out of things to study."

"There are others who can undertake those tasks," Crysta said, referring to a group of scholars from Zovaria they'd seen the day before. The studious group was only one of many who'd ventured in already, looking to exchange information with the Laatu.

"Your point being?" Hefra inquired.

"I mean, I want to stay, too… But I think Balstei is onto something greater. Maybe I could help him. Maybe I'll find Lago there with him, who knows?"

"Look at you, sweetheart, turning into a thrill-seeking wayfarer all of a sudden. I understand what you are saying, I'm feeling that itch as well. I'd like to see how the convoys handle all those species, how the shamans make them work together. And Alúma said they travel with the Nu'irg, which I'm very curious to study as well. So, when are we heading out?"

"You want to come with me?"

"An adventurous spirit won't save your pretty face out there, you'd die in a matter of hours." She scanned Crysta up and down with a disapproving look, focusing on how she kept her elbows off the root bridge to avoid dirtying her silk shirt, which she had begun to wear once more. "I think you could use a hand, a new wardrobe, and my cutlass."

"We should ask Alúma if we could borrow a smilodon for our trip," Hefra said to Crysta the next day, as she stuffed her monstrous pack for their journey.

Alúma did not let them borrow a smilodon.

It was out of the question for the queen—the cats were on a mission, with strict roles, not there to serve the whims of New World visitors, no matter how honorable they were. The queen offered them a guide to help them reach the southern wall and gifted them vials of soot to trade. She wished them well but warned them they would be on their own once they left the Moordusk Dome.

Once they reached the port city of Nebush, they witnessed the intermixing of the races, sometimes on amiable terms, sometimes not so hospitably. There was tension in the air, but also a sense that a favoring wind was soon to bring a wholesome change.

They purchased supplies, including more appropriate clothing for Crysta, chosen by Hefra. They also bought two horses using their vials of soot. The farmer who sold them the horses was extremely grateful for the trade, but Hefra warned him to hurry to resell his soot before the powder devalued, telling him the supply of aetheric carbon would soon increase exponentially for all realms.

It took them over a month of constant travel to reach the Udarbans Forest; over the bridges of New Karst and Barnoy, past Alluviar and Alderstead, then following the coast of the Esduss Sea away from the singing sand dunes of Dunewaar. Eventually, they reached the untamed wilderness tucked between the sea, the scablands, and the long spine of the Stelm Sajal. They spotted smilodons in a wide clearing, and simple huts demarcating a lively village near recently plowed fields. Among the hairless and bare-chested citizens of this newly formed settlement, a man stood out with his striped doublet and his carefully trimmed gray beard.

Balstei was working a hoe into the fields. He saw the horses approach, wiped the sweat from his forehead, shaded his eyes with a calloused hand, and said, "What in Takh's two names are you wearing, Crysta?"

Chapter Fifty-Eight

Rilgsilv

Monarch Hallow's plan to take the Bighorn Dome was well underway.

The salt miners of Brinelaar and the potash miners of Caerlye had been hard at work for months, casting and firing pipe segments to allow Hallow's army to easily enter the dome. The pipes did not need to seal tightly; they only needed to hold together until the vines wrapped around them and locked them in place. Quantity over precision.

Before sending his army in, the monarch had ventured into the dome discreetly, followed by his private guard of arbalisters, whom he sent to scout the internal periphery to find the best locations to install his pipes.

The inside of the Bighorn Dome was an enormous valley trapped between the sierras of the Stelm Rilgéreo and Stelm Rilganesh. The vines that grew at those elevations did so more sideways instead of straight up, rooting at the summits of tall mountains. Luckily for the Negians, none of the citizens of the dome lived near the walls, so Fjorna and her arbalisters were able to safely scout from the perimeter.

Ferocious species of caprids inhabited this dome, many of which were extinct in the New World; they could be seen grazing in the valley, climbing up the steep cliffs, and herding by the expansive lakes and rivers. There were the corkscrew-horned markhors, gold-furred takins, and thick-humped makapanias. There were also graceful oryxes, impalas, and serows. But the mightiest of all were the companion species: the Rashúrian ibexes and bighorn sheep—

both of which had grown to nearly the size of horses—and the thick-helmed bootheriums, also known as helmeted muskoxen, who were thrice as large.

A ring-shaped lake marked the center of Rilgdrolom, and from it a black mountain arose, so tall that it seemed to graze the top of the dome. The volcanic prominence was cracked in half, with the central trunk of the dome wedged between the mirrored halves. The beauty of it was incomparable, though neither the monarch nor his subjects paid attention to such things.

The Red Stag waited with Crescu Valaran, sitting in a secluded boulder field while discussing Crescu's training—it had not gone as well as they had hoped.

"I can do it, partially," Crescu said, nervously tapping his fingers over Krostsilv, which he held in his lap. "They will obey me, as I showed you last week. But once they get hurt, once I feel their pain, I lose it."

The Red Stag sucked on his cheeks, visibly disappointed. "Why do you care if they hurt? They are mere weasels, badgers, raccoons—no offense. They're worth even less than the soldiers we send to die for our cause, yet you've shown no qualms about directing a platoon into the frontlines. You have to free your mind from these thoughts. Focus on our goals, not on their insignificant lives."

"I have been trying, Monarch Hallow. But the mask… it has affected the way I see things." He smiled as Dishu, the yellow-throated marten that he kept as a pet, wormed her way out of his sleeve and perched atop his mask. "It's just… I feel the way they feel," he continued as he petted the mustelid. "And the mask creates this connection where I begin to care for—"

"Nonsense," the Red Stag said, backhanding the marten off the mask. Dishu yelped as she landed on the dirt, then squirmed behind a rock.

Crescu tensed up, wanting to react but unwilling to defy his monarch.

"That hurt you as well, didn't it?" the Red Stag asked. "Yet Krostsilv is not covering your stupefied face. Do not blame the mask for your flaws, Crescu. Whatever hypocritical feelings you have are yours to own. You are a good general, you know how to command your legion. Now learn how to control your fucking pets, or by the Shade of Yza, I will find myself a different Silv-Thaar who can."

"Is that why you hired those shaman mercenaries?"

The Red Stag leaned back and remained silent. He used his quaar-shafted spear to poke absentmindedly at a dead grasshopper. As a masterful spearman, Crescu was jealous of the majestic replica of the Spear of Undoing the Red Stag wielded and was irked that his monarch hadn't even used it once—he merely had it for display.

"So, it's true," Crescu pressed. "It's not the generals who will be next in line."

"Not in the way you think, Crescu. Yes, the twelve shamans Urcai sent are invaluable to keep in communication with Hestfell, given they each control multiple heralds. They were trained in Wastyr, and are indispensable for this mission, but they are also loyal to the Empire. But what matters is that, given their background, they should be able to learn to wield the masks and control their animals much quicker than any of us."

He locked eyes with Crescu, then softened a little. "I'm not looking to replace you, if that is what you are wondering. My goal has always been to gift the masks to our generals—though perhaps not all of them—before anyone else. But soon we will have more masks than active generals following us, and we'll need to make quick use of them. We can't waste weeks learning to wield them—the new Silv-Thaars will need to take hold of their beasts immediately, even during battle. But even if—"

Footsteps. Their heads rose. The Red Stag placed his hand on the hilt of his sword; Crescu readied his spear. They relaxed as they saw it was just Fjorna and Aurélien. The women had just returned from a two-day trip north, where they had approached a village from which a cloud of dust and smoke had billowed recently.

"Monarch Hallow," Fjorna said, stopping in front of the men. "A positive development, perhaps. This dome is peculiar—it's not one tribe inhabiting it, but two, perhaps more. They are at war with each other."

The Red Stag tipped his rack to signal for her to continue.

"The tribe that lives west of the lake was being attacked by those huge muskoxen, and hundreds of infantry as well. The caprids worked too well with each other, without suffering the odd spams the mindlocked creatures get. I think they were doing it out of their own free will. The tribe controlling the mask seems to be trying to keep the western folk at bay, pushing their territory back, but they don't seem interested in killing them outright. They could've easily trampled them to bits with so many animals at their disposal, but instead just tore down their village."

"Interesting," he mulled over her words. "How strong are the legions of this western tribe?"

"It's hard to know where their territory begins or ends, as it goes up into the mountains. But given the quantity of settlements and roads we've seen, their numbers must be vast."

"It's a much greater force than those at Anglass and Lequa," Aurélien said. "They seem smarter, making better use of their resources than the other Miscam. It's hard to tell from this distance, but the eastern half of the dome seems less populated, covered in wilderness."

"Perhaps the ones controlling the mask are protecting that territory," the Red Stag hypothesized, scratching at his dewlap. "We could take advantage of this situation, but we need more information. Fjorna, I want you to capture a member of this western tribe and bring them to me. Treat them with respect. I don't want them to distrust us, but do not let them alert anyone. You mustn't be seen, and you must leave no tracks."

And so Fjorna did. Three days later, she returned with a farmer named Uldan. Helped by Aurélien, who knew enough Miscamish to interpret between them, the Red Stag persuaded Uldan to tell the story of his tribe's recent struggles.

The Miscam tribes in this dome were named the Ikhel. The Western Ikhel had been at war with the Eastern Ikhel for hundreds of years. The Western Ikhel wanted to open up the dome and live in the outside world, believing it was time to walk freely under the blue sky once more, but the Eastern Ikhel were too strong, holding command of all the caprids in the vast dome. They ignored the pleas of their western cousins, having chosen to wait the entire two thousand years Noss had commanded them to wait.

Refusing to follow the rules imposed by the ancients, the Western Ikhel began to seize control of the lands, making use of them as they saw fit, birthing many more children than was allowed by their laws. They were growing stronger, but still could not compete with the strength of Rilgsilv and the loyal companion species. Although Uldan did not describe them as such, the Eastern Ikhel had been merciful, leniently pushing their enemies westward and limiting their lands so that they could breed no further, though sometimes that required killing some of them.

Uldan was spellbound as he recounted his story. He had only seen the Rilgfröa from far away once, and now he was talking with the Urgfröa and the Krostfröa, who said they had come from the outside to free this dome from its doom and were promising power and wealth not just for Uldan, but for the entire Western Ikhel tribe.

One new thing that the Red Stag learned from Uldan's tale was that the Silvesh could be used to open the domes in their entirety. The monarch didn't know how to go about doing that—and the farmer clearly didn't know either—but it was something he was very interested in discovering.

A meeting between the leader of the Western Ikhel and the Red Stag was arranged in utmost secrecy, thanks to Uldan's discreet aid. Luhásu was the chief's name. She met the Red Stag in the privacy of a dark basalt cave, by the warmth of a crackling fire.

To prepare for the meeting, the Red Stag had ordered his servants to paint his muzzle, antlers, and brows in an intimidating and striking red pattern, brushing off all the fur clumps. He was wearing his red leather armor, decorated with golden studs sprouting over spiraling filigrees. His silver pauldrons gleamed, rimmed in black, encrusted with rhodonite crystals in the shape and color of his sigil. He held in one hand Ockam's quaar shield, which he called Gaönir-Bijeor, like the legendary Shield of Creation; and in the other, his new quaar-shafted Spear of Undoing, Tor-Reveo.

Luhásu was formidable. She had warrior's blood and showed neither fear nor respect when entering the cave, even in the presence of the Urgfröa and Krostfröa. The Red Stag liked that.

Luhásu had brown skin and yellow eyes and was dressed in an armor of bones and metal plates held by many belts. She wielded a shield made from the helmeted skull of a bootherium as well as a long-shafted ice axe that had a sharp blade on one end and a piercing pick on the other. She spoke of the centuries of oppression her tribe had suffered, how the Eastern Ikhel held strong, keeping her tribe from expanding and enjoying the bounty of their limited terrain.

That evening, the Red Stag took Luhásu out to see the vastness of the lands outside the Bighorn Dome. Luhásu froze at the utter madness of the vast sky of blue that shone while her dome slept, of the unreachable new horizons. "I knew it all along," she whispered in awe while Aurélien interpreted. "My blood told me so, it pumped hard to tell me that the time to see the world of the ancients was at hand."

"There is much more beyond these hills and mountains," the Red Stag said. "An entire sea spreads beyond where your eyes can see. A massive continent past that." He waited, never pushing, knowing full well what Luhásu would request of him next.

"I propose to you an alliance," Luhásu said at last. "I will lead you through Rilgdrolom and help you vanquish the Eastern Ikhel, but in return I shall become the wielder of Rilgsilv."

"Just the Silv in exchange for your aid?" the Red Stag questioned, as if confounded by such a small request. He believed in Luhásu, and he needed her help. He wasn't concerned if she changed her mind at some point, as he could easily kill her, take the mask, and move on. But she showed promise, strength, ambition, and most of all, ruthlessness, which was something lacking in Silv-Thaar Valaran.

"It is all we Western Ikhel wish for," Luhásu said.

The Red Stag paced around, pretending to consider. "Most of the Miscam were misguided in their ways," he said. "The land they worked so hard to upkeep, to control, ended up controlling them, as was the case with your eastern cousins. You have lived for generations in a constrained world. Let me propose something in return, Luhásu, daughter of Neithua, born of the True Ikhel. Take control of Rilgsilv, but join me in liberating the other domes that remain sealed. Command a legion of caprid beasts and help me take the lands others have squandered. Conquer in the name of the Negian Empire and expand the reach of the Ikhel race to lands thousandfold richer and more fertile than any you've yet witnessed."

Chapter Fifty-Nine

Hold

Sterjall was awoken by a soft rustle. He cracked his eyelids open and saw Kulak furtively leaving his root-woven bed at the 'tween deck, headed upstairs.

Where is he off to? he wondered. He got out of bed silently and wrapped his cloak over his tunic as he exited into the early morning light. His piercing amber eyes glowed eerily from within the compound shadows of his black-and-gray fur and hood.

He shivered as he stepped onto the deck. It was cold out at sea. He was beginning to regret having let Alaia cut holes in his hood so his ears could pop out—although it was comfortable, the modifications did a poor job of holding the cold at bay. They were only as far north as Withervale, but the Quiescent Ocean was always frigid, and it brought with it a cold snap whenever the western winds blew into the Isdinnklad, freezing Teslurkath and Fjordsulf even as early as Autumn.

He nodded at a couple of sailors and at Kenondok, who had just come down the ratlines, then scanned around for Kulak, but could not spot him. Kenondok soon returned with something in his hands. "Do not understand why you so cold, under so much fur," the brawny man said. "But take this. Helps stay dry." He held open a green oilskin coat of the kind all the sailors were wearing and wrapped it over the wolf's shoulders.

"Th-thank you," Sterjall replied, cinching the coat's belt. He felt immediate relief under the light garment, which draped down to his ankles and was fully waterproof and better at resisting the unrelenting sea spray.

"Khuron is at stern," Kenondok said, noticing Sterjall's searching eyes, then left in the opposite direction.

Sterjall joined Kulak atop the quarterdeck, standing shoulder to shoulder to absorb a bit of heat from him. Kulak was wearing the same kind of oilskin coat, while his head was covered with a gray knit cap with embroidered holes cut for his ears. His black ear tufts slapped around in the changing winds, like flags trying to send out a warning signal.

"Looks good on you," Kulak observed, glancing to his side. He scooted even closer, taking a handpaw out of his pocket only to place it inside Sterjall's own pocket, where no one could see their fingers brushing over each other.

Sterjall noticed Kulak's eyes were caught by the curve of the receding Moordusk Dome; it looked as if it was sinking into the Isdinnklad's waters. "They'll be alright," he murmured.

"My scalp knows. But it wonders when I see home once more. Long time, it might be." He inhaled a cold breath, then asked, "How long until Nagradrolom?"

"Hud Ilsed said that with these wind conditions, it'll take us two full days or so. But it should become visible soon enough." He kept staring at Kulak, who looked beautiful in a melancholy sort of way.

"I thought you'd be happier, leaving the dome again," Sterjall said.

"My scalp can be both happy and sad. But more happy, when with you."

Sterjall smiled, feeling Kulak's handpaw tighten around his. He felt the prince shiver. "Hey," he said abruptly, "it's too cold and gloomy up here. Come with me."

"Come where?"

"Just follow me," Sterjall said, and led Kulak down the steps to the 'tween deck. He saw Kitjári and Alaia still asleep, and continued down to the orlop deck, where a handful of sailors were drinking braaw while most snored next to munnji crates. No one paid attention to the two young men, who continued deeper still into the hold, which was packed with provisions for the long journey.

Sterjall wordlessly guided Kulak toward the farthest corner of the hold. Only a hint of light shone this deep into the ship, coming from where the stairs opened in the ceiling. On a wide platform a few feet off the ground were the backup sails, hiding beneath a tangle of ropes. Sterjall stopped there and faced Kulak.

"Last time we were down here, your eyes told me you were planning something," Sterjall said. "Well, before Alaia interrupted us."

"Maybe I was testing waters," Kulak admitted.

"You've been pushy... but I'm glad of that. You told me to tell you what I want, once I'm ready. Well..." He didn't know how to finish that sentence, and it didn't seem necessary to finish it anyway. In a playful but rough manner, he grabbed Kulak and pushed him down onto the platform, making him land on the ropes and soft sails, then jumped on top of him and brought their muzzles together.

He spread Kulak's coat open and ran his handpaws over the prince's soft chest fur, then his claws slid lower and flipped Kulak's kilt up. It felt unnecessary to undress him further: the shodog was already open at the front, and the kilt offered easy access to his wandering paws.

For the first time, Sterjall explored the mystery between Kulak's legs. The caracal's crotch was covered in short, silky fur, with pink skin warmly blushing underneath; it was wildly different from Aio's perfectly smooth crotch, yet it had equally sensual curves. The wolf pushed the tight sheath down to reveal the small and strangely barbed cock, which reminded him of Kulak's tongue. He puckered his muzzle around it while his claws teased the tiny, fuzz-covered balls.

Kulak suppressed a moan.

Sterjall widened his maw and enveloped the entirety of Kulak's crotch, working his tongue around all of it, sliding the slick muscle up the underside to then wrap around the hardened cock. Kulak tensed at the feeling of the sharp teeth—but they weren't pressing down, just holding him in place.

Sterjall pulled his muzzle back, panting. He hurriedly cast his coat off, then unfastened his brooch and hurled it and his cloak away. He unbuckled his belt and dropped his trousers.

He admired the body in front of him, but only for a single breath. He moved his hips closer to Kulak, who regarded him with a mix of anxiety and eagerness. The wolf did not need to tease his cock from its sheath, it was already out and throbbing. He pressed it between the caracal's asscheeks and—

"—Khuron? *Je väujun imirr sa hiennat!*" a deep voice called. "*Khienn elluss ma mad?*"

Sterjall quickly pulled his trousers up, feeling the shadows move as a lantern brightened the hold behind him. Kulak hurried to his feet as well, having a much easier time by simply letting his kilt drape down. He walked away from Sterjall, as if pacing around the hold while nonchalantly fixing his knit cap back into place.

"I am here, Kenondok," he replied in Miscamish.

"The captain is looking for you," Kenondok repeated. "What are you doing down here?"

"Showing Sterjall where we keep the spare sails," Kulak said.

The weaponsmith lifted his lantern and spotted the wolf in the back of the hold, fumbling with his brooch. Sterjall circled around some barrels and hurried past him, nodding awkwardly.

"She is in her quarters," Kenondok said, walking deeper into the hold while the young men headed up the stairs. "Lago-Sterjall!" he then called.

Sterjall froze.

Kenondok walked to him and tossed him his coat. "Forgot this," he said with an expression as hard and flat as a brick.

"Thank you," Sterjall mumbled, then hurried up the stairs.

Chapter Sixty

A Flower of Deep Time

The Fjordlands Dome loomed monumentally tall and imposing before *Drolvisdinn*. Even in the haze, something about its color was eerie, the dome seeming bluer than it should be. Its snowcap was unbalanced, thicker on the western side, where the Quiescent Ocean's gelid winds struck hardest. *It looks too white for this early in the season*, Sterjall thought—but that was the way of the frozen lands of the northwest.

This far into the Isdinnklad, they could even see what they believed to be the top of the Varanus Dome, far to the southwest. It was barely an edge of an immaterial silhouette, which might have been a distant cloud, but there was something too still and unnerving about it for it to be merely a cloud.

Hud Ilsed calculated they'd reach their destination that afternoon.

Sterjall came up from the 'tween deck and immediately began to shiver from the cold. He pulled out the brime cube Kulak had gifted to him and held it like one would hold a hot mug, feeling quite thankful for its warmth. He looked up—Sunu was sitting cross-legged in the crow's nest, with Olo hovering above them. The wolf looked around the ship and saw Kitjári at the stern, who had borrowed his binoculars to scout for potential threats. He passed by Alaia, who was brushing Pichi's beach-colored fur; Pichi was loving the distraction, for the brushing made her temporarily forget about her seasickness. Kulak was there too, trying to comfort Blu, who was curled around the mainmast, also not feeling his best. Sterjall took the steps up to the bow and spotted Mamóru—the Nu'irg was holding so still that a gull had landed on the tusks of his dark mask, which hung by his hip. *Perhaps the gull thinks him a new figurehead,* Sterjall thought as he approached.

"Aren't you cold?" he asked, his misty breath blowing away quickly. The western breeze carried a frigid spray of seawater, yet Mamóru was only wearing his usual white robe. His braided beard sparkled with salty droplets.

"Very cold," Mamóru replied. "Extremely cold, I would say, but I haven't felt this alive in so, so long."

"Were you a sailor?"

Mamóru smiled. He took out his long-stemmed pipe and opened one of the four mistleaf pouches that dangled from his belt. He packed the pipe carefully with pinches of a spicier mistleaf this time, one with hints of cardamom.

"Not a sailor, no," he said, lighting his pipe. "I never learned the ropes. But I traveled aboard many a ship before, journeying far and away to study cultures much different from any I had encountered before. I feel as if the more one can understand and connect with others, the more alive one is—and I always had a fondness for living."

"Well, you've done it longer than anyone else, so I guess you found what you were looking for."

"Perhaps, agnurf son, perhaps." The spicy smoke drifted out from between his chapped lips.

Sterjall stared at the still-healing scabs on the old man's face, then said, "Banook told us the Nu'irgesh were supposed to heal fast. We even saw him mangle his toes and fully recover in just a couple of days. It's been weeks, but your injuries are still showing."

"I will mend, it will merely take me longer. I don't have the means Banook or the other Nu'irgesh have. We are, in a sense, the embodied wholes of our kinds. When we shapeshift, when we heal, it is the energy of our kindred that we tap into. Now I have to depend on my own cells and metabolism, and the meager energy Momsúndosilv provides me with. Humans, unfortunately, cannot feed me in the way my own clade could."

"I've been wondering," Sterjall continued, "why do some Nu'irgesh take a human form, but not forms from any other clades? Or does that happen as well?"

"Not that I know of," the old man answered. "Humans are... I don't know how to explain it—there is something fascinating about you. Forgive me if I speak in the third person, for I am human as well, but not in the exact same way you are. Humans are deeply flawed, yet there's a spark within them that makes them... alluring."

"I don't know," the wolf muttered, staring at his footpaws. "We seem to simply bring trouble. There's not much that is special about us, we can't even mindspeak."

"Yet many of you share that passion for discovery, that hunger for knowledge. That is a charm other species have not, or if they do, they have it to a smaller degree." He let smoke flow out of his nostrils, allowing the wind to tease it away from him. "It is the reason I chose to take a human form. The quest for understanding the nature of the forces that make us who we are has kept my flame burning for all these years. Yet I don't know what makes humans special, truly. Perhaps there is a threshold they crossed at some point in their endless making, a gap bridged not by becoming something superior or righteous, but simply by developing an enhanced potential. Now that I think of it, perhaps humans aren't special at all, not in the grand scheme of things—they are merely consequential."

Mamóru smirked, wandering through a memory, then shook his head. "Did I ever tell you how intensely the Acoapóshi disliked me?"

"Disliked you? Are you joking?"

"I jest not. They had a severe aversion to me for no other reason than my having taken the form of a man. Well, perhaps there were a few other reasons... I liked to question their customs, and influenced the Toldask Miscam away from the Acoapóshi way of life. The greatest flawed belief the Acoapóshi held to their chests was that they were superior to the other seventeen tribes, and thus they wanted to change them in their own image."

"But what was so wrong about you being a human?"

"In their minds, it was unnatural. They could not tolerate that I'd dare intrude into the clade of 'their' Nu'irg, Buujik. Not that she'd give it a moment's thought... she didn't care much for the Acoapóshi either way. Strange people, those in that tribe. But they performed the greatest of goods. They saved us all, in the end."

"Did they hate Banook for it too, then?"

"I don't think they ever found out. Banook didn't take his human form until much later, when the tribes were far from one another growing their domes. They wouldn't have approved, is my guess. They were far too obstinate."

They both kept their eyes on the approaching curve of the Fjordlands Dome.

"Do you ever miss the way things were before the Downfall?" Sterjall asked, unprompted.

"I always do. But those moments still live within me every time I remember them, so they are not truly gone, not until my own spark flickers out. And even then, they will live on—albeit in a much lesser form—in the writings I left at the Istrilm Sanctum. All these stories, all these friends, lovers, and enemies we lose, are never truly gone."

"That sounds comforting," Sterjall said. "But I honestly have a hard time believing it. When someone dies, they truly die, unless you believe in the Takh Codex or some other stupid text."

"It sounds to me like you are thinking of someone in particular."

Sterjall remained quiet. The sound of the gulls, the ruffling of his fur by the Isdinnklad's breeze, they had made him recall being on the catamaran with Ockam's body by his side. He could feel the presence of the bear's eyes, those deep black eyes that had stared straight into his soul until the bear's last breath was exhaled. Sterjall put a handpaw over his Sceres-shaped brooch, sighing at the sense of loss that accompanied those memories.

Mamóru shivered, apparently feeling the cold for the first time. "This person you are thinking of, do you miss them?" he asked.

"Yes. I miss him."

"Did you miss him before you met him?"

"What do you mean?"

"Before the two of you met. Assuming you hadn't known him for your entire life. Did you have this feeling of longing and loss about him before he came into your life?"

"But that's not how things work. What is it that you are getting at?"

"Say you are strolling on a breezy mountain path, and you come upon an exquisite, golden flower. It is the most beautiful flower your eyes have ever beheld. Stupefied, you stop and gaze upon its perfection, rejoicing in its uniqueness and splendor. But one day, the flower withers and dies, slowly crumbling into the sands and rocks that once fed it."

The puff of smoke coming out of Mamóru's mouth was pulled quickly from bow to stern, vanishing as if it had never been there. He continued, "There was a period in time in which there was no flower, then a moment in which it existed and brought you happiness, followed by yet another period in which the flower was no more and you began to miss it. Both the stretch of time before and the one after are equally infinite. That moment in the middle—in which the flower brought you so much joy—only existed for the briefest of times, immeasurably short when compared to the eternities before and after. Why is it then, Lago-Sterjall, that you only miss the flower for that one particular infinite stretch that lies ahead of you? Why do you not feel downcast and forlorn during all that time before, when the flower also did not exist?"

"I'm not entirely sure I follow. The past is in the past. Missing someone is about now and about what comes later, not before."

"For you, that may be the case, because you live in the present, and your limited brain thinks it only moves forward in time. But that doesn't mean that the entirety of reality operates in the same way your brain perceives it. Imagine you live in a dark and empty universe, one that is infinitely vast and vacant. One day, as you travel through the nothingness of the cosmos, you find that same magnificent golden flower. It is the only thing you've ever seen, as the universe itself holds nothing more than you, the flower, and endless space. You know this golden flower is immortal—it's been there forever before and will perdure an eternity into the future. Would you feel sad if you had to walk away from it?"

"Not as sad as with the previous example," Sterjall replied almost immediately.

"Why so?"

"I think... because I would know the flower is still out there, somewhere, even if I'm not next to it."

"Yet space is only one more dimension, just as time is. You moving away from the flower in one or all dimensions of space does not make you as sad, does not leave you hopeless. Yet time makes you feel as if only the closeness of now matters, and perhaps an extremely shortsighted number of days or years in the near future. Why should time hold that much power over you? Did the flower in my former example not live through only the briefest moment in time, which is as insignificantly small as the amount of space the flower occupied in the vastness of the latter example?"

"This is no longer as comforting as I thought it was."

"It is not necessarily meant to be. This person you miss so much... after you die, even after we all die and the Endfall sucks away the light of all stars, he will always and *forever* have been that person you loved in that one stretch of time, and *that* is unchanging and eternal. Just because you are unable to travel back in time—as you could have walked through space to see that golden flower in the empty cosmos—it does not mean that those moments did not happen and are not there throughout eternity."

Mamóru's eyes narrowed imperceptibly. "We are extremely limited beings, only able to perceive an inadequate portion of all that surrounds us. In the same way that we never even knew that our own planet—the very ground we stepped, spat, bled, and shat on—was alive the whole time, in that same way we still don't see the whole picture when it comes to the incomprehensible vastness of deep time."

"I think I understand what you are trying to say," Sterjall said. "Yes, I'm limited, we all are. That's the problem. I have to live with these limitations, and within these limitations I miss Ockam, and there's nothing I can do to help it. I don't believe in an afterlife, and your parables are but a cold substitute to those fragile self-delusions."

Sterjall turned away, ashamed of his abrasive tone. He averted Mamóru's gaze, looking down at the fast-moving water.

The old man continued smoking. "Yet you've seen your limitations withdraw, agnurf son, in very recent times. I don't believe you'll ever overcome the dark chasm that deep time carves in front and behind us, but with the help of Agnargsilv, you've experienced things your own mind could not have imagined prior to wielding it. These new qualia you've experienced, these new ways of perception are now a part of you. And thus I feel there is yet hope. Perhaps the experience of deep time is merely another layer of qualia we have not yet uncovered, one that our minds are not yet ready to experience or are not complex enough to process."

Mamóru unhooked the mask from his belt and held it in front of him.

"These masks are wonderful tools that let us glimpse into new concepts such as we've discussed. We learn how our finite senses are attuned to only a narrow strip of data while so much more awaits beyond our means of perception. What does it feel like to see empathy? To be different inside and out? How do the qualia that a human experiences compare to those of a wolf, an elephant, a fish, a tree, a rock? I know a few of these from my experience as a Nu'irg, you do through being the Agnargfröa.

"Perhaps therein lies the answer to grasping the mysteries of the cosmos, in learning to understand our extended family of beings—whether those similar to us or wildly unlike us—and thus learning to understand ourselves. Only through that effort shall we further expand our consciousnesses."

Mamóru's pipe had gone cold. He relit it, and in a cloud of spicy smoke exhaled one final thought. "These ideas will not bring your friend, Ockam, back from the dead. Nothing will. But perhaps there is a momentary breath of solace to be found once we understand that our limitations don't define reality, and that eternity—even if unreachable to us—exists within the briefest moments in time."

Chapter Sixty-One

Fjordlands

"That peninsula must be Fel Spur," Kitjári said, as *Drolvisdinn* approached a rocky landmass extending south from the Fjordlands Dome. She nodded to Hud Ilsed. "Let's keep west of it, away from the inhabited islands."

They had seen plenty of fishing vessels earlier in the day, always in the direction of Koroberg and the many islands southeast of the dome, so they had sailed west to find a more furtive way to enter it.

Ilsed directed her crew to circle around the peninsula, then to continue north in the open waters between Fel Spur and Feli'i Spur. Their green sails hurried them in their final approach toward the dome.

"Ship comes! Northwest!" Abjus yelled from the foredeck.

Ilsed spied it with the binoculars. "Sails blue like New World sky," she informed them.

"Khaar Du merchants," Kitjári said. "They're headed directly toward us. Sail past them. Move the smilodons below deck."

They did as she commanded and veered slightly, but the blue-flagged ship matched their course to intercept them. The Silvfröash shifted to their human forms and hid their masks.

"They are probably wondering what nethervoid we spawned from," Jiara mused. "They are just curious, not necessarily dangerous."

"But they could bring trouble back to us," Lago said.

The incoming ship was a classic Khaar Du galley, with sails promptly being reefed, its passengers all waving politely. *Drolvisdinn* rudely blew past it. Yells and whistles came from the galley, from sailors both curious and upset at the ship that ignored them. But one thing was for certain: the Khaar Du would remember this encounter. *Drolvisdinn* was a wonder to behold, its construction like nothing the northern tribe had ever seen before.

"Khest, they are turning around," Jiara swore. The galley had extended oars to more quickly shift course.

"Blue-sailed ship is too heavy," Ilsed remarked, "it cannot outsail *Drolvisdinn*."

"They can't outsail us," Jiara agreed, "but we can't let them see us go into the dome. Head to those islands, over there."

Drolvisdinn performed a quick maneuver around a rocky headland. The galley's sails billowed behind them, in sluggish pursuit, but soon the Laatu ship had moved behind cover. They meandered around another jagged point, then changed course again, now making directly for the vines. Sails were reefed, and oars rowed backward, slowing them down. The Silvfröash returned to their half-forms, getting ready.

"Don't slow too much!" Sterjall said. "We'll open the vines from a distance, keep moving!" With Leif held in his outstretched hand, he began opening a tunnel into the dome's wall long before they were close enough to enter it, but it was much too narrow. "Help me out," he called to the others.

Kulak took out a quaar conduit from his disassembled blowgun, while Alaia handed one of hers to Kitjári. Together the Silvfröash aimed their empathic focus, widening the path to let *Drolvisdinn* glide in. The crew used their push poles to keep the vessel from snagging on the vines to either side.

Once the entire ship was inside the tunnel, Sterjall rushed to the stern and willed the vines to close behind them. As the vines contracted like a light-frightened pupil, Sterjall spotted the galley through the closing circle. *I hope they didn't see us sail through the vines.*

Lamps were lit, illuminating a cathedral of thorns. The splashing water did not echo around them but faded strangely on the textured walls.

Drolvisdinn moved in deeper to explore the depths of Nagradrolom, the Fjordlands Dome.

When nearly half a mile of wall had been breached, the waters began to rock them up and down, sending *Drolvisdinn* dangerously close to the vines. Push poles pressed hard, trying to stabilize the vessel.

"What is happening?" Alaia screamed as the sound of the water splashing was joined by a strange howling that rumbled from beyond the vines. Then they heard the crack of thunder.

"A storm brews within the dome," Mamóru explained. "If we stay here, our hull might shatter. Either we continue in, or we turn around."

A flash lit up vines right in front of them. Thunder reverberated three heartbeats later.

"We are almost inside!" Ilsed exclaimed. Then, in Miscamish, she addressed her crew, "Push away from white blood vines. Push, unrelenting as the tides!"

The world tumbled and flashed. They exited the vines into a torrent of rain. A gale was forcing the waves high, aiming to hurl the ship back against the wall. Gusts of wind and water slapped at them frenetically. Luckily, their sails had already been reefed, as otherwise the strain would have shattered the masts.

"Should we try to go back inside?" Sterjall suggested, though no one was listening. Either way, it would be no easy feat to reenter the vine tunnel while the ship bobbed up, down, and sideways. Staying close to the vines was too treacherous, so the Laatu rowed north against the enormous waves, with almost no visibility to aid them.

"Rocks off the starboard beam!" Ilsed warned.

It wasn't just rocks, but a monolithic vertical wall, reaching so high that even when lit by lightning, its cloud-veiled top could not be glimpsed. They veered to port, trapping themselves in a channel between the rock wall and the vine wall.

"Into the wind!" Ilsed commanded.

The oars pulled hard and redirected the ship to prevent it from tipping over. The keel sliced a foamy streak behind them, while the prow lifted and dropped like a sledgehammer onto the waves. The ship was heavy with cargo in the hold, so it held its position and was able to face the wind. Green sails loosened their bindings and flapped madly, threatening to succumb to the tempest. Sailors tried to wrangle the canvas under control, risking being tossed overboard.

A mighty wave hurled the vessel to port, and although *Drolvisdinn* did not tip over, the tallest masthead snagged on a vine that pulled it in. Lines from the mainsail tangled and snapped, sending the boom flying sideways, but releasing them from the trap. Sailors rowed hard while more of them battled to restrain the swinging boom. The vessel floated further northwest, away from the wall of the dome. Soon they found themselves safe from rock and vine, but waves were still trying to swallow them while rain bucketed down upon them.

Drolvisdinn's crew was alert, operating without the need for instructions. They withstood the storm's ire for two more hours, until the sea and the wind gave up, and all was calm again. Brief flashes of lightning revealed the dreary nightscape: nothing but water and steep walls.

As they sailed into the unknown, an icy-white glow became apparent atop the cliffs to starboard. The light abruptly vanished behind clouds.

"Did you see that?" Sterjall asked.

"My eyes saw it," Ilsed answered. "Perhaps a lighthouse? Yet very dim."

The glow returned, but this time upon a completely different cliff and as four separate dots. The lights were as cool as the icebergs of the Ash Sea and held a wide aura of softness due to the cloud enveloping them.

For the next several hours they rowed, trying to follow the bright apparitions that materialized and vanished atop the cliffs. The lights were often lined up in horizontal rows, sometimes a dozen visible at once, but the mists only let them glimpse transient smears, nothing more defined.

Although hiding behind miles of clouds, the trunk of the Fjordlands Dome lit up some time later. As the day brightened—albeit not by much—the cold beacons became harder to spot. The dim daylight let the ship's crew finally assess the destruction the storm had caused. They set out to fix what they could.

"Hold carries storm sails," Hud Ilsed said. "If only our scalps had known better. Sail battens become broken. Mending and rigging sails much laborious, time-consuming. For now, oars and foresail help us get to shore."

The rain had replenished the headlands, and they were emptying out now, bathing the fjords in myriad waterfalls that descended in thunderous fogs. Some falls were but mere tendrils of thin white, some were veils that evaporated before hitting the waves, while others were unstoppable deluges of white and brown rainwater.

A dozen miles in, the fjord they were entering split into three passages. Northward it cut much deeper between the cliffs, with the distant horizon partially hidden by one of the supporting vine columns. To the west a shallower but wider channel headed back toward the dome's wall. To the east an inlet extended for a handful of miles, with rocky headlands on either side that descended to a slope where the fjord was fed by a foaming creek.

"My eyes see more glowing lights toward the inlet," Kulak said, "shining within standing stones."

Kitjári asked for the binoculars. "What are they?" she asked. "They remind me of the streetlights of Zovaria."

Mamóru squinted at the distant forms. "Lodestones," he replied. "They are markers, pathways to follow."

"Like cairns?" Sterjall asked.

"Like cairns," Mamóru agreed, "only brighter. But I have never seen ones burning with such cold fires—the ones I once saw in these lands burned with orange flames."

"Stones lead to inlet's bottom," Ilsed said. "Waters are calm, and *Drolvisdinn* eager to rest."

As they entered the inlet, they got a better view of the standing stones. Like perpetual sentinels, the lodestones stood along the entire edge of the cliffs, about a stone's throw apart from each other. They were of varied heights, some only half as tall as a person, some up to five times as tall. At the top of each, a cold light burned.

"We are followed," Kenondok warned, pointing his lips toward shapes drifting along the lodestone path. They were hulking hogs, larger than any pigs or boars they had ever seen, with tusks rivaling those of proboscideans. The suids were curious, weaving between the lights while keeping a safe distance.

The ship reached the end of the inlet, where a cascading stream emptied its overfilled bladder onto rocks that groaned and foamed. They were separated from the stream by a rock platform that cradled a quieter, still pool of water—the remains of an ancient pier that was now too eroded and covered in barnacles. On the shore to starboard, splintering masts and shards of rotten hulls stuck out from the sharp rocks, with guillemots, gannets, and pelicans nesting among the debris.

They rowed into the placid pool until *Drolvisdinn* softly leaned on the side of the pier. The crew tied the ship to the few still-standing pillars, then lowered the ramp.

Hud Ilsed stepped down and checked for signs of wear on the rocks. "This pier is forgotten," she said. "No feet have walked on it, no ship has docked on it, for many cycles of the seasons."

"We should climb up the hill," Sterjall recommended, "perhaps follow the lodestones."

They packed Pichi's harness with their bags, and everyone but the ship's crew headed out to explore. Mamóru was too weak to walk at the speed of the others, so they let him ride on Blu. Both smilodons were ecstatic to be back on dry land—or rather, very wet land—so much so that Kulak had to scold Blu for rushing off in a gallop too joyfully, nearly hurling Mamóru off the pier.

It had begun to softly drizzle, making it hard to see, but the weather at least helped keep mosquitoes away. At the end of the long pier, the gigantic boars snorted, showing their angled silhouettes and disappearing once the wayfarers got too close. The pier ended in carved stone steps which were cascading softly with rainwater. They took care ascending the slippery steps, until they reached the line of lodestones.

"Look, it's not fire," Sterjall said, approaching one of the lower stones, which had its concave top at chest level. "What is this glowing thing?" He walked around the carved boulder and could not understand what he was seeing.

Suspended by a braided copper armature above the lodestone's hollowed top was a white-glowing object about the size of an apple. The object reflected into the water pooled at the lodestone's top, shining doubly, and also refracted thousandfold from droplets that had landed over it. Softened by distance and fog, its glow had seemed dim, but up close it was too bright to gaze at directly. Sterjall reached out with a handpaw to touch it, squinting all the while.

"Hey, be careful!" Alaia said. "It might be hot or dangerous."

"It's not hot, I can feel it," Sterjall said, hovering his handpaws close to the glowing object. He lightly rubbed a paw pad on the rough, knapped surface—it felt and looked as cold as the drizzle that coated it. "How are they glowing without fire?" he asked. "They aren't attached to anything, other than these wires."

"Not fire, but a different kind of alchemical reaction is what sets them aglow," Mamóru answered from atop Blu. He took a short puff from his pipe and let the oaky smoke become one with the mists. "These stones are known as pharoliths."

"Pharoliths?" Sterjall asked. "Like the one Dravéll wielded against the tailless scorpion inside the Ashen Dome?"

"Excuse me, agnurf son?" Mamóru asked.

"Oh, of course... It's a story from the *Barlum Saga*, by Loregem. But that was written only a hundred years ago, you couldn't have heard of it. Dravéll, the protagonist, he uses the Pharolith of Rakk to defeat the scorpion by tricking him into swallowing it, burning the netherbeast from the inside. But this pharolith isn't hot like the one in the story."

"They are never hot, I'm afraid," Mamóru said. "They are rocks made of aetheric phosphorus, or *pharos*, found deep within the aching hearts of mountains. I saw a few in my younger days, and even held one that belonged to King Raminin Stunnward, in the ancient Kingdom of Nisos."

"As in *the* Fel Nisos?" Kitjári asked. "Where the Republic of Lerev now rules?"

"The same one, if the map you once drew was correct. Pharoliths were known to be the treasures of royalty in the remote, southwestern isles. Some may still be preserved."

"Why does pharos glow like that?" Sterjall asked.

"We do not know why any of the aetheric elements do what they do." He leaned down on Blu's saddle and tapped the ammonite-encrusted handle of his cane into the concave top of the lodestone, disturbing the reflection of the pharolith into bouncing concentric rings. Beneath the water were sharp pebbles, like grains waiting to be crushed in a heavy mortar. "Pharolith knappings," the old man said. "After pharoliths are mined from their underground cradles, exposure to air or water creates a reaction that sets them alight.

But they eventually oxidize and turn back to darkness. You can strike their crust clean to make them glow once more, until the rock is too small to knap further and its light is forever extinguished. Rocks the size of the one in front of us could be kept alight for many years, even decades, if carefully knapped down."

Sterjall sank a handpaw into the water and removed a handful of cold, sharp knappings—they looked like the wings of dead beetles.

"To prevent the light from fading," Mamóru continued, "pharoliths were kept wrapped in oil-soaked cloths, so that neither air nor water would taint them. I well remember old King Stunnward's folly. He feared the dark, so every evening he removed the oily cloth from his pharolith, to light his bedchamber as he slept. Though he wanted the light to last forever, one day it was extinguished, and soon his own life was extinguished as well. Pharoliths were exceedingly valuable in those times. It seems that this land has a vast resource of them."

"Can we take some, then?" Sterjall asked.

"Leave them alone, Gwoli," Alaia said. "It might not be kind to disturb them. What if they mark tombs or something? We can ask about them once we meet the locals."

"Alaia says truth," Kulak said. "Let us keep our legs moving. There are many more pharoliths on the roads ahead. Let them guide us."

The lodestone path took them east through mossy highlands. The enormous boars trotted alongside them, sometimes as shadows in the mists, sometimes lit by the pharoliths' lights.

"Should we be afraid of them?" Alaia asked. "Because I'm a bit afraid of them."

"My scalp thinks they are more afraid of our cats," Kulak replied. And then, so that everyone in their group would hear, he added, "Blu, Pichi, do not feed on suids, eat nothing with tusks. If your bellies hunger, hunt for deer or sheep. This is nagra's home. We treat suids like we would expect guests to treat felids in Mindreldrolom."

Blu blinked slowly. Pichi huffed and flashed her enormous, serrated fangs.

It was windier up in the highlands, and the vapors were capricious, sometimes clearing the view for miles ahead, and at other times sinking them into a fog so dense they could barely see their own feet. Without the icy glow of the pharoliths, it would have been quite easy to get lost. The trunk had remained obscured, though they caught glimpses of a vertical dimness through the clouds, giving them a sense of the general direction they should aim for.

Vast and fertile lands broadened around them, where sheep and deer grazed, blanketed in dew. To the east the landscape dropped to what they guessed was another fjord, and to the north the lodestone path continued into a thick forest of hazel and birch, which rippled up and down a complex terrain of hillocks and green canyons. The clouds at last parted and granted them a sweeping view into the distance.

"There's the trunk," Sterjall noted as they kept walking.

"And a most magnificent mountain beneath it," Mamóru added. "That is Stelm Shäerath, also known as the Tricolored Mountain."

Stelm Shäerath was tall and sharp, like a stretched pyramid with a serrated top, rising beneath the center of the dome. The steep mountain was triple-banded. It was black at the jagged top, though much of the summit was white-capped. Its middle was a rusty band of gneiss rock which had eroded faster, making the concave belt narrower. The base was of light-gray granite, offering a solid foundation. Luckily, the trunk was not sprouting from the top of the four-mile-tall mountain, but slightly to the east of it, closer to where the black pinnacle joined the reddish mid-section.

"I hiked around the mountain's ruddy core once," Mamóru said, "in times before the domes were grown."

"How did you get to travel so much?" Sterjall inquired, walking alongside Blu but keeping his eyes on the Tricolored Mountain. "If as a Nu'irg you have to stay close to those of your own kind, does that mean there were elephants all the way up here?"

"Not elephants," Mamóru replied. "Mastodons were common in these territories. Mammoths lived in the steppes in the northeast, while elephants roamed the areas near the scablands and into the far east, in what you call the Bayanhong lands. Proboscideans were not common everywhere, so I did not get to travel wherever I wanted, but I got to see quite a lot in my time."

"What's the one place you always wanted to visit, but could not?" Alaia asked.

"Hmm. I think that would have to be the place you now call the Wastyr Triumvirate, though back when I knew of it, it used to be three kingdoms—Yorkab, Fesh-Ahiir, and Nijugwa. The entirety of Fel Yorkab never had proboscideans, so I was never able to sail there."

He puffed his pipe once more. "Wastyr has the best varietals of silver-tipped mistleaf anyone can find," he continued. "Though luckily, they are exported, so I've been able to taste them without having to travel there. I heard that mistleaf grows best there, for they only have four seasons."

"Only four seasons?" Sterjall questioned. "How is that possible?"

"The mists of Umbra never cloud their great island, although it is misty nearly year-round. Warm mists, mind you, not cold. And they do not get snow, other than upon their tallest peaks, so there is no Thawing season to speak of. The weather makes for a bizarre land where quite peculiar animals roam."

"What sorts of animals?" Alaia asked, intrigued.

"Kinds that did not inhabit the mainland, or if they do or did, only in small numbers. There is a clade of humped ungulates called camels, and long-necked ones they call giraffes. Their cats are even stranger, as they are not the felids we know, but a different clade, the viverroids. Meerkats are some of their kind, as well as hyenas, mongooses, civets, and aardwolves."

"I've only heard a few of those names before," Sterjall admitted. "Did you mention a wolf?"

"Aardwolf. Not a wolf, not a cat, somewhere in-between, or more likely somewhere on the side. They even have armored tree-climbers called pangolins. I've seen a few of these species with my own eyes, though they had been caged for the pleasure of heartless kings and vicious queens."

"Why didn't the Miscam make Silvesh for these creatures?" Sterjall asked.

"I'm not certain," Mamóru said. "Perhaps because there is no camelid Nu'irg, or one for the viverroids. If there were, I likely would have felt their presence."

"How come they don't get their own Nu'irgesh?" Alaia complained. "That doesn't sound fair."

"This is just my assumption, not a fact," the old man said, "but I believe we Nu'irgesh come into existence at some critical threshold which may be related to the number of individuals within our species, or to the branchings within our clades, or to the vastness of our territories. Perhaps it's related to all of those variables and others I am too simple-minded to envision."

Alaia thought for a moment, lifted a finger to speak, then put it back down. She pondered some more, then finally said, "Wouldn't that mean that there should be Nu'irgesh for insects? Or maybe for fish? Or trees? There are more of them, and they are more widespread than any other kinds."

"Ah, a clever gal you are," Mamóru said, tipping his pipe to her. "This is something few are aware of. Let me tell you about one encounter I had millennia ago, when sailing across the Alommo Sea. I stopped to explore Feli'i Oskrud, an island on the western side of the placid sea. I was there to witness a wonderful natural phenomenon—the yearly migration of lilac crabs."

"What is special about crabs migrating?" Sunu asked.

"Their numbers, for starters," the old man answered. "In Umbra, during Fogdawn, on an evening when the Ilaadrid Shard shines, all crabs emerge from their burrows at the same time and hurry to the ocean to spawn. Millions and millions of them march along in a lilac cascade of chitinous claws. That night I was there in my human form, as otherwise I would've been unable to avoid stomping on dozens of them at a time, given that the entire ground gets covered in nothing but scurrying shells. And that was when I saw him…"

They all waited for Mamóru to exhale his twirls of smoke and continue.

"Flowing with the torrent of lilac crabs was one that stood out, as it was not of the same species. It was an elbow crab, with an arrowhead-shaped shell encrusted with so many carcinized bumps that it looked more like a triangular shard of dried-up corals and barnacles. I stared at the pointed shell, and it stopped. As if time itself had frozen still, all the crabs that were flowing in the deluge stopped as well and turned to face me. I saw him then, and I knew he was the spirit of all crabs, the Nu'irg ust Fraans. But despite that, despite us recognizing each other, we were unreachable to one another. I could not mindspeak with him the way I can with Nelv or any of my other Nu'irgesh friends. The crab stared at me, confused, perhaps even more so because I was in my human form. He wiped his eyestalks with his claws and shapeshifted into a lilac crab like all the rest. He restarted his sideways march, and all the other millions of shells followed an instant later. Among the incomprehensible numbers, the Nu'irg was quickly lost to my sight."

"Why couldn't you mindspeak with him?" Sterjall asked. "Aren't all Nu'irgesh related, able to communicate with one another?"

"Not all. Some of us are more closely related than others. The qualia of being a crab are as alien to me as that of being a leech, or a siphonophore. There may be countless more Nu'irgesh among us, from kinds just so queer to us that we don't even notice them, and they may remain forever beyond our reach."

"The Acoapóshi should've made a mask for them too," Sterjall said. "Maybe that way we'd be able to understand them better."

"Perhaps, perhaps, but it would not be as simple as that. Your anatomy as a human is analogous to that of a wolf. A crab, however, would be no easy task, in the same way that it'd be hard to conceive anatomical relationships between you and a velvet worm, or a sagebrush. The Acoapóshi did the best they could with the knowledge Noss granted them."

"This all makes me wonder," Alaia said, "what if we inadvertently kill a Nu'irg, from time to time? When we step on an ant, or eat a piece of lettuce without even giving it a moment's thought."

"That is why I respect all living things equally," Mamóru said, "no matter how big or small."

"But I saw you swatting mosquitoes all the way here," Alaia rebutted.

"Well…" the old man muttered, inhaling a bit more smoke. "They had been getting on my nerves."

Chapter Sixty-Two

Tusks and Axes

The lodestones led them to the edge of the forest and continued deeper still, cutting through the green while following what seemed to be the only obvious path toward the trunk.

"It seems your road is laid before you," Hud Ilsed said to Kulak. "The ship needs repairs, the crew needs guidance. This fertile land will provide for us. Worry not, Khuron, no suid shall be poisoned by our darts. In how long should we seek for you if you do not return?"

Kulak discussed with his friends. They concluded that a journey through unknown lands could take a handful of days to a few weeks, depending on the terrain and condition of the roads. They would also have to convince the inhabitants to open up their dome and have the wielder of Nagrasilv agree to come with them. Kulak promised Ilsed that Sunu would be sending Olo weekly to keep her informed, so that she could have *Drolvisdinn* ready to depart when they returned.

"If you hear not from Olo for two weeks," Kulak said, "then there is trouble. Come and search for us."

As the strongest of their warriors, Hod Abjus volunteered to stay with Hud Ilsed to offer protection.

Once Ilsed and Abjus left, the wayfarers continued into the overgrown forest, where the hefty hogs did not follow. The lodestones still delineated a semblance of a path, even if many were swallowed inside gnarly tree trunks and would have been invisible if it had not been for the pharoliths shining atop them.

It began to rain again, forcing them to trudge sluggishly. A few miles into the woods, they arrived at a portentous dolmen of six lodestones supporting a flat slab of rock, which kept the ground below it mostly dry. The dolmen was large, but larger still were the old trees enveloping it under their mossy canopy, as if embracing a primeval shrine. Encrusted in the runic patterns carved on the rocks were shards of pharoliths, setting them aglow.

As the dome was dimming, the travelers decided to stop, strike a brime cube to light a fire, and share a warm meal. They readied their camp and sent the smilodons to hunt. Pichi returned only moments later, dropped a slender deer at their feet, and scampered away again to find something meatier for herself.

"Boars would been tastier," Kenondok grumbled as he butchered the deer. "There are so many of them." His scalp had been repainted before the trip, this time with concentric circles. His moist head glistened under the light of the glowing runes.

"Imagine if you had found us at Mindreldrolom with a dead jaguar next to our camp," Sterjall told him. "I don't think you would've been happy to see that."

"Is not same," Kenondok said. "Pigs and boars are good flavor. Jaguar meat is tough, pungent, not good." He finished cutting off the deer's head and tossed it to the side.

They roasted the deer over a bonfire. The rain came and went, but the dolmen kept them dry as they fell asleep.

Sterjall awoke thinking he must still be dreaming. He was submerged in a deep, low mist. In front of him was a silhouette of a creature that could not be real—a suid of some kind, but with upper jaw tusks that shot upward and bent in such an inconvenient curve that they ended up piercing the animal's own forehead.

He yelped as the creature's cold nose sniffed his footpaws. The suid squealed and fled into the fog.

"Babirusa," Mamóru explained. "They are harmless."

"Did we wake up on an entirely different planet?" Sterjall said, sitting up. The air was swarming with a fluttering of lacewings, like forest sprites made of the essence of translucency. The rain had stopped, but there was a new rattling sound all around them; loud, foreign, and permeating. A churning mist gathered at their feet, sliding into the undergrowth. Kenondok was nearby, squatting over the fire as he heated munnji cakes for breakfast, feet and knees invisible in the milky fog.

They ate quietly, observing the thousands of nearly invisible wings hover about them, then packed up and walked away from the dolmen, kicking off plumes of vapors and listening to the cacophony of forest sounds.

As they walked, they thought they saw mice scurrying beneath the foggy blanket. Sterjall aimed his keen ears with a cock of his head, located a target, and dropped to grab it. From the mist he pulled out not a rodent, but a mouse-sized isopod that had curled into a perfect ball to protect its numerous legs with its chitinous exoskeleton. The creature clacked its shell as a warning, so Sterjall let it go.

"They are all over the trees," Alaia said. "Look at that one." An old kapok tree was covered with so many of the creatures that it looked as if it had a shifting and contorting bark. When the isopods snapped their shells in a *shht-shht-clack* pattern, their calls were quickly responded to by the adjacent ones, rippling out a wave of motion and sound.

By midmorning, they had arrived at a clearing that rose to a grassy hill capped by a bucolic village. The buildings were bluestone cabins with bone-shingled roofs with steep angles that would easily shed the constant rains and the heavy Winter snows. Lodestones snaked out from the village in spiraling patterns, scattering all the way into the shadows of the forest, each topped with a glowing pharolith.

They took cover at the edge of the forest, behind a toppled lodestone big as a petrified giant. Many villagers meandered about; running chores, working the fields, or simply playing among the rocks.

Sterjall took out his binoculars to get a better view. *What on Noss am I seeing?* he wondered. "There's... something peculiar about these people," he murmured. "Their faces, take a look." He passed the binoculars around.

"It's not just their faces," Kitjári said, "their hands, skin. Are those tusks? Are they all in half-forms?"

Kulak looked next. "They look like less than half-forms to my eyes," he said.

Each and every villager, from the youngest toddler to the most wrinkled elder, had partial characteristics from species of suids. Some grew triangular, furry ears; some had curly tails with poofy tufts at their ends; some had faces with strange protrusions, as if their cheekbones had been pulled out like clay. Wiry fur and heart-shaped noses were common, and many villagers—perhaps most—had tusks of one sort or another.

When it was Kenondok's turn to spy through the binoculars, he recoiled from what he saw.

"Loathsome!" he cried out in Miscamish. "It is clear what this means. They have broken their oath to Nagrasilv, to human and suidkind. These creatures are unnatural, sinful."

"Perhaps Nagradrolom has different laws," Kulak said. "We are not here to judge the ways of the Puqua Miscam."

"But Khuron Kulak," Kenondok complained, "it does not matter which tribe they belong to. They have been mixing their blood with pig's blood. Every one of them is born in transgression."

"Perhaps they found the laws to be unnecessary," Kulak retorted, "and antiquated."

"Khuron!"

"My ears will hear no more of it. We will honor their ways and seek for their aid, which is what we came here for. Are we in agreement?" he said, looking only at the members of his own tribe.

Sunu slowly closed and opened their eyes to show they had no quarrel.

Kenondok stood firm and said, "My lips will remain sealed, but that does not mean I am tolerant of their disrespect."

"Fair," Kulak said. "They do not need to be tolerant of your disrespect either. Remain quiet."

Sterjall waited until tempers had cooled, then said, "Keep your weapons ready, but out of your hands. We don't want to scare them."

"I shall handle the greeting," Mamóru said. "Follow me." He put his pipe away and rode Blu toward the village, following a line of lodestones.

They were immediately spotted.

Children cried. Adults grabbed them and fled toward the center of the village. A commotion rose all around, first caused by the sight of the smilodons, then worsened once the villagers saw the animal people traveling with the beasts.

A band of big-boned and rough-looking villagers came trotting down the hill, shakily pointing axes at the newcomers to form a wall in their path. Despite their show of bravado, they did not look like trained warriors. Their axes—although beautifully inlaid with pharoliths—were functional tools for chopping firewood, not forged for war. Despite the unreadiness of the villagers, their tusks, demeanor, and varied body characteristics made them all appear fierce.

Mamóru straightened atop Blu's saddle, appearing powerful despite his frail state. He raised his dark cane and spoke the Miscamish greeting, loud and clear. "*Oset fin uth halvet.*"

One of the Puqua villagers pointed an axe directly at Blu's face, then said, "*Ugça noyyo mush? Ugçim azzo ung mogaxo ummaënolth, klog ung she fjonne? Lummya akte!*"

"*Ejienn enuss Miscamish?*" Mamóru inquired, wondering whether anyone was understanding him.

"*Dalaxo Miscam nawesh!*" was the forceful reply. "*Najash!*"

"Do you know what language they are speaking?" Sterjall asked in Common.

"I'm afraid not," Mamóru said. "I don't recognize the tongue, but it might be the old—"

"Speak Commun?" a gravelly voice spoke up. A stocky man walked in front of the axes, flashing four prominent tusks, trying to suck in his bulging belly to seem fiercer. A mixture of warthog and human features competed over his face, blending in a strange realm between the two. His arms were covered in bristly brown hairs, and his oddly shaped fingers ended in miniature hooves, as if he was wearing dark, triangular thimbles at each fingertip.

"Who are ye?" the thick villager asked. "What sort uf demun has crawled out uf our fjordesh?" His thick accent was filled with exchanged vowels and contractions.

"Demons we are not," Mamóru answered. "My name is Mamóru, and with me travel the Mindrelfröa, Agnargfröa, and Urnaadifröa. We have traveled to your realm with news from the world beyond Nagradrolom. We come hoping for aid, seeking your wise counsel."

The citizens were stricken by a mixture of reverence and fear, but were still cautious enough not to lower their weapons. Their faces glowed with uncertainty, illuminated by pharolith rings they wore on their tusks, ears, and noses.

The warthog man snorted. "Then how'd ye travel to Onbar, if demuns ye aren't? D'*sgørmenn* is sealed, d'world beyond still unreachable."

"We sailed through the dome's wall, and our Silvesh granted us passage," Mamóru said, lifting Momsúndosilv for all to see. "The time to open the domes has come, but Noss has lost their voice. This is why we came to seek the Nagrafröa's aid."

"*Umeggro muz!*" the warthog-faced man said. The others all rested their axes on their shoulders, yet seemed no more at ease. "I know not if ye bear glad or dire tidings, but welcome ye, Mamóru, n'*Meçua* who with ye travel. Yer name's d'same as d'Nu'irg uf legends who could take a human form."

"It is I, the Nu'irg ust Momsúndo."

The Puqua all gasped in unison, but their leader seemed dubious. "Cannot be so," he argued, "them legends spoke uf a young man, not uf a beard uf gray, or uf a fanged beast like d'one ye ride."

"The legends speak of times past. I have aged plenty since then. My body has grown weak and unable to carry me to where I need to go, though my spirit remains potent. Who do we have the honor of speaking to?"

"I'm Cap'n Siffo," he said, bowing to one knee. "I am *zonnomen* in d'city uf Ôllomuy, capital uf Gwur Laçam. If Nagrafröa ye seek, to Krûn ye must travel, in pruvince uf Gwur Atzo. I can show ye d'path, but I need t'ask ye tell us mour, if ye'd be kind enough t'join us in d'longhouse."

They agreed to follow and were soon escorted into the village of Onbar. Captain Siffo sent a handful of emissaries ahead to tell the gathering citizens not to fear, but also to warn them not to disturb the guests. Crowds peered at them curiously. Children hid behind standing stones, peeked out of windows, or held on to their parents' cloven-hoofed legs.

"What was that language you were speaking earlier?" Sterjall asked Captain Siffo.

"Our native tongue, Puqua. D'old Puqua tongue is spoken mostly in d'fjords, not as much inland, where Cummon is more cummon."

"How come you don't speak Miscamish?" Alaia asked.

"Many Miscamish wurds we still speak, but d'tongue's unly used by shamans n'few clans who keep to d'old traditions. We've moved past it, same as we moved past some uf d'old laws d'Acoapóshi Miscam tried t'lock us into."

The longhouse was at the north end of the village. It was an oval-shaped building supported by a dozen lodestones on each long side. It was spacious; a place for crowded town hall gatherings and parties. An oval table decorated the center, illuminated by a complex chandelier of hundreds of teardrop-shaped pharoliths, like a frozen rain of light.

The seven wayfarers took their seats and were joined by a dozen perplexed representatives from the tribe. The villagers who had earlier pointed their axes at them stood by the walls, listening in, fascinated by the newcomers. After introductions, Siffo asked for drinks and food to be brought in.

"You drink braaw as well?" Kulak asked as the drinks were poured for them. He could smell the fermented, pineapple-like scent emanating from the fizzy drink.

"Uf course!" Siffo answered. "Finest braaw there is, d'braaw frum Esçarsúl."

Kulak tasted it and winced. It was strong, mighty strong, harder than rum and nothing like the softer drink he was used to. He dragged his whiskers up in a forced smile.

The elder chief of Onbar, a long-snouted woman named Malnûvi, joined them at the table. She was older than most of the other tribespeople, spoke a cleaner Common than Siffo, and had no tusks in her long, pig-like snout. "Would ye now tell us yer story, please?" she kindly asked.

The travelers recounted their tale briefly, as they knew the complete tale would have to be told soon enough. They explained why they needed the Nagrafröa's help and why it was important to avoid delays.

"D'story ye tell us is grave n'cuncerning," Siffo said. "Our shaman shell send their owl to d'city uf Krûn, so that d'Nagrafröa can be informed uf yer coming n'be ready to greet ye. Her name is Nalaníri. I'll ask mine friends to pack what is needed fur d'road. We may wait in here n'palaver while them preparations take place, as I am much curious 'bout many matters."

"And so are we," Sterjall said. "I... I hope you don't mind, but there's something we all want to ask about. It's about how, um, different you all look?"

Captain Siffo grunted, then said, "This be one uf d'things I's curious 'bout as well. Except fur ye in yer half-forms, ye are all so plain-skinned, n'have unly bare hands, feet, n'faces. Why's it that yer tribes haven't yet took d'features uf yer kindred clades?"

"*A uth wucaff*," Kenondok mumbled under his breath. Then, speaking up for the first time since the earlier introductions, he said, "Only Silvfröash are meant to hold the sacred half-forms."

Kulak glared at him.

Siffo's brow tightened into a bristly knot. "But what then's d'point uf d'Silvesh, if not t'share d'glory uf them sacred species with d'rest uf d'tribe? How do yer people find kinship with d'felids, canids, n'uther kinds?"

"Sunu uses soot to find kinship with all kinds," Sunu answered, caressing Olo's feathers. "Sunu uses empathy and needs not take the forms of mindrel, for that is the honor reserved to the Mindrelfröa. But this is Sunu's path, and no one else's."

"Though we don't know much about them," Kitjári said, "I don't believe the Wutash—northern or southern—had anyone but their chosen Silvfröash take half-forms either."

"Nor did the Toldask Miscam," Mamóru agreed.

Malnûvi tilted her head, drooping one of her long, fuzzy ears toward the table, and seemed earnestly sad for them. She sighed an affirmative grunt, then said, "I am much surprised. Some uf us share mour commonalities with d'suids. Some clans are still mostly plain-skinned, though none as plain as yerselves. It is our main goal, generation after generation, fur us all t'become closer to d'nagra half-forms. Yer saying that's not what yer tribes intended?"

"Not for the tribes we know of," Kitjári said. "But how do you do this? How do you become closer to the forms the Nagrafröa takes?"

"In d'most obvious way, uf course," Siffo said. "Nagrasilv is passed to a different family every cycle. Them conceive new children whilst in them half-forms, so that d'bloodline is strong, so that unique suid aspects are bred each time. Them are qualities we treasure n'have been striving to develop since d'time uf d'Downfall."

Kenondok looked utterly disgusted but managed to keep his thoughts to himself.

"Your laws are certainly different," Kitjári said. "Perhaps this goal is something unique to your tribe, and not something the other tribes were attempting. Or have you heard of this before, Mamóru?"

Mamóru shook his head. "I have not. All the Miscam tribes I knew had the same laws against this, but the laws came not from their own elders but from the Acoapóshi tribe who created the Silvesh."

"Them Acoapóshi were strict n'closed-minded, if ye ask me," Malnûvi said. "Them tried t'enforce many rules, but them could not do much mour enforcing once d'domes a-closed."

"There is much mour I'd like t'ask ye," Siffo said, "but I know yer story's long n'it's d'Nagrafröa who shell hear it. Would ye let me join ye? I can at least travel with ye to d'Tricolored Mountain, but would be much happy t'join ye n'Nalaníri after we find her. I'm a well-traveled cap'n n'can tell ye mour 'bout our lands."

"We'd be honored to have you," Mamóru said. "We could use the company, and your knowledge as well. I presume it will be a long trip, and we have much to discuss."

"Before we depart," Kulak added, "we must tell you we have friends waiting. Our sailors could use help, food, and company. Storms tore our sails, and they need mending. It would be a kindness to tell them we are fine, tell them we are on our way to the Nagrafröa."

Kulak described the path they took and what the stone pier looked like.

A babirusa-faced woman named Befnu raised a hoofed finger in acknowledgment and with her guttural accent said, "Ye camest thru d'old pier uf Mâscarmush, which not in decades has been used. There be a shmall villige un d'southern headland, where I's froum. I shell take cares uf it, a-helpin' yer friends n'yer tattered ship."

"Be mindful of them," Kulak said. "They are Laatu Miscam, from my lands. Their eyes might not see as yours see, their scalps may frighten from your appearance. Tell them Khuron Kulak sent you. Perhaps then they will listen and not fear. My scalp apologizes if they behave in unfriendly ways."

"I's aware uf d'problem," Befnu said. "Centuries past, same struggles we faced. Many a clan cared not fur d'new laws. I shell handle it as certain as d'kenzir is aglow."

A thundering sound like the call of a humpback whale rattled the chandelier, making the shadows tremble.

"Was that a whale?" Alaia said. "Aren't we far from—"

"*Kubas* are ready t'depart!" an emissary yelled, holding open the door of the longhouse.

"What's a kuba?" Alaia asked.

"Them kubanochoeruses," Malnûvi answered. "Largest uf our companion species. Them help us travel long distances n'move heavy stones 'round." Malnûvi studied Alaia, then said, "Ye, young Lurr, have been much quiet. Yet ye seem cunfident, n'beautiful. Are ye sure ye aren't part nagra?"

"I'm quite sure?" Alaia said, blushing.

"Because ye have d'most unique little tusk a-growin' un yer forehead."

"It's not a tusk, it's a spur. I'm from a race called the Oldrin. We grow these bones in different parts of our bodies, and mine just happened to grow here"—she pointed to her nub—"and also on my back."

"Well, watch yerself *ugimeld*, fur our kind treasures traits unique as yers, n'our men might be smitten by such an outrageous display uf beauty."

Alaia beamed. Other than from other Oldrin, she had rarely heard anyone speak about her spurs in a positive way.

"I am envious," Malnûvi continued, "I can't even grow tusks in mine mouth. But let us go now n'ride to Krûn—our *kubas* await."

Enormous beasts waited outside the longhouse. The kubanochoeruses were the size Mamóru had been in his steppe mammoth primal form, and though they had cloven hooves like their suid cousins, theirs were flattened and broad to better distribute the heavy load of their bodies. They were proportionally more long-legged than other suids, and had a single, forward-pointed horn stretching from the center of their foreheads. This long, bony projection was covered in thick leather and velvety fur. Two more horns they also had, if one could call them that, as they were merely pointed brows that extended into sharp edges, like triangles of bone over the orbits of their eyes.

Three kubas had been readied: a black one, a gray one, and one with light-brown colors like Pichi's coat, except in wiry bristles instead of soft fur. All three kubas were now vocalizing to each other, in pulses and oscillating groans very similar to those of the largest cetaceans, though rougher on the edges. Saddled over their wide backs were colorful howdahs with covered seats that allowed half a dozen riders to comfortably ride while protected from the elements.

"I told our smilodons to follow," Kulak said to Siffo. Noticing the hesitation in Siffo's tightened face, he added, "Do not let your scalp worry, they are kind, friendly."

On the side of the longhouse was an ascending ramp. From there they stepped onto the howdahs and took their seats. Malnûvi and Siffo joined them, as well as two villagers who had been sitting at the oval table, and two of the ones who had pointed their axes at them.

"D'light uf d'kenzir is with ye," a villager called out as the kubas stomped away.

"N'so it shines within us all!" Captain Siffo answered, riding on.

Chapter Sixty-Three

The Tricolored Mountain

The kubas swung their long, tireless legs and took the wayfarers toward the snowy peak of Stelm Shäerath.

The ride was steady and breezy. The kubas traversed a wide road lined with pharolith-topped lodestones. The path was slightly elevated, placing the howdahs at the level of the canopy. From that perspective, the dense forest flowed alongside them as if they were sailing over a sea of leaves.

Their three kubas had to move to a pullout for a moment, to make room for another kuba stomping in the opposite direction, hauling an oversized wagon. Even in the broad daylight, the wagon's cargo illuminated their faces as it passed by: it was a single pharolith block the size of a cabin, roughly cut and recently quarried. The pharolith was marbled with dark stripes, from inclusions and impurities, but even so it shone as bright as the sun reflecting on an icy lake. The lead kuba vocalized a guttural tremolo that made the dangling decorations of the howdah shimmer, then stomped onward.

"Could you tell us more about the pharoliths?" Alaia asked Siffo.

"Them whats?"

"Pharoliths, the glowing rocks, like the one that just passed us by, or these decorating your tusks. Glowing rocks are not something you see in the New World."

"Oh, ye mean them kenzir stones. I guess them weren't cummon 'ere neither 'fore d'dome a-closed. D'kenzir are mined at Erne Brumm, far north, at d'skirts uf Laaja Deulmosk. D'kenzir seams were discovered 'bout six hundred years to date. Beautiful mines we have there, with all d'walls set aglow. Them are so bright ye need t'wear a veil over yer eyes or ye'll be struck by a headache as painful as when ye go fogblind. Can never run out uf kenzir stones, we keep un diggin' n'mour veins keep a-finding. We hardly need t'burn fire fur light no mour."

Siffo reached below his seat and brought out an egg-shaped metal container about the size of his hairy fist. "Take a look," he said.

Alaia examined the artifact. It felt hollow, made of thin, overlapping metal plates. It had a flat, circular bottom, and when she spun it as if trying to unscrew it, the metal plates spread open like the petals of a lotus flower. Cradled inside was a briolette-cut pharolith, multifaceted in its elongated, sparkling shape. The inside surfaces of the petals had been polished to a mirror and now reflected all the light straight into Alaia's face. It was blinding.

"Open it up some mour," Siffo encouraged her, showing her how to spin the bottom to further spread the petals, widening the beam of light until it fully blossomed.

"This is gorgeous!" Alaia gasped, squinting at the kenzir stone.

"Ye can have it if ye like," Siffo said. "It lights up yer horn like a jewel."

"Are you sure?" Alaia asked, too entranced to pick up on Siffo's flirty tone.

"Ya, it's yers, *ugimeld*."

"Don't feel so flattered, these be cummon lamps," Malnûvi said to Alaia, earning a venomous glance from Siffo. "Cheap at any uf d'Krûn bazaars. We'll fetch mour fur all uf ye."

As the forest transitioned into mossy highlands, a fjord opened up to their right. Sterjall dared to look over the edge of their howdah, straight down into a vertical drop, but Alaia was afraid that the whole structure might loosen, tip over, and hurl them down into the frigid waters.

The fjord was teeming with vessels of all sizes, all with billowing sails of black or dark grays. Captain Siffo pointed to an extensive port reflecting at the head of the fjord and said, "D'city up ahead's named Arho. It's an important trade city fur d'western pruvinces, largest exporter uf blood cakes, hence all d'ships."

"Blood cakes?" Sterjall asked.

"Them food of the vines."

"You mean munnji?" Kulak asked, overhearing the conversation.

"No idea what them words mean, cat Lorr. D'silos west uf Arho make them blood cakes that feed most uf our species. It's a similar variety uf blood cakes what's made these 'ere kubas grow so maddeningly huge. Makes them wicked smart, too, though Gurruhøf here is not d'smartest uf d'bunch."

The kuba they were riding suddenly shook her back, as if trying to rid herself of a pestering fly.

"We do the same, at Mindreldrolom," Kulak said, holding on tight. "We call cakes that companion species eat *idshall-munnji,* and just *munnji* for cakes we and the other species eat."

"Ye eat them bloody cakes yerselves?" Siffo grumbled, tightening his soft nose in a disgusted knot. "Them are fur d'suids unly!"

"Aren't you a suid?" Alaia countered.

"Ye know what I mean, *ugimeld*. Them taste acrid n'foul, like a carcass left t'rot in a hot, humid Summer."

"Perhaps you did not learn how to prepare them properly," Sunu said. "We can teach you, and will gladly allow you to partake from our own supply."

Siffo snorted twice, shaking his warthog head.

"Which species other than kubas have you grown as companions?" Kulak asked.

"We've got them *celebochoeruses* in most farms, or *celebs* fur short, n'domestic pigs around d'cities. Them grew quite large since our dome a-closed. Friendly, lovely creatures them are, unlike them irritable kubas."

Gurruhøf shook her back again, this time nearly tossing them off, howdah and all.

Once the captain took control once more, he continued, "Ye'll see them companion pigs around Arho, them are everywhere. But won't stay there we won't, we'll keep un to d'village uf Adaami, where our tusks can rest, n'then continue to d'mountain at morning's break."

Arho had a charming beauty to it. The houses were mostly constructed out of bluestone and companion suid bones, but mixed heavy logs into their structures. The roads were paved with dark red bricks, and there were streetlights that shone day and night. Alaia pointed out that the population of Arho seemed different from that of Onbar: in Onbar the suid traits mostly resembled those of warthogs, while in Arho they were more akin to wild boars.

The smilodons trotting alongside the kubas terrified the locals, feral and human alike. Never in this dome had anyone seen such gigantic, ferocious predators.

From up atop a tall balcony, an old woman cried out, "*Und yuëroça dir Miscam maimegwål fum ishtamik, unk ferego yurunwål fum shimik!*"

"*Unk ferego yurunwål fum shimik!*" the crowd chanted in reply.

"What are they saying?" Kitjári asked Malnûvi.

"Them say, *D'faces uf d'Miscam have come t'bless us, them gods have returned to us.*"

The dome was completely dark by the time they reached Adaami—not even the blue glow of night penetrated the mists that had formed. The forest road had no pharoliths to light it, but that was no problem, as the Puqua had attached massive pharolith lanterns to the forehead horns of each of their kubas.

The locals were honored that their quaint village had been chosen as a resting stop for such a momentous occasion. They were a humble people mostly of the bushpig variety, very hospitable, who offered them a variety of food and drink as well as comfortable beds.

In the morning, they continued ascending toward Stelm Shäerath. Now that they were closer, they could truly appreciate the geological grandeur of the Tricolored Mountain. The rusty central band of gneiss rock was exposed at these elevations, cutting through the forest and slowly being molded by erosion. It created confusing marbled patterns, making the rocks seem soft and wavy. The gray-colored lodestones had been supplanted by ruddy gneiss boulders carved with softened edges, matching the natural patterns of the striations. The pharoliths at their concave tops reflected an autumnal glow, like torches burning unflickering flames.

As the kubas scaled the road, the forest around them changed colors. The aspens shone in vain golds, the maples in ardent reds, the oaks in scalding oranges, and the alders in chromatic transitions of all warm colors. The road dipped through marbled gneiss canyons, where the rusty colors blended perfectly with the changing leaves that accumulated in cracks and crevices.

"It's so early in the season for Autumn colors," Alaia noted, though they were already feeling the change in temperature.

"These northern lands are chilled by the Quiescent Ocean," Mamóru explained, "and we are climbing to higher elevations." He exhaled a blissful sigh. "I can't begin to tell you how my soul rejoices at the sight of each and every leaf that falls or hangs to display its luminance. It has been so many centuries since I've seen a forest dressed in fire and gold."

They arrived at Krûn in the early afternoon. The city flourished to the east of the trunk, just past the gneiss canyons, rising on a prominent cliff of granite. The view was phenomenal, even more so from atop the kubas. Extensive fjords propagated to the north, east, and south of them, all streaked with vertical lines from the numerous waterfalls that drenched their cliffsides. Tiny dots of cold lights delineated paths along treacherous cliffsides, and sea stacks proudly displayed lighthouses with tops carved from single pharolith blocks. It was a complex landscape that mixed defiant islands, sheer drops, shimmering beacons, and tangled patterns of land, mist, and sea.

The city of Krûn was similar to Arho, though it lacked a port. Instead of using bone, in Krûn the roofs were covered with rock shingles that blended black, rust, and gray colors, trying to mimic the tricolored nature of the mountain home. The streets were green with dew-drenched moss and lined on both sides with white-barked trees.

The plaza at the center of the city was marked by a monumental lodestone five times taller than any of the kubas, capped by a pharolith pyramid. The kubas veered around the monolith and approached a ramp at the north end of the plaza, next to the Guildhall of Krûn. As the riders were about to dismount, a woman at the ramp yelled something at them in Puqua. Siffo leaned over to have a conversation with her, which brewed into an argument, leaving the captain exasperated. He turned toward his guests and said, "Mine apologies. It seems Nalaníri wasn't in town when d'message was received, n'since d'message was addressed to her alone, no soul dared read it. Mine friend tells me she's somewhere in d'Slømmon Forest. Knowing her, she's probably a-hunting fur honey truffles."

"What are honey truffles?" Alaia asked.

"Them are much a rare delicacy that a-grows un d'sides uf d'mountains. Nalaníri is an accomplished chef, n'seems to sometimes furget 'bout her responsibilities to d'Krûn Temple, preferring t'spend time in d'woods a-searching fur unique ingredients. Furgive me fur blabbering in this manner, but she tends t'be a bit hard t'work with."

"When will she return?" Sterjall asked.

Siffo snorted. "It could take her days or weeks. We know she'll be here by d'first day uf Dewrest, to follow through with her monthly temple duties, but that's still a-weeks away. If ye'd be comfortable with it, I could take ye to d'Slømmon Forest. I think I know where we'll find her, but we might have t'take a small hike." After some consultation, the wayfarers agreed.

The kubas swung their legs once more, crossing through the colorful bazaar of Krûn. Other giant suids treaded heavily about, pulling carts filled with goods; they were the bison-sized domestic pigs and celebochoeruses Malnûvi had told them about. The suids and partially suid humans all made way for the stomping convoy.

"D'forest is right behind d'trunk," Siffo said, pointing ahead.

A double line of standing stones framed the wide path toward the trunk. The kubas strode between the lodestones, which kept growing taller as they neared the mile-wide tower of vines. Two pig-faced priests stood guard by the entrance of Ommo ust Nagra; they stared at the party with confused eyes, uncertain of what creatures they saw atop the howdahs, and fearful of the sharp-toothed ones following the kubas.

Over the temple's archway hung the skull of a kubanochoerus, one with massive tusks not quite as large as those of mammoths, yet more numerous—

six in total. Carved deeply into the skull, right over the forehead horn, was the suid glyph—it shone in a mosaic of perfectly cut kenzir stones.

The entire perimeter of the trunk was surrounded by a forest of changing colors, raining fiery leaves that accumulated in soft beds. The kubas continued along a road that arced left at the temple's steps, traversing the forest in a shallow curve around the trunk until they arrived at the opposite side of the immense column, from where trails spiderwebbed into the forest, ascending toward the steep, rising mountain.

"This's d'Slømmon Forest," Siffo said.

"What are those things?" Alaia asked.

The landscape was adorned with bizarre rock formations: sharp black rocks—some as big as the kubas—suspended over thinner columns of marbled rock. Since the reddish columns blended with the fiery forest, the black tops seemed to be hovering in midair, right above the canopy.

Siffo explained that the formations were hoodoos: hard rocks from the upper, darker band of the mountain that had been stranded atop the softer gneiss rock, which had eroded faster, leaving only narrow columns to hold up the black tops. It created a mystical landscape of totem-like formations, all hiding in the red forest of white barks.

"Come to think of it," Mamóru pondered, "the entire black top of Stelm Shäerath is one enormous, snow-capped hoodoo. Let's hope it doesn't come toppling down anytime soon."

Siffo asked the four villagers who had traveled with them to wait by the kubas, warning them that they might have to spend the night in the forest.

"I'm much sorry to make ye hike like this," Siffo said to the foreigners, "but if time is uf d'essence, this'll be d'fastest way t'talk to d'Nagrafröa. I know d'area where them honey truffles a-grow. I hope we can find her there. Fullow right behind me, if ye please."

They packed a few supplies on Pichi's harness and ventured into the forest, with Mamóru riding on Blu once more.

The Slømmon Forest was as confounding as it was beautiful. Incessant insect-like calls permeated through it from what appeared to be enormous cicadas clinging to tall branches. All the trees were wrapped in bright bark, from the papery birches, to the geometrically textured silver poplars, to the lush and majestic opal sycamores, which were rare but impossible to miss. From this white and gold forest the rusty marbled pillars rose suddenly out of the soil, like smoothened tree trunks, merging into the leaves above. The ground rippled into hillocks and mounds of brightly colored mulch.

Occasionally, quaar-black boulders would poke out from the fiery leaves, looking like portals to the nethervoids of a sunless land.

Siffo called out Nalaníri's name. His voice was deep, full, raspy. Despite his powerful lungs and controlled release, the undulating hills, countless hoodoos, and forest critters swallowed his voice. The only creatures who noticed Siffo's calls were the many isopods hiding in the mulch, who scurried away from his thunderous voice, leaving leafy wakes behind them.

"Them are called quoll-quolls," Captain Siffo told them, noticing their curious looks. "Them are much delicious, ye shell try them. Many a kind breeds in these forests. Like them noisy ones up there."

They looked to where Siffo pointed his tusks and realized that what they had thought were cicadas were actually a different kind of quoll-quoll, longer and more slender, who rubbed the segments of their chitinous shells to produce the buzzing and humming sound that filled the forest.

The trail ended at a grandiose hoodoo which was topped by a pointed black rock, distinguishing itself from the more common rectangular or irregular tops of the other hoodoos. The base of this hoodoo was supported by three striated arches, looking almost like fingers sprouting from the ground to grasp the tall pillar.

Siffo stepped underneath the arches, where he kicked at the cold remains of a recent fire. Flakes of pharolith knappings shimmered among the charcoal like discarded, iridescent elytra. "It seems someone was 'round here recently. Frum this point un, there's not a trail t'fullow, n'it's farther into d'forest that them honey truffles a-grow. I suggest we split up t'find Nalaníri, n'meet back here 'fore darkness falls. It'll be easy t'find yer way, simply walk up any uf d'hills n'look fur Tur-Reveok, d'pointed hoodoo right above us, n'fullow it back. There aren't no dangers in this forest."

"Tur-Reveok?" Kitjári said. "Sounds just like Tor-Reveo, Takhamún's Spear of Undoing."

"It is named after a spear, uf sorts," Siffo agreed. "'Twas the name of Lûr-rumaag's forehead horn, d'kuba goddess who carved them twelve fjords with her tusks."

"More stories of old that influenced the new," Mamóru said. "Some of the stories we are creating today will live on in other forms too, shifting like the sands of time."

They split up to search for Nalaníri. Sterjall chose to go with Alaia, and Kulak went with Kenondok. Siffo, Malnûvi, Kitjári, and Sunu went their own ways, though Sunu always had Olo for company. Mamóru was tired and decided to stay under the three arches of Tur-Reveok and wait for them, keeping Blu and Pichi company, who were happy to lounge around for a while.

Chapter Sixty-Four

Nalaníri of the Nagra

"Bear would've gone into a frenzy chasing after these things," Sterjall said to Alaia, trying to catch one of the speeding quoll-quolls. "Imagine him seeing the leaves move like that, he'd bark his brains out. I miss that nubhead of a dog."

"Me too," she said. "I wonder how he's doing. He seemed to really like Frud, though Sabikh still scared him."

"I'm sure Banook is taking good care of him." Sterjall began to hum a melody, lost in his own thoughts. *I wonder what he's doing right now.*

"Is that the mountain song again?" Alaia asked. "You have to teach me the lyrics sometime. I only remember a few parts."

Sterjall's upper body contorted in a self-conscious shrug. "I'm actually adding some new verses," he shyly admitted. "Banook had already changed it a bit to add me into it. I thought it'd be nice to contribute some of my own stanzas. Banook once said that stories are alive and ever changing, and so I thought it would be fitting."

"You wrote your own? Now you *have* to sing them to me!"

"I've barely started. I don't know how to rhyme the same way he does. It's not easy."

"You'll have time to fix things. Now sing it. I'm not taking no for an answer."

Sterjall smiled with embarrassment, but he actually did want to show off his work; he had been thinking hard about it. "Alright, it's only two stanzas so far. I haven't figured out how to continue it. And don't laugh."

Alaia nodded eagerly and forced a serious expression.

Sterjall cleared his throat, and while pulling at his chin whiskers he sang:

> The wolf cub takes the poet's quill and dips the tip in verse,
>
> His paw is nowhere near as skilled yet hopes he'll be no worse.
>
> Their tale in rhyming couplets grows, adventure calls again,
>
> Though he'd be happier writing prose, he pens a fresh qua*train*.

> Wayfarers leave the—

"Wait, wait. Those last two don't rhyme," Alaia interrupted.
"Of course they do!"
"It's pronounced *qua*train, not qua*train*, it does not rhyme with *again*."
"See? Now you've gone and ruined it for me."
"Sorry! I just thought you'd like some input."
"How do you even know that?"
Alaia huffed. "What, because I'm a mine worker I can't know this sort of stuff?"
"I didn't mean—"
"I'm kidding. Some of the poetry books you borrowed from Crysta, I sometimes took them to the mines, and Ebaja and I would read them together. Her father was a writer, you know? Anyway, I'll be quiet now. Sing me the rest."
Sterjall cowered between his shoulders.
"Stop that," she demanded. "Really, it's good! Sing it!"
Sterjall seemed doubtful. While squinting at her as a warning, he went on.

> …he pens a fresh qua*train*.

> Wayfarers leave the cabin's sight and turn away from home,
>
> Da'áju's vast and endless ice caldera they must roam.
>
> Between crevasses deep and cold they reach the ancient room,
>
> Urnaadi's mask, as legends told, is freed from its cursed tomb.

Alaia applauded. "I love it so much! In such short a time we've gone all the way to Da'áju and out."

"Thank you." Sterjall smiled. "And after that... Well, it's just hard to write the next part, but once I get through those sad moments, the song will get back to adventures again."

"Must have felt like that for Banook. He had to find beautiful words to sing about the end of many of his kind, yet he found them. But like you say, there's a lot of fun after you get through that one moment. Though won't it be awkward? Because you will have to write about Aio *inside* Banook's poem." She shoulder-bumped him and laughed. "It will be a story filled with jealousy, secrets, and unrequited love!"

"What do you mean 'unrequited'?"

"Well... Be honest, Gwoli. I know you like him, but from what you've told me, you don't quite like him the same way you like Banook."

"Yeah... I know it's different, but more has happened since that last time with the fireflies."

"Were you sneaking around in the dark hulls of *Drolvisdinn* again?"

"Just once. But again, we got interrupted."

"No! Who?"

"Kenondok. I don't think he saw anything though, it was too dark. But he looked a bit... intense."

"He can't help it with that face," she chuckled, swinging joyfully around a tree trunk. "But Aio. What about Aio?"

"I guess I'm growing fond of him. But it's not the same as with Banook. Nothing could be, anyhow."

"Why does it have to be the same? As long as you two are happy. And not causing any trouble. Poor Kenondok's head seems to be about to explode with what the Puqua are doing here. I don't want to see what happens if you present him with a puppy-kitten of your making."

Sterjall glared at her. "This is your first and only warning..."

"Would it purr? Or howl? Or could it do both? And I'm not up for breast-feeding, so don't you look at me for help with—"

Sterjall jumped at her and pinched her sides, making her drop onto the leaves, laughing uncontrollably and making a dozen quoll-quolls flee in terror.

"Fuck, st-stop! Fine, f-fine, let me breathe!"

They lay there atop the leaves for a while, catching their breath.

"Just like old times," he said.

"Except you are a wolf now," she squawked. "You can tickle, but your claws are also fucking sharp." She slapped at his arm, then checked her sides for scratches.

"Good," he said with a smug smile.

Alaia sat up and shook a rain of orange leaves off her hair. "It's scary. It truly hasn't been that long. Khest, it was just a year ago that we left home. Whatever *home* means."

"Right now, home is this forest, and I must say it's quite a beautiful home." Sterjall rose to his feet and helped Alaia up. "Let's keep going, we don't have much time till dark."

They walked side by side among the hoodoos, spotting new creatures and plants they could never have dreamed of before. Sterjall bounced his muzzle to an internal beat.

"Hey, how about this?" he asked after a while.

Their tale in rhyming couplets grows alongside best of friends,

Though he'd be happier writing prose a *qua*train next he pens.

"That's the one!" Alaia shouted. She put an arm around him as they walked. "Best of friends."

Kulak meandered ahead of Kenondok, his footpaws rustling over the orange leaves.

"I cannot wait to leave this cursed dome," Kenondok muttered, following behind him. He had gotten used to speaking in Common, but when he was alone with Kulak, he felt he needed to use Miscamish to fully express himself.

"Hmm..." Kulak said. He'd asked Kenondok to come with him, but he was paying little attention to him. He was instead picturing what his life might've been like if he'd been born in a place like this. He imagined his dead brother walking beside him, picturing him in his half-form—or perhaps quarter form—of a tiger. He could've been holding his handpaw, he thought. His big brother's handpaw.

"Ashaskem..." he mumbled.

"Huh?" Kenondok asked, barely hearing the breathed words.

"Nothing," Kulak said. "Help me up, my eyes can see better from above."

Kenondok boosted Kulak up onto a craggy hoodoo. The caracal scanned above the canopy, hearing Kenondok still complaining below him.

"The forest is too dense," Kulak said, hopping down to the soft ground. "But there is a clearing ahead, that way." He pointed with his whiskers.

"As I was saying," Kenondok went on, "Siffo is a captain. Maybe they can bring their own ship and crew. We do not need their kind on our ship."

"Why is this such a big problem with you?" Kulak questioned, finally too bothered by the running blabbering to continue ignoring it.

"Not just me. Ilsed will not like it, Abjus will not like it, all the sailors will not like it. My scalp knows we need this woman—"

"Ierun, she is Ierun in this land. Get used to referring to her that way."

"Fine. We need this *Ierun* for the mission, but she and her people are sinful, and *Drolvisdinn* is a sacred ship."

"What is so sacred about it? It is a pile of wood and cloth."

"Khuron!"

"This is why I asked you to come with me. Because your scalp cannot stop thinking in backward ways. And who knows what careless things you would say to Siffo or Malnûvi, or Noss forbid, to Nalaníri herself, if left alone with them."

Kenondok's face reddened, partly from embarrassment, but mostly from anger. "Your mother would not have thought this way. She is wiser."

Kulak froze, his voice flat and quiet when he replied, "You have no idea of the things Mother has done. Or worse yet, Father. Do not talk like you know them, because you do not."

"What is it you speak of? I've known them for longer than you have been alive."

"You do not know them well enough. And you do not know me. If you did, you would not have wanted me—nor others you consider friends—aboard *Drolvisdinn* either."

"Speak clearly, Khuron," Kenondok demanded while crossing his arms and lifting his chin.

"I do not take orders from you, Weaponsmith." Kulak turned away and kept walking. "Your scalp can figure it out."

Sunu walked alone.

They had let Olo fly free, to explore the forest on their own.

Sometimes they could feel the ghost of Olo's claws where he normally perched on their shoulder, but Olo was not there.

It felt like a part of them was missing. But not Olo; it was something else.

The isopods blared a droning alarm, unceasing, unnerving.

Sunu walked alone and found a toppled black rock. Their violet-cast eyes looked up the rusty column it had fallen from and found the topless top, sitting lonesome with no blackness to shelter it.

They climbed atop the black rock and from it leapt to grab the exposed edge of the broken hoodoo, then pulled themself up to the barren top.

Sunu sat alone, cross-legged, atop the incomplete column.

Lacewings hovered around them, forming a translucent-green spiral.

They closed their eyes and listened to the forest.

The forest spoke to them.

Kitjári was the first to scent a clear trail. It was not a fair competition, as the others did not have her extraordinary sense of smell or her tracking skills. She followed her nose. *Smells smokey, musky, with a hint of worn leather*, she thought, and then breathed in a pungent and sweet tinge. She formed synesthetic mental images from the varied smells she caught—their qualia were infinitely complex and descriptive to her bear senses.

She circled around a toppled hoodoo, finding nothing behind it, but she leaned down and smelled the black rock: hints of sandalwood, oakmoss, and salty sweat. *It smells good*, she thought.

She found a pocket of disturbed leaves and compared the moisture of the leaves that had been flipped around to those that remained untouched. She ran her paw pads over parallel scrapes on the side of a hoodoo, and near them found two wiry white hairs, disguised against the light bark of a silver poplar. She put one in her muzzle to taste it.

She stood straight then, feeling foolish as she realized she had been following her nose and tracking instincts too much, and not focusing Urnaadisilv's sight. As she consciously brought the sense to life, the threads of the forest revealed themselves in their infinite complexity. She tried to perceive the threads farther ahead of her rather than wider to her sides, but the forest was so filled with life that it became confusing, so she went back to her own way of doing things.

She prowled over the mulch and undergrowth, following an invisible trail that to her bear nose smelled like... like... *Like a sunbeam made of snowflakes?* She did not understand why she'd thought that—her senses made no sense sometimes—but she could follow the trail nonetheless.

Something tingled in the periphery of Urnaadisilv's sight, from a direction she was not expecting: up over the canopy, on top of a smooth hoodoo, she could feel the characteristic glow of a Silv. The aura had an opalescent pink color, like a crystallized soap bubble refracting rosy petals.

She approached in silence and saw someone climbing down in a strange fashion, using a rope wrapped around a wide pillar of marbled rock with one end tied to her belt, the other tight in her grasp as she leaned backward to force the weight of her sharp-hoofed feet against the rock, as if walking down a wall. From this angle, Kitjári could only see the boar's feet and curly, tufted tail coming out of her leather trousers, but there was no doubt this was Nalaníri.

Nalaníri kept dropping slowly by giving a bit of slack to her rope before tensing it again. She paused, as if feeling something was out of place.

Kitjári called from below, "Excuse me, are you Ierun Nalan—"

"*Møg yomach?!*" Nalaníri bellowed. She pulled too tightly on the rope, making her legs too vertical, losing friction. She toppled down.

Kitjári rushed to aid and didn't quite catch her—Nalaníri would've been too heavy for that—but did soften her landing, tumbling sideways with her to roll atop a soft bed of leaves.

From the pile of autumnal colors, Nalaníri sprang up in utter confusion, screaming, "*Fûggun ishk nim yeg nëaggo! Zhu yeg hant—*"

And then she went quiet, seeing Kitjári, sensing Urnaadisilv's golden aura, and perhaps understanding the implications.

She brushed off leaves from between her white shirt and Spring-green vest, then stood on uncertain, flexible hooves, unsure of how hard she must've hit her head on the way down.

"I'm sorry if I startled you. I don't speak Puqua," Kitjári said. "My name is Kitjári, my friends and I—"

Nalaníri leaned in uncomfortably close to Kitjári's face, scrutinizing. Kitjári crossed her beady eyes to stare at the boar's heart-shaped nose: the septum was pierced by a horseshoe-shaped nosering with two pharolith beads at the ends.

Nalaníri was in her half-form of a wild boar, though some of her softer features more closely resembled those of a domestic pig. She was a pear-shaped woman with strong, hairy arms. Her body was portly, covered in random spots of white and black fur, with gray tones fringing the edges.

"What sort uf creature are ye?" she asked. "Why d'ye glow like a field of barley? Have I lost mine senses?" She leaned in and touched her nose to Kitjári's, in her own manner of greeting.

Kitjári startled back, confused. "I am the Urnaadifröa," she said, wiping her nose. She shapeshifted into her human form and took off the mask for Nalaníri to see. "We came here looking for you, from far-distant lands. We need your help."

Nalaníri's eyes widened. Her amiable lips awkwardly smiled to uncover two small, glossy tusks protruding upward from her lower jaw. Even with her snout fully closed, the tiny tusks lightly lifted her lips, making it seem as if she was constantly smiling. She softly caressed the mask that Jiara held in front of her and said, "Urnaadifröa, I am beyond honored! But I'm mostly confused. How'd ye come t'be in d'Slømmon Forest? Shell ye not be in Urnaadidrolom, awaiting fur Noss's call?"

"How to say this…" Jiara took a deep breath. "We came looking for you, Ierun Nalaníri, because the—"

Nalaníri snorted and belly laughed. "Ierun? I'm no ierun, m'dear. I'm jis' a chef who happens t'be a-wearing a fancy mask."

"Ierun, chief, either way—"

"Not chief, m'dear, *chef*. We have no ierenesh in Nagradrolom. I'm sorry, I did not mean t'interrupt ye. Do go on."

"Honestly, it's a long and complicated story, and one better told with the help of the other Silvfröash who travel with me."

Nalaníri looked around. "Uther Silvfröash? I see them not."

"They are spread around the forest trying to find you, like I was. We are to meet back at Tur-Reveok before the sun sets. I mean, before it gets dark."

"Well, ye arrived jis' in time then, Kitjári, voice uf d'ursids," Nalaníri said. She bundled her rope, placed a hoofed hand on Jiara's shoulder, and began walking. "Jis' in time, 'cause up un that hoodoo, I harvested four delicious honey truffles, n'them were d'last ingredient I needed t'prepare a most sumptuous dinner. Ye all shell join me n'tell me yer story, though I'm much too curious n'will ask ye questions d'entire time we walk there."

"That sounds fair to me, as I'm feeling quite hungry," Jiara said as she followed. "And my name is Jiara, Jiara Ascura, when I'm not wearing the Silv."

Nalaníri stopped, mortified by her mistake and her lack of courtesy. She shapeshifted, took her own mask off, and said, "A pleasure to meet ye, Jiara Ascura. This's d'uther me. Name's Prikka, though ye won't see me in this form much often."

In her human form, Prikka had only one suid-like trait: her skin was half pink and half black, divided in splotches matching the patterns of her half-form's fur. Her short-trimmed hair was half white and half black, depending on the skin color beneath it.

Her skin is like a maze of light and dark, Jiara thought.

Prikka tensed uncomfortably at the stare. She put Nagrasilv back on and shapeshifted into her wild boar half-form again. The glowing nosering had stayed put on her bulbous nose the entire time.

Jiara followed suit, turning back into the cinnamon-furred bear.

"Now tell me, Kitjári uf d'Urnaadi, what news have ye brought frum d'world outside them impenetrable walls?"

They strode side by side while Kitjári explained all she could. Nalaníri would get distracted often, as she would smell mushrooms or herbs and go pluck them, then store them in the many pockets of her vest. She explained to Kitjári that the honey truffles she was searching for grew only in a thin layer of fertile sediment compressed between the rusty columns and their black tops. They were hard to find, and one always had to climb to get to them.

They took a minor detour so that Nalaníri could retrieve her gear. Her camp was at the end of a box canyon eroded in the marbled rock. Nalaníri entered the secluded chamber and gasped as she stared down. Her backpack was on the ground, the top was open, and over it a wiry-haired javelina was munching on the quoll-quolls that had spilled out.

"Probo! Get yer hairy balls uff mine ingredients! Shush!" Nalaníri chased after the javelina, who shapeshifted into a tiny pygmy hog and escaped with a shrill squeal through a crack in the wall.

"Was that... the Nu'irg ust Nagra?"

Nalaníri grunted twice. "D'one n'unly. He's such a pest, no respect at all. It's not like he can't a-find his own food, or eat blood cakes like d'rest uf his kind." She pushed the isopods and herbs that did not have too much drool on them back into the bag, then hauled it over her thick shoulders. "N'he'll be back," she added. "He's certainly smelled mine honey truffles by now. It's d'one food he can't get un his own, not 'til he learns to tie ropes 'round that selfish pot belly uf his."

An axe was stuck into a log, its blade encrusted with a complex pattern of pharoliths, making it sparkle with an icy light. The sharp blade was opposed by equally sharp twin tusks of ivory white. Nalaníri unwedged the axe from the log.

"What a beautiful weapon," Kitjári whispered, leaning in to stare at the delicate figures the pharoliths drew upon the blade.

Nalaníri snorted. "Weapon? It's a tool, m'dear. T'chop wood n'remove quoll-quoll shells. Why would anyone be a-carrying a weapon in these here peaceful forests?" She tucked the axe in a scabbard by her side, the lights from it vanishing beneath the cover.

Kitjári continued with her story as they approached their destination.

Probo didn't take too long to return, being at first hesitant and shy in a warthog shape, then hopping along next to them in his javelina primal form. Kitjári admired Probo's spiked, bristly hairs, and the delicate white collar that formed around his neck. His aura shared the same opalescent rosiness as Nalaníri's, though his felt more erratic. Kitjári also could not help but notice Probo's enormous, bouncing testicles. She bowed to him and offered a bearish smile. Probo grunted, content even if still distrustful.

"Are you mindspeaking to him to explain what is happening?" Kitjári asked.

"He's asking me to, but I'm not a-giving him d'satisfaction. Let him wunder fur a while."

Kitjári and Nalaníri were the first to arrive back at Tur-Reveok. As they neared it, Probo stopped and sniffed the air. He hopped around, searching. In front of the three arches, he saw Mamóru, standing with arms outstretched. He hesitated, recognizing his old friend while still finding him much too different from how he remembered him. He rushed to meet Mamóru's embrace, then rubbed noses with him as he squealed. Probo then noticed Blu and Pichi sitting under the arches and gave them a dismissive huff. Blu ignored him, but Pichi retorted with a saber-sharp hiss. It was fine; not everyone needed to like each other.

Kitjári introduced Mamóru to the Nagrafröa. Noses were rubbed, then Nalaníri took out her cooking implements and ingredients, asking Kitjári to bring wood and paper birch bark so she could make a fire under the arches. Kitjári showed Nalaníri how to light a fire using a cube of brime, making her snort at the white-hot sparks it produced, then sneer disapprovingly at the rotten-egg smell they left behind.

As the dome darkened, the others returned.

When Sterjall and Alaia arrived, Nalaníri rubbed noses with the wolf, then pulled on his whiskers to peer at his piercing canines in an unintentionally rude fashion, making Sterjall laugh nervously and eye Alaia for help. After rubbing noses with Alaia, she quickly reached to scratch at her nub and smelled it up close, squealing happily with approval, then returned to her cooking duties.

She was confused when she smelled Sunu, though she could not tell why. Olo *eihnk-eihnk*ed when Nalaníri got too close, and she responded with an exhaling huff and slight shake of her head, in a similar attitude to Probo when meeting the smilodons.

Then came Siffo, with Malnûvi close behind him. They knew the Nagrafröa and exchanged pleasantries with her. They helped Nalaníri hang pharolith lamps around the camp, illuminating the inside of the three arches with the cold symmetry of the effulgent flowers.

When Kulak and Kenondok arrived, Nalaníri played with the black tufts on Kulak's ears, then went on to touch noses with Kenondok, who backed off in revulsion and stood defensively.

"*Gmorgee thuspt!*" she muttered in Puqua, shaking her head. She slowly turned around, snorted at Kenondok, then went back to cooking.

The dinner was opulent and slow-cooked. Nalaníri assigned roles to a few people, as she needed help if the courses were to be ready at the proper times. Once the cooking was done, she served a plate for each of them—including ones for Probo, Blu, and Pichi—of a sumptuous meal of three different species of quoll-quolls stuffed with opaltusk mushrooms and infused with a blackcurrant balsamic reduction. The three isopods were served next to a side of honey truffle wild rice, topped with crushed nuts, and decorated with water hyssop leaves and flowers. And there was plenty of acorn flatbread to go with the course.

Nalaníri insisted the Silvfröash try the meal in their half-forms *and* in their human forms, to taste the differences in flavors the qualia of the Silvesh provided. They humored her, and could taste the difference, but they missed a lot of the delicate notes Nalaníri kept going on about. Just like how Sterjall's hearing, Kulak's sight, and Kitjári's sense of smell were exceptional, so was Nalaníri's sense of taste.

It was chilly that night. After cleaning up, they sat around a bonfire. They had finally finished telling Nalaníri their full story and were waiting for her reply.

"I've no reason t'doubt yer story or yer motives," she said as she munched on fresh berries—as simple a dessert as she could concoct after that complex dinner.

"I'll join ye into Kruwendrolom, n'I hope we can have a good chat with old Noss. As fur Nagradrolom, if d'world outside is green n'lush, I agree it's time t'open it. It'll help Noss t'become mour connected if we can spread suidkind across them lands. But mine tusks a-worry. Ye say war's a-brewing, that them want t'take d'Silvesh away. Would them not come after d'Puqua? Will it be safe to do as ye ask?"

"It won't be as complicated as with the Laatu," Kitjári said. She reached over and plucked a few huckleberries from a bowl, then while chewing, said, "The lands around the Fjordlands Dome are not densely populated. Koroberg is a big city, part of Zovaria, but it doesn't have any military bases. And the Khaar Du up north are a peaceful kind. You would still do well to be careful, to set boundaries and expect skirmishes, but the war won't reach you here."

"We'll help you plan the best routes," Sterjall added. "And as far as Nagrasilv, you are right—they will come after it, after you. But if we stick together, we will protect one another."

"Thank ye, wulfy," Nalaníri said as she reheated a piece of flatbread over the fire, holding it in her hoofed fingers, seemingly unbothered by the flames. "In d'morning we can return to Krûn, n'we'll summon d'chiefs uf all d'pruvinces. Ye shell explain it all again, n'them will take charge uf d'preparations fur d'dome t'open. We've been ready fur this moment, though we never thought d'day would arrive. There's a plan we can set in motion. It'll take 'bout a week, then we can sail away."

"We can bring our own ship," Siffo said, to Kenondok's relief. "Mineself n'mine crew shell volunteer t'help. I'm d'cap'n uf d'fastest vessel in Ôllomuy, as our four trophies frum d'pooning regatta can attest to. We could depart together, frum Mâscarmush."

Malnûvi nodded and said, "I will take care uf gathering d'Krûn shamans as early as possible in d'morrow, to send messages to all d'chiefs."

Nalaníri grunted her approval. "In d'morrow, Nagradrolom's end will be set underway, n'a new life fur d'Puqua shell begin! D'light uf d'kenzir shell show us d'way, n'we shell fullow!"

Chapter Sixty-Five

Hêsshogo's Bow

After an unnecessarily elaborate but delicious breakfast, the wayfarers walked out of the forest, boarded the kubanochoeruses, and made their way back to Krûn.

Upon their return to the capital, Siffo gave each of them a rib-crushing hug, rubbed noses with them to bid them farewell, and departed for Ôllomuy to ready his ship. Sunu sent Olo to Ilsed and Abjus, to let them know of their plans and to warn them to expect Siffo and his vessel.

The Puqua chiefs met at the Guildhall of Krûn after two cycles of the arudinn. As the head chef of the guildhall, Nalaníri had been busy preparing a feast for the proceedings. While the chiefs asked their questions, Nalaníri walked around the enormous table handing out a sumptuous dessert of live grubs crawling on a spiced fruit salad.

"We can set a perimeter uf warriors un d'eastern lands," an almost entirely plain-skinned chief recommended. "Two mour at the great bays with our fleet, but d'northwest shell need no aid."

"Keep your pharoliths hidden from foreigners," Kulak warned, "as we Laatu kept our brime and soot mines secret. Use the stones of light for trade, but only after your scalps get to know your new neighbors."

"That shell be d'hardest uf our tasks, it seems," an old chief with a drooping snout said. "Protecting our perimeter we can handle, but living without our kenzir stones?"

"It's unly fur a few months," Nalaníri said, taking a seat at the table once more. "We need t'develop relationships, learn who can be trusted. Now eat yer grubs before them crawl out of yer bowls."

With not much hesitation, the chiefs agreed to move forward with the plan and begin opening the dome in one week's time. The Puqua were well organized, and the process was expedient and well rehearsed. The chiefs would have a lot of work to do, but the citizens were already spreading the gossip, stowing away or covering all pharoliths, assembling their fleet and warriors for protection, and gathering all the companion suids that would help with the transition into the new epoch.

Once the preparations were underway, Nalaníri's cooks, waiters, and other helpers began to pack up and prepare for the opening. She felt sorrowful seeing her empty kitchen, not knowing when she might return to this land she for so long had called home.

Without the guildhall kitchen to worry about, Nalaníri's duties were limited: other than meeting daily with representatives from distant towns and talking with people on the streets to ease their worries and anxieties, she spent most of her time cooking for her guests and inquiring more about their adventures. The travelers had been staying in Nalaníri's home, a simple dwelling with most of the cramped space dedicated to her kitchen.

A few days after the meeting with the chiefs, three guests showed up for dinner at Nalaníri's home: a boy named Rushun and a girl named Pau—both teenagers—who'd come from the distant mining town of Barushem, accompanied by their father, a much older man named Odask, who did not seem very friendly. Nalaníri rubbed noses with the two youths but not with the old man.

The three guests spoke only Puqua, but with the aid of Agnargsilv, Sterjall gathered that the teenagers were Nalaníri's children, yet he was uncertain of what relationship Nalaníri had with Odask. The boy and girl wanted to travel north with a caravan as soon as the dome opened, so they'd come to say their farewells to Nalaníri. Odask said he would stay in Barushem, as he was too old and tired for new adventures.

After Odask and the children left, Nalaníri would say no more about them, and no one felt comfortable enough to pry into her private matters.

On the morning of the twenty-eighth day of Fireleaf, Nalaníri led her guests to the Krûn Temple. The Nagrafröa was more welcoming here than Alúma had been at Mindreldrolom, and without hesitation invited those who did not wield a Silv—Alaia, Sunu, Kenondok, and even Blu and Pichi—to join in and watch as she set the opening of the dome in motion. All but Kenondok accepted the invitation, as for him the sacred temple had been forbidden at home and so was forbidden here as well. He waited outside, standing uncomfortably next to the pig-headed guards.

Nalaníri led them underneath the massive kuba skull, to the long, shallow ramp of the pharolith-decorated hallway. The inside of the temple was lit by radiant suid sculptures of glass with pharolith hearts that shone at their cores. The sculptures glowed so brightly that colorful lacquers had been painted over them to diffuse their light.

The smooth core vine climbed up from the central dais, and in front of it the marble throne waited, tusked hundredfold, in a tangle of curves that did not look comfortable for hinds or backs. Nalaníri took her place upon the throne and expediently directed the threads to collapse the quaar lattice inward. The conduits and joints above her folded with mathematical precision, like a kaleidoscope of shadows. The lattice tightened, forming an armor around the core vine, then a powerful signal of invisible threads shot upward and permeated throughout the dome. The vine and its quaar shield sank slowly underground, leaving only a hole that soon filled with white sap. A rumble tore through the temple, followed by a pervasive feeling like that of static electricity. Vines rustled and crawled, signaling the beginning of the end of Nagradrolom.

It would take some time for the dome to open enough for people to travel in and out, but the wayfarers would not wait to depart. With the deed almost too unceremoniously completed, they walked out, mounted on Blu, Pichi, and a few giant domestic pigs—who were less comfortable, but much nimbler than the kubas—and followed the marbled canyons down toward the fjords, following the lodestone path. Probo pranced near them all the while, taking the shapes of many different suids and somehow always managing to show up ahead of them, then disappear behind, and then show up ahead once more.

At noon of the following day, they arrived at the pier of Mâscarmush, where Hud Ilsed, Hod Abjus, and Captain Siffo greeted them. *Drolvisdinn* was accompanied by Siffo's ship. White of hull and black of sails, the seaworthy vessel relied upon magsteel-strong kuba bones as part of the construction of its deck and hull. The ship's name was *Fjummomurr*, which in Puqua meant *tusked whale*, and its skeletal bow was decorated with a prominent figurehead in the shape of a narwhal with a twirling tusk painted in silver. *Fjummomurr* was illuminated by dozens of pharolith lamps, and dozens more were stowed in its hold, to be traded for valuable goods in the New World.

As captain of the radiant Puqua ship, Siffo looked the part, having transformed his bulky figure with a leather tailcoat suit and a colorful tricorne hat.

He had decorated his upper tusks with pharolith rings and the lower ones with pharolith caps, although he would remove them at night so they would not hinder his sight in the dark. He strolled proudly upon his deck, issuing quick orders to his dependable Puqua sailors, readying them to cast off all lines.

Ilsed, Abjus, and the *Drolvisdinn* crew seemed to have adjusted to the suid-like strangers. When Kulak inquired as to how they had fared, Ilsed confessed that she was not comfortable with the Puqua boarding her ship, and they had refused assistance with fixing their torn sails, but they did accept the Puqua's materials to craft replacement battens and repair the hull damage. Ilsed agreed to make an exception for Nalaníri, who wanted to travel with the rest of the Silvfröash. Kenondok sulked at this decision, quiet in his displeasure and his inability to overrule the captain's orders.

It was a bright day when they departed, with cumulus clouds clinging like snowy canopies to the tops of the supporting columns and the trunk. Nalaníri said goodbye to Probo, who would lead suidkind out from the dome to help with the migrations, just as Nelv was doing with the felids. The wind was moderate and steady, and the time to depart was at hand.

"D'light uf d'kenzir is with ye!" Malnûvi hollered from the barnacled pier.

"N'so it shines within us all!" Captain Siffo and Nalaníri replied from their ships.

The two vessels sailed west from Mâscarmush, through the same fjords *Drolvisdinn* had traversed previously. Probo followed at the cliff's edge, weaving left and right around the lodestones.

"I shell miss that rotten yam uf a suid," Nalaníri said, waving goodbye to the Nu'irg while also mindspeaking tender words of farewell to him.

"Seems like he'll miss you too," Kitjári said. "Look at him go."

The javelina followed fast and swift, until the headland ended, and he could follow no longer. He let out a shrill squeal and turned around.

Alaia came closer. "Hey, Nalaníri, I was curious about something," she said.

"Yes, m'dear?"

"Since many of the Puqua are close to being in their half-forms... Does that mean you can mindspeak with each other?"

Nalaníri laughed from the depths of her belly, then slapped Alaia right on her back spurs. "Wouldn't that be awful!" she said. "Thank d'Tricolored Mountain we cannot. Imagine having t'hear all them rowdy sailors even when them are not a-singing. No, mine dear, that we cannot do. I can mindspeak with mine feral suids unly because Nagrasilv acts as a bridge fur it."

"It's strange," Alaia thought aloud. "Shouldn't it be natural for all humans to mindspeak, like it is with every other species?"

"Mayhaps," Nalaníri answered, "but humans lost them voices long ago, before them fjords were carved by d'mighty tusks uf Lûrrumaag."

"Lost their voices?" Alaia asked. "How? What do you mean?"

"Ye ask me questions like I'm some sort uf sage, but d'only sage I know I use t'cook with. How shell I know? It's jis' d'way things are. D'rest be myths, legends, n'bedtime stories."

"Something was indeed lost by humankind," Mamóru quietly added, "while something else was gained. This happened even before my time, and how or why no one can truly tell."

"The Tsing codices speak of some of that," Kitjári offered. "We had a Tsing soldier at Thornridge who told us a weird story about monkeys who swallowed stars. Made no sense at all. But she believed in it, she thought it was the reason humans lost their voices."

"I wonder if we'll regain that ability one day," Alaia mused.

"There may be hope still," Nalaníri said. "If them Acoapóshi n'Noss were able t'craft these here Silvesh, perhaps there is some way t'restore what we lost."

Dusk was settling by the time they reached the edge of Nagradrolom. They let Nalaníri begin the parting of the vines so that she could understand how the empathic focus worked on them, and she picked it up right away, just as Kulak had.

"It's jis' like asking d'lattice t'collapse," she observed. "Nagrasilv asks kindly, n' d'vines a-listen."

With the combined strength of the Silvesh, the vines opened even wider than before, allowing the two ships to fit through easily, with *Drolvisdinn* at the head and *Fjummomurr* close behind. They expected to encounter bright sunlight when they breached through, but instead they were met by a gray morning with a light rain.

"Rain again?" Kitjári complained, putting on an oilskin coat. "Why does it have to be the exact opposite on the other side for this dome?"

"I have t'admit, it's a bit disappointing," Nalaníri said. "I truly wanted t'see d'blue sky ye all keep babbling about. So far it looks jis' d'same as d'Keldris Allastirg in d'Umbra season."

"Give it time," Sterjall said, looking up at the low clouds. The vapors were shifting fast, and spreading.

They were all gathered atop *Drolvisdinn*'s quarterdeck, watching for any signs from Sunnokh.

The air brightened.

Kulak pointed straight up and said, "Nalaníri, look," but rather than looking up himself, he watched Nalaníri's expression. The sky had opened up, revealing a patch of perfect blue above them. Nalaníri's face spread wide with joy, and Kulak's did the same, seeing in Nalaníri what his expression must have been like the first time he'd seen the blue sky, or the stars. Behind them, they heard the crew of *Fjummomurr* hollering and grunting with delight.

The drizzling mist around them turned yellow. The clouds that had been enveloping them pushed west with the warmer, eastern winds, filling their sails with warmth and light. The cloud finally moved past them, revealing the perfect blue sky and the glorious face of Sunnokh reflecting over the Isdinnklad. They stared eastward, entranced. *Fjummomurr*'s crew went silent, while Nalaníri leaned so far over the edge of *Drolvisdinn*'s railings that the others were afraid she'd tumble snout first into the sea.

"D'bow uf Hêshoggo has come t'bless our sails!" came a call from the bow of the other ship. It was Captain Siffo, projecting his powerful voice across. "Behold d'colors uf d'hero's mighty bow!"

They all turned and saw that the drizzling cloud that had just passed them carried with it a perfect rainbow. Nalaníri squealed with delight, and Kulak tightly embraced Sterjall when he saw the arched beauty, which he had only known about from spritetales. They held each other and stared at the bow of all colors, sailing fast toward it, though it would remain forever unreachable.

Chapter Sixty-Six

Sea Shanties

"What are they singing about now?" Sterjall asked Nalaníri.

Fjummomurr's crew had felt their hearts so full that they'd been compelled to belt out their joy, singing sea shanties aft and fore till their throats ran sore. The latest shanty was in Puqua, though even those in Common had been very hard for Sterjall to understand.

"This one's a song fur hauling cargo," Nalaníri said. "Them lazy hogs aren't hauling a thing, but shanties sometimes are good jis' fur d'joy uf singing. Each uf them songs serves a different purpose, t'keep them rhythms a-going, t'call out instructions, t'replenish them spirits."

Captain Siffo had been leading the singing, but with his throat now sore, he tapped on the shoulders of both his shantyman and shantywoman, who carried on with a much more vulgar tune. The shantyman began, aided by responses from the men among the crew:

Mine callused old phallus is callous as gallows,

Sink that twisting eel! Ho!

It sniffs fur yer palace but don't mean no malice,

Make them hogwives squeal! Yo!

Don't care that yer chalice a-stinks like old scallops.

Force them down to kneel! Ho!

Mine callused old phallus is callous as gallows.

Plunge that twisting eel! Yo!

The shantywoman led next, with the women responding to her chant:

Yer numb prick be downcast n'seasick, ye won't last.

Hack your flaccid eel! Hey!

Yer foreskin be vast as d'sails uf d'foremast.

Dice it down with steel! Ay!

Ye don't blast n'sore gast, this boar hast ye bored fast!

Bugger off or we'll—hey!

Yer numb prick be downcast n'seasick, ye won't last.

Chop your flaccid eel! Ay!

Sterjall ears were pricked up. "Are they really singing about—"

"Yes, m'dear wulfy," Nalaníri cut in. "About how t'properly dice n'cook eels, nothing mour."

By late afternoon, the Varanus Dome appeared on the distant horizon, poking through gray clouds.

"It's hard to see any details," Alaia said, gazing through the binoculars. "But I can see some of the bigger vines poking out from it, like scraggly hairs."

"I can't wait for it to get dark," Sterjall said. "I've been wanting to see the Varanus wisps ever since Crysta told me about them. Have you traveled there before?" he asked Mamóru. "Is it true there are dragons living there?"

"There once were, dragons of a sort," Mamóru said. "Fel Varanus used to be inhabited by giant lizards, which the Mo'óto Miscam tribe called *varanus dragons*. I don't know whether they survived the Downfall, but I presume they must still survive somewhere within the dome."

No proper sunset welcomed them that day. Billowing clouds had been congregating suspiciously in the west, obscuring the last hours of sunlight and any view of the Varanus Dome. Still, Nalaníri thought it was most beautiful, and she held her breath when she saw patches of gray sky briefly turn rosy pink—the color of her aura—before bleeding into darkness.

Right before the morning twilight, when the sky was at its darkest shade of ultramarine, Sterjall was awoken by a shaking of his shoulders.

"Gwoli, you should come out and see this."

"What is it?" he mumbled, drool sticking his whiskers to his muzzle.

"I think you probably guessed by now," Alaia said. "Jiara is up there already. Bring your kitty."

Sterjall shook Kulak awake. They climbed abovedeck and joined the others atop the forecastle. Sterjall came to a stop next to Alaia. Kulak came behind them and placed his soft chin on the wolf's shoulder, letting his whiskers tickle the longer fur at his neck. Sterjall peered uncomfortably around, then relaxed when he saw that no Laatu crew members could spot the risky gesture.

Alaia and Jiara were there staring at the dome, which was now much closer and much more menacing-looking. The clouds had all receded, revealing a sky that was clear and star-studded. Sceres was setting in the west, casting an eerie rim of Amethyst light on the northern edges of the dome, which terminated in an incomprehensible silhouette of a million unruly tentacles. Despite its terrifying shapes, the dome was beautiful.

And it glowed.

Wisps sprouted from it, dozens of them, and in the humid and salty air the lights looked like needles of heavenly light splitting cracks into the darkness.

Sterjall caressed Kulak's head as they stood in silence.

For so many years I dreamed of seeing this, Sterjall thought. *It's both beautiful and terrifying. I hope Crysta found a way into the Moordusk Dome. She deserves to experience all of this, and more.* He glanced toward Alaia. "Thank you for waking me up."

"How could I not? I remember you obsessing over wisps ever since you first looked through that damn telescope. It all changed for you then. No turning back."

"It's true," he admitted. *No turning back.*

Jiara had been keeping watch with the binoculars all night. She handed them back to Sterjall. "Check out the one on the top left, the streaky one. I think it's about to vanish," she said.

As Sterjall looked at it, the wisp flickered and abruptly disappeared.

"They've been doing that all night," Jiara said. "Some show up, others vanish. They tend to shimmer before it happens."

Sterjall was surprised to see Jiara and not Kitjári; she had been keeping her bear half-form almost all the time lately. Her long hair was blowing westward, as if trying to touch the last beams of purple moonlight.

"You haven't slept?" he asked her.

"Dozed off a few times. Don't worry, kid, I'll go to bed soon."

Sterjall followed Jiara's gaze as she looked toward the stern. Sitting at the edge of the quarterdeck's railing was Nalaníri, keeping her eyes fixed on Sceres, waiting for her to set. Mamóru was leaning beside her, having a conversation that might have lasted all night.

"I've been standing watch and talking to Nalaníri," Jiara added. "She's so excited about everything, it's a wonder to behold. I don't believe she's blinked once since we saw the rainbow."

"My scalp cannot blame her," Kulak said to Sterjall. "The first time you took me outside Mindreldrolom, I also wanted to stay out and watch Sceres all night."

"Was that the time you rascals escaped to the beach instead of going to Parjuul?" Jiara asked slyly.

Sterjall's eyes widened. "Hey, how do you...? Alaia! I told you not to—"

"It was not Alaia. I told Jiara," Kulak confessed. "I had to tell someone. It was special. It always will be special."

"Yeah," Sterjall nervously agreed. "Just... don't tell anyone else, please."

"Mother is not here, she cannot ground me from across the sea. Let us enjoy the view. My eyes have not yet seen Sceres going to sleep in the waves. She seems ready for it."

Sceres dipped her trembling toes in the frigid waters of the Quiescent Ocean. The white caps lit up purple, streaking until the moon's light blinked and vanished. Though her shining presence was no longer directly visible, her rays were still illuminating the insurmountable dome and would continue to do so until the glow of Sunnokh took over.

Mamóru approached, the mistleaf from his pipe smoking up in purple veils. "Well, that was exquisite, but now I need to lie down. Would one of you please take care of Nalaníri? Perhaps you'll be better at convincing her to get some rest."

"I'll join you," Jiara told him. "Ilsed is taking next watch."

Alaia followed them as well, while Sterjall and Kulak joined Nalaníri at the quarterdeck. As always, with her tiny tusks pushing her upper lips up, it was hard to tell if Nalaníri was smiling, but her eyes told them she was indeed happy. The two beads on her nosering dimly lit up her pink nose, like twin stars.

"Endless beauty," she sighed. "One wunder after anuther." With the moon gone, she was now looking up at the brightening constellations. "This world offers so many a miracle, n'I've not been out here fur even a full day. I'm glad ye all came to me n'trusted me t'help ye. N'I will, I'll do all I can to let d'other tribes meet d'fullness uf this world."

"Your world is beautiful too," Sterjall said. "I'd never seen fjords before, or kubas, or pharoliths, or a majestic mountain of three colors. And I never tasted anything as delicious as those quoll-quolls you prepared."

She grunted happily. "N'now you've got me thinking uf all d'flavors n'delicacies I've been a-missing. How much mour there is to learn n'explore! It fills mine heart with joy n'mine belly with a demanding emptiness."

A green meteor slashed across the western sky.

"Did you see that?" Sterjall asked. Kulak and Nalaníri nodded.

"I've seen a dozen mour t'night," Nalaníri said. "Mamóru explained t'me what them are. I can't keep mine eyes uff d'sky, I don't know how any uf ye ever sleep. Ye have to teach me 'bout d'stars, wulfy. Jiara told me ye can read them, that them tell ye stories n'show ye where to go."

"I can teach you about a few of them, if you promise me you'll get some sleep right after."

"But what 'bout sunrise? I can't a-miss sunrise."

"There are still many hours till Sunnokh rises. How about this? I'll teach you about some of the stars and constellations, but then we both get some rest, and I'll ask Ilsed to wake us up in time for sunrise."

Nalaníri accepted the offer. Kulak stayed up with them for the lessons—he could never get enough of Sterjall talking about the stars.

Chapter Sixty-Seven

Sea Serpents

"I don't think we'll find a wall this time," Sterjall said, staring at the chaotic bramble they were headed toward. "It's like the vines just snake in and out of the water. There's no beginning or end to these tendrils."

The wind blew to the northwest, providing a beam reach on their tight sails, which they needed to trim a bit to avoid going too fast—vines could come up from nowhere now, and they could not risk snagging on them.

"My eyes see a way in," Ilsed remarked. "Left of the island off the starboard bow."

Kitjári spied through the binoculars. "Looks mostly open that way. Sterjall, what do you think?"

But before Sterjall could answer, they heard a piercing whistle, then a warthog-headed sailor yelled something in Puqua from the crow's nest of *Fjummomurr*.

"Ships to d'southeast," Nalaníri warned.

Kitjári aimed the binoculars behind them and quickly spotted the threat. "Shit. Pink sails. And they have a downwind run to us. They must've seen us by now."

"Can we outsail them?" Sterjall asked.

Hud Ilsed looked at her leaf-shaped sails. "Not with the wind blowing as it wills, not unless we change course away from Kruwendrolom."

"Some of those are scouting trimarans," Kitjári said. "They are fast and maneuver swiftly. But perhaps we could lose them among the vines."

"Do you think that's Admiral Grinn?" Alaia asked.

Kitjári shrugged. "I guess we'll find out soon enough. Nalaníri, let Cap'n Siffo know his crew should ready their weapons."

"D'Puqua sailors are not warriors, m'dear."

"Don't care. Tell them to hurl pharoliths if they must, but *Fjummomurr* needs to be ready."

Nalaníri removed her tusked axe from its scabbard, letting the inlaid pharoliths shine again, and said, "If a battle them want, a battle them shell have." She held the axe up high and vociferously called out instructions to the other ship.

"Let Pichi and Blu out from belowdecks," Kitjári said. "We might need their help."

"They are drowsy from the swaying," Kulak noted. "They will not be able to do much."

"But they will look intimidating. The Zovarians have already seen them fight once, they will think twice before attacking us with them on board."

Four ships closed in on them.

Drolvisdinn was arriving at the first gnarls of the dome, and now they saw how myths of dragons could easily be born in these waters: some of the large vines sank into the water and then curved back up, and down, and up again, looking like enormous sea serpents forming thorny arches above and below the whitecapped sea. Some of those tendrils extended for miles, while others were dense like thickets and clustered in cancerous clumps. They were entering the domain of dragons now, having to weave their way around the thorn-covered curves, praying to the sprites of wind and luck.

"Two ships are changing course," Ilsed notified them. "Under that vine!"

"They will cut in front of us," Kitjári said.

"Not if their sails are gone," Kulak said, rushing to starboard. "Come with me!"

A blaring horn blew in front of them as the two ships that had cut around appeared ahead of them, slightly to starboard.

Kulak pulled out a quaar conduit from his blowgun and aimed it up at the tangle of vines curving over the ships. Kitjári and Sterjall quickly followed his lead, with Nalaníri still confused as to what was happening. The vines lowered at their command like sluggish fingers, but just fast enough to catch the tip of a trimaran's sail.

The ship snagged and nearly flipped over, spinning with its momentum and leaving ragged pink tears of cloth on the thorns. The other trimaran cleared the threat, and now that it was no longer under the arch of green thorns, it began to match their heading while trying to wedge them closer to two more pink-sailed ships.

"Keep pushing, they'll move out of the way," Sterjall said.

Kitjári shook her head. "No, those hulls are reinforced with iron. They could take a hit and we'd be the ones in trouble. Pull slightly to port, but don't let them divert us entirely off-course."

The pink-sailed trimaran soon sailed right by their starboard side, still trying to force them to veer off.

"Tie up your sails and prepare to be boarded!" a voice yelled. The ship was close enough for them to see the soldiers' faces.

"Stay out of our way or we'll crash into you!" Sterjall yelled back.

"We can take that hit, but you may not!" their captain called out. "Tie up your sails now, under orders of Arch Sedecim Bervenisk of Holv-Umarion, or you will suffer the full force of the Centennial Fleet!"

"Is that you, Lago?" a higher-pitched voice called out. "Or Sterjall, I guess."

It was Kedra, climbing up the ratlines to get a better view.

"You rancid taint!" Alaia yelled. "You betrayed us!"

"Quiet, spur," she said, then focused on Sterjall again. "I knew I'd find you lurking around these domes. Was that you who was spotted around Koroberg a few weeks back? Where is Balstei? Admiral Grinn would like a word with him—his ship will reach us any moment now. Who are the ugly pig people in the other ship?"

"You ask too many questions," Kitjári said. "Now let us pass. If you sink our ship, the masks will sink with us."

"Or maybe they'll float, we'll see. Is that voice... Jiara?" Kedra asked, revealing the gap in her teeth through a wide smile. "You look different!" Her smile faded. "Those masks don't belong to you, and you know it. We are at war, and without them, the Zovarian Union will soon be doomed, and the rest of the realms will fall with us. Monarch Hallow is amassing a huge force, we *need* to fight back. You should help us instead of going around trying to—"

A metallic *clang* and then a *crack* stopped Kedra's words. They all looked back and saw a heavy rope extending from *Fjummomurr*'s prow, connecting to the Zovarian ship's rudder. Another *clang!* resounded as a second whaling harpoon launched from Siffo's ship, tying another rope to the rudder. The ropes were attached to heavy barrels and chains, which the Puqua crew pushed overboard to anchor the Zovarian vessel. *Fjummomurr* moved out of the way as the Zovarian ship snagged on the weight of the barrels—its rudder loosened and then broke off, sending them tumbling away.

"Bye, cunt!" Alaia yelled as Kedra's ship was lost behind them.

"Quickly, weave around those vines!" Ilsed called to her crew.

The other two ships were close, but now that they sailed under the same wind, the Zovarians began to lag behind. *Drolvisdinn* and *Fjummomurr* sailed almost side by side, coordinating their course. They approached a gnarl of huge vines, passed underneath an arch, and circled around two columns to lose their pursuers. But the enemy ships chose a narrow heading in a straight line and quickly closed the distance.

"Just keep pushing toward the dome," Sterjall suggested. "If we open a path in the vines, we can lose them."

"We cannot approach at full speed," Ilsed warned. "Vines will not open fast enough, *Drolvisdinn* would crash. We lose them in these waters, or they will catch up."

They kept weaving under the serpentine tangles, trying to outperform the two Zovarian ships. They made some headway, but were still miles from the proper edge of the dome.

As they passed between the snaking curves of yet another vine, they heard a loud creaking sound. Suddenly the ship jolted, hard enough that everyone fell to the deck.

Drolvisdinn slowed to a stop, while *Fjummomurr* barely avoided hitting them and kept sailing forward.

"We are snagged on an underwater vine!" a Laatu sailor reported.

The Silvfröash tried to combine their empathic focus to will the vine out of the way, but the vine was of the larger kind, and obstinate as a sleeping giant, it would not budge. The sailors took out their push poles to shift the pressure on the keel, but there were not enough points of contact to gain leverage. They would have to tie the sails and row in the opposite direction to free themselves, but there was not enough time to do that: a Zovarian ramship had already taken position on their port side, and the pink-clad soldiers were getting ready to board *Drolvisdinn*.

"Surrender now and we'll spare your lives!" called a blue-caped figure wearing shining bronze armor. Admiral Grinn. While standing on the edge of his ornate ramship and holding on to the rigging, the admiral felt a metallic clinking against his armor. He peered down and saw a small dart sticking out from his breastplate. Then a soldier toppled over unconscious next to him, then another fell overboard as more darts from the Laatu flew at them.

"Take them down! Board!" Grinn ordered.

Hooks were cast, ramps were pushed, and dozens of soldiers rushed toward *Drolvisdinn*. Kitjári released five arrows in quick succession, each aimed with deadly precision, but as the fight came to them, she leapt to the front, slicing and parrying with her sword as soldiers tried to reach the deck. A spear swung by her muzzle, and she bit the arm holding it, spinning with its force and hurling the spearman into the sea. Another Zovarian jumped her—she swiped at him with her claws, letting him topple onto the deck with his chest ripped open.

"Hold them back!" she yelled, but like ants, the Zovarians kept on coming.

Sterjall used Leif to cut as many ropes as he could, while Kulak stood by his side to protect him, shooting darts with his quaar blowgun. Alaia was up on the ratlines, wearing the quaar helm Banook had gifted her, taking her time to aim her blowgun at those enemies wearing the least amount of plated armor.

Kenondok, Abjus, and Sunu focused on detaching the ramps, but they were barbed and too heavy for them to pull back up. As the soldiers ran over the platforms, Sunu spun their long halberd in a Maelstrom Gale, then followed it with a Chitin Claw, aiming for their legs, cracking tibias and fibulas and sending the soldiers tumbling in pinwheels before they slammed into the sea. Those who made it across were met by Abjus's and Kenondok's blades and fists.

Both Pichi and Blu were flashing their saber-like teeth, but the constant swaying of the ship made them tumble off balance. The Zovarians tried to keep their distance, but they were met with the smilodons' full ferocity if they drew close.

The Laatu had an advantage at a distance, but as soon as their foes were within close range, most were hopelessly unprepared and outnumbered.

"Siffo is coming back!" Sterjall said, trying to keep his hopes up. *Fjummomurr* was turning, but it would take some time for the ship to maneuver around the vines—their aid would not arrive soon enough.

Nalaníri dodged a spear and stood bewildered, not knowing what to do. She was not a fighter like the others, yet Nagrasilv gave her the advantage of foreseeing attacks. She brandished her tusked axe when she could and body slammed a careless attacker or two, but mostly stayed out of the way. She heard Mamóru call her name and gladly went to him.

"I need your help," the old man told her, his eyes on a trimaran approaching from starboard.

Drolvisdinn jolted as the trimaran scraped against its side. It was a smaller ship, yet still filled with well-armed soldiers. Before the new enemies had a chance to board, Nalaníri grabbed onto Mamóru and jumped with him toward the triple prow of the Zovarian vessel, landing in a roll to protect the frail man. The ship tilted as Mamóru shapeshifted into a squalid yet still powerful steppe mammoth. He trumpeted thunderously, the deck cracking beneath him and sending the soldiers off balance. Angered sailors tried to push the mammoth off their ship, piercing his columnar legs with their swords and spears and making him topple to his side, nearly sinking the vessel. The mammoth called out in pain, and from *Drolvisdinn* the call was heard. Pichi, despite her drowsy state, leapt aboard the trimaran, landing atop the soldiers who were fighting the mammoth.

Mamóru regained his footing and swung his tusks as he trampled toward the stern of the ship, taking down one mast before loosening another. As the second mast fell, it snagged in the curl of Mamóru's left tusk and it pulled down, snapping the ivory and sending the tusk spinning away. The heavy pull threw the mammoth off balance again. His legs buckled; the deck cracked. He collapsed sideways, breaking two of the ship's triple hulls and sinking through the wooden boards. The remains of the ship listed heavily as water rushed in.

Mamóru attempted to free himself from the wreckage, yet he only managed to tangle in the ship's lines. Soldiers dove into the cold water to save themselves from the sinking hulk. As the Zovarian trimaran split to pieces, Nalaníri and Pichi were swallowed into the sea along with the mammoth.

Soldiers from the wreck climbed up *Drolvisdinn*'s hull, helped by others who tossed down ropes for them. Sunu picked them off at a safe distance, slashing with the sharp end of their halberd and bludgeoning with the blunt end. A soldier made it across, but the shaman strangled her with a Deathlock Vine, then searched for Nalaníri and Mamóru, spotting no sign of them.

Sterjall rushed past Sunu, slicing Leif into shoulder blades and ankles, piercing kidneys and lungs, never hesitating. He was trying to get closer to help Laatu sailors who'd been trapped in a corner, when he suddenly froze as a heavily armored sedecim peacekeeper landed in front of him, brandishing a spiked mace. Sterjall suddenly recalled the mace-wielding wolverine who'd broken his arm in Withervale, and froze in fear. The peacekeeper swung his heavy mace down, splintering the boards by Sterjall's legs. The wolf tried to crawl away, but a second swing was incoming.

"No!" Kulak cried out, slamming his small body against the peacekeeper's side, throwing his aim off by just enough to prevent it from smashing Sterjall's skull. Sterjall rolled out of the way and sliced the ligament behind the peacekeeper's knee, making him fall to his side, but before the wolf could strike a deadly blow, a Union guard slammed him with her shield and shoved him to the ground.

Kulak was on top of the peacekeeper. He had lost his knife in another soldier's ribs, so he scratched at the helm with his claws and smashed down uselessly with his elbows. The heavily armored knight rolled over, trapping Kulak beneath him.

"I'm coming!" Sterjall cried out, but the woman with the shield had him pinned beneath her weight. "Kulak, watch out!"

The peacekeeper lifted a heavy fist, and though Kulak could see the blow coming, he could do nothing to avoid it. The gauntlet smashed into the caracal's face, then more slams came from the armored knuckles of the other hand, splattering blood onto the deck. Sterjall screamed and with a kick hurled the guard off him, but she held onto his tunic and pulled him even farther from Kulak.

The peacekeeper lifted both his fists at once, ready to crush Kulak's skull. As he lowered his arms, they were taken inside Blu's jaws, who chomped down and tore them off at the elbows, flinging the knight out of the way. Blu tipped off balance, blood foaming between his long fangs.

More soldiers kept boarding *Drolvisdinn*. The Laatu sailors were trapped in a corner, trying to use push poles and oars to keep the attackers at bay. Abjus protected them, parrying against a piercing lance and dodging a fast-swinging sword, taking two soldiers down. A Union guard hurled his spear, and Abjus dodged it by leaning backward, but before he could recover, a wounded soldier who lay on the floorboards grabbed onto his shodog and pulled him down, wrapping a strangling arm around his neck. As Abjus tried to free himself, the Union guard jumped at him with a knife, slicing his abdomen. Kenondok heard Abjus's cry and rushed to help him, but could find no way through the wall of Zovarians.

Another jolt shook the vessel as Captain Siffo's ship slammed into Admiral Grinn's ramship, then sent his partial-suid crew to board. The Zovarian soldiers had been warned about the Silvfröash—a few of them were survivors from the battle at the Siltlands—so they knew to be wary when fighting the half-forms, but they had not expected dozens more half-beasts to suddenly appear. Although the Puqua sailors were not trained warriors, or even truly half-formed, the Zovarians did not know the difference, and their fear told them that each and every one of these pig, boar, and hog creatures was carrying one of the mystical masks of the Miscam and would be as invincible as the others they had been battling. It became a self-fulfilling prophecy, as their fear betrayed them.

The Puqua quickly pushed through Admiral Grinn's ship, slashing their axes or slamming with oars, then jumped aboard *Drolvisdinn*.

Kenondok used the distraction to drag Abjus to safety, though he knew his friend would likely not survive the wound. He took cover with the rest of the Laatu crew, who were being forced toward the bow of the ship. In a chaotic roar, a barrage of squealing Puqua sailors trampled their way toward the prow, terrorizing the Zovarian soldiers and breaking their formation, giving the Laatu a chance to take out their blowguns once more. Sunu joined them, twirling their halberd like a tornado of bones.

Sterjall helped Kulak up. The caracal's lips were bleeding, one of his eyes was swollen shut, and he was unable to walk on his own. Sterjall pulled Kulak's arm over his shoulders and carried him away from the core of the battle. Blu followed them, half-stumbling as he protected them. *Please, stay up, walk with me,* Sterjall thought, unable to speak the words, his breath failing him in the struggle.

They inched toward the stern of the ship, where Kitjári and Ilsed were defending injured sailors. Sterjall heard a roar; he turned to see that Blu had been trapped beneath a heavy net. The smilodon slashed to get free, only tangling himself further. A piercing battlecry followed: Admiral Grinn was running toward them, brandishing a baselard sword much like the one Balstei had once stolen from him. Sterjall had to throw Kulak away from him, making him stumble face down as he dodged the admiral's sharp strike.

"You selfish dog!" the admiral screeched, readying a new attack. "The power you wield could be used for the good of all of us, for the future of the Union!" He swung, slicing a clean cut into the mizzenmast. Sterjall did not overreact; he remembered Sunu's teachings and readied himself in the Stalking Jaguar stance. Grinn pulled his sword back and lunged again, but the wolf was ready—he scraped Leif's pommel over his brime bracer, shooting a torrent of sparks into the admiral's face, then advanced quickly to strike.

Although the sparks were a good distraction, in the daytime they were not enough to blind the admiral. Grinn hesitated for a moment but understood the strategy and quickly shifted from a direct strike to a parrying one, deflecting Sterjall's dagger.

Sterjall tried again, releasing two Brime Strikes in a row, but the admiral wasn't impressed by the lights any longer; he even ignored the sparks that had begun to burn holes into his cape. Sterjall tried once more anyway, then rushed to sneak in a stab with Leif, but the admiral was a much better swordsman and knew how to position his legs and blade to keep an advantageous distance. Grinn advanced slowly, pushing Sterjall back, letting him take the steps up to the quarterdeck. The higher ground gave Sterjall some hope, but belatedly he realized what the admiral was doing. Grinn let Sterjall climb to safety before turning around to attack Kulak, who was helplessly crawling on the deck.

No... Sterjall thought as Admiral Grinn lifted his sword. *I left him, I failed him, I should've—*

A shrill cry exploded above the admiral. He looked up to see Alaia dropping from the rigging. She smashed like an angry hammer onto Grinn's head, then pulled hard at his smoking cape, tumbling then kicking as they rolled onto the deck, making the admiral lose his helm. Alaia stabbed her small blade through the admiral's thigh, then broke away from him. While Grinn was trying to remove the blade, a dart from Ilsed found its way into his neck. He toppled like a wet sack of grain.

Sterjall was rushing back to help Kulak when Alaia stopped him. "I'll take care of him, you go help the others," she said. He bolted toward the Puqua, who were surrounding the remaining enemy soldiers.

Kitjári was shooting her last arrows when she heard a roaring cry for help. She looked over the bulwark and saw Pichi clawing on *Drolvisdinn*'s hull, and near the smilodon swam Nalaníri, trying to fight off soldiers while protecting Mamóru, who was once again an old man, holding onto a barrel. Kitjári grabbed a rope and dove into the water with her sword pointed down.

"Lower your weapons and we'll let you live," Sterjall commanded the Zovarians, who had been parrying against the pig-headed monsters on one end and against the smooth-skinned freaks on the other. When they saw the dark-faced wolf approach, they lost all hope. They slowly complied, but not all of them; a few tried to fight back and were quickly disabled by immobilizing darts.

"Tie them down," Sterjall said. The Puqua and Laatu crews got to work.

The Puqua had suffered only three casualties, but the Laatu had lost more than half of their crew, including Hod Abjus. Khuron Kulak was badly concussed and bleeding. Pichi had crawled back up onto the deck, where she collapsed, utterly exhausted and fervently hating the sea. Kitjári was helping Nalaníri up the ropes, and pulled Mamóru up with them, who was barely conscious, had a broken femur, was missing a tooth, and had been left feeble and shivering.

The Silvfröash kneeled next to Mamóru and with their Silvesh took his pain into their own bodies, sharing it, making it bearable. They would have to do so again many times over the following days, as Mamóru's wounds were dire and his body too brittle.

Sterjall felt his leg throb after aiding Mamóru. He stood weakly and walked toward the surviving Zovarians. "What you did was not just careless, but cruel," he said to them.

"And what you are doing is selfish," an anonymous voice spoke from within the crowd. But Sterjall could feel the fear in his threads and spotted the speaker. He pushed the others aside and faced the soldier.

"You know nothing," he said, muzzle close to the man's quivering ear. "You are murderers, cowards."

The man sucked in a breath of courage and answered, "There is a war, Lorr Vaari, which you are running away from. Yet you claim we are the cowards? The Union cannot fight alone, and you are deserting it, deserting your own people." He spat, leaving his saliva dangling on Sterjall's whiskers.

Sterjall wiped it off and pulled Leif out, holding it a hairbreadth away from the man's eye. "You have no inkling of what our mission is."

"Right. Kill me for speaking truth. Do it, Lorr Vaari, and show everyone which side you are on."

Kitjári stepped closer. "Well I do think we should kill this rhoidnibbler, it'll make it much easier to—"

"Stop," Alaia interjected, hurrying to stand between them. "Just let these assholes back onto their own ship, there's no need to spill more blood."

"And what will that accomplish?" Kitjári asked. "They'll just chase after us."

"Tear down their sails, then," Alaia said. "None of these ships will travel much farther." She peeked over her shoulder toward Kedra's ship, which was still visible as a pink dot in the distance, left floundering with no rudder. "Either way, the Union has plenty more ships, there's nothing we can do about that. But these idiots were merely following orders. Let them go, let them talk, and maybe those self-righteous Arch Sedecims will learn something."

"I'm with d'smart *ugimeld* un this one," Nalaníri said, also barging in. "Siffo's crew can help disable d'enemy ship. We'll be a-sailing into where them can't fullow anyway."

Sterjall pulled his dagger away, then noticed a mocking smile on the soldier's face. He looked to Alaia and said, "This is going to get us nowhere. I don't think it's smart to—"

"I don't care," Alaia said, taking command. She stood atop a barrel, removed her quaar helm, and directed her voice toward the enemy survivors. "Those of you who fell by darts were the lucky ones," she said. "We did not use a lethal poison, we only aimed to disable you. Your sleepy friends and your shit-faced admiral will wake up tomorrow. The rest of them, well, they got what they deserved. Go back home to Zovaria, go and fight against the Red Stag's army. Stop chasing after us, you nubheads. We have our own mission, one you could not begin to understand. Now get off our fucking ship."

As the bound soldiers were made to walk back to Admiral Grinn's ramship, all the dead, dying, or unconscious enemy soldiers were moved there as well, including Grinn himself. The Puqua took any weapons and shields into *Fjummomurr*, then set to tearing down the Zovarian ship's sails, but left the spare sailcloth in the hold, knowing it would take the Zovarians at least a full day to replace them.

Kitjári was dragging a dead sedecim peacekeeper across a ramp, the one with no arms. "This wangmonger is heavy," she muttered to Sterjall, dropping the body onto the ramship's deck. "We should check the captain's quarters. I'm sure they would not miss a few things."

Atop an ample mahogany dresser, they found three maps: a wide one of the two continents, one of Fel Varanus and the surrounding islands, and one of the stars. They also found a sextant, a spyglass, the captain's logbook, and a declination table.

"Not feeling particularly guilty about stealing some of these things," Sterjall said, picking up all the instruments and papers.

Drolvisdinn's surviving sailors were too few to operate the complex ship. Captain Siffo offered Ilsed part of his crew, and although she still felt their presence as polluting to her sacred vessel, she was forced to accept. The Laatu quickly showed the Puqua how to work their leaf-shaped sails, then unsnagged themselves from the underwater vines, and once more drifted toward the dome, leaving the Zovarians to tend to their disabled ship.

As the voyagers cruised the waters, they prepared their dead for a burial at sea. Too many had been lost. They sewed a hammock around each body, weighed them down, and let the deep waters of the Isdinnklad carry them to the Six Gates of Felsvad. Inside the mouths of each of the deceased, a cube of brime had been placed, so that even in the deepest cold of the sea they would carry with them the warmth of a hearth.

Not long after, they found themselves blocked by too many tangles of green thorns. The Silvfröash took care of not only moving the vines out of the way, but of sensing how deep the water went to avoid snagging the vessel on obstacles again.

Slow and steady as the flow of Teslurkath's mighty glaciers, *Drolvisdinn* and *Fjummomurr* began their journey into the Varanus Dome.

Chapter Sixty-Eight

Hallow

The eyes of the Red Stag shimmered in sharp, venomous yellow, reflecting the sapfire-lit boulders hurled by a dozen trebuchets. The massive stones crashed against a munnji silo right above Mankar Enos, a village in the southwestern mountains of the Bighorn Dome.

As the boulders tore through the sacred silos, the yellow sapfire was engulfed by the green-flaming sap, which spilled like a waterfall toward the village. The entire supporting column shimmered brightly above its skirt of flames—a perfect beacon that would be seen as far as Runa, the Ikhel capital.

"That should be enough to get their attention," the Red Stag said, watching from a nearby mesa. He looked at Luhásu, chief of the Western Ikhel, and said, "Go now, finish off the rest of the villagers, but let enough of them run away and call for aid."

Aurélien Knivlar interpreted the words, but her efforts were not needed—Luhásu well knew the strategy and was committed to it. She would lure the Eastern Ikhel army into the trap, then flee directly into a nearby lake, knowing that the Red Stag would send his cervids with instructions to kill anything on land.

The Red Stag watched Luhásu mount a well-trained muskox and rush downhill to meet her legion, then he walked toward his pavilion. "Knivlar. Fetch me Silv-Thaar Valaran. I need a word with him."

"At once, Monarch Hallow," the red-haired shaman replied crisply.

The Red Stag pushed the tarp entrance open and found dinner waiting for him—venison shanks and roasted quail, accompanied by a bottle of fine-aged wine. He was halfway through his meal when Valaran entered the pavilion.

"Apologies, Lorr," the raccoon general began. "I did not mean to interrupt—"

"At ease, Valaran. Come, sit, we have a few hours to spare before the Eastern Ikhel arrive."

Valaran pushed his striped tail out of the way as he sat, eyeing the monarch's long muzzle as it tore the last bits of venison from a bone. He found it gruesome to see the Red Stag eating meat. It reminded him of the time he'd spotted a deer eating a young rabbit; he hadn't known that cervids could do such a thing, yet the beast had swallowed it whole.

The bone clinked on a silver plate. The mighty elk wiped his muzzle clean, then said, "Luhásu is on her way. Before dawn, that mask will be ours."

Valaran smiled conspiratorially. "So you are sending her into a trap, then?"

The elk cocked his head, confused. "What is it you mean?"

"I… I simply thought… Well, to be frank, Lorr, not just me, but most of the soldiers I've spoken to think you are sending the Ikhel chief to her death, and that you'll gift the recovered mask to General Baneras, or General dus Fer, perhaps."

The Red Stag chuckled. "Do they take me to be so callous? Well, who can blame them? What you hypothesized is not entirely the truth. If Luhásu dies—and the odds are positively against her—that will be on her. But if she lives, she will have earned her mask and her place in our army. We shall soon see."

"Then I better not mention that to the generals, or they'll loose arrows on her at once," Valaran said lightheartedly.

The Red Stag smiled, a gesture that vanished as quickly as it appeared. "Are your beasts ready?" he asked.

"Yes, down by the canyon's mouth, well hidden."

"Are they still in their cages?"

"They are," Valaran replied, seemingly embarrassed to admit it. "Until it's time to strike. To avoid unnecessary risks."

"I am all for caution, so I will not force you to do otherwise. But it still concerns me. You've managed to control them at last, but…" he looked away, pretending to be suddenly interested in the flickering flames of the candelabra.

"But what, Monarch Hallow?"

The Red Stag pushed his plate away and rose to his feet. He refilled his goblet with dark-red wine, then poured a second glass, offering it to Valaran.

Valaran shook his head, "I'd rather not drink before the—"

"Take it," the Red Stag demanded, holding the goblet forward. Valaran did as he was told. "I heard rumors," the monarch continued. "Rumors that your wolverines still go wild in their cages, trying to break free."

"It's the reason I prefer to keep them caged."

"And they just happen to go wild only at night, and almost every night."

"Perhaps Krostsilv doesn't keep the mindlock as tight when I sleep."

"Odd, isn't it? But who could say? It's not like Urcai and I tested all of this out long before taking risks with our beasts. How strange that such issues never bothered me or Jaxon."

The raccoon tightened his grip on his goblet as the Red Stag continued, now facing him directly. "But that can't be it, can it? Another possibility is that you are willfully taking your mask off. Or will you deny it?"

Valaran shrunk in his fur, staring up at the arresting cervid. He felt the power of Urgsilv tasting his threads, probing his emotions for a lie, and he dared not lie. "I... No, I will not deny it, Lorr. But not always, only when I know it's safe to do so."

The Red Stag slapped Valaran's goblet away, splashing the red fluid over the raccoon's fur and armor. "You babble about avoiding unnecessary risks, yet you do this? And while defying my direct orders?"

Valaran's head dropped. "I'm most ashamed of my behavior, Monarch Hallow. There is no excuse, and it will not happen again. I believe I am finally at ease with the mask's influence, and I shan't need to take my human form any longer. I will gladly take any punishment you wish to inflict upon me, for I deserve—"

"Please shut that rotten rat mouth at once. Scorch my balls, don't be so pathetic. Stand up."

Valaran stood at once, his back straight as his spear.

The Red Stag looked him in the eyes, holding the stare like a crushing vise. "There is strength in certain kinds of weakness," he snarled, "but not the kinds you practice. You are loyal, yet foolish. You are strong, yet reckless. There is potential in you, but you are so quick to waste it." He placed his hoofed fingertips under the raccoon's chin, forcing him to turn his head this way and that.

Valaran expected a dagger to suddenly stab his kidneys, but instead the Red Stag let go of him with a small shove and said, "Leave now, and get your legion ready. Do not fail me tonight, Valaran."

Silv-Thaar Valaran hurried toward the exit, then stopped and turned. He remained quiet for three full breaths, then asked, "Why, Lorr?"

The Red Stag waited for him to elaborate.

"Why are you so lenient on me?"

"Speak your mind, General."

"Since... Since the moment you gifted me this mask, I... I was not of rank, I was not deserving of it. Anyone would've guessed you'd choose Chief Daro over me, or any of the generals. Why me? And why are you so quick to forgive my mistakes?"

"Another show of weakness," the Red Stag said. "But this is the good kind. Come, let me show you something." He walked to a corner of the room. There, his quaar shield and spear had been tossed carelessly onto a rug, but upon a magsteel stand rested his wave-bladed longsword. He unclasped the scabbard and removed the sword—the crests and troughs appeared one by one, no sound escaping from the fur-lined interior. The blade glinted with a teal tinge, as if it had captured a beam of stray moonlight. He held the sword with the point down and lifted the crossguard to Valaran's masked face. "What do you see?" he asked.

A fluid script of inlaid gold shimmered across the crossguard.

"Your name, Lorr," Valaran answered. "Your family's name."

"My family's name," the Red Stag repeated with a scowl. He lowered the sword and paced around the general. "Why do you think I do what I do, Silv-Thaar Valaran? Why go through all this trouble to gather allies, conquer lands, capture masks?"

"For the Empire, of course."

"Scorch the fucking Empire!"

Valaran tensed, holding his breath.

"If loyalty to the Empire was my priority, I would not have skewered that wimp of an emperor. I would have been following his orders until he set all nine states to burn. Think again, Valaran, and think hard."

"For... Um... For your legacy, then, for your name. Is that what you mean?"

The Red Stag stopped his pacing, tapping the tip of his blade against his hooves. "I had no family name, once. I was only Alvis. And you did not either. *Crescu of the Khull Ford.* I heard your story. You fought your way out of that nightmare, alone. You survived, made a new name for yourself in the army."

"You had no family name? You are Bergsulfi as well, then?"

"No. I'm the son of a duchess from Frishnea. Some cunt with too big a castle who died a decade ago, suffocated in her wealth. Only women become heirs in their backward manners—men are expendable and are granted no more than their given names."

Valaran remained quiet, waiting for the Red Stag to collect his thoughts.

"She sold me. To work at a leather tannery for a fat pig of a feudal lord." He held his sword horizontally, looking down at the sinuous highlights it captured from the candles. "I worked in that stink hole for years, gaining the trust of the owner, bringing the deliveries straight into his home. This sword was hanging as a trophy in his manor. I took it, then sliced that useless man's fatty throat before escaping. I took it because it was mine to take, because it was the freedom my hard work had earned. And with it, I took its name."

He sheathed the sword and placed it back on the stand.

"People like you, Valaran," he continued, "you understand what it is like to be nothing, to know no one is destined to save you, no one other than yourself. You understand the pain it brings. You've lived through the injustices committed under selfishness and cowardice, yet you endured, you thrived. This is the only reason why I haven't yet sliced your throat like I did with that swine so many years back." He grabbed onto Valaran's wrist then, grip tightened. "But one thing you still need to grasp, Valaran, is that when you are offered a drink, you don't just accept the glass, you take the damn bottle."

He let go and stared the general down.

"I... I thank you, Monarch Hallow, for your—"

"If you dare say *mercy*, I will be forced to reconsider."

"No. It's not mercy. Thank you for your foresight. For your understanding. I can see clearly now, and I will not fail you."

The Red Stag nodded, leading Valaran toward the exit. "It is why I also trust Luhásu," he said. "She was born Eastern, but chose her own path. Whether she lives or not is up to her. We shall soon see what comes of this battle, so make your troops ready now."

Valaran walked out of the pavilion but held the tarp open. He peered over his shoulder.

"Lorr..." he said. "Your son... When he is born, he will be in good hands."

Chapter Sixty-Nine

Bayanhong Wars

Not only did Luhásu survive the battle into which she had lured the Eastern Ikhel, but it was by her ice axe that the Rilgfröa fell. Luhásu did not wait—she claimed her prize and put the caprid mask on even before the Red Stag could personally congratulate her.

Within the span of a dozen days, Luhásu learned to control the Silv's power and found her half-form of a markhor: a goat of formidable strength and intimidating screw-shaped horns. Her hide was thick, covered by her long-draping chest fur. Her armor of bone and metal plates protected her thick arms and her cloven-hoofed legs, which were stronger than a mule's.

As Luhásu had no family name, and the Miscam naming traditions had been forbidden by the Red Stag, she simply added the Mask Vanguard title to her own half-form species, becoming Silv-Thaar Markhor.

Markhor taught the Red Stag of the power the Silvesh had to open up the domes in their entirety, and though she wanted to demonstrate the ability at Ommo ust Rilg, the monarch stopped her. He believed it wiser to keep his resources secured; this way he could make sure the Eastern Ikhel would not escape through the mountains, and he could command the flow of supplies by keeping the pipe tunnels fortified, perpetually under his control.

With Silv-Thaar Markhor's new legion of goats, wildebeest, takins, oryxes, muskoxen, and countless other caprids, the Negian Empire quickly overthrew and enslaved the Eastern Ikhel, then carried on with their next goal by leaving the Bighorn Dome through pipes installed in the eastern wall and attacking the Bayani capital of On Khurderen, taking them entirely by surprise. Silv-Thaar Markhor led the attack, riding on the back of Beiféren, the Nu'irg ust Rilg. The unlucky Nu'irg had been mindlocked, forced to fight in his primal form of a mammoth-sized bootherium—a helmeted muskox—all the while being aware he was committing unforgivable atrocities.

Once the fortress city of On Khurderen was taken, war came to the Negians from the north. But those reinforcements came too late; the Negian Empire now controlled strategic lands, key resources, and even the Bayani capital. The Bayanhong Tribes had no way to combat the strength of all the Negian soldiers, especially now that they were combined with the unstoppable force of the horns and antlers of the cervids and caprids.

Silv-Thaar Valaran's musteloids, on the other hand, had not performed as well as the monarch had expected.

"Why the *fuck* did you falter at the last moment?" the Red Stag spat. He shot to his feet, shoving his chair out of the way. "It cost us hundreds of elk and soldiers, and now we'll need to rebuild the bastion's outer wall."

"I will get it under control, I swear by the Shade of Yza," Silv-Thaar Valaran moped, keeping his eyes sunken in shadows. "It was merely a momentary lapse."

The Red Stag paced around the war room. "It took Luhásu mere weeks to master what you've had months to learn. I should rip that damn mask off your face and give it to someone who will do as they are told."

"Monarch Hallow, please," Valaran pleaded. "We took care of it. The north flank is ours, we can hold it easily now and keep moving south. The Dorhond are already fleeing their lands, we could—"

"I know! We have no time to waste if we want to pick up enough Oldrin slaves. If it wasn't for that, I'd be willing to give Krostsilv to one of the shamans, or to General Broadleaf. After all, it was he who shouldered the burden of bringing those jarv wolverines for you."

Silv-Thaar Valaran leaned back in his chair, for once unafraid to express his utter disappointment toward his monarch. "I take responsibility for my mistakes," he replied stiffly. "But Behler Broadleaf? You know better than that. He wants Fjarmallen, the northern coasts, nothing more."

The Red Stag slammed his hoofed hands on the table. "I know!" he huffed, irked at having to agree with Valaran.

The debriefing was taking place in the On Khurderen Citadel, a tight fortress no longer commanded by the Bayani. Silv-Thaar Markhor was not present, but Fjorna Daro stood guard at a respectful distance, silently irritated that her name was never brought up even as a joke when speaking of who could be the next Silv-Thaar.

The Red Stag rubbed his muzzle and began pacing once more. "I don't have faith in some of the generals," he confided in a seething mumble. He trusted Valaran, despite his flaws. "They have too many vested interests in the Loorian lands. Korten, perhaps, or Gino—they are the only two I can trust to follow through. The rest don't see the potential of the Jerjan Continent. I think they are afraid of the Tsing Empire, of Afhora, even of the Tharma-fucking-Federation. Scorching cowards."

He dropped into a chair, looking defeated. He sighed deeply. "A cormorant from Hestfell arrived today. This is what is getting me in such a mood," he admitted.

"What does Urcai have to say?"

"He says more domes are opening in the far west, but we can't get good information. The Zovarian army is too secretive, but after their fleet left the Moordusk Dome, the Fjordlands Dome began to open up. And I can fucking guarantee you the Varanus Dome will be next. I think the Zovarians are in possession of those masks and they are following our very same strategy."

"Shit," Valaran muttered. He rubbed his claws through his chin fur.

"If they got the old canid mask, as well as that bear one that apparently came from the middle of an ice field, perhaps by now they have five in their possession. Two more than we do."

"They can't have as large an army, though."

The mighty elk sneered. "But they have a powerful fleet, and they could potentially ally with Bauram, likely even with the Republic. What worries me, Valaran, is that this is a complex game where time is the most important variable. The realm that takes the domes the fastest will command the two continents. Those Zovarian maggots can't be the winners in this war, yet they seem to be ahead somehow."

"We've been moving as fast as humanly possible, Lorr."

"Yet it is still taking us too long," the Red Stag said. He stood once more, leaned over the table, and tapped on a map of the continents where the domes were circled in red. "Take a look here, General, and tell me… What would you do?"

"Well, past the Dorhond Range, we have the Archstone Dome. That's the one for bovids?"

"No, bovids are on Tsing lands. Archstone is the dome of perissodactyls—horses, rhinos and such."

"Right, horses. And the next nearest one is quite out of the way to the east, the Moonrise Dome. Seals, walruses."

"Correct, quite out of the way," the Red Stag agreed, feigning a yawn.

Silv-Thaar Valaran leaned back again. "Monarch Hallow, I know what you want to ask of me. I agree. We need to take these domes faster, and we'll only do so if we can cover more ground. Let me prove to you that I am worthy of Krostsilv. Let me take the Moonrise Dome for you. If I could enter it, then find a way to open the dome like Luhásu taught us, I could attack by land while our fleet surprises them by sea. You have nearly no use for the ships anymore, other than to push supplies over the Ophidian. The core of your army must march by land."

"You read my thoughts well, General. The pinniped mask will not be as useful when the real war is being fought on land, but it would still offer a significant advantage to the general wielding it. Opening the Moonrise Dome is a sound strategy, yet that would release the resources within it. If we want to properly contain them, the Elmaren Queendom needs to first be securely under our control. I don't think your legion is enough to take on the city of white towers. I will ask Silv-Thaar Markhor to go with you, but it will be *your* battle to win."

The raccoon nodded.

"Monarch Hallow, if I may?" Fjorna interjected from a dark corner of the room.

"Yes, Chief Daro? Step closer."

Fjorna drifted into the light, yet kept the deformed half of her face in shadow. "Apologies for the impudence, but you don't seem to have need of our protection any longer. I think Markhor can serve you best, while I could protect Valaran with my arbalisters. We know each other better, and we can take most of our archers with us. You have not needed to attack from range, not since you've resorted to sending the cervids to the frontlines, and now you have the caprids as well. Archers are rarely within range to be of use to you."

"This is true," the Red Stag agreed.

"If you'll allow," Fjorna continued, "I'll provide Valaran with all his needs. Armsmaster Shea Lu can help with the naval attack."

"Fjorna is right," Valaran said. "Shea would be the perfect woman for this job. The admirals trust her and would die for her sixteen times over. And you could use Markhor to fight the Graalman Horde. Besides, she has no experience at sea. I don't think she even knows what a sea is."

"So you agree this is a sound plan?" the Red Stag asked. "It will make it harder on you. You will have fewer soldiers, no caprids."

"I will have the people I trust," Valaran said. "And I will take Gwonlesilv for you. I promise."

"Then tomorrow we'll meet with the other generals and work on splitting our resources. I trust you, Silv-Thaar Valaran, but this is your last chance."

"I will not fail you, Monarch Hallow."

"That was a solid strategy," Valaran said to Fjorna as they left the On Khurderen Citadel. "And I don't lie when I say I trust you," he added, "perhaps more than anyone." He stopped and checked their surroundings.

"But..." Fjorna prompted.

"But... Khest be damned. It's hard to say this, but as much as I admire her skills, and I would've died for her in the past, I don't think I trust Shea any longer. I think Osef got to her, and now she thinks I've planned on taking this mask all along, as if I betrayed you all. I tried talking to her, but it's useless. She pretends there's nothing wrong, but I can see it in her eyes. I know her way too well."

"Let me deal with Shea. She will listen to me."

"Thank you." Valaran's shoulders relaxed. "Tell me something, honestly. You would've been much safer with Hallow. You didn't need to volunteer for this mission. I know I'm fucked, but I have to do this to prove myself to him. Why are you doing this?"

"Ever since..." Her thoughts trailed off, for a moment rekindling the memory of a wolf-masked beast clawing senselessly at her face. Her bones had never settled in the right way, and even breathing was still painful. "Ever since that mongrel took our brothers, our sisters from us, it's become more important for those of us who still live to stick together." She faced him, aiming her good eye straight at him, and added, "It does not matter how big your legion gets, or how ugly a skunk you become, we are still the same old, tiny squad. We are family, and I'm not leaving you behind."

Fjorna tried to hold her stare, but her face contorted unconsciously, revealing a glimpse of frustration.

"And..." Valaran prompted.

"And... I know you probably noticed by now, but I am sick of Monarch Hallow. I dislike his strategy, more so every day. He was an inspiration to us all when he claimed the throne, when he took the Anglass and Lequa domes from those savages. But he has become too blind to the needs of the lands we are conquering. The power of Urgsilv is getting to him. He's bloodthirsty. He mindlessly sacrifices his cervids, seeing no other value in them than war. But those same elk and deer are meant to feed the cities of the Empire, they are not expendable. We are burning through our resources and leaving nothing but barren lands behind us. I don't think he will ever stop, even after he has every single mask there is to be had. At this rate, he'll soon be the ruler of all Noss and have no one to rule over."

"I partially agree," Valaran said with indecision veiling his frown. "Though I think he does have the wellbeing of his people in mind. He's just too focused on his mission. This war comes first, it's bigger than any of us. And even if I entirely disagreed with him—like you said, there's no stopping him. We are either with him, or we die by his hands. Claws. Hooves, whatever."

"It's something we could further discuss," Fjorna whispered. "But not here. Not now. Let's get back to the barracks and tell the others about our upcoming trip to the land where the moon rises."

Chapter Seventy

Into the Dragon's Lair

The Varanus Dome was unbalanced, untamed.

The interior of the wall of vines was a tangle that spread chaotically, never truly beginning or ending. Even when deep within the thicket, the light of sunset filtered in. Contrary to how the vines grew at the other domes—mostly vertically—here they grew in every which direction. This made the parting of them slower and the finding of passages to travel through much more precarious.

Nalaníri was on *Drolvisdinn*'s deck, moving vines out of the way and helping Hud Ilsed navigate. Kulak was helping too, though only a little bit: he was still suffering from the blows he took to his face, which had left him unable to keep his balance.

Alaia was belowdecks, comforting Blu and Pichi while Sunu cared for their injuries.

Mamóru slept in the comfortable bed in *Drolvisdinn*'s captain's quarters, wounded and drained. Sterjall and Kitjári sat near him, at a table upon which were the items they'd stolen from Admiral Grinn's ship.

"Seems Grinn got word about us from the Khaar Du," Kitjári said, leafing through the logbook. "They reported a green-sailed ship near Koroberg. That's when he began patrolling these waters, waiting for us to come out."

"How did the Zovarians know that was us?" Sterjall asked.

"They didn't, at the time. It was just an odd report. But I bet once they saw other green-sailed ships leaving the Moordusk Dome, they put it all together."

She quickly scanned more pages. "Ship sightings, weather reports, repairs. What's this?"—she pointed to a recent entry—"Stationed by the 'cove,' whatever that means. They have more ships there. Do you see that on the maps?"

They searched the maps but could not find any place by that name.

"And here," Kitjári continued reading, "there's mention of another fleet at Yanan." She looked at the world map and pointed to Holv-Yanan, the lone Zovarian state at the northern end of Fel Baubór, just south of Fel Varanus. "If we end up going south, we need to be careful with them."

"Well, at least we'll have tools to navigate with, if and when we go that way," Sterjall said, playing with the sextant.

"Plenty of new toys," Kitjári agreed, extending the collapsible spyglass. "I'm keeping this one, if you don't mind."

Nalaníri stepped into the room. "Ye both done a-playing? We could use some help. Some uf d'vines are taking too long t'move out, some don't want t'move at all."

"You stay here and take care of Mamóru," Kitjári said to Sterjall.

"It's like half uf wulfy's eye toy," Nalaníri said, glancing toward the spyglass as they both left the captain's quarters.

Sterjall noticed Mamóru stirring, so he moved to sit next to him.

The old man looked feeble and in so much pain. His crusted eyes cracked open. He was warm, but still shivering. He made a gesture toward the side table.

Sterjall saw a cup of tea there, already cold. He handed it to him. "I'll brew a fresh pot for you," he said, then walked to the cabin's stove to set water to boil.

While Mamóru drank the cold tea, Sterjall focused on the Nu'irg's broken femur, taking some of the pain for himself.

Mamóru placed a hand on Sterjall's forearm. "Thank you for that kindness, agnurf son, but don't overdo it. You will need your wits and energy for what lies ahead."

"It's alright, I can take some of it. How is the leg?"

"Old, broken, useless. Like the rest of my body," he joked, flashing a smile now missing a tooth.

"You didn't seem so useless during the fight. If it wasn't for you, we would've been overrun by that other ship. You saved us, again."

"It was the least I could do. I care greatly for you all, but you are very good at getting into trouble. Yet I still feel bad for all the Zovarians who had to die because of me."

"They deserved it, though."

"Perhaps, but I'm never quick to cast judgment. Tolerance is dangerous if given away unconditionally, yet we can still hold empathy for those who do not deserve our tolerance. Most of those soldiers knew not what they were doing, whose wellness they were serving, or why such orders had been given to them. Alas, knowingly or not, they were in the wrong and needed to be stopped. They suffered greatly, and it hurt me to make them suffer, even if it was for the greater good."

Sterjall pulled on his whiskers as he pondered. "The first time I had to… kill someone, it was when the Negians attacked Withervale. It was to save my friend Ockam, but I guess also to save myself. I felt terrible for days. I kept seeing that man's bloodied neck, hearing the crunching of my blade in his spine. Then we got into more trouble at Thornridge, and it felt wrong and vile to kill again, but I had no other choice. It was us or them. And since then it's happened again, and again, and every time it gets easier. And… that scares me."

"We must stop our enemies without losing ourselves in the process. You are aware of your own struggle, and that tells me you will choose a righteous path. There is more than individual lives at stake. The Silvesh in the wrong hands could be devastating for the planet themself. It's like a cancer, where every cell that becomes corrupted will take many more with them, and cutting the tumor out is the only way to prevent the entire organism from dying, as much as the cut might hurt."

Sterjall heard the water boiling; he tried to ignore it. "Sometimes I think I'd rather not feel as much. It'd make things easier."

"Dissociating yourself from the pain is necessary, but only good up to a point. Agnargsilv has given you a gift, that of feeling as others do no matter how different they may be from you, and with that gift of extended empathy comes suffering. Sometimes we must remain islands to avoid over-encumbering our emotions, because we still need to function and serve higher purposes than ourselves. Don't let the weight of the world sink you down, agnurf son, for your friends need you, and Noss might need you just as much."

Hours passed.

Though the ships had not yet reached the dome's interior, they encountered a vine mottled in shining arudinn, like an elongated specter signaling to the darkness. More arudinn-covered vines they soon encountered, some even underwater with their little bulbs flickering on and off or pulsating in odd waves as if the lights were traveling down the vines, then bouncing back to interfere with their own rippling patterns.

There was no moment when they finally reached the inside of the dome—it was a gradual transition. Even miles in, the vines wove in such disorder that the wayfarers could rarely see the domed sky, and instead saw a tangle that continued to an uncertain horizon. Some vines from that tangle flickered menacingly, others were dark, like carbonized serpents.

"Wind's a-blowing once mour!" Captain Siffo called from *Fjummomurr*, which had been following close behind *Drolvisdinn*. Both ships shifted from oars to sails.

It was supposed to be midmorning, but it felt more like dusk. At these depths, the dome had a heavy density of creatures and plants, but not much diversity, as if a handful of species had taken over most of the resources and spread uncontained.

The waterway became even more complicated to navigate, always needing at least a couple of Silvfröash at the bow to push vines out of their way and watch for dangers beneath.

Drolvisdinn suddenly jolted. "Did we snag un something?" Nalaníri asked. They looked over the railings and spotted an enormous shape swimming below them.

"The Khest is that?" Sterjall asked.

Nalaníri followed the slithering shape with her mask's gaze. "Looks somewhere 'tween a snake n'a gator, but longer than either uf them. This land's a dangerous one."

They veered west, searching for a clear course to the shores of the mainland, but it proved difficult. After a dozen more miles, they found their way into a canyon where the tall walls prevented the vines from taking over the waters. They traversed it swiftly, unable to see much due to the cliffs blocking the view.

As they reached the end of the canyon, a lush shore flattened to port, thick with ferns the size of cottages. Beyond the shore was a tall hill, and on top of it was a building slathered in moss, so green that it would have remained unnoticed if it hadn't been for the conspicuous square holes on its five sides.

"We should investigate that," Sterjall said.

Ilsed's crew readied the cockboat. Sterjall, Kitjári, and Nalaníri headed out to explore, rowing to the rocky shore and tying the cockboat to a tangle of lianas.

"This's like no forest from our world," Nalaníri said.

"Never seen anything like it either," Sterjall agreed. "Not even in Mindreldrolom, and that dome felt overgrown and wild to me."

Next to them, a tangle of thorny vines suffered spasms of light. Nalaníri touched the sickly bulbs; they flickered, the glow traveling through the entire vine like a shiver of perturbed light. "D'arudinn are unwell. Why's them doing this? Why's them spread so far over d'land?"

More vines tangled above them. They had to duck beneath some and step over many more. Their thorns grew in clusters of three, five, or seven instead of the usual single thorns, giving them a more threatening, cactus-like appearance. The jungle was filled with reptiles and amphibians of all sorts, crawling from every hole, cleverly disguising their bodies with green against green or by remaining still and dark like bark.

Sterjall ducked beneath a pulsating vine and found a puddle behind it. To cross it, he held on to a liana and pulled his weight up, but the liana suddenly detached and snapped back at him with a hiss and a chomp of pink gums.

"Snake!" he yapped, jolting backward and almost piercing his back on a clump of thorns. The snake fell into the puddle and wriggled away, hiding among ferns.

"That was a huge snake!" Kitjári exclaimed. "But it didn't seem venomous."

"I don't care," Sterjall grumbled, fur standing on end. "I'm not grabbing on to any more anythings from here on."

They noticed a stepped pattern on the side of the hill they were climbing, as if it had once been terraced.

"This is not a hill, it's a pyramid," Kitjári said, finding an exposed corner of rock. "And if it's overgrown like this, it must've been abandoned long ago. Let's keep going, we are almost at the top."

The mossy rock structure at the summit consisted of five wide pillars holding up a flat top. Orchids and bromeliads decorated every crack in violet, maroon, peach, and lime colors. The structure reminded Nalaníri of the dolmens that served as shrines throughout her lands, though these rocks were much more cleanly cut and lacked the light of the kenzir stones.

Sterjall found a circular hole at the center of the structure. "There used to be an entrance here, steps that went down. All collapsed now."

"N'bones. Right here, by mine hooves, rotten n'forgotten," Nalaníri said.

They crossed under the structure, exiting on the southern side, from where they had a clearer view of the vast dome. The canyon they had been sailing through joined a large waterway that continued due south, cutting toward a central mountain range. Two peaks stood out among the prominent mountains, and from a saddle at the center of these two peaks, the central trunk extended upward. Rather than growing into a perfect column, the trunk untangled itself into a jungle of tendrils, creating a ceiling that was more maze-like than dome-like.

The binoculars showed them dozens of other human-made structures, all of them overgrown and falling to pieces. The vines kept pulsing unsteadily in their field of view.

"This is going to give me a headache," Sterjall said.

"Our best shot will be to investigate the trunk," Kitjári said.

"Aye," Nalaníri agreed. "If there's anyone 'round, or d'mask is anywhere t'be found, it's mour likely t'be by d'temple."

They returned to the ship and sailed toward the wide waterway. A sandy beach with occasional mangroves opened to starboard. Sterjall was suddenly distracted by a cloud of white sand kicking up at the shore. "What in Noss is that?"

Fighting on the land were two massive reptiles, toppling over each other and hissing violently. They looked like giant monitor lizards, each twenty feet in length, spinning and snapping as they tried to bite one another. Their legs were compact, powerfully muscled and clawed; their long heads were supported by bulky necks covered in scaled skin as thick as any armor. From the pink depths of their maws dripped a sticky mucus, tinted red with blood and rage.

"Those must be the varanus dragons Mamóru was talking about," Kitjári said.

Kulak had gotten up and joined them. His left eye was still swollen shut, and his black feline lips had a puffy cut on them. "Look there," he pointed. "That moose is what they fight for."

"They killed a moose?" Alaia whimpered.

"No, the moose yet lives," Sunu observed, entranced by the gory spectacle. The moose was missing a leg, and part of his ribcage had been eaten, but he was still very much alive, trying to crawl away. "That helpless creature is suffering," Sunu said, taking out their blowgun. Before they were out of range, they shot a dart to grant the moose a quicker ending.

The ships drifted past the horror. More dragons treaded the long shore, some much larger than the two they'd seen fighting, prowling coldly while flicking their bifurcated tongues.

"These dragons are loathsome and cruel," Sunu declared. "They lack compassion. Our felids know how to eat, how to fight, while suffering is minimized. This place lacks guidance. Sunu does not believe anyone is speaking to these scaled beasts. Much was lost in here, much needs fixing."

Ruins towered in disrepair to either side, filled with slitted, unblinking eyes. Entire villages—long deserted—hunkered next to lowlands that might once have been good for farming. Not a sign of recent habitation could be found. They sailed by old docks and piers with abandoned ships decomposing like green bones from rotting whales.

Night in the dome was about to begin. Unlike the healthier domes, in Varanus the transition to dusk was not a smooth one. Some vines went dark too early, others flickered uncontrollably, and a stubborn few never darkened at all. By the time it was deep in what should have been nighttime, the dome was lit by blindingly bright beams of sunlight—reverse wisps breaching through. These beams did not last long, given that the motion of Sunnokh let them only exist for a moment at most, but they constantly reappeared in new areas. It was a confusing spectacle, but at least the angle and color of the wisps gave Sterjall a sense of the time of day outside the dome.

The next morning, they reached a set of stone piers at the base of the two tall peaks that embraced the trunk. A great city sprawled there, or what was left of it—most was flooded or swallowed by the jungle.

"These piers look safe enough to dock at," Kitjári said. "I think this is as close to the trunk as we'll get by water."

"My eyes see an old path that snakes between the two mountains," Kulak said, looking through his one good eye. "If Blu and Pichi take us, we can make it to the trunk before nightfall."

"You should stay," Sterjall told him. "You aren't well yet, you can barely stay on your feet."

Kulak shook his head. "Our quest is to find the Kruwenfröa, I cannot do that from aboard the ship."

"But there are dangerous creatures lurking underwater that only the Silvesh can see," Sterjall countered, not sounding entirely convincing. "The sailors need someone to look after them."

"Perhaps you should stay to spoil this old man with Mindrelsilv's healing tricks," Mamóru interrupted as he came alongside them. He had walked out assisted by crutches. Kulak immediately went to him, helping the Nu'irg sit on the bench that encircled *Drolvisdinn*'s mainmast.

"Thank you, mindahim son. Let your friends go, and stay here to protect us."

"But the Kruwenfröa—"

"I do not think we will find a Kruwenfröa in these forsaken lands. Something has gone awry here, and we need to find out what."

"What do we do if we find nothing but skeletons?" Sterjall asked.

"You set the scorched place to open," Alaia answered. The others stared at her. "If you find no one else, you open this dome up and let these poor creatures leave."

"But them beasts be wild!" Nalaníii objected.

"We're on an island," Alaia said. "They won't mess with the mainland, not yet. And birds and other flying species can find a better home. We can't let them rot in here forever, whatever happened is not their fault."

"Alaia may be right," Mamóru said. "If no Mo'óto Miscam remain to fulfill their oath to Noss, it becomes our duty to see it through."

"I'll stay here and explore the nearby ruins with Kulak and the others," Alaia said. "You should go before it gets dark. If it ever gets dark." She stood behind Kulak, and while placing a hand on his shoulder looked straight to Sterjall. "I'll take care of him," she mouthed. Sterjall nodded his thanks.

After packing a few supplies and disembarking, Sterjall and Sunu mounted Blu, while Kitjári extended a handpaw to help Nalaníri atop Pichi.

"I'm not so sure 'bout this," Nalaníri muttered, trying to find a way to sit on Pichi's harness, which was better fitted for carrying goods than people. "Ye certain she won't be bothered? We're both a bit un d'heavier side."

Kitjári shook her head. "Pichi can haul twenty of you, and she is the sweetest." As she said that, Pichi turned and flashed her serrated fangs—though she did so lovingly, Nalaníri did not feel the love.

Chapter Seventy-One

The Drowned Palace

The smilodons bolted through the half-sunken city. Built from lustrous, masterfully cut rock, most of the majestic metropolis had remained standing, but even rocks succumbed to the pressure of roots growing underneath, or ice expanding within their cracks. Towers that had been hundreds of feet tall were now hundreds of feet wide. Homes, temples, and ancient halls were swallowed by ponds and cascading streams.

Hungry varanus dragons roamed the old city. The dangerous reptilians would have been a much greater threat if the wayfarers had been traveling on foot. Some ignored them, others chased after them, but while the dragons could move fast, they were still too slow to be a threat to the agile cats.

Where the city walls ended, a path rose into the forested mountains, often impeded by collapsed bridges and roaring falls. Dutifully they ascended the path, jumping over chasms, beneath abandoned buildings, and through tunnels that cut straight into the rock of the mountain, until they reached the saddle between the two peaks. From both steep mountains, thundering waterfalls fell. The saddle held a concave valley that had once been the foundation of another powerful city, now flooded by the streams that fed it, with only the tops of buildings poking out. The untangling mess of the trunk reflected over the flooded realm, shining eerily with uncertain lights.

"Maybe we can cross by jumping between the rooftops," Sterjall said.

"We'll get wet," Kitjári said, "but I think the cats should be able to handle it."

They directed Blu and Pichi to an embankment that cut through most of the lake. From the end of that ridge, they hopped across toppled columns, walls, and roofs that were still above water. Around them, countless eyes stared, blinking whitely through their nictitating membranes. Scaled spines sliced through the waters, where conspicuous logs floated with thousands of patient teeth.

The smilodons jumped from stone to stone, sometimes high up on tall buildings, sometimes with paws splashing in shallow waters, moving fast before the crocodilian residents had a chance to swim toward them.

They found a high road circling the trunk and followed it toward the temple's archway, taking cascading steps back down toward the water. From that vantage point, they could see—but not reach—the half-submerged entrance. The braided patterns carved around it resembled knotted snakes, twisting sinuously up to an indented reptilian glyph, which was half-broken and dripping with moss.

"The only way to get in would be to swim," Kitjári said, frowning.

"Well, at least we know d'ramp goes up, so d'rest uf d'temple won't be underwater," Nalaníri said, trying to sound hopeful. "Can them kitties paddle?"

"They don't like it much, but they are good swimmers," Sterjall answered. "We should move. There are too many eyes in the water, and though they look still, I think they are slowly drifting toward us."

"Sounds like d'perfect way t'get trapped!" Nalaníri said a bit too cheerfully. "Let's take d'plunge before we overthink it n'change our minds."

The two smilodons jumped in and swam toward the portal. The water was almost icy, making the smilodons swim faster. They crossed the dripping threshold and paddled up the vaulted hallway until their paws touched solid ground, the water leveling with the ramp.

Each of the wayfarers had brought a pharolith lamp, which they now spread open, filling the hallway with a radiant, cold light. The ramp itself was an endless cascade, fed by cracks in the walls and by springs sprouting from beneath the stone bricks. Though the angle was not steep, it took a daunting effort by the smilodons to claw their way up the slippery surface.

"Reminds me of the ice ramp at Da'áju," Sterjall commented, holding tight to Blu's saddle.

"Yeah," Kitjári said, nervously peeking back the way they'd come. "Except that instead of a black pit of death, we could slide into the jaws of giant gators. Not sure which one I hate the most."

The half-mile tunnel finally ended, but even before entering the temple, they knew no Kruwenfröa or Kruwensilv was to be found here: there was no aura, no glow. The pharoliths lit up a circular room very much like the ones in the Moordusk and Fjordlands domes, except that here there were three waterfalls discharging right out of the walls, turning the floor into a shallow pool. The marble throne—this one decorated with one too many pointed teeth—was still above water, rising on the central pedestal alongside a pile of disconnected bones. The wayfarers hopped down from their cats, splashing their feet, hooves, and footpaws into the water. Sterjall walked up the steps and picked up one of the green bones, an ulna, searching for clues.

"I don't think we'll find anyone alive in here," he said, both frustrated and demoralized. "If the Silv is not in this temple, it could take us years to find it among the ruins, if it's still even in this dome."

Kitjári stepped behind the throne and caressed the core vine. It was moist and slick; it seemed healthy. "Despite the water damage, the temple seems fine, and the lattice above it is—shit!" she yelped, looking up. A wide ledge encircled the room, and at the edges of it, stuck on the thorns of the columnar vines, draped what looked like a long, translucent sheet.

"What is that?" Sterjall asked.

"It's... a snakeskin," Kitjári whispered, then swallowed thickly. "I don't think I want to loiter around this cursed place any longer. We are not going to find any answers here, as much as it hurts to admit it. It's time we consider what Alaia suggested. Are we setting this place to open? Do you all think that's a good idea?"

"It must be done," Sunu agreed.

"Seems like we have no uther choice," Nalaníri said. "It shell work jis' d'same with any uf d'Silvesh."

"Could I try it this time?" Sterjall asked, feeling a bit self-conscious.

Kitjári shrugged.

"It's much easier than it seems," Nalaníri said. "Once ye get it started, it goes all un its own. But don't delay now, wulfy, get un it."

Sterjall somewhat regretted his decision when he had to place his tail and back upon the slimy throne. He ignored the icky feeling and focused on the lattice. Despite the unruly state of the dome, the vines at the temple had not gone out of shape, perhaps due to the lattice's proximity. The temple was in good working order.

Though it might not have been anything extraordinary to someone like Nalaníri or Kulak, who sat at their temples' thrones every month to help the vines grow properly, the experience was exquisitely savored by Sterjall. When he focused on the lattice above him, his perception of the space he was in expanded. As Kulak had once described to him, he could sense the entire dome at once, as if every vine was visible miles above and around him, even down to the roots that dug deep into Noss's crust.

Seeing it as a whole, he could even sense the dome's own glow, and understood it to be not just one simple organism, but something much more complex. The dome's aura was a waxy green, like the vines themselves, but it appeared eaten by holes with darker edges, reminding him of burnt paper. The threads that his consciousness bound to were not ones of health, but of pain, of uncertainty and chaos. He saw the twisted gnarls of all twenty-three supporting columns and the unkempt tangles of the trunk right above them, and sensed how the vines extended their tentacles to the skies for answers but found none, so they kept on growing, knowing not what their purpose was.

The pain struck him all at once. Feeling the enormity of the anguish of such a creature was beyond him. His jaw slackened; his eyes widened. For a moment, he thought he would collapse, perhaps die, but soon his mind came to understand that the pain was not his to bear, and he allowed it to seep into the back of his perception. He felt sad for this plant, this macroorganism of purposelessness, and felt inclined to heal it, to offer a bit of himself to make it feel better, if it could indeed feel anything at all. He knew it was Agnargsilv embedding that nurturing instinct into his mind, making him feel the need to heal the dome as the mask had done for centuries at the Heartpine Dome. But the time for healing the Varanus Dome was long gone—it wasn't comfort that it needed; it was undoing, unbeing, rest.

Sterjall pictured the end, and with his empathic focus exponentially increased by the lattice, he willed the quaar formation to collapse.

The lattice obeyed.

The tessellated form shifted and contorted its polygonal form, reducing its volume and compressing toward the center. It wrapped its quaar segments around the core vine, and while veiling it in blackness, lowered it into the heart of the mountain, sending out an alleviating signal that the entire dome would understand. A pool of sap formed over the hole the vine sank into, leaving a perfect circle of whiteness.

With no fanfare, the end of the Varanus Dome began.

"That... That wasn't so hard," Sterjall said. "The mask, it showed me how to do it." As he rose from the slimy throne, an earthquake shook the temple. "We better get back to the others now."

As they were about to mount the smilodons, another tremor struck them, but this one felt different, being followed by a slithering sound that rumbled from the only exit.

"Get back!" Kitjári warned, just as an enormous creature, over fifty feet long, crept into the circular room. The snake's head rose, and her tongue flicked out to smell her soon-to-be meals. She focused on the two smilodons, who hissed while they slunk backward to find cover. The snake's eyes followed them, her pit organs sensing the warmth of their blood.

Blades were drawn. Sunu took out their blowgun. "Move to the far end, away from the exit," they said. "Maybe the guardian will leave us be, if we let it escape."

But the snake remained by the exit, with her sight still focused on the cats. The more snake that crawled into the temple, the more the exit became obstructed. They had entered her nest, and she was not happy about the intrusion. The snake tentatively lunged, hissed, and spat, snapping her jaws in defiance, more afraid of the pharoliths than of the negligible size of her enemies.

"It's too big to fight!" Kitjári exclaimed.

"Sunu, your darts!" Sterjall cried out.

But Sunu shook their head. "Sunu has no darts for something that size. It will only make the guardian mad. Be still, hold your lights up, and attack only if the guardian attacks first."

The snake coiled defensively, building a wall of slippery scales that seemed impossible to defeat. She lunged at Blu, but he jumped behind one of the thorn-covered columns, which the serpent refused to touch. Sunu jumped in to aid the felid, blowing a dart at the snake's face, but it simply bounced off her thick scales. The snake attacked again, this time going for Pichi, but Sterjall quickly hurled his pharolith lamp in an arc. The creature pounced at the flying object and snapped her jaws around it, finding nothing, then turned with her maw open, shining bright and pink with the pharolith sitting on her tongue. Sunu blew a dart straight into the snake's glowing mouth. It hit her gums and made her writhe in pain, instantly pulling back.

Blu saw a chance and attacked the giant. He leapt and landed right in the middle of the tangle of scales. The snake's body was as wide as the enormous cat, but Blu did not care. He clawed, then bit down deeply with his saber-teeth. The serpent coiled her tail around Blu's body and lifted him up. Pichi rushed to defend Blu while he kept biting, tearing, and howling for help.

"Leave him alone!" Sterjall cried, tightening his grip on Leif. The moment the wolf began to heroically—or stupidly—charge toward the giant beast, the temple grounds were shaken by a massive stomping, making him lose his balance. From the exit hidden behind the snake, a giant alligator shoved his tapered jaws forward, tossing the serpent into the air, then rushing underneath her to enter the temple. The gator turned around at full speed, and as he did so, he shapeshifted into a frill-necked lizard only three feet in length, stopping atop the toothed throne at the center of the room. The snake landed with a massive splash, and the small reptile gaped his mouth at her, hissing as he spread out his cartilaginous frill.

The snake curled tight in shame at the lizard's ire, letting go of Blu. She looked hesitantly toward the exit, then slithered down the wet ramp as fast as she could.

The lizard jumped off the throne and in midair turned into a double-crested basilisk. With barely any splashing, he ran atop the water on his two back claws, bolting toward a wall. He grabbed onto the rock and climbed until he reached a safe ledge far above them, next to the dangling snakeskin. From there the reptile stared down patiently, like a green gargoyle.

Sterjall hurried to comfort Blu, who seemed stunned and scared and might have been crushed to death if help had not arrived. Pichi stood guard by the exit, staring into the dark hallway, but the serpent would not return anytime soon, not after having been chastised by the Nu'irg ust Kruwen himself.

"His name's Ishke'ísuk," Nalaníri told the others, aiming a pharolith lamp a bit rudely at the perching basilisk. "Mamóru was a-telling me 'bout him d'uther night. It's a good sign he's still 'round here. Almost as old a creature as Mamóru himself. Almost."

Sterjall looked up at the Nu'irg, tasting his distinctive aura; it gave him the impression of a polychromatic lilac color, like an uncertain oil slick of tremorous violets, bashful pinks, and undying amaranthines. "Thank you, Ishke'ísuk," he said, hoping the Nu'irg could understand at least those words.

The basilisk remained motionless.

"The Nu'irg must have felt the dome opening," Sunu conjectured. "We were lucky he found us."

"Why is he perching there?" Kitjári asked. "What does he want?"

Nalaníri shrugged. "No way fur us t'know. Can't talk to reptiles without d'reptilian mask."

"Sunu could," Sunu said, approaching Ishke'ísuk. "In the manner Sunu talks to Olo. Lizards are not much different from birds."

"But you wouldn't hear him back," Sterjall noted.

"No," Sunu said. "Speaking is easy, listening is harder. Though some shamans such as Klaawich have managed, or at least that is what they claim. But Nu'irgesh are smart as companion species. Ishke'ísuk's eyes are purposeful and have the same questioning authority as Nelv's."

Ishke'ísuk had remained still as the rocky ledge he perched upon until he heard Nelv's name. At that moment, his head tilted slightly, and he blinked, but that was all.

"It's worth trying," Sterjall conceded.

Sunu walked toward the wall and looked up. They asked Nalaníri to widen the beam of her pharolith, to avoid blinding the Nu'irg, then picked out a seedpod filled with soot from their necklaces, inhaled the powder, and closed their eyes. The roars of the flowing waters made it easier for Sunu to concentrate. They felt with their mind and tried to reach the consciousness of the Nu'irg.

Sterjall closed his eyes too, paying attention only to Sunu and Ishke'ísuk. Sunu's head swam with threads that did not belong to them, attracting them with the influence of the aetheric carbon particles they had inhaled while extending the Nu'irg's lilac aura toward themself. The shaman opened their dilated eyes and looked up at the basilisk, and though Sterjall could not hear any words, he felt the essence of ideas being communicated.

After a long-drawn moment, the basilisk jumped down and ran atop the water toward the exit. He slid down the water ramp, letting the current take him far out of sight.

"What did he say?" Kitjári asked.

"Sunu's scalp cannot know what the Nu'irg said. But Sunu asked for him to show us answers. We should follow."

They mounted their cats and followed Ishke'ísuk down the ramp, sliding clumsily most of the way. The double-crested basilisk was waiting at the flooded bottom. Once the others reached him, he ran atop the water once more and stopped right on top of an alligator's head, framed by its protruding eyes.

Sunu focused on the basilisk again. "Sunu asked if it is safe. Nu'irg blinked. It must be safe."

Sterjall tapped on Blu's shoulder blades. "Come on Blu, it's not too far." The smilodon growled, upset by this repeated, soaking humiliation, and also concerned about those floating eyes, but after a long moment he, and then Pichi, splashed in and swam side by side, exiting the long tunnel. Around them gathered dozens of reptilian eyes, measuring them with cold curiosity.

Ishke'ísuk led the way, keeping ahead of them, bolting over the water and stopping on the backs of gators, crocodiles, or turtles to make sure the others were keeping up. Once the smilodons swam close enough to him, he darted weightlessly to his next scaly platform. The reptiles followed them, sometimes swimming below them, making the cats tense uncomfortably.

They were headed toward a five-sided pyramid, very similar to the structure they had climbed after entering the dome, but this one was sticking partially out of the lake and partially from the very mountain, dangerously close to one of the largest waterfalls. Other than by water, there seemed to be no access to this palace, as its lower floors had been flooded along with the rest of the city.

The capitals of an old colonnade rose from the water, delineating a clear path toward the pyramid. Ishke'ísuk took off again at full speed, leaving a thin wake behind his brisk back claws. He reached the shore and turned to wait like a statue.

The explorers reached dry land and dismounted, letting the cats shake themselves off ungracefully.

"Follow," Sunu demanded, as Ishke'ísuk darted ahead in a green flash, not even giving them time to wring out their trousers.

Ishke'ísuk stopped atop a pedestal. As they approached him, he sprinted once more, in a perpetual state of stillness contrasted by fast motion, making them uncertain of his patience or lack thereof. The double-crested basilisk climbed two levels higher on the pyramid, then disappeared into one of the entrances.

Spreading open their pharolith lamps, they entered a narrow and tall opening, noticing the corroded flagpoles flanking them, imagining what this palatial sanctuary might have looked like in ages past. The constricting passage widened into a great hall. They could not see Ishke'ísuk directly anymore, but the Silvfröash could sense his lilac aura at the end of the ample room. Water had not seeped directly into this chamber, but the moisture could not be stopped: all the surfaces were blanketed in black and yellow slime molds, while blueish algae brewed in puddles at the corners. The black and yellow forms crawled up the legs of stone tables and wove around the carved columns, even covering most of the dripping, buttressed ceiling.

White patches poked out of the slime in clumpy heaps. Nalaníri kicked at a mound, which broke apart to reveal a brittle ribcage covered by a dissolving cloth. "Skeletons. By d'light uf d'kenzir, there are so many uf them, hundreds."

"Seems like a dining hall. What do you think happened here?" Sterjall asked Kitjári.

Kitjári sniffed with her keen bear nose. With the tip of her short sword, she pushed the remains around. Her nose quickly detected the metals of old blades, chalices, trays, rings. Most of the dead were slumped at the tables, where she found plates and moldy silverware beneath their arms and skulls.

"None of the weapons I see are unsheathed," she said, puzzled by the scene. "There was no struggle here, they died while dining. The porcelain plates are kingly, and so are the carvings in these columns. This seems like the phantom of a great feast."

Aside from the dead mounds, there were also many eyes watching them. Red they were, and patiently immobile, from amphibians and reptiles who had nested within the bones. Their retinas reflected the light of the pharoliths like rubies under moonlight.

At the end of the hall was a staircase where Ishke'ísuk waited, perched on a rusty handrail.

"Wait here," Sterjall said to Blu and Pichi, noticing the spiraling steps would be too narrow for their huge bodies. "I hope we won't be long."

The wayfarers followed the basilisk to a lower level.

"This kitchen's bigger than d'one at d'guildhall," Nalaníri observed, immediately recognizing the arrangement of tables, sinks, and racks. "Not as many dead bodies as up above."

Running water echoed in the room, but the basilisk ignored the kitchen and disappeared further down the stairway. They heard a splash.

The steps ended in frothy water, where Ishke'ísuk waited as a blind skink, wriggling pink and eyeless like an overgrown earthworm. Sunu focused on the skink, asking a question with their mind. The skink flailed, swam deeper, and waited there.

"Sunu thinks Ishke'ísuk wants us to follow in water," Sunu said. "Your Silvesh can see better. Sunu will wait with Olo. You follow."

"I'm not diving into that green muck," Sterjall complained. "We don't even know how deep that goes."

Sunu made themself comfortable, sitting on a wide step and leaning against the wall. "Follow the Nu'irg. The path is open before you."

"Look through that wall with your Silv," Kitjári said, pulling on Sterjall's shoulder. "See that hollow area? It must be a pocket of air in the next level down. We can go together, help each other see the way forward."

"Well, 'twas good while it lasted," Nalaníri said. "Let's go drown in this muldy water, no reason t'wait any longer." She took off her vest, made sure her glowing axe and lamp were firmly secured to her belt, and jumped into the water.

Kitjári and Sterjall removed their excess clothing and dove in, also carrying their weapons and lights. The water was cold, though they didn't feel the shock immediately, as their legs had already been wet.

They swam down the spiral steps, following their Silvesh's sights more than the pharolith lights, which barely shone through the muck. Sterjall was not used to the increased pressure, and once they reached a dozen feet below the water, his ears began to hurt. The steps flattened there, and a passage opened to their side. As soon as they crossed into the next room, they swam upward and gasped for air in a pocket just big enough for their heads to surface. The stale air felt refreshing. They ignored the Nu'irg for a moment while they studied their surroundings.

The steps had led them to the center of a long hallway, with the floor twenty feet below them. Massive statues served as columns, depicting anthropomorphized snakes, dragons, turtles, crocodiles, iguanas, geckos, and tegus.

Ishke'ísuk floated at the far end of the long hall of statues. They paddled toward him with their heads above water, pushing off the floating debris and algae at the surface. The hallway ended in a wall, but below the waterline was a large archway framing a closed double door. It was made of thick wood and looked heavy. The blind skink found a small hole under the doors to wriggle through, and swam to the other side, waiting as an impatient lilac glow.

"Let's hope d'doors are unlocked," Nalaníri said before diving down. She struggled with the doorknob, pulling it up and pushing it down, until she ran out of air and swam back up.

Kitjári tried next, placing her footpaws on the submerged floor and pushing up until she felt the doorknob give, but she only managed to sever it, tearing off a piece of the rotting wood along with it.

"Sorry, I think I broke it," she said once she resurfaced. "But the wood is weak. Maybe we can break through it."

"You two go ahead," Sterjall said. "That's too deep for me. My ears were already hurting during the last swim."

Nalaníri swam down and swung her glowing axe, failing miserably as the water prevented her from picking up speed. Kitjári swam below her and wedged her sword between two boards, loosening them and using her thick claws to rip out parts of the decayed wood. Nalaníri followed her lead, placing her thicker blade in the newly opened crack and pulling on it like a lever, tearing off a large plank.

They swam up for air and then down again, carving out a bit at a time. After a dozen or so dives, they at last saw through to the other side. Kitjári reached her arm through the hole and found a metal bolt, pulled it hard, and unlocked the doors. She kicked them both open.

She resurfaced and gasped, "Alright, they are open, there's air on the other side. Let's go."

The next room was much taller, soaring so far above them that the ceiling was lost beyond the reach of their lights. The constant percussion of dripping water made the room feel even bigger.

Sterjall felt the lilac aura up ahead, but then noticed it splitting. He cocked his head and realized there had been two glows waiting. As they waded toward the twin auras, they could feel the ground slowly rising, until steps rose out the water to an elevated platform that was crowned by a heavy throne of rusted iron and copper, one much more extravagant and menacing than the marble throne at the temple. Slumbering upon the throne, unperturbed for untold centuries, rested the skeleton of an ancient queen, still wearing the black countenance of Kruwensilv.

Sterjall shook himself dry and jumped up and down a few times to get the water out of his ears. He climbed up the steps in silence, following the others.

He shivered with cold, holding his arms tight and his shoulders high, leaving a wet trail behind him.

The old queen seemed so at peace, as if she had died in her sleep, lounging in her finest clothes. She was holding a goblet of gold adorned with fine jewels and slimy mold.

Sterjall's footpaws accidentally kicked something. "What is this thing?" he asked aloud, reaching down to touch a long, cone-shaped artifact. He could sense that the object interacted strangely with the surrounding threads, aligning them in perfect, crystalline angles. "It's made of quaar. Looks like a piece of armor."

Kitjári scraped off some of the slime growing on it. "It has multiple joints, as if made for a thick tail. And look at these sharp studs on the tip."

The long piece of armor was made of twelve articulated segments of quaar, which could clasp down to hold any size tail. Though the quaar weighed nearly nothing at all, the last segment at the tip was fitted with heavy steel spikes, like the head of a mace.

They stepped around the tail armor to get a closer look at Kruwensilv. It seemed more complex than the masks they wore, with filaments woven into geometric scales across the entirety of the mask. It also seemed more menacing than their counterparts, with narrower eyes, no ears, and an army of pointed teeth interlaced with one another.

Sterjall hovered a handpaw close to the mask, never touching it, uncertain whether perturbing the remains of the dead queen would be proper. "Is it okay if we—"

"To d'netherflames with it," Nalaníri interrupted, pulling the mask off the dead body. The skull made a cracking sound, tipped over, and clonked its way down the steps until it splashed in the water, making Sterjall wince. "She's as dead as d'dust uf our ancestors. I don't believe she'd mind if we take this. Little Ishke seems t'want us t'have it anyhow."

The blind skink seemed content, if a skink could portray such a mood. As soon as he felt the reptilian mask was in the wayfarers' hands, he swam toward the exit.

Nalaníri picked up the tail armor and shook off as much slime as she could. "Let's take this as well, fur whoever ends up wielding d'mask. As long as them don't end up as a turtle or something tailless like it—that'd be quite a waste."

They took a last look around the throne room. Though the throne was elevated, most of the chamber remained underwater, and there was not much more to be found above the water's surface. The queen was wearing precious adornments, and the jewels upon her goblet would likely be worth fortunes, but they decided not to disturb those artifacts.

"Let's get out of here," Kitjári said. "We should make camp before night arrives. Night, or whatever in Khest you call it when the arudinn pulsate like that."

"Yes please," Sterjall agreed through chattering teeth.

Ishke'ísuk led the way back along the same underwater path, then perched on a giant fiddlehead once they had made their way outside the drowning pyramid.

"What should we do with the mask?" Sterjall asked, striking his brime bracer to make a fire, his top priority. "Who is going to wear it?"

"We should consult with Mamóru," Kitjári said, sitting by the lake, scraping the hardened mold off the mask and tail armor. "But now, we need rest. We'll chat with the old mammoth tomorrow."

When morning unevenly arrived, Sunu inhaled a small dose of soot and looked at Ishke'ísuk's expressionless, basilisk face. "Nu'irg ust Kruwen seems thankful," Sunu said. "Sunu told him Mamóru awaits. Sunu could hear no answer, but thinks he understood, felt his happiness."

Ishke'ísuk suddenly bolted atop the water, then stopped on a drowning column.

"Better fullow d'eager lizard," Nalanírí said.

They mounted the cats and trailed behind the Nu'irg, hopping between the toppled ruins, finding the driest path out of the lake. While they trotted down the mountain, Ishke'ísuk led as a lined gliding lizard, flying from tree to tree, extending his yellow patagia to catch the air and float carefree to the lower levels of the path. Once they reached the city at the bottom, Ishke'ísuk ran next to them as a perentie, a type of spotted monitor lizard that surprised them with its speed, effortlessly matching the cats' fast pace.

Reaching the stone piers, the wayfarers stumbled upon an ongoing skirmish: a troop of Puqua and Laatu sailors were trying to board their ships, but a handful of varanus dragons refused to leave the pier, sniffing for a way into the vessels.

Ishke'ísuk outran the cats, transformed into a frill-necked lizard, and hissed the dragons away. The huge reptiles hurled themselves into the water in fear of the tiny creature.

"Ishke'ísuk!" Mamóru called from a chair atop the deck of *Drolvisdinn*.

The lizard stopped and stared, his frills slackening with his surprise.

"My friend, it is I!" Mamóru called. "What joy to see your scales once more, what joy!"

Ishke'ísuk shifted to his primal form, jumped onto the ship, and curled his overjoyed tail around Mamóru's neck and beard.

Chapter Seventy-Two

Kruwenfröa

Mamóru was carried on his chair into the abandoned city and placed at the center of a series of concentric rings of stones. The boulders were of different sizes; some standing, some on their sides, all carved with cryptic runes and draped in moss. Everyone had left the ships to gather around the toppled rocks; even varanus dragons lurked at the periphery, hissing and stomping, but with Ishke'ísuk present, none of them dared bother the newcomers.

Kruwensilv and the tail armor were displayed atop a rune-covered pedestal at the center of the ring of stones. Mamóru sat next to the pedestal, with Ishke'ísuk perching on the ammonite handle of his blackthorn cane. The old man did his best to convey strength, though little of it resided within him any longer. He signaled for his friends to join him and asked them to recount their recent adventure. Once their story had been told, Sterjall, Kitjári, Nalaníri, and Sunu left the center of the ring and went to sit at the stones with the others, leaving only the two Nu'irgesh in the center.

Mamóru picked up the reptilian mask and said, "The six Silvesh have at last been gathered. Three domes have now begun to open, returning their white blood into the arteries of Noss. We have journeyed this far to find a way to speak with our planet, but they will entertain no audience with us unless six speakers are present. Ishke'ísuk tells me no Mo'óto Miscam remain alive, but their tragic story is one for another time. A new voice for the reptilians must be chosen, and volunteers must come forward."

"I volunteer for this honor," Hud Ilsed said. She stood proudly, lifting her tanned breasts. She stepped into the central ring and kneeled.

"I do as well," Kenondok offered, following her lead, "though my scalp believes Hod Abjus would have been best fitted for this honor." He lowered his deep-blue head in remembrance.

"Why don't you give it a try?" Sterjall whispered to Alaia.

"Khest no," she whispered back. "You want me to be a slimy snake? Really, ever since you put that thing on, I've been afraid of them. And I'm happy with who I am, thank you very much."

A handful of Puqua and Laatu sailors also stepped forward. In the end, seven volunteers kneeled within the ring of stones.

Mamóru regarded them and judged their commitment.

"I thank you all for offering to undertake this responsibility. I feel you are all truthful in your commitment, but it is not my duty to choose. The Nu'irg ust Kruwen should make the choice, in honor of the Mo'óto Miscam who lost their lives to safeguard his kind. What say you, Ishke'ísuk? Who do you believe will lead reptiliankind in honor and help fulfill our oath to Noss?"

Mamóru held his cane out, with the basilisk perching on top of it. The lizard stood so still that they all doubted he had heard the question. After an endless pause, Ishke'ísuk blinked, then his head lightly turned. After another prolonged moment, he ran at full speed and wrapped himself around Sunu's freckled neck, surprising Olo, who flew off their shoulders with an annoyed screech.

"I am afraid Sunu has not volunteered," Mamóru said to the Nu'irg. "The Kruwenfröa must be willing to accept their obligations."

Ishke'ísuk wrapped himself tighter around Sunu's neck, then hissed at Mamóru.

"Sunu is sorry," Sunu said, to the lizard and to all around them. "Laatu law does not allow allgenders to be the voices of the animals. Sunu will not defy their own tribe's rules."

Ishke'ísuk climbed atop Sunu's bald head and spat. Sunu's purple scalp pigments had almost all faded by now—only a memory of the leaf-like patterns remained. The basilisk held on tight, digging his claws in deeply enough that they drew blood.

"Sunu is sorry," Sunu repeated with genuine regret, blood streaking down the bridge of their nose.

"Ishke'ísuk," Mamóru called out, reprimanding the basilisk with a stare. He mindspoke something more to him, something he did not want to say aloud.

"We are no longer in Mindreldrolom," Sterjall muttered. "Why should we be bound by Laatu traditions?"

"An ignorant, disrespectful comment," Hud Ilsed said. "You may not care about our traditions, but the Laatu do."

"But Sunu is a shaman," Kitjári said. "Whoever wields this mask needs to be able to do so quickly. It took me months to learn, as I was not ready, but Sunu already knows how to talk to other species and has even talked to Ishke'ísuk. Sunu is the most qualified, the one who would learn the fastest among any of us."

"My nose has used ustlas too, many a time!" Kenondok complained, back on his feet.

"Not in same ways a shaman does," Kulak retorted. "If Ishke'ísuk picked you, Kenondok, my eyes would be happy to see you wear Kruwensilv. But Nu'irg ust Kruwen chose Sunu, who is as fearless a fighter as you, as honorable a leader as Ilsed, as trustworthy a companion as any of the volunteers."

"Khuron disregards too many sacred laws," Kenondok said. "We should honor wisdom of our past voices. This way is not proper."

"There's no precedent fur any uf this," Nalaníri said. "We must a-find our own ways. I know Puqua laws be foreign to most uf ye, but them did work well enough in them own way. We didn't pass Nagrasilv to our children, but to an heir uf our choosing, picked by d'community. Our laws—"

Ilsed huffed and cut her off. "Your kind chose plain-skinned families to force them to inherit suid blood. We are Laatu. We need not honor your ways."

"What I was a-meaning t'say," Nalaníri continued, raising an eyebrow, "is that our laws all differ. Who knows what laws them had in this dome 'fore doom struck them? Mayhaps Mo'óto priests cast runestones into d'mud n'guessed at them furtunes, or read d'smearing entrails uf a smitten warrior. But that matters no longer, fur we do know d'wishes uf d'Nu'irg. We'll always have customs that'll differ frum one anuther, no matter our similarities."

"Then respect our differences," Kenondok snapped. "Sunu is Laatu, they follow Laatu law. If allgenders cannot make children, they should not wield a sacred Silv, or their line dies with them."

Kulak rose to his feet and loudly voiced, "Allgenders have no children *because* our laws do not allow them to, not because they are unable. If having children was required for Laatu to wield a Silv, then I would not have been Mindrelfröa. Yet here I stand as Kulak, not as Aio."

Sterjall shifted uncomfortably, watching carefully out of the corner of his eye, keeping his handpaws pressed between his knees.

"This is not true, Khuron," Hud Ilsed said with a confused twist at the edges of her red lips. "Once we return to Mindreldrolom, you will be given a chance to foster an heir. The six provinces have already chosen candidates for you."

Kulak shook his head. "We travel to new worlds together, we fight and bleed together, yet your scalps do not know your Khuron." He sat back down and put an arm around Sterjall's shoulder. "I am not going to have children, as my heart is not in love with a woman, and I do not believe it ever will be."

All the Laatu tensed up and grew still, some with faces of disgust, some with mere confusion. The Puqua didn't seem quite as concerned and only looked entertained behind their tusks. Sterjall wished he could put Kruwensilv on himself, turn into a turtle, and hide in his thick shell.

"Khuron Kulak, be careful with your words," Kenondok warned.

"I do not have to be, and I do not have to hide from you any longer." He reached for Sterjall's handpaws and managed to pull one free, interlacing their fingers in the open. Sterjall felt a jolt of pride in the gesture, a feeling that was quickly overshadowed by terror and embarrassment.

Kulak continued to speak, raising his voice. "Many Silvfröash choose ways of life different from what is expected of them. Wearing the Silvesh lets us see more ways of being, and all ways are valid, all must be respected. I love Sterjall, and I choose to be with him, despite what the Laatu will say about us."

Kenondok opened his mouth to speak, but Kulak interrupted him.

"Not as your Khuron, but as Mindrelfröa, I am responsible for shaping Laatu laws, which were never meant to remain frozen like the top of Stelm Humenath, but to change in times of need like the shifting waters of the Stiss Regu-Omen. Mother still enforces laws, being the eldest, but the Mindrelfröa decides when to change them. Mindreldrolom has opened, a new epoch begins, the time for change is here. If Sunu wishes to bear this honor, new Laatu law will allow them to. And if Sunu chooses to find love, and wishes to raise children in the future, be that as it may. It is none of our concern, but theirs, and new Laatu law will allow them to as well."

Sunu lowered their head in a sad smile, their violet-cast eyes conflicted, the basilisk still perched upon their crown.

Kenondok's scalp was boiling, dripping sweat. "This is most disrespectful to our—"

"Not a word more, Kenondok. Fröa ust Mindrel has spoken," Kulak said. "We cannot decide. Sunu must decide. If they do not wish to take this honor, that is up to them, and we will respect their choice."

The gathering went quiet as a funeral.

"Sunu, the choice is yours alone," Mamóru finally spoke into the silence.

Sunu raised their head to look toward Kulak. "If the Mindrelfröa's new laws allow it, Sunu will be most honored to shoulder the burden of

Kruwensilv. Thank you, Khuron." As Sunu bowed, Ishke'ísuk jumped off their head and went to perch on Mamóru's cane once more.

"Then the voice of the reptilians shall be one with your own," Mamóru proclaimed, pointing at the mask on the pedestal.

Sunu walked into the circle and picked up the mask.

Kenondok stomped out of the ring but stopped before he could go very far, as too many dragons still prowled on the periphery.

Sunu held the Silv in front of them, trying to find an aspect of themself in the confounding teeth and scales. "If you will so allow, Sunu will wait until nightfall to wear the mask of pain. Time is needed to make Sunu ready."

Kulak agreed with a nod, then added, "And the proper ceremony, the Laatu Tarvio Loom Tikhálv, shall be performed in your honor."

The Laatu returned to their ship, whispering to each other and sneaking furtive looks back at Kulak. The Puqua also returned to their ship, but in a better mood, having been wildly amused by the proceedings. Sunu stayed with Mamóru and Ishke'ísuk to ask for their advice. The rest of them walked around the ruins to converse.

"The Laatu don't seem very happy about this," Alaia told them. "Are you boys alright?"

"I guess. I'll be fine," Sterjall said without much confidence. "I just didn't expect—"

"My scalp wishes to apologize," Kulak interrupted. "I was very afraid, but my scalp thinks it was the right thing to do. I do not want to live in hiding anymore."

"It's alright," Sterjall lied, "it just took me by surprise. The Laatu won't trust us now. It might make things harder."

"Not t'worry, mine furry friends," Nalaníri told them. "What ye did was mighty brave. D'Puqua sailors were fascinated by d'drama unfolding in front uf them. Hollering shanties shell be written 'bout them awkward moments we witnessed."

Sterjall cringed at the idea, while Kulak blushed under his fur.

Nalaníri went on. "I had a hunch down in mine belly a-telling me there was something going un between ye two. Ye make d'most adorable couple."

Kulak smiled through his cut lips and held tighter onto Sterjall's handpaw, but Sterjall just felt embarrassed and out of place.

That evening, dozens of pharolith lamps were placed among the concentric rings of stones, summoning clouds of spiraling moths as well as eager Puqua and Laatu onlookers who waited for the ceremony to begin. The night was yet stranger than the preceding ones; now that the dome was opening, the light of the arudinn fluctuated with more uncertainty, and the shuffling of the vines had begun to birth more sporadic and numerous wisps. Adding to the anomalous atmosphere were the constant tremors.

As the Mindrelfröa, Aio would do the honors for Sunu, as his mother had performed the ceremony for him when he turned fifteen. He instructed Puqua sailors to help him carry the pedestal out from the center of the ring and to cover the area with sand. Lago, Prikka, and Jiara were also in their more appropriate human forms, as it was not their night to celebrate.

Some distance from the stone circle, Prikka had lit a fire and was preparing a special meal for the occasion. Jiara helped her out, entranced by seeing Prikka in her human form, which she had only glimpsed for one brief moment the day they had met, when Prikka had fallen into her arms. Jiara found Prikka's blotchy skin alluring in the firelight, seeing only the pink side of her while the blacks blended seductively with the darkness. Prikka noticed the stare, and being too self-conscious of her rarely seen human self, she distractedly burned her fingers on a pan.

"*Fûggun!*" she swore, sucking on her fingers. "Them blasted things! I understand why them want us in our human forms, but it's so undignified. I jis' don't get how yer people cook with them floppy sausages. Mine hooves were much easier t'work with. It's been a while since I spent so long in this wretched form, I'd be mighty afraid t'handle a chopping knife!" She snorted her derision.

"I'll help you with anything with blades," Jiara said. "Keep your sausages attached to you, please." She began to chop the fresh-picked water chestnuts.

Alaia sat next to Lago, waiting by a bonfire away from the main circle of patient spectators. Lago was biting at his nails, watching the embers flicker short-lived images.

"Now will you tell me what's happening in that head of yours?" Alaia asked quietly. "Maybe as a human you'll have it more figured out."

"What do you mean?"

"How uncomfortable you were with Kulak, with all that happened. I know you are shy about some things, but that looked a bit more awkward than I expected."

Lago focused on the embers, feeling his eyes dry up from the heat. "I don't know how to explain it."

"Just say it."

"It's not as much about him. It's more about… He said he loves me."

"And do you—"

"And I *don't*... want to... fall in love with him." Lago looked away, trying to hide his face from the orange light.

"Does that mean you *are* falling in love with him?"

"How could I not? He's grown so much, and he is much braver than I am, and he takes care of me, and—I was okay just playing around, just a bit of fun here and there, but this isn't right."

"Why is it not right?"

"You know..."

Alaia put an arm around Lago and pinched his smooth cheek from the far side. "Look, Gwoli, I'm not the smartest when it comes to relationships. I've barely had a few flings in my life, and I don't even get what the appeal of sex is. Whatever I've learned has been from watching your mess-ups, from trying to understand what makes your creaky gears turn, but I still learned quite a bit from that alone."

She pulled her legs up and leaned into him. "There's nothing that says you can only love one person. You can love a big bear for one reason, a kitty for an entirely different one. Some of those reasons might overlap, and how you handle your relationship is between you two, you three, you sixteen, whatever you want. I think that in his ten thousand years of life, Banook has probably figured that out too, and would not blame you for loving someone else."

"Sixty thousand..."

"Right, making my point."

"I just... Maybe I do love Aio, but I don't think I could love him as much as I love Banook. That's so unfair. For Aio, I mean. He feels more for me, and I don't think I can match that."

"And who is counting? It's not some Qupi chips you are trading, it is what it is. If it makes you happy, why not enjoy it however much you can both enjoy it?"

Lago pulled at his curls. "Wouldn't he get jealous?"

"Banook could never be—"

"Not Banook, but Aio. I try not to talk about Banook around him, because I don't want him to feel uncomfortable. But then I'm hiding a part of myself that is very important. That's dishonest. It feels like I'm pushing Aio away, like I'm not giving myself entirely to him."

Alaia rose to her feet. "Well, like every problem you've encountered before, it's not going to solve itself by you sulking and not speaking your mind. Talk to Aio, see where it takes you."

Lago stared at grayish pebbles on the ground.

"When you are ready, of course," she added. "Come now, the ceremony is about to start. We should be there for Sunu."

Over the now sand-covered center of the ring of stones, Aio had drawn the glyph that represented the clade of reptiles. From atop a flowering tree, Ishke'ísuk watched in the form of an ahaetulla whip snake. The light of the pharoliths made his keyhole-shaped pupils and lime-green scales glisten like cut emeralds.

Lago slouched next to Alaia. They both had no clue what the Laatu Tarvio Loom Tikhálv entailed, but Aio had told them it was a simple ceremony, yet warned them it could get intense if Sunu did not learn how to wear the mask quickly. If that happened, they would have to perform the ceremony again the following night, and again, until Sunu learned to tolerate the pain. Aio was not concerned—the older one was, the easier it became to internalize the pain, and Sunu was nearly twice his age.

Only two Laatu sailors had agreed to chant for the ceremony. The rest—including Ilsed and Kenondok—watched more out of curiosity than respect. The chants were low, dissonant, oscillating with ragged overtones. Though Lago could hear a few Miscamish words here and there, he could not follow what the song said.

Sunu stood outside the circle while Aio finished decorating the glyph, placing colorful leaves in the indentations he had drafted. The glyph had been drawn for Sunu, not for the crowd, and it seemed upside down to Lago, with the sharp tip of the large triangle pointing almost straight at him. Aio placed the last few leaves to embellish the triangle's tip, lowered Kruwensilv over it, then moved out of the way without perturbing the sand.

Sunu removed their long-sleeve shodog, unclasped their necklaces, and dropped their tailcoat kilt. Fully naked, they approached the mask and knelt at the center of the triangle. The entirety of Sunu's exposed body was as smooth and freckled as the parts Lago had seen before, but Lago had never seen anyone with Sunu's particular anatomy. Sunu was intersex; their small breasts were ambiguous enough to pass for either male or female, but their genitals shared the same ambiguity. They had a small penis, but instead of testicles, labia spread around a slit that rose halfway up their shaft. Their crotch was all-encompassing and confusing to Lago, and it made him wonder whether many of the allgenders in the Laatu tribe were this way.

Aio walked behind Sunu and handed them a mortar and pestle. Sunu ground a clumpy powder while Aio joined in the chant. Sunu then held the mortar above and in front of their bald head. Aio poured water into the mix and stirred it. Instead of using the blue kupógo grinesht pigments, he used the purple kupógo gringralv, the color appropriate for allgenders.

Though he was not as skilled as his mother, Aio tried his best. He dipped a flexible stick in the mortar and used it to draw line after line over Sunu's scalp, starting by drawing the reptilian glyph on their forehead, then branching knotted patterns out from it. He tried to preserve Sunu's preference for leaf-like patterns on their right side and mushroom-like imprints on their left. It was his first time doing this, and he might have messed up here and there, but overall he did a respectable job, covering Sunu's scalp with an impressive and powerful design.

Aio put the mortar away and returned to kneel behind Sunu. He grabbed on to their shoulders and continued chanting. Sunu readied themself to put on the mask.

"We could've used our own masks to take some of their pain away," Lago whispered in Alaia's ear.

"That's not part of their ritual."

"But it's so painful. I don't want to see them suffer."

"They need to learn it on their own. Shh, I think they are ready."

The chanting suddenly stopped.

Sunu picked up Kruwensilv and placed it on their face without hesitation. As the mask conformed to their facial features, Sunu contorted backward and convulsed, but Aio was there to hold their shoulders. Sunu struggled. This land was filled with pain, a pain that had been trapped and seething for far too long. Sunu took it all in and understood the plight of all the creatures of the dome. They understood the shame the Laatu felt as they saw them take on the mask, as they saw them unmake their sacred laws. They understood the anguish that Ishke'ísuk carried from the loss of the tribe that had once been in charge of keeping the dome in a healthy balance. They understood their own sorrows, which paled in comparison to all that they now felt. Sunu did not push the pain away, but embraced it, and let despair fill their body as they shook in the sand and unmade the glyph.

Aio was no longer able to hold on to Sunu's shoulders. In this situation, the ritual called for him to remove the mask and repeat the ritual the next day. He tried to pull the mask off, but Sunu held it tight to their face with both hands, then curled protectively into a ball and began to weep. Their shaking suddenly stopped, and all that was left was sobs, tears, and grief.

Aio stood, then walked to the edge of the circle, letting Sunu discover the pain of this moment on their own, just as his mother had once done for him.

Chapter Seventy-Three

The Lashing Ichor

Mamóru wrapped a blanket over his legs, then looked to Sunu. "How does the mask feel now, Kruwenfröa?" he asked, sitting in his chair in front of a bonfire the sailors had lit for him at the city's crumbling harbor.

"More… bearable," Sunu replied haltingly, wearing the mask for the fourth time now. Sunu had been training since the previous day, to get themself ready. "Olo likes Sunu better this way," they said, and Olo replied with *eihnk-eihnk!* "Olo is clearer to Sunu now, though a bit of soot is still needed to talk to him. Still, Sunu is sad that even with Kruwensilv, even once Sunu finds their half-form, they will never hear Olo's own voice."

"Does Sunu need to be in their half-form for us to talk to Noss?" Sterjall asked Mamóru.

"That shan't be necessary," Mamóru answered. "Just as when the Acoapóshi first talked to Noss, using their graphite masks that held no powers of transformation, these Silvesh don't require we take those forms. We are not going to communicate in the languages of those clades of animals, but in our own. Yet Sunu needs to be comfortable wearing the mask for a longer period. It would be wise to wait until at least tomorrow."

Kitjári approached, not hiding her concerned expression. "What will happen to all the animals in here?" she asked. She quickly glanced at Ishke'ísuk, who had been basking on a rock by Mamóru's chair. "The dome is quickly opening, and we don't have the people to help like we did at the Fjordlands and Moordusk domes."

"Not much can be done for these creatures, not yet," Sunu said. "Kruwendrolom births from an island. Birds and insects will take flight on translucent and feathered wings. Sea creatures will flap their fins and tails to new waters. Land animals will spread their claws to the rest of the island, perhaps to nearby islands, but not much farther. Sunu will come back after our mission is over and help species return to the mainland. Months, perhaps years this job will take, and resources we do not yet have, but Sunu promises to see it through upon their return."

"There is more to learn about this forgotten land," Mamóru said. "Gather around, children. Ishke'ísuk has a tale he wishes to tell us." He tapped on his shoulder, and the basilisk came to perch on it. "He has waited many centuries to share this story. I will help interpret for him."

The wayfarers sat around the fire, joined by many Puqua sailors, who loved to hear stories and would likely turn this one into a shanty one day. Ishke'ísuk pushed his chest up and lifted the crests of his back to full display, ready for his audience.

Mamóru reached to a pouch on his belt and picked out a silver-tipped mistleaf variety he had not yet smoked. He lit his pipe and took three puffs. The smoke rose in swirling forms that described shapes yet unknown. The tones of the complex scents spoke of grasslands, of musky caverns, and of hot chocolate on Winter nights.

Mamóru began to interpret the soundless words. "Beyond six lands, beneath six seas, this island was known as Ashgwemar, and the home of the Mo'óto tribe it was. The Nu'irg ust Kruwen tells me that the great capital city of Macu, and many more like it, had already been built long before the domes were sprouted. The Mo'óto grew their dome over their island and felt safe, knowing their old cities would be protected from the life-ending threat of the Downfall.

"During the last days when the dome was closing, a small boat from a northern tribe sailed between the vines, seeking refuge. All non-Mo'óto had been denied entrance, but through an unguarded channel, the foreigners found their way and settled near the walls. Ishke'ísuk tells me a Mo'óto villager found the stowaways, took pity on them, and hid them until the dome finished closing. This would prove to be their doom. Everyone's doom."

The listeners leaned in closer.

"The northerners brought with them the lashing ichor, a dreadful disease the Mo'óto could not fight against, as the only plant known to cure it could only be found in the northern fjords, a place now as inaccessible to them as the craters of Sceres. The lashing ichor showed no effects for months, then very slowly it began to tint the skin of the infected in a ghastly purple, and inevitably ended their lives as their pores and veins suppurated and burst, leaving them convulsing over pools of their own blood. Their last breaths ended in unspeakable agony. The disease spread from small villages to large cities. Each province knew when death had come knocking, for they could see the purple skin of their citizens and knew even those showing no symptoms would soon perish. Most chose to take their lives once they saw their skin change color, avoiding the excruciating end. In an attempt to contain the spread of the disease, the borders of the provinces were closed. That worked, for a while. For decades, the Mo'óto lived in isolation, protecting themselves from each other. But no matter the precautions, the lashing ichor found its way in again."

Ishke'ísuk looked through the sparks of the bonfire, straight at Sunu.

"The Kruwenfröa at the time, Ierun Teifréru, saw her people's numbers dwindling. The disease had not yet come to Macu, but she knew it was only a matter of time. Ierun Teifréru chose to travel west past Klad Eramar, and in her cayman half-form walk through the vines to see if the world outside was yet habitable. Perhaps reopening the dome would be their only chance at surviving, or perhaps she could find the medicine that was needed. She crossed the wall of vines and at its end found a wall of ice as thick as the ocean is deep. She walked back into the dome, crestfallen and frostbitten, and there she collapsed. Ishke'ísuk was there with her, and tried to keep her warm, but his kind is of cold blood, and he could not do much to help her. So he searched for aid. He found an old woman who took Teifréru into her hut, served her warm food, and gave her woolly clothes to wear."

Ishke'ísuk closed his eyes and lowered his head.

"To this day, Ishke'ísuk regrets having searched for help. The clothes the old woman gave to Ierun Teifréru had the seeds of the lashing ichor in them. When the queen returned to Macu, she unknowingly carried the disease with her. It wasn't long until most of the citizens of Macu grew purple skin and realized their days were counted. The queen ordered a great banquet to be prepared, to splurge to an extreme never before seen in any realm. They feasted, all the while knowing that the food had been poisoned and would allow them all quick passage to the Six Gates."

Mamóru exhaled the grassy, musky smoke and let it blow upward as if releasing ghosts. The smoke lifted, dancing and spiraling with the bonfire's sparks.

"Ishke'ísuk says the palace was quiet the next morning. Some of the other villages lasted for a few more decades, but eventually they all succumbed to the lashing ichor. The dome became unsteady after that. With a mind of its own, Kruwendrolom encroached inward, and unbeknownst to the reptiles within, outward as well.

"Within the chaos, the reptiles found a new balance. Much of what they had tried to preserve was lost, but some precious parts remained. Ishke'ísuk did his best to protect them. The great cities of Ashgwemar had stood for thousands of years, but once the humans were gone, in mere decades they were buried under the green, or sunken under the blue."

Ishke'ísuk's tail curled tightly.

"That is the story of this tragic realm," Mamóru concluded, dangling the long stem of his pipe from his chapped lips. "Ishke'ísuk is mighty glad to see we came for him and his kind. He had lost all hope. He knows our quest is important, and just as we are helping them, he kindly asks we allow him to travel with us, so that he might help us in return. Thread unravels, cut, and sewn, and so the story goes."

Sunu bowed in front of the basilisk. "Sunu's scalp shares your sorrow. Sunu does not comprehend how acts of kindness can end in such tragedy. What was lost cannot be brought back, but what remains, Sunu vows to protect."

Chapter Seventy-Four

Braided Threads

For the rest of the day, Sunu worked to better understand Kruwensilv's powers, accompanied by the basilisk, who would often perch upon their left shoulder, opposite Olo.

While Sunu meditated and practiced with their mask, Kulak asked Sterjall to join him in exploring the ruins of the Mo'óto Miscam city. They walked side by side, with Sterjall still apprehensive about the dragons who lurked nearby, even though Ishke'ísuk had asked them not to eat any of the two-legged folk.

"Kenondok and I spoke earlier this morning," Kulak said as he balanced on the scaled back of a giant sculpture of a gharial. He moved in a light-hearted manner, but something about his posture was tense.

Sterjall waited for him to continue.

Kulak stopped at the end of the crocodilian's long, narrow snout, scaring a frog away from the prominent nostrils. "Kenondok says he has lost trust in us. In me." His tufted ears flicked as if swatting away a fly.

"Who the fuck cares what Kenondok thinks?" Sterjall asked more loudly than he intended, holding a handpaw up to help Kulak hop down.

"Laatu sailors do. Hud Ilsed, too." Kulak puckered his black lips. "Mother does too. Kenondok is wise, in his own ways, even if not in every way. Perhaps I should have been more careful. Perhaps my outburst endangered our mission."

"It wasn't an outburst. You were protecting Sunu."

"Part of it, yes. But part of it was protecting us." He snuck a handpaw over Sterjall's crotch, groping softly. "I am tired of lying, of hiding," he said. "My scalp wants more. Perhaps I am only selfish. Always selfish."

Despite his sudden arousal, Sterjall didn't want to venture too deeply into that conversation. He had felt too uncomfortable with Kulak using the word *love*, and did not want to even acknowledge it had happened. *It is easier this way*, he thought, and remained silent.

Kulak sensed the tension and removed his handpaw, then guided him through a desolate alley, following an old water canal. "This is the one," he said, glad to change the subject, arriving at a pentagonal stupa more than half-buried in roots and flowering ivies.

"Looks like a temple," Sterjall said, following Kulak beneath a crumbling archway.

Five spiraling stone buttresses held together a vaulted ceiling. The stained-glass oculus at the top was partially collapsed, letting vegetation, moisture, and a tenuous light drip in. Carved friezes covered the walls, inset with runes that would have once been shining with gold paint, but now grew dark lichens within them.

"My scalp knew you would like this place," Kulak said, eyeing Sterjall's awed expression. "Old ruins. Forsaken, but always beautiful." He had explored this area while the others were fighting giant snakes and looting skeletal queens in underwater palaces.

"This is where my scalp thinks they chopped off their heads," Kulak said, stopping at a central altar where a rusty, crescent-shaped dagger rested.

"Chopped off their heads?" Sterjall asked as he watched Kulak handling the blade.

"Yes. Sacrifices to appease gods, if the Mo'óto Miscam believed in any. Or perhaps they chopped vegetables. We cannot know for sure." He dropped the dagger and went to climb a nearby toppled column.

He's acting so elusive and strange, Sterjall mulled. *Or maybe he's just being playful.*

While Kulak tried reaching what used to be an interior balcony, Sterjall approached one of the five walls of the stupa, where a niche opened up. It seemed as though a statue should have occupied the space, but only a pillow of moss filled the hollow.

"It is so quiet in here," Sterjall said, hearing only his muted echo and the staccato dripping of water. He looked down at the moss, removed his cloak, then called, "Kulak, come take a look."

Kulak slid down a leaning column, walked behind a wall that was more roots than rocks, and found Sterjall next to the niche. He could tell something was amiss—Sterjall was pulling his threads inward, making himself unreadable.

"What is wrong?" he asked.

"Come closer," Sterjall said, tensing up.

Kulak advanced with cat-like silence, but Sterjall's sensitive ears could hear his beating heart. Once Kulak was close enough, he noticed Sterjall's cloak was spread over the pillow of moss. Before he could ask what was happening, Sterjall was grabbing on to him and pushing him into the niche, straddling the caracal.

"What are you—"

"If you want more, we can have more," Sterjall said, then bound his long muzzle to the prince's shorter one. He felt his tongue scrape over Kulak's sharp fangs, then against his rough tongue, and pulled back. "We've been interrupted enough times. And Kenondok won't find us here."

"True," Kulak said, his breathing hastened as much as his palpitations. He tried to get up to remove his clothing, but Sterjall pushed him back down.

"Stay there," Sterjall said. "Let me look at you." He leaned back farther and flipped Kulak's kilt up. The caracal was already hard, his tiny cock bouncing to match his pulse.

You are beautiful, Sterjall thought, but for some reason did not want to say it out loud. *But what am I doing?* He wanted Kulak, he needed to be inside of him, but he did not want to ruin the moment with his own insecurities. "Stay like that," he ordered, pulling his own tunic off and tossing it to the side. "Let me have you," he added, "all of you."

Kulak nodded and lightly whimpered.

Sterjall's amber eyes narrowed. He leaned down once more, first kissing his lover, then holding his arms down. He wrapped his maw around Kulak's neck, like a predator would, forcing him to bend his spine back and hold his breath in ecstasy. *He is the exact opposite of Banook,* Sterjall thought, not wanting to think about Banook but unable to stop himself. With his big bear, he felt protected, intimidated, embraced by his enormous girth. Now he was on top, being dominant, enveloping a smaller body. He tried to push the thought of Banook aside and focus on what he had in front of him, what he needed at that moment. *But this is merely sex, not love,* he told himself. *This is not the same.*

Holding down his soft bite, the wolf unbuttoned his trousers and forced Kulak to spread his legs. Without much warning, the wolf mounted the caracal, sliding halfway inside him.

"Wait, slow," Kulak pleaded breathlessly.

Sterjall pulled back and released his bite so he could see Kulak's eyes. A bit more gently, he pushed forward again.

Kulak moaned. "I... I don't know if I can..." he mumbled, holding Sterjall back a bit.

Sterjall held back for a breath. *But this is what I want, right now.* He leaned in and pressed deeper, but the caracal clenched his thighs to keep him from going too far.

Kulak's breath was jagged, tremorous. He clawed at the wolf's back, tense and quivering.

Sterjall panted, his eyes locked on the caracal's, not letting him go. He tried finding a way in once more but was stopped yet again. He pulled out, dripping, frustrated. Kulak closed his eyes and seemed to relax. He then cracked his eyes open and softly asked, "Do you really want me?"

Sterjall stiffened, hoping his desperate look was answer enough.

"Say it," Kulak said. "Do you want to be one with me?"

The wolf panted, eyes wide and ecstatic.

"Say it," Kulak demanded. "Say that you want me."

"Yes, fuck, I want you," Sterjall admitted.

Then abruptly, while taking in a deep breath, Kulak wrapped his legs around Sterjall's back and pulled him all the way in until the wolf's sheath compressed against his hole.

Sterjall was too shocked, too eager and frenzied. Without warning, unable to stop himself, his erection grew larger and bulged at the base of its shaft, tying them together.

Kulak growled, then bit on his knuckles to silence himself.

"Sorry, I'm sorry," Sterjall said, not sure whether he should try to pull out. "I didn't think it... I've never... What should I—"

"Stay inside me," Kulak groaned, pulling their chests together. "Stay. Hold me."

Sterjall held him, feeling Kulak's pulse thunder through him. He then felt Kulak tighten and whine lightly. A sudden warmth washed over his belly as Kulak tensed and ejaculated.

"Stay," Kulak whispered. "Stay..."

Sterjall let his weight down fully onto his lover, then focused on his breathing, slowing it until they were nearly synchronized.

In that moment of focus, of silence, they both saw themselves more clearly. *It is as if our threads are looping and merging into one, just like our bodies,* Sterjall thought, and for a handful of heartbeats he could see no distinction between wolf and caracal—all they were was a braid of eager threads knotted with each other, glowing inside an aura of liquid sapphires and emeralds.

Sterjall had been relaxed, yet was struck by a sudden surge of ecstasy. Surprised, he pushed his upper body up. He panted, tongue dripping onto Kulak's chest as his shaft tightened, his muscles strained. He let his impulses take over, pushed deeper, and released himself into Kulak.

His throbbing quickly subsided, his grip loosened, but he did not pull out. Feeling light-headed, he dropped his weight back onto the caracal.

Kulak began to purr.

"What... I've never heard you do that before," Sterjall whispered, an ear pressed to Kulak's chest.

"Happens rarely. Not something my scalp controls. It comes on its own, and when it does, it feels wonderful."

Despite the purring, Sterjall sensed that Kulak was feeling embarrassed. "Why are you so flustered?" he asked.

Kulak stared up toward the broken oculus of stained glass—like a jagged pupil, it seemed to stare back. "It is... because I have never done this," he admitted. "Not with Mindrelsilv."

"Truly? By the way you've been pushing me, I thought you must've had a lot of experiences like this before."

"Like this? Certainly never done it with a wolf!" Kulak laughed. "But honestly, no. As much as my scalp always wanted to, I never had the courage." He let Sterjall pull out so they could lie side by side. "The Silvesh make the experience intimate, truthful. Seeing our threads combined, seeing our bodies tied as one, was beautiful."

"It was... beautiful," Sterjall said. *You are beautiful,* he thought once more, in silence.

Chapter Seventy-Five

A Candle in the Dark

Mamóru sat alone in his chair on *Drolvisdinn*'s deck, wrapped in a cotton quilt, watching the pulsing arudinn in the night sky and the wisps of sunlight that penetrated more and more often now. Lago pulled up a bench and slouched next to him.

"I think that's my favorite of the mistleaf scents," Lago said off-handedly as a thin cloud of smoke wafted by his face.

"You should try the tannic smokefronds of Wastyr someday, if you care to taste a golden bazaar of spices and faraway lands. Or rather, forget I said that. These leaves can be deadly for your kind, if you smoke them for long enough."

"I only like the smells, don't worry. How are you feeling?"

"Wonderful. There are few spectacles such as this that one can claim to have witnessed, even for someone as old as myself. In mere weeks, day and night will blend into one, and it will all change once again."

"It is spectacular," Lago agreed, "but I was asking about your legs. And the rest of yourself, I guess."

"Oh, my old body is not doing so well, but that's to be expected after all that has occurred. Tell me, agnurf son, why are you not in your half-form? You seem most comfortable as a wolf, most of the time."

"I often feel as if wearing Agnargsilv is like prying too much. I wanted to ask you some questions, and didn't feel it was right if I got the answers in a way that was not you telling me yourself."

"That's thoughtful of you," Mamóru said. "What questions do you have?"

"I'm... I just feel. I don't know what will happen if we do this tomorrow. You said that wearing Momsúndosilv might be the end... for you."

"I am afraid it might be, Lago-Sterjall. But my end is not the end of all things. The world will go on, with or without me."

"Is there something we can do? Maybe we can use the other Silvesh to make you feel better and help you through it, and you will be able to—"

Mamóru put a frail hand on Lago's shoulder. "I said it *might* be just to reassure you all, so that you would let me make this choice on my own. I *know* it will be the end for me, but I have committed myself to this path. It will be hard for a youth like yourself to understand, but despite all the glory I'm still witnessing to this very moment, life has lost its spark for me. I am lonely, Lago. I have been lonely for far too long. I don't want to remain the last of my kind for thousands more years—we all must end either way, someday. And very few of us get to choose how we go."

Mamóru tightened the quilt around his neck and sighed a wispy cloud that smelled of old leather in a forest filled with mushrooms.

"I am so tired," he added. "I have seen so much that I feel as if my life has not been in vain. I have left my writings on the wall, and my legacy for others to protect, and that gives solace to my heart. Noss needs me, more than you or our friends need me. My memory is, in part, Noss's memory, and this final act is not just necessary, but inevitable."

"What will happen to you? I mean, if you are gone. What happens to a Nu'irg then?"

"The same that happens to all of us. I will cease to exist in that moment in time, and for the time ahead of it. We are all the same, Lago. You, and I, and the planet, and each bacterium that swims in the waters below us. Even our planet's life is but a heartbeat in the infinite history of our universe, and they will also one day cease to be. There is nothing wrong with dying, as long as we've given it our all, taken care of one another, and made sure we have lived in a way that has made the best of every moment that was entrusted to our care."

"What will the rest of us do next? After talking to Noss? After you..."

"That, agnurf son, is for you to decide."

Lago was no longer looking at the wisps. He stared down at the wooden deck, noticing the broken pattern of his breath. A chill ran through his skin. He felt a latent guilt for never having said goodbye to Ockam, and an urge to express his feelings overcame him. He stood and embraced Mamóru. "I don't want you to leave," he said, tears filling his eyes.

Mamóru embraced him back. "It will be alright, Lago-Sterjall. Remember that golden flower I once told you about? That flower in the infinitude of time? I will be like that. Once I was not, now here I am, and tomorrow I will cease to be. But I will always be there in that past moment in time, during which I hope to have made a difference in this sometimes-too-cruel world. And that past self of me will remember you too, Lago, and be proud of you. So don't despair."

"I wish there was a way," he sobbed. "Some way to stop this pattern. I can't exist in the past, memories are not the same as the real thing. I don't care if you've been around for tens of thousands of years, it's still too short a time."

"It is, relatively. But I am happy with the way my life went, and it makes me happy to see that you will head in the right direction in your own life. I might not be around to see it, but I can be proud now, knowing in my heart that you will go on to do great things."

Mamóru kept his arms around the young man. He exhaled a cloud of white smoke. The scents clung to Lago's curly hair, to his clothes.

"A life is like a candle, shining in the dark," the old man said. "Eventually, it will be extinguished, but the memory of it remains, like a scent dancing in the last trail of smoke it exhaled, ingrained in the memories of those lives it touched. That is, perhaps, what afterlife is about. It is a pattern, a memory, an influence left behind by the deeds one performed during the time allotted to them. As ephemeral as that pattern is, and even if no longer conscious, it is still valid and casts its influence into the future. You have that light within you, agnurf son. It shines shyly like a trembling star at twilight. It may still be dim, but even the smallest spark can ignite to greatness and inspire the many. Noss will remember me, and you will remember me, and I will leave with a smile, and that will be enough."

"I don't know how I'll be able to go on," Lago cried.

Mamóru wiped Lago's cheeks and said, "Just follow your heart, and always remember the flower."

Chapter Seventy-Six

Noss

The day for the audience with Noss had arrived. The Silvfröash knew of no ritual or any established protocol, but they thought it proper to fulfill some sort of formality before such a consequential moment. The six gathered at the innermost of the rings of stones, where the sand had been spread flat once more, with a wide circle to represent Noss drawn at the center. Around this circle they drew the six glyphs for each of their clades, then sat cross-legged in front of them, with their Silvesh on their laps. Mamóru could not cross his broken legs, so he sat in his chair, higher than any of them.

A single pharolith glowed at the center of the circle, like a lotus flower of luminescence.

Puqua and Laatu alike gathered around to spectate, sitting on the outermost of the concentric rings of stones, not wanting to perturb the ceremony, but not daring to miss it.

Mamóru was wearing his white robes. His beard was not braided, but flowed loose and smooth over the brightly embroidered garment. He cleared his throat and tapped his blackthorn cane on the ground, quieting the spectators. He had already instructed the crowd not to disturb them throughout the process, no matter what happened, no matter how long it took. He regarded those sitting on the sand before him.

"Once our masks embrace our faces, I will ask you all to pay attention to the threads of those around you and to the auras of your Silvesh. You must use your empathic focus to make them all flow into one, to bind, to combine, to create. Though each of us will retain their own mind and awareness, we will also form a new consciousness, together. Keep our consciousness as one, and focus until the very end. Do not break the cycle."

Mamóru signaled to Alaia, who promptly came to him. "Would you mind keeping a hold of my cane, dear?" he asked. Alaia took the cane and walked away. Then she turned back, embraced Mamóru, kissed his cheek, and quickly walked out of the ring, covering her eyes.

"Do you remember the chanting words I taught you?" Mamóru asked. They all nodded. "They are not magical words, at least no more magical than any other words are. The Miscam chanted these six words to help them concentrate, to keep their minds in synchrony. Try to keep the same pace and the same tone as those around you." He straightened his back on the chair and looked at the person sitting to his left. "It is time. Prikka of the Nagra, would you be the first?"

Prikka grunted twice. "Yes Lorr. Let's hope this works, or I'll ask ye all to make up a good excuse fur me if I go home with empty hooves. Thank ye, greatly, old fellow." She nodded to Mamóru, then put Nagrasilv on and shapeshifted into Nalaníri.

Mamóru continued clockwise, nodding to Jiara.

"It's been an honor," she said in a bit too much of a defeatist, yet realistic tone. She donned the bear mask, and Kitjári wood-claw sat her heavy haunches in Jiara's stead.

Next came Sunu, seated directly across from Mamóru. They looked up to the tree where Ishke'ísuk and Olo waited. The basilisk blinked his approval. "Sunu is ready," Sunu said. "Sunu is ready to listen to the planet." They put on the mask of dark teeth and scales and remained Sunu, though able to see much more.

"Mindrelfröa, I ask for your blessing," Mamóru proceeded.

Aio lifted the felid mask to his face and became Kulak. "My scalp will remember your words of wisdom," the caracal said. "Thanks to your kindness, the planet will know themself once more." He swallowed, then slowly blinked.

Mamóru's head turned slightly. "Lago Vaari of Withervale, it is now your turn."

"I don't feel like I'm *of Withervale* any longer," Lago said.

"You were of Withervale once, and now you are of much more, but the Lago you once were is and always will be as well. Would you do me the honor?"

Lago stared at his mask, knowing full well what the implications would be once he put it on. His eyes felt heavy, and the knot at his throat tightened. He put the mask on, yet kept his human form for a little longer. "Thank you. I will remember the flower," he said and choked up, but the dark mask hid his tears.

Mamóru stared at him with compassion and warmth.

I will remember the flower, Lago thought. *Every time I smell the woody scents of mistleaf, you will be with me, and I will recall everything you've ever taught me. I will remember, and that will be enough.*

Lago wiped his tears and stared at his nails, which he had lacquered with a translucent varnish for the occasion. He felt the lacquers crackle and fall into shimmering dust as he shifted into Sterjall.

Mamóru looked around through narrowed, wrinkled eyes, satisfied. He lifted Momsúndosilv and placed it on his face. Though he had never worn a Silv before, it seemed a most natural process to him, as if he did not feel the pain the others had felt; or perhaps he did feel it, but did not show it. He had lived through millennia of so much joy, pain, fear, doubt, and pleasure that the experience brought forth by the mask paled in comparison. He sat there, placid and determined, his mask like a tusked void of blackness hovering above marble-like white robes; he was an effigy of contrasts, nobility, and timelessness.

"Ah, just as I had thought," Mamóru sighed, gazing upon the threads of consciousness, the colorful auras, and the forces of empathy that had always enveloped them yet he had never sensed with such clarity before. "What a wonderful way to experience and understand this complex world of ours."

Without hesitation, yet with savored unhurriedness, Mamóru expertly shapeshifted into his half-form. He knew better than anyone else who he was, and the change felt as natural as breathing.

Sterjall was transfixed by how the dark tusks of the mask reshaped in the foggy cloud of the transformation, one of them elongating into a sensual curve that then turned into glossy ivory, the other shrinking into a jagged, broken tusk. The black trunk that had been so stylized and faceted became soft and organic, curling like a snake covered in patchy fur. Within the figure, the pearlescent white auras flowed through each other, feeding the sparkling glow in an endless loop. Mamóru had turned into a beautiful half-steppe mammoth. His thick fur was dark gray with splashes of brown warmth, with added sprinkles of white that provided texture and an air of maturity and intellect. His eyes were small and peaceful, and a bit sad. His large head expanded in a domed top, almost looking like a bowl-shaped haircut. His strange ears draped down and flattened to the side of his neck, and seemed to be made of dangling fur alone. His entire body gave the impression of being much bigger, as if he had suddenly gained a lot of weight, all due to the very long, wiry fur that piled under his bright robe.

The one-tusked mammoth stared at his wrinkled and leathery half-human hands. He lifted his arms up, and the world went quiet—not a murmur or sigh dared perturb the moment. As he lowered his arms, he began to chant, "*Hum che velm isk enn gwum, hum che velm isk enn gwum, hum che velm isk enn gwum…*"

The six Silvfröash closed their eyes and chanted in unison.

"*… Hum che velm isk enn gwum…*"

Their Silvesh showed them the threads of their very awareness and the colorful auras that made up the higher levels of complexity of their masks. With their empathic focus, they willed their threads and auras to flow and blend into one. Emerald greens and indigos of twilight braided knots around one another while opalescent pinks exploded with golden sun streaks and lilac tendrils swam into white shimmers of pearl. There was no shape to this weaving; it was all around them, all through them, as if the fabric of space itself was infused with their colorful presence, and their presence became the space they inhabited. The mixed colors narrowed into a circle that focused around their heads, propelling the auras back into themselves in an endless loop. They felt their awareness expand, witnessing the event from all six viewpoints at once, as their minds interwove into one.

Suddenly, the glowing complexities of the auras collapsed, as if now that they had reassembled themselves at a higher level, the masks appeared simpler, looking like the threads they could better understand, although ones of a different hue, or tone, or flavor. Even their own presence as a single consciousness was no longer an aura of mixed colors, but a web of threads amalgamated from all the pieces that made them up. This tapestry was woven from their six combined consciousnesses, from the six Silvesh, from their own individual human and animal selves, from the cells that formed their bodies, from the bacteria that inhabited their guts, from the organelles performing ceaseless functions within those cells, from the intricate forms their carbon particles assembled into, from their relationship to their environment and all living things around them.

Sterjall was now many, and he was one. He/they examined the mental space they had created. It felt as if the six of them were sitting in a room made of light. When one of them looked around, the other five looked with them, as they were all tied to one will, yet they still retained their own sense of selves. All around them was a higher-level entity. Rather than visualizing it as an aura, they saw it as a shimmering membrane, like a soap bubble of infinitely shifting hues. Sterjall could feel the pressure changes as the thin surface oscillated, though he was not touching it. He was right next to the membrane, and infinitely far from it at the same time. The membrane knew not of space, size, color, or shape—it simply was, and they were a part of it, as much as apart from it.

Sterjall heard himself say words, though he wasn't the one saying them. He knew it was Mamóru who was putting the sentences together, but it felt to him as if he had made the conscious decision to speak them.

"The six in one have gathered for an audience with the cradle of our kinds. Long has it been. Do you heed our call?"

The membrane vibrated between dimensions, flickering back and forth. The vibrations shaped themselves into thoughts that flooded their minds.

«Who... am I?...» they mindspoke deep within the awareness of the six.

"You are Noss, our planet," Mamóru said. "We are those who walk on your continents and swim in your oceans. We are the Silvfröash, the voices of the animals."

The membrane oscillated with uncertainty. «Nossssss... There is a vague memory, but most of it is veiled, lost.»

Is this what mindspeech feels like? Sterjall wondered, also wondering whether the other five were sharing the same thought. He could no longer tell the difference between thoughts, the mindspeech of Noss, and the words Mamóru had spoken for the six.

The membrane compressed and entangled itself with them, projecting images into their minds, as if the bubble had become a spherical window through which they could see what Noss wanted them to see. They saw a murky blackness pricked by smeared dots. A green-blue dot moved closer in an instant, and as it approached it grew exponentially, and they sank through its clouds to witness the gnarled tentacles of the Varanus Dome from the skies. The view passed through the tangled vines and paused directly above the ring of stones, where they saw themselves sitting, though the image was wispy and unclear. Despite being vague and unfocused, the images the membrane conjured carried with them more meaning than what they directly saw, as if peering into a dream.

«I see you,» the membrane communicated. «Noss perished.» The consciousness seemed confused. «I was birthed anew from the loss of the past. I am not Noss. Yet I am still Noss.»

Noss's membrane scintillated and showed them a faint image of a long-veiled comet hurtling toward them. They watched as the comet passed through them, incinerating everything in its path before flashing atop a distant peak. They did not see individual animals dying, but rather the essence of the species being torn apart, their threads snapping and dissolving, and the all-consuming fire cleansing the land and boiling the seas. As if speeding through time, they saw the land turn white. As it thawed, new threads emerged and combined in ever-increasing complexity, until the land was covered with a blanket of new threads that rippled over the surface of the two continents. The blanket shimmered in all colors until it became a membrane, a new organism, a new consciousness. A new Noss.

«Why?» the consciousness asked, and though they manifested the question as a single, voiceless word, it carried more complexities within it. «Why are you here? How is it you can talk to me? What are you asking of me?» they implied.

"We are communicating with you through the Silvesh," Sterjall said as the six. "Six of the eighteen masks you once helped create. Do you—"

«Silvesh.» The membrane compressed space and oscillated, showing them filaments of quaar coalescing into a recognizable, almost skull-like shape: Hoombusilv—the first Silv—they all knew it to be, though only Mamóru had seen it before. Noss attempted to show images of other masks being formed, but they were foggy and incomplete. «I barely remember the Silvesh,» they expressed. «My past self thought them into being, long ago. I remember so little of this past.» The amorphous images vanished. «Why are you here?»

They all replied together, uncertain of who was leading the words. "Centuries ago, you helped us build the domes, the drolomesh, in order to safeguard our species and protect yourself from the Downfall, caused by the comet you seem to clearly remember. The lands have healed now, yet you have not sent a signal for the domes to reopen, as you promised to do. Why have you not spoken to the temples? Why do the domes remain closed?"

The membrane vibrated furiously and showed them an aerial view of the two continents, a view which Sterjall quickly recognized: it was the same as the carved map they had found at Da'áju. Not just similar, but exactly as he remembered it. He realized then—as the other five did—that Noss was showing them images from their own minds, sometimes from their imaginations, constructing with the pieces they could find, assembling new concepts with fragments borrowed from the whole. In this constructed liminal space, the domes that had been opened were clearly visible and had threads spreading outward, mingling and interlacing themselves with the membrane that covered the entirety of the land. The domes that had not yet opened, however, were circles of emptiness; they were not black, but spaces of non-being, like blind spots, a complete absence of sensory input. It felt painful to gaze upon them, as their brains could not comprehend not seeing something they were staring directly at. They felt Noss's anger at these blind spots. They felt their frustration.

«They are unreachable to me,» Noss communicated. «I do not remember how. I knew nothing of the past beyond the Downfall, not until the three domes were opened. Your actions, your presence, they are helping me remember, but only so little.»

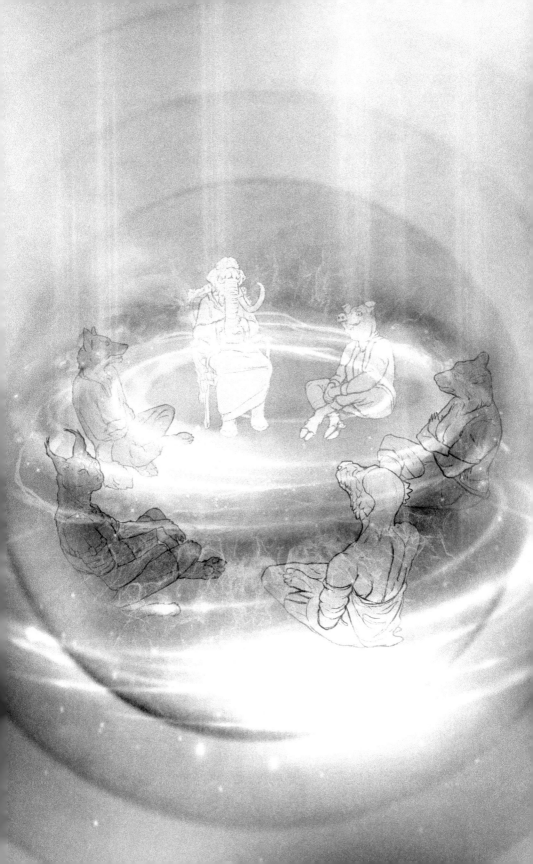

Mamóru took control of the voice once more. "I can help you remember more. I was alive long before the Downfall, and though my memory is limited, it is well preserved."

The membrane seemed to pass through them, tasting them, exploring them from the inside. «I remember you, Nu'irg ust Momsúndo. The Silvesh were not made for your kind.»

"Proboscideans are no more. I am the last that remains, and thus I wield my clade's Silv as a last resort."

«With the proboscideans, a part of old Noss perished as well. Your memory will help me see better, ancient one. Tell me your story.»

"I will," Mamóru said. "But first, another story we must tell you."

The six spoke together, telling their story from the breaching of the Heartpine Dome through the present time. They explained how they had come upon the Silvesh, why they had decided to open the three domes, and discussed the threat the Red Stag posed with the masks he had already taken into his possession. They spoke at length, with each word carrying further meanings, as the planet could read their emotions and intentions, and they quickly understood the peril in which they found themself. The retelling seemed to go on for hours, though they could not discern how time passed or did not pass within this mental realm.

Once the core part of their story had been recounted, Mamóru said, "My memory reaches much further into the past, and I will share it with you, but it will be the last thing for me to do before we leave you, for the story is much too long. We have told you all that we know about the most pressing matters. Uncertainty clouds our judgment. We need clarity as to which course of action will be best to help you, to help ourselves."

«The remaining domes must be opened,» the membrane communicated, showing no hesitation. «The three you freed have helped me see into the past, but darkly. I urge you to continue to release my trapped memories. Help the animals spread, if you can, or leave them be and they will spread in due time.» The membrane vibrated with a sense of urgency and formed itself into shapes of jagged mountains. Sterjall recognized the Stelm Ca'éli. As the view moved south, the membrane showed them a conflicting image of the Heartpine Dome. Noss could see partially within it, while other parts were obscured to their senses and memory. More parts of the dome had collapsed since they last saw it. «Loss,» they lamented. «What was lost here cannot be recovered.»

"Why not?" Sterjall dared ask, feeling his words lacking. It was as if Noss's mindspeech was pure, eternal, full of meanings, while his meager words were mere sounds, or perhaps only the idea of sounds.

«The temple is broken,» Noss explained. «The lattice is no more, and thus Agnargdrolom cannot be saved from its fate. This cradle will collapse, and its life, its memory, will be lost.»

Sterjall felt a surge of pain in his chest, feeling impotent, but fully understanding the impossibility of saving Heartpine from its doom.

«But not all yet is lost,» Noss explained. The view moved to the Anglass Dome, and then to the Lequa Dome, and although both domes were in a blind spot for Noss, the Silvfröash could sense the dread and tragedy wafting from within them.

The membrane obscured itself and reappeared as a perfectly white sphere between them. «These other domes that our enemy has ransacked will also fall unless they are freed. You must hasten to these lands as well and open these domes, or they could soon be no more.»

Noss made the membrane resonate in a deafening pulse. It opalesced and wobbled, seeming to grow in every dimension at once, becoming the lands of the Negian Empire as seen from above. The threads there were broken and torn, like a suppurating gash that spread fast and far toward the southeast.

«Cancer. It spreads,» the intonations lamented. «Much damage is being perpetrated, and the wound will worsen unless you stop them. It is painful. Will you help me?»

"We will help in every way we can," the six said as one. "Is there anything you can do to aid us in this quest?"

The membrane fogged up and held still while Noss considered. «In the same way you cannot influence a specific cell in your bodies, I cannot change what happens over my crust, within my oceans, in the small bumps of my sierras. I can do nothing. All I can offer is answers, information. Ask, and I shall answer, if the memory is within my grasp.»

Kitjári took the initiative, and as the six she said, "Where is the Red Stag now? Can you tell us anything about him?"

Noss shaped their membrane into tendrils, extending outward as if searching for answers. Soon the membrane quivered and showed them a view of the Jerjan Continent, right over a blind spot that they knew to be the Bighorn Dome. A gangrenous gash cut through Noss's membrane and passed through the dome, continuing east, toward the lands of the Bayanhong Tribes. «My body is hurting here, and the wound is stretching east. I cannot sense individuals. I can see no further.»

"Can the power of Urgsilv be stopped? Can we prevent the Red Stag from using it?" Kulak asked.

«I do not remember how the Silvesh work,» was the unfortunate answer. «They were not made by me, but by the Noss who perished, who knew much that I have forgotten.»

"But you are still that same Noss," Kulak implored, trying to pull some threads of hope.

«I am not. The Noss who perished lived for billions of years, growing smart and cunning with time. I have not even been alive for fifteen centuries. The memories you have recovered for me are like fragments of pages from a torn book. I must piece them together, read them, understand them, and make new memories from them.»

Sterjall wondered for a moment how Noss could understand what a book was, and then realized he himself had formed that mental image—Noss had only retrieved it and used it to explain themself.

"Can ye tell us who else can aid us in this quest?" Nalaníri asked. "Who shell we ask fur help?" The other five felt themselves speaking as Nalaníri, taking her accents and intonations and briefly experiencing gentle tusks lifting their lips.

«The Nu'irgesh can help. They are powerful,» the vibrations echoed. «Other Silvfröash can help, but I do not know them, as they are hidden within other domes. I do not know your realms, your people. You must help each other.»

"Could you tell us anything else about the Silvesh?" Sterjall inquired. "Even if you don't know how they work, could you tell us why they were made in the first place?"

Noss's membrane scintillated and wobbled in an exerted manner. It seemed to be thinking, probing, feeling frustrated. «Little can I recall about them. Their complexity astounds me. I am just as curious as to why my old self undertook the effort to construct them. But I will try to see more.» The Silvfröash felt as if the membrane passed through them, reaching inside each cell of their bodies, rummaging through and palpating the Silvesh that were parts of their half-forms. All but Sunu felt this invasion into their bodies, though Sunu felt their friends' uncomfortableness.

The membrane detached from their marrows, then loosened itself into a rippling mist. «There is an aspect of the Silvesh I can sense, I can taste, that seems to be beyond your grasp.» The membrane pulled away and settled around them as a perfect, all-colored sphere. «Your feral forms are inaccessible to you, except to the wise Momsundofröa. This knowledge was hidden as a safeguard, as it is dangerous for you to take your animal forms, as you risk losing yourselves in them. But they could prove useful to you, as long as you are mindful whenever you choose to undertake this change, as long as you take the proper precautions.»

"Would you show us how to do this?" Sterjall asked haltingly, pained at the sudden memory of Ockam that flashed through his thoughts.

«I will, if you are wary of the peril.» The membrane turned dark and wispy and invasively passed through the awareness of the six once more, touching too closely, manipulating, tasting. Noss was showing them a process that was impossible to put into words. The permeating membrane taught them how to forget about the threads they manipulated when shifting into their half-forms and instead focus on a less intellectual, purely visceral instinct. It was less about shaping with the masks, and more about letting the masks shape themselves, about surrendering to their impulses. The process was similar to how they internalized the pain to wear the Silvesh, but rather than just accepting what the masks showed them, it required them to embrace it and let the compulsions take over. They all understood, even Sunu, who had not yet experienced the process of transformation.

«Take heed of the risks,» Noss warned them, «and retain your full awareness when you make use of this knowledge. You must give in to the impulses of the Silvesh, but do not give in so far as to forget yourselves. Remaining close to those you love, hearing their voices or seeing their faces, that will help you safely transition back. But do not attempt it while alone, or you may lose your humanity in the process.»

The six nodded and thanked Noss for the new knowledge.

«There is nothing more I can teach you about the Silvesh,» Noss communicated. «If there is more to know, it is not within my reach, at least not until more of my memory is returned to me. Open more domes, then ask me again after I have had time to learn and ponder.»

Sterjall was about to ask another question, but Noss interrupted him, flashing with a sense of urgency. «Although only moments have elapsed in your minds, your consciousnesses are tied to mine. An instant within this realm could be hours, days in your own short-lived cycles. Your bodies will soon fail you, and you will die. Ask no more of me.»

They all sensed that Noss had no further answers anyway, not the kind of answers that would be helpful to them. They did not argue, and dared not waste another heartbeat, which could be a whole day.

«Now it is your turn to share knowledge,» Noss commanded with a low rumble. «Wise Nu'irg ust Momsúndo, tell me the rest of your story, our story, from as far back as you can recall.»

Mamóru looked around at his friends, and they could all see themselves through his eyes. They felt through him, and within him was a great hollowness, a deep exhaustion. They knew then why Mamóru had chosen to end himself, and though the hollowness remained, they felt some comfort from gaining that understanding.

"My story will take many days to be properly told," Mamóru said to his friends. "You need nourishment and rest, and I will need you to look after me while I tell Noss all that I have learned through my long life."

"We can wait here with you," Sterjall said.

"No, agnurf son. By the time my tale is told, I will be gone. If it offers any comfort, many of my memories will reside within Noss's consciousness and will outlive any and all of you, as with the writings I left on the lava tubes. These memories will not be me, but I am proud to know that all the learning I've worked toward across the millennia has not been for naught."

Mamóru extricated himself from the other five and became his own self within the mindspace they inhabited. The loop he created between his aura and that of his Silv kept feeding itself, maintaining his consciousness at a higher level where he could still communicate with the planet.

Mamóru's figure in the mental space seemed to be drifting away, his edges becoming less defined. "You have a great task ahead of you," he said to them all, but each felt he was talking to them singularly. "I am certain you will make us all proud. Do not let sorrow consume you. You have each other, you have friends you have not yet met, and you will have greater sorrows to overcome in due time. Hold on to each other, and remember."

"We'll remember you, always," Sterjall spoke, but it was truly all five of them saying it together.

"Go now," Mamóru commanded. "Go, and find a path to open the other domes. Travel south, and travel east. Stop the cancer from spreading and recover our planet's lost memories. Go now, and find yourselves."

Mamóru closed his eyes and separated his mind from theirs. The membrane around them shifted through unknown dimensions, it oscillated in a tuneless hum and collapsed into itself. They felt their bodies weighing down upon them. Their minds separated, leaving only their singular beings, detached and alone with their own thoughts.

They opened their eyes and saw themselves still sitting among the stones, with most of the sand where they had drawn their glyphs long since blown away by the wind. Their legs ached, their bellies grumbled, their necks were sore. They felt utterly drained, as if they had used up every last dollop of energy and had not slept in months.

It was late at night within Kruwendrolom, but with the dome well on its way to opening, the wisps above them had grown so numerous that the light was like that of twilight moments after the sun sets. Mamóru sat next to them in his chair, breathing slowly, eyes closed. Through the Silvesh, they saw the half-mammoth's intense, dazzling aura looping through itself in an endless knot, while his threads seeped downward, merging into the crust of the planet. His presence pulsated to the rhythm of his beating heart.

Sterjall stood on weakened legs. His first impulse was to reach for Mamóru, but Kulak grabbed his arm and stopped him.

"He needs to focus," Kulak whispered with a weak but determined voice. "We will keep watch over him."

"Hey, you are up!" they heard Alaia call out. She had been sleeping on the stones, waiting for them. She came rushing to Sterjall and saw that he was crying. "Is everything okay?"

"I..." he looked at Alaia, then looked at all his friends. "We have to..." Sterjall suppressed a sob. He focused his eyes on Mamóru peacefully sitting in his chair. He was not yet gone, but would soon be. *I can't do this,* he thought, *why couldn't he stay a bit longer? Why does he need to go?*

"Gwoli?" Alaia prompted.

"I don't want him to leave," he rasped out. He embraced Alaia and let it all out. He cried for the pointlessness of it all, for his lack of understanding of his own purpose, for his selfishness in not wanting to go on, for his fear of being left alone. He cried for the love he felt for others, and for the impermanence of life itself.

Chapter Seventy-Seven

Full Change

All five of them were ravenous. Alaia told them they had been in communion with Noss for two and a half days, not moving a finger. Mamóru had been adamant about not interrupting the process, and so they had silently guarded the six from outside the circle. The five emissaries had no energy left in them. They ate the quickest of meals and collapsed for the night.

After a late breakfast the next day, everyone gathered by the outermost of the rings of stones, keeping their distance from Mamóru, their voices no more than whispers. The five told the others what they had learned from the new Noss, what paths of action Noss had recommended, and what would become of Mamóru. They did not know how long Mamóru would take to tell his story to the planet, but all agreed they'd keep watch over him until the very end.

"Noss felt it was urgent that we open the domes in the Negian Empire," Kitjári said, addressing the entire group. "But those domes are far away, and we have no way to fight the Negian numbers, not unless we work with the Union."

"We shouldn't look t'fight," Nalaníri said, "but to go by unnoticed. We can enter d'domes, sneak into d'temples, n'collapse them lattices 'fore anyone can stop us. If we do it in secret n'avoid a-fighting, we could prevent what happened t'Agnargdrolom."

"The Negians would have thousands of soldiers in there," Kitjári rebutted. "They'd spot us, sooner or later."

"Mayhaps," Nalaníri dismissed her. "Noss has taught us how t'take our feral forms. As plain-old animals, we could move without being noticed."

"Or we could get shot at by a random hunter, then served on a platter," Sterjall half-joked. He still felt very tired and knew it might take days to recover from the exertion. "But you are right, Nalaníri, once we learn to control those forms, they will come in handy. And it seems we'll need to split up, as much as it hurts me to say. Some of us will have to go south, some will have to go back through Zovaria, then farther east."

"N'we need t'help spread our animals as much as we can," Nalaníri said. "I believe I shell go back to Nagradrolom, find Probo, n'travel east through d'mountains. This could be a safe way t'get to d'Negian Empire without a-risking being seen by yer Zovarian friends."

Siffo tipped his tricorne hat, acknowledging he was eager to help with anything Nalaníri needed.

"Noss said the Nu'irgesh can help us," Kitjári said. "The Red Stag controls Sovath, the cervid Nu'irg, and we don't know what became of the musteloid Nu'irg from the Lequa Dome... But we do know where to find Probo, Nelv, and also Banook. And Banook said Safis was now with him."

Sterjall's heart pumped with vigor. "We could go see him! But... But he can't leave the northern territories."

"Not unless the bears go with," Kitjári said. "I think it's time for the bears to leave the mountains. They will follow Urnaadisilv's call. Once I learn how to do that, I mean."

"I can't wait to see him again!" Sterjall said a bit too loudly, to which Kulak tensed up, his tail suddenly slapping under his kilt.

Alaia gave Sterjall an awkward smile. "Gwoli, I think you should travel south, to the Azurean Dome. Nalaníri is going north because she needs Probo. Kitjári is needed there because of Urnaadisilv, otherwise the bears won't move. We can't all go back that way, the other domes need to be opened too."

"You and Kulak work best together," Kitjári said, putting a handpaw on each of their shoulders. "You both should go south, with Sunu to protect you—they are as great a warrior as you could ask for, and I'm sure even more so once they find their half-form. Nalaníri and I can travel to the Wujann peaks, letting the bears move ahead of us while we make a plan with Probo, Banook, and Safis."

Nalaníri grunted twice. "T'gether we shell hunt down them bears!" She poked an elbow into Kitjári's ribs. "Not in a bad way, mind ye."

Kitjári awkwardly smiled, and Sterjall noticed. He was certain she was blushing underneath all that fur, but did not comment on it.

"Then we go together," Kulak declared, elbowing Sterjall to mimic Nalaníri.

Sterjall was unhappy with this decision, but he knew it to be the right one. Kulak stood right next to him for comfort, but he didn't feel comforted enough.

"I'll go with you guys," Alaia said to the two of them, sticking her head over their shoulders. "I don't know how useful I can be, but I'm not leaving you behind."

"If Nu'irgesh we need, Nelv we should seek," Sunu said.

Kulak nodded uncertainly and said, "Nelv is helping felids spread. She could be near Mindreldrolom, or very far away by now."

"If Khuron requests, I could ask a shaman to speak a message to Nelv," Kenondok said. "Some of us wish returning home. Many things our scalps are not comfortable with. Our task is completed, we are not required to do more, but we can help sail whoever needs to go back."

Sterjall and Kulak looked toward Ilsed and the other Laatu who stood behind her. She nodded gravely, confirming what they had feared: the Laatu were not willing to join them on the next stage of their long mission.

Kulak chose not to acknowledge their decision and simply said, "Captain Siffo, will *Fjummomurr* and its crew be willing to travel south with us?"

The captain grunted twice. "Till d'Endfall n'beyond. We've already gone to d'land uf dragons, why not see what else lurks in d'faraway waters uf yer plain-skinned realms?" Siffo gazed at his crew, and they all hollered in agreement. Siffo shushed them, pointing toward Mamóru, who still needed to focus.

After much more debating, they arrived at several decisions. Under Captain Siffo's command, *Fjummomurr* would take Sterjall, Kulak, Sunu, Ishke'ísuk, and Alaia to the south, in search of the Azurean Dome of the Ji Miscam, the dome of the extinct clade of marsupials that was tucked between the Azure, Cobalt, and Cerulean deserts of the Kingdom of Bauram. They hoped to find the Quajufröa there, as well as Ëalcor, the Nu'irg ust Quaju, and ask them to join their cause. Blu and Pichi would be needed for speed on land, and would travel with them as well. Later, they would venture southeast to the Republic of Lerev, an island where instead of Takhísh and Takhamún it was Noss themself that the Lerevi worshipped, as well as their eighteen animal spirits. There they would try to enter the Nisos Dome, home of the Sehján Miscam; that was the land of the clade known as the glires, encompassing rodents and lagomorphs, and Okrisilv was their mask. Their path beyond that point was uncertain, but it would likely take them past the Gulf of Erjilm.

Under Hud Ilsed's command, *Drolvisdinn* would sail north back to the Fjordlands Dome, where Nalaníri would find Probo, and together with Kitjári they would venture east in search of Banook and Safis. Their mission would be to infiltrate the lands of the Negian Empire, breach the domes the Red Stag had ransacked, and open them before they suffered the same fate as the Varanus Dome; or even worse, before they collapsed like the Heartpine Dome.

After dropping off Nalaníri and Kitjári, Ilsed would sail *Drolvisdinn* back to the Moordusk Dome. Kenondok would ask for the whereabouts of Nelv and pass on a message. He was tasked with telling her that once she finished helping with the felid migrations, she was to travel south, past the scablands and the Udarbans Forest, all the way to the Taring Peninsula at the very bottom of the Gulf of Erjilm. Twice a month, on the nights in which Sceres shone bright with the Ilaadrid Shard, she was to walk to the headlands at the end of the peninsula and search for a skeletal-white ship with black sails. Sterjall's party did not know how long it would take them to get that far into their journey, so there would be no hurry yet for Nelv.

"Kenondok, I'd ask for one more favor," Sterjall said. "Could you ask Hud Quoda to search for my friend, Crysta? I told Crysta to travel to her province to witness the dome opening. She might be there, or she might not, but if she is, I'd like to send one last letter to her."

Kenondok nodded. Despite his apprehensions about all the broken rules, he still felt a sense of duty toward the mission. "Crysta of the Withering Vale sent us missive that helped greatly," he replied. "She is honorable woman, and I will return the favor. My own hands may deliver the message if I find your friend."

They paused for a moment, all thinking the same thing.

"What about Mamóru?" Sterjall finally asked, looking toward the mammoth, who was still sitting in the same position, still connected to Noss.

"I guess we'll have to wait and see what happens," Kitjári said quietly.

Over the next couple of days, they took turns watching over Mamóru. Other than a few moths, insects didn't seem to approach him, and there was no rain other than a soft drizzle. Hour by hour, Mamóru was changing. He was still in his half-form, but as time passed, his shape became smokey and translucent, as if he was somewhere in the process of shapeshifting. As the hours passed, his figure became ever more ethereal, first diluting into smoke and dark threads, then leaving nothing but a dark mask suspended above white robes, with only a feeble smoke wearing them.

On the third day, while Siffo and Alaia watched over Mamóru, the five Silvfröash walked to the far end of the ruins of the Mo'óto city. They were discussing the new understanding they had recently gained, that of how to shapeshift into their feral forms.

"As long as we are not alone, Noss said it would be safe to attempt this," Sterjall said. "I think it's better if we learn now, before we split ways. I feel much safer with all of you around."

"So does my scalp," Kulak agreed as they entered the five-sided stupa that he and Sterjall had recently visited. They gathered at the center of the building and stood around the central altar.

"Seems like them chopped uff heads here," Nalaníri said, picking up the crescent-shaped dagger at the altar.

"Told you," Kulak mumbled to Sterjall.

The broken oculus above them shone a bright beam of light right between them.

"So, shell we attempt it?" Nalaníri asked, dropping the rusty dagger. "Who'll be d'lucky one to start?"

"Certainly not Sunu," Sunu said, being there mostly for learning and support. They would not be able to attempt this yet, not until they knew their half-form.

Kitjári took a step forward. "I'll give it a try first. Just stay close, okay? Keep me sane, keep me with you." She unlatched her dark-walnut cloak and let it drop to the ground, followed by her gray leather armor, her tunic, and her undergarments. Her cinnamon-colored fur glistened in velvety waves, obscuring her six breasts. She clinked the claws of her footpaws on the mosaicked tiles, nervously readying herself.

She recalled Noss's instructions and gave in to Urnaadisilv's commands. It was not hard for her to do, as Noss had implanted the knowledge directly into their memories; it was more akin to remembering something she had already done before. She dropped forward. With her twenty claws on the ground, her proportions began to shift. None of the mysterious smoke formed this time, as her external body parts were already ursine. Instead, her fur quivered and reshaped, bulging and contorting, until she lost her humanoid expressions and musculature as well as aspects of her human mind.

It took her a forceful moment to fully shapeshift, but at last, there she was— a gorgeous black bear of cinnamon color, as feral and wild-looking as any that roamed the Stelm Wujann.

Her little button eyes scanned around, like curious berries. She felt the world with new qualia, enhanced by her fully transitioned anatomy. The scents she could perceive were deeper, more complex, and colorful. Standing on four paws felt perfectly natural and comfortable. She walked around, feeling her shoulder blades bounce up and down in a way she had never felt before. She smelled her own clothes and pushed the fabrics with her nimble nose and muzzle, entirely forgetting that hands were supposed to serve the function of grabbing and probing.

Despite her increased sensitivity with certain senses, others were missing. She could no longer see the threads of consciousness, though she could still feel them in a different way, like a field of electricity tingling her fur. She no longer had access to the extended empathic focus that Urnaadisilv provided, though she still possessed her natural empathy, as she ever would, with or without the mask. She was a bear now, in the truest sense—not a human, not something in-between. All that remained of her as a human were her memories and her will.

She heard noises around her. Noises. Voices? Her friends were talking, but it was difficult to understand their words. "Kitjári...—you—back—instead—" Some of the words made sense, like her name. She was Kitjári, and she said so by growling loud and clear for all of them to hear. Her growl did not sound like the words her friends were uttering, but she knew they meant the same thing. "Kitjári!" they called again, but she wasn't paying attention to her ears now, but to her keen nose, using it to taste her environment.

She sniffed at a trail of recent footprints, which led her to a tangle of plants that only her nose knew guarded a rotten skeleton. She followed the scent into a niche in the back of the stupa, and on top of a soft, plushy pile of moss smelled something familiar. It smelled like Kulak, like Sterjall. She suddenly remembered her friends' names and turned her head around, noticing they were still calling for her. The bear snapped back to her senses and recalled why she was there. She trotted back to the center of the chamber, nodded in a mostly human gesture, huffed, and balanced on two legs. She sharply took control of Urnaadisilv's impulses and let her proportions shift back, but her fear at the loss of control pushed her beyond her half-form, summoning the tendrils and smoke that took her back to her human self. She ripped the mask right off her face.

"By Soroley's frozen tears, that scared me for a moment," Jiara said, hyperventilating, feeling a chill breeze on her bare skin. She put her clothes back on while she explained her experience.

"It was quite something how crisp all scents were," she concluded. "I could smell everything that's happened here, in clear detail," she added, glancing toward Sterjall.

Sterjall's eyes avoided hers, finding a sudden fascination with the tiles at his footpaws.

"Well, now I'm mour curious than ever," Nalaníri said. "Once I learn t'do this, I shell be able t'match Probo's incessant pestering. What a delightful surprise it'll be next time I see him."

She dropped her pocketed vest, her baggy shirt, her leather trousers, her loose undergarments. Jiara had never seen Nalaníri's naked body before, and felt strangely aroused by the patterns of white and black, and by the incredible display of an entire dozen teats, which weren't hidden under fur like Kitjári's breasts, and were nowhere near as large either. Nalaníri had perky, pink nipples, with small areolas supporting them, and right below the two columns of six nipples, Jiara locked her eyes on—

"—un my hooves first? Hey, are ye listening, m'dear?"

"H-huh?" Jiara stammered.

"I was asking if I shell drop un mine hooves 'fore I start it."

"I kind of did it during? The entire, I mean, the whole time," Jiara fumbled.

"Just try it, it's not as hard as when you first changed into your half-form."

Nalaníri grunted and focused. She began her change while standing on two hooves, then dropped to all fours once her shifting proportions made it hard to stand upright. Her tusks grew bigger in her full wild boar form, though they were still relatively small. The feral boar was more sizable than anyone expected: as tall as Kitjári as a black bear, but heftier. She had the same white and black fur, but on her back now blossomed a wiry mane that spiked like quills from a porcupine.

The boar wriggled her heart-shaped nose, noticing she had forgotten to take off her glowing nosering. She shrugged it off, suspecting it looked good on her in whichever form she took.

She wished she'd prepared a great dish to taste while in this new form; it was something she would have to experience later. She didn't lose herself as deeply as Kitjári had, and could understand words more easily, though they still became vague and abstract to her. She grunted as she pranced around the circle to sample the scents of her friends. She lifted her snout and grunted in front of Kulak.

"What is it?" Kulak asked.

"She wants to greet you, I think," Jiara guessed. "In the Puqua way."

Kulak squatted and rubbed noses with her. The boar then greeted Sterjall, Sunu, and Jiara in the same manner. She then stood over her clothes, shook her wiry mane in excitement, and got up on two hooves.

"A most wunderful experience!" Nalaníri said, returning to her half-form. She pulled her undergarments up while looking toward the two young men, lifting an encouraging eyebrow.

Kulak and Sterjall glanced at each other. Sterjall was trembling.

"Do you want to try it at the same time?" Kulak asked.

"I think… Yeah, maybe, that might make it easier."

Sterjall felt his old shame return. He had never been naked in front of Nalaníri or Sunu before, and with all eyes on him, he felt inescapably exposed. He was surprised and encouraged by how easily Kulak removed his shodog and kilt, standing proudly in front of the others, seeing no reason to feel ashamed of his sandstone fur or his tiny, dangling testicles.

Sterjall awkwardly removed his tunic and dropped his trousers, covering his sheath with his handpaws, but that very gesture only served to make him more embarrassed.

Kulak scrutinized his moves and offered a sympathetic smile. "Do you want to—"

"I'm fine," Sterjall said. "Just give me a breath."

Sterjall closed his eyes, feeling the anxiety burn through his veins. In his mind, he recited Ockam's litany. *A young tree I am, the old forest I am not, yet forest and tree are of one soul. A small fish I am, the vast ocean I am not, yet ocean and fish are of one mind. A frail wolf I am, the strong pack I am not,* "yet pack and wolf are of one heart," he finished the last words in a whisper and opened his eyes.

He took a deep breath, uncovered his crotch, and loosened his shoulders.

"Ready?" Kulak prompted.

Sterjall nodded.

They both dropped forward at the same time. Kulak was the first to shift: his body shrank quickly, his shoulder blades flexed, his mostly human-shaped hands compressed into tighter paws. His body turned slender and regal, his curved back undulated sensually, his black ear tufts perked up like antennae. As a feral caracal, he was substantially larger than a housecat—at least the ones in the New World, not the giant cat companions of Mindreldrolom—but he still was less than half the size of his human form. He noticed Sterjall struggling mid-transformation and tried to speak a word of encouragement, but only managed an odd, chirping sort of mew. The dark bundle of fur contorted in front of him.

Sterjall's legs shifted in a similar way to how Kulak's had, growing more angular, attaching at a new angle to his hips and chest, while his handpaws shrunk into more compact, real paws. His black tail grew fuller, his neck thicker, his rib cage more forward-pointed, his teeth sharper. The colors and patterns of his fur remained the same as before: quaar-black head and limbs, dusky-gray body with rosettes easing the transition, and a lighter belly and chest. The burn scars upon his left leg remained patchy, as they did in any of his forms. Instead of decreasing in size, Sterjall grew a bit larger, morphing into a sizable timber wolf.

The wolf took an indecisive step toward the caracal and sniffed. He then chewed on the felid's face in the way wolves did to greet each other—the caracal tried to say "stop," but instead he hissed.

They were aware of the way their expressions had shifted, yet they could not help themselves. Their reactions felt natural, and they only noticed any strangeness when they looked at themselves with the human portion of their awareness that still resided within them. Like Kitjári and Nalaníri before them, they found it hard to understand their friends, who had furrowed brows and seemed to be asking questions; the two young animals simply couldn't be bothered to try to decipher their friends' words.

The caracal and the wolf let themselves go, forgetting for a glorious moment about their responsibilities, their sorrows, their worries. They chased after one another through the toppled columns, like a puppy and a kitten in a friendly scuffle, dropping on their backs to kick at each other's bellies, biting at each other's tails. The wolf was aware of his strength and took care not to hurt the smaller caracal, pretending to lose his balance and letting him bite at his neck.

The caracal shook the wolf's neck fluff, then triumphantly leapt atop a column too high for the wolf to reach. The dejected canid looked up and half-whined. His muzzle opened, and out came an awkward woof, somewhere between a bark and a howl. He surprised himself with the loudness of his voice, which echoed in the great stupa and made him look around. He then saw the worried faces of his friends. The realization made him suddenly recall his human essence, and he figured it must be time to turn back.

The wolf reverted into his half-form, with his tail still excitedly wagging. The caracal followed right after, smiling sharply and laughing fully.

"We must try that again!" Kulak exclaimed.

Sterjall chuckled, reaching for his clothes. "We must. But promise me we'll do it only when we are together. I almost lost myself in there, it was too much fun!"

"My scalp promises," Kulak said. "You looked so big as a real wolf. And I was so small, so helpless."

"Helpless? Your claws!" Sterjall countered. "I feel ever-so-slightly mauled here." He looked down to find droplets of blood on his belly, and he was sure there must be more scratches on his back.

"Sunu is glad you enjoyed yourselves," Sunu said, "and excited to see what form the future holds for them."

Chapter Seventy-Eight

The Journey Ahead

Sterjall and Alaia were up in *Drolvisdinn*'s crow's nest, gazing at the evolving spectacle of the Varanus Dome's lights.

"Twelve teats? What a hoarder," Alaia chuckled.

"And I caught Jiara peeking at them," Sterjall said. "I have a feeling she likes her."

"You were peeking at them too, though. You even counted them."

"Couldn't help myself, they were a bit hard to miss," he said and leaned back. "But it was such a good time. Scary, but wonderful." He sighed. "It's odd, that it happened to be today, of all days."

"That what happened? What is odd?"

"That today was my first time experiencing my feral form. Think of the date. Does it seem familiar?"

"I honestly can't figure out what month it is anymore, especially with this jumbled dome that doesn't know the difference between day and night."

"It's the twelfth. Of Dewrest?" he said, lifting his furry eyebrows.

"Gwoli! Happy birthday! I mean, happy Sterjall day. Happy furday? Happy half-formth day? I don't know what to call this, but of course I remember! You little toddler you, one year old already. So proud of you." She pulled on his whiskers and kissed his wet nose.

"Hey, stop that or I *will* bite. But yes, it's exactly one year later, and now I've learned how to take on a new form. In another year, maybe I'll turn into a jumping spider, or a chinchilla. Who knows what's coming?" He inhaled deeply, as if smelling a memory of campfires and granite. "At this time last year, it was just beginning to get cold in the mountains, and I would wear his oversized shirt while practicing, and then we'd warm up by the fireplace, and..."

Alaia scooted closer. "By Pliwe. What good times those were back at his cabin. I miss that fat bundle of joy."

"I do too. Every day."

Alaia elbowed his side. "You should write to him. Tell him what's been going on. He'll get to see Kitjári soon enough, and she can take the letter for you."

"That's a great idea! I—I just... I just wouldn't know what to say."

"As always, you'll figure it out," she said. "And as always, it's better if you are honest about things."

He understood; she didn't need to say more.

After dinner that night, Lago entered *Drolvisdinn*'s captain's quarters and placed Agnargsilv on the bed Mamóru had used. It was empty and cleanly made up. He pulled up a chair next to the nightstand, ripped a piece of paper from Ockam's old notebook, and dipped a quill in ink. While Agnargsilv watched him, he wrote:

> Dear Banook,
> Today is the twelfth day of Dewrest. Do you remember that date? It's the day Sterjall was born. I'm one year old today, though I feel much older.

Lago paused to dip the quill again, breathed in the camphor fumes, thought for a while, and then continued writing.

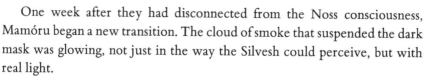

One week after they had disconnected from the Noss consciousness, Mamóru began a new transition. The cloud of smoke that suspended the dark mask was glowing, not just in the way the Silvesh could perceive, but with real light.

Mamóru's friends gathered around him that afternoon. The sky was dark outside the dome, and they could see patches of it through the newly opened holes. The opening vines had never ceased pulsating in strange patterns, and Mamóru seemed to palpitate with them. His white robes incandesced from within. The radiant fog held up the quaar mask—a hovering visage of darkness suspended within luminous beams.

They sat in the stone circle. Kulak and Sterjall held handpaws. Alaia leaned against Kitjári, who offered a comforting bear embrace. Sunu and Nalaníri sat side by side, speculating about what this all could mean.

The brilliant light flickered, then shone ever brighter until they could no longer look directly at it. In an instant, they were struck by a blinding, effulgent burst that then faded into an afterimage. Mamóru's robes collapsed onto the chair, leaving nothing behind, then the dark Silv fell weightlessly atop the robes, making no noise at all.

Through teary eyes, Sterjall looked around, and Agnargsilv let him see one last glimpse: the pearlescent aura that had made up the Nu'irg's consciousness spread outward like a slow-moving shockwave, rippling through every living being that surrounded them.

Mamóru was gone.

A thousand miles to the east, Banook was sauntering through the Stelm Wujann with the company of Safís and Bear. He stopped, looked up to the tusked constellation of the Nu'irg ust Momsúndo, and felt his heart crumple and shatter. Next to him, Safís let out a piercing howl. Bear, too, howled, though he knew not why.

"You should carry it," Kitjári told Sterjall the next morning. She handed him Mamóru's mask, but he couldn't bring himself to touch it.

"I can't. It still glows, like he is still in there. It's too hard."

"It's Momsúndosilv's own aura, not Mamóru's. And even if it no longer works, it could become useful later." Despite the seemingly sacrilegious nature of the experiment, after Mamóru's passing, the Silvfröash had briefly attempted wearing the proboscidean Silv to see if any of its powers remained—the mask had turned entirely inert.

Kitjári shoved the mask closer. "Take it."

Sterjall took the mask and put it in his bag, out of sight, though he could still sense the dim glow and could smell the scent of mistleaf that permeated it.

The sailors were gathering food and resources, filling the ships' wooden casks with a supply of fresh water. It had been two weeks since they had set the dome to open, and they guessed they would be able to sail out easily, perhaps without much help from the Silvesh.

Sunu was sad to depart this wretched dome: despite its chaos, they had grown fond of the reptiles. They had grown more acquainted with

Kruwensilv, and although still unsure of their path, they felt a particular fascination toward turtles, as some days they wished they could hide deep in a shell and forget about the struggles of the world around them.

Now that Mamóru was gone, there was no direct way to communicate with Ishke'ísuk, not until Sunu found their half-form and gained their reptilian qualia. Before the end, Mamóru had explained to Ishke'ísuk what he could do to help his friends, and he'd agreed to join Sunu on their journey. The migration of the reptiles would have to wait—Sunu and Ishke'ísuk would have to return at some later date to finish their personal quest in Fel Varanus, once the dome was no more.

The wayfarers shared one last feast together, expertly cooked by Nalaníri, then walked toward the stone piers to board their separate ships.

"I wish I could go with you," Sterjall told Kitjári, walking by her side. "I even thought that... No, forget about it."

"You thought what?" she asked. "Come on, kid, don't be shy."

"I thought that... that maybe we could trade masks. I could learn to be a bear, you know?"

"Don't think that thought hasn't occurred to all of us. But the truth is, now that I found my form, it is an intrinsic part of me, and always will be. Even if I found a new side of me later, this bear is the part I will always feel the closest to—it would tear my soul apart to lose it."

"Yeah, I understand. If I had first put Urnaadisilv on, it might have been different. But I'm a wolf now, it's who I am. The mask shaped me to be this way and I could never see myself giving it up."

"It pains me to think that some Miscam had to hand off their masks to their successors before they died. Like Alúma did for Aio."

"It's probably not so bad if it's for your own children, but I bet it still hurt."

They kept walking. Sterjall contemplated his footpaws as they traversed the cold stones.

Kitjári playfully bumped his shoulder. "Hey, stop worrying, kid. I will give Banook the biggest of bear hugs for you, I promise."

"Thank you. Oh, before I forget, would you mind also giving him this?" He produced an envelope that was sealed with stamped wax. He had used the pommel of Leif, which Banook had carved, to stamp the vibrant-blue wax with the heads of a bear and a wolf touching noses together.

"What's this?" she asked. "Oh, sorry, I shouldn't pry into these things. You don't need to tell me." She took a deep whiff of the envelope and slyly added, "You are clear. It only smells like you, and not like Kulak's cum."

"Don't say shit like that out loud!" Sterjall barked while glancing around, mortified. "Could you really smell—"

"Oh yes, that stupa smelled like a whorehouse. But don't worry, I don't think anyone but me would've noticed. I will hand this to Banook and send him your love. Cheer up, cub," she said, using the pet name only Banook ever called him. "You'll get to see him again. All our paths will cross farther ahead, somewhere."

"I hope so," Sterjall said, then jumped in to embrace her. Kitjári gave the best hugs when in her half-form—Sterjall savored the moment, sinking deep between her ample breasts.

"That's enough, puppy," she said, holding him at arm's length. "Don't go making Banook jealous now. And don't worry, though we'll be apart, we are still one team. Just like when Dravéll and Ishkembor had to part ways in the *Barlum Saga*."

"Wayfarers of the Sixteen Realms," Sterjall said.

The wayfarers said their farewells and boarded their vessels.

As the ships pulled away from the pier of the lost city, *Drolvisdinn* drifted north, headed through the same passage they had used when they entered the dome, while *Fjummomurr* sailed east through a water channel they believed would connect them to the Esduss Sea.

Sunu sat cross-legged in *Fjummomurr*'s crow's nest and waved. Olo perched on their right shoulder, while Ishke'ísuk sat on their left.

"May the moon light your path!" Sterjall hollered, choked up.

"May the stars guide your heart!" he heard Kitjári call back.

"Find some exotic ingredients fur me, fur d'feast we shell have once we meet again!" Nalaníri yelled, her loud voice already fading in the distance. "D'light uf d'kenzir is with ye!"

"N'so it shines within us all!" Captain Siffo's thunderous voice replied.

"We'll miss you!" Alaia screamed at the top of her lungs, dangling from the ratlines.

Sterjall held tightly to Kulak's handpaw. Their eyes followed Kitjári and Nalaníri as they receded in the haze. They watched until their friends were no longer in sight, and they were left alone, with each other.

End of Book 2

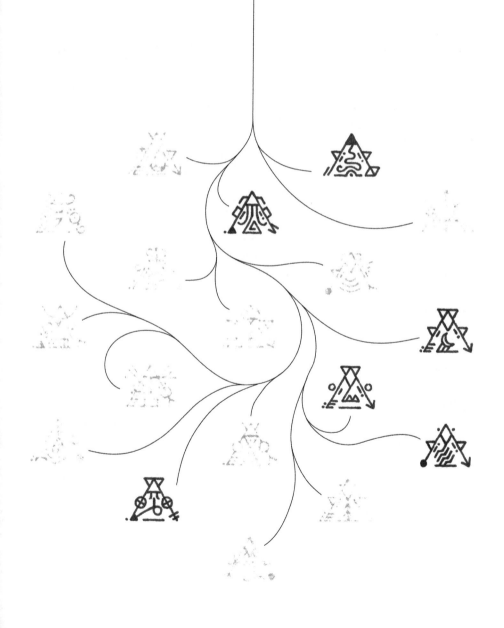

THE NOSS SAGA
CONTINUES
ON BOOK 3

LEARN MORE AT
JoaquinBaldwin.com/book3/buy

Appendices

All the materials found in these appendices can also be found online with much cleaner formatting and with additional goodies, such as a complete Miscamish dictionary, full-resolution maps, and updated illustrations. They are included here for your convenience, but I recommend you check them out on the official website.

Scan this QR code or type in the following URL to access the extras:

JoaquinBaldwin.com/book2/extras

To keep updated on new book releases and to gain access to unreleased illustrations, deleted chapters, tutorials, and lots more, sign up to my mailing list in the following link:

JoaquinBaldwin.com/list

The Rules of Minquoll

Excerpt from *Wayfaring Field Notes* by Hefra Boarmane, published in 1461 A.D.

Field Styles
- **Tournament (Gwur Ali):** 6x4 conifers, branches highly reinforced with companion-species bones.
- **Freestyle (Gwur Aalpe):** Around 30 conifers not in a grid. Fields are sometimes round. Protruding rocks count as valid contact points.
- **Uprooted (Gwur Pantuul):** Played over mangroves. Not as much height, but significantly slipperier and wetter.
- **Leafstorm (Gwur Ŭrĕath):** Played among fire maples, best during Autumn. Branches are wildly chaotic.
- **Sheijir (Gwur Esmukh):** Exclusive to the Arsaash Forest, where banyan roots are grown into a field like the tangles of a funnel-web spider.
- **Aloof (Gwur Gomosh):** Played aboard Gorgámmu, a stadium raft with twenty-four masts and excessive amounts of taut lines.

Core Rules and Terminology
- **Ring:** Score on the smaller, top hoop, worth 6 points.
- **Bangle:** Score on the middle hoop, worth 4 points.
- **Hoop:** Score on the larger, bottom hoop, worth 2 points.
- **Bearer:** The player holding the ball. Only allowed to move on their current tree. They must pass or launch in order to regain free movement (they can do so while leaping to their next tree).
- **Sprinter:** Player not holding the ball. They are allowed to move freely, but if they traverse on the ground (go rogue) outside of their turn, a point is deducted from their team, unless they do so to retrieve a drop.
- **Ward:** Name for the hoop guard, the ocelot (lynxes sometimes play as wards, though rarely).
- **Rogue:** A player who purposely runs on the ground to take a strategic position. Rogues take turns. After one team goes rogue and returns, the other team can choose to go rogue as well without a point deduction, or hold their move to prevent their enemy from using the same advantage. Whenever the ball drops, each team can send one rogue to recover it, and the last to leave the ground cedes the rogue turn to the

- enemy team. Rogues can move freely but must pass the ball without moving upon catching it.
- **Drop**: When the ball falls to the ground. A point is deducted from the last team who touched it, unless it was by a ward. The player retrieving the ball cannot go rogue with it and must pass immediately or climb back up the same tree. A drop does not hold the game unless the ball leaves the playing field.
- **Launch**: Hurling the ball toward a hoop.
- **Assault**: Hurling the ball at an enemy player to make it bounce into a drop. An easy way to score a single point, but risks losing the ball. Teams often use an assault while accompanied by a shadowing rogue to recover the ball.
- **Parry**: When a ward blocks and the ball drops, which incurs no point deduction and grants the ball to the ward's team.
- **Backstab**: It is possible to score a point from the back side of the hoops, although the launch area is quite limited. A backstab adds an extra point to the score value.
- **Maul**: When the ball is torn to pieces by two felids biting and pulling at it. The team trying to steal the ball from the bearer during a maul is handed the next ball once the game resumes.

Species

- **Snow leopards**: Team captains. Excellent blockers due to their long tails and not being encumbered by riders. They mindspeak to their team to strategize moves.
- **Ocelots**: Wards. Agile and energetic. Mostly stay by their hoops, but can rush into the field for strategic moves.
- **Lynxes**: sometimes used as wards. They are great at stealing directly from bearers, but not as good at blocking in midair.
- **Jaguars**: Best climbers. Can snake to the smaller branches on top to make plays from above.
- **Tigers**: Most powerful. Can hold a position without risking someone stealing the ball.
- **Black panthers**: They tend to stay low and out of sight. Superb rogues.
- **Mountain lions**: Fastest for horizontal offense when rushing on the lower branches.
- **Humans**: Useless bipedal parasites on the backs of the agile felids.

The Eighteen Clades

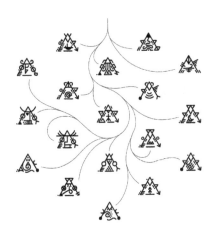

Avian - Kroowin

Kroowinsilv: finished in the year 8003 B.D.
Location: Yenwu Dome
Tribe: Murtégo Miscam
Nu'irg: Skugge (great gray owl, A)

Bovid - Trommo

Trommosilv: finished in the year 8018 B.D.
Location: Ashen Dome
Tribe: Tjardur Miscam
Nu'irg: Pamúnn (nyala, M)

Canid - Agnarg

Agnargsilv: finished in the year 8077 B.D.
Location: Heartpine Dome
Tribe: Southern Wutash Miscam
Nu'irg: Safis (tundra wolf, F)

Caprid - Rilg

Rilgsilv: finished in the year 8017 B.D.
Location: Bighorn Dome
Tribe: Ikhel Miscam (Western and Eastern)
Nu'irg: Beiféren (bootherium, M)

Cervid - Urg

Urgsilv: finished in the year 8015 B.D.
Location: Anglass Dome
Tribe: Teldebran Miscam
Nu'irg: Sovath (chital, F)

Cetacean - Amá'a

Amá'asilv: finished in the year 8023 B.D.
Location: Seafaring Dome
Tribe: Isdinnuk Miscam
Nu'irg: Allamónea (sperm whale, F). Deceased.

Chiropteran - Balast

Balastsilv: finished in the year 8082 B.D.
Location: Scoria Dome
Tribe: Bikhéne Miscam
Nu'irg: Fuuriseth (white leaf-nosed bat, F)

Felid - Mindrel

Mindrelsilv: finished in the year 8062 B.D.
Location: Moordusk Dome
Tribe: Laatu Miscam
Nu'irg: Nelv (clouded leopard, F)

Glires - Okri

Okrisilv: finished in the year 8127 B.D.
Location: Nisos Dome
Tribe: Ji Miscam
Nu'irg: Gwit (hazel dormouse, M)

Marsupial - Quaju

Quajusilv: finished in the year 8012 B.D.
Location: Azurean Dome
Tribe: Sehján Miscam
Nu'irg: Ëalcor (thylacine, M)

Musteloid - Krost

Krostsilv: finished in the year 8040 B.D.
Location: Lequa Dome
Tribe: Jojek Miscam
Nu'irg: Muri (honey badger, M)

Perissodactyl - Almel

Almelsilv: finished in the year 8029 B.D.
Location: Archstone Dome
Tribe: Alampaari Miscam
Nu'irg: Estriéggo (white rhinoceros, M)

Pinniped - Gwonle

Gwonlesilv: finished in the year 8033 B.D.
Location: Moonrise Dome
Tribe: Khardok Miscam
Nu'irg: Däo-Varjak (ribbon seal, F)

Primate - Hoombu

Hoombusilv: finished in the year 8232 B.D.
Location: Tarpits Dome
Tribe: Acoapóshi Miscam
Nu'irg: Buujik (red-shanked douc, F)

Proboscidean - Momsúndo

Momsúndosilv: finished in the year 8097 B.D.
Location: Brasha'in Scablands
Tribe: Toldask Miscam
Nu'irg: Mamóru (steppe mammoth, M)

Reptilian - Kruwen

Kruwensilv: finished in the year 8006 B.D.
Location: Varanus Dome
Tribe: Mo'óto Miscam
Nu'irg: Ishke'ísuk (double-crested basilisk, M)

Suid - Nagra

Nagrasilv: finished in the year 8027 B.D.
Location: Fjordlands Dome
Tribe: Puqua Miscam
Nu'irg: Probo (javelina, M)

Ursid - Urnaadi

Urnaadisilv: finished in the year 8041 B.D.
Location: Da'áju Caldera
Tribe: Northern Wutash Miscam
Nu'irg: Kerjaastórgnem (arctotherium, M)

Glossary of Commonly Used Miscamish Words

Parts of speech:
adj. adjective *adv.* adverb *art.* article
conj. conjunction *det.* determiner *interj.* interjection
nan. animate noun *nina.* inanimate noun *num.* numeral
prep. preposition *pron.* pronoun *v.* verb

Animate nouns, pronouns, and determiners come in six levels, indicated by the numbers 1-6. An *s* is for singular, *p* for plural.

> **Key**
> **spelling** - approx. pronunciation /IPA/ (part of speech) - definition(s)

agnarg AG-narg /ˈagnarg/ (nan4) - canid, canine

Agnargfröa ag-narg-FRO-ah /ˌagnargˈfro.a/ (nan5) - voice of the canids

Agnargsilv AG-narg-silv /ˈagnargsɪlv/ (nan5) - mask of canids

agnist AG-nist /ˈagnɪst/ (nan3) - fox

agnurf AG-noo-rf /ˈagnurf/ (nan3) - wolf

allastirg AH-last-irg /ˈallastɪrg/ (nina) - south

almel AL-mehl /ˈalmɛl/ (nan4) - perissodactyl, equine

amá'a ah-MAH-'ah /aˈmaʔa/ (nan4) - cetacean

ankrov ANKH-rohv /ˈankrov/ (adj) - rusty

arambukh AH-rahm-boo-kh /ˈarambuχ/ (nina) - money, coin

arudinn AH-roo-dihn /ˈarudɪnn/ (nan2) - seedlight

ash ash /aʃ/ (adj) - white, blank

baakiag BAA-key-ag /ˈbaːkɪag/ (adv) - please

balast BAH-last /ˈbalast/ (nan4) - chiropteran

bir beer /bɪr/ (nina) - home

braaw bra /braːw/ (nina) - mead

ca'éli kah-'EH-lee /kaʔˈɛli/ (nan3) - pilgrim

dinn dihn /dɪnn/ (nan1) - light

drolom DROH-lom /ˈdrolom/ (nan5) - dome
drolv drolv /drolv/ (nan2) - wing
drolvis DROL-vis /ˈdrolvɪs/ (nina) - eternity
enwenn EN-when /ˈɛnwɛnn/ (nina) - graphite
ĕovad EH-oh-vahd /ˈɛ.ovad/ (nan1) - fire
esht esht /ɛʃt/ (adj) - blue
far far /far/ (nan3) - pine, conifer
fel fell /fɛl/ (nina) - island
frŏa FRO-ah /ˈfro.a/ (nan6) - voice
gralv grah-lv /gralv/ (adj) - purple
grest grest /grɛst/ (interj) - no
grin grin /grɪn/ (nina) - paint, color, hue
gwonle WON-leh /ˈgwonlɛ/ (nan4) - pinniped
gwur gwoor /gwur/ (nina) - province, territory
hed head /hɛd/ (nan3) - chief (allgender)
hod hohd /hod/ (nan3) - chief (male)
hoombu HOH-OHM-boo /ˈhoːmbu/ (nan4) - primate, ape, monkey
hud hood /hud/ (nan3) - chief (female)
idash EE-dash /ˈɪdaʃ/ (adj) - clear, transparent
ieren YEH-rehn /ˈjɛrɛn/ (nan3) - royal (allgender ruler)
ieron YEH-rohn /ˈjɛron/ (nan3) - king, emperor
ierun YEH-roon /ˈjɛrun/ (nan3) - queen
isdinn IS-dihn /ˈɪsdɪnn/ (nan1) - sea
Iskimesh IS-key-mesh /ˈɪskɪmɛʃ/ (nan6) - Enchantress, third planet from Sunnokh
jall jahl /dʒall/ (nan2) - heart
keldris KEHL-dris /ˈkɛldrɪs/ (nina) - bay, harbor, cove, port
Khumen KHOO-men /ˈχumɛn/ (nan6) - Dawn Pilgrim, first planet from Sunnokh
khuren KHOO-rehn /ˈχurɛn/ (nan3) - prince (allgender)
khuron KHOO-rohn /ˈχuron/ (nan3) - prince (male)
khurun KHOO-roon /ˈχurun/ (nan3) - princess
klad clad /klad/ (nan1) - lake
klannath KLA-nath /ˈklannath/ (nina) - north
kriss chris /krɪss/ (nina) - iron
kroovieth KROH-vee-eth /ˈkroːvɪɛθ/ (nan3) - starling
kroowin CROW-win /ˈkroːwɪn/ (nan4) - avian

krost crossed /krɒst/ (nan4) - musteloid, mustelid
kruwen CREW-when /'kruwɛn/ (nan4) - reptilian, reptile
kupógo coo-POH-goh /kuˈpogo/ (nan3) - snail
laaja LAH-jah /'laːdʒa/ (nan1) - volcano
leif LAY-f /'leɪf/ (nan2) - fang
lerr LEH-rr /lɛrr/ (nan3) - liege (allgender honorific)
lerrkin LEH-rr-kin /'lɛrrkɪn/ (adj) - bisexual
loomdinn LOOM-dihn /'loːmdɪnn/ (nina) - east (birth-light)
lorr lore /lorr/ (nan3) - lord, sir, mister
lorrkin LORE-kin /'lorrkɪn/ (adj) - gay, attracted to men
lurr LOO-rr /lurr/ (nan3) - lady, madam, miss
lurrkin LOO-rr-kin /'lurrkɪn/ (adj) - lesbian, attracted to women
maarg mah-arg /maːrg/ (adj) - red
malpa MAHL-pah /'malpa/ (adj) - great
mindahim MIHN-dah-him /'mɪndahɪm/ (nan3) - caracal
mindílli minh-DEE-lee /mɪnˈdɪlli/ (nan3) - sand cat
mindrégo mihn-DREH-goh /mɪnˈdrɛgo/ (nan3) - saber-toothed cat, smilodon
mindrel MIHN-drehl /'mɪndrɛl/ (nan4) - felid, feline
mindu MIHN-doo /'mɪndu/ (nan3) - black panther
minnéllo mih-NEH-loh /mɪˈnnɛllo/ (nan1) - waterfall
minquoll MIHN-kwol /'mɪnkwoll/ (nina) - catball
Miscamish MISS-kah-mih-sh /'mɪskamɪʃ/ (nina) - Miscamish
momsúndo mom-SOON-doh /momˈsundo/ (nan4) - proboscidean
nagra NAH-grah /'nagra/ (nan4) - suid
ninn nihn /nɪnn/ (nina) - pass
nokh noh-kh /noχ/ (nan1) - sky
Noss noss /noss/ (nan6) - second planet from Sunnokh
nu'irg NOO-ˈee-rg /'nuʔɪrg/ (nan5) - ghost, spirit, soul
okri OH-kree /'okrɪ/ (nan4) - glires, rodent, lagomorph
okruwil OH-kroo-will /'okruwɪl/ (nan3) - pacarana
okruwom OH-kroo-wohm /'okruwom/ (nan3) - castoroides (giant beaver)
ommo OH-moh /'ommo/ (nina) - temple, church
Ongumar ON-goo-mar /'ongumar/ (nan6) - Amberlight, fifth planet from Sunnokh
quaar kwaar /'kwaːr/ (nina) - soot (crystalline, durable form)
quaju KWA-joo /'kwadʒu/ (nan4) - marsupial

quas kwas /kwas/ (nina) - canyon
rilg reel-g /rɪlg/ (nan4) - caprid
rilganesh REEL-gah-nesh /ˈrɪlganɛʃ/ (nan3) - sheep (big horned)
rilgéreo reel-GEH-reh-oh /rɪlˈgɛrɛo/ (nan3) - goat
sajal SAH-jahl /ˈsajal/ (adj) - foreboding
Sceres SEH-rehs /ˈssɛrɛs/ (nan6) - moon (the moon)
senstregalv SENS-treh-gal-v /ˈsɛnstrɛgalv/ (nina) - obsidian (special)
Senstrell SENS-trell /ˈsɛnstrɛll/ (nan6) - obsidian, fourth planet from Sunnokh
shisendinn SHE-sen-dihn /ˈʃɪsɛndɪnn/ (nina) - west (death-light)
shodog SHO-dog /ˈʃodog/ (nina) - jacket (open-chested)
Silv silv /sɪlv/ (nan5) - mask
Silvfröa silv-FRO-ah /sɪlvˈfro.a/ (nan5) - voice of the mask
stelm stelm /stɛlm/ (nina) - mountain
ster stare /stɛr/ (nan6) - star
stiss stiss /stɪss/ (nan1) - river
sulf soo-lf /sulf/ (nina) - land
sun soon /sun/ (nan1) - flame
Sunnokh SOO-noh-kh /ˈsunnoχ/ (nan6) - sun (sky-flame)
tago TAH-goh /ˈtago/ (adj) - gray
telm telm /tɛlm/ (nina) - valley
thaar tha-ar /ˈθaːr/ (nan3) - vanguard
trell trell /trɛll/ (adj) - black
trod troh-d /trod/ (nina) - peak
trommo TROM-moh /ˈtrommo/ (nan4) - bovid, bovine
urg oorg /urg/ (nan4) - cervid
urgei OOr-gay /ˈurgeɪ/ (nan3) - elk
urnaadi oor-NAH-dee /urˈnaːdɪ/ (nan4) - ursid, ursine, bear
ust oo-st /ust/ (prep) - of, of the
ustlas OO-st-lahs /ˈustlas/ (nan1) - soot
welkil WEHL-kihl /ˈwɛlkɪl/ (nan3) - aphid (resin making beetle)
wujann WOO-jan /ˈwudʒann/ (adj) - icy

Characters, Gods, Items, Tribes

Abjus *(M) AB-juice*
Chief of Gwur Esmukh in Mindreldrolom. Fiercest Laatu warrior.

Acoapóshi / *ah-kowa-POH-shee*
Miscam tribe in the Tarpits Dome. Stewards of Hoombusilv, the mask of primates.

Aio *(M) EYE-oh*
Kulak's human form. Prince of Mindreldrolom. Ierun Alúma's son.

Alaia *(F) ah-LAY-uh*
Lago's best friend. Worker at the Withervale coal mines.

Alampaari / *alam-PAH-ree*
Miscam tribe at Archstone Dome. Stewards of Almelsilv, mask of perissodactyls.

Allamónea *(F) ala-MOH-nea*
Cetacean Nu'irg. Sperm whale primal form. Died in times before the Downfall.

Alúma-Farshálv *(F) ah-LOO-mah far-SHALL-v*
Queen of Mindreldrolom. Khuron Aio-Kulak's mother. Tigress half-form.

Alvis Hallow *(M) AHL-vis HAL-low*
Red Stag's human form. Monarch of the Negian Empire.

Ansko Loregem *(M) ANS-koh LORE-gem*
Writer of the Barlum Saga and the Chronicles of Aubellekh.

Ardof Zaom-Zinemog *(M) ARD-of ZAH-om ZEE-neh-mog*
A ranger informant who frequents Brimstowne to gather information.

Ashaskem *(M) ASH-as-kem*
Kulak's brother who was killed as a baby for being born part tiger.

Aurélien Knivlar *(F) aw-REH-lee-en knee-VLAR*
Shaman in Fjorna's arbalister squad. Commands Aness and Islav, magpie heralds.

Balstei Woodslav *(M) BAHLL-stay WOOD-slav*
An artificer who studies the aetheric elements.

Banook *(M) bah-NOOK*
A mountain of a man who lives alone in the mountains.

Bear *(M) bear*
Lago's mostly mutt, barely shepherd dog.

Behler Broadleaf *(M) BEH-lehr BROAD-leaf*
General of the Fifth Legion of the Negian Empire. Snub-nosed.

Beiféren *(M) bay-FEH-ren*
Caprid Nu'irg. Bootherium (helmeted muskox) primal form.

Bikhéne / *bee-KHEH-neh*
Miscam tribe in the Scoria Dome. Stewards of Balastsilv, the mask of chiropterans.

Blu *(M) blue*
Kulak's companion smilodon.

Bonmei *(M) BON-may*
Heir to Agnargsilv. Son of Mawua, grandson of Sontai. Ockam's adoptive son.

Buil *(M) boo-ill*
Chief of Gwur Úrëath in Mindreldrolom. Lives in Humenath. Short and stocky.

Buujik *(F) BOO-jick*
Primate Nu'irg. Red-shanked douc primal form. Can take the form of a woman.

Corben Holt *(M) CORE-ben holt*
Crysta's youngest son. Works at the shipyard and sails a catamaran.

Crescu Valaran *(M) KREHS-coo VAH-lah-ran*
Armsmaster in Fjorna's arbalister squad.

Crone of Ukhagar *(F) crone of OO-kha-gar*
Trickster character from spritetales.

Crysta Holt *(F) CHRIS-tuh holt*
Lago's professor. Works at the Mesa Observatory for the Zovarian military.

Däo-Varjak *(F) DAH-oh VAR-jack*
Pinniped Nu'irg. Ribbon seal primal form.

Dashal *(M) DAH-shll*
Scholar who operates the sunnograph at Zovaria's School of Cosmology.

Dravéll *(M) drah-VEHLL*
Character in the Barlum Saga. Main hero.

Drolvisdinn / *DROLL-vis-dihn*
Ilsed's leaf-sailed ship with a hull of knotted roots.

Dunokh Sull / *DOO-nokh sool*
"The Arc of the Night Sky." A legendary quaar bow. Also a constellation.

Ëalcor *(M) EH-al-core*
Marsupial Nu'irg. Thylacine primal form.

Edmar Helm *(M) ED-muhr helm*
General of the First Legion of the Negian Empire.

Estriéggo *(M) ess-tree-EH-goh*
Perissodactyl Nu'irg. Woolly rhinoceros primal form.

Esum *(F) EH-soom*
Havengall monk who works with the sunnograph.

Fingrenn *(A) FIN-gren*
Laatu interpreter who tutors the travelers.

Fjorna Daro *(F) FYOR-nah DAHR-oh*
Chief Arbalister from a specialist squad of the Negian Empire.

Fjummomurr / *FEW-moh-murr*
Siffo's black-sailed whaling ship with a hull reinforced with kuba bones.

Frud *(M) frood*
Bear from the Stelm Wujann. Sabikh's cub. Also a Barlum Saga character.

Fulm *(M) fool-m*
Night-furred smilodon with a hissy attitude.

Fuuriseth *(F) FOO-ree-seth*
Chiropteran Nu'irg. White leaf-nosed bat primal form.

Gaönir-Bijeor / *gah-OH-neer BEE-jeh-or*
"Shield of Creation." Takhísh's legendary shield.

Gino Baneras *(M) GEE-no bah-NEH-rahs*
General of the Fourth Legion of the Negian Empire. Longbowman.

Givra *(F) GIVE-rah*
Laatu warrior who befriends Alaia.

Grinn *(M) grinn*
Admiral of Zovaria's Centennial Fleet. Bashed in the head by Balstei.

Gweshkamir *(M) WESH-kah-mere*
Prophet. Writer of the Takh Codex.

Gwil *(M) gwill*
Chaplain at the Withervale chapter of the Havengall Congregation.

Gwit *(M) gWIT*
Glires (rodent and lagomorph) Nu'irg. Hazel dormouse primal form.

Gwoli *(M) WOH-lee*
"Younger brother" in Oldrin. Pet name Alaia has for Lago.

Hefra Boarmane *(F) HEH-fruh BOAR-main*
Naturalist who specializes in ornithology and entomology.

Holfster *(A) HOLEf-str*
Botanist from Bauram. Has a nursery in Withervale.

Ikhel / *EE-hell*
Miscam tribe in the Bighorn Dome. Stewards of Rilgsilv, the mask of caprids.

Ilaadrid Shard / *ee-LAH-drihd shard*
The beacon that shines on Sceres's face twice a month.

Ilsed *(F) ILL-sed*
Chief of Gwur Gomosh in Mindreldrolom. Captain of Drolvisdinn.

Isdinnuk / *IS-dih-nook*
Miscam tribe in the Seafaring Dome. Stewards of Amá'asilv, the mask of cetaceans.

Ishke'ísuk *(M) ish-keh-'EE-sook*
Reptilian Nu'irg. Double-crested basilisk primal form.

Iskimesh *(F) IS-key-mesh*
Enchantress. Third planet from Sunnokh.

Jaxon Remon *(M) JACK-son REE-mon*
General of the Third Legion of the Negian Empire. Missing his left arm.

Ji / *gee*
Miscam tribe in the Azurean Dome. Stewards of Quajusilv, the mask of marsupials.

Jiara Ascura *(F) gee-AH-rah as-COO-rah*
Platoon commander in the Free Tribelands.

Jiu Zezi *(F) gee-oo ZEH-zee*
Yenwu cosmologist who discovered the comet that would cause the Downfall.

Jojek / *JOE-jeck*
Miscam tribe in the Lequa Dome. Stewards of Krostsilv, the mask of musteloids.

Kedra *(F) KEH-drah*
Zovarian scout who works for Crysta.

Kenondok *(M) KEH-non-dock*
Laatu weaponsmith who specializes in blowguns and darts.

Kenzir stone / *KEN-sr*
Pharoliths. Glowing rocks made with the aetheric element of pharos.

Kerjaastórgnem *(M) ker-jah-STORE-gnem*
Ursid Nu'irg. Arctotherium primal form. Can take the form of a man. Banook.

Khardok / *KHAR-dock*
Miscam tribe in the Moonrise Dome. Stewards of Gwonlesilv, mask of pinnipeds.

Khopto *(M) KHOP-toh*
Havengall monk who works with soot and specializes in "seeing the threads."

Khumen *(M) KHOO-men*
Dawn Pilgrim. First planet from Sunnokh.

Kitjári *(F) kit-JAH-ree*
Translates to "wood-claw" in Miscamish.

Klaawich *(A) KLAA-which*
Laatu shaman who has an albatross companion.

Kobos *(M) COH-bohs*
Smilodon-tiger hybrid with powerful muscles.

Korten dus Fer *(M) COURT-en doos fair*
General of the Sixth Legion of the Negian Empire.

Kulak *(M) COO-lack*
Mindrelfröa. Khuron Aio's caracal half-form.

Laatu / *LAH-AH-too*
Miscam tribe in the Moordusk Dome. Stewards of Mindrelsilv, the mask of felids.

Lago Vaari *(M) LAH-goh VAH-ree*
Sterjall's human form. Young man from Withervale who inherits Agnargsilv.

Leif / *LAY-f*
"Fang." Lago's dagger.

Lettáni *(A) leh-TA-nee*
Chief of Gwur Aalpe in Mindreldrolom. Wears long, colorful shodog.

Luhásu *(F) loo-HA-soo*
Western Ikhel leader who allies with the Red Stag to obtain Rilgsilv.

Lummukem *(A) LOO-moo-kem*
A winged dragon from spritetales. Also a constellation.

Luras Varum *(M) LURE-us VAH-ruhm*
Lago's name when he wants to go by incognito.

Malazzari *(M) mah-lah-ZA-ree*
Graalman god of fertility. Hung horse. Also a constellation.

Malnûvi *(F) mal-NOO-vee*
Puqua elder chief from the village of Onbar.

Mamóru *(M) mah-MOH-roo*
Proboscidean Nu'irg. Steppe mammoth primal form. Can take the form of a man.

Mauvenel *(A) MA-OO-vin-el*
Legendary hero who wielded Dunokh Sull.

Mo'óto / *moh-'OH-toh*
Miscam tribe in the Varanus Dome. Stewards of Kruwensilv, the mask of reptilians.

Muri *(M) MOO-ree*
Musteloid Nu'irg. Honey badger primal form.

Muriel Clawwick *(F) MEW-ree-el CLAW-wick*
Arbalister in Fjorna's squad. Waldomar's sister.

Murtégo / *moor-TEH-goh*
Miscam tribe in the Yenwu Dome. Stewards of Kroowinsilv, the mask of avians.

Nalaníri *(F) nah-lah-NEE-ree*
Nagrafröa. Prikka's boar half-form. Puqua chef.

Nelv *(F) nelv*
Felid Nu'irg. Clouded leopard primal form.

Noss *(A) noss*
Second planet from Sunnokh.

Ockam Radiartis *(M) OCK-uhm ra-dee-AR-tiss*
Sylvan scout from the Free Tribelands. Bonmei's adoptive father.

Odask *(M) ODD-ask*
The father of Nalaníri's two children.

Olo *(M) OH-loh*
Sunu's azure-hooded jay herald.

Ongumar *(M) ON-goo-mar*
Amberlight. Fifth planet from Sunnokh.

Osef Windscar *(M) OW-sehf WIND-scar*
Arbalister in Fjorna's squad.

Pamúnn *(M) pah-MOON*
Bovid Nu'irg. Nyala primal form.

Pau *(F) pow*
Nalaníri's teenaged daughter.

Pellámbri *(F) peh-LUHM-bree*
The Lodestar. A pink nebula at the heart of the Sword of Zeiheim.

Pian-Thi *(F) pee-an TEA*
Empress of the Tsing Empire.

Pichi *(F) PEE-chee*
Largest of smilodons, who usually carries all the gear.

Prikka *(F) PREE-kah*
Nalaníri's human form. Puqua chef.

Probo *(M) PROH-boh*
Suid Nu'irg. Javelina primal form.

Puqua / *POO-kwa*
Miscam tribe in the Fjordlands Dome. Stewards of Nagrasilv, the mask of suids.

Quggon / *KYOO-gone*
A cube made of 9 chips that add up to a value of one hundred Qupi.

Quoda *(F) KWO-dah*
Chief of Gwur Pantuul in Mindreldrolom. Lives in Panjuul. Dreadlock wig.

Qupi / *KYOO-pee*
Chevron-shaped chips used as currency units.

Red Stag *(M) red stag*
Alvis Hallow's elk half-form when wearing Urgsilv.

Rowan Holt *(M) ROW-uhn holt*
Crysta's husband.

Rushun *(M) ROO-shoon*
Nalaníri's teenaged son.

Sabikh *(F) sah-BEE-kh*
Bear from the Stelm Wujann. Frud's mother. Barlum Saga character.

Safis *(F) sah-FEES*
Canid Nu'irg. Tundra wolf primal form.

Sceres *(F) SEH-rehs*
Noss's moon.

Sehján / *seh-JAHN*
Miscam tribe in the Nisos Dome. Stewards of Okrisilv, the mask of glires.

Senstrell *(F) SENS-trell*
"Obsidian." Fourth planet from Sunnokh.

Shea Lu *(F) SHEH-ah loo*
Arbalister in Fjorna's squad.

Siffo *(M) SEE-foh*
Puqua captain of Fjummomurr, the Tusked Whale. Quarter warthog.

Skugge *(A) SKOO-geh*
Avian Nu'irg. Great gray owl primal form. Only allgender Nu'irg.

Skyfarer / *SKY-farer*
Corben's swift catamaran. Also a winged ship constellation.

Sontai *(F) SON-tie*
Bonmei's grandmother. Gives Agnargsilv to Lago. Gray fox half-form.

Sovath *(F) SOH-vahth*
Cervid Nu'irg. Chital primal form. Often seen as a megaloceros next to the Red Stag.

Sterjall *(M) STARE-jahl*
Agnargfröa. Lago's timber wolf half-form.

Sunnokh *(M) SOO-noh-kh*
"Sky-flame." The sun.

Sunu *(A) SOO-noo*
Laatu shaman warrior trained both in the arts of healing and battle.

Suque *(A) SOO-kwe*
Oldest Laatu interpreter. Historian.

Sword of Zeiheim / *ZEI-hime*
Legendary weapon crafted of lightning. Also a constellation.

Takhamún *(M) ta-kha-MOON*
The Unmaker, god of destruction from the Takh Codex.

Takhísh *(M) ta-KHEE-sh*
The Demiurge, god of creation from the Takh Codex.

Teldebran / *TELL-the-brahn*
Miscam tribe in the Anglass Dome. Stewards of Urgsilv, the mask of cervids.

Thurann Embercut *(F) THOO-rahn EM-br-cut*
Marshal of the Zovarian Ninth Battalion, stationed in Nebush.

Tjardur / *CHAR-dure*
Miscam tribe in the Ashen Dome. Stewards of Trommosilv, the mask of bovids.

Toldask / *TOLD-ask*
Miscam tribe at Brasha'in Scablands. Held Momsúndosilv, mask of proboscideans.

Tor-Reveo / *tore REH-vee-oh*
"Spear of Undoing." Takhamún's legendary spear.

Tremor *(M) TREH-mr*
Jartadi steed the Red Stag rides. Black velvet coat.

Trevin Gobbar *(M) TREH-vinn GOH-bar*
Arbalister in Fjorna's squad. Long nose.

Ulle dus Grei *(F) OO-leh doos gray*
Emperor Uvon dus Grei's sister, who the Red Stag impregnates.

Urcai *(M) OOR-ky*
Crafty artificer from the Negian Empire.

Uvon dus Grei *(M) OO-von doos gray*
Young emperor of the Negian Empire. Son of Grei dus Gauno.

Wutash, Northern / *WOO-tash*
Miscam tribe in the Da'áju Caldera. Stewards of Urnaadisilv, the mask of ursids.

Wutash, Southern / *WOO-tash*
Miscam tribe in the Heartpine Dome. Stewards of Agnargsilv, the mask of canids.

Yza *(F) IT-suh*
Demigoddess whose shade blesses all it touches.

Locations

Abrasion Bay
Bay with rough waters and occasional icebergs southwest of the Fjordlands Dome.

Afhora, Kingdom of / *ah-FOR-uh*
One of the sixteen realms. Its capital is Sundhollow.

Agnargdrolom / *AG-narg-droh-lom*
Heartpine Dome. Located between the Free Tribelands and the Negian Empire.

Allathanathar / *ala-THA-na-thar*
Capital of the Kingdom of Bauram.

Almeldrolom / *AL-mehl-droh-lom*
Archstone Dome. Located between the Dorhond Tribes and the Graalman Horde.

Amá'adrolom / *ah-MAH-'ah-droh-lom*
Seafaring Dome. Located in the Capricious Ocean, locked to an atoll.

Anglass / *AN-glass*
Negian fortress on the south-east perimeter of the Anglass Dome.

Anglass Dome / *AN-glass*
Urgdrolom. Dome located in the Negian Empire, north of the Stiss Malpa.

Archstone Dome
Almeldrolom. Dome located between the Dorhond Tribes and the Graalman Horde.

Arho / *AR-hoh*
Port city in the Fjordlands Dome.

Arjum / *AR-joom*
Capital of the Laatu Miscam, province of Gwur Ali, in Mindreldrolom, the Moordusk Dome.

Arjum Promenade / *AR-joom*
Public walkway around Mindreldrolom's trunk.

Ash Sea
"White Sea." Northern sea teeming with icebergs.

Ashen Dome
Trommodrolom. Dome in southern Tsing Empire, with a top that constantly smokes.

Ashgwemar / *ASH-gwe-mahr*
Old Mo'óto name for Fel Varanus.

Azash / *ah-ZAH-sh*
Capital of the Elmaren Queendom.

Azurean Dome / *ah-ZUR-ean*
Quajudrolom. Dome located in the Kingdom of Bauram, surrounded by blue sands.

Balastdrolom / *BAH-last-droh-lom*
Scoria Dome. Located between Afhoran, Tharman, and Graalman lands.

Barnoy / *BAR-noy*
Zovarian city with a bridge crossing the Stiss Tungeo.

Barushem / *BAH-roo-shem*
Soot mining town in the northern edges of the Fjordlands Dome.

Bauram, Kingdom of / *bau-RAHM*
One of the sixteen realms. Its capital is Allathanathar.

Bayanhong Tribes / *BAH-jann-hong*
One of the sixteen realms. Its capital is On Khurderen.

Baysea Beyenaar / *BAY-eh-nahr*
Often frozen bay in the Khaar Du territories.

Bergsulf / *BERG-sulf*
Land of indep. colonies in the Unclaimed Territories, north of the Fractured Range.

Bighorn Dome
Rilgdrolom. Dome between the peaks of the Stelm Rilgéreo and Stelm Rilganesh.

Brasha'in Scablands / *brah-sha-'EEN*
Volcanic wasteland in the western Zovarian Union.

Brightbay Run
Wide river in the Zovarian Union, crossing by the city of New Karst.

Brimstowne / *BRIMs-town*
Mining frontier town in an independent Bergsulfi colony by the Stelm Wujann.

Brinelaar / *BRINE-lar*
Salt mining town west of the Bighorn Dome.

Brumm / *broom*
Kenzir stone mines in the Fjordlands Dome.

Caerlye / *CARE-lie*
Potash mining town west of the Bighorn Dome.

Capricious Ocean
Southernmost of the four oceans, known for its unpredictable waters.

Corundum Monolith
Enormous crystal worshipped by the Khaar Du.

Da'áju Caldera / *da-'AH-joo*
Vast, static cirque glacier in the Stelm Wujann.

Dakhud / *DAH-hood*
Capital of the province of Gwur Aalpe in the Moordusk Dome.

Dathereol Princedom / *dah-THEE-ree-ol*
One of the sixteen realms. Its capital is Therimark.

Dimbali / *dim-BAH-lee*
Negian city on the Topaz Beck.

Doralghon / *DOH-ralg-hone*
Capital of the Graalman Horde.

Dorhond Range / *DOOR-hund*
Ragged sierras separating the White Desert from the Archstone Dome.

Dorhond Tribes / *DOOR-hund*
One of the sixteen realms. Its capital is Oskirin.

Drann Trodesh / *drahn TROH-desh*
Sawtoothed mountains wrapping around Unemar Lake.

Druhal / *droo-HAL*
Capital of the Wastyr Triumvirate. One of three.

Dunewaar / *DUNE-war*
Vast land of sand dunes where the old Dunewaar Queendom once stood.

Elanúbril / *ella-NOO-breel*
Capital of the Khaar Du Tribes.

Elmaren Queendom / *EL-ma-ren*
One of the sixteen realms. Its capital is Azash.

Emen Ruins / *EH-men*
Dorvauros ruins with hot springs resting within a lava tube.

Esçarsúl / *es-char-SOOL*
City in the Fjordlands Dome with a fine braaw.

Esduss Sea / *ES-doos*
Sea separating Fel Baubór from the Loorian mainland.

Eyes of the Great Spider
Range of craters west of Baysea Beyenaar worshipped by the Khaar Du.

Farjall / *FAR-jall*
Negian fortress on the south-east perimeter of the Heartpine Dome.

Farkhalum / *far-KHA-loom*
Capital of the Wastyr Triumvirate. One of three.

Farsulf Forest / *far-SOOLF*
"Pine Land." Forest north of the Heartpine Dome, south of the Stelm Ca'éli.

Fel Baubór / *fell bau-BORE*
Continent-sized island of blue sands, mostly belonging to the Kingdom of Bauram.

Fel Mellanolv / *fell MEH-la-nohlv*
Bayani island on the far east.

Fel Nisos / *fell NY-sus*
Great island of the Republic of Lerev.

Fel Oskrud / *fel OS-crude*
Largest island in the Alommo Sea.

Fel Shinn / *fell sheen*
Island north of Fel Varanus.

Fel Ukhagar / *fell OO-khah-gar*
Island of the Charred Wastes. Claimed by Dathereol.

Fel Varanus / *fell VAH-rah-noose*
Zovarian island on which the Varanus Dome spreads its tendrils.

Fel Yorkab / *fell YOR-cab*
Continent-sized island of the Wastyr Triumvirate, on the southern reaches of Noss.

Firefalls
"Minnelvad." Steaming waterfalls in the Stelm Wujann, northwest of Brimstowne.

Fjarmallen Peninsula / *fee-ar-MAH-lehn*
Loosely inhabited lands on the fast southwest of the Dathereol Princedom.

Fjordlands Dome
Nagradrolom. Dome located between the Zovarian Union and Khaar Du Tribes.

Fjordsulf / *FJORD-soolf*
Cold land of fjords and icebergs of the Khaar Du Tribes.

Free Tribelands
One of the sixteen realms. Its capital is Klemes.

Graalman Horde / *GROWL-mahn*
One of the sixteen realms. Its capital is Doralghon.

Gulf of Erjilm / *ERR-juhlm*
Circular gulf at the split between the two great continents.

Gwonledrolom / *WON-leh-droh-lom*
Moonrise Dome. Located in the far east, in the Elmaren Queendom.

Hashan / *ha-SHUN*
Capital of the Tsing Empire. Also called the "City of Bridges."

Heartpine Dome
Agnargdrolom. Dome located between the Free Tribelands and the Negian Empire.

Hestfell / *HEST-fell*
Capital of the Negian Empire.

Hoombudrolom / *HOH-OHM-boo-droh-lom*
Tarpits Dome. Located in the Tsing Empire, by the Khonn Tar Pits.

Hum Khaabash / *whom KHAA-bash*
"Six Widows." Monolithic rocks overlooking the Isdinnklad in the Moordusk Dome.

Humenath / *WHO-men-ath*
Capital of the province of Gwur Úrëath in the Moordusk Dome.

Illenev / *EE-leh-nehv*
Capital of the Wastyr Triumvirate. One of three.

Isdinnklad / *IS-dihn-clad*
"Sea Lake." Long, tapering sea splitting the Loorian Continent.

Jerjan Continent / *JER-jann*
Named after Laaja Jerja, tallest peak at 38,264 feet.

Karst Forest
Forest south of the Moordusk Dome.

Kayamur / *CAH-yah-moore*
Negian port city in the only Negian state in the Jerjan Continent.

Keldris Allastirg / *KEL-dris AH-last-ihrg*
"Southern Bay" in the Fjordlands Dome.

Keldris Klannath / *KEL-dris CLAH-nuth*
"Northern Bay" in the Fjordlands Dome.

Khaar Du Tribes / *khar doo*
One of the sixteen realms. Its capital is Elanúbril.

Khaar Du Wastes / *khar doo*
Icy wastelands of the north.

Khoomalith / *WHO-ma-lith*
Negian port city on the Ophidian Sea.

Klemes / *CLEM-uhs*
Capital of the Free Tribelands, west of the Klad Senet.

Koroberg / *COH-roh-berg*
Zovarian port city southwest of the Fjordlands Dome.

Kroowindrolom / *CROW-win-droh-lom*
Yenwu Dome. Located in the Yenwu Peninsula.

Krostdrolom / *CROSSED-droh-lom*
Lequa Dome. Located in the eastern Negian Empire, by Bayanhong settlements.

Krûn / *croon*
Capital of the Puqua Miscam in Nagradrolom, the Fjordlands Dome.

Kruwendrolom / *CREW-when-droh-lom*
Varanus Dome. Located in Fel Varanus, a far western island of the Zovarian Union.

Laaja Deulmosk / *LA-AH-jah DEWL-mosque*
Volcano in the Fjordlands Dome very close to the kenzir stone mines.

Laaja Jerja / *LA-AH-jah JIR-jah*
Volcano. Tallest peak of the Jerjan Continent at 38,264 feet.

Laaja Khem / *LA-AH-jah khem*
Volcano northwest of the Da'áju Caldera with old Dorvauros mines.

Laaja Khenukh / *LA-AH-jah KHEH-nookh*
Volcano on the eastern edge of the Brasha'in Scablands.

Lamanni / *la-MA-nee*
Negian City. Main Negian road also named after it.

Lequa Dome / *LEH-kwa*
Krostdrolom. Dome located in the eastern Negian Empire.

Lequa Sea / *LEH-kwa*
Northeastern sea that funnels into the Ophidian. Dome is named after it.

Lerev, Republic of / *luh-REHV*
One of the sixteen realms. Its capital is Normouth.

Loorian Continent / *LOO-ree-anne*
Named after Mount Loor, tallest peak at 35,167 feet.

Macu / *MA-coo*
Old Mo'óto capital at the center of the Varanus Dome.

Mâscarmush / *MASS-car-moosh*
Ruined port at the end of a fjord in the Fjordlands Dome.

Mindreldrolom / *MIHN-drehl-droh-lom*
Moordusk Dome. Located in the Zovarian Union, near Zovaria.

Minnelvad / *ME-nell-vahd*
"Firefalls." Steaming waterfalls in the Stelm Wujann, northwest of Brimstowne.

Mirefoot
Zovarian industrial town where they mine peat and harness the bog gasses.

Montano / *mon-TAH-no*
Negian port city in the only Negian state in the Jerjan Continent.

Moonbow Timberlands
Vast Zovarian forest south of the Moordusk Dome, north of the Stelm Sajal.

Moonrise Dome
Gwonledrolom. Dome located in the far east, in the Elmaren Queendom.

Moordusk Bogs
Wetlands east of the Moordusk Dome, where peat is harvested.

Moordusk Dome
Mindreldrolom. Dome located in the Zovarian Union, near Zovaria.

Mount Fogra / *FOG-rah*
Tallest peak of the Stelm Wujann. Home of the Wujann Observatory.

Mount Loor / *lure*
Tallest peak of the Loorian Continent at 35,167 feet.

Muskeg
Zovarian town on the southeast of the Moordusk Dome.

Nagradrolom / *NAH-grah-droh-lom*
Fjordlands Dome. Located between the Zovarian Union and the Khaar Du Tribes.

Nebush / *NEH-bush*
Zovarian port town on the southwest of the Moordusk Dome.

Needlecove
Small Zovarian town with chalk promontories close to the Northlock Strait.

Negian Empire / *NEE-jann*
One of the sixteen realms. Its capital is Hestfell.

New Karst
Zovarian city on the Old Pilgrim's Road.

Ninn Tago / *nihn TAH-goh*
"Gray Pass." Road cutting over the Stelm Ca'éli, connecting Withervale to Knife Point.

Nisos Dome / *NY-sus*
Okridrolom. Dome located in the Republic of Lerev, in the island of Fel Nisos.

Nool / *nool*
Negian city close to Withervale.

Normouth / *NOR-muth*
Capital of the Republic of Lerev.

Northlock Strait
Narrow passage separating the Isdinnklad Sea from the Isdinnklad Lake.

Oälpaskist / *oh-AL-pass-kissed*
Capital of the province of Gwur Gomosh in the Moordusk Dome.

Okridrolom / *OH-kree-droh-lom*
Nisos Dome. Located in the Republic of Lerev, in the island of Fel Nisos.

Old Karst
Zovarian city on the Old Pilgrim's Road.

Old Pilgrim's Road
Longest road in the Loorian Continent, running from Umarion to Wyrmwash.

Öllomuy / *OH-low-moo-ee*
Port city in the Fjordlands Dome where Siffo is from. They harvest very sweet figs.

On Khurderen / *on khur-DEH-rehn*
Capital of the Bayanhong Tribes.

Onbar / *ON-bar*
Village in the Fjordlands Dome where first contact with the Puqua happens.

Ophidian Sea
Snaking sea separating the Loorian and Jerjan continents.

Oskirin / *OSS-kih-ruhn*
Capital of the Dorhond Tribes.

Parjuul / *par-JOOL*
Capital of the province of Gwur Pantuul in the Moordusk Dome.

Quajudrolom / *KWA-joo-droh-lom*
Azurean Dome. Located in the Kingdom of Bauram, surrounded by blue sands.

Quas Trell / *kwas trell*
"Black Canyon." Capital of the province of Gwur Esmukh in the Moordusk Dome.

Quiescent Ocean
Westernmost of the four oceans, known for its calm waters.

Rilgdrolom / *REEL-g-droh-lom*
Bighorn Dome. Located between the peaks of the Stelm Rilgéreo and Stelm Rilganesh.

Sajal Crater / *SAH-jall*
Round crater in the volcanic lands of the Stelm Sajal. Known for its warm waters.

Scoria Dome
Balastdrolom. Dome located between Afhoran, Tharman, and Graalman lands.

Seafaring Dome
Amá'adrolom. Dome located in the Capricious Ocean, locked to an atoll.

Shaderift
Negian city on the southwest of the Lequa Dome.

Shaderift Aqueduct
Conduit built to carry water from the Klad Enturg to the fortress of Shaderift.

Sharr Helm / *shahr helm*
Capital of the Tharma Federation.

Slømmon Forest / *SLOW-muhn*
Forest in the Stelm Shäerath of the Fjordlands Dome, known for its hoodoos.

Spine Bay
Inner saltwater bay northeast of the Fjordlands Dome.

Stelm Bir / *stelm beer*
"Home Mountain." Central peak inside the Heartpine Dome.

Stelm Ca'éli / *stelm cah-'EH-lee*
"Pilgrim Sierras." Range that splits the Zovarian Union and the Free Tribelands.

Stelm Humenath / *stelm WHO-men-ath*
Highest peak inside the Moordusk Dome.

Stelm Khull / *stelm khool*
"Graveyard Mountains." Mountains extending east from the Stelm Wujann.

Stelm Rilganesh / *stelm REEL-gah-nesh*
"Bighorn Sheep Mountains." Range north of the Bighorn Dome.

Stelm Rilgéreo / *stelm reel-GEH-reh-oh*
"Goat Mountains." Range south of the Bighorn Dome.

Stelm Sajal / *stelm SAH-jall*
"Foreboding Mountains." Volcanic range east of the Brasha'in Scablands.

Stelm Shäerath / *stelm SHAH-eh-rath*
The Tricolored Mountain, peak at the Fjordlands Dome from where the trunk grows.

Stelm Tai-Du / *stelm tai-DOO*
"Night-Snow Mountains." Range north of the Tarpits Dome.

Stelm Wujann / *stelm WOO-jann*
"Icy Mountains." Vast sierras in the northern Loorian Continent.

Steps of Odrásmunn / *oh-DRAS-moon*
Columnar basalt formation that runs on the north of the Brasha'in Scablands.

Stiss Fulvéni / *stiss fool-VEH-nee*
Eastern river in the Moordusk Dome, full of waterfalls.

Stiss Khull / *stiss khool*
"Graveyard River." Glacier-fed river extending east from the Stelm Wujann.

Stiss Malpa / *stiss MAHL-pah*
River that empties into the tip of the Isdinnklad Lake, right at Withervale.

Stiss Regu-Omen / *stiss REH-goo omen*
Main river that crosses through the capital and trunk of the Moordusk Dome.

Sundhollow / *SUHND-hollow*
Capital of the Kingdom of Afhora.

Taring / *TAH-ring*
Pre-Downfall ruins at the Taring Peninsula, southwest of the Gulf of Erjilm.

Tarpits Dome
Hoombudrolom. Dome located in the Tsing Empire, by the Khonn Tar Pits.

Teslurkath / *TESS-lure-cath*
Iceberg-covered shores on the frigid, northwestern frontiers of Noss.

Tharma Federation / *THAHR-mah*
One of the sixteen realms. Its capital is Sharr Helm.

Therimark / *THEH-ree-mark*
Capital of the Dathereol Princedom.

Thicket Island
Large island east of Fel Varanus, wrapped by unruly vines from the Varanus Dome.

Thirteen Peaks
Mountains separating the White Desert of Dorhond from the archlands of the Horde.

Thornridge Lookout
Free Tribelands fortress protecting the perimeter road around the Heartpine Dome.

Trommodrolom / *TROM-moh-droh-lom*
Ashen Dome. Located in the southern Tsing Empire, with a top that constantly smokes.

Tsenhanuur / *zen-hah-NOOR*
Graalman city in the archlands.

Tsing Empire / *zing*
One of the sixteen realms. Its capital is Hashan.

Tumultuous Ocean
Easternmost of the four oceans, known for its rough waters.

Udarbans Forest / *OO-dar-bans*
Uninhabited forest southwest of the Brasha'in Scablands.

Umarion / *oo-MA-ree-on*
Far western Zovarian city at the end of the Old Pilgrim's Road.

Unclaimed Territories
Areas not claimed by any of the sixteen realms.

Unemar Lake / *OO-neh-mar*
Placid lake surrounded by the five peaks of Drann Trodesh.

Unthawing Ocean
Northernmost of the four oceans, known for its icesheets and icebergs.

Urgdrolom / *OORG-droh-lom*
Anglass Dome. Located in the Negian Empire, wrapped by the Stiss Malpa.

Varanus Dome / *VAH-rah-noose*
Kruwendrolom. Dome located in Fel Varanus, a far western island of the Zovarian Union.

Wastyr Triumvirate / *was-TIER*
One of the sixteen realms. Its capital is Illenev.

White Desert
Expansive desert of white sands speckled with Dorhond temples.

Withervale
Easternmost Zovarian city, on the border with the Negian Empire.

Wuhir Peak / *WOO-here*
"Leafy Peak." Prominent peak in the Karst Forest.

Wyrmwash
Negian port city at the mouth of the Stiss Negii.

Yanan / *YA-nun*
Zovarian city in Holv-Yanan, the only Zovarian state in Fel Baubór.

Yenmai / *YEN-my*
Capital of the Yenwu State.

Yenwu Dome / *YEN-woo*
Kroowindrolom. Dome located in the Yenwu Peninsula.

Yenwu State / *YEN-woo*
One of the sixteen realms. Its capital is Yenmai.

Zovaria / *zoh-VAH-ree-uh*
Capital of the Zovarian Union.

Zovarian Union / *zoh-VAH-ree-uhn*
One of the sixteen realms. Its capital is Zovaria.

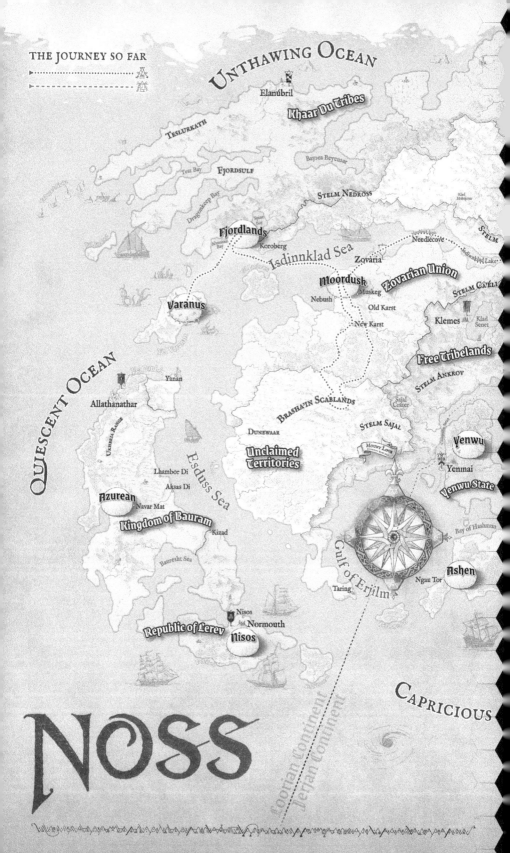

Acknowledgments

As I started doing in Book 1 of this series, I planned for the credits to remain about the same for all books, given that I wrote them simultaneously. Some new names (such as those of my generous beta readers) might be added from book to book, but most of the thanks I wish to give are to the same people and groups. So, let the core of these acknowledgments stand sixfold, for each of the volumes of the *Noss Saga*.

I was spoiled by my parents, Angélica Delgado and Juan Carlos Baldwin. They would let me buy any book I wanted, encouraging me to devour Bradbury, Sagan, Tolkien, Allende, Márquez, Vasconcelos, Gaiman, Asimov, Borges, and so much more. All my passions sprout from their unrelenting support—it is all their fault. Gracias, a él y ella.

Writing can be a lonesome endeavor, but I had my husband, Timothy, always here beside me, to whom I could blabber incoherent thoughts at random intervals, like a bouncing board for spittle and nonsense. Too many of the best ideas for this saga came from me spouting something massively stupid, only to hear him correct me or point out a different route I had not the foresight to envision.

Awfully prematurely, when I was merely in the planning stages of the first book, I had begun to envision the covers. Since the very start I knew I wanted Ilse Gort to lend her skillful hands for the illustrations. I was terrified to ask for her help. I was so happy when she said yes, and happier still when she proposed ideas that were much better than my own.

My editor, Andrew Corvin, was instrumental in fixing up my messes with a barrage of thoughtful suggestions. His notes were not just simple grammar and typo corrections, but offered insights on the characters' motivations, flow of sentences, word choice, and even broader story notes that truly helped focus the work and keep the voice consistent.

On the audiobook side, Magnus Carlssen did a fantastic job adding his own flavor to the narration, even getting all my tricky pronunciations right. I ran a poll among the beta readers to see which voice they preferred, and Magnus landed right at the top for a reason. And teaming him Iain James Armour (Fox Amoore), who wrote the melodies for each of the lyrics, has been such a blessing—the first time I heard a work in progress of one of the songs, I squealed.

I had the luck to count with a thoughtful and diverse group of beta readers and proofreaders, who gave me a ton of notes to work with. Thank you for believing in me and for offering your help—this book is far better thanks to you, Abs M Rice, Alejandro Renteria, Alex Mui, Amanda Leigh, Angie Lee Camp, Arthur Huang, BirdsongChoir, Blackquill, Brian Jackson, Carlos A. Luna Aranguré, Charlie McGrew, Colleen Maloney, Conor Davitt, Cosmo, David "Professor Jefe" Jones, Edwin Herrell, Elliot D. Brown, Erik Tye, Fana, FFAT, Franz Anthony, Guephren, Jack Sanderson, Jul, Kiko, Kyle Branch, Kyle Dolloff, Louis D.S, Marco Nowak, Marián Sulák, Marcus Rodriguez, Markus Lundberg, Marston Jones, Matt Morgan, Matthew Green, Max Sjöblom, Miguel Ángel García García, Miles Fox, Nora Rogers, North, Reverie Benedetto, Rosalea Barker, Ross Blocher, Rourkie, Ryan Tye, Sandra Malpica, Santi Rowe, Scurrow, Sean Wenzel, Shadow Worfu, Skiriki, Solomon H., Streuhund, Ted Sawyer, Tiberius Rings, Timothy Dahlum, Victor Hugo Guadagnin, and a couple of anons.

One thing I never lacked during this process was encouragement. As an introvert, having an online community I can count on has been a true blessing. I truly appreciate everyone in social media who has been hitting little heart icons to trigger tiny releases of dopamine in my brain. In particular, thank you to my fervent furry following, who taught me to be courageous enough to be myself, to write a story that speaks my truth. You inspire me.

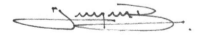

About the Author

Joaquín Baldwin was born in Paraguay, where he first found his love of books by picking up every volume by Ray Bradbury he could get his hands on, and then by submerging himself into a single-bound copy of the Lord of the Rings trilogy—but it wasn't until much later that he'd acquire a taste for writing.

At age 19, he moved to the US to study film and animation, where he received a BFA from CCAD and an MFA from UCLA. He was the recipient of a full scholarship from the Jack Kent Cooke Foundation.

His short films have won over 100 awards and honors at festivals and competitions such as Cannes, the Student Academy Awards, Cinequest, and USA Film Festival. Soon after receiving his masters, he began working at the Walt Disney Animation Studios as a CG Layout Artist, and later as a Director of Cinematography, working on films such as Zootopia, Encanto, Wreck-It Ralph, Frozen, Raya, and Moana.

Never content with sticking to his lane, Joaquín has experience as a professional photographer, illustrator, comic artist, web designer, and 3D designer. His varied skillset came in handy when developing his fantasy saga, allowing him to create his own illustrations, maps, 3D models, book covers, website, and even his own language (phonetics, runes, and all).

Since the 2020 pandemic hit, he's been spending every second of his free time forging the complex world of Noss.

Sign up to Joaquín's mailing list:
`JoaquinBaldwin.com/list`

Connect with Joaquín on social media:
`Search for @joabaldwin to find him on most sites, such as Bluesky, Mastodon, Facebook, Twitter, and Instagram.`

Printed in the USA
CPSIA information can be obtained
at www.ICGtesting.com
LVHW090911160624
783312LV00029B/638/J